Ken Follett was only twenty-seven when he wrote the award-winning novel *Eye of the Needle* which became an international bestseller. He has since written several equally successful novels, including *Code to Zero* and *Jackdaws.* He is also author of the non-fiction bestseller *On Wings of Eagles.* He lives with his family in London and Hertfordshire.

Visit the Ken Follett website at
http://www.ken-follett.com

THE THIRD TWIN
AND
PAPER MONEY

Also by Ken Follett

The Modigliani Scandal
Eye of the Needle
Triple
The Key to Rebecca
The Man from St Petersburg
On Wings of Eagles
Lie Down with Lions
The Pillars of the Earth
Night Over Water
A Dangerous Fortune
A Place Called Freedom
The Hammer of Eden
Code to Zero
Jackdaws

KEN FOLLETT

THE THIRD TWIN AND PAPER MONEY

PAN BOOKS

The Third Twin first published 1996 by Macmillan.
First published in paperback 1997 by Pan Books
Paper Money first pubished 1996 by Macmillan
First published in paperback 1996 by Pan Books

This omnibus edition published 2003 by Pan Books
an imprint of Pan Macmillan Ltd
Pan Macmillan, 20 New Wharf Road, London N1 9RR
Basingstoke and Oxford
Associated companies throughout the world
www.panmacmillan.com

ISBN 0 330 42100 X

1 3 5 7 9 8 6 4 2

A CIP catalogue record for this book is available from
the British Library.

Printed and bound in Great Britain by
Mackays of Chatham plc, Chatham, Kent

THE THIRD TWIN

To my stepchildren:
Jann Turner, Kim Turner and Adam Broer
with love

SUNDAY

CHAPTER ONE

A HEATWAVE lay over Baltimore like a shroud. The leafy suburbs were cooled by a hundred thousand lawn sprinklers, but the affluent inhabitants stayed inside with the air-conditioning on full blast. On North Avenue, listless hookers hugged the shade and sweated under their hairpieces, and the kids on the street corners dealt dope out of the pockets of baggy shorts. It was late September, but fall seemed a long way off.

A rusty white Datsun, the broken lens of one headlight fixed in place with an X of electrician's tape, cruised through a white working-class neighbourhood north of downtown. The car had no air-conditioning, and the driver had rolled down all the windows. He was a handsome man of twenty-two wearing cut-off jeans, a clean white T-shirt and a red baseball cap with the word SECURITY in white letters on the front. The plastic upholstery beneath his thighs was slippery with his perspiration, but he did not let it bother him. He was in a cheerful mood. The car radio was tuned to 92Q—'Twenty jams in a row!' On the passenger seat was an open binder. He glanced at it occasionally, memorizing a typed page of technical terms for a test tomorrow.

Learning was easy for him, and he would know the material after a few minutes of study.

At a stop light, a blonde woman in a convertible Porsche pulled alongside him. He grinned at her and said: 'Nice car!' She looked away without speaking, but he thought he saw the hint of a smile at the corners of her mouth. Behind her big sunglasses she was probably twice his age: most women in Porsches were. 'Race you to the next stop light,' he said. She laughed at that, a flirtatious musical laugh, then she put the stick shift into first with a narrow, elegant hand and tore away from the light like a rocket.

He shrugged. He was only practising.

He drove by the wooded campus of Jones Falls University, an Ivy League college much swankier than the one he attended. As he passed the imposing gateway, a group of eight or ten women jogged by in running clothes: tight shorts, Nikes, sweaty T-shirts and halter tops. They were a field hockey team in training, he guessed, and the fit-looking one in front was their captain, getting them in shape for the season.

They turned into the campus, and suddenly he was overwhelmed, swamped by a fantasy so powerful and thrilling that he could hardly see to drive. He imagined them in the locker room—the plump one soaping herself in the shower, the redhead towelling her long copper-coloured hair, the black girl stepping into a pair of white lace panties, the dikey team captain walking around naked, showing off her muscles—when something happened to terrify them. Suddenly they were all in a panic, wide eyed with dread, screaming and crying, on the edge of hysteria. They ran this way and that, crashing into one another. The fat girl fell over and lay there weeping helplessly while the others trod on her, unheeding, as they tried desperately to hide, or find the door, or run away from whatever was scaring them.

He pulled over to the side of the road and put the car in neutral. He was breathing hard and he could feel his heartbeat hammering. This was the best one he had ever had. But a little piece of the fantasy was missing. What were they frightened of? He hunted about in his fertile imagination for the answer, and gasped with desire when it came to him: a fire. The place was ablaze, and they were terrified by the flames. They coughed and choked on the smoke as they milled about, half naked and frenzied. 'My God,' he whispered, staring straight ahead, seeing the scene like a movie projected on to the inside of the Datsun's windshield.

After a while he calmed down. His desire was still strong, but the fantasy was no longer enough: it was like the thought of a beer when he had a raging thirst. He lifted the hem of his T-shirt and wiped the sweat from his face. He knew he should try to forget the fantasy, and drive on; but it was too wonderful. It would be terribly dangerous—he would go to jail for years if he were caught—but danger had never stopped him doing anything in his life. He struggled to resist temptation, though only for a second. 'I want it,' he murmured, and he turned the car around and drove through the grand gateway into the campus.

He had been here before. The university spread across a hundred acres of lawns and gardens and woodland. Its buildings were mostly made of a uniform red brick, with a few modern concrete-and-glass structures, all connected by a tangle of narrow roads lined with parking meters.

The hockey team had disappeared, but he found the gymnasium easily: it was a low building next to a running track, and there was a big statue of a discus thrower outside. He parked at a meter but did not put a coin in: he never put money in parking meters. The muscular captain of the hockey team was standing on the steps of the gym, talking to a guy in a ripped sweatshirt. He ran up the steps, smiling at the captain as he passed her, and pushed through the door into the building.

The lobby was busy with young men and women in shorts and headbands coming and going, rackets in their hands and sports bags slung over their shoulders. No doubt most of the college teams trained on Sundays. There was a security guard behind a desk in the middle of the lobby, checking people's student cards; but at that moment a big group of runners came in together and walked past the guard, some waving their cards and others forgetting, and the guard just shrugged his shoulders and went on reading *The Dead Zone.*

The stranger turned and looked at a display of silver cups in a glass case, trophies won by Jones Falls athletes. A moment later a soccer team came in, ten men and a chunky woman in studded boots, and he moved quickly to fall in with them. He crossed the lobby as part of their group and followed them down a broad staircase to the basement. They were talking about their game, laughing at a lucky goal and indignant about an outrageous foul, and they did not notice him.

His gait was casual but his eyes were watchful. At the foot of the stairs was a small lobby with a Coke machine and a pay phone under an acoustic hood. The men's locker room was off the lobby. The woman from the soccer team went down a long corridor, heading presumably for the women's locker room, which had probably been added as an afterthought by an architect who imagined there would never be many girls at Jones Falls, back in the days when 'coeducational' was a sexy word.

The stranger picked up the pay phone and pretended to search for a quarter. The men filed into their locker room. He watched the woman open a door and disappear. That must be the women's locker room. They were all in there, he thought excitedly, undressing and showering and rubbing themselves with towels. Being so close to them made him feel hot. He wiped his brow with the back of his hand. All he had to do to complete the fantasy was get them all scared half to death.

He made himself calm. He was not going to spoil it by haste. It needed a few minutes' planning.

When they had all disappeared, he padded along the corridor after the woman.

Three doors led off it, one on either side and one at the end. The door on the right was the one the woman had taken. He checked the end door and found that it led to a big, dusty room full of bulky machinery: boilers and filters, he guessed, for the swimming pool. He stepped inside and closed the door behind him. There was a low, even electrical hum. He pictured a girl delirious with fright, dressed only in her underwear—he imagined a bra and panties with a pattern of flowers—lying on the floor staring up at him with terrified eyes as he unbuckled his belt. He savoured the vision for a moment, smiling to himself. She was just a few yards away. Right now she might be contemplating the evening ahead: maybe she had a boyfriend, and was thinking of letting him go all the way tonight; or she could be a freshman, lonely and a little shy, with nothing to do on Sunday night but watch *Columbo*; or perhaps she had a paper to deliver tomorrow and was planning to stay up all night finishing it. *None of the above, baby. It's nightmare time.*

He had done this kind of thing before, though never on such a scale. He had always loved to frighten girls, ever since he could remember. In high school there was nothing he liked better than to get a girl on her own, in a corner somewhere, and threaten her until she cried and begged for mercy. That was why he kept having to move from one school to another. He dated girls sometimes, just to be like the other guys, and have someone to walk into the bar on his arm. If they seemed to expect it he would bone them, but it always seemed kind of pointless.

Everyone had a kink, he figured: some men liked to put on women's clothing, others had to have a girl dressed in leather walk all over them with spike heels. One guy he knew thought the sexiest part of a woman was her feet: he got a hard-on standing in the women's footwear section of a department store, watching them put on shoes and take them off again.

His kink was fear. What turned him on was a woman trembling with fright. Without fear, there was no excitement.

Looking around methodically, he took note of a ladder fixed to the wall, leading up to an iron hatch bolted on the inside. He went quickly up the ladder, slid back the bolts, and pushed up the hatch. He found himself staring at the tyres of a Chrysler New Yorker in a parking lot. Orienting himself, he figured he was at the back of the building. He closed the hatch and climbed down.

He left the pool machine room. As he walked along the corridor, a woman coming the other way gave him a hostile stare. He suffered a moment of anxiety: she might ask him what the hell he was doing hanging around the women's locker room. An altercation like that was not in his scenario. At this point it could spoil his plan. But her eyes lifted to his cap and took in the word SECURITY, and she looked away and turned into the locker room.

He grinned. He had bought the cap for $8.99 in a souvenir store. But people were used to seeing guards in jeans at rock concerts, detectives who looked like criminals until they flashed their badges, airport police in sweaters; it was too much trouble to question the credentials of every asshole who called himself a security guard.

He tried the door opposite the women's locker room. It opened into a small storeroom. He hit the light switch and closed the door behind him.

Obsolete gym equipment was stacked around him on racks: big black medicine balls, worn rubber mats, Indian clubs, mouldy boxing gloves, and splintered wooden folding chairs. There was a vaulting horse with burst upholstery and a broken leg. The room smelled musty. A large silver pipe ran along the ceiling, and he guessed it provided ventilation to the locker room across the corridor.

He reached up and tried the bolts that attached the pipe to what looked like a fan. He could not turn them with his fingers, but he had a wrench in the trunk of the Datsun. If he could detach the pipe, the fan would draw air from the storeroom instead of from the outside of the building.

He would make his fire just below the fan. He would get a can of gasoline and pour some into an empty Perrier bottle and bring it down here along with some matches and a newspaper for kindling and that wrench.

The fire would grow quickly and produce huge billows of smoke. He would tie a wet rag over his nose and mouth and wait until the storeroom was full of it. Then he would detach the ventilator pipe. The fumes would be drawn into the duct and pumped out into the women's locker room. At first no one would notice. Then one or two would sniff the air and say: 'Is someone smoking?' He would open the storeroom door and let the corridor fill with smoke. When the girls realized something was seriously wrong, they would open the locker room door and think the whole building was on fire, and they would all panic.

Then he would walk into the locker room. There would be a sea of brassieres and stockings, bare breasts and asses and pubic hair. Some would be running out of the showers, naked and wet, fumbling for towels; others would be trying to pull on clothes; most would be running around searching for the door, half blinded by smoke. There would be screams and sobs and shouts of fear. He would continue to pretend to be a security guard, and yell orders at them: 'Don't stop to dress! This is an emergency! Get out! The whole building is blazing! Run, run!' He would smack their bare asses, shove them around, snatch their clothes away, and feel them up. They would know something was badly wrong but most of them would be too crazy to figure it out. If the muscular hockey captain was still there she might have the presence of mind to challenge him, but he would just punch her out.

Walking around, he would select his main victim. She would be a pretty girl with a vulnerable look. He would take her arm, saying: 'This way, please, I'm with security.' He would lead her into the corridor then turn the wrong way, to the pool machine room. There, just when she thought she was on the way to safety, he would smack her face and punch her in the gut and throw her on the dirty concrete floor. He would watch her roll and turn and sit upright, gasping and sobbing and looking at him with terror in her eyes.

Then he would smile and unbuckle his belt.

CHAPTER TWO

Mrs Ferrami said: 'I want to go home.'

Her daughter Jeannie said: 'Don't you worry, Mom, we're going to get you out of here sooner than you think.'

Jeannie's younger sister, Patty, shot Jeannie a look that said: *How the hell do you think we're going to do that?*

The Bella Vista Sunset Home was all Mom's health insurance would pay for, and it was tawdry. The room contained two high hospital beds, two closets, a couch and a TV. The walls were painted mushroom brown and the flooring was a plastic tile, cream streaked with orange. The window had bars, but no curtains, and it looked out onto a gas station. There was a washbasin in the corner and a toilet down the hall.

'I want to go home,' Mom repeated.

Patty said: 'But Mom, you keep forgetting things, you can't take care of yourself any more.'

'Of course I can, don't you *dare* speak to me that way.'

Jeannie bit her lip. Looking at the wreck that used to be her mother, she wanted to cry. Mom had strong features: black eyebrows, dark eyes, a straight nose, a wide mouth and a strong chin. The same pattern was repeated in both Jeannie and Patty, although Mom was small and they were both tall like Daddy. All three of them were as strong-minded as their looks suggested: *formidable* was the word usually used to describe the Ferrami women. But Mom would never be formidable again. She had Alzheimer's.

She was not yet sixty. Jeannie, who was twenty-nine, and Patty, twenty-six, had hoped she could take care of herself for a few more years, but that hope had been shattered this morning at five a.m., when a Washington cop had called to say he had found Mom walking along 18th Street in a grubby nightdress, crying and saying she could not remember where she lived.

Jeannie had got in her car and driven to Washington, an hour from Baltimore on a quiet Sunday morning. She picked Mom up from the precinct house, took her home, got her washed and dressed then called Patty. Together the two sisters made arrangements for Mom to check into Bella Vista. It was in the town of Columbia, between Washington and Baltimore. Their Aunt Rosa had spent her declining years here. Aunt Rosa had had the same insurance policy as Mom.

'I don't like this place,' Mom said.

Jeannie said: 'We don't either, but right now it's all we can afford.' She intended to sound matter-of-fact and reasonable, but it came out harsh.

Patty shot her a reproving look and said: 'Come on, Mom, we've lived in worse places.'

It was true. After their father went to jail the second time, the two girls and Mom had lived in one room with a hotplate on the dresser and a water tap in the corridor. Those were the welfare years. But Mom had been a lioness in adversity. As soon as both Jeannie and Patty were in school she found a trustworthy older woman to mind the girls when they came home, she got a job—she had been a hairdresser, and she was still good, if old-fashioned—and she moved them to a small apartment with two bedrooms in Adams-Morgan, which was then a respectable working-class neighbourhood.

She would fix French toast for breakfast and send Jeannie and Patty to school in clean dresses, then do her hair and make up her face—you had to look smart, working in a salon—and always leave a spotless kitchen with a plate of cookies on the table for the girls when they came back. On Sundays the three of them cleaned the apartment and did the laundry together. Mom had always been so capable, so reliable, so tireless, it was heartbreaking to see the forgetful, complaining woman on the bed.

Now she frowned, as if puzzled, and said: 'Jeannie, why have you got a ring in your nose?'

Jeannie touched the delicate silver band and gave a wan smile. 'Mom, I had my nostril pierced when I was a kid. Don't you remember how mad you got about it? I thought you were going to throw me out on the street.'

'I forget things,' Mom said.

'I sure remember,' said Patty. 'I thought it was the greatest thing ever. But I was eleven and you were fourteen, and to me everything you did was bold and stylish and clever.'

'Maybe it was,' Jeannie said with mock vanity.

Patty giggled. 'The orange jacket sure wasn't.'

'Oh, God, that jacket. Mom finally burned it after I slept in it in an abandoned building and got fleas.'

'I remember that,' Mom said. 'Fleas! A child of mine!' She was still indignant about it, fifteen years later.

Suddenly the mood was lighter. Reminiscing had reminded them of how close they were. It was a good moment to leave. 'I'd better go,' Jeannie said, standing up.

'Me too,' said Patty. 'I have to make dinner.'

However, neither woman moved toward the door. Jeannie felt she was abandoning her mother, deserting her in a time of need. Nobody here loved her. She should have family to look after her. Jeannie and Patty should stay with her, and cook for her, and iron her nightdresses and turn the TV to her favourite show.

Mom said: 'When will I see you?'

Jeannie hesitated. She wanted to say, *Tomorrow, I'll bring you your breakfast and stay with you all day.* But it was impossible: she had a busy week at work. Guilt flooded her. *How can I be so cruel?*

Patty rescued her, saying: 'I'll come tomorrow, and bring the kids to see you, you'll like that.'

Mom was not going to let Jeannie get off that easily. 'Will you come too, Jeannie?'

Jeannie could hardly speak. 'As soon as I can.' Choking with grief, she leaned over the bed and kissed her mother. 'I love you, Mom. Try to remember that.'

The moment they were outside the door, Patty burst into tears.

Jeannie felt like crying too, but she was the older sister, and she had long ago gotten into the habit of controlling her own emotions while she took care of Patty. She put an arm around her sister's shoulders as they walked along the antiseptic corridor. Patty was not weak, but she was more accepting than Jeannie, who was combative and wilful. Mom always criticized Jeannie and said she should be more like Patty.

'I wish I could have her at home with me, but I can't,' Patty said woefully.

Jeannie agreed. Patty was married to a carpenter called Zip. They lived in a small row house with two bedrooms. The second bedroom was shared by her three boys. Davey was six, Mel four and Tom two. There was nowhere to put a grandma.

Jeannie was single. As an assistant professor at Jones Falls University she earned thirty thousand dollars a year—a lot less than Patty's husband, she guessed—and she had just taken out her first mortgage and bought a two-room apartment and furnished it on credit. One room was a living room with a kitchen nook, the other a bedroom with a closet and a tiny bathroom. If she gave Mom her bed she would have to sleep on the couch every night; and there was no one at home during the day to keep an eye on a woman with Alzheimer's. 'I can't take her either,' she said.

Patty showed anger through her tears. 'So why did you tell her we would get her out of there? We can't!'

They stepped outside into the torrid heat. Jeannie said: 'Tomorrow I'll go to the bank and get a loan. We'll put her in a better place and I'll top up the insurance money.'

'But how will you ever pay it back?' said Patty practically.

'I'll get promoted to associate professor, then full professor, and I'll be commissioned to write a textbook and get hired as a consultant by three international conglomerates.'

Patty smiled through her tears. 'I believe you, but will the bank?'

Patty had always believed in Jeannie. Patty herself had never been ambitious. She had been below average at school, and had married at nineteen and settled down to raise children without any apparent regrets. Jeannie was the opposite. Top of the class and captain of all sports teams, she had been a tennis champion and had put herself through college on sports scholarships. Whatever she said she was going to do, Patty never doubted her.

But Patty was right, the bank would not make another loan so soon after financing the purchase of her apartment. And she had only just started as assistant professor: it would be three years before she was considered for promotion. As they reached the parking lot Jeannie said desperately: 'Okay, I'll sell my car.'

She loved her car. It was a twenty-year-old Mercedes 230C, a red two-door sedan with black leather seats. She had bought it eight years ago, with her prize money for winning the Mayfair Lites College Tennis Challenge, five thousand dollars. That was before it became chic to own an old Mercedes. 'It's probably worth double what I paid for it,' she said.

'But you'd have to buy another car,' Patty said, still remorselessly realistic.

'You're right.' Jeannie sighed. 'Well, I can do some private tutoring. It's against JFU's rules, but I can probably get forty dollars an hour teaching remedial statistics one-on-one with rich students who have flunked the exam at other universities. I could pick up three hundred dollars a week, maybe; tax free if I don't declare it.' She looked her sister in the eye. 'Can you spare anything?'

Patty looked away. 'I don't know.'

'Zip makes more than I do.'

'He'll kill me for saying this, but we might be able to chip in seventy-five or eighty a week,' Patty said at last. 'I'll get him to put in for a raise. He's kind of timid about asking, but I know he deserves it, and his boss likes him.'

Jeannie began to feel more cheerful, although the prospect of spending her Sundays teaching backward undergraduates was dismal. 'For an extra four hundred a week we might get Mom a room to herself with her own bathroom.'

'Then she could have more of her things about her, ornaments and maybe some furniture from the apartment.'

'Let's ask around, see if anyone knows of a nice place.'

'Okay.' Patty was thoughtful. 'Mom's illness is inherited, isn't it? I saw something on TV.'

Jeannie nodded. 'There's a gene defect, AD3, that's linked to early-onset Alzheimer's.' It was located at chromosome 14q24.3, Jeannie recalled, but that would not mean anything to Patty.

'Does that mean you and I will finish up like Mom?'

'It means there's a good chance we will.'

They were both silent for a moment. The thought of losing your mind was almost too grim to talk about.

'I'm glad I had my children young,' Patty said. 'They'll be old enough to look after themselves by the time it happens to me.'

Jeannie noted the hint of reproof. Like Mom, Patty thought there was something wrong with being twenty-nine and childless. Jeannie said: 'The fact that they've found the gene is also hopeful. It means that by the time we're Mom's age, they may be able to inject us with an altered version of our own DNA that doesn't have the fatal gene.'

'They mentioned that on TV. Recombinant DNA technology, right?'

Jeannie grinned at her sister. 'Right.'

'See, I'm not so dumb.'

'I never thought you were dumb.'

Patty said thoughtfully: 'The thing is, our DNA makes us what we are, so if you change my DNA, does that make me a different person?'

'It's not just your DNA that makes you what you are. It's your upbringing too. That's what my work is all about.'

'How's the new job going?'

'It's exciting. This is my big chance, Patty. A lot of people read the article I wrote about criminality and whether it's in our genes.' The article, published last year while she was still at the University of Minnesota, had borne the name of her supervising professor above her own, but she had done the work.

'I could never figure out whether you said criminality is inherited or not.'

'I identified four inherited traits that *lead* to criminal behaviour: impulsiveness, fearlessness, aggression and hyperactivity. But my big theory is that certain ways of raising children counteract those traits and turn potential criminals into good citizens.'

'How could you ever prove a thing like that?'

'By studying identical twins raised apart. Identical twins have the same DNA. And when they're adopted at birth, or split up for some other reason, they get raised differently. So I look for pairs of twins where one is a criminal and the other is normal. Then I study how they were raised and what their parents did differently.'

'Your work is really important,' Patty said.

'I think so.'

'We *have* to find out why so many Americans nowadays turn bad.'

Jeannie nodded. That was it, in a nutshell.

Patty turned to her own car, a big old Ford station wagon, the back full of brightly coloured kiddie junk: a tricycle, a folded-down stroller, an assortment of rackets and balls, and a big toy truck with a broken wheel.

Jeannie said: 'Give the boys a big kiss from me, okay?'

'Thanks. I'll call you tomorrow after I see Mom.'

Jeannie got her keys out, hesitated, then went over to Patty and hugged her. 'I love you, Sis,' she said.

'Love you, too.'

Jeannie got in her car and drove away.

She felt jangled and restless, full of unresolved feelings about Mom and Patty and the father who was not there. She got on I-70 and drove too fast, weaving in and out of the traffic. She wondered what to do with the rest of the day, then remembered that she was supposed to play tennis at six then go for beer and pizza with a group of graduate students and young faculty from the psychology department at Jones Falls. Her first thought was to cancel the entire evening. But she did not want to sit at home brooding. She would play tennis, she decided: the vigorous exercise would make her feel better. Afterwards she would go to Andy's Bar for an hour or so, then have an early night.

But it did not work out that way.

*

Her tennis opponent was Jack Budgen, the university's head librarian. He had once played at Wimbledon and, though he was now bald and fifty, he was still fit, and all the old craft was there. Jeannie had never been to Wimbledon. The height of her career had been a place on the US Olympic tennis team while she was an undergraduate. But she was stronger and faster than Jack.

They played on one of the red clay tennis courts on the Jones Falls campus. They were evenly matched, and the game attracted a small crowd of spectators. There was no dress code, but out of habit Jeannie always played in crisp white shorts and a white polo shirt. She had long dark hair, not silky and straight like Patty's but curly and unmanageable, so she tucked it up inside a peaked cap.

Jeannie's serve was dynamite and her two-handed cross-court backhand smash was a killer. There was not much Jack could do about the serve, but after the first few games he made sure she did not get many chances to use the backhand smash. He played a sly game, conserving his energy, letting Jeannie make mistakes. She played too aggressively, serving double faults and running to the net too early. On a normal day, she reckoned, she could beat him; but today her concentration was shot, and she could not second-guess his game. They won a set each, then the third went to 5–4 in his favour and she found herself serving to stay in the match.

The game went to two deuces, then Jack won a point and the advantage was to him. Jeannie served into the net, and there was an audible gasp from the little crowd. Instead of a normal, slower second service, she threw caution to the winds and served again as if it was a first service. Jack just got his racket to the ball and returned it to her backhand. She smashed it and ran to the net. But Jack was not as off-balance as he had pretended to be, and he returned a perfect lob that sailed over her head and landed on the back line to win the match.

Jeannie stood looking at the ball, hands on her hips, furious with herself. Although she had not played seriously for years, she retained the unyielding competitiveness that made it hard to lose. Then she calmed her feelings and put a smile on her face. She turned around. 'Beautiful shot!' she called. She walked to the net and shook his hand, and there was a ragged round of applause from the spectators.

A young man approached her. 'Hey, that was a great game!' he said with a broad smile.

Jeannie took him in at a glance. He was a hunk: tall and athletic, with curly fair hair cut short, and nice blue eyes, and he was coming on to her for all he was worth.

She was not in the mood. 'Thanks,' she said curtly.

He smiled again, a confident, relaxed smile that said most girls were happy when he talked to them, regardless of whether he was making any sense. 'You know, I play a little tennis myself, and I was thinking—'

'If you only play a *little* tennis, you're probably not in my league,' she said, and she brushed past him.

Behind her, she heard him say in a good-humoured tone: 'Should I assume that a romantic dinner followed by a night of passion is out of the question, then?'

She could not help smiling, if only at his persistence, and she had been ruder than necessary. She turned her head and spoke over her shoulder without stopping. 'Yes, but thanks for the offer,' she said.

She left the court and headed for the locker room. She wondered what Mom was doing now. She must have had dinner by this time: it was seven thirty, and they always fed people early in institutions. She was probably watching TV in the lounge. Maybe she would find a friend, a woman of her own age who would tolerate her forgetfulness and take an interest in her photographs of her grandchildren. Mom had once had a lot of friends—the other women at the salon, some of her customers, neighbours, people she had known for twenty-five years—but it was hard for them to keep up the friendship when Mom kept forgetting who the hell they were.

As she was passing the hockey pitch she ran into Lisa Hoxton. Lisa was the first real friend she had made since arriving at Jones Falls a month ago. She was a technician in the psychology laboratory. She had a science degree but did not want to be an academic. Like Jeannie, she came from a poor background, and was a little intimidated by the Ivy League hauteur of Jones Falls. They had taken to one another instantly.

'A *kid* just tried to pick me up,' Jeannie said with a smile.

'What was he like?'

'He looked like Brad Pitt, but taller.'

'Did you tell him you had a friend more his age?' Lisa said. She was twenty-four.

'No.' Jeannie glanced over her shoulder, but the man was nowhere in sight. 'Keep walking, in case he follows me.'

'How could that be bad?'

'Come on.'

'Jeannie, it's the creepy ones you run away from.'

'Knock it off!'

'You might have given him my phone number.'

'I should have handed him a slip of paper with your bra size on it, that would have done the trick.' Lisa had a big bust.

Lisa stopped walking. For a moment Jeannie thought

she had gone too far, and offended Lisa. She began to frame an apology. Then Lisa said: 'What a great idea! *I'm a 36D, for more information call this number.* It's so subtle, too.'

'I'm just envious, I always wanted hooters,' Jeannie said, and they both giggled. 'It's true, though, I prayed for tits. I was practically the last girl in my class to get my period, it was so embarrassing.'

'You actually said *Dear God, please make my tits grow,* kneeling beside your bed?'

'Actually I prayed to the Virgin Mary, I figured it was a girl thing. And I didn't say tits, of course.'

'What did you say, breasts?'

'No, I figured you couldn't say breasts to the Holy Mother.'

'So what did you call them?'

'Bristols.'

Lisa burst out laughing.

'I don't know where I got that word from, I must have overheard some men talking. It seemed like a polite euphemism to me. I never told anyone that before in my life.'

Lisa looked back. 'Well, I don't see any good-looking guys following us. I guess we shook off Brad Pitt.'

'It's a good thing. He's just my type: handsome, sexy, over-confident and totally untrustworthy.'

'How do you know he's untrustworthy? You only met him for twenty seconds.'

'All men are untrustworthy.'

'You're probably right. Are you coming to Andy's tonight?'

'Yeah, just for an hour or so. I have to shower first.' Her shirt was wet through with perspiration.

'Me too.' Lisa was in shorts and running shoes. 'I've been training with the hockey team. Why only for an hour?'

'I've had a heavy day.' The game had distracted Jeannie, but now she winced as the agony came flooding back. 'I had to put my mom into a home.'

'Oh, Jeannie, I'm sorry.'

Jeannie told her the story as they entered the gymnasium building and went down the stairs to the basement. In the locker room Jeannie caught sight of their reflection in the mirror. They were so different in appearance that they almost looked like a comedy act. Lisa was a little below average height, and Jeannie was almost six feet. Lisa was blonde and curvy, whereas Jeannie was dark and muscular. Lisa had a pretty face, with a scatter of freckles across a pert little nose, and a mouth like a bow. Most people described Jeannie as striking, and men sometimes told her she was beautiful, but nobody ever called her pretty.

As they climbed out of their sweaty sports clothes Lisa said: 'What about your father? You didn't mention him.'

Jeannie sighed. It was the question she had learned to dread, even as a little girl; but it invariably came, sooner or later. For many years she had lied, saying Daddy was dead or disappeared or remarried and gone to work in Saudi Arabia. Lately, however, she had been telling the truth. 'My father's in jail,' she said.

'Oh, my God. I shouldn't have asked.'

'It's okay. He's been in jail most of my life. He's a burglar. This is his third term.'

'How long is his sentence?'

'I don't remember. It doesn't matter. He'll be no use when he comes out. He's never looked after us and he's not about to begin.'

'Did he never have a regular job?'

'Only when he wanted to case a joint. He would work as janitor, doorman, security guard for a week or two before robbing the place.'

Lisa looked at her shrewdly. 'Is that why you're so interested in the genetics of criminality?'

'Maybe.'

'Probably not.' Lisa made a tossing-aside gesture. 'I hate amateur psychoanalysis anyway.'

They went to the showers. Jeannie took longer, washing her hair. She was grateful for Lisa's friendship. Lisa had been at Jones Falls just over a year, and she had shown Jeannie around when she arrived here at the beginning of the semester. Jeannie liked working with Lisa in the lab because she was completely reliable; and she liked hanging out with her after work because she felt she could say whatever came into her mind without fear of shocking her.

Jeannie was working conditioner into her hair when she heard strange noises. She stopped and listened. It sounded like squeals of fright. A chill of anxiety passed through her, making her shiver. Suddenly she felt very vulnerable: naked, wet, underground. She hesitated, then quickly rinsed her hair before stepping out of the shower to see what was going on.

She smelled burning as soon as she got out from under the water. She could not see a fire, but there were thick clouds of black and grey smoke close to the ceiling. It seemed to be coming through the ventilators.

She felt afraid. She had never been in a fire.

The more cool-headed women were snatching up their bags and heading for the door. Others were getting hysterical, shouting at one another in frightened voices and running here and there pointlessly. Some asshole of a security man, with a spotted handkerchief tied over his nose and mouth, was making them more scared by walking up and down shoving people and yelling orders.

Jeannie knew she should not stay to get dressed, but she could not bring herself to walk out of the building naked. There was fear running through her veins like ice water, but she made herself calm. She found her locker. Lisa was nowhere to be seen. She grabbed her clothes, stepped into her jeans and pulled her T-shirt over her head.

It took only a few seconds, but in that time the room emptied of people and filled with fumes. She could no longer see the doorway and she started to cough. The thought of not being able to breathe scared her. I know where the door is, and I just have to keep calm, she told herself. Her keys and money were in her jeans pockets. She picked up her tennis racket. Holding her breath, she walked quickly through the lockers to the exit.

The corridor was thick with smoke, and her eyes began to water so that she was almost blind. Now she wished to heaven that she had gone naked and gained a few precious seconds. Her jeans did not help her see or breathe in this fog of fumes. And it did not matter being naked if you were dead.

She kept one shaky hand on the wall to give her a sense of direction as she rushed along the passage, still holding her breath. She thought she might bump into other women but they all seemed to have got out ahead of her. When there was no more wall, she knew she was in the small lobby, although she could not see anything but clouds of smoke. The stairs had to be straight ahead. She crossed the lobby and crashed into the Coke machine. Was the staircase to the left now, or the right? The left, she thought. She moved that way, then came up against the door to the men's locker room and realized she had made the wrong choice.

She could not hold her breath any longer. With a groan she sucked in air. It was mostly smoke, and it made her cough convulsively. She staggered back along the wall, racked with coughing, her nostrils burning, eyes streaming, barely able to see her own hands in front of her. With all her being she longed for one breath of the air she had been taking for granted for twenty-nine years. She followed the wall to the Coke machine and stepped around it. She knew she had found the staircase when she tripped over the bottom step. She dropped her racket and it slid out of sight. It was a special one—she had won the Mayfair Lites Challenge with it—but she left it behind and scrambled up the stairs on hands and knees.

The smoke thinned suddenly when she reached the spacious ground-floor lobby. She could see the building doors, which were open. A security guard stood just outside, beckoning her and yelling: 'Come on!' Coughing and choking, she staggered across the lobby and out into the blessed fresh air.

She stood on the steps for two or three minutes, bent double, gulping air and coughing the smoke out of her lungs. As her breathing at last began to return to normal, she heard the whoop of an emergency vehicle in the distance. She looked around for Lisa but could not see her.

Surely she could not be inside? Still feeling shaky, Jeannie moved through the crowd, scanning the faces. Now that they were out of danger, there was a good deal of nervous laughter. Most of the students were more or less undressed, so there was a curiously intimate atmosphere. Those who had managed to save their bags were lending spare clothes to others less fortunate. Naked women were grateful for their friends' soiled and sweaty T-shirts. Several people were dressed only in towels.

Lisa was not in the crowd. With mounting anxiety Jeannie returned to the security guard at the door. 'I think my girlfriend may be in there,' she said, hearing the tremor of fear in her own voice.

'I ain't going after her,' he said quickly.

'Brave man,' Jeannie snapped. She was not sure what she wanted him to do but she had not expected him to be completely useless.

Resentment showed on his face. 'That's their job,' he said, and he pointed to a fire truck coming down the road.

Jeannie was beginning to fear for Lisa's life, but she did not know what to do. She watched, impatient and helpless, as the firemen got out of the truck and put on breathing apparatus. They seemed to move so slowly that she wanted to shake them and scream: 'Hurry, hurry!' Another fire truck arrived, then a white police cruiser with the blue-and-silver stripe of the Baltimore Police Department.

As the firemen dragged a hose into the building, an officer buttonholed the lobby guard and said: 'Where do you think it started?'

'Women's locker room,' the guard told him.

'And where is that, exactly?'

'Basement, at the back.'

'How many exits are there from the basement?'

'Only one, the staircase up to the main lobby, right here.'

A maintenance man standing nearby contradicted him. 'There's a ladder in the pool machine room that leads up to an access hatch at the back of the building.'

Jeannie caught the officer's attention and said: 'I think my friend may be inside there still.'

'Man or woman?'

'Woman of twenty-four, short, blonde.'

'If she's there, we'll find her.'

For a moment Jeannie felt reassured. Then she realized he had not promised to find her alive.

The security man who had been in the locker room was nowhere to be seen. Jeannie said to the fire officer: 'There was another guard down there, I don't see him anywhere. Tall guy.'

The lobby guard said: 'Ain't no other security personnel in the building.'

'Well, he had a hat with SECURITY written on it, and he was telling people to evacuate the building.'

'I don't care what he had on his hat—'

'Oh, for Pete's sake, stop arguing!' Jeannie snapped. 'Maybe I imagined him, but if not his life could be in danger!'

Standing listening to them was a girl wearing a man's khaki pants rolled up at the cuffs. 'I saw that guy, he's a real creep,' she said. 'He felt me up.'

The fire officer said: 'Keep calm, we'll find everyone. Thank you for your cooperation.' He walked off.

Jeannie glared at the lobby guard for a moment. She felt the fire officer had dismissed her as a hysterical woman because she had yelled at the guard. She turned away in disgust. What was she going to do now? The firemen ran inside in their helmets and boots. She was barefoot and wearing a T-shirt. If she tried to go in with them they would throw her out. She clenched her fists, distraught. Think, think! Where else could Lisa be?

The gymnasium was next door to the Ruth W. Acorn Psychology Building, named after the wife of a benefactor but known, even to faculty, as Nut House. Could Lisa have gone in there? The doors would be locked, on Sunday, but she probably had a key. She might have run inside to find a laboratory coat to cover herself, or just to sit at her desk and recover. Jeannie decided to check. Anything was better than standing here doing nothing.

She dashed across the lawn to the main entrance of

Nut House and looked through the glass doors. There was no one in the lobby. She took from her pocket the plastic card that served as a key and swiped it through the card reader. The door opened. She ran up the stairs, calling: 'Lisa! Are you there?' The laboratory was deserted. Lisa's chair was neatly tucked under her desk and her computer screen was a grey blank. Jeannie tried the women's restroom at the end of the corridor. Nothing. 'Damn!' she said frantically. 'Where the hell are you?'

Panting, she hurried back outside. She decided to make a tour of the gymnasium building in case Lisa was just sitting on the ground somewhere catching her breath. She ran around the side of the building, passing through a yard full of giant garbage cans. At the back was a small parking lot. She saw a figure jogging along the footpath, heading away. It was too tall to be Lisa and she was pretty sure it was a man. She thought it might be the missing security guard, but he disappeared around the corner of the Student Union before she could be sure.

She continued around the building. At the far side was the running track, deserted now. Coming full circle, she arrived at the front of the gym.

The crowd was bigger, and there were more fire engines and police cars, but she still could not see Lisa. It seemed almost certain that she was still in the burning building. A sense of doom crept over Jeannie, and she fought it. *You can't just let this happen!*

She spotted the fire officer she had spoken to earlier. She grabbed his arm. 'I'm almost certain Lisa Hoxton is in there,' she said urgently. 'I've looked everywhere for her.'

He gave her a hard look and seemed to decide she was reliable. Without answering her, he put a two-way radio to his mouth. 'Look out for a young white female believed to be inside the building, named Lisa, repeat Lisa.'

'Thank you,' Jeannie said.

He nodded curtly and strode away.

Jeannie was glad he had listened to her but still she could not rest. Lisa might be stuck in there, locked in a toilet or trapped by flames, screaming for help unheard; or she might have fallen and struck her head and knocked herself out, or succumbed to the fumes, and be lying unconscious with the fire creeping closer by the second.

Jeannie remembered the maintenance man saying there was another entrance to the basement. She had not seen it as she ran around the outside of the gym. She decided to look again. She returned to the back of the building.

She saw it immediately. The hatch was set into the ground close to the building, partly hidden by a grey Chrysler New Yorker. The steel trapdoor was open, leaning against the building wall. Jeannie knelt by the square hole and leaned down to look inside.

A ladder led down to a dirty room lit by fluorescent tubes. She could see machinery and lots of pipes. There were wisps of smoke in the air, but not thick clouds: it must be closed off from the rest of the basement. Nevertheless the smell of the smoke reminded her of how she had coughed and choked as she searched blindly for the staircase, and she felt her heart beat faster at the memory.

'Is anybody there?' she called.

She thought she heard a sound but she could not be sure. She shouted louder. 'Hello?' There was no reply.

She hesitated. The sensible thing to do would be to return to the front of the building and grab a fireman, but that could take too long, especially if the fireman decided to question her. The alternative was to go down the ladder and take a look.

The thought of re-entering the building made her legs weak. Her chest still hurt from the violent spasms of coughing caused by the smoke. But Lisa might be down there, hurt and unable to move, or trapped by a fallen timber, or just passed out. She had to look.

She steeled her nerve and put a foot on the ladder. Her knees felt weak and she almost fell. She hesitated. After a moment she felt stronger, and she took a step down. Then a breath of smoke caught in her throat, making her cough, and she climbed out again.

When she had stopped coughing, she tried again.

She went down one rung, then two. If the smoke makes me cough, I'll just come right out again, she told herself. The third step was easier, and after that she went down quickly, jumping off the last rung on to the concrete floor.

She found herself in a big room full of pumps and filters, presumably for the swimming pool. The smell of smoke was strong, but she could breathe normally.

She saw Lisa right away, and the sight made her gasp.

She was lying on her side, curled up in the foetal position, naked. There was a smear of what looked like blood on her thigh. She was not moving.

For a moment Jeannie was rigid with fear.

She tried to get hold of herself. 'Lisa!' she shouted. She heard the shrill overtone of hysteria in her own voice, and took a breath to keep calm. *Please, God, let her be all right.* She made her way across the room, through the tangle of pipework, and knelt beside her friend. 'Lisa?'

Lisa opened her eyes.

'Thank God,' Jeannie said. 'I thought you were dead.'

Slowly Lisa sat up. She would not look at Jeannie. Her lips were bruised. 'He . . . he raped me,' she said.

Jeannie's relief at finding her alive was replaced by a sick feeling of horror that gripped her heart. 'My God. Here?'

Lisa nodded. 'He said this was the way out.'

Jeannie closed her eyes. She felt Lisa's pain and humiliation, the sense of being invaded and violated and soiled. Tears came to her eyes and she held them back fiercely. For a moment she was too weak and nauseated to say anything.

Then she tried to pull herself together. 'Who was he?'

'A security guy.'

'With a spotted scarf over his face?'

'He took it off.' Lisa turned away. 'He kept smiling.'

It figured. The girl in khaki pants had said a security guard felt her up. The lobby guard was sure there were no other security people in the building. 'He was no security guard,' Jeannie said. She had seen him jogging away just a few minutes ago. A wave of rage swept over her at the thought that he had done this dreadful thing right here, on the campus, in the gymnasium building, where they all felt safe to take off their clothes and shower. It made her hands shake, and she wanted to chase after him and strangle him.

She heard loud noises: men shouting, heavy footsteps and the rush of water. The firemen were operating their hoses. 'Listen, we're in danger here,' she said urgently. 'We have to get out of this building.'

Lisa's voice was a dull monotone. 'I don't have any clothes.'

We could die in here! 'Don't worry about clothes, everyone's half naked out there.' Jeannie scanned the room hastily and saw Lisa's red lace brassiere and panties in a dusty heap beneath a tank. She picked them up. 'Put your underwear on. It's dirty, but it's better than nothing.'

Lisa remained sitting on the floor, staring vacantly.

Jeannie fought down a feeling of panic. What could she do if Lisa refused to move? She could probably lift Lisa, but could she carry her up that ladder? She raised her voice. 'Come on, get up!' Taking Lisa's hands she pulled her to her feet.

At last Lisa met her eyes. 'Jeannie, it was horrible,' she said.

Jeannie put her arms around Lisa's shoulders and hugged her hard. 'I'm sorry, Lisa, I'm so sorry,' she said.

The smoke was becoming more dense, despite the heavy door. Fear replaced pity in her heart. 'We have to get out of here—the place is burning down. For God's sake put these on!'

At last Lisa began to move. She pulled up her panties and fastened her bra. Jeannie took her hand and led her to the ladder on the wall, then made her go up first. As Jeannie followed, the door crashed open and a fireman entered in a cloud of smoke. Water swirled around his boots. He looked startled to see them. 'We're all right, we're getting out this way,' Jeannie yelled to him. Then she went up the ladder after Lisa.

A moment later they were outside in the fresh air.

Jeannie felt weak with relief: she had got Lisa out of the fire. But now Lisa needed help. Jeannie put an arm around her shoulders and led her to the front of the building. There were fire trucks and police cruisers parked every which way across the road. Most of the women in the crowd had now found something with which to cover their nakedness, and Lisa was conspicuous in her red underwear. 'Does anyone have a spare pair of pants, or anything at all?' Jeannie begged as they made their way through the crowd. People had given away all their spare clothing. Jeannie would have given Lisa her own sweatshirt, but she had no bra on underneath.

Finally a tall black man took off his button-down and gave it to Lisa. 'I'll want it back, it's a Ralph Lauren,' he said. 'Mitchell Waterfield, math department.'

'I'll remember,' Jeannie said gratefully.

Lisa put the shirt on. She was short, and it reached to her knees.

Jeannie felt she was getting the nightmare under control. She steered Lisa to the emergency vehicles. Three cops stood leaning against a cruiser, doing nothing. Jeannie spoke to the oldest of the three, a fat white man with a grey moustache. 'This woman's name is Lisa Hoxton. She's been raped.'

She expected them to be electrified by the news that a major crime had been committed, but their reaction was surprisingly casual. They took a few seconds to digest the information, and Jeannie was getting ready to snap at them, when the one with the moustache levered himself off the hood of the car and said: 'Where did this happen?'

'The basement of the burning building, in the pool machine room at the back.'

One of the others, a young black man, said: 'Those firemen will be hosing away the evidence right now, Sarge.'

'You're right,' the older man replied. 'You better get down there, Lenny, and secure the crime scene.' Lenny hurried away. The sergeant turned to Lisa. 'Do you know the man who did this, Ms Hoxton?' he said.

Lisa shook her head.

Jeannie said: 'He's a tall white man wearing a red baseball cap with the word SECURITY on the front. I saw him in the women's locker room soon after the fire broke out, and I think I saw him running away just before I found Lisa.'

The cop reached into the car and pulled out a radio microphone. He spoke into it for a while then hung it up again. 'If he's dumb enough to keep the hat on we may catch him,' he said. He spoke to the third cop. 'McHenty, take the victim to hospital.'

McHenty was a young white man with spectacles. He said to Lisa: 'You want to sit in the front or the back?'

Lisa said nothing but looked apprehensive.

Jeannie helped her out. 'Sit in the front, you don't want to look like a suspect.'

A terrified look crossed Lisa's face and she spoke at last. 'Aren't you coming with me?'

'I will if you like,' Jeannie said reassuringly. 'Or I could swing by my apartment and pick up some clothes for you, and meet you at the hospital.'

Lisa looked at McHenty worriedly.

Jeannie said: 'You'll be all right now, Lisa.'

McHenty held open the door of the cruiser and Lisa got in.

'Which hospital?' Jeannie asked him.

'Santa Teresa.' He got in the car.

'I'll be there in a few minutes,' Jeannie called through the glass as the car sped away.

She jogged to the faculty parking lot, already regretting that she had not gone with Lisa. Her expression as she left had been frightened and wretched. Of course she needed clean clothes, but maybe she had a more urgent need for another woman to stay with her and hold her hand and reassure her. Probably the last thing she wanted was to be left alone with a macho man with a gun. As she jumped into her car Jeannie felt she had screwed up. 'Jesus, what a day,' she said as she tore out of the parking lot.

She lived not far from the campus. Her apartment was the upper storey of a small row house. Jeannie double-parked and ran inside.

She washed her hands and face hurriedly then threw on some clean clothes. She thought for a moment about which of her clothes would fit Lisa's short, rounded figure. She pulled out an oversize polo shirt and a pair of sweatpants with an elastic waistband. Underwear was more difficult. She found a baggy pair of man's boxer shorts that might do, but none of her bras would fit. Lisa would have to go without. She added deck shoes, stuffed everything into a duffel, and ran out again.

As she drove to the hospital her mood changed. Since the fire broke out she had been focused on what she had to do: now she began to feel enraged. Lisa was a happy, garrulous woman, but the shock and horror of what had happened had turned her into a zombie, frightened to get into a police car on her own.

Driving along a shopping street, Jeannie started to look for the guy in the red cap, imagining that if she saw him she would swing the car up on the sidewalk and run him down. But in fact she would not recognize him. He must have taken off the bandanna, and probably the hat too. What else had he been wearing? It shocked her to realize she could hardly remember.

Some kind of T-shirt, she thought, with blue jeans or maybe shorts. Anyway, he might have changed his clothes by now, as she had.

In fact it could be any tall white man on the street: that pizza delivery boy in the red coat; the bald guy walking to church with his wife, hymn books under their arms; the handsome bearded man carrying a guitar case; even the cop talking to a bum outside the liquor store. There was nothing Jeannie could do with her rage and she gripped the steering wheel tighter until her knuckles turned white.

Santa Teresa was a big suburban hospital near the northern city limits. Jeannie left her car in the parking lot and found the emergency room. Lisa was already in bed, wearing a hospital gown and staring into space. A TV set with the sound off was showing the Emmy awards ceremony: hundreds of Hollywood celebrities in evening dress drinking champagne and congratulating one another. McHenty sat beside the bed with his notebook on his knee.

Jeannie put down the duffel. 'Here are your clothes. What's happening?'

Lisa remained expressionless and silent. She was still in shock, Jeannie figured. She was suppressing her feelings, fighting to stay in control. But at some point she had to show her rage. There would be an explosion sooner or later.

McHenty said: 'I have to take down the basic details of the case, Miss—would you excuse us for a few more minutes?'

'Oh, sure,' Jeannie said apologetically. Then she

caught a look from Lisa and hesitated. A few minutes ago she had been cursing herself for leaving Lisa alone with a man. Now she was about to do it again. 'On the other hand,' she said, 'maybe Lisa would prefer me to stay.' Her instinct was confirmed when Lisa gave a barely perceptible nod. Jeannie sat on the bed and took Lisa's hand.

McHenty looked irritated but he did not argue. 'I was asking Miss Hoxton about how she tried to resist the assault,' he said. 'Did you scream, Lisa?'

'Once, when he threw me on the floor,' she said in a low voice. 'Then he pulled the knife.'

McHenty's voice was matter-of-fact, and he looked down at his notebook as he spoke. 'Did you try to fight him off?'

She shook her head. 'I was afraid he would cut me.'

'So you really didn't put up any resistance after that first scream?'

She shook her head and began to cry. Jeannie squeezed her hand. She wanted to say to McHenty, *What the hell was she supposed to do?* But she kept silent. Already today she had been rude to a boy who looked like Brad Pitt, made a bitchy remark about Lisa's boobs and snapped at the lobby guard in the gym. She knew she was not good at dealing with authority figures and she was determined not to make an enemy of this policeman, who was only trying to do his job.

McHenty went on: 'Just before he penetrated you, did he force your legs apart?'

Jeannie winced. Surely they should have female cops to ask these questions?

Lisa said: 'He touched my thigh with the point of the knife.'

'Did he cut you?'

'No.'

'So you opened your legs voluntarily.'

Jeannie said: 'If a suspect pulls a weapon on a cop, you generally shoot him down, don't you? Do you call that *voluntary*?'

McHenty gave her an angry look. 'Please leave this to me, miss.' He turned back to Lisa. 'Do you have any injuries at all?'

'I'm bleeding, yes.'

'Is that as a result of the forced intercourse?'

'Yes.'

'Where are you injured, exactly?'

Jeannie could not stand it any longer. 'Why don't we let the doctor establish that?'

He looked at her as if she were stupid. 'I have to make the preliminary report.'

'Then let it say she has internal injuries as a result of the rape.'

'I'm conducting this interview.'

'And I'm telling you to back off, mister,' Jeannie said, controlling the urge to scream at him. 'My friend is in distress and I don't think she needs to describe her internal injuries to you when she's going to be examined by a doctor any second now.'

McHenty looked furious but he moved on. 'I noticed you had on red lace underwear. Do you think that had any effect on what happened?'

Lisa looked away, her eyes full of tears.

Jeannie said: 'If I reported my red Mercedes stolen, would you ask me whether I had provoked the theft by driving such an attractive car?'

McHenty ignored her. 'Do you think you might have met the perpetrator before, Lisa?'

'No.'

'But the smoke must have made it difficult for you to see clearly. And he wore a scarf of some kind over his face.'

'At first I was practically blind. But there wasn't much smoke in the room where . . . he did it. I saw him.' She nodded to herself. 'I saw him.'

'So you would recognize him if you saw him again.'

Lisa shuddered. 'Oh, yes.'

'But you've never seen him before, like in a bar or anything.'

'No.'

'Do you go to bars, Lisa?'

'Sure.'

'Singles bars, that kind of thing?'

Jeannie boiled over. 'What the *hell* kind of question is that?'

'The kind defence lawyers ask,' McHenty said.

'Lisa isn't on trial—she's not the perpetrator, she's the victim!'

'Were you a virgin, Lisa?'

Jeannie stood up. 'Okay, that's enough. I do not believe this is supposed to happen. You're not supposed to ask these invasive questions.'

McHenty raised his voice. 'I'm trying to establish her credibility.'

'One hour after she was violated? Forget it!'

'I'm doing my job—'

'I don't believe you know your job. I don't think you know shit, McHenty.'

Before he could reply, a doctor walked in without knocking. He was young and looked harassed and tired. 'Is this the rape?' he said.

'This is Ms Lisa Hoxton,' Jeannie said icily. 'Yes, she was raped.'

'I'll need a vaginal swab.'

He was charmless, but at least he provided an excuse to get rid of McHenty. Jeannie looked at the cop. He stayed put, as if he thought he was going to supervise the taking of the swab. She said: 'Before you do that, doctor, perhaps Patrolman McHenty will excuse us?'

The doctor paused, looking at McHenty. The cop shrugged and went out.

The doctor pulled the sheet off Lisa with an abrupt gesture. 'Lift your gown and spread your legs,' he said.

Lisa began to cry.

Jeannie could hardly believe it. What was it with these men? 'Excuse me, sir,' she said to the doctor.

He glared at her impatiently. 'Have you got a problem?'

'Could you please try to be a little more polite?'

He reddened. 'This hospital is full of people with traumatic injuries and life-threatening illnesses,' he said. 'Right now in the emergency room there are three children who have been in a car wreck, and they're all going to die. And you're complaining that I'm not being *polite* to a girl who got into bed with the wrong man?'

Jeannie was flabbergasted. 'Got into bed with the wrong man?' she repeated.

Lisa sat upright. 'I want to go home,' she said.

'That sounds like a hell of a good idea,' Jeannie said. She unzipped her duffel and began to put the clothes out on the bed.

The doctor was dumbstruck for a moment. Then he said angrily: 'Do as you please.' He went out.

Jeannie and Lisa looked at one another. 'I can't believe that happened,' Jeannie said.

'Thank God they've gone,' Lisa said, and she got out of bed.

Jeannie helped her take off the hospital gown. Lisa pulled on the fresh clothes quickly and stepped into the shoes. 'I'll drive you home,' Jeannie said.

'Would you sleep over at my apartment?' Lisa said. 'I don't want to be alone tonight.'

'Sure. I'll be glad to.'

McHenty was waiting outside. He seemed less confident. Perhaps he knew he had handled the interview badly. 'I still have a few more questions,' he said.

Jeannie spoke quietly and calmly. 'We're leaving,' she said. 'Lisa is too upset to answer questions right now.'

He was almost scared. 'She has to,' he said. 'She's made a complaint.'

Lisa said: 'I wasn't raped. It was all a mistake. I just want to go home now.'

'You realize it's an offence to make a false allegation?'

Jeannie said angrily: 'This woman is not a criminal—she's the victim of a crime. If your boss asks why she's withdrawing the complaint, say it's because she was brutally harassed by Patrolman McHenty of the Baltimore Police Department. Now I'm taking her home. Excuse us, please.' She put her arm around Lisa's shoulders and steered her past the cop toward the exit.

As they left she heard him mutter: 'What did I do?'

CHAPTER THREE

Berrington Jones looked at his two oldest friends. 'I can't believe the three of us,' he said. 'We're all close to sixty years old. None of us has ever made more than a couple of hundred thousand dollars a year. Now we're being offered sixty million *each*—and we're sitting here talking about turning the offer down!'

Preston Barck said: 'We were never in it for the money.'

Senator Proust said: 'I still don't understand it. If I own one third of a company that's worth a hundred and eighty million dollars, how come I'm driving around in a three-year-old Crown Victoria?'

The three men had a small private biotechnology company, Threeplex Inc. Preston ran the day-to-day business, Jim was in politics and Berrington was an academic. But the takeover was Berrington's baby. On a plane to San Francisco he had met the CEO of Landsmann, a German pharmaceuticals conglomerate, and had got the man interested in making a bid. Now he had to persuade his partners to accept the offer. It was proving harder than he had expected.

They were in the den of a house in Roland Park, an affluent suburb of Baltimore. The house was owned by

Jones Falls University and loaned to visiting professors. Berrington, who had professorships at Berkeley in California and at Harvard as well as Jones Falls, used the house for the six weeks of the year he was in Baltimore. There was little of his in the room: a laptop computer, a photograph of his ex-wife and their son, and a pile of new copies of his latest book, *To Inherit the Future: How Genetic Engineering Will Transform America.* A TV set with the sound turned down was showing the Emmy ceremonies.

Preston was a thin, earnest man. Although he was one of the most outstanding scientists of his generation, he looked like an accountant. 'The clinics have always made money,' Preston said. Threeplex owned three fertility clinics that specialized in *in vitro* conception—test-tube babies—a procedure made possible by Preston's pioneering research in the seventies. 'Fertility is the biggest growth area in American medicine. Threeplex will be Landsmann's way into this big new market. They want us to open five new clinics a year for the next ten years.'

Jim Proust was a bald, suntanned man with a big nose and heavy spectacles. His powerful, ugly face was a gift to the political cartoonists. He and Berrington had been friends and colleagues for twenty-five years. 'How come we never saw any money?' Jim asked.

'We always spent it on research.' Threeplex had its own labs, and also gave research contracts to the biology and psychology departments of universities. Berrington handled the company's links with the academic world.

Berrington said in an exasperated tone: 'I don't know why you two can't see that this is our big chance.'

Jim pointed at the TV. 'Turn up the sound, Berry—you're on.'

The Emmys had given way to *Larry King Live,* and Berrington was the guest. He hated Larry King—the man was a red-dyed liberal, in his opinion—but the show was an opportunity to talk to millions of Americans.

He studied his image, and he liked what he saw. He was in reality a short man, but television made everyone the same height. His navy suit looked good, the sky-blue shirt matched his eyes, and the tie was a burgundy red that did not flare on the screen. Being super-critical, he thought his silver hair was too neat, almost bouffant: he was in danger of looking like a television evangelist.

King, wearing his trademark braces, was in aggressive mood, his gravelly voice challenging. 'Professor, you've stirred up controversy again with your latest book, but some people feel this isn't science, it's politics. What do you say to that?'

Berrington was gratified to hear his own voice sounding mellow and reasonable in reply. 'I'm trying to say that political decisions should be based on sound science, Larry. Nature, left to itself, favours good genes and kills off bad ones. Our welfare policy works against natural selection. That's how we're breeding a generation of second-rate Americans.'

Jim took a sip of whisky and said: 'Good phrase—a generation of second-rate Americans. Quotable.'

On TV, Larry King said: 'If you have your way, what happens to the children of the poor? They starve, right?'

Berrington's face on the screen took on a solemn look. 'My father died in 1942, when the aircraft carrier *Wasp* was sunk by a Japanese submarine at Guadalcanal. I was six years old. My mother struggled to raise me and send me to school. Larry, I *am* a child of the poor.'

It was close enough to the truth. His father, a brilliant engineer, had left his mother a small income, enough so that she was not forced to work or remarry. She had sent Berrington to expensive private schools and then to Harvard—but it *had* been a struggle.

Preston said: 'You look good, Berry—except maybe for the country-western hairstyle.' Barck, the youngest of the trio at fifty-five, had short black hair that lay flat on his skull like a cap.

Berrington gave an irritated grunt. He had had the same thought himself, but it annoyed him to hear it from someone else. He poured himself a little more whisky. They were drinking Springbank, a single malt.

On the screen, Larry King said: 'Philosophically speaking, how do your views differ from those of, say, the Nazis?'

Berrington touched the remote control and turned the set off. 'I've been doing this stuff for ten years,' he said. 'Three books and a million crappy talk shows later, what difference has it made? None.'

Preston said: 'It has made a difference. You've made genetics and race an issue. You're just impatient.'

'Impatient?' Berrington said irritably. 'You bet I'm

impatient! I'll be sixty in two weeks. We're all getting old. We don't have much time left!'

Jim said: 'He's right, Preston. Don't you remember how it was when we were young men? We looked around and saw America going to hell: civil rights for Negroes, Mexicans flooding in, the best schools being swamped by the children of Jewish Communists, our kids smoking pot and dodging the draft. And boy, were we right! Look what's happened since then! In our worst nightmares we never imagined that illegal drugs would become one of America's biggest industries and that a third of all babies would be born to mothers on Medicaid. And we're the only people with the guts to face up to the problems—us and a few like-minded individuals. The rest close their eyes and hope for the best.'

They did not change, Berrington thought. Preston was ever cautious and fearful, Jim bombastically sure of himself. He had known them so long he looked fondly on their faults, most of the time anyway. And he was accustomed to his role as the moderator who steered them on a middle course.

Now he said: 'Where are we with the Germans, Preston? Bring us up to date.'

'We're very close to a conclusion,' Preston said. 'They want to announce the takeover at a press conference one week from tomorrow.'

'A week from tomorrow?' Berrington said with excitement in his voice. 'That's great!'

Preston shook his head. 'I have to tell you, I still have doubts.'

Berrington made an exasperated noise.

Preston went on: 'We've been going through a process called disclosure. We have to open our books to Landsmann's accountants, and tell them about anything that might affect future profits, such as debtors who are going bust, or pending lawsuits.'

'We don't have any of those, I take it?' Jim said.

Preston gave him an ominous look. 'We all know this company has secrets.'

There was a moment of silence in the room. Then Jim said: 'Hell, that's a long way in the past.'

'So what? The evidence of what we did is out there walking around.'

'But there's no way Landsmann can find out about it—especially in a week.'

Preston shrugged as if to say *Who knows?*

'We have to take that risk,' Berrington said firmly. 'The injection of capital we'll get from Landsmann will enable us to accelerate our research programme. In a couple of years' time we will be able to offer affluent white Americans who come to our clinics a genetically engineered perfect baby.'

'But how much difference will it make?' Preston said. 'The poor will continue to breed faster than the rich.'

'You're forgetting Jim's political platform,' Berrington said.

Jim said: 'A flat income tax rate of ten per cent, and compulsory contraceptive injections for women on welfare.'

'Think of it, Preston,' Berrington said. 'Perfect babies for the middle classes, and sterilization for the poor. We could start to put America's racial balance right again. It's what we always aimed for, ever since the early days.'

'We were very idealistic then,' Preston said.

'We were right!' Berrington said.

'Yes, we were right. But as I get older, more and more I start to think the world will probably muddle along somehow even if I don't achieve everything I planned when I was twenty-five.'

This kind of talk could sabotage great endeavours. 'But we can achieve what we planned,' Berrington said. 'Everything we've been working toward for the last thirty years is within our grasp now. The risks we took in the early days, all these years of research, the money we've spent—it's all coming to fruition at last. Don't get an attack of nerves at this point, Preston!'

'I don't have bad nerves, I'm pointing out real, practical problems,' Preston said peevishly. 'Jim can propose his political platform, but that doesn't mean it's going to happen.'

'That's where Landsmann comes in,' Jim said. 'The cash we'll get for our shares in the company will give us a shot at the biggest prize of all.'

'What do you mean?' Preston looked puzzled, but Berrington knew what was coming, and he smiled.

'The White House,' Jim said. 'I'm going to run for president.'

CHAPTER FOUR

A FEW MINUTES before midnight, Steve Logan parked his rusty old Datsun on Lexington Street in the Hollins Market neighbourhood of Baltimore, west of downtown. He was going to spend the night with his cousin Ricky Menzies, who was studying medicine at the University of Maryland in Baltimore. Ricky's home was one room in a big old house tenanted by students.

Ricky was the greatest hellraiser Steve knew. He loved to drink, dance and party, and his friends were the same. Steve had been looking forward to spending the evening with Ricky. But the trouble with hellraisers was that they were inherently unreliable. At the last minute Ricky got a hot date and cancelled, and Steve had spent the evening alone.

He got out of the car, carrying a small sports bag with fresh clothes for tomorrow. The night was warm. He locked the car and walked to the corner. A bunch of youngsters, four or five boys and a girl, all black, were hanging out by a video store, smoking cigarettes. Steve was not nervous, although he was white: he looked as if he belonged here, with his old car and his faded blue jeans; and anyway he was a couple of inches taller than the biggest of them. As he passed, one of them said quietly but distinctly: 'Wanna buy some blow, wanna buy some rock?' Steve shook his head without pausing in his stride.

A very tall black woman was walking towards him, dressed to kill in a short skirt and spike-heeled shoes, hair piled high, red lipstick and blue eyeshadow. He could not help staring at her. As she came closer she said: 'Hi, handsome,' in a deep masculine voice, and Steve realized it was a man. He grinned and walked on.

He heard the kids on the corner greet the transvestite with easy familiarity. 'Hey, Dorothy!'

'Hello, boys.'

A moment later he heard tyres squeal and glanced back. A white police car with a silver-and-blue stripe was pulling up at the corner. Some of the kids melted away into the dark streets; others stayed. Two black patrolmen got out, in no hurry. Steve turned around to watch. Seeing the man called Dorothy, one of the patrolmen spat, hitting the toe of a red high-heeled shoe.

Steve was shocked. The act was so gratuitous and unnecessary. However, Dorothy hardly paused in his stride. 'Fuck you, asshole,' he muttered.

The remark was barely audible, but the patrolman had good ears. He grabbed Dorothy by the arm and slammed him against the window of the store. Dorothy tottered in the high heels. 'Don't *ever* speak to me that way, you piece a shit,' the cop said.

Steve felt indignant. What did the guy expect if he went around spitting at people, for Christ's sake?

An alarm bell started ringing in the back of his mind. *Don't get in a fight, Steve.*

The cop's partner stood leaning on the car, watching, his face a blank.

'What's the matter, brother?' Dorothy said seductively. 'Do I *disturb* you?'

The patrolman punched him in the stomach. The cop was a beefy guy and the punch had all his weight behind it. Dorothy doubled over, gasping.

'The hell with this,' Steve said to himself, and he strode to the corner.

What are you doing, Steve?

Dorothy was still bent over, gasping. Steve said: 'Good evening, officer.'

The cop looked at him. 'Vanish, motherfucker,' he said.

'No,' Steve said.

'What did you say?'

'I said no, officer. You leave that man alone.' *Walk away, Steve, you damn fool, walk away.*

His defiance made the kids cocky. 'Yeah, thass right,' said a tall, thin boy with a shaved head. 'You got no call to fuck with Dorothy, he ain't broke no law.'

The cop pointed an aggressive finger at the boy. 'You want me to frisk you for dope, you just keep talking that way.'

The boy lowered his eyes.

'He's right, though,' Steve said. 'Dorothy isn't breaking any laws.'

The cop came over to Steve. *Don't hit him, whatever*

you do, don't touch him. Remember Tip Hendricks. 'You blind?' the cop said.

'What do you mean?'

The other cop said: 'Hey, Lenny, who gives a shit. Let's go.' He seemed uncomfortable.

Lenny ignored him and spoke to Steve. 'Can't you see? You're the only white face in the picture. You don't belong here.'

'But I've just witnessed a crime.'

The cop stood close to Steve, too close for comfort. 'You want a trip down town?' he said. 'Or do you want to get the fuck out of here, now?'

Steve did not want a trip down town. It was so easy for them to plant a little dope in his pockets, or beat him up and say he had resisted arrest. Steve was at law school: if he were convicted of a crime he could never practise. He wished he had not taken this stand. It was not worth throwing away his entire career just because a patrolman bullied a transvestite.

But it was *wrong*. Now two people were being bullied, Dorothy and Steve. It was the *cop* who was breaking the law. Steve could not bring himself to walk away.

But he adopted a conciliatory tone of voice. 'I don't want to make trouble, Lenny,' he said. 'Why don't you let Dorothy go, and I'll forget that I saw you assault him.'

'You *threatening* me, fuckhead?'

A punch to the stomach and a left-and-right to the head. One for the money, two for the show. The cop would go down like a horse with a broken leg.

'Just making a friendly suggestion.' This cop seemed to want trouble. Steve could not see how the confrontation could be defused. He wished Dorothy would walk quietly away now, while Lenny's back was turned; but the transvestite stood there, watching, with one hand gently rubbing his bruised stomach, enjoying the cop's fury.

Then luck intervened. The patrol car's radio came to life. Both cops froze, listening. Steve could not make out the jumble of words and number codes, but Lenny's partner said: 'Officer in trouble. We're out of here.'

Lenny hesitated, still glaring at Steve, but Steve thought he saw a hint of relief in the cop's eyes. Maybe he, too, had been rescued from a bad situation. But there was only malice in his tone. 'Remember me,' he said to Steve. ''Cause I'll remember you.' With that he jumped into the vehicle and slammed the door, and the car tore away.

The kids clapped and jeered.

'Whew,' Steve said gratefully. 'That was scary.'

It was also dumb. You know how it could have gone. You know what you're like.

At that moment his cousin Ricky came along. 'What happened?' Ricky asked, looking at the disappearing patrol car.

Dorothy came over and put his hands on Steve's shoulders. 'My hero,' he said coquettishly. 'John Wayne.'

Steve was embarrassed. 'Hey, c'mon.'

'Any time you want a walk on the wild side, John Wayne, you come to me. I'll let you in free.'

'Thanks all the same . . .'

'I'd kiss you, but I can see you're bashful, so I'll just say goodbye.' He waggled red-tipped fingers and turned away.

'Bye, Dorothy.'

Ricky and Steve went in the opposite direction. Ricky said: 'I see you've already made friends in the neighbourhood.'

Steve laughed, mainly with relief. 'I almost got in bad trouble,' he said. 'A dumbass cop started beating up on that guy in the skirt and I was fool enough to tell him to stop.'

Ricky was startled. 'You're lucky you're *here*.'

'I know it.'

They reached Ricky's house and went in. The place smelled of cheese, or maybe it was stale milk. There was graffiti on the green-painted walls. They edged around the bicycles chained up in the hallway and went up the stairs. Steve said: 'It just makes me mad. Why should Dorothy get punched in the gut? He likes to wear miniskirts and make-up: who gives a damn?'

'You're right.'

'And why should Lenny get away with it because he's wearing a police uniform? Policemen should have *higher* standards of behaviour, because of their privileged position.'

'Fat chance.'

'That's why I want to be a lawyer. To stop this kind of shit from happening. Do you have a hero, someone you want to be like?'

'Casanova, maybe.'

'Ralph Nader. He's a lawyer. That's my role model. He took on the most powerful corporations in America—and he won!'

Ricky laughed and put his arm around Steve's shoulders as they entered his room. 'My cousin, the idealist.'

'Ah, hell.'

'Want some coffee?'

'Sure.'

Ricky's room was small and furnished with junk. He had a single bed, a battered desk, a sagging couch and a big TV set. On the wall was a poster of a naked woman marked with the names of every bone in the human skeleton, from the parietal bone of the head to the distal phalanges of the feet. There was an air-conditioner but it did not seem to be working.

Steve sat on the couch. 'How was your date?'

'Not as hot as advertised.' Ricky put water in a kettle. 'Melissa is cute, all right, but I wouldn't be home this early if she was as crazy for me as I was led to believe. How about you?'

'I looked around the Jones Falls campus. Pretty classy. I met a girl, too.' Remembering, he brightened. 'I saw her playing tennis. She was terrific—tall, muscular, fit as hell. A service like it was fired out of a fucking bazooka, I swear to God.'

'I never heard of anyone falling for a girl because of her tennis game,' Ricky grinned. 'Is she a looker?'

'She's got this really strong face.' Steve could see it now. 'Dark brown eyes, black eyebrows, masses of dark hair . . . and this delicate little silver ring through her left nostril.'

'No kidding. Unusual, huh?'

'You said it.'

'What's her name?'

'I don't know.' Steve smiled ruefully. 'She gave me the brush-off without breaking stride. I'll probably never see her again in my life.'

Ricky poured coffee. 'Maybe it's for the best—you have a steady date, don't you?'

'Sort of.' Steve had felt a little guilty, being so attracted to the tennis player. 'Her name is Celine,' he said. 'We study together.' Steve went to school in Washington, DC.

'You sleeping with her?'

'No.'

'Why not?'

'I don't feel that level of commitment.'

Ricky looked surprised. 'This is a language I don't speak. You have to feel committed to a girl before you fuck her?'

Steve was embarrassed. 'It's just the way I feel, you know?'

'Have you always felt that way?'

'No. When I was at high school I did whatever girls would let me do, it was like a contest or something, I would bone any pretty girl who would take her panties off . . . but that was then, and this is now, and I'm not a kid any more. I think.'

'How old are you, twenty-two?'

'Right.'

'I'm twenty-five, but I guess I'm not as grown up as you.'

Steve detected a note of resentment. 'Hey, it's not a criticism, okay?'

'Okay.' Ricky did not seem seriously offended. 'So what did you do, after she gave you the brush-off?'

'Went to a bar in Charles Village and had a couple beers and a hamburger.'

'That reminds me—I'm hungry. Want something to eat?'

'What have you got?'

Ricky opened a cupboard. 'Boo Berry, Rice Krispies or Count Chocula.'

'Oh, boy, Count Chocula sounds great.' Ricky put bowls and milk on the table and they both tucked in.

When they had finished, they rinsed their cereal bowls and got ready for bed. Steve lay on the couch in his undershorts: it was too hot for a blanket. Ricky took the bed. Before they went to sleep, Ricky said: 'So what are you going to do at Jones Falls?'

'They asked me to be part of a study. I have to have psychological tests and stuff.'

'Why you?'

'I don't know. They said I was a special case, and they would explain everything when I get there.'

'What made you say yes? Sounds like kind of a waste of time.'

Steve had a special reason, but he was not going to tell Ricky. His answer was part of the truth. 'Curiosity, I guess. I mean, don't you wonder about yourself? Like, what kind of person am I really, and what do I want in life?'

'I want to be a hotshot surgeon and make a million bucks a year doing breast implants. I guess I'm a simple soul.'

'Don't you ask yourself what's it all for?'

Ricky laughed. 'No, Steve, I don't. But you do. You were always a thinker. Even when we were kids, you used to wonder about God and stuff.'

It was true. Steve had gone through a religious phase at about age thirteen. He had visited several different churches, a synagogue and a mosque, and earnestly questioned a series of bemused clergymen about their beliefs. It had mystified his parents, who were both unconcerned agnostics.

'But you were always a little bit different,' Ricky went on. 'I never knew anyone score so high in tests without breaking a sweat.'

That was true, too. Steve had always been a quick study, effortlessly coming top of the class, except when the other kids teased him and he made deliberate mistakes just to be less conspicuous.

But there was another reason why he was curious about his own psychology. Ricky did not know about it. Nobody at law school knew. Only his parents knew.

Steve had almost killed someone.

He was fifteen at the time; already tall, but thin. He was captain of the basketball team. That year, Hillsfield High made it to the city championship semi-final. They played against a team of ruthless street fighters from a Washington slum school. One particular opponent, a boy called Tip Hendricks, fouled Steve all through the match. Tip was good, but he used all his skill to cheat. And every time he did it he would grin, as if to say, *Got you again, sucker!* It drove Steve wild, but he had to keep his fury inside. All the same he played badly and the team lost, missing their chance at the trophy.

By the worst of bad luck, Steve ran into Tip in the parking lot, where the buses were waiting to take the teams back to their schools. Fatally, one of the drivers was changing a wheel, and had a tool kit open on the ground.

Steve ignored Tip, but Tip flicked his cigarette butt at Steve, and it landed on his jacket.

That jacket meant a lot to Steve. He had saved up his earnings from working Saturdays at McDonald's, and he had bought the damn thing the day before. It was a beautiful tan blouson made of soft leather the colour of butter, and now it had a burn mark right on the chest, where you could not help but see it. It was ruined. So Steve hit him.

Tip fought back fiercely, kicking and butting, but Steve's rage numbed him and he hardly felt the blows. Tip's face was covered in blood by the time his eye fell on the bus driver's tool kit and he picked up a tyre iron. He hit Steve across the face with it twice. The blows really hurt, and Steve's rage became blind. He got the iron away from Tip—and he could remember nothing, after that, until he was standing over Tip's body, with the bloodstained iron bar in his hand, and someone else was saying, *Jesus Christ Almighty, I think he's dead.*

Tip was not dead, though he did die two years later, killed by a Jamaican marijuana importer to whom he owed eighty-five dollars. But Steve had wanted to kill him, had *tried* to kill him. He had no real excuse: he had struck the first blow, and although Tip had been the one to pick up the tyre iron, Steve had used it savagely.

Steve was sentenced to six months in prison, but the sentence was suspended. After the trial he went to a different school and passed all his exams as usual. Because he had been a juvenile at the time of the fight, his criminal record could not be disclosed to anyone, so it did not prevent his getting into law school. Mom and Dad now thought of it as a nightmare that was over. But Steve had doubts. He knew it was only good luck and the resilience of the human body that saved him from a murder trial. Tip Hendricks was a human being, and Steve had almost killed him for a *jacket.* As he listened to Ricky's untroubled breathing across the room, he lay awake on the couch and thought: *What am I?*

MONDAY

CHAPTER FIVE

'DID YOU ever meet a man you wanted to marry?' Lisa said.

They were sitting at the table in Lisa's apartment, drinking instant coffee. Everything about the place was pretty, like Lisa: flowered prints, china ornaments, and a teddy bear with a spotted bow tie.

Lisa was going to take the day off, but Jeannie was dressed for work in a navy skirt and white cotton blouse. It was an important day, and she was jumpy with tension. The first of her subjects was coming to the lab for tests. Would he fit in with her theory or flout it? By the end of the afternoon she would either feel vindicated or be painfully reappraising her ideas.

However, she did not want to leave until the last possible moment. Lisa was still very fragile. Jeannie figured the best thing she could do was sit and talk to her about men and sex the way they always did, help her get on the road back to normality. She would have liked to stay here all morning, but she could not. She was really sorry Lisa would not be at the lab to help her today, but it was out of the question.

'Yeah, one,' Jeannie said in answer to the question. 'There was one guy I wanted to marry. His name was

Will Temple. He was an anthropologist. Still is.' Jeannie could see him now, a big man with a fair beard, in blue jeans and a fisherman's sweater, carrying his ten-speed bicycle through the corridors of the university.

'You've mentioned him before,' Lisa said. 'What was he like?'

'He was great.' Jeannie sighed. 'He made me laugh, he took care of me when I was sick, he ironed his own shirts and he was hung like a horse.'

Lisa did not smile. 'What went wrong?'

Jeannie was being flip, but it hurt her to remember. 'He left me for Georgina Tinkerton Ross.' As if by way of explanation, she added: 'Of the Pittsburgh Tinkerton Rosses.'

'What was she like?'

The last thing Jeannie wanted to do was recall Georgina. However, this was taking Lisa's mind off the rape, so she forced herself to reminisce. 'She was perfect,' she said, and she disliked the bitter sarcasm she heard in her own voice. 'Strawberry blonde, hour-glass figure, impeccable taste in cashmere sweaters and crocodile shoes. No brain, but a hell of a big trust fund.'

'When did all this happen?'

'Will and I lived together for a year when I was doing my doctorate.' It had been the happiest time she could remember. 'He moved out while I was writing my article on whether criminality is genetic.' *Great timing, Will. I just wish I could hate you more.* 'Then Berrington offered me a job at Jones Falls and I jumped at it.'

'Men are creeps.'

'Will isn't really a creep. He's a beautiful guy. He fell

for someone else, that's all. I think he showed really bad judgement in his choice. But it's not like we were married or anything. He didn't break any promises. He wasn't even unfaithful to me, except maybe once or twice before he told me.' Jeannie realized she was repeating Will's own words of self-justification. 'I don't know, maybe he was a creep after all.'

'Maybe we should return to Victorian times, when a man who kissed a woman considered himself engaged. At least girls knew where they were.'

Right now Lisa's perspective on relationships was pretty skewed, but Jeannie did not say so. Instead she asked: 'What about you? Did you ever find one you wanted to marry?'

'Never. Not one.'

'You and I have high standards. Don't worry, when Mr Right comes along he'll be wonderful.'

The entry phone sounded, startling them both. Lisa jumped up, bumping the table. A porcelain vase fell to the floor and shattered, and Lisa said: 'God *damn* it.'

She was still right on the edge. 'I'll pick up the pieces,' Jeannie said in a soothing voice. 'You see who's at the door.'

Lisa picked up the handset. A troubled frown crossed her face, and she studied the image on the monitor. 'All right, I guess,' she said dubiously, and she pressed the button that opened the building door.

'Who is it?' Jeannie asked.

'A detective from the Sex Crimes Unit.'

Jeannie had been afraid they would send someone to bully Lisa into cooperating with the investigation.

She was determined they would not succeed. The last thing Lisa needed now was more intrusive questions. 'Why didn't you tell him to fuck off?'

'Maybe because she's black,' Lisa said.

'No kidding?'

Lisa shook her head.

How clever, Jeannie thought as she swept shards of porcelain into her cupped hand. The cops knew she and Lisa were hostile. If they had sent a white male detective he would not have got through the door. So they sent a black woman, knowing that two middle-class white girls would bend over backwards to be polite to her. Well, if she tries to push Lisa around I'll throw her out of here just the same, Jeannie thought.

She turned out to be a stocky woman of about forty, smartly dressed in a cream blouse with a colourful silk scarf, carrying a briefcase. 'I'm Sergeant Michelle Delaware,' she said. 'They call me Mish.'

Jeannie wondered what was in the briefcase. Detectives usually carried guns, not papers. 'I'm Dr Jean Ferrami,' Jeannie said. She always used her title when she thought she was going to quarrel with someone. 'This is Lisa Hoxton.'

The detective said: 'Ms Hoxton, I want to say how sorry I am about what happened to you yesterday. My unit deals with one rape a day, on average, and every single one is a terrible tragedy and a wounding trauma for the victim. I know you're hurting and I understand.'

Wow, Jeannie thought, this is different from yesterday.

'I'm trying to put it behind me,' Lisa said defiantly, but tears came to her eyes and betrayed her.

'May I sit down?'

'Of course.'

The detective sat at the kitchen table.

Jeannie studied her warily. 'Your attitude seems different from the patrolman's,' she said.

Mish nodded. 'I'm also deeply sorry about McHenty and the way he treated you. Like all patrolmen he has received training on how to deal with rape victims, but he seems to have forgotten what he was taught. I'm embarrassed for the entire police department.'

'It was like being violated all over again,' Lisa said tearfully.

'It's not supposed to happen any more,' Mish said, and a note of anger crept into her voice. 'This is how so many rape cases end up in a drawer marked "Unfounded". It's not because women lie about rape. It's because the justice system treats them so brutally that they withdraw the complaint.'

Jeannie said: 'I can believe that.' She told herself to be careful: Mish might talk like a sister, but she was still a cop.

Mish took a card from her purse. 'Here's the number of a volunteer centre for victims of rape and child abuse,' she said. 'Sooner or later, every victim needs counselling.'

Lisa took the card, but she said: 'Right now all I want is to forget it.'

Mish nodded. 'Take my advice, put the card in a

drawer. Your feelings go through cycles, and there will probably come a time when you're ready to seek help.'

'Okay.'

Jeannie decided that Mish had earned a little courtesy. 'Would you like some coffee?' she offered.

'I'd love a cup.'

'I'll make some fresh.' Jeannie got up and filled the coffee maker.

Mish said: 'Do you two work together?'

'Yes,' Jeannie replied. 'We study twins.'

'Twins?'

'We measure their similarities and differences, and try to figure out how much is inherited and how much is due to the way they were raised.'

'What's your role in this, Lisa?'

'My job is to find the twins for the scientists to study.'

'How do you do that?'

'I start with birth records, which are public information in most states. Twinning is about one per cent of births, so we get a set of twins for every hundred birth certificates we look at. The certificate gives the date and place of birth. We take a copy, then track down the twins.'

'How?'

'We have every American phone book on CD-ROM. We can also use driving licence registries and credit reference agencies.'

'Do you always find the twins?'

'Goodness, no. Our success rate depends on their age. We track down about ninety per cent of ten-year-olds, but only fifty per cent of eighty-year-olds. Older people are more likely to have moved house several times, changed their names or died.'

Mish looked at Jeannie. 'And then you study them.'

Jeannie said: 'I specialize in identical twins who have been raised apart. They're much more difficult to find.' She put the coffee pot on the table and poured a cup for Mish. If this detective was planning to put pressure on Lisa, she was taking her time about it.

Mish sipped her coffee then said to Lisa: 'At the hospital, did you take any medication?'

'No, I wasn't there long.'

'They should have offered you the morning-after pill. You don't want to be pregnant.'

Lisa shuddered. 'I sure don't. I've been asking myself what the hell I'd do about it.'

'Go to your own doctor. He should give it to you, unless he has religious objections—some Catholic physicians have a problem with it. In that case the volunteer centre will recommend an alternate.'

'It's so good to talk to someone who knows all this stuff,' Lisa said.

'The fire was no accident,' Mish went on. 'I've talked to the fire chief. Someone set light to a storage room next to the locker room—and he unscrewed the ventilation pipes to make sure the smoke was pumped into the locker room. Now, rapists are not really interested in sex: it's fear that turns them on. So I think the fire was all part of this creep's fantasy.'

Jeannie had not thought of that possibility. 'I assumed he was just an opportunist who took advantage of the fire.'

Mish shook her head. 'Date rape is usually opportunistic: a guy finds that the girl is too stoned or drunk to fight him off. But men who rape strangers are different. They're planners. They fantasize the event, then work out how to make it happen. They can be very clever. It makes them more scary.'

Jeannie felt even angrier. 'I nearly died in that goddamn fire,' she said.

Mish said to Lisa: 'I'm right in thinking you had never seen this man before? He was a total stranger?'

'I think I saw him about an hour earlier,' she replied. 'When I was out running with the field hockey team, a car slowed right down and the guy stared at us. I have a feeling it was him.'

'What kind of a car?'

'It was old, I know that. White, with a lot of rust. Maybe a Datsun.'

Jeannie expected Mish to write that down, but she carried on talking. 'The impression I get is of an intelligent and completely ruthless pervert who will do whatever it takes to get his kicks.'

Jeannie said bitterly: 'He should be locked away for the rest of his life.'

Mish played her trump card. 'But he won't be. He's free. And he will do it again.'

Jeannie was sceptical. 'How can you be sure of that?'

'Most rapists are serial rapists. The only exception is the opportunistic date-rapist I mentioned before: that type of guy might offend only once. But men who rape strangers do it again and again—until they're caught.'

Mish looked hard at Lisa. 'In seven to ten days' time, the man who raped you will put another woman through the same torture—unless we catch him first.'

'Oh, my God,' Lisa said.

Jeannie could see where Mish was heading. As Jeannie had anticipated, the detective was going to try to talk Lisa into helping with the investigation. Jeannie was still determined not to let Mish bully or pressure Lisa. But it was hard to object to the kind of things she was saying now.

'We need a sample of his DNA,' Mish said.

Lisa made a disgusted face. 'You mean his sperm.'

'Yes.'

Lisa shook her head. 'I've showered and taken a bath and douched myself. I hope to God there's nothing left of him inside me.'

Mish was quietly persistent. 'Traces remain in the body for forty-eight to seventy-two hours afterwards. We need to do a vaginal swab, a pubic-hair combing and a blood test.'

Jeannie said: 'The doctor we saw at Santa Teresa yesterday was a real asshole.'

Mish nodded. 'Doctors hate dealing with rape victims. If they have to go to court, they lose time and money. But you should never have been taken to Santa Teresa. That was one of McHenty's many mistakes. Three hospitals in this city are designated Sexual Assault Centers, and Santa Teresa isn't one of them.'

Lisa said: 'Where do you want me to go?'

'Mercy Hospital has a Sexual Assault Forensic Examination unit, we call it the SAFE unit.'

Jeannie nodded. Mercy was the big downtown hospital.

Mish went on: 'You'll see a Sexual Assault Nurse Examiner, who is always a woman. She's specially trained in dealing with evidence, which the doctor you saw yesterday was not—he would probably have screwed up anyway.'

Mish clearly did not have much respect for doctors.

She opened her briefcase. Jeannie leaned forward, curious. Inside was a laptop computer. Mish lifted the lid and switched it on. 'We have a program called E-FIT, for Electronic Facial Identification Technique. We like acronyms.' She gave a wry smile. 'Actually it was devised by a Scotland Yard detective. It enables us to put together a likeness of the perpetrator, without using an artist.' She looked expectantly at Lisa.

Lisa looked at Jeannie. 'What do you think?'

'Don't feel pressured,' Jeannie said. 'Think about yourself. You're entitled. Do what makes you feel comfortable.'

Mish shot her a hostile glare, then said to Lisa: 'There's no pressure on you. If you want me to leave, I'm out of here. But I'm asking you. I want to catch this rapist, and I need your help. Without you, I don't stand a chance.'

Jeannie was lost in admiration. Mish had dominated and controlled the conversation ever since she walked into the room, yet she had done it without bullying or manipulation. She knew what she was talking about, and she knew what she wanted.

Lisa said: 'I don't know.'

Mish said: 'Why don't you take a look at this computer program? If it upsets you, we'll stop. If not, I will at least have a picture of the man I'm after. Then, when we're done with that, you can think about whether you want to go to Mercy.'

Lisa hesitated again, then said: 'Okay.'

Jeannie said: 'Just remember, you can stop any time you feel upset.'

Lisa nodded.

Mish said: 'To begin, we'll get a rough approximation to his face. It won't look like him, but it will be a basis. Then we'll refine the details. I need you to concentrate hard on the perpetrator's face, then give me a general description. Take your time.'

Lisa closed her eyes. 'He's a white man about my age. Short hair, no particular colour. Light eyes, blue I guess. Straight nose . . .'

Mish was operating a mouse. Jeannie got up and stood behind the detective so she could see the screen. It was a Windows program. In the top right-hand corner was a face divided into eight sections. As Lisa named features, Mish would click on a section of the face, pulling down a menu, then check items on the menu based on Lisa's comments: hair short, eyes light, nose straight.

Lisa went on: 'Kind of a square chin, no beard or moustache . . . how am I doing?'

Mish clicked again and an entire face came on the main screen. It showed a white man in his thirties with regular features, and it might have been any one of a thousand guys. Mish turned the computer around so that Lisa could see the screen. 'Now, we're going to change the face bit by bit. First, I'll show you this face with a whole series of different foreheads and hairlines. Just say yes, no or maybe. Ready?'

'Sure.'

Mish clicked the mouse. The face on the screen changed, and suddenly the forehead had a receding hairline.

'No,' Lisa said.

She clicked again. This time the face had a straight fringe like an old-fashioned Beatle haircut.

'No.'

The next haircut was wavy, and Lisa said: 'That's more like it. But I think he had a part.'

The next was curly. 'Better still,' Lisa said. 'This is better than the last one. But the hair is too dark.'

Mish said: 'After we've looked at them all, we'll come back to the ones you liked and pick the best. When we have the whole face we can carry on improving it using the retouch feature: making the hair darker or lighter, moving the part, making the whole face older or younger.'

Jeannie was fascinated, but this was going to take an hour or more, and she had work to do. 'I've got to go,' she said. 'Are you okay, Lisa?'

'I'm fine,' Lisa said, and Jeannie could tell it was the truth. Maybe it would be better for Lisa to get involved in hunting the man down. She caught Mish's eye and saw a flash of triumph in her expression. Was I wrong, Jeannie wondered, to be hostile to Mish and defensive of Lisa? Mish was certainly *sympa.* She had all the right words. Just the same, her priority was not to help Lisa, but to catch the rapist. Lisa still needed a true friend, someone whose main concern was for her.

'I'll call you,' Jeannie said to her.

Lisa hugged Jeannie. 'I can't thank you enough for staying with me,' she said.

Mish held out her hand and said: 'Good to meet you.'

Jeannie shook hands. 'Good luck,' she said. 'I hope you catch him.'

'So do I,' said Mish.

CHAPTER SIX

STEVE PARKED in the large student parking lot in the south-west corner of the hundred-acre Jones Falls campus. It was a few minutes before ten o'clock, and the campus was thronged with students in light summer clothes on their way to the first lecture of the day. As he walked across the campus he looked out for the tennis player. The chances of seeing her were slender, he knew, but he could not help staring at every tall dark-haired woman to see if she had a nose ring.

The Ruth W. Acorn Psychology Building was a modern four-storey structure in the same red brick as the older, more traditional college buildings. He gave his name in the lobby and was directed to the laboratory.

In the next three hours he underwent more tests than he could have imagined possible. He was weighed, measured and fingerprinted. Scientists, technicians and students photographed his ears, tested the strength of his grip, and assessed his startle reflex by showing him pictures of burn victims and mutilated bodies. He answered questions about his leisure-time interests, his religious beliefs, his girlfriends and his job aspirations. He had to state if he could repair a doorbell, whether he considered himself well groomed, would he spank his children and did certain music make him think of pictures or changing colour patterns? But no one told him why he had been selected for the study.

He was not the only subject. Also around the lab were two little girls and a middle-aged man wearing cowboy boots, blue jeans and a western shirt. At midday they all gathered in a lounge with couches and a TV, and had pizza and Cokes for lunch. It was then Steve realized there were in fact two middle-aged men in cowboy boots: they were twins, dressed the same.

He introduced himself, and learned that the cowboys were Benny and Arnold, and the little girls were Sue and Elizabeth. 'Do you guys always dress the same?' Steve asked the men as they ate.

They looked at each other, then Benny said: 'Don't know. We just met.'

'You're twins, and you just met?'

'When we were babies we were both adopted—by different families.'

'And you accidentally dressed the same?'

'Looks like it, don't it?'

Arnold added: 'And we're both carpenters, and we both smoke Camel Lights, and we both have two kids, a boy and a girl.'

Benny said: 'Both girls are called Caroline, but my boy is John and his is Richard.'

Arnold said: 'I wanted to call my boy John, but my wife insisted on Richard.'

'Wow,' Steve said. 'But you can't have inherited a taste for Camel Lights.'

'Who knows?'

One of the little girls, Elizabeth, said to Steve: 'Where's your twin?'

'I don't have one,' he replied. 'Is that what they study here, twins?'

'Yes.' Proudly she added: 'Sue and me are dizygotic.'

Steve raised his eyebrows. She looked about eleven. 'I'm not sure I know that word,' he said gravely. 'What does it mean?'

'We're not identical. We're fraternal twins. That's why we don't look the same.' She pointed at Benny and Arnold. 'They're monozygotic. They have the same DNA. That's why they're so alike.'

'You seem to know a lot about it,' Steve said. 'I'm impressed.'

'We've been here before,' she said.

The door opened behind Steve, and Elizabeth looked up and said: 'Hello, Dr Ferrami.'

Steve turned and saw the tennis player.

Her muscular body was hidden beneath a knee-length white laboratory coat, but she moved like an athlete as she walked into the room. She still had the air of focused concentration that had been so impressive on the tennis court. He stared at her, hardly able to believe his luck.

She said hello to the little girls and introduced herself to the others. When she shook Steve's hand she did a double-take. 'So you're Steve Logan!' she said.

'You play a great game of tennis,' he said.

'I lost, though.' She sat down. Her thick, dark hair swung loosely around her shoulders, and Steve noticed, in the unforgiving light of the laboratory, that she had one or two grey hairs. Instead of the silver ring she had a plain gold stud in her nostril. She was wearing make-up today, and the mascara made her dark eyes even more hypnotic.

She thanked them all for giving up their time in the service of scientific enquiry and asked if the pizzas were good. After a few more platitudes she sent the girls and the cowboys away to begin their afternoon tests.

She sat close to Steve, and for some reason he had the feeling she was embarrassed. It was almost as if she were about to give him bad news. She said: 'By now you're wondering what this is all about.'

'I guessed I was picked because I've always done so well in school.'

'No,' she said. 'True, you score very high on all intellectual tests. In fact your performance at school understates your abilities. Your IQ is off the scale. You probably come top of your class without even studying hard, am I right?'

'Yes. But that's not why I'm here?'

'No. Our project here is to ask how much of people's make-up is predetermined by their genetic inheritance.' Her awkwardness vanished as she warmed to her subject. 'Is it DNA that decides whether we're intelligent, aggressive, romantic, athletic? Or is it our upbringing? If both have an influence, how do they interact?'

'An ancient controversy,' Steve said. He had taken a philosophy course at college and he had been fascinated by this debate. 'Am I the way I am because I was born like it? Or am I a product of my upbringing and the society I was raised in?' He recalled the catchphrase that summed up the argument: 'Nature or nurture?'

She nodded, and her long hair moved heavily, like the ocean. Steve wondered how it felt to the touch. 'But we're trying to resolve the question in a strictly scientific way,' she said. 'You see, identical twins have the same genes—exactly the same. Fraternal twins don't, but they are normally brought up in exactly the same environment. We study both kinds, and compare them with twins who are brought up apart, measuring how similar they are.'

Steve was wondering how this affected him. He was also wondering how old Jeannie was. Seeing her run around the tennis court yesterday, with her hair hidden in a cap, he assumed she was his age; but now he could tell she was nearer thirty. It did not change his feelings about her, but he had never before been attracted to someone so old.

She went on: 'If environment was more important, twins raised together would be very alike, and twins raised apart would be quite different, regardless of whether they were identical or fraternal. In fact we find the opposite. Identical twins resemble one another, regardless of who raised them. Indeed, identical twins raised apart are more similar than fraternal twins raised together.'

'Like Benny and Arnold?'

'Exactly. You saw how alike they are, even though they were brought up in different homes. That's typical. This department has studied more than a hundred pairs of identical twins raised apart. Of those two hundred people, two were published poets, and they were a twin pair. Two were professionally involved with pets—one was a dog trainer and the other a breeder—and they were a twin pair. We've had two musicians—a piano teacher and a session guitarist—also a twin pair. But those are just the more vivid examples. As you've seen this morning, we do scientific measurements of personality, IQ and various physical dimensions, and these often show the same pattern: the identical twins are highly similar, regardless of their upbringing.'

'Whereas Sue and Elizabeth seem quite different.'

'Right. Yet they have the same parents, the same home, they go to the same school, they've had the same diet all their lives, and so on. I expect Sue was quiet all through lunch, but Elizabeth told you her life story.'

'As a matter of fact, she explained the word "monozygotic" to me.'

Dr Ferrami laughed, showing white teeth and a flash of pink tongue, and Steve felt inordinately pleased that he had amused her.

'But you still haven't explained my involvement,' he said.

She looked awkward again. 'It's a little difficult,' she said. 'This has never happened before.'

Suddenly he realized. It was obvious, but so surprising that he had not guessed until now. 'You think I have a twin that I don't know about?' he said incredulously.

'I can't think of any gradual way to tell you,' she said with evident chagrin. 'Yes, we do.'

'Wow.' He felt dazed: it was hard to take in.

'I'm really sorry.'

'Nothing to apologize for, I guess.'

'But there is. Normally people know they're twins before they come to us. However, I've pioneered a new way of recruiting subjects for this study, and you're the first. Actually, the fact that you don't know you have a twin is a tremendous vindication of my system. But I didn't foresee that we might be giving people shocking news.'

'I always wanted a brother,' Steve said. He was an only child, born when his parents were in their late thirties. 'Is it a brother?'

'Yes. You're identical.'

'An identical twin brother,' Steve murmured. 'But how could it happen without my knowledge?'

She looked mortified.

'Wait a minute, I can work it out,' Steve said. 'I could be adopted.'

She nodded.

It was an even more shocking thought: Mom and Dad might not be his parents.

'Or my twin could have been adopted.'

'Yes.'

'Or both, like Benny and Arnold.'

'Or both,' she repeated solemnly. She was gazing intently at him with those dark eyes. Despite the turmoil in his mind he could not help thinking how lovely she was. He wanted her to stare at him like this for ever.

She said: 'In my experience, even if a subject doesn't know he or she is a twin, they normally know they were adopted. Even so, I should have guessed you might be different.'

Steve said painfully: 'I just can't believe Mom and Dad would have kept adoption a secret from me. It's not their style.'

'Tell me about your parents.'

He knew she was making him talk to help him work through the shock, but that was okay. He collected his thoughts. 'Mom's kind of exceptional. You've heard of her, her name's Lorraine Logan.'

'The lonely hearts columnist?'

'Right. Syndicated in four hundred newspapers, author of six bestsellers about women's health. Rich and famous, and she deserves it.'

'Why do you say that?'

'She really cares about the people who write to her. She answers thousands of letters. You know, they basically want her to wave a magic wand—make their unwanted pregnancies vanish, get their kids off drugs, turn their abusive men into kindly and supportive husbands. She always gives them the information they need and tells them it's their decision what to do, trust your feelings and don't let anyone bully you. It's a good philosophy.'

'And your father?'

'Dad's pretty ordinary, I guess. He's in the military, works at the Pentagon, he's a colonel. He does public relations, writes speeches for generals, that kind of thing.'

'A disciplinarian?'

Steve smiled. 'He has a highly developed sense of duty. But he's not a violent man. He saw some action in Asia, before I was born, but he never brought it home.'

'Did you require discipline?'

Steve laughed. 'I was the naughtiest boy in class, all through school. Constantly in trouble.'

'What for?'

'Breaking the rules. Running in the hallway. Wearing red socks. Chewing gum in class. Kissing Wendy Prasker behind the Biology shelf in the school library when I was thirteen.'

'Why?'

'Because she was so pretty.'

She laughed again. 'I meant, why did you break all the other rules?'

He shook his head. 'I just couldn't be obedient. I did what I wanted to do. The rules seemed stupid, and I got bored. They would have thrown me out of school, but I always got good grades, and I was usually captain of one sports team or another: football, basketball, baseball, track. I don't understand myself. Am I a weirdo?'

'Everybody's weird in their own way.'

'I guess so. Why d'you wear the nose ring?'

She raised her dark eyebrows, as if to say *I ask the questions around here,* but she answered him just the same. 'I went through a punk phase when I was about fourteen: green hair, ripped stockings, everything. The pierced nostril was part of that.'

'It would close up and heal over if you let it.'

'I know. I guess I keep it because I feel that total respectability is deadly dull.'

Steve smiled. My God, I like this woman, he thought, even if she is too old for me. Then his mind switched back to what she had told him. 'What makes you so sure I have a twin?'

'I've developed a computer program that searches medical records and other databases for pairs. Identical twins have similar brainwaves, electrocardiograms, fingerprint ridge counts, and teeth. I scanned a large database of dental X-rays held by a medical insurance company, and found someone whose teeth measurements and arch forms are the same as yours.'

'It doesn't sound conclusive.'

'Maybe not, although he even has cavities in the same places you do.'

'So who is he?'

'His name is Dennis Pinker.'

'Where is he now?'

'Richmond, Virginia.'

'Have you met him?'

'I'm going to Richmond to see him tomorrow. I'll do many of the same tests on him, and take a blood sample so we can compare his DNA with yours. Then we'll know for sure.'

Steve frowned. 'Do you have a particular area that you're interested in, within the field of genetics?'

'Yes. My specialty is criminality and whether it's inherited.'

Steve nodded. 'I get it. What did he do?'

'Pardon me?'

'What did Dennis Pinker do?'

'I don't know what you mean.'

'You're going to visit him, instead of asking him to come here, so obviously he's incarcerated.'

She coloured faintly, as if she had been caught out in a deception. With her cheeks flushed she looked sexier than ever. 'Yes, you're right,' she said.

'What's he in jail for?'

She hesitated. 'Murder.'

'Jesus!' He looked away from her, trying to take it in. 'Not only do I have an identical twin brother, but he's a murderer! Jesus Christ!'

'I'm sorry,' she said. 'I've handled this badly. You're the first subject like this I've ever studied.'

'Boy. I came here hoping to learn something about myself, but I've learned more than I wanted to know.' Jeannie did not know, and never would know, that Steve had almost killed a boy called Tip Hendricks.

'And you're very important to me.'

'How so?'

'The question is whether criminality is inherited. I published a paper which said that a certain type of personality is inherited—a combination of impulsiveness, daring, aggression and hyperactivity—but that whether or not such people become criminals depends on how their parents deal with them. To prove my theory I have to find pairs of identical twins, one of whom is a criminal and the other a law-abiding citizen. You and Dennis are my first pair, and you're perfect: he's in jail and you, forgive me, you're the ideal all-American boy. To tell you the truth, I'm so excited about it I can hardly sit still.'

The thought of this woman being too excited to sit still made Steve restless too. He looked away from her, afraid his lust would show in his face. But what she had told him was painfully disturbing. He had the same DNA as a murderer. What did that make him?

The door opened behind Steve, and she looked up. 'Hi, Berry,' she said. 'Steve, I'd like you to meet Professor Berrington Jones, the head of the twins study here at JFU.'

The professor was a short man in his late fifties, handsome with sleek silver hair. He wore an expensive-looking suit of grey-flecked Irish tweed and a red bow tie with white dots, and he looked as neat as if he had just come out of a bandbox. Steve had seen him on TV a few times, talking about how America was going all to hell. Steve did not like his views, but he had been brought up to be polite, so he stood up and held out his hand to shake.

Berrington Jones started as if he had seen a ghost. 'Good God!' he said, and his face turned pale.

Dr Ferrami said: 'Berry! What is it?'

Steve said: 'Did I do something?'

The professor said nothing for a moment. Then he seemed to collect his wits. 'I'm sorry, it's nothing,' he said, but he still seemed shaken to the core. 'It's just that I suddenly thought of something . . . something I've forgotten, a most dreadful mistake. Please excuse me.' He went to the door, still muttering: 'My apologies, forgive me.' He went out.

Steve looked at Dr Ferrami.

She shrugged and spread her hands in a gesture of helplessness. 'Beats the hell out of me,' she said.

CHAPTER SEVEN

BERRINGTON SAT at his desk, breathing hard.

He had a corner office, but otherwise his room was monastic: plastic tiled floor, white walls, utilitarian file cabinets, cheap bookshelves. Academics were not expected to have lavish offices. The screen-saver on his computer showed a slowly revolving strand of DNA twisted in the famous double-helix shape. Over the desk were photographs of himself with Geraldo Rivera, Newt Gingrich and Rush Limbaugh. The window overlooked the gymnasium building, closed because of yesterday's fire. Across the road, two boys were using the tennis court, despite the heat.

Berrington rubbed his eyes. 'Damn, damn, damn,' he said with feeling.

He had persuaded Jeannie Ferrami to come here. Her paper on criminality had broken new ground by focusing on the components of the criminal personality. The question was crucial to the Threeplex project. He wanted her to continue her work under his wing. He had induced Jones Falls to give her a job and had arranged for her research to be financed by a grant from Threeplex.

With his help she could do great things, and the fact that she came from a poor background only made her achievement more impressive. Her first four weeks at Jones Falls had confirmed his judgement. She had hit the ground running and her project got under way fast. Most people liked her—although she could be abrasive: a ponytailed lab technician who thought he could get away with sloppy work had suffered a scorching rebuke on her second day.

Berrington himself was completely smitten. She was as stunning physically as she was intellectually. He was torn between a fatherly need to encourage and guide her, and a powerful urge to seduce her.

And now this!

When he had caught his breath he picked up the phone and called Preston Barck. Preston was his oldest friend: they had met at MIT in the sixties, when Berrington was doing his doctorate in psychology and Preston was an outstanding young embryologist. Both had been considered odd, in that era of flamboyant lifestyles, with their short haircuts and tweed suits. They soon discovered that they agreed about all sorts of things: modern jazz was a fraud, marijuana was the first step on the road to heroin, the only honest politician in America was Barry Goldwater. The friendship had proved more robust than either of their marriages. Berrington no longer thought about whether he liked Preston: Preston was just there, like Canada.

Right now Preston would be at Threeplex's headquarters, a cluster of neat low-rise buildings overlooking a golf course in Baltimore County, north of the city.

Preston's secretary said he was in a meeting, and Berrington told her to connect him anyway.

'Good morning, Berry—what's up?'

'Who else is there?'

'I'm with Lee Ho, one of the senior accountants from Landsmann. We're going over the final details of Threeplex's disclosure statement.'

'Get him the fuck out of there.'

Preston's voice faded as he moved the phone away from his face. 'I'm sorry, Lee, this is going to take a while. I'll catch up with you later.' There was a pause, and he spoke into the mouthpiece again. Now his voice was peevish. 'That was Michael Madigan's right-hand man I just threw out. Madigan is the CEO of Landsmann, in case you've forgotten. If you're still as keen on this takeover as you were last night, we'd better not—'

Berrington ran out of patience and interrupted him. 'Steven Logan is here.'

There was a moment of stunned silence. 'At Jones Falls?'

'Right here in the psychology building.'

Preston immediately forgot Lee Ho. 'Jesus Christ, how come?'

'He's a subject, he's undergoing tests in the laboratory.'

Preston's voice went up an octave. 'How the hell did that happen?'

'I don't know. I ran into him five minutes ago. Imagine my surprise.'

'You just recognized him?'

'Of course I *recognized* him.'

'Why's he being tested?'

'It's part of our twins study.'

'Twins?' Preston yelled. '*Twins?* Who's the other goddamn twin?'

'I don't know yet. Look, something like this was sure to happen sooner or later.'

'But now of all times! We'll have to pull out of the Landsmann deal.'

'Hell, no! I'm not going to let you use this as an excuse for going wobbly on the takeover, Preston.' Now Berrington wished he had not made this call. But he had needed to share his shock with someone. And Preston could be an astute strategic thinker. 'We just have to find a way to control the situation.'

'Who brought Steve Logan into the university?'

'The new associate professor we just hired, Dr Ferrami.'

'The guy who wrote that terrific paper on criminality?'

'Yes, except it's a woman. A very attractive woman, as a matter of fact—'

'I don't care if she's Sharon fucking Stone—'

'I assume she recruited Steven to the project. She was with him when I met him. I'll check.'

'That's the key to it, Berry.' Preston was calming down now and focusing on the solution, not the problem. 'Find out how he was recruited. Then we can begin to assess how much danger we're in.'

'I'll get her in here right away.'

'Call me right back, okay?'

'Sure.' Berrington hung up.

However, he did not call Jeannie immediately. Instead he sat and collected his thoughts.

On his desk was an old monochrome photograph of his father as a second lieutenant, resplendent in his white naval uniform and cap. Berrington had been six years old when the *Wasp* went down. Like every small boy in America, he hated the Japs and played games in which he slaughtered them by the dozen in his imagination. And his daddy was an invincible hero, tall and handsome, brave and strong and all-conquering. He could still feel the overpowering rage that had gripped him when he found out the Japs had killed Daddy. He had prayed to God to make the war go on long enough for him to grow up and join the navy himself and kill a million Japs in revenge.

He had never killed anyone. But he had never hired a Japanese employee or admitted a Japanese student to a school or offered a Japanese psychologist a job.

A lot of men, faced with a problem, asked themselves what their father would have done about it. Friends had told him this: it was a privilege he would never have. He had been too young to get to know his father. He had no idea what Lieutenant Jones would have done in a crisis. He had never really had a father, just a superhero.

He would question Jeannie Ferrami about her recruitment methods. Then, he decided, he would ask her to have dinner with him.

He called Jeannie's internal number. She picked up right away. He lowered his voice and spoke in a tone that his ex-wife, Vivvie, used to call furry. 'Jeannie, it's Berry,' he said.

She was characteristically direct. 'What the heck is going on?' she said.

'Could I talk to you for a minute, please?'

'Sure.'

'Would you mind stepping into my office?'

'I'll be right there.' She hung up.

As he waited for her, he wondered idly how many women he had bedded. It would take too long to recall them one by one, but maybe he could approximate scientifically. It was more than one, more than ten certainly. Was it more than a hundred? That would be two point five per year since he was nineteen: he had certainly had more than that. A thousand? Twenty-five per year, a new woman every two weeks for forty years? No, he had not done that well. During the ten years he had been married to Vivvie Ellington he had probably had no more than fifteen or twenty adulterous liaisons in total. But he had made up for it afterwards. Somewhere between a hundred and a thousand, then. But he was not going to take Jeannie to bed. He was going to find out how the hell she had come into contact with Steven Logan.

Jeannie knocked at the door and came in. She was wearing a white laboratory coat over her skirt and blouse. Berrington liked it when the young women wore those coats as dresses, with nothing else but their underwear. He found it sexy.

'Good of you to come by,' he said. He drew out a chair for her, then pulled his own chair around from behind his desk so there would not be a barrier between them.

His first task was to give Jeannie some plausible explanation for his behaviour on meeting Steven Logan. She would not be easy to fool. He wished he had given it more thought instead of counting up his conquests.

He sat down and gave her his most disarming grin. 'I want to apologize for my weird behaviour,' he said. 'I've been downloading some files from the University of Sydney, Australia.' He gestured at his desktop computer. 'Just as you were about to introduce me to that young man, I realized I had left my computer on and forgotten to hang up the phone line. I just felt kind of foolish, that's all, but I was pretty rude.'

The explanation was thin, but she seemed to accept it. 'I'm relieved,' she said candidly. 'I thought I had done something to offend you.'

So far, so good. 'I was on my way to talk to you about your work,' he went on smoothly. 'You've certainly got off to a flying start. You've only been here four weeks and your project is well under way. Congratulations.'

She nodded. 'I had long talks with Herb and Frank over the summer, before I officially started,' she said. Herb Dickson was the department head and Frank Demidenko a full professor. 'We figured out all the practicalities in advance.'

'Tell me a little more about it. Have any problems come up? Anything I can help with?'

'Recruitment is my biggest problem,' she said.

'Because our subjects are volunteers, most of them are like Steve Logan, respectable middle-class Americans who believe that the good citizen has a duty to support scientific enquiry. Not many pimps and dope dealers come forward.'

'A point our liberal critics haven't failed to make.'

'On the other hand, it's not possible to find out about aggression and criminality by studying law-abiding middle-American families. So it was absolutely crucial to my project that I solved the recruitment problem.'

'And have you?'

'I think so. It occurred to me that medical information about millions of people is nowadays held on huge databases by insurance companies and government agencies. That includes the kind of data we use to determine whether twins are identical or fraternal: brainwaves, electrocardiograms, and so on. If we could search for pairs of similar electrocardiograms, for example, it would be a way of identifying twins. And if the database were big enough, some of those pairs would have been raised apart. And here's the kicker: *Some of them might not even know they were twins.*'

'It's remarkable,' Berrington said. 'Simple, but original and ingenious.' He meant it. Identical twins reared apart were very important to genetics research, and scientists went to great lengths to recruit them. Until now the main way to find them had been through publicity: they read magazine articles about twin studies and volunteered to take part. As Jeannie said, that process gave a sample that was predominantly respectable middle-class, which was a disadvantage in general and a crippling problem to the study of criminality.

But for him personally it was a catastrophe. He looked her in the eye and tried to hide his dismay. This was worse than he had feared. Only last night Preston Barck had said *We all know this company has secrets.* Jim Proust had said no one could find them out. He had not reckoned with Jeannie Ferrami.

Berrington clutched at a straw. 'Finding similar entries in a database is not as easy as it sounds.'

'True. Graphic images use up many megabytes of space. Searching such records is vastly more difficult than running Spelcheck on your doctoral thesis.'

'I believe it's quite a problem in software design. So what did you do?'

'I wrote my own software.'

Berrington was surprised. 'You did?'

'Sure. I took a Master's in computer science at Princeton, as you know. When I was at Minnesota, I worked with my professor on neural-network-type software for pattern recognition.'

Could she be that smart? 'How does it work?'

'It uses fuzzy logic to speed up pattern matching. The pairs we're looking for are similar, but not absolutely identical. For example, X-rays of identical teeth, taken by different technicians on different machinery, are not exactly the same. But the human eye can see that they're the same, and when the X-rays are scanned and digitized and stored electronically, a computer equipped with fuzzy logic can recognize them as a pair.'

'I imagine you'd need a computer the size of the Empire State Building.'

'I figured out a way to shorten the process of pattern matching by looking at a small portion of the digitized image. Think about it: to recognize a friend, you don't need to scan his whole body—just his face. Automobile enthusiasts can identify most common cars from a photograph of one headlight. My sister can name any Madonna track after listening to about ten seconds of it.'

'That's open to error.'

She shrugged. 'By not scanning the entire image, you risk overlooking some matches. I figured out that you can radically shorten the search process with only a small margin of error. It's a question of statistics and probabilities.'

All psychologists studied statistics, of course. 'But how can the same program scan X-rays and electrocardiograms and fingerprints?'

'It recognizes electronic patterns. It doesn't care what they represent.'

'And your program works?'

'It seems to. I got permission to try it out on a database of dental records held by a large medical insurance company. It produced several hundred pairs. But of course I'm only interested in twins who have been raised apart.'

'How do you pick them out?'

'I eliminated all the pairs with the same surname, and all the married women, since most of them have taken the husband's name. The remainder are twins with no apparent reason for having different surnames.'

Ingenious, Berrington thought. He was torn between admiration of Jeannie and fear of what she could find out. 'How many were left?'

'Three pairs—kind of a disappointment. I was hoping for more. In one case, one of the twins had changed his surname for religious reasons: he had become a Muslim and taken an Arab name. Another pair had disappeared without trace. Fortunately, the third pair are just what I was looking for: Steven Logan is a law-abiding citizen and Dennis Pinker is a murderer.'

Berrington knew that. Late one evening, Dennis Pinker had cut the electric power to a cinema in the middle of a *Friday the Thirteenth* movie. In the ensuing panic he had molested several women. One girl had apparently tried to fight him off, and he had killed her.

So Jeannie had found Dennis. Christ, he thought, she's dangerous. She could ruin everything: the takeover, Jim's political career, Threeplex, even Berrington's academic reputation. Fear made him angry: how could everything he had ever worked for be threatened by his own protégée? But there was no way he could have known what would happen.

Her being here at Jones Falls was lucky, in that he had early warning of what she was up to. However, he saw no way out. If only her files could be destroyed in a fire, or she could be killed in a car wreck. But that was fantasy.

Might it be possible to undermine her faith in her

software? 'Did Steven Logan know he was adopted?' he said with hidden malice.

'No.' Jeannie's brow wrinkled in a troubled frown. 'We know that families often lie about adoption, but he thinks his mother would have told him the truth. But there may be another explanation. Suppose they were unable to adopt through the normal channels, for some reason, and they bought a baby. They might lie about that.'

'Or your system could be flawed,' Berrington suggested. 'Just because two boys have identical teeth doesn't guarantee they're twins.'

'I don't think my system is flawed,' Jeannie said briskly. 'But I am worried about telling dozens of people that they might be adopted. I'm not even sure I have the right to invade their lives in that way. I've only just realized the magnitude of the problem.'

He looked at his watch. 'I'm running out of time, but I'd love to discuss this some more. Are you free for dinner?'

'Tonight?'

'Yes.'

He saw her hesitate. They had had dinner together once before, at the International Congress of Twin Studies, where they had first met. Since she had been at JFU they had had drinks together once, in the bar of the Faculty Club on campus. One Saturday they had met by accident in a shopping street in Charles Village, and Berrington had shown her around the Baltimore Museum of Art. She was not in love with him, not by a long way, but he knew she had enjoyed his company on those three occasions. Besides, he was her mentor: it was hard for her to refuse him.

'Sure,' she said.

'Shall we go to Hamptons, at the Harbor Court Hotel? I think it's the best restaurant in Baltimore.' It was the swankiest, anyway.

'Fine,' she said, standing up.

'Then I'll pick you up at eight?'

'Okay.'

As she turned away from him, Berrington was visited by a sudden vision of her naked back, smooth and muscular, and her flat ass and her long, long legs; and for a moment his throat went dry with desire. Then she shut the door.

Berrington shook his head to clear his mind of lascivious fantasy, then called Preston again. 'It's worse than we thought,' he said without preamble. 'She's written a computer program that searches medical databases and finds matched pairs. First time she tried it out, she found Steven and Dennis.'

'Shit.'

'We've got to tell Jim.'

'The three of us should get together and decide what the hell we're going to do. How about tonight?'

'I'm taking Jeannie to dinner.'

'Do you think that may solve the problem?'

'It can't hurt.'

'I still think we'll have to pull out of the Landsmann deal in the end.'

'I don't agree,' Berrington said. 'She's pretty bright,

but one girl isn't going to uncover the whole story in a week.'

However, as he hung up he wondered if he should be so sure.

CHAPTER EIGHT

THE STUDENTS in the Human Biology Lecture Theater were restive. Their concentration was poor and they fidgeted. Jeannie knew why. She, too, felt unnerved. It was the fire and the rape. Their cosy academic world had been destabilized. Everyone's attention kept wandering as their minds went back again and again to what had happened.

'Observed variations in the intelligence of human beings can be explained by three factors,' Jeannie said. 'One: different genes. Two: a different environment. Three: measurement error.' She paused. They all wrote in their notebooks.

She had noticed this effect. Any time she offered a numbered list, they would all write it down. If she had simply said *Different genes, different environments and experimental error* most of them would have written nothing. Since she had first observed this syndrome, she included as many numbered lists as possible in her lectures.

She was a good teacher—somewhat to her surprise. In general, she felt her people skills were poor. She was impatient, and she could be abrasive, as she had been this morning with Sergeant Delaware. But she was a good communicator, clear and precise, and she enjoyed explaining things. There was nothing better than the kick of seeing enlightenment dawn in a student's face.

'We can express this as an equation,' she said, and she turned around and wrote on the board with a stick of chalk:

$$Vt = Vg + Ve + Vm$$

'Vt being the Total variance, Vg the Genetic component, Ve the Environmental, and Vm the Measurement error.' They all wrote down the equation. 'The same may be applied to any measurable difference between human beings, from their height and weight to their tendency to believe in God. Can anyone here find fault with this?' No one spoke, so she gave them a clue. 'The sum may be greater than the parts. But why?'

One of the young men spoke up. It was usually the men: the women were irritatingly shy. 'Because genes and the environment act upon one another to multiply effects?'

'Exactly. Your genes steer you towards certain environmental experiences and away from others. Babies with different temperaments elicit different treatment from their parents. Active toddlers have different experiences than sedentary ones, even in the same house. Daredevil adolescents take more drugs than choirboys in the same town. We must add to the right-hand side of the equation the term Cge, meaning gene–environment covariation.' She wrote it on the board then looked at the Swiss Army watch on her wrist. It was five to four. 'Any questions?'

For a change it was a woman who spoke up. She was Donna-Marie Dickson, a nurse who had gone back to school in her thirties, bright but shy. She said: 'What about the Osmonds?'

The class laughed, and the woman blushed. Jeannie said gently: 'Explain what you mean, Donna-Marie. Some of the class may be too young to remember the Osmonds.'

'They were a pop group in the seventies, all brothers and sisters. The Osmond family are all musical. But they don't have the same genes, they're not twins. It seems to have been the family environment that made them all musicians. Same with the Jackson Five.' The others, who were mostly younger, laughed again, and the woman smiled bashfully and added: 'I'm giving away my age here.'

'Ms Dickson makes an important point, and I'm surprised no one else thought of it,' Jeannie said. She was not surprised at all, but Donna-Marie needed to have her confidence boosted. 'Charismatic and dedicated parents may make all their children conform to a certain ideal, regardless of their genes, just as abusive parents may turn out a whole family of schizophrenics. But these are extreme cases. A malnourished child will be short in stature, even if its parents and grandparents are all tall. An over-fed child will be fat even if it has thin ancestors. Nevertheless, every new study tends to show, more conclusively than the last, that it is predominantly the genetic inheritance, rather than the environment or style of upbringing, that determines the nature of the child.' She paused. 'If there are no more questions, please read Bouchard et al. in *Science*, 12 October 1990, before next Monday.' Jeannie picked up her papers.

They began packing up their books. She hung around for a few moments, to create an opportunity for students too timid to ask questions in open class to approach her privately. Introverts often became great scientists.

It was Donna-Marie who came up to the front. She had a round face and fair curly hair. Jeannie thought she must have been a good nurse, calm and efficient. 'I'm so sorry about poor Lisa,' Donna-Marie said. 'What a terrible thing to happen.'

'And the police made it worse,' Jeannie said. 'The cop who drove her to the hospital was a real asshole, frankly.'

'That's too bad. But maybe they'll catch the guy who did it. They're passing out flyers with his picture all over the campus.'

'Good!' The picture Donna-Marie was talking about must have been produced by Mish Delaware's computer program. 'When I left her this morning she was working on the picture with a detective.'

'How's she feeling?'

'Still numb . . . but jumpy, too.'

Donna-Marie nodded. 'They go through phases, I've seen it before. The first phase is denial. They say: "I just want to put it all behind me and get on with my life." But it's never that easy.'

'She should talk to you. Knowing what to expect might help her.'

'Any time,' Donna-Marie said.

Jeannie walked across the campus towards Nut House. It was still hot. She found herself looking around watchfully, like a nervous cowboy in a western movie, expecting someone to come around the corner of the freshmen's residence and attack her. Until now the campus of Jones Falls had seemed like an oasis of old-fashioned tranquillity in the desert of a modern American city. Indeed, JFU was like a small town, with its shops and banks, sports fields and parking meters, bars and restaurants, offices and homes. It had a population of five thousand, of whom half lived on campus. But it had been turned into a dangerous landscape. That guy has no *right* to do this, Jeannie thought bitterly; to make me feel afraid in my own place of work. Maybe a crime always had this effect, causing the solid ground to seem unsteady beneath your feet.

As she entered her office she started thinking about Berrington Jones. He was an attractive man, very attentive to women. Whenever she had spent time with him she had enjoyed herself. She was also indebted to him, for he had given her this job.

On the other hand, he was a bit oily. She suspected that his attitude to women might be manipulative. He always made her think of the joke about a man who says to a woman: 'Tell me all about yourself. What's your opinion of, for example, me?'

In some ways he did not seem like an academic. But Jeannie had observed that the real go-getters of the university world noticeably lacked the vague, helpless air of the stereotype absent-minded professor. Berrington looked and acted like a powerful man. He had not done great scientific work for some years, but that was normal: brilliant original discoveries, such as the double helix, were usually made by people under thirty-five. As scientists got older they used their experience and instincts to help and direct younger, fresher minds. Berrington did that well, with his three professorships and his role as conduit for Threeplex's research money. He was not as respected as he might have been, however, because other scientists disliked his involvement in politics. Jeannie herself thought his science was good and his politics were crap.

At first she had readily believed Berrington's story about downloading files from Australia, but on reflection she was not so sure. When Berry looked at Steven Logan he had seen a ghost, not a phone bill.

Many families had parenthood secrets. A married woman might have a lover, and only she would know who was the real father of her child. A young girl might have a baby and give it to her mother, pretending to be an older sister, the whole family conspiring to keep the secret. Children were adopted by neighbours, relatives and friends who concealed the truth. Lorraine Logan might not be the type to make a dark secret of a straightforward adoption, but she could have a dozen other reasons for lying to Steven about his origins. But how was Berrington involved? Could he be Steven's real father? The thought made Jeannie smile. Berry was handsome, but he was at least six inches shorter than Steven. Although anything was possible, that particular explanation seemed unlikely.

It bothered her to have a mystery. In every other respect, Steven Logan represented a triumph for her. He was a decent law-abiding citizen with an identical twin brother who was a violent criminal. Steve vindicated her computer search program and confirmed her theory of criminality. Of course, she would need another hundred pairs of twins like Steven and Dennis before she could talk about proof. All the same, she could not have had a better start to her program of research.

Tomorrow she would see Dennis. If he turned out to be a dark-haired dwarf, she would know something had gone badly wrong. But if she were right, he would be Steven Logan's double.

She had been shaken by the revelation that Steve Logan had no idea he might be adopted. She was going to have to work out some procedure for dealing with this phenomenon. In future she could contact the parents, and check how much they had told, before approaching the twins. It would slow her work, but it had to be done: she could not be the one to reveal family secrets.

That problem was soluble, but she could not lose the sense of anxiety caused by Berrington's sceptical questions and Steven Logan's incredulity, and she began to think anxiously of the next stage of her project. She was hoping to use her software to scan the FBI's fingerprint file.

It was the perfect source for her. Many of the twenty-two million people on file had been suspected or convicted of crimes. If her program worked, it should yield hundreds of twins including several raised-apart pairs. It could mean a quantum leap forward in her research. But first she had to get the Bureau's permission.

Her best friend at school had been Ghita Sumra, a math wizard of Asian-Indian descent who now had a top job managing information technology for the FBI. She worked in Washington, DC but lived here in Baltimore. Ghita had already agreed to ask her employers to cooperate with Jeannie. She had promised a decision by the end of this week, but now Jeannie wanted to hurry her. She dialled her number.

Ghita had been born in Washington but her voice still held a hint of the Indian subcontinent in its softness of tone and roundness of vowels. 'Hey, Jeannie, how was your weekend?' she said.

'Awful,' Jeannie told her. 'My mom finally flipped and I had to put her in a home.'

'I'm sorry to hear that. What did she do?'

'She forgot it was the middle of the night, got up, forgot to get dressed, went out to buy a carton of milk, and forgot where she lived.'

'What happened?'

'The police found her. Fortunately she had a cheque from me in her purse, and they were able to track me down.'

'How do you feel about it?'

That was a female question. The men—Jack Budgen, Berrington Jones—had asked what she was going to do.

It took a woman to ask how she felt. 'Bad,' she said. 'If I have to take care of my mother, who's going to take care of me? You know?'

'What kind of place is she in?'

'Cheap. It's all her insurance will cover. I have to get her out of there, as soon as I can find the money to pay for something better.' She heard a pregnant silence at the other end of the line, and realized that Ghita thought she was being asked for money. 'I'm going to do some private tutoring on the weekends,' she added hastily. 'Did you talk to your boss about my proposal yet?'

'As a matter of fact I did.'

Jeannie held her breath.

'Everyone here is real interested in your software,' Ghita said.

That was neither a yes nor a no. 'You don't have computer scanning systems?'

'We do, but your search engine is faster by far than anything we've got. They're talking about licensing the program from you.'

'Wow. Maybe I won't need to do private tuition at the weekends after all.'

Ghita laughed. 'Before you open the champagne, let's make sure the program actually works.'

'How soon can we do that?'

'We'll run it at night, for minimal interference with normal use of the database. I'll have to wait for a quiet night. It should happen within a week, two at most.'

'No faster?'

'Is there a rush?'

There was, but Jeannie was reluctant to tell Ghita of her worries. 'I'm just impatient,' she said.

'I'll get it done as soon as possible, don't worry. Can you upload the program to me by modem?'

'Sure. But don't you think I need to be there when you run it?'

'No, I don't, Jeannie,' Ghita said with a smile in her voice.

'Of course, you know more about this kind of stuff than I do.'

'Here's where to send it.' Ghita read out an E-mail address and Jeannie wrote it down. 'I'll send you the results the same way.'

'Thanks. Hey, Ghita?'

'What?'

'Am I going to need a tax shelter?'

'Get out of here,' Ghita laughed, and she hung up.

Jeannie clicked her mouse on America Online and accessed the Internet. As her search program was uploading to the FBI, there was a knock at her door and Steven Logan came in.

She looked at him appraisingly. He had been given disturbing news, and it showed in his face; but he was young and resilient, and the shock had not brought him down. He was psychologically very stable. If he had been a criminal type—as his brother Dennis presumably was—he would have picked a fight with someone by now. 'How are you doing?' she asked him.

He closed the door behind him with his heel. 'All finished,' he said. 'I've undergone all the tests and completed each examination and filled out every questionnaire that can be devised by the ingenuity of humankind.'

'Then you're free to go home.'

'I was thinking of staying in Baltimore for the evening. As a matter of fact, I wondered if you'd care to have dinner with me.'

She was taken by surprise. 'What for?' she said ungraciously.

The question threw him. 'Well, uh . . . for one thing, I'd sure like to know more about your research.'

'Oh. Well, unfortunately I have a dinner engagement already.'

He looked very disappointed. 'Do you think I'm too young?'

'For what?'

'To take you out.'

Then it struck her. 'I didn't know you were asking me for a *date*,' she said.

He was embarrassed. 'You're kind of slow to catch on.'

'I'm sorry.' She *was* being slow. He had come on to her yesterday, on the tennis court. But she had spent all day thinking of him as a subject for study. However, now that she thought about it, he *was* too young to take her out. He was twenty-two, a student; she was seven years older; it was a big gap.

He said: 'How old is your date?'

'Fifty-nine or sixty, something like that.'

'Wow. You like *old* men.'

Jeannie felt bad about turning him down. She owed him something, she thought, after what she had put him through. Her computer made a doorbell sound to tell her that the program had finished uploading. 'I'm through here for the day,' she said. 'Would you like to have a drink in the Faculty Club?'

He brightened immediately. 'Sure, I'd love to. Am I dressed okay?'

He was wearing khakis and a blue linen shirt. 'You'll be better dressed than most of the professors there,' she smiled. She exited and turned her computer off.

'I called my mom,' Steven said. 'Told her about your theory.'

'Was she mad?'

'She laughed. Said I wasn't adopted, nor did I have a twin brother who was put out for adoption.'

'Strange.' It was a relief to Jeannie that the Logan family was taking all this so calmly. On the other hand, their laid-back scepticism made her worry that perhaps Steven and Dennis were not twins after all.

'You know . . .' She hesitated. She had said enough shocking things to him today. But she plunged on. 'There is another possible way you and Dennis could be twins.'

'I know what you're thinking,' he said. 'Babies switched at the hospital.'

He was very quick. This morning she had noticed more than once how fast he worked things out. 'That's right,' she said. 'Mother number one has identical twin boys, mothers two and three each have a boy. The twins are given to mothers two and three, and their babies are given to mother number one. As the children grow up, mother number one concludes that she has fraternal twins who bear one another remarkably little resemblance.'

'And if mothers two and three don't happen to be acquainted, no one ever observes the startling resemblance between babies two and three.'

'It's the old staple of the romance writers,' she admitted. 'But it's not impossible.'

'Is there a book on this twin stuff?' he said. 'I'd like to know more about it.'

'Yeah, I have one . . .' She looked along her bookshelf. 'No, it's at home.'

'Where do you live?'

'Close by.'

'You could take me home for that drink.'

She hesitated. This one is the normal twin, she reminded herself, not the psychopath.

He said: 'You know so much about me, after today. I'm curious about you. I'd like to see where you live.'

Jeannie shrugged. 'Sure, why not? Let's go.'

It was five o'clock, and the day was at last beginning to cool as they left Nut House. Steve whistled when he saw the red Mercedes. 'What a neat car!'

'I've had it for eight years,' she said. 'I love it.'

'My car's in the parking lot. I'll come up behind you and flash my lights.'

He left. Jeannie got into her car and started it. A few minutes later she saw headlights in her rear-view mirror. She pulled out of her parking space and drove off.

As she left the campus she noticed a police cruiser tuck in behind Steve's car. She checked her speedometer and slowed down to thirty.

It seemed Steven Logan was smitten with her. Although she did not reciprocate his feelings, she was kind of pleased. It was flattering to have won the heart of a handsome young hunk.

He stayed on her tail all the way home. She pulled up outside her house and he parked right behind her.

As in many old Baltimore streets, there was a row stoop, a communal front porch that ran the length of the row, where neighbours had sat cooling themselves in the days before air-conditioning. She crossed the stoop and stood at her door, getting out her keys.

Two cops exploded out of the patrol car, guns in their hands. They took up firing positions, their arms stretched out stiffly, their guns pointed directly at Jeannie and Steve.

Jeannie's heart stopped.

Steven said: 'What the *fuck—*'

Then one of the men yelled: 'Police! Freeze!'

Jeannie and Steve both raised their hands.

But the police did not relax. 'On the floor, mother-fucker!' one of them screamed. 'Face down, hands behind your back!'

Jeannie and Steve both lay face down.

The policemen approached them as cautiously as if they were ticking bombs. Jeannie said: 'Don't you think you'd better tell us what this is about?'

'You can stand up, lady,' said one.

'Gee, thanks.' She got to her feet. Her heart was beating fast, but it seemed obvious the cops had made some kind of dumb mistake. 'Now that you've scared me half to death, what the hell is going on?'

Still they did not reply. They both kept their guns pointed at Steve. One of them knelt beside him and, with a swift, practised motion, handcuffed him. 'You're under arrest, cocksucker,' the cop said.

Jeannie said: 'I'm a broad-minded woman, but is all this cursing really necessary?' Nobody took any notice of her. She tried again. 'What's he supposed to have done, anyway?'

A light blue Dodge Colt screeched to a halt behind the police cruiser and two people got out. One was Mish Delaware, the detective from the Sex Crimes Unit. She had on the same skirt and blouse she had worn this morning, but she wore a linen jacket that only partly concealed the gun at her hip.

'You got here fast,' said one of the patrolmen.

'I was in the neighbourhood,' she replied. She looked at Steve, lying on the floor. 'Get him up,' she said.

The patrolman took Steve by the arm and helped him stand.

'It's him all right,' Mish said. 'This is the guy who raped Lisa Hoxton.'

'Steven did?' Jeannie said incredulously. *Jesus, I was about to take him into my apartment.*

'Rape?' Steven said.

'The patrolman spotted his car leaving the campus,' Mish said.

Jeannie noticed Steve's car for the first time. It was a tan Datsun, about fifteen years old. Lisa had thought she saw the rapist driving an old white Datsun.

Her initial shock and alarm began to give way to rational thought. The police suspected him: that did not make him guilty. What was the evidence? She said: 'If you're going to arrest every man you see driving a rusty Datsun . . .'

Mish handed Jeannie a piece of paper. It was a flyer bearing a computer-generated black-and-white picture of a man. Jeannie stared at it. It did look something like Steven. 'It might be him and it might not,' Jeannie said.

'What are you doing with him?'

'He's a subject. We've been doing tests on him at the lab. I can't believe he's the guy!' Her test findings showed that Steven had the inherited personality of a potential criminal—but they also showed he had *not* developed into an actual criminal.

Mish said to Steven: 'Can you account for your movements yesterday between seven and eight p.m.?'

'Well, I was at JFU,' Steven said.

'What were you doing?'

'Nothing much. I was supposed to go out with my cousin Ricky, but he cancelled. I came here to check out where I had to be this morning. I had nothing else to do.'

It sounded lame even to Jeannie. Maybe Steve was the rapist, she thought with dismay. But if he was, her entire theory was shot.

Mish said: 'How did you spend your time?'

'I watched the tennis for a while. Then I went to a bar in Charles Village and spent a couple of hours. I missed the big fire.'

'Can anyone corroborate what you say?'

'Well, I spoke to Dr Ferrami, although at that point I didn't actually know who she was.'

Mish turned to Jeannie. Jeannie saw hostility in her eyes, and recalled how they had clashed, this morning, when Mish was persuading Lisa to cooperate.

Jeannie said: 'It was after my tennis game, a few minutes before the fire broke out.'

Mish said: 'So you can't tell us where he was when the rape took place.'

'No, but I'll tell you something else. I've spent all day giving this man tests, and he doesn't have the psychological profile of a rapist.'

Mish looked scornful. 'That's not evidence.'

Jeannie was still holding the flyer. 'Nor is this, I guess.' She balled it up and dropped it on the sidewalk.

Mish jerked her head at the cops. 'Let's go.'

Steven spoke in a clear, calm voice. 'Wait a minute.'

They hesitated.

'Jeannie, I don't care about these guys, but I want to tell you that I didn't do this, and I never would do anything of the kind.'

She believed him. She asked herself why. Was it just that she needed him to be innocent for her theory? No: she had the psychological tests to show that he had none of the characteristics associated with criminals. But there was something else: her intuition. She felt safe with him. He gave out no wrong signals. He listened when she talked, he did not try to bully her, he did not touch her inappropriately, he showed no anger or hostility. He liked women and he respected her. He was not a rapist.

She said: 'Do you want me to call someone? Your parents?'

'No,' he said decisively. 'They'd worry. And it will all be over in a few hours. I'll tell them then.'

'Aren't they expecting you home tonight?'

'I said I might stay with Ricky again.'

'Well, if you're sure,' she said dubiously.

'I'm sure.'

'Let's go,' Mish said impatiently.

'What's the damn hurry?' Jeannie snapped. 'You have some other innocent people to arrest?'

Mish glared at her. 'Do you have anything more to say to me?'

'What happens next?'

'There'll be a line-up. We'll let Lisa Hoxton decide whether this is the man that raped her.' With facetious deference Mish added: 'Is that okay with you, Dr Ferrami?'

'That's just fine,' Jeannie said.

CHAPTER NINE

They took Steve down town in the pale blue Dodge Colt. The woman detective drove and the other one, a heavy-set white man with a moustache, sat beside her, looking cramped in the little car. No one spoke.

Steve quietly seethed with resentment. Why the hell should he be riding in this uncomfortable car, his wrists in handcuffs, when he ought to be sitting in Jeannie Ferrami's apartment with a cold drink in his hand? They had just better get this over with quickly, that was all.

Police headquarters was a pink granite building in Baltimore's red-light district, among the topless bars and porn outlets. They drove up a ramp and parked in the internal garage. It was full of police cruisers and cheap compacts like the Colt.

They took Steve up in an elevator and put him in a room with yellow-painted walls and no windows. They took off his handcuffs then left him alone. He assumed they locked the door: he did not check.

There was a table and two hard plastic chairs. On the table was an ashtray containing two cigarette butts, both filter tips, one with lipstick on. Set into the door was a pane of opaque glass: Steve could not see out but he guessed they could see in.

Looking at the ashtray, he wished he smoked. It would be something to do here in this yellow cell. Instead he paced up and down.

He told himself he could not really be in trouble. He had managed to get a look at the picture on the flyer, and although it was more or less like him, it was not *him*. No doubt he resembled the rapist, but when he stood in the line-up with several other tall young men, the victim would not pick him out. After all, the poor woman must have looked long and hard at the bastard who did it: his face would be burned into her memory. She would not make a mistake.

But the cops had no right to keep him waiting like this. Okay, they had to eliminate him as a suspect, but they did not have to take all night about it. He was a law-abiding citizen.

He tried to look on the bright side. He was getting a close-up view of the American justice system. He would be his own lawyer: it would be good practice. When in the future he represented a client accused of a crime, he would know what the person was going through in police custody.

He had seen the inside of a precinct house once before, but that had felt very different. He was only sixteen. He had gone to the police with one of his teachers. He had admitted the crime immediately, and told the police candidly everything that had happened. They could see his injuries: it was obvious the fight had not been one-sided. His parents had come to take him home.

That had been the most shameful moment of his life. When Mom and Dad walked into that room, Steve wished he were dead. Dad looked mortified, as if he had suffered a great humiliation; Mom's expression showed grief; they both looked bewildered and wounded. At the time, it was all he could do not to burst into tears, and he still felt choked up whenever he recalled it.

But this was different. This time he was innocent.

The woman detective came in carrying a cardboard file folder. She had taken off her jacket but she still wore the gun on her belt. She was an attractive black woman of about forty, a little on the heavy side, and she had an I'm-in-charge air.

Steve looked at her with relief. 'Thank God,' he said.

'For what?'

'That something is happening. I don't want to be here all damn night.'

'Would you sit down, please?'

Steve sat.

'My name is Sergeant Michelle Delaware.' She took a sheet of paper from the folder and put it on the table. 'What's your full name and address?'

He told her, and she wrote it on the form. 'Age?'

'Twenty-two.'

'Education?'

'I have a college degree.'

She wrote on the form then pushed it across to him. It was headed:

Police Department
Baltimore, Maryland

EXPLANATION OF RIGHTS
Form 69

'Please read the five sentences on the form then write your initials in the spaces provided beside each sentence.' She passed him a pen.

He read the form and started to initial.

'You have to read aloud,' she said.

He thought for a moment. 'So that you know I'm literate?' he asked.

'No. It's so that you can't later *pretend* to be illiterate and claim that you were not informed of your rights.'

This was the kind of thing they did not teach you in law school.

He read: 'You are hereby advised that: One, you have the absolute right to remain silent.' He wrote *SL* in the space at the end of the line, then read on, initialling each sentence. 'Two, anything you say or write may be used against you in a court of law. Three, you have the right to talk with a lawyer at any time, before any questioning, before answering any questions, or during any questioning. Four, if you want a lawyer and cannot afford to hire one, you will not be asked any questions, and the court will be requested to appoint a lawyer for you. Five, if you agree to answer questions, you may stop at any time and request a lawyer, and no further questions will be asked of you.'

'Now sign your name, please.' She pointed to the form. 'Here, and here.'

The first space for signature was underneath the sentence:

I HAVE READ THE ABOVE EXPLANATION OF MY RIGHTS, AND I FULLY UNDERSTAND IT.

____

Signature

Steve signed.

'And just below,' she said.

I am willing to answer questions, and I do not want any attorney at this time. My decision to answer questions without having an attorney present is free and voluntary on my part.

____

Signature

He signed, and said: 'How the hell do you get *guilty* people to sign that?'

She did not answer him. She printed her name, then signed the form.

She put the form back in the folder and looked at him. 'You're in trouble, Steve,' she said. 'But you seem like a regular guy. Why don't you just tell me what happened?'

'I can't,' he said. 'I wasn't there. I guess I just look like the jerk that did it.'

She sat back, crossed her legs, and gave him a friendly smile. 'I know men,' she said in an intimate tone. 'They have urges.'

If I didn't know better, Steve thought, I'd read her body language and say she was coming on to me.

She went on: 'Let me tell you what I think. You're an attractive man, she took a shine to you.'

'I've never met this woman, Sergeant.'

She ignored that. Leaning across the table, she covered his hand with her own. 'I think she provoked you.'

Steve looked at her hand. She had good nails, manicured, not too long, varnished with clear nail polish. But the hand was wrinkled: she was older than forty, maybe forty-five.

She spoke in a conspiratorial voice, as if to say, *This is just between you and me.* 'She was asking for it, so you gave it to her. Am I right?'

'Why the hell would you think that?' Steve said with irritation.

'I know what girls are like. She led you on then, at the last minute, she changed her mind. But it was too late. A man can't just *stop*, just like that, not a real man.'

'Oh, wait, I get it,' Steve said. 'The suspect agrees with you, imagining that he's making it look better for himself; but in fact he's admitted that intercourse took place, and half of your job is done.'

Sergeant Delaware sat back, looking annoyed, and Steve figured he had guessed right.

She stood up. 'Okay, smartass, come with me.'

'Where are we going?'

'The cells.'

'Wait a minute. When's the line-up?'

'As soon as we can reach the victim and bring her in here.'

'You can't hold me indefinitely without some court procedure.'

'We can hold you for twenty-four hours without *any* procedure, so button your lip and let's go.'

She took him down in the elevator and through a door into a lobby that was painted a dull orange-brown. A notice on the wall reminded officers to keep suspects handcuffed while searching them. The turnkey, a black policeman in his fifties, stood at a high counter. 'Hey, Spike,' said Sergeant Delaware. 'Got a smartass college boy for you.'

The turnkey grinned. 'If he's so smart, how come he's in here?'

They both laughed. Steve made a mental note not to tell cops, in future, when he had second-guessed them. It was a failing of his: he had antagonized his school-teachers the same way. Nobody likes a wise guy.

The cop called Spike was small and wiry, with grey hair and a little moustache. He had a perky air but there was a cold look in his eyes. He opened a steel door. 'You coming through to the cells, Mish?' he said. 'I got to ask you to check your weapon if so.'

'No, I'm finished with him for now,' she said. 'He'll be in a line-up later.' She turned and left.

'This way, boy,' the turnkey said to Steve.

He went through the door.

He was in the cell block. The walls and floor were the same muddy colour. Steve thought the elevator had stopped at the second floor, but there were no windows, and he felt as if he were in a cavern deep underground, and it would take him a long time to climb back to the surface.

In a little anteroom was a desk and a camera on a stand. Spike took a form from a pigeonhole. Reading it upside-down, Steve saw it was headed:

Police Department
Baltimore, Maryland

PRISONER ACTIVITY REPORT
Form 92/12

The man took the cap off a ballpoint pen and began to fill out the form.

When it was done he pointed to a spot on the ground and said: 'Stand right there.'

Steve stood in front of the camera. Spike pressed a button and there was a flash.

'Turn sideways.'

There was another flash.

Next Spike took out a square card printed in pink ink and headed:

Federal Bureau of Investigation,
United States Department of Justice
Washington, D.C. 20537

Spike inked Steve's fingers and thumbs on a pad then pressed them to squares on the card marked *1.R.THUMB, 2.R.INDEX*, and so on. Steve noticed that Spike, though a small man, had big hands with prominent veins. As he did so, Spike said conversationally: 'We have a new Central Booking Facility over at the city jail on Greenmount Avenue, and they have a computer that takes your prints without ink. It's like a big photocopy machine: you just press your hands on the glass. But down here we still using the dirty old system.'

Steve realized he was beginning to feel ashamed, even though he had not committed a crime. It was partly the grim surroundings, but mainly the feeling of powerlessness. Ever since the cops burst out of the patrol car outside Jeannie's house, he had been moved around like a piece of meat, with no control over himself. It brought a man's self-esteem down fast.

When his fingerprints were done he was allowed to wash his hands.

'Permit me to show you to your suite,' Spike said jovially.

He led Steve down the corridor with cells to the left and right. Each cell was roughly square. On the side that gave on to the corridor there was no wall, just bars, so that every square inch of the cell was clearly visible from outside. Through the bars Steve could see that each cell had a metal bunk fixed to the wall and a stainless-steel toilet and washbasin. The walls and bunks were painted orange-brown and covered with graffiti. The toilets had no lids. In three or four of the cells a man lay listlessly on the bunk, but most of them were empty. 'Monday's a quiet day here at the Lafayette Street Holiday Inn,' Spike joked.

Steve could not have laughed to save his life.

Spike stopped in front of an empty cell. Steve stared inside as the cop unlocked the door. There was no privacy. Steve realized that if he needed to use the toilet he would have to do it in full view of anyone, man or woman, who happened to be walking along the corridor. Somehow that was more humiliating than anything.

Spike opened a gate in the bars and ushered Steve inside. The gate crashed shut and Spike locked it.

Steve sat on the bunk. 'Jesus Christ Almighty, what a place,' he said.

'You get used to it,' Spike said cheerfully, and he went away.

A minute later he came back carrying a styrofoam package. 'I got a dinner left,' he said. 'Fried chicken. You want some?'

Steve looked at the package, then at the open toilet, and shook his head. 'Thanks all the same,' he said. 'I guess I'm not hungry.'

CHAPTER TEN

BERRINGTON ORDERED champagne.

Jeannie would have liked a good slug of Stolichnaya on the rocks, after the kind of day she had had, but drinking hard liquor was no way to impress an employer, and she decided to keep her desire to herself.

Champagne meant romance. On previous occasions when they had met socially he had been charming rather than amorous. Was he now going to make a pass at her? It made her uneasy. She had never met a man who could take rejection with good grace. And this man was her boss.

She did not tell him about Steve, either. She was on the point of doing so several times during their dinner, but something held her back. If, against all her expectations, Steve did turn out to be a criminal, her theory would start to look shaky. But she did not like to anticipate bad news. Before it was proved she would not foster doubts. And she felt sure it would all turn out to be an appalling mistake.

She had talked to Lisa. 'They've arrested Brad Pitt!' she had said. Lisa was horrified to think that the man had spent the entire day at Nut House, her place of work, and that Jeannie had been on the point of taking him into her home. Jeannie had explained that she was sure Steve was not really the perpetrator. Later she realized she probably should not have made the call: it might be construed as interfering with a witness. Not that it would make any real difference. Lisa would look at a row of young white men, and either she would see the man who raped her or she would not. It was not the kind of thing she would make a mistake about.

Jeannie had also spoken to her mother. Patty had been there today, with her three sons, and Mom talked animatedly about how the boys had raced around the corridors of the home. Mercifully, she seemed to have forgotten that it was only yesterday she moved into Bella Vista. She talked as if she had lived there for years, and reproached Jeannie for not visiting more often. After the conversation Jeannie felt a little better about her mother.

'How was the sea bass?' Berrington said, interrupting her thoughts.

'Delicious. Very delicate.'

He smoothed his eyebrows with the tip of his right index finger. For some reason the gesture struck her as self-congratulatory. 'Now I'm going to ask you a question, and you have to answer honestly.' He smiled, so that she would not take him too seriously.

'Okay.'

'Do you like dessert?'

'Yes. Do you take me for the kind of woman who would pretend about a thing like that?'

He shook his head. 'I guess there's not much you do pretend about.'

'Not enough, probably. I have been called tactless.'

'Your worst failing?'

'I could probably do better if I thought about it. What's your worst failing?'

Berrington answered without hesitation. 'Falling in love.'

'That's a failing?'

'It is if you do it too often.'

'Or with more than one person at a time, I guess.'

'Maybe I should write to Lorraine Logan and ask her advice.'

Jeannie laughed, but she did not want the conversation to get on to Steven. 'Who's your favourite painter?' she said.

'See if you can guess.'

Berrington was a super-patriot, so he must be sentimental, she figured. 'Norman Rockwell?'

'Certainly not!' He seemed genuinely horrified. 'A vulgar illustrator! No, if I could afford to collect paintings I'd buy American Impressionists. John Henry Twachtman's winter landscapes. I'd love to own *The White Bridge*. What about you?'

'Now *you* have to guess.'

He thought for a moment. 'Joan Miró.'

'Why?'

'I imagine you like bold splashes of colour.'

She nodded. 'Perceptive. But not quite right. Miró's too messy. I prefer Mondrian.'

'Ah, yes, of course. The straight lines.'

'Exactly. You're good at this.'

He shrugged, and she realized he had probably played guessing games with many women.

She dipped a spoon into her mango sorbet. This was definitely not a business dinner. Soon she would have to make a firm decision about what her relationship with Berrington was going to be.

She had not kissed a man for a year and a half. Since Will Temple walked out on her she had not even been on a date until today. She was not carrying a torch for Will: she no longer loved him. But she was wary.

However, she was going crazy living the life of a nun. She missed having someone hairy in bed with her; she missed the masculine smells—bicycle oil and sweaty football shirts and whisky—and most of all she missed the sex. When radical feminists said the penis was the enemy, Jeannie wanted to reply, *Speak for yourself, sister.*

She glanced up at Berrington, delicately eating caramelized apples. She liked the guy, despite his nasty politics. He was smart—her men *had* to be intelligent—and he had winning ways. She respected him for his scientific work. He was slim and fit looking, he was probably a very experienced and skilful lover, and he had nice blue eyes.

All the same, he was too old. She liked mature men, but not that mature.

How could she reject him without ruining her career? The best course might be to pretend to interpret his attention as kindly and paternal. That way she might avoid spurning him outright.

She took a sip of champagne. The waiter kept

refilling her glass and she was not sure how much she had drunk, but she was glad she did not have to drive.

They ordered coffee. Jeannie asked for a double espresso to sober her up. When Berrington had paid the bill, they took the elevator to the parking garage and got in his silver Lincoln Town Car.

Berrington drove along the harbour side and got on to the Jones Falls Expressway. 'There's the city jail,' he said, pointing to a fortress-like building that occupied a city block. 'The scum of the earth are in there.'

Steve might be in there, Jeannie thought.

How had she even contemplated sleeping with Berrington? She did not feel the least warmth of affection for him. She felt ashamed that she had even toyed with the idea. As he pulled up to the kerb outside her house, she said firmly: 'Well, Berry, thank you for a charming evening.' Would he shake hands, she wondered, or try to kiss her? If he tried to kiss her, she would offer her cheek.

But he did neither. 'My phone at home is out of order, and I need to make one call before I go to bed,' he said. 'May I use your phone?'

She could hardly say, *Hell, no, stop by a pay phone.* It looked as if she was going to have to deal with a determined pass. 'Of course,' she said, suppressing a sigh. 'Come on up.' She wondered if she could avoid offering him coffee.

She jumped out of the car and led the way across the row stoop. The front door gave on to a tiny lobby with two more doors. One led to the ground-floor apartment, occupied by Mr Oliver, a retired stevedore. The other, Jeannie's door, opened on to the staircase that led up to her second-floor apartment.

She frowned, puzzled. Her door was open.

She went inside and led the way up the stairs. A light was on up there. That was curious: she had left before dark.

The staircase led directly into her living room. She stepped inside and screamed.

He was standing at her refrigerator with a bottle of vodka in his hand. He was scruffy and unshaven, and he seemed a little drunk.

Behind her, Berrington said: 'What's going on?'

'You need better security in here, Jeannie,' the intruder said. 'I picked your locks in about ten seconds.'

Berrington said: 'Who the hell is he?'

Jeannie said in a shocked voice: 'When did you get out of jail, Daddy?'

CHAPTER ELEVEN

THE LINE-UP room was on the same floor as the cells.

In the anteroom were six other men of about Steve's age and build. He guessed they were cops. They did not speak to him and avoided his gaze. They were treating him like a criminal. He wanted to say, *Hey, guys, I'm on your side, I'm not a rapist, I'm innocent.*

They all had to take off their wristwatches and jewellery and put on white paper coveralls over their clothes. While they were getting ready, a young man in a suit came in and said: 'Which of you is the suspect, please?'

'That's me,' Steve said.

'I'm Lew Tanner, the public defender,' the man said. 'I'm here to make sure the line-up is run correctly. Do you have any questions?'

'How long will it take me to get out of here afterwards?' Steve said.

'Assuming you're not picked out of the line-up, a couple of hours.'

'Two hours!' Steve said indignantly. 'Do I have to go back in that fucking cell?'

'I'm afraid so.'

'Jesus Christ.'

'I'll ask them to handle your discharge as fast as possible,' Lew said. 'Anything else?'

'No, thanks.'

'Okay.' He went out.

A turnkey ushered the seven men through a door onto a stage. There was a backdrop, with a graduated scale that showed their height, and positions numbered one to ten. A powerful light shone on them, and a screen divided the stage from the rest of the room. The men could not see through the screen, but they could hear what was going on beyond it.

For a while there was nothing but footsteps and occasional low voices, all male. Then Steve heard the unmistakable sound of a woman's steps. After a moment a man's voice spoke, sounding as if he were reading from a card or repeating something by rote.

'Standing before you are seven people. They will be known to you by number only. If any of these individuals have done anything to you, or in your presence, I want you to call out their number, and number only. If you would like any of them to speak, say any form of specific words, we will have them say those words. If you would like to have them turn around or face sideways, then they will do that as a group. Do you recognize any one of them who has done anything to you or in your presence?'

There was a silence. Steve's nerves were wound up tight as guitar strings, even though he was sure she would not pick him out.

A low female voice said: 'He had a hat on.'

She sounded like an educated middle-class woman of about his own age, Steve thought.

The male voice said: 'We have hats. Would you like them all to put on a hat?'

'It was more of a cap. A baseball cap.'

Steve heard anxiety and tension in her voice but also determination. There was no hint of falseness. She sounded like the kind of woman that would tell the truth, even when distressed. He felt a little better.

'Dave, see if we have seven baseball caps in that closet.'

There was a pause of several minutes. Steve ground his teeth in impatience. A voice muttered: 'Jeeze, I didn't know we had all this stuff . . . eyeglasses, moustaches—'

'No chitchat, please, Dave,' the first man said. 'This is a formal legal proceeding.'

Eventually a detective came onto the stage from the side and handed a baseball cap to each man in the line-up. They all put them on and the detective left.

From the other side of the screen came the sound of a woman crying.

The male voice repeated the form of words used earlier. 'Do you recognize any one of them who has done anything to you or in your presence? If so call out their number and number only.'

'Number four,' she said with a sob in her voice.

Steve turned and looked at the backdrop.

He was number four.

'No!' he shouted. 'This can't be right! It wasn't me!'

The male voice said: 'Number four, did you hear that?'

'Of course I heard it but I didn't do this!'

The other men in the line-up were already leaving the stage.

'For Christ's sake!' Steve stared at the opaque screen, his arms spread wide in a pleading gesture. 'How could you pick me out? I don't even know what you look like!'

The male voice from the other side said: 'Don't say anything, mam, please. Thank you very much for your cooperation. This way out.'

'There's something wrong here, can't you understand?' Steve yelled.

The turnkey Spike appeared. 'It's all over, son, let's go,' he said.

Steve stared at him. For a moment he was tempted to knock the little man's teeth down his throat.

Spike saw the look in his eye and his expression hardened. 'Let's have no trouble, now. You got nowhere to run.' He took Steve's arm in a grip that felt like a steel clamp. It was useless to protest.

Steve felt as if he had been bludgeoned from behind. This had come from nowhere. His shoulders slumped and he was seized by helpless fury. 'How did this happen?' he said. 'How did this happen?'

CHAPTER TWELVE

BERRINGTON SAID: 'Daddy?'

Jeannie wanted to bite off her tongue. It was the dumbest thing she could have said: *When did you get out of jail, Daddy?* Only minutes ago Berrington had described the people in the city jail as the scum of the earth.

She felt mortified. It was bad enough her boss finding out that her father was a professional burglar. Having Berrington meet him was even worse. His face had been bruised by a fall and he had several days' growth of beard. His clothes were dirty and he had a faint but disgusting smell. She felt so ashamed she could not look at Berrington.

There had been a time, many years ago, when she was not ashamed of him. Quite the reverse: he made other girls' fathers seem boring and tiresome. He had been handsome and fun loving, and he would come home in a new suit, his pockets full of money. There would be movies and new dresses and ice-cream sundaes and Mom would buy a pretty nightdress and go on a diet. But he always went away again, and around about the age of nine she found out why.

Tammy Fontaine told her. She would never forget the conversation.

'Your jumper's horrible,' Tammy had said.

'Your nose is horrible,' Jeannie had replied wittily, and the other girls broke up.

'Your mom buys you clothes that are really, like, gruesome.'

'Your mom's fat.'

'Your daddy's in jail.'

'He is not.'

'He is so.'

'He is NOT!'

'I heard my daddy tell my mommy. He was reading the newspaper. *I see old Pete Ferrami's back in jail again*, he said.'

'Liar, liar, pants on fire,' Jeannie had chanted, but in her heart she believed Tammy. It explained everything: the sudden wealth, the equally sudden disappearances, the long absences.

Jeannie never had another of those taunting schoolgirl conversations. Anyone could shut her up by mentioning her father. At the age of nine, it was like being crippled for life. Whenever something went missing at school, she felt they all looked accusingly at her. She never shook the guilty feeling. If another woman looked in her purse and said: 'Darn, I thought I had a ten-dollar bill,' Jeannie would flush crimson. She became obsessively honest: she would walk a mile to return a cheap ballpoint, terrified that if she kept it the owner would say she was a thief like her father.

Now here he was, standing there in front of her boss,

dirty and unshaven and probably broke. 'This is Professor Berrington Jones,' she said. 'Berry, meet my father, Pete Ferrami.'

Berrington was gracious. He shook Daddy's hand. 'Good to meet you, Mr Ferrami,' he said. 'Your daughter is a very special woman.'

'Ain't that the truth,' Daddy said with a pleased grin.

'Well, Berry, now you know the family secret,' she said resignedly. 'Daddy was sent to jail, for the third time, on the day I graduated *summa cum laude* from Princeton. He's been incarcerated for the last eight years.'

'It could have been fifteen,' Daddy said. 'We had guns on that job.'

'Thank you for sharing that with us, Dad. It's sure to impress my boss.'

Daddy looked hurt and baffled, and she felt a stab of pity for him, despite her resentment. His weakness hurt him as much as it hurt his family. He was one of nature's failures. The fabulous system that reproduced the human race—the profoundly complex DNA mechanism Jeannie studied—was programmed to make every individual a little bit different. It was like a photocopier with a built-in error. Sometimes the result was good: an Einstein, a Louis Armstrong, an Andrew Carnegie. And sometimes it was a Pete Ferrami.

Jeannie had to get rid of Berrington fast. 'If you want to make that call, Berry, you can use the phone in the bedroom.'

'Uh, it'll keep,' he said.

Thank God for that. 'Well, thank you for a very special evening.' She held out her hand to shake.

'It was a pleasure. Good night.' He shook hands awkwardly and went out.

Jeannie turned to her father. 'What happened?'

'I got time off for good behaviour. I'm free. And naturally, the first thing I wanted was to see my little girl.'

'Right after you went on a three-day drunk.' He was so transparently insincere, it was offensive. She felt the familiar rage rise inside her. Why couldn't she have a father like other people's?

He said: 'Come on, be nice.'

Anger turned into sadness. She had never had a real father and she never would. 'Give me that bottle,' she said. 'I'll make coffee.'

Reluctantly he handed her the vodka and she put it back in the freezer. She put water in the coffee maker and turned it on.

'You look older,' he said to her. 'I see a little grey in your hair.'

'Gee, thanks.' She put out mugs, cream and sugar.

'Your mother went grey early.'

'I always thought you were the cause of that.'

'I went to her place,' he said in tone of mild indignation. 'She doesn't live there any more.'

'She's in Bella Vista now.'

'That's what the neighbour told me. Mrs Mendoza. She gave me your address. I don't like to think of your mother in a place like that.'

'Then take her out of there!' Jeannie said indignantly. 'She's still your wife. Get yourself a job and a decent apartment and start taking care of her.'

'You know I can't do that. I never could.'

'Then don't criticize me for not doing it.'

His tone became wheedling. 'I didn't say anything about you, honey. I just said I don't like to think of your mother in an institution, that's all.'

'I don't like it either, nor does Patty. We're going to try to raise the money to get her out of there.' Jeannie felt a sudden surge of emotion, and she had to fight back tears. 'God damn it, Daddy, this is tough enough without having you sit there complaining.'

'Okay, okay,' he said.

Jeannie swallowed hard. *I shouldn't let him get to me this way.* She changed the subject. 'What are you going to do now? Do you have any plans?'

'I'll look around for a while.'

He meant he would scout for a place to rob. Jeannie said nothing. He was a thief, and she could not change him.

He coughed. 'Maybe you could let me have a few bucks to get me started.'

That made her mad again. 'I'll tell you what I'm going to do,' she said in a tight voice. 'I'll let you shower and shave while I put your clothes through the washer. If you keep your hands off that vodka bottle, I'll make you some eggs and toast. You can borrow some pyjamas and sleep on my couch. But I'm not giving you any cash. I'm desperately trying to find the money to pay for Mom to stay someplace where they'll treat her like a human being and I don't have a dollar to spare.'

'Okay, sweetie,' he said, putting on a martyred air. 'I understand.'

She looked at him. In the end, when the turmoil of shame and anger and pity died down, all she felt was longing. She wished with all her heart that he could take care of himself, could stay in one place more than a few weeks, could hold down a normal job, could be loving and supportive and stable. She yearned for a father who would be a father. And she knew she would never, ever have her wish. There was a place in her heart for a father, and it would always be empty.

The phone rang.

Jeannie picked it up. 'Hello.'

It was Lisa, sounding upset. 'Jeannie, it was him!'

'Who? What?'

'That guy they arrested with you. I picked him out of the line-up. He's the one that raped me. Steven Logan.'

'He's the rapist?' Jeannie said incredulously. 'Are you sure?'

'There's no doubt, Jeannie,' Lisa said. 'Oh, my God, it was horrible seeing his face again. I didn't say anything at first, because he looked different with no hat. Then the detective made them all put on baseball caps, and I knew for certain sure.'

'Lisa, it can't be him,' Jeannie said.

'What do you mean?'

'His tests are all wrong. And I spent time with him, I have a feeling.'

'But I *recognized* him.' Lisa sounded annoyed.

'I'm amazed. I can't understand it.'

'This spoils your theory, doesn't it? You wanted one twin to be good and the other bad.'

'Yes. But one counter-example doesn't disprove a theory.'

'I'm sorry if you feel your project is threatened by this.'

'That's not the reason I'm saying it's not him.' Jeannie sighed. 'Hell, maybe it is. I don't know any more. Where are you now?'

'At home.'

'Are you okay?'

'Yes, I'm fine, now he's locked up in jail.'

'He seems so nice.'

'They're the worst kind, Mish told me. The ones that seem perfectly normal on the surface are the cleverest and most ruthless, and they enjoy making women suffer.'

'My God.'

'I'm going to bed, I'm exhausted. I just wanted to tell you. How was your evening?'

'So-so. I'll tell you all about it tomorrow.'

'I still want to go to Richmond with you.'

Jeannie had planned to take Lisa to help her interview Dennis Pinker. 'Do you feel up to it?'

'Yes, I really want to carry on living a normal life. I'm not sick, I don't need to convalesce.'

'Dennis Pinker will probably be Steve Logan's double.'

'I know. I can handle it.'

'If you're sure.'

'I'll call you early.'

'Okay. Goodnight.'

Jeannie sat down heavily. Could Steven's engaging nature be no more than a mask? I must be a bad judge of character if that's so, she thought. And maybe a bad scientist too: perhaps all identical twins will turn out to be identically criminal. She sighed.

Her own criminal ancestry sat beside her. 'That professor is a nice-looking guy, but he must be older than me!' he said. 'You having a thing with him, or what?'

Jeannie wrinkled her nose. 'The bathroom's through there, Daddy,' she said.

CHAPTER THIRTEEN

STEVE WAS back in the interrogation room with the yellow walls. The same two cigarette butts were still in the ashtray. The room had not changed, but he had. Three hours ago he had been a law-abiding citizen, innocent of any crime worse than driving at sixty in a fifty-five zone. Now he was a rapist, arrested and identified by the victim and accused. He was in the justice machine, on the conveyor. He was a criminal. No matter how often he reminded himself that he had done nothing wrong, he could not shake the feeling of worthlessness and ignominy.

Earlier he had seen the woman detective, Sergeant Delaware. Now the other one, the man, came in, also carrying a blue folder. He was Steve's height but much broader and heavier, with iron-grey hair cut short and a bristling moustache. He sat down and took out a pack of cigarettes. Without speaking, he tapped out a cigarette, lit it, and dropped the match in the ashtray. Then he opened the folder. Inside was yet another form. This one was headed:

DISTRICT COURT OF MARYLAND FOR ....
(City/County)

The top half was divided into two columns headed **COMPLAINANT** and **DEFENDANT**. A little lower down it said:

STATEMENT OF CHARGES

The detective began to fill out the form, still without speaking. When he had written a few words he lifted the white top sheet and checked each of four attached carbon copies: green, yellow, pink and tan.

Reading upside-down, Steve saw that the victim's name was Lisa Margaret Hoxton. 'What's she like?' he said.

The detective looked at him. 'Shut the fuck up,' he said. He drew on his cigarette and continued writing.

Steve felt demeaned. The man was abusing him and he was powerless to do anything about it. It was another stage in the process of humiliating him, making him feel insignificant and helpless. You bastard, he thought, I'd like to meet you outside of this building, without your damn gun.

The detective began filling in the charges. In box number one he wrote Sunday's date, then *at Jones Falls University gymnasium, Balto., MD.* Below he wrote *Rape, 1st degree.* In the next box he put the place and date again, then *Assault with intent to rape.*

He picked up a continuation sheet and added two more charges: *Battery* and *Sodomy.*

'Sodomy?' Steve said in surprise.

'Shut the fuck up.'

Steve was ready to punch him out. This is deliberate,

he told himself. The guy wants to provoke me. If I throw a punch at him, he has an excuse to call three other guys in here to hold me down while he kicks the shit out of me. Don't do it, don't do it.

When he finished writing, the detective turned the two forms around and pushed them across the table at Steve. 'You're in bad trouble, Steve. You've beaten and raped and sodomized a girl—'

'No, I haven't.'

'Shut the fuck up.'

Steve bit his lip and remained silent.

'You're scum. You're shit. Decent people don't even want to be in the same room as you. You've beaten and raped and sodomized a girl. I know it's not the first time. You've been doing it a while. You're sly, and you plan, and you've always got away with it in the past. But this time you've been caught. Your victim has identified you. Other witnesses place you near the scene at the time. In an hour or so, just as soon as Sergeant Delaware has gotten a search or seizure warrant from the court commissioner on duty, we're going to take you over to Mercy Hospital and do a blood test and comb through your pubic hair and show that your DNA matches what we found in the victim's vagina.'

'How long does that take—the DNA test?'

'Shut the fuck up. You're nailed, Steve. Do you know what's going to happen to you?'

Steve said nothing.

'The penalty for first-degree rape is life imprisonment. You're going to jail, and you know what's going to happen there? You're going to get a taste of what you've been dishing out. A good-looking youngster like you? No problem. You're going to be beaten and raped and sodomized. You're going to find out how Lisa felt. Only in your case it will go on for years and years and years.'

He paused, picked up the cigarette packet, and offered it to Steve.

Surprised, Steve shook his head.

'By the way, I'm Detective Brian Allaston.' He lit a cigarette. 'I really don't know why I'm telling you this, but there is a way you can make it better for yourself.'

Steve frowned, curious. What was coming now?

Detective Allaston got up, walked around the table, and sat on its edge, with one foot on the floor, intimately close to Steve. He leaned forward and spoke in a softer voice. 'Let me lay it out for you. Rape is vaginal intercourse, using force or the threat of force, against the will or without the consent of the woman. For it to be first-degree rape, there has to be an aggravating factor such as kidnapping, disfigurement, or rape by two or more persons. The penalties for second-degree rape are lower. Now, if you can persuade me that what you did was only second degree, you could do yourself a great big favour.'

Steve said nothing.

'Do you want to tell me how it happened?'

At last Steve spoke. 'Shut the fuck up,' he said.

Allaston moved very fast. He came off the table, grabbed Steve by the front of his shirt, lifted him out of the chair and slammed him against the cinderblock wall. Steve's head jerked back and hit the wall with a painful bang.

He froze, clenching his fists at his sides. Don't do it, he said to himself, don't fight back. It was hard. Detective Allaston was overweight and out of condition and Steve knew he could lay the bastard out in no time. But he had to control himself. All he had to hold on to was his innocence. If he beat up a cop, no matter how he had been provoked, he would be guilty of a crime. And then he might as well give up. He would lose heart if he did not have that sense of righteous indignation to buoy him up. So he stood there, rigid, his teeth clenched, while Allaston pulled him off the wall and slammed him back twice, three times, four times.

'Don't ever speak to me like that again, you punk,' Allaston said.

Steve felt his rage ebb away. Allaston was not even hurting him. This was theatre, he realized. Allaston was acting a part, and doing it badly. He was the tough guy and Mish was the nice one. In a while she would come in and offer him coffee and pretend to be his friend. But she would have the same aim as Allaston: to persuade Steve to confess to the rape of a woman he had never met called Lisa Margaret Hoxton. 'Let's cut the crap, Detective,' he said. 'I know you're a tough son of a bitch with hairs growing out of your nostrils, and you know that if we were somewhere else and you didn't have that gun on your belt I could beat the shit out of you, so let's stop trying to prove ourselves.'

Allaston looked surprised. No doubt he had expected Steve to be too scared to speak. He let go of Steve's shirt front and walked to the door.

'They told me you were a smartass,' he said. 'Well,

let me tell you what I'm going to do for your education. You're going back to the cells for a while, but this time you'll have company. You see, all the forty-one empty cells down there are somehow out of commission, so you're going to have to share with a guy called Rupert Butcher, known as Porky. You think you're a big motherfucker, but he's bigger. He's coming down from a three-day crack party, so he has a headache. Last night, around the time you were setting fire to the gymnasium and sticking your nasty dick into poor Lisa Hoxton, Porky Butcher was stabbing his lover to death with a gardening fork. You should enjoy one another. Let's go.'

Steve was scared. All his courage ebbed away as if a plug had been pulled, and he felt defenceless and defeated. The detective had humiliated him without really threatening to hurt him badly, but a night with a psychopath was seriously dangerous. This Butcher character had already committed a murder: if he were capable of rational thought he would know that he had little to lose by committing another.

'Wait a minute,' Steve said shakily.

Allaston turned back slowly. 'Well?'

'If I confess, I get a cell to myself.'

Relief showed in the detective's expression. 'Sure,' he said. His voice had suddenly become friendly.

The change of tone caused Steve to burn with resentment. 'But if I don't, I get murdered by Porky Butcher.'

Allaston spread his hands in a helpless gesture.

Steve felt his fear turn to hatred. 'In that case, Detective,' he said, 'fuck you.'

The surprised look came back into Allaston's face. 'You bastard,' he said. 'We'll see if you're so goddamn feisty in another couple of hours. Come on.'

He took Steve to the elevator and escorted him to the cell block. Spike was still there. 'Put this creep in with Porky,' Allaston told him.

Spike raised his eyebrows. 'That bad, huh?'

'Yeah. And by the way—Steve here has nightmares.'

'That so?'

'If you hear him cry out—don't worry about it, he's just dreaming.'

'I get you,' Spike said.

Allaston left and Spike took Steve to his cell.

Porky was lying on the bunk. He was about Steve's height but a lot heavier. He looked like a bodybuilder who had been in a car wreck: his bloodstained T-shirt was stretched tight over bulging muscles. He lay on his back, head toward the rear of the cell, feet hanging over the end of the bunk. He opened his eyes when Spike unlocked the gate and let Steve in.

It crashed shut and Spike locked it.

Porky opened his eyes and stared at Steve.

Steve stared back for a moment.

'Sweet dreams,' Spike said.

Porky closed his eyes again.

Steve sat on the floor, with his back to the wall, and watched Porky sleep.

CHAPTER FOURTEEN

Berrington Jones drove home slowly. He felt disappointed and relieved at the same time. Like a dieter who wrestles with temptation all the way to the ice-cream parlour then finds it closed, he had been saved from something he knew he ought not to do.

He was no closer to solving the problem of Jeannie's project and what it might uncover, however. Maybe he should have spent more time questioning her and less having fun. He frowned in perplexity as he parked outside the house and went in.

The place was quiet: Marianne, the housekeeper, must have gone to bed. He went into the den and checked his answering machine. There was one message.

'Professor, this is Sergeant Delaware from the Sex Crimes Unit calling on Monday night. I appreciate your cooperation today.' Berrington shrugged. He had done little more than confirm that Lisa Hoxton worked at Nut House. She went on: 'As you are Ms Hoxton's employer and the rape took place on campus, I thought I should tell you we have arrested a man this evening. In fact he was a subject at your laboratory today. His name is Steven Logan.'

'Jesus!' Berrington burst out.

'The victim picked him out at the line-up so I'm sure the DNA test will confirm that he is the man. Please pass this information on to any others at the college who you think appropriate. Thank you.'

'No!' Berrington said. He sat down heavily. 'No,' he said more quietly.

Then he began to weep.

After a moment he got up, still crying, and closed the study door, for fear the maid might come in. Then he returned to his desk and buried his head in his hands.

He stayed that way for some time.

When at last the tears dried up, he lifted the phone and called a number he knew by heart.

'Not the answering machine, please, God,' he said aloud as he listened to it ring out.

A young man answered. 'Hello?'

'This is me,' Berrington said.

'Hey, how are you?'

'Desolate.'

'Oh.' The tone was guilty.

If Berrington had any doubts, that note in the voice swept them away. 'You know what I'm calling about, don't you.'

'Tell me.'

'Don't play games with me, please. I'm talking about Sunday night.'

The young man sighed. 'Okay.'

'You goddamn fool. You went to the campus, didn't you? You—' He realized he should not say too much on the phone. 'You did it again.'

'I'm sorry—'

'You're sorry!'

'How did you know?'

'At first I didn't suspect you—I thought you'd left town. Then they arrested someone who looks just like you.'

'Wow! That means I'm . . .'

'You're off the hook.'

'Wow. What a break. Listen . . .'

'What?'

'You wouldn't say anything. To the police, or anything.'

'No, I won't say a word,' Berrington said with a heavy heart. 'You can rely on me.'

TUESDAY

CHAPTER FIFTEEN

THE CITY OF Richmond had an air of lost grandeur, and Jeannie thought Dennis Pinker's parents fitted right in. Charlotte Pinker, a freckled redhead in a whispering silk dress, had the aura of a great Virginia lady even though she lived in a frame house on a narrow lot. She said she was fifty-five, but Jeannie guessed she was probably nearer sixty. Her husband, whom she referred to as 'the Major', was about the same age, but he had the careless grooming and unhurried air of a man who had long retired. He winked roguishly at Jeannie and Lisa and said: 'Would you girls like a *cocktail*?'

His wife had a refined Southern accent, and she spoke a little too loudly, as if she were perpetually addressing a meeting. 'For Mercy's sake, Major, it's ten o'clock in the morning!'

He shrugged. 'Just trying to get the party off to a good start.'

'This is no party—these ladies are here to *study* us. It's because our son is a murderer.'

She called him *our son*, Jeannie noted; but that did not mean a lot. He might still have been adopted. She was desperate to ask about Dennis Pinker's parentage.

If the Pinkers admitted that he was adopted, that would solve half the puzzle. But she had to be careful. It was a delicate question. If she asked too abruptly, they were more likely to lie. She forced herself to wait for the right moment.

She was also on tenterhooks about Dennis's appearance. Was he Steven Logan's double or not? She looked eagerly at the photographs in cheap frames around the little living room. All had been taken years ago. Little Dennis was pictured in a stroller, riding a tricycle, dressed for baseball, and shaking hands with Mickey Mouse in Disneyland. There were no pictures of him as an adult. No doubt the parents wanted to remember the innocent boy before he became a convicted murderer. In consequence, Jeannie learned nothing from the photographs. That fair-haired twelve-year-old might now look exactly like Steven Logan, but he could equally well have grown up ugly and stunted and dark.

Both Charlotte and the Major had filled out several questionnaires in advance, and now they had to be interviewed for about an hour each. Lisa took the Major into the kitchen and Jeannie interviewed Charlotte.

Jeannie had trouble concentrating on the routine questions. Her mind kept wandering to Steve in jail. She still found it impossible to believe he could be a rapist. It was not just because that would spoil her theory. She liked the guy: he was smart and engaging, and he seemed kind. He also had a vulnerable side: his bafflement and distress at the news that he had a psychopathic twin had made her want to put her arms around him and comfort him.

When she asked Charlotte if any other family members had ever been in trouble with the law, Charlotte turned her imperious gaze on Jeannie and drawled: 'The men in my family have always been terribly violent.' She breathed in through flared nostrils. 'I'm a Marlowe by birth, and we are a hot-blooded family.'

That suggested that Dennis was not adopted, or that his adoption was not acknowledged. Jeannie concealed her disappointment. Was Charlotte going to deny that Dennis could be a twin?

The question had to be asked. Jeannie said: 'Mrs Pinker, is there any chance Dennis might have a twin?'

'No.'

The response was flat: no indignation, no bluster, just factual.

'You're sure.'

Charlotte laughed. 'My dear, that's one thing a mother could hardly make a mistake about!'

'He definitely isn't adopted.'

'I carried that boy in my womb, may God forgive me.'

Jeannie's spirits fell. Charlotte Pinker would lie more readily than Lorraine Logan, Jeannie judged, but all the same it was strange and worrying that they should both deny their sons were twins.

She felt pessimistic as they took their leave of the Pinkers. She had a feeling that when she met Dennis she would find he looked nothing like Steve.

Their rented Ford Aspire was parked outside. It was a hot day. Jeannie was wearing a sleeveless dress with a jacket over it for authority. The Ford's air-conditioner groaned and pumped out tepid air. She took off her pantyhose and hung her jacket on the rear-seat coat hook.

Jeannie drove. As they pulled onto the highway, heading for the prison, Lisa said: 'It really bothers me that you think I picked the wrong guy.'

'It bothers me, too,' Jeannie said. 'I know you wouldn't have done it if you didn't feel sure.'

'How can you be so certain I'm wrong?'

'I'm not certain about anything. I just have a strong feeling about Steve Logan.'

'It seems to me that you should weigh a feeling against an eyewitness certainty, and believe the eyewitness.'

'I know. But did you ever see that Alfred Hitchcock show? It's in black-and-white, you catch reruns sometimes on cable.'

'I know what you're going to say. The one where four people witness a road accident and each one sees something different.'

'Are you offended?'

Lisa sighed. 'I ought to be, but I like you too much to be mad at you about it.'

Jeannie reached across and squeezed Lisa's hand. 'Thanks.'

There was a long silence, then Lisa said: 'I hate it that people think I'm weak.'

Jeannie frowned. 'I don't think you're weak.'

'Most people do. It's because I'm small, and I have a cute little nose, and freckles.'

'Well, you don't *look* tough, it's true.'

'But I am. I live alone, I take care of myself, I hold down a job, and nobody fucks with me. Or so I thought, before Sunday. Now I feel people are right: I *am* weak. I can't take care of myself at all! Any psychopath walking around the streets can grab me and hold a knife at my face and do what he wants with my body and leave his sperm inside me.'

Jeannie looked across at her. Lisa was white faced with passion. Jeannie hoped it was doing her good to get these feelings out. 'You're not weak,' she said.

'*You're* tough,' Lisa said.

'I have the opposite problem—people think I'm invulnerable. Because I'm six feet tall and I have a pierced nostril and a bad attitude, they imagine I can't be hurt.'

'You don't have a bad attitude.'

'I must be slipping.'

'Who thinks you're invulnerable? I don't.'

'The woman who runs the Bella Vista, the home my mom's in. She said to me, straight out, *Your mother will never see sixty-five.* Just like that. *I know you'd prefer me to be honest,* she said. I wanted to tell her that just because there's a ring in my nose it doesn't mean I have no goddamn feelings.'

'Mish Delaware says rapists aren't really interested in sex. What they enjoy is having power over a woman, and dominating her, and scaring her, and hurting her. He picked someone who looked as if she would be easily frightened.'

'Who wouldn't be frightened?'

'He didn't pick you, though. You probably would have slugged him.'

'I'd like the chance.'

'Anyway, you would have fought harder than I did and you wouldn't have been helpless and terrified. So he didn't pick you.'

Jeannie saw where all this was heading. 'Lisa, that may be true, but it doesn't make the rape your fault, okay? You're not to blame, not one iota. You were in a train wreck: it could have happened to anyone.'

'You're right,' Lisa said.

They drove ten miles out of town and pulled off the interstate at a sign marked 'Greenwood Penitentiary'. It was an old-fashioned prison, a cluster of grey stone buildings surrounded by high walls with razor wire. They left the car in the shade of a tree in the visitors' parking lot. Jeannie put her jacket back on but left off her pantyhose.

'Are you ready for this?' Jeannie said. 'Dennis is going to look just like the guy who raped you, unless my methodology is all wrong.'

Lisa nodded grimly. 'I'm ready.'

The main gate opened to let out a delivery truck, and they walked in unchallenged. Security was not tight, Jeannie concluded, despite the razor wire. They were expected. A guard checked their identification and escorted them across a baking-hot courtyard where a handful of young black men in prison fatigues were throwing a basketball.

The administration building was air-conditioned.

They were shown into the office of the warden, John Temoigne. He wore a short-sleeved shirt and a tie, and there were cigar butts in his ashtray. Jeannie shook his hand. 'I'm Dr Jean Ferrami from Jones Falls University.'

'How are you, Jean?'

Temoigne was obviously the type of man who found it hard to call a woman by her surname. Jeannie deliberately did not tell him Lisa's first name. 'And this is my assistant, Ms Hoxton.'

'Hi, honey.'

'I explained our work when I wrote to you, Warden, but if you have any further questions I'd be glad to answer them.' Jeannie had to say that, even though she was itching to get a look at Dennis Pinker.

'You need to understand that Pinker is a violent and dangerous man,' said Temoigne. 'Do you know the details of his crime?'

'I believe he attempted to sexually assault a woman in a cinema, and killed her when she tried to fight him off.'

'You're close. It was at the old Eldorado movie theatre down in Greensburg. They were all watching some horror movie. Pinker got into the basement and turned off the electric power. Then, while everyone was panicking in the dark, he ran round feeling girls up.'

Jeannie exchanged a startled look with Lisa. It was so similar to what had happened at JFU on Sunday. A diversion had created confusion and panic, and given the perpetrator his opportunity. And there was a similar hint of adolescent fantasy about the two scenarios: feeling up all the girls in the darkened cinema, and seeing the women running naked out of the changing room. If Steve Logan was Dennis's identical twin, it seemed they had committed very similar crimes.

Temoigne went on: 'One woman unwisely tried to resist him, and he strangled her.'

Jeannie bridled. 'If he had felt you up, Warden, would you have *unwisely* tried to resist him?'

'I ain't a girl,' Temoigne said with the air of one who plays a winning card.

Lisa tactfully intervened. 'We should get started, Dr Ferrami—we have a lot of work to do.'

'You're right.'

Temoigne said: 'Normally you would interview the prisoner through a grille. You've specially asked to be in the same room with him, and I have orders from above to let you. All the same I urge you to think again. He is a violent and dangerous criminal.'

Jeannie felt a tremor of anxiety, but she stayed outwardly cool. 'There will be an armed guard in the room all the time we're with Dennis.'

'There sure will. But I'd be more comfortable if there was a steel mesh separating you from the prisoner.' He gave a sickly grin. 'A man doesn't even have to be a psychopath to suffer temptation with two such attractive young girls.'

Jeannie stood up abruptly. 'I appreciate your concern, Warden, I really do. But we have to carry out certain procedures, such as taking a blood sample, photographing the subject and so on, which can't be done through bars. Furthermore, parts of our interview are intimate and we feel it would compromise our results to have such an artificial barrier between us and the subject.'

He shrugged. 'Well, I guess you'll be okay.' He stood up. 'I'll walk you along to the cell block.'

They left the office and crossed a baked-earth yard to a two-storey concrete blockhouse. A guard opened an iron gate and let them in. The interior was as hot as the outside. Temoigne said: 'Robinson here will take care of you from now on. Anything else you girls need, just holler.'

'Thank you, Warden,' Jeannie said. 'We appreciate your cooperation.'

Robinson was a reassuringly tall black man of about thirty. He had a pistol in a buttoned holster and an intimidating-looking nightstick. He showed them into a small interview room with a table and half a dozen chairs in a stack. There was an ashtray on the table and a water cooler in the corner, otherwise the room was bare. The floor was tiled in grey plastic and the walls were painted a similar shade. There was no window.

Robinson said: 'Pinker will be here in a minute.' He helped Jeannie and Lisa arrange the table and chairs. Then they sat down.

A moment later the door opened.

CHAPTER SIXTEEN

Berrington Jones met with Jim Proust and Preston Barck at The Monocle, a restaurant close to the Senate office building in Washington. It was a power lunch venue, full of people they knew: congressmen, political consultants, journalists, aides. Berrington had decided there was no point in trying to be discreet. They were too well known, especially Senator Proust with his bald head and big nose. If they had met in an obscure location, some reporter would have spotted them and written a gossip item asking why they were holding secret meetings. Better to go where thirty people would recognize them and assume they were having a routine discussion about their legitimate mutual interests.

Berrington's aim was to keep the Landsmann deal on the rails. It had always been a risky venture, and Jeannie Ferrami had made it downright dangerous. But the alternative was to give up their dreams. There would be only one chance to turn America around and put her back on the course of racial integrity. It was not too late, not quite. The vision of a law-abiding, churchgoing, family oriented white America could be made a reality. But they were all around sixty years of age: they were not going to get another chance after this.

Jim Proust was the big personality, loud and blustering; but although he often annoyed Berrington, he could usually be talked around. Mild-mannered Preston, much more likeable, was also stubborn.

Berrington had bad news for them, and he got it out of the way as soon as they had ordered. 'Jeannie Ferrami is in Richmond today, seeing Dennis Pinker.'

Jim scowled. 'Why the hell didn't you stop her?' His voice was deep and harsh from years of barking orders.

As always, Jim's overbearing manner irritated Berrington. 'What was I supposed to do, tie her down?'

'You're her boss, aren't you?'

'It's a university, Jim, it's not the fucking army.'

Preston said nervously: 'Let's keep our voices down, fellas.' He wore narrow spectacles with a black frame: he had been wearing the same style since 1959, and Berrington had noticed that they were now coming back into fashion. 'We knew this might happen sometime. I say we take the initiative, and confess everything right away.'

'Confess?' Jim said incredulously. 'Are we supposed to have done something wrong?'

'It's the way people might see it—'

'Let me remind you that when the CIA produced the report that started all this, *New Developments in Soviet Science,* President Nixon himself said it was the most alarming news to come out of Moscow since the Soviets split the atom.'

Preston said: 'The report may not have been true—'

'But we thought it was. More importantly, our president believed it. Don't you remember how goddamn scary that was back then?'

Berrington certainly remembered. The Soviets had a breeding programme for human beings, the CIA had said. They were planning to turn out perfect scientists, perfect chess players, perfect athletes—and perfect soldiers. Nixon had ordered the US Army Medical Research Command, as it then was, to set up a parallel programme, and find a way to breed perfect American soldiers. Jim Proust had been given the job of making it happen.

He had come immediately to Berrington for help. A few years earlier Berrington had shocked everyone, especially his wife, Vivvie, by joining the army just when anti-war sentiment was boiling up among Americans of his age. He had gone to work at Fort Detrick, in Frederick, Maryland, studying fatigue in soldiers. By the early seventies he was the world's leading expert in the heritability of soldierly characteristics such as aggression and stamina. Meanwhile Preston, who had stayed at Harvard, had made a series of breakthroughs in understanding human fertilization. Berrington had talked him into leaving the university and becoming part of the great experiment with him and Proust.

It had been Berrington's proudest moment. 'I also remember how exciting it was,' he said. 'We were at the leading edge of science, we were setting America right, and our *president* had asked us to do this job for him.'

Preston toyed with his salad. 'Times have changed. It's no longer an excuse to say: "I did it because the president of the United States asked me to." Men have gone to jail for doing what the president told them.'

'What was wrong with it?' Jim said testily. 'It was secret, sure. But what's to *confess*, for God's sake?'

'We went undercover,' Preston said.

Jim flushed beneath his tan. 'We transferred our project into the private sector.'

That was sophistry, Berrington thought, though he did not antagonize Jim by saying so. Those clowns from the Committee to Re-Elect the President had got caught breaking into the Watergate Hotel and all of Washington ran scared. Preston set up Threeplex as a private limited corporation, and Jim gave it enough bread-and-butter military contracts to make it financially viable. After a while the fertility clinics became so lucrative that its profits paid for the research programme without help from the military. Berrington moved back into the academic world, and Jim went from the army to the CIA and then into the Senate.

Preston said: 'I'm not saying we were wrong—although some of the things we did in the early days were against the law.'

Berrington did not want the two of them to take up polarized positions. He intervened, saying calmly: 'The irony is that it proved impossible to *breed* perfect Americans. The whole project was on the wrong track. Natural breeding was too inexact. But we were smart enough to see the possibilities of genetic engineering.'

'Nobody had even heard the goddamn *words* back then,' Jim growled as he cut into his steak.

Berrington nodded. 'Jim's right, Preston. We should

be proud of what we did, not ashamed. When you think about it, we've performed a miracle. We set ourselves the task of finding out whether certain traits, such as intelligence and aggression, are genetic; then identifying the genes responsible for those traits; and finally engineering them into test-tube embryos—and we're on the brink of success!'

Preston shrugged. 'The entire human biology community has been working on the same agenda—'

'Not quite. We were more focused, and we placed our bets carefully.'

'That's true.'

In their different ways Berrington's two friends had let off steam. They were so predictable, he thought amiably; maybe old friends always were. Jim had blustered and Preston had whined. Now they might be calm enough to take a cool look at the situation. 'That brings us back to Jeannie Ferrami,' Berrington said. 'In a year or two she may tell us how to make people aggressive without turning them into criminals. The last pieces of the jigsaw are falling into place. The Landsmann takeover offers us the chance to accelerate the entire programme and get Jim into the White House too. *This is no time to draw back.*'

'That's all very well,' said Preston. 'But what are we going to do? The Landsmann organization has a goddamn ethics panel, you know.'

Berrington swallowed some snapper. 'The first thing to realize is that we do not have a *crisis* here, we just have a *problem,*' he said. 'And the problem is not Landsmann. Their accountants won't discover the truth in a hundred years of looking at our books. Our problem is Jeannie Ferrami. We have to stop her learning anything more, at least before next Monday, when we sign the takeover documents.'

Jim said sarcastically: 'But you can't *order* her, because it's a university, not the fucking army.'

Berrington nodded. Now he had them both thinking the way he wanted. 'True,' he said calmly. 'I can't give her orders. But there are more subtle ways to manipulate people than those used by the military, Jim. If you two will leave this business in my hands, I'll deal with her.'

Preston was not satisfied. 'How?'

Berrington had been turning this question over and over in his mind. He did not have a plan, but he had an idea. 'I think there's a problem around her use of medical databases. It raises ethical questions. I believe I can force her to stop.'

'She must have covered herself.'

'I don't need a *valid* reason, just a pretext.'

'What's this girl like?' Jim said.

'About thirty. Tall, very athletic. Dark hair, ring in her nose, drives an old red Mercedes. For a long time I thought very highly of her. Last night I discovered there's bad blood in the family. Her father is a criminal type. But she's also clever, feisty and stubborn.'

'Married, divorced?'

'Single, no boyfriend.'

'A dog?'

'No, she's a looker. But hard to handle.'

Jim nodded thoughtfully. 'We still have many loyal

friends in the intelligence community. It wouldn't be so difficult to make such a girl *vanish.*'

Preston looked scared. 'No violence, Jim, for God's sake.'

A waiter cleared away their plates, and they fell silent until he had gone. Berrington knew he had to tell them what he had learned from last night's message from Sergeant Delaware. With a heavy heart, he said: 'There's something else you need to know. On Sunday night a girl was raped in the gym. The police have arrested Steve Logan. The victim picked him out of a line-up.'

Jim said: 'Did he do it?'

'No.'

'Do you know who did?'

Berrington looked him in the eye. 'Yes, Jim, I do.'

Preston said: 'Oh, shit.'

Jim said: 'Maybe we should make the boys *vanish.*'

Berrington felt his throat tighten up as if he were choking, and he knew he was turning red. He leaned over the table and pointed his finger at Jim's face. 'Don't you ever let me hear you say that again!' he said, jabbing his finger so close to Jim's eyes that Jim flinched, even though he was a much bigger man.

Preston hissed: 'Knock it off, you two, people will see!'

Berrington withdrew his finger but he was not through yet. If they had been in a less public place he would have got his hands around Jim's throat. Instead he grabbed a fistful of Jim's lapel. 'We gave those boys life. We brought them into the world. Good or bad, they're our responsibility.'

'All right, all right!' Jim said.

'Just understand me. If one of them is even hurt, so help me Christ, I'll blow your fucking head off, Jim.'

A waiter appeared and said: 'Would you gentlemen like dessert?'

Berrington let go of Jim's lapel.

Jim smoothed his suit coat with angry gestures.

'Goddamn,' Berrington muttered. 'Goddamn.'

Preston said to the waiter: 'Bring me the check, please.'

CHAPTER SEVENTEEN

STEVE LOGAN had not closed his eyes all night.

Porky Butcher had slept like a baby, occasionally giving a gentle snore. Steve sat on the floor watching him, fearfully observing every movement, every twitch, thinking about what would happen when the man woke up. Would Porky pick a fight with him? Try to rape him? Beat him up?

He had good reason to tremble. Men in jail were beaten up all the time. Many were wounded, a few killed. The public outside cared nothing, figuring that if jailbirds maimed and slaughtered one another they would be less able to rob and murder law-abiding citizens.

At all costs, Steve kept telling himself shakily, he must try not to look like a victim. It was easy for people to misread him, he knew. Tip Hendricks had made that mistake. Steve had a friendly air. Although he was big, he looked as if he would not hurt a fly.

Now he had to appear ready to fight back, though without being provocative. Most of all he should not let Porky sum him up as a clean-living college boy. That would make him a perfect target for gibes, casual blows, abuse and finally a beating. He had to appear a hardened criminal, if possible. Failing that, he should puzzle and confuse Porky by sending out unfamiliar signals.

And if none of that worked?

Porky was taller and heavier than Steve, and might be a seasoned street fighter. Steve was fitter and could probably move faster, but he had not hit anyone in anger for seven years. In a bigger space, Steve might have taken Porky out early and escaped without serious injury. But here in the cell it would be bloody, whoever won. If Detective Allaston had been telling the truth, Porky had proved, within the last twenty-four hours, that he had the killer instinct. Do I have the killer instinct, Steve asked himself? Is there any such thing as the killer instinct? I came close to killing Tip Hendricks. Does that make me the same as Porky?

When he thought of what it would mean to win a fight with Porky, Steve shuddered. He pictured the big man lying on the floor of the cell, bleeding, with Steve standing over him the way he had stood over Tip Hendricks, and the voice of Spike the turnkey saying *Jesus Christ Almighty, I think he's dead.* He would rather be beaten up.

Maybe he should be passive. It might actually be safer to curl up on the floor and let Porky kick him until the man tired of it. But Steve did not know if he could do that. So he sat there with a dry throat and a racing heart, staring at the sleeping psychopath, playing out fights in his imagination, fights he always lost.

He guessed this was a trick the cops played often. Spike the turnkey certainly did not appear to think it unusual. Maybe, instead of beating people up in interrogation rooms to make them confess, they let other suspects do the job for them. Steve wondered how many people confessed to crimes they had not committed just to avoid spending a night in a cell with someone like Porky.

He would never forget this, he swore. When he became a lawyer, defending people accused of crimes, he would never accept a confession as evidence. He saw himself in front of a jury. 'I was once accused of a crime I did not commit, but I came close to confessing,' he would say. 'I've been there, I *know*.'

Then he remembered that if he were convicted of this crime he would be thrown out of law school and would never defend anyone at all.

He kept telling himself he was not going to be convicted. The DNA test would clear him. Around midnight he had been taken out of the cell, handcuffed, and driven to Mercy Hospital, a few blocks from police headquarters. There he gave a blood sample from which they would extract his DNA. He asked the nurse how long the test took, and was dismayed to learn that the results would not be ready for three days. He returned to the cells dispirited. He was put back in with Porky, who was mercifully still asleep.

He guessed he could stay awake for twenty-four hours. That was the longest they could hold him without court sanction. He had been arrested at about six p.m., so he could be stuck here until the same time tonight. Then, if not before, he must be given an opportunity to ask for bail. That would be his chance to get out.

He struggled to recall his law school lecture on bail.

'The only question the court may consider is whether the accused person will show up for trial,' Professor Rexam had intoned. At the time it had seemed as dull as a sermon; now it meant everything. The details began to come back to him. Two factors were taken into account. One was the possible sentence. If the charge was serious, it was more risky to grant bail: a person was more likely to run away from an accusation of murder than one of petty theft. The same applied if he had a record, and faced a long sentence in consequence. Steve did not have a record: although he had once been convicted of aggravated assault, that was before he was eighteen, and it could not be used against him. He would come before the court as a man with a clean sheet. However, the charges he faced were very grave.

The second factor, he recollected, was the prisoner's 'community ties': family, home, and job. A man who had lived with his wife and children at the same address for five years and worked around the corner would get bail, whereas one who had no family in the city, had moved into his apartment six weeks ago and gave his occupation as unemployed musician would probably be refused. On this score Steve felt confident. He lived with his parents and he was in his second year at law school: he had a lot to lose by running away.

The courts were not supposed to consider whether the accused man was a danger to the community. That would be prejudging his guilt. However, in practice they did. Unofficially, a man who was involved in an ongoing violent dispute was more likely to be refused bail than someone who had committed one assault. If

Steve had been accused of a series of rapes, rather than one isolated incident, his chances of getting bail would have been close to zero.

As things stood he thought it could go either way, and while he watched Porky he rehearsed increasingly eloquent speeches to the judge.

He was still determined to be his own lawyer. He had not made the phone call he was entitled to. He wanted desperately to keep this from his parents until he was able to say he had been cleared. The thought of telling them he was in jail was too much to bear: they would be so shocked and grieved. It would be comforting to share his plight with them, but each time he was tempted he remembered their faces when they had walked into the precinct house seven years ago after the fight with Tip Hendricks, and he knew that telling them would hurt him more than Porky Butcher ever could.

Throughout the night more men had been brought into the cells. Some were apathetic and compliant, others loudly protested their innocence, and one struggled with the cops and got professionally beaten up as a result.

Things had quietened down around five o'clock in the morning. At about eight, Spike's replacement brought breakfast in styrofoam containers from a restaurant called Mother Hubbard's. The arrival of food roused the inmates of the other cells, and the noise woke Porky.

Steve stayed where he was, sitting on the floor, gazing vacantly into space but anxiously watching Porky out of the corner of his eye. Friendliness would be seen as a sign of weakness, he guessed. Passive hostility was the attitude to take.

Porky sat up on the bunk, holding his head and staring at Steve, but he did not speak. Steve guessed the man was sizing him up.

After a minute or two Porky said: 'The fuck you doin' in here?'

Steve set his face in an expression of dumb resentment, then let his eyes slide over until they met Porky's. He held his gaze for a few moments. Porky was handsome, with a fleshy face that had a look of dull aggression. He gazed speculatively at Steve with bloodshot eyes. Steve summed him up as dissipated, a loser, but dangerous. He looked away, feigning indifference. He did not answer the question. The longer it took Porky to figure him out, the safer he would be.

When the turnkey pushed the food through the slit in the bars, Steve ignored it.

Porky took a tray. He ate all the bacon, eggs and toast, drank the coffee, then used the toilet noisily, without embarrassment.

When he had done he pulled up his pants, sat on the bunk, looked at Steve, and said: 'What you in here for, white boy?'

This was the moment of greatest danger. Porky was feeling him out, taking his measure. Steve now had to appear to be anything but what he was, a vulnerable middle-class student who had not been in a fight since he was a kid.

He turned his head and looked at Porky as if noticing him for the first time. He stared hard for a long moment before answering. Slurring a little, he said: 'Motherfucker started fuckin' me around so I fucked him up, but good.'

Porky stared back. Steve could not tell whether the man believed him or not. After a long moment Porky said: 'Murder?'

'Fuckin'-A.'

'Me, too.'

It seemed Porky had bought Steve's story. Recklessly, Steve added: 'Motherfucker ain't gonna fuck me around no fuckin' more.'

'Yeah,' said Porky.

There was a long silence. Porky seemed to be thinking. Eventually he said: 'Why they put us in together?'

'They got no fuckin' case against me,' Steve said. 'They figure, if I waste you in here, they got me.'

Porky's pride was touched. 'What if I waste you?' he said.

Steve shrugged. 'Then they got you.'

Porky nodded slowly. 'Yeah,' he said. 'Figures.'

He seemed to have run out of conversation. After a while he lay down again.

Steve waited. Was it all over?

After a few minutes, Porky seemed to go back to sleep.

When he snored, Steve slumped against the wall, weak with relief.

After that, nothing happened for several hours.

Nobody came to speak to Steve, no one told him what was going on. There was no Customer Service Desk where you could get information. He wanted to know when he would get the chance to ask for bail but no one told him. He tried speaking to the new turnkey but the man simply ignored him.

Porky was still asleep when the turnkey came and opened the cell door. He fitted Steve with handcuffs and leg irons then woke Porky and did the same to him. They were chained to two other men, taken a few steps to the end of the cell block and ushered into a small office.

Inside were two desks, each with a computer and laser printer. Before the desks were rows of grey plastic chairs. One desk was occupied by a neatly dressed black woman of about thirty years. She glanced up at them, said 'Please sit down,' and carried on working, tapping her keyboard with manicured fingers.

They shuffled along the row of chairs and sat. Steve looked around. It was a regular office, with steel file cabinets, noticeboards, a fire extinguisher and an old-fashioned safe. After the cells it looked beautiful.

Porky closed his eyes and appeared to go back to sleep. Of the other two men, one stared with an unbelieving expression at his right leg, which was in a plaster cast, while the other smiled into the distance, plainly having no idea where he was, seeming either high as a kite or mentally disturbed, or both.

Eventually the woman turned from her screen. 'State your name,' she said.

Steve was first in line, so he replied: 'Steven Logan.'

'Mr Logan, I'm Commissioner Williams.'

Of course: she was a court commissioner. He now remembered this part of his criminal procedure course. A commissioner was a court official, much lowlier than a judge. She dealt with arrest warrants and other minor procedural matters. She had the power to grant bail, he recalled; and his spirits lifted. Maybe he was about to get out of here.

She went on: 'I'm here to tell you what you're charged with, your trial date, time and location, whether you will have bail or be released on your own recognizance and if released, any conditions.' She spoke very fast, but Steve picked up the reference to bail that confirmed his recollection. This was the person whom he had to persuade that he could be relied on to show up at his trial.

'You are before me on charges of first-degree rape, assault with intent to rape, battery and sodomy.' Her round face was impassive as she detailed the horrible crimes he was accused of. She went on to give him a trial date three weeks ahead, and he remembered that every suspect must be given a trial date not more than thirty days away.

'On the rape charge you face life imprisonment. On the assault with intent to rape, two to fifteen years. Both these are felonies.' Steve knew what a felony was, but he wondered if Porky Butcher did.

The rapist had also set fire to the gymnasium, he recalled. Why was there no charge of arson? Perhaps because the police had no evidence directly linking him to the fire.

She handed him two sheets of paper. One stated that he had been notified of his right to be represented, the second told him how to contact a public defender. He had to sign copies of both.

She asked him a series of rapid-fire questions and keyed the answers into her computer: 'State your full name. Where do you live? And your phone number. How long have you lived there? Where did you live prior to that?'

Steve began to feel more hopeful as he told the commissioner that he lived with his parents, he was in his second year at law school, and he had no adult criminal record. She asked if he had a drug or alcohol habit and he was able to say no. He wondered if he would get the chance to make some kind of statement appealing for bail, but she spoke fast and appeared to have a script she had to follow.

'For the charge of sodomy I find lack of probable cause,' she said. She turned from her computer screen and looked at him. 'This does not mean that you did not commit the offence, but that there is not enough information here, in the detective's statement of probable cause, for me to affirm the charge.'

Steve wondered why the detectives had put that charge in. Perhaps they hoped he would deny it indignantly and give himself away, saying, *That's disgusting, I fucked her but I didn't sodomize her, what do you think I am?*

The commissioner went on: 'But you must still stand trial for the charge.'

Steve was confused. What was the point of her finding if he still had to stand trial? And if he, a second-year-law student, found all this hard to follow, what was it like for the average person?

The commissioner said: 'Do you have any questions?'

Steve took a deep breath. 'I want to apply for bail,' he began. 'I'm innocent—'

She interrupted him. 'Mr Logan, you are before me on felony charges, which fall under rule 638B of the court. Which means that I, as a commissioner, cannot make a bail decision upon you. Only a judge can.'

It was like a punch in the face. Steve was so disappointed he felt ill. He stared at her unbelievingly. 'Then what's the point of this whole farce?' he said angrily.

'At this time you are being held at a no-bail status.'

He raised his voice. 'So why have you asked me all these questions and raised my hopes? I thought I could get out of this place!'

She was unmoved. 'The information you've given me about your address and so on will be checked by a pre-trial investigator who will report to the court,' she said calmly. 'You go for bail review tomorrow and the judge will make the bail decision.'

'I'm being kept in a cell with him!' Steve said, pointing at the sleeping Porky.

'The cells are not part of my responsibility—'

'The guy is a murderer! The only reason he hasn't killed me yet is that he can't stay awake! Now I'm formally complaining to you, as a court official, that I'm being mentally tortured and my life is in danger.'

'When the cells are full you have to share—'

'The cells aren't full, look out your door and you can see. Most of them are empty. They put me in with him so he would beat me up. And if he does I'm taking action against you, personally, Commissioner Williams, for letting it happen.'

She softened a little. 'I'll look into it. Now I'm handing you some papers.' She gave him the charge summary, the probable cause statement, and several other papers. 'Please sign each one and take a copy.'

Frustrated and downhearted, Steve took the ballpoint she offered and signed the papers. As he was doing so, the turnkey prodded Porky and woke him up. Steve handed the papers back to the commissioner. She put them in a folder.

Then she turned to Porky. 'State your name.'

Steve buried his head in his hands.

CHAPTER EIGHTEEN

JEANNIE STARED at the door of the interview room as it slowly opened.

The man who walked in was Steven Logan's double.

Beside her, she heard Lisa gasp.

Dennis Pinker looked so like Steven that Jeannie would never be able to tell them apart.

The system worked, she thought triumphantly. She was vindicated. Even though the parents vehemently denied that either of these two young men could possibly have a twin, they were as alike as her two hands.

The curly fair hair was cut the same way: short, with a part. Dennis rolled the sleeves of his prison fatigues the same neat way Steven did the cuffs of his blue linen shirt. Dennis closed the door behind him with his heel, the way Steven had when he walked into Jeannie's office in Nut House. He gave her an engaging, boyish smile just like Steven's as he sat. She could hardly believe this was not Steven.

She looked at Lisa. She was staring bug-eyed at Dennis, her face pale with fear. 'It's him,' she breathed.

Dennis looked at Jeannie and said: 'You're going to give me your panties.'

Jeannie was chilled by his cool certainty, but she was

also intellectually excited. Steven would never say a thing like that. Here it was, the same genetic material transformed into two completely different individuals—one a charming college boy, the other a psychopath. But was the difference merely superficial?

Robinson, the guard, said mildly: 'Now behave yourself and be nice, Pinker, or you'll be in bad trouble.'

Dennis gave that boyish grin again, but his words were scary. 'Robinson won't even know it's happened, but you'll do it,' he said to Jeannie. 'You'll walk out of here with the breeze blowing on your bare ass.'

Jeannie made herself calm. This was empty bragging. She was smart and tough: Dennis would not have found it easy to attack her even if she had been alone. Having a tall prison guard standing next to her with a nightstick and a gun, she was perfectly safe.

'Are you okay?' she murmured to Lisa.

Lisa was pale, but her mouth was set in a determined line, and she said grimly: 'I'm fine.'

Like his parents, Dennis had filled out several forms in advance. Now Lisa began on the more complex questionnaires, which could not be completed simply by ticking boxes. As they worked, Jeannie reviewed the results and compared Dennis with Steven. The similarities were astonishing: psychological profile, interests and hobbies, tastes, physical skills—all were the same. Dennis even had the same astonishingly high IQ as Steven.

What a waste, she thought. This young man could become a scientist, a surgeon, an engineer, a software designer. Instead he's in here, vegetating.

The big difference between Dennis and Steven was in their socialization. Steven was a mature man with above-average social skills—comfortable meeting strangers, prepared to accept legitimate authority, at ease with his friends, happy to be part of a team. Dennis had the interpersonal skills of a three-year-old. He grabbed anything he wanted, he had trouble sharing, he was frightened of strangers, and if he could not get his way he lost his temper and became violent.

Jeannie could remember being three years old. It was her earliest memory. She saw herself leaning over the cot in which her new baby sister lay sleeping. Patty had been wearing a pretty pink sleepsuit with pale blue flowers embroidered on the collar. Jeannie could still feel the hatred that had possessed her as she stared at the tiny face. Patty had stolen her mommy and daddy. Jeannie wanted with all her being to kill this intruder who had taken so much of the love and attention previously reserved for Jeannie alone. Aunt Rosa had said: 'You love your little sister, don't you?' and Jeannie replied: 'I hate her, I wish she would die.' Aunt Rosa had slapped her, and Jeannie had felt doubly mistreated.

Jeannie had grown up, and so had Steven, but Dennis never had. Why was Steven different from Dennis? Had he been saved by his upbringing? Or did he just seem different? Were his social skills no more than a mask for the psychopath beneath?

As she watched and listened, Jeannie realized there was another difference. She was afraid of Dennis. She could not put her finger on the exact cause, but there was menace in the air all around him. She had the sense he would do anything that came into his head, regardless of the consequences. Steven had not given her that feeling for one moment.

Jeannie photographed Dennis and took close-ups of both ears. In identical twins the ears were normally highly similar, especially the attachment of the ear lobes.

When they were almost done, Lisa took a blood sample from Dennis, something she had been trained to do. Jeannie could hardly wait to see the DNA comparison. She was certain Steven and Dennis had the same genes. That would prove beyond doubt that they were identical twins.

Lisa routinely sealed the phial and signed the seal, then she went to put it in the cool box in the trunk of the car, leaving Jeannie to finish the interview on her own.

As Jeannie completed the last set of questions, she wished she could get Steven and Dennis in the laboratory together for a week. But that was not going to be possible for many of her twin pairs. In studying criminals she would constantly face the problem that some of her subjects were in jail. The more sophisticated tests, involving laboratory machinery, would not be done on Dennis until he got out of jail, if ever. She just had to live with that. She would have plenty of other data to work with.

She finished the last questionnaire. 'Thank you for your patience, Mr Pinker,' she said.

'You didn't give me your panties yet,' he said coolly.

Robinson said: 'Now, Pinker, you been good all afternoon, don't spoil it.'

Dennis threw the guard a look of sheer contempt. Then he said to Jeannie: 'Robinson's scared of rats, did you know that, lady psychologist?'

Suddenly Jeannie felt anxious. There was something going on that she did not understand. She began hurriedly to tidy up her papers.

Robinson looked embarrassed. 'I hate rats, it's true, but I ain't scared of them.'

'Not even of that big grey one in the corner?' Dennis said, pointing.

Robinson whirled around. There was no rat in the corner, but when Robinson's back was turned Dennis reached into his pocket and whipped out a tightly wrapped package. He moved so quickly that Jeannie did not guess what he was doing until it was too late. He unfolded a blue spotted handkerchief to reveal a fat grey rat with a long pink tail. Jeannie shuddered. She was not squeamish, but there was something profoundly creepy about seeing the rat cupped lovingly in the hands that had strangled a woman.

Before Robinson could turn around again, Dennis had released the rat.

It ran across the room. 'There, Robinson, there!' Dennis cried.

Robinson turned around, saw the rat and paled. 'Shit,' he growled, and he drew his nightstick.

The rat ran along the floor moulding, looking for somewhere to hide. Robinson went after it, lashing out with his nightstick. He made a series of black marks on the wall but missed the rat.

Jeannie watched Robinson with a warning alarm ringing in her mind. There was something wrong here, something that did not make sense. This was a humorous jape. Dennis was not a practical joker, he was a sexual pervert and a murderer. What he had done was uncharacteristic. Unless, she realized with a tremor of dread, this was a diversion, and Dennis had some other purpose—

She felt something touch her hair. She turned around in her chair, and her heart stopped.

Dennis had moved and was standing up close to her. In front of her face he held what looked like a home-made knife: it was a tin spoon with the bowl flattened and sharpened to a point.

She wanted to scream but she felt strangled. A second ago she had thought herself perfectly safe: now she was being threatened by a murderer with a knife. How could it have happened so quickly? The blood seemed to drain out of her head and she could hardly think.

Dennis grabbed her hair with his left hand and moved the point of the knife so close to her eye that she could not focus on it. He bent over and spoke in her ear. His breath was warm on her cheek and he smelled sweaty. His voice was so low that she could hardly hear him over the noise Robinson was making. 'Do as I say or I'll slice your eyeballs.'

She melted with terror. 'Oh, God, no, don't make me blind,' she pleaded.

Hearing her own voice speak in such an alien tone of grovelling surrender brought her to her senses somewhat. She tried desperately to pull herself together and think. Robinson was still chasing the rat: he had no idea what Dennis was up to. Jeannie could hardly believe this was happening. They were in the heart of a state prison and she had an armed guard, yet she was at Dennis's mercy. How glibly she had thought, a few short hours ago, that she would give him a hard time if he attacked her! She began to tremble with fear.

Dennis jerked painfully on her hair, pulling up, and she shot to her feet.

'Please!' she said. Even as she spoke, she hated herself for begging in this humiliating way, but she was too terrified to stop. 'I'll do anything!'

She felt his lips on her ear. 'Take off your panties,' he murmured.

She froze. She was ready to do whatever he wanted, no matter how shaming, in order to escape; but to take off her panties might be as dangerous as to defy him. She did not know what to do. She tried to see Robinson. He was out of her field of view, behind her, and she did not dare turn her head because of the knife next to her eye. However, she could hear him cursing the rat and swiping at it with his club, and it was evident he still had not seen what Dennis was doing.

'I don't have much time,' Dennis murmured in a voice like an icy wind. 'If I don't get what I want, you'll never see the sun shine again.'

She believed him. She had just finished three hours of psychological interviews with him and she knew what he was like. He had no conscience: he was not capable of guilt or remorse. If she frustrated his wishes, he would maim her without hesitation.

But what would he do after she had taken off her panties, she thought desperately? Would he be satisfied and take the blade away from her face? Would he slash her anyway? Or would he want something more?

Why couldn't Robinson kill the damned rat?

'Quickly!' Dennis hissed.

What could be worse than blindness? 'All right,' she groaned.

She bent awkwardly, with Dennis still holding her hair and pointing the knife at her. Fumbling, she pulled up the skirt of her linen dress and pushed down her K mart white cotton briefs. Dennis grunted, deep in his throat like a bear, as they dropped to her ankles. She felt ashamed, even though reason told her this was not her fault. Hurriedly she worked her dress back down, covering her nakedness. Then she stepped out of her panties and kicked them away across the grey plastic-tiled floor.

She felt dreadfully vulnerable.

Dennis released her, snatched up the panties, and pressed them to his face, breathing in, his eyes closed in ecstasy.

Jeannie stared at him, aghast at this forced intimacy. Even though he was not touching her, she shuddered in disgust.

What would he do next?

Robinson's nightstick made a revolting, squashing sound. Jeannie turned and saw that at last he had struck the rat. His stick had smashed the rear half of its fat body, and there was a red smear across the grey plastic tiles. It could no longer run, but it was still alive, its eyes open and its body moving as it breathed. Robinson hit it again, smashing its head. It stopped moving and a grey slime seeped out of the crushed skull.

Jeannie looked back at Dennis. To her surprise he was sitting at the table, as he had all afternoon, looking as if he had never moved. He wore an innocent air. The knife and her panties had disappeared.

Was she out of danger? Was it all over?

Robinson was panting with exertion. He directed a suspicious glare at Dennis and said: 'You didn't *bring* that vermin in here, Pinker, did you?'

'No, sir,' Dennis said glibly.

Jeannie formed in her mind the words *Yes, he did!* But for some reason she did not say them.

Robinson went on: ''Cause if I thought you done a thing like that, I would . . .' The guard shot a sideways look at Jeannie and decided not to say exactly what he would do to Dennis. 'I believe you know I'd make you regret it.'

'Yes, sir.'

Jeannie realized she was safe. But relief was followed immediately by anger. She stared at Dennis, outraged. Was he going to pretend that nothing had happened?

Robinson said: 'Well, you can get a bucket of water and clean this place up, anyway.'

'Right away, sir.'

'That is, if Dr Ferrami is finished with you.'

Jeannie tried to say, *While you were killing the rat,*

Dennis stole my panties, but the words would not come out. They seemed so foolish. And she could imagine the consequences of saying them. She would be stuck here for an hour while the allegation was investigated. Dennis would be searched and her underwear found. It would have to be shown to Warden Temoigne. She imagined him examining the evidence, handling her panties and turning them inside out, with a strange look on his face . . .

No. She would say nothing.

She suffered a pang of guilt. She had always scorned women who suffered assault and then kept quiet about it, letting the offender get away with it. Now she was doing the same thing.

She realized that Dennis was counting on that. He had foreseen how she would feel and gambled that he could get away with it. The thought made her so indignant that for a moment she contemplated putting up with the hassle just to thwart him. Then she envisioned Temoigne and Robinson and all the other men in this jail looking at her and thinking, *She doesn't have any panties on*, and she realized it would be too humiliating to be borne.

How clever Dennis was: as clever as the man who had set fire to the gymnasium and raped Lisa, as clever as Steve . . .

'You seem a little shook,' Robinson said to her. 'I guess you don't like rats any more than I do.'

She pulled herself together. It was over. She had survived with her life and even her eyesight. What happened that was so bad? she asked herself. I might have been mutilated or raped. Instead I just lost my underwear. Be grateful. 'I'm fine, thank you,' she said.

'In that case, I'll take you out.'

The three of them left the room together.

Outside the door Robinson said: 'Go get a mop, Pinker.'

Dennis smiled at Jeannie, a long, intimate smile, as if they were lovers who had spent the afternoon in bed together. Then he disappeared into the interior of the jail. Jeannie watched him go with immense relief, but it was tinged with continuing revulsion, for he had her underwear in his pocket. Would he sleep with her panties pressed to his cheek, like a child with a teddy bear? Or would he wrap them around his penis as he masturbated, pretending that he was fucking her? Whatever he chose to do she felt she was an unwilling participant, her privacy violated and her freedom compromised.

Robinson walked her to the main gate and shook her hand. She crossed the hot parking lot to the Ford, thinking, *I'll be glad to drive out of this place.* She had a sample of Dennis's DNA, that was the most important thing.

Lisa was at the wheel, running the air-conditioning to cool the car. Jeannie slumped into the passenger seat.

'You look beat,' Lisa said as she pulled away.

'Stop at the first shopping strip,' Jeannie said.

'Sure. What do you need?'

'I'll tell you,' Jeannie replied. 'But you're not going to believe it.'

CHAPTER NINETEEN

AFTER LUNCH Berrington went to a quiet neighbourhood bar and ordered a martini.

Jim Proust's casual suggestion of murder had shaken him. Berrington knew he had made a fool of himself by grabbing Jim's lapel and yelling. But he did not regret the fuss. At least he could be sure Jim knew exactly how he felt.

It was nothing new for them to fight. He remembered their first great crisis, in the early seventies, when the Watergate scandal broke. It had been a terrible time: conservatism was discredited, the law-and-order politicians turned out to be crooked, and any clandestine activity, no matter how well intentioned, was suddenly viewed as an unconstitutional conspiracy. Preston Barck had been terrified, and wanted to give up the whole mission. Jim Proust called him a coward, angrily argued there was no danger, and proposed to carry it on as a joint CIA–Army project, perhaps with tighter security. No doubt he would have been ready to assassinate any investigative journalist who pried into what they were doing. It had been Berrington who suggested setting up a private company and distancing themselves from the government. Now once again it was up to him to find a way out of their difficulties.

The place was gloomy and cool. A TV set over the bar showed a soap opera, but the sound was turned down. The cold gin calmed Berrington. His anger at Jim gradually evaporated, and he focused his mind on Jeannie Ferrami.

Fear had caused him to make a rash promise. He had recklessly told Jim and Preston that he would deal with Jeannie. Now he had to fulfil that imprudent undertaking. He had to stop her asking questions about Steve Logan and Dennis Pinker.

It was maddeningly difficult. Although he had hired her and arranged her grant, he could not simply give her orders: as he had told Jim, the university was not the army. She was employed by JFU, and Threeplex had already handed over a year's funding. In the long term, of course, he could easily pull the plug on her; but that was not good enough. She had to be stopped immediately, today or tomorrow, before she learned enough to ruin them all.

Calm down, he thought, calm down.

Her weak point was her use of medical databases without the permission of the patients. It was the kind of thing the newspapers could make into a scandal, regardless of whether anyone's privacy was genuinely invaded. And universities were terrified of scandal: it played havoc with their fund-raising.

It was tragic to wreck such a promising scientific project. It went against everything Berrington stood for. He had encouraged Jeannie, and now he had to undermine her. She would be heartbroken, and with reason. He told himself that she had bad genes and would have got into trouble sooner or later; but all the same he wished he did not have to be the cause of her downfall.

He tried not to think about her body. Women had always been his weakness. No other vice tempted him: he drank in moderation, never gambled, and could not understand why people took drugs. He had loved his wife, Vivvie, but even then he had not been able to resist the temptation of other women, and Vivvie had eventually left him because of his fooling around. Now when he thought of Jeannie he imagined her running her fingers through his hair and saying, *You've been so good to me, I owe you so much, how can I ever thank you?*

Such thoughts made him feel ashamed. He was supposed to be her patron and mentor, not her seducer.

As well as desire he felt burning resentment. She was just a girl, for God's sake: how could she be such a threat? How could a kid with a ring in her nose possibly jeopardize him and Preston and Jim when they were on the brink of achieving their lifetime ambitions? It was unthinkable they should be thwarted now: the idea made him dizzy with panic. When he was not imagining himself making love to Jeannie, he had fantasies of strangling her.

All the same he was reluctant to start a public outcry against her. It was hard to control the press. There was a chance they would begin by investigating Jeannie and finish up investigating him. This would be a dangerous strategy. But he could think of no other, short of Jim's wild talk of murder.

He drained his glass. The bartender offered him another martini but he declined. He looked around the bar and spotted a pay phone next to the men's room. He swiped his American Express card through the card reader and called Jim's office. One of Jim's brash young men answered: 'Senator Proust's office.'

'This is Berrington Jones—'

'I'm afraid the senator is in a meeting right now.'

He really should train his acolytes to be a little more charming, Berrington thought. 'Then let's see if we can avoid interrupting him,' he said. 'Does he have any media appointments this afternoon?'

'I'm not sure. May I ask why you need to know, sir?'

'No, young man, you may not,' Berrington said with exasperation. Self-important assistants were the curse of Capitol Hill. 'You may answer my question, or you may put Jim Proust on the phone, or you may lose your goddamn job, now which is it to be?'

'Please hold.'

There was a long pause. Berrington reflected that wishing Jim would teach his aides to be charming was like hoping a chimpanzee would teach its young table manners. The boss's style spread to the staff: an ill-mannered person always had rude employees.

A new voice came on the phone. 'Professor Jones, in fifteen minutes the senator is due to attend a press conference to launch Congressman Dinkey's book *New Hope for America*.'

That was just perfect. 'Where?'

'The Watergate Hotel.'

'Tell Jim I'll be there, and make sure my name is on

the guest list, please.' Berrington hung up without waiting for a reply.

He left the bar and got a cab to the hotel. This would need to be handled delicately. Manipulating the media was hazardous: a good reporter might look past the obvious story and start asking why it was being planted. But each time he thought of the risks, he reminded himself of the rewards and steeled his nerve.

He found the room where the press conference was to be held. His name was not on the list—self-important assistants were never efficient—but the book's publicist recognized his face and welcomed him as an additional attraction for the cameras. He was glad he had worn the striped Turnbull & Asser shirt that looked so distinguished in photographs.

He took a glass of Perrier and looked around the room. There was a small lectern in front of a blow-up of the book's cover, and a pile of press releases on a side table. The TV crews were setting up their lights. Berrington saw one or two reporters he knew, but none he really trusted.

However, more were arriving all the time. He moved around the room making small talk, keeping an eye on the door. Most of the journalists knew him: he was a minor celebrity. He had not read the book, but Dinkey subscribed to a traditionalist right-wing agenda that was a mild version of what Berrington shared with Jim and Preston, so Berrington was happy to tell reporters that he endorsed the book's message.

At a few minutes past three, Jim arrived with Dinkey. Close behind them was Hank Stone, a senior *New York*

Times man. Bald, red nosed, bulging over the waistband of his pants, shirt collar undone, tie pulled down, tan shoes scuffed, he had to be the worst-looking man in the White House press corps.

Berrington wondered if Hank would do.

Hank had no known political beliefs. Berrington had met him when he did an article about Threeplex, fifteen or twenty years ago. Since getting the Washington job he had written about Berrington's ideas once or twice and Jim Proust's several times. He treated them sensationally, rather than intellectually, as newspapers inevitably did, but he never moralized in the pious way liberal journalists would.

Hank would treat a tip-off on its merits: if he thought it was a good story he would write it. But could he be trusted not to dig deeper? Berrington was not sure.

He greeted Jim and shook hands with Dinkey. They talked for a few minutes while Berrington looked out hopefully for a better prospect. But none came and the press conference started.

Berrington sat through the speeches, containing his impatience. There was just not enough time. Given a few days he could find someone better than Hank, but he did not have a few days, he had a few hours. And an apparently fortuitous meeting like this was so much less suspicious than making an appointment and taking the journalist to lunch.

When the speeches were over there was still no one better than Hank in view.

As the journalists dispersed Berrington buttonholed

him. 'Hank, I'm glad I ran into you. I may have a story for you.'

'Good!'

'It's about misuse of medical information on databases.'

He made a face. 'Not really my kind of thing, Berry, but go on.'

Berrington groaned inwardly: Hank did not seem to be in a receptive mood. He ploughed on, working his charm. 'I believe it *is* your kind of thing, because you'll see potential in it that an ordinary reporter might overlook.'

'Well, try me.'

'First of all, we're not having this conversation.'

'That's a little more promising.'

'Secondly, you may wonder why I'm giving you the story, but you're never going to ask.'

'Better and better,' Hank said, but he did not make a promise.

Berrington decided not to push him on it. 'At Jones Falls University, in the psychology department, there's a young researcher called Dr Jean Ferrami. In her search for suitable subjects to study, she scans large medical databases without the permission of the people whose records are on the files.'

Hank pulled at his red nose. 'Is this a story about computers, or about scientific ethics?'

'I don't know, you're the journalist.'

He looked unenthusiastic. 'It isn't much of a scoop.'

Don't start playing hard to get, you bastard. Berrington

touched Hank's arm in a friendly gesture. 'Do me a favour, make some enquiries,' he said persuasively. 'Call the university president, his name is Maurice Obell. Call Dr Ferrami. Tell them it's a big story, and see what they say. I believe you'll get some interesting reactions.'

'I don't know.'

'I promise you, Hank, it will be worth your time.' *Say yes, you son of a bitch, say yes!*

Hank hesitated, then said: 'Okay, I'll give it a whirl.'

Berrington tried to conceal his satisfaction behind an expression of gravity, but he could not help a little smile of triumph.

Hank saw it, and a suspicious frown crossed his face. 'You're not trying to use me, are you, Berry? Like to frighten someone, maybe?'

Berrington smiled and put an arm around the reporter's shoulders. 'Hank,' he said. 'Trust me.'

CHAPTER TWENTY

JEANNIE BOUGHT a three-pack of white cotton panties at a Walgreen in a strip mall just outside Richmond. She slipped a pair on in the ladies' restroom of the neighbouring Burger King. Then she felt better.

Strange how defenceless she had felt without underwear. She had hardly been able to think of anything else. Yet when she was in love with Will Temple she had liked to go around with no panties on. It made her feel sexy all day. Sitting in the library, or working in the lab, or just walking down the street, she would fantasize that Will showed up unexpectedly, in a fever of passion, saying, *There isn't much time but I've got to have you, now, right here,* and she was ready for him. But without a man in her life she needed her underwear like she needed shoes.

Properly dressed again, she returned to the car. Lisa drove them to the Richmond-Williamsburg airport, where they checked their rental car and caught the plane back to Baltimore.

The key to the mystery must lie with the hospital where Dennis and Steven were born, Jeannie mused as they took off. Somehow, identical twin brothers had ended up with different mothers. It was a fairytale scenario but something like it must have happened.

She looked through the papers in her case and checked the birth information on the two subjects. Steven's birthday was August 25th. To her horror she found that Dennis's birthday was September 7th—almost two weeks later.

'There must be a mistake,' she said. 'I don't know why I didn't check this before.' She showed Lisa the conflicting documents.

'We can double check,' Lisa said.

'Do any of our forms ask which hospital the subject was born at?'

Lisa gave a rueful laugh. 'I believe that's one question we didn't include.'

'It must have been a military hospital, in this case. Colonel Logan is in the army, and presumably "the Major" was a soldier at the time Dennis was born.'

'We'll check.'

Lisa did not share Jeannie's impatience. For her it was just another research project. For Jeannie it was everything. 'I'd like to call right away,' she said. 'Is there a phone on this plane?'

Lisa frowned. 'Are you thinking of calling Steven's mother?'

Jeannie heard the note of disapproval in Lisa's voice. 'Yes. Why shouldn't I?'

'Does she know he's in jail?'

'Good point. I don't know. Damn. I shouldn't be the one to break the news.'

'He may have called home already.'

'Maybe I'll go see Steven in jail. That's allowed, isn't it?'

'I guess so. But they might have visiting hours, like hospitals.'

'I'll just show up and hope for the best. Anyway, I can call the Pinkers.' She waved at a passing stewardess. 'Is there a phone on the plane?'

'No, I'm sorry.'

'Too bad.'

The stewardess smiled. 'Don't you remember me, Jeannie?'

Jeannie looked at her for the first time and recognized her immediately. 'Penny Watermeadow!' she said. Penny had done her doctorate in English at Minnesota alongside Jeannie. 'How are you?'

'I'm great. How are you doing?'

'I'm at Jones Falls, doing a research project that's running into problems. I thought you were going after an academic job.'

'I was, but I didn't get one.'

Jeannie felt embarrassed that she had been successful where her friend had failed. 'That's too bad.'

'I'm glad, now. I enjoy this work and it pays better than most colleges.'

Jeannie did not believe her. It shocked her to see a woman with a doctorate working as a stewardess. 'I always thought you'd be such a good teacher.'

'I taught high school for a while. I got knifed by a student who disagreed with me about Macbeth. I asked myself why I was doing it—risking my life to teach Shakespeare to kids who couldn't wait to go back out on the streets and get on with stealing money to buy crack cocaine.'

Jeannie remembered the name of Penny's husband. 'How's Danny?'

'He's doing great, he's area sales manager now. It means he has to travel a lot, but it's worth it.'

'Well, it's good to see you again. Are you based in Baltimore?'

'Washington, DC.'

'Give me your phone number, I'll call you up.' Jeannie offered a ballpoint and Penny wrote her phone number on one of Jeannie's file folders.

'We'll have lunch,' Penny said. 'It'll be fun.'

'You bet.'

Penny went forward.

Lisa said: 'She seemed bright.'

'She's very clever. I'm horrified. There's nothing wrong with being a stewardess, but it's kind of a waste of twenty-five years of education.'

'Are you going to call her?'

'Hell, no. She's in denial. I'd just remind her of what she used to hope for. It would be agony.'

'I guess. I feel sorry for her.'

'So do I.'

As soon as they landed, Jeannie went to a pay phone and called the Pinkers in Richmond, but their line was busy. 'Damn,' she said querulously. She waited five minutes then tried again, but she got the same infuriating tone. 'Charlotte must be calling her violent family to tell them all about our visit,' she said. 'I'll try later.'

Lisa's car was in the parking lot. They drove into the city and Lisa dropped Jeannie at her apartment. Before getting out of the car Jeannie said: 'Could I ask you a great big favour?'

'Sure. I'm not saying I'll do it, though.' Lisa grinned.

'Start the DNA extraction tonight.'

Her face fell. 'Oh, Jeannie, we've been out all day. I have to shop for dinner—'

'I know. And I have to visit the jail. Let's meet at the lab later, say at nine o'clock?'

'Okay.' Lisa smiled. 'I'm kind of curious to know how the test turns out.'

'If we start tonight, we could have a result by the day after tomorrow.'

Lisa looked dubious. 'Cutting a few corners, yes.'

'Attagirl!' Jeannie got out of the car and Lisa drove away.

Jeannie would have liked to get right into her car and drive to police headquarters, but she decided she should check on her father first, so she went into the house.

He was watching *Wheel of Fortune.* 'Hi, Jeannie, you're home late,' he said.

'I've been working, and I haven't finished yet,' she said. 'How was your day?'

'A little dull, here on my own.'

She felt sorry for him. He seemed to have no friends. However, he looked a lot better than he had last night. He was clean and shaved and rested. He had warmed up a pizza from her freezer for his lunch: the dirty dishes were on the kitchen counter. She was about to ask him who the hell he thought was going to put them in the dishwasher, but she bit back her words.

She put down her briefcase and began to tidy up. He did not turn off the TV.

'I've been to Richmond, Virginia,' she said.

'That's nice, honey. What's for dinner?'

No, she thought, this can't go on. He's not going to treat me like he treated Mom. 'Why don't you make something?' she said.

That got his attention. He turned from the TV to look at her. 'I can't cook!'

'Nor can I, Daddy.'

He frowned, then smiled. 'So we'll eat out!'

The expression on his face was hauntingly familiar. Jeannie flashed back twenty years. She and Patty were wearing matching flared denim jeans. She saw Daddy with dark hair and sideburns, saying: 'Let's go to the carnival! Shall we get cotton candy? Jump in the car!' He had been the most wonderful man in the world. Then her memory jumped ten years. She was in black jeans and Doc Marten boots, and Daddy's hair was shorter and greying, and he said: 'I'll drive you up to Boston with your stuff, I'll get a van, it'll give us a chance to spend time together, we'll eat fast food on the road, it'll be such fun! Be ready at ten!' She had waited all day, but he never showed up, and the next day she took a Greyhound.

Now, seeing the same old let's-have-fun light in his eyes, she wished with all her heart that she could be nine years old again and believe every word he said.

But she was grown up now, so she said: 'How much money do you have?'

He looked sullen. 'I don't have any, I told you.'

'Me either. So we can't eat out.' She opened the refrigerator. She had an iceberg lettuce, some fresh corn on the cob, a lemon, a pack of lamb chops, one tomato and a half-empty box of Uncle Ben's rice. She took them all out and put them on the counter. 'I tell you what,' she said. 'We'll have fresh corn with melted butter as an appetizer, followed by lamb chops with lemon zest accompanied by salad and rice, and ice cream for dessert.'

'Well, that's just great!'

'You get it started while I'm out.'

He stood up and looked at the food she had put out.

She picked up her briefcase. 'I'll be back soon after ten.'

'I don't know how to cook this stuff!' He picked up a corn cob.

From the shelf over the refrigerator she took *The Reader's Digest All-the-Year-Round Cookbook*. She handed it to him. 'Look it up,' she said. She kissed his cheek and went out.

As she got into her car and headed down town she hoped she had not been too cruel. He was from an older generation, the rules had been different in his day. Still, she could not be his housekeeper even if she had wanted to: she had to hold down her job. By giving him a place to lay his head at night she was already doing more for him than he had done for her most of her life. All the same she wished she had left him on a happier note. He was inadequate, but he was the only father she had.

She put her car in a parking garage and walked through the red-light district to police headquarters. There was a swanky lobby with marble benches and a mural depicting scenes from Baltimore history. She told the receptionist she was here to see Steven Logan, who was in custody. She expected to have to argue about it, but after a few minutes' wait a young woman in uniform took her inside and up in the elevator.

She was shown into a room the size of a closet. It was featureless except for a small window set into the wall at face level and a sound panel beneath it. The window looked into another similar booth. There was no way to pass anything from one room to the other without making a hole in the wall.

She stared through the window. After another five minutes Steven was brought in. As he entered the booth she saw that he was handcuffed and his feet were chained together, as if he were dangerous. He came to the glass and peered through. When he recognized her, he smiled broadly. 'This is a pleasant surprise!' he said. 'In fact it's the only nice thing that's happened to me all day.'

Despite his cheerful manner he looked terrible: strained and tired. 'How are you?' she said.

'A little rough. They've put me in a cell with a murderer who has a crack hangover. I'm afraid to go to sleep.'

Her heart went out to him. She reminded herself that he was supposed to be the man who raped Lisa.

But she could not believe it. 'How long do you think you'll be here?'

'I have a bail review before a judge tomorrow. Failing that, I may be locked up until the DNA test result comes through. Apparently that takes three days.'

The mention of DNA reminded her of her purpose. 'I saw your twin today.'

'And?'

'There's no doubt. He's your double.'

'Maybe *he* raped Lisa Hoxton.'

Jeannie shook her head. 'If he had escaped from jail at the weekend, yes. But he's still locked up.'

'Do you think he might have escaped then returned? To establish an alibi?'

'Too fanciful. If Dennis got out of jail, nothing would induce him to go back.'

'I guess you're right,' Steven said gloomily.

'I have a couple of questions to ask you.'

'Shoot.'

'First I need to double-check your birthday.'

'August 25th.'

That was what Jeannie had written down. Maybe she had Dennis's date wrong. 'And do you happen to know where you were born?'

'Yes. Dad was stationed at Fort Lee, Virginia, at the time, and I was born in the army hospital there.'

'Are you sure?'

'Certain. Mom wrote about it in her book *Having a Baby*.' He narrowed his eyes in a look that was becoming familiar to her. It meant he was figuring out her thinking. 'Where was Dennis born?'

'I don't know yet.'

'But we share a birthday.'

'Unfortunately, he gives his birthday as September 7th. But it might be a mistake. I'm going to double-check. I'll call his mother as soon as I get to my office. Have you spoken to your parents yet?'

'No.'

'Would you like me to call them?'

'No! Please. I don't want them to know until I can tell them I've been cleared.'

She frowned. 'From everything you've told me about them, they seem the kind of people who would be supportive.'

'They would. But I don't want to put them through the agony.'

'Sure it would be painful for them. But they might prefer to know, so they can help you.'

'No. Please don't call them.'

Jeannie shrugged. There was something he was not telling her. But it was his decision.

'Jeannie . . . what's he like?'

'Dennis? Superficially, he's like you.'

'Does he have long hair, short hair, a moustache, dirty fingernails, acne, a limp—'

'His hair is short just like yours, he has no facial hair, his hands are clean and his skin is clear. It could have *been* you.'

'Jeeze.' Steven looked deeply uncomfortable.

'The big difference is his behaviour. He doesn't know how to relate to the rest of the human race.'

'It's very strange.'

'I don't find it so. In fact it confirms my theory. You were both what I call wild children. I stole the phrase from a French film. I use it for the type of child who is fearless, uncontrollable, hyperactive. Such children are very difficult to socialize. Charlotte Pinker and her husband failed with Dennis. Your parents succeeded with you.'

This did not reassure him. 'But underneath, Dennis and I are the same.'

'You were both born wild.'

'But I have a thin veneer of civilization.'

She could see he was profoundly troubled. 'Why does it bother you so much?'

'I want to think of myself as a human being, not a housetrained gorilla.'

She laughed, despite his solemn expression. 'Gorillas have to be socialized too. So do all animals that live in groups. That's where crime comes from.'

He looked interested. 'From living in groups?'

'Sure. A crime is a breach of an important social rule. Solitary animals don't have rules. A bear will trash another bear's cave, steal its food and kill its young. Wolves don't do those things: if they did, they couldn't live in packs. Wolves are monogamous, they take care of one another's young, and they respect each other's personal space. If an individual breaks the rules they punish him: if he persists, they either expel him from the pack or kill him.'

'What about breaking unimportant social rules?'

'Like farting in an elevator? We call it bad manners. The only punishment is the disapproval of others. Amazing how effective that is.'

'Why are you so interested in people who break the rules?'

She thought of her father. She did not know whether she had his criminal genes or not. It might have helped Steve to know that she, too, was troubled by her genetic inheritance. But she had lied about Daddy for so long that she could not easily bring herself to talk about him now. 'It's a big problem,' she said evasively. 'Everyone's interested in crime.'

The door opened behind her and the young woman police officer looked in. 'Time's up, Dr Ferrami.'

'Okay,' she said over her shoulder. 'Steve, did you know that Lisa Hoxton is my best friend in Baltimore?'

'No, I didn't.'

'We work together: she's a technician.'

'What's she like?'

'She's not the kind of person who would make a wild accusation.'

He nodded.

'All the same, I want you to know that I don't believe you did it.'

For a moment she thought he was going to cry. 'Thank you,' he said gruffly. 'I can't tell you how much it means to me.'

'Call me when you get out.' She told him her home number. 'Can you remember that?'

'No problem.'

Jeannie was reluctant to leave. She gave him what she hoped was an encouraging smile. 'Good luck.'

'Thanks, I need it in here.'

She turned away and left.

The policewoman walked her to the lobby. Night was falling as she returned to the parking garage. She got on to the Jones Falls Expressway and flicked on the headlights of the old Mercedes. Heading north, she drove too fast, eager to get to the university. She always drove too fast. She was a skilful but somewhat reckless driver, she knew. But she did not have the patience to go at fifty-five.

Lisa's white Honda Accord was already parked outside Nut House. Jeannie eased her car alongside it and went inside. Lisa was just turning on the lights in the lab. The cool box containing Dennis Pinker's blood sample stood on the bench.

Jeannie's office was right across the corridor. She unlocked her door by passing her plastic card through the card reader and went in. Sitting at her desk, she called the Pinker house in Richmond. 'At last!' she said when she heard the ringing tone.

Charlotte answered. 'How is my son?' she said.

'He's in good health,' Jeannie replied. He hardly seemed like a psychopath, she thought, until he pulled a knife on me and stole my panties. She tried to think of something positive to say. 'He was very cooperative.'

'He always had beautiful manners,' Charlotte said in the Southern drawl she used for her most outrageous utterances.

'Mrs Pinker, may I double-check his birthday with you?'

'He was born on the seventh of September.' Like it should be a national holiday.

It was not the answer Jeannie had been hoping for. 'And what hospital was he born in?'

'We were at Fort Bragg, in North Carolina, at the time.'

Jeannie suppressed a disappointed curse.

'The Major was training conscripts for Vietnam,' Charlotte said proudly. 'The Army Medical Command has a big hospital at Bragg. That's where Dennis came into the world.'

Jeannie could not think of anything more to say. The mystery was as deep as ever. 'Mrs Pinker, I want to thank you again for your kind cooperation.'

'You're welcome.'

She returned to the lab and said to Lisa: 'Apparently, Steven and Dennis were born thirteen days apart and in different states. I just don't understand it.'

Lisa opened a fresh box of test tubes. 'Well, there's one incontrovertible test. If they have the same DNA, they're identical twins, no matter what anyone says about their birth.' She took out two of the little glass tubes. They were a couple of inches long. Each had a lid at the top and a conical bottom. She opened a pack of labels, wrote 'Dennis Pinker' on one and 'Steven Logan' on the other, then labelled the tubes and placed them in a rack.

She broke the seal on Dennis's blood and put a

single drop in one test tube. Then she took a phial of Steven's blood out of the refrigerator and did the same.

Using a precision-calibrated pipette—a pipe with a bulb at one end—she added a tiny measured quantity of chloroform to each test tube. Then she picked up a fresh pipette and added a similarly exact amount of phenol.

She closed both test tubes and put them in the Whirlimixer to agitate them for a few seconds. The chloroform would dissolve the fats and the phenol would disrupt the proteins, but the long coiled molecules of deoxyribonucleic acid would remain intact.

Lisa put the tubes back in the rack. 'That's all we can do for the next few hours,' she said.

The water-dissolved phenol would slowly separate from the chloroform. A meniscus would form in the tube at the boundary. The DNA would be in the watery part, which could be drawn off with a pipette for the next stage of the test. But that would have to wait for the morning.

A phone rang somewhere. Jeannie frowned: it sounded as if it was coming from her office. She stepped across the corridor and picked it up. 'Yes?'

'Is this Dr Ferrami?'

Jeannie hated people who called and demanded to know your name without introducing themselves. It was like knocking on someone's front door and saying: 'Who the hell are you?' She bit back a sarcastic response and said: 'I'm Jeannie Ferrami. Who is this calling, please?'

'Naomi Freelander, *New York Times.*' She sounded like a heavy smoker in her fifties. 'I have some questions for you.'

'At this time of night?'

'I work all hours. It seems you do too.'

'Why are you calling me?'

'I'm researching an article about scientific ethics.'

'Oh.' Jeannie thought immediately about Steve not knowing he might be adopted. It was an ethical problem, though not an insoluble one—but surely the *Times* did not know about it? 'What's your interest?'

'I believe you scan medical databases looking for suitable subjects to study.'

'Oh, okay.' Jeannie relaxed. She had nothing to worry about on this score. 'Well, I've devised a search engine that scans computer data and finds matching pairs. My purpose is to find identical twins. It can be used on any kind of database.'

'But you've gained access to medical records in order to use this program.'

'It's important to define what you mean by access. I've been careful not to trespass on anyone's privacy. I never see anyone's medical details. The program doesn't print the records.'

'What does it print?'

'The names of the two individuals, and their addresses and phone numbers.'

'But it prints the names in pairs.'

'Of course, that's the point.'

'So if you used it on, say, a database of electroencephalograms, it would tell you that John Doe's brainwaves are the same as Jim Fitz's.'

'The same or similar. But it would not tell me anything about either man's health.'

'However, if you knew previously that John Doe was a paranoid schizophrenic, you could conclude that Jim Fitz was, too.'

'We would never know such a thing.'

'You might know John Doe.'

'How?'

'He might be your janitor, anything.'

'Oh, come on!'

'It's possible.'

'Is *that* going to be your story?'

'Maybe.'

'Okay, it's theoretically possible, but the chance is so small that any reasonable person would discount it.'

'That's arguable.'

The reporter seemed determined to see an outrage, regardless of the facts, Jeannie thought; and she began to worry. She had enough problems without getting the damn newspapers on her back. 'How real is all this?' she said. 'Have you actually found anyone who feels their privacy has been violated?'

'I'm interested in the potentiality.'

Jeannie was struck by a thought. 'Who told you to call me, anyway?'

'Why do you ask?'

'Same reason you've been asking me questions. I'd like to know the truth.'

'I can't tell you.'

'That's interesting,' Jeannie said. 'I've talked to you at some length about my research and my methods. I have nothing to hide. But you can't say the same. You appear to be, well, *ashamed*, I guess. Are you ashamed of the way you found out about my project?'

'I'm not ashamed of anything,' the reporter snapped.

Jeannie felt herself getting cross. Who did this woman think she was? 'Well, someone's ashamed. Otherwise why won't you tell me who he is? Or she?'

'I have to protect my sources.'

'From what?' Jeannie knew she should lay off. Nothing was to be gained by antagonizing the press. But the woman's attitude was insufferable. 'As I've explained, there's nothing wrong with my methods and they don't threaten anyone's privacy. So why should your informant be so secretive?'

'People have reasons—'

'It looks as if your informant was malicious, doesn't it?' Even as she said it, Jeannie was thinking, *Why should anyone want to do this to me?*

'I can't comment on that.'

'No comment, huh?' she said sarcastically. 'I must remember that line.'

'Dr Ferrami, I'd like to thank you for your cooperation.'

'Don't mention it,' Jeannie said, and she hung up.

She stared at the phone for a long moment. 'Now what the hell was that all about?' she said.

WEDNESDAY

CHAPTER TWENTY-ONE

BERRINGTON JONES slept badly.

He spent the night with Pippa Harpenden. Pippa was a secretary in the physics department, and a lot of professors had asked her out, including several married men, but Berrington was the only one she dated. He had dressed beautifully, taken her to an intimate restaurant, and ordered exquisite wine. He had basked in the envious glances of men his own age dining with their ugly old wives. He had brought her home and lit candles and put on silk pyjamas and made love to her slowly until she gasped with pleasure.

But he woke up at four o'clock and thought of all the things that could go wrong with his plan. Hank Stone had been sucking down the publisher's cheap wine yesterday afternoon: he might just forget all about his conversation with Berrington. If he remembered it, the editors of the *New York Times* might still decide not to follow up the story. They might make some enquiries and realize there was nothing much wrong with what Jeannie was doing. Or they could simply move too slowly and start looking into it next week, when it would be too late.

After he had been tossing and turning for a while, Pippa mumbled: 'Are you all right, Berry?'

He stroked her long, blond hair, and she made sleepily encouraging noises. Making love to a beautiful woman was normally consolation for any amount of trouble, but he sensed it would not work now. He had too much on his mind. It would have been a relief to talk to Pippa about his problems—she was intelligent, and she would be understanding and sympathetic—but he could not reveal such secrets to anyone.

After a while he got up and went running. When he returned she had gone, leaving a thank-you note wrapped in a sheer black nylon stocking.

The housekeeper arrived a few minutes before eight and made him an omelette. Marianne was a thin, nervy girl from the French Caribbean island of Martinique. She spoke little English and was terrified of being sent back home, which made her very biddable. She was pretty, and Berrington guessed that if he told her to blow him she would think it was part of her duties as a university employee. He did no such thing, of course: sleeping with the help was not his style.

He took a shower, shaved, and dressed for high authority in a charcoal-grey suit with a faint pinstripe, a white shirt and a black tie with small red dots. He wore monogrammed gold cuff links, he folded a white linen handkerchief into his breast pocket, and he buffed the toecaps of his black Oxfords until they gleamed.

He drove to the campus, went to his office, and turned on his computer. Like most superstar academics, he did very little teaching. Here at Jones Falls he gave one lecture per year. His role was to direct and supervise the research of the scientists in the department and to add the prestige of his name to the papers they wrote. But this morning he could not concentrate on anything, so he looked out of the window and watched four youngsters play an energetic game of doubles on the tennis court while he waited for the phone to ring.

He did not have to wait long.

At nine thirty the president of Jones Falls University, Maurice Obell, called. 'We've got a problem,' he said.

Berrington tensed. 'What's up, Maurice?'

'Bitch on the *New York Times* just called me. She says someone in your department is invading people's privacy. A Dr Ferrami.'

Thank God, Berrington thought jubilantly; Hank Stone came through! He made his voice solemn. 'I was afraid of something like this,' he said. 'I'll be right over.' He hung up and sat for a moment, thinking. It was too soon to celebrate victory. He had only begun the process. Now he had to get both Maurice and Jeannie to behave just the way he wanted.

Maurice sounded worried. That was a good start. Berrington had to make sure he stayed worried. He needed Maurice to feel it would be a catastrophe if Jeannie did not stop using her database search program immediately. Once Maurice had decided on firm action, Berrington had to make sure he stuck to his resolve.

Most of all, he had to prevent any kind of compromise. Jeannie was not much of a compromiser by nature, he knew, but with her whole future at stake she would probably try anything. He would have to fuel her outrage and keep her combative.

And he must do all that while trying to appear well intentioned. If it became obvious that he was trying to undermine Jeannie, Maurice might smell a rat. Berrington had to seem to defend her.

He left Nut House and walked across campus, past the Barrymore Theater and the Faculty of Arts to Hillside Hall. Once the country mansion of the original benefactor of the university, it was now the administration building. The university president's office was the magnificent drawing room of the old house. Berrington nodded pleasantly to Dr Obell's secretary and said: 'He's expecting me.'

'Go right in, please, Professor,' she said.

Maurice was sitting in the bay window overlooking the lawn. A short, barrel-chested man, he had returned from Vietnam in a wheelchair, paralysed from the waist down. Berrington found him easy to relate to, perhaps because they had a background of military service in common. They also shared a passion for the music of Mahler.

Maurice often wore a harassed air. To keep JFU going he had to raise ten million dollars a year from private and corporate benefactors, and consequently he dreaded bad publicity.

He spun his chair around and rolled to his desk. 'They're working on a big article on scientific ethics, she says. Berry, I can't have Jones Falls heading that article with an example of unethical science. Half our big donors would have a cow. We've got to do something about this.'

'Who is she?'

Maurice consulted a scratch pad. 'Naomi Freelander. She's the Ethics Editor. Did you know newspapers had ethics editors? I didn't.'

'I'm not surprised the *New York Times* has one.'

'It doesn't stop them acting like the goddamn Gestapo. They're about to go to press with this article, they say, but yesterday they got a tip-off about your Ferrami woman.'

'I wonder where the tip came from?' Berrington said.

'There are some disloyal bastards around.'

'I guess so.'

Maurice sighed. 'Say it's not true, Berry. Tell me she doesn't invade people's privacy.'

Berrington crossed his legs, trying to appear relaxed when he was in fact wired taut. This was where he had to walk a tightrope. 'I don't believe she does anything wrong,' he said. 'She scans medical databases and finds people who don't know they're twins. It's very clever, as a matter of fact—'

'Is she looking at people's medical records without their permission?'

Berrington pretended to be reluctant. 'Well . . . sort of.'

'Then she'll have to stop.'

'The trouble is, she really needs this information for her research project.'

'Maybe we can offer her some compensation.'

Berrington had not thought of bribing her. He doubted it would work, but there was no harm in trying. 'Good idea.'

'Does she have tenure?'

'She started here this semester, as an assistant professor. She's six years away from tenure, at least. But we could give her a raise. I know she needs the money, she told me.'

'How much does she make now?'

'Thirty thousand dollars a year.'

'What do you think we should offer her?'

'It would have to be substantial. Another eight or ten thousand.'

'And the funding for that?'

Berrington smiled. 'I believe I could persuade Threeplex.'

'Then that's what we'll do. Call her now, Berry. If she's on campus, get her in here right away. We'll settle this thing before the Ethics Police call again.'

Berrington picked up Maurice's phone and called Jeannie's office. It was answered right away. 'Jeannie Ferrami.'

'This is Berrington.'

'Good morning.' Her tone was wary. Had she sensed his desire to seduce her on Monday night? Maybe she wondered if he was planning to try again. Or perhaps she had already got wind of the *New York Times* problem.

'Can I see you right away?'

'In your office?'

'I'm in Dr Obell's office at Hillside Hall.'

She gave an exasperated sigh. 'Is this about a woman called Naomi Freelander?'

'Yes.'

'It's all horseshit, you know that.'

'I do, but we have to deal with it.'

'I'll be right over.'

Berrington hung up. 'She'll be here momentarily,' he told Maurice. 'It sounds as if she's already heard from the *Times*.'

The next few minutes would be crucial. If Jeannie defended herself well, Maurice might change his strategy. Berrington had to keep Maurice firm without seeming hostile to Jeannie. She was a hot-tempered, assertive girl, not the type to be conciliatory, especially when she thought she was in the right. She would probably make an enemy of Maurice without any help from Berrington. But just in case she was uncharacteristically sweet and persuasive, he needed a fall-back plan.

Struck by inspiration, he said: 'We might rough out a press statement while we're waiting.'

'That's a good idea.'

Berrington pulled over a pad and began scribbling. He needed something that Jeannie could not possibly agree to, something that would injure her pride and make her mad. He wrote that Jones Falls University admitted mistakes had been made. The university apologized to those whose privacy had been invaded. And it promised that the program had been discontinued as of today.

He handed his work to Maurice's secretary and asked her to put it through her word processor right away.

Jeannie arrived fizzing with indignation. She was wearing a baggy emerald-green T-shirt, tight black jeans and the kind of footwear that used to be called engineer boots but were now a fashion statement. She had a silver ring in her pierced nostril and her thick dark hair was tied back. She looked kind of cute, to Berrington, but her outfit would not impress the university president. To him she would appear the kind of irresponsible junior academic who might get JFU into trouble.

Maurice invited her to sit down and told her about the call from the newspaper. His manner was stiff. He was comfortable with mature men, Berrington thought: young women in tight jeans were aliens to him.

'The same woman called me,' Jeannie said with irritation. 'This is ludicrous.'

'But you do access medical databases,' Maurice said.

'I don't look at the databases, the computer does. No human being sees anyone's medical records. My program produces a list of names and addresses, grouped in pairs.'

'Even that . . .'

'We do nothing further without first asking permission of the potential subject. We don't even tell them they're twins until after they've agreed to be part of our study. So whose privacy is invaded?'

Berrington pretended to back her. 'I told you, Maurice,' he said. 'The *Times* has it all wrong.'

'They don't see it that way. And I have to think of the university's reputation.'

Jeannie said: 'Believe me, my work is going to enhance that reputation.' She leaned forward, and Berrington heard in her voice the passion for new knowledge that drove all good scientists. 'This is a project of critical importance. I'm the only person who has figured out how to study the genetics of criminality. When we publish the results it will be a sensation.'

'She's right,' Berrington put in. It was true. Her study would have been fascinating. It was heartbreaking to destroy it. But he had no choice.

Maurice shook his head. 'It's my job to protect the university from scandal.'

Jeannie said recklessly: 'It's also your job to defend academic freedom.'

That was the wrong tack for her to take. Once upon a time, no doubt, university presidents had fought for the right to the unfettered pursuit of knowledge, but those days were over. Now they were fund-raisers, pure and simple. She would only offend Maurice by mentioning academic freedom.

Maurice bristled. 'I don't need a lecture on my presidential duties from you, young lady,' he said stiffly.

Jeannie did not take the hint, to Berrington's delight. 'Don't you?' she said to Maurice, warming to her theme. 'Here's a direct conflict. On the one hand is a newspaper apparently bent on a misguided story; on the other a scientist after the truth. If a university president is going to buckle under that kind of pressure, what hope is there?'

Berrington was exultant. She looked wonderful, cheeks flushed and eyes flashing, but she was digging her own grave. Maurice was antagonized by every word.

Then Jeannie seemed to realize what she was doing, for she suddenly changed tack. 'On the other hand, none of us wants bad publicity for the university,' she said in a milder voice. 'I quite understand your concern, Dr Obell.'

Maurice softened immediately, much to Berrington's chagrin. 'I realize this puts you in a difficult position,' he said. 'The university is prepared to offer you compensation, in the form of a raise of ten thousand dollars a year.'

Jeannie looked startled.

Berrington said: 'That ought to enable you to get your mother out of that place you're so worried about.'

Jeannie hesitated only for a moment. 'I'd be deeply grateful for that,' she said, 'but it wouldn't solve the problem. I still have to have criminal twins for my research. Otherwise there's nothing to study.'

Berrington had not thought she could be bribed.

Maurice said: 'Surely there must be another way to find suitable subjects for you to study?'

'No, there's not. I need identical twins, raised apart, at least one of whom is a criminal. That's a tall order. My computer program locates people who don't even know they're twins. There's no other method of doing that.'

'I hadn't realized,' Maurice said.

The tone was becoming perilously amicable. Then Maurice's secretary came in and handed him a sheet of paper. It was the press release Berrington had drafted. Maurice showed it to Jeannie, saying: 'We need to be able to issue something like this today, if we're to kill this story off.'

She read it quickly, and her anger returned. 'But

this is bullshit!' she stormed. 'No mistakes have been made. No one's privacy has been invaded. No one has even complained!'

Berrington concealed his satisfaction. It was paradoxical that she was so fiery, yet she had the patience and perseverance to do lengthy and tedious scientific research. He had seen her working with her subjects: they never seemed to irritate or tire her, even when they messed up the tests. With them, she found bad behaviour as interesting as good. She just wrote down what they said and thanked them sincerely at the end. Yet outside the lab she would go off like a firecracker at the least provocation.

He played the role of concerned peacemaker. 'But, Jeannie, Dr Obell feels we have to put out a firm statement.'

'You can't say the use of my computer program has been discontinued!' she said. 'That would be tantamount to cancelling my entire project!'

Maurice's face hardened. 'I can't have the *New York Times* publishing an article that says Jones Falls scientists invade people's privacy,' he said. 'It would cost us millions in lost donations.'

'Find a middle way,' Jeannie pleaded. 'Say you're looking into the problem. Set up a committee. We'll develop further privacy safeguards, if necessary.'

Oh, no, Berrington thought. That was dangerously sensible. 'We have an ethics committee, of course,' he said, playing for time. 'It's a subcommittee of the senate.' The senate was the university's ruling council and consisted of all the tenured professors, but the work was done by committees. 'You could announce that you're handing over the problem to them.'

'No good,' Maurice said abruptly. 'Everyone will know that's a stall.'

Jeannie protested: 'Don't you see that by insisting on immediate action you're practically ruling out any thoughtful discussion!'

This would be a good time to bring the meeting to a close, Berrington decided. The two were at loggerheads, both entrenched in their positions. He should finish it before they started to think about compromise again. 'A good point, Jeannie,' Berrington said. 'Let me make a proposal here—if you permit, Maurice.'

'Sure, let's hear it.'

'We have two separate problems. One is to find a way to progress Jeannie's research without bringing a scandal down upon the university. That's something Jeannie and I have to resolve, and we should discuss it at length, later. The second question is how the department and the university present this to the world. That's a matter for you and me to talk about, Maurice.'

Maurice looked relieved. 'Very sensible,' he said.

Berrington said: 'Thank you for joining us at short notice, Jeannie.'

She realized she was being dismissed. She got up with a puzzled frown. She knew she had been outmanoeuvred, but she could not figure out how. 'You'll call me?' she said to Berrington.

'Of course.'

'All right.' She hesitated, then went out.

'Difficult woman,' Maurice said.

Berrington leaned forward, clasping his hands together, and looked down, in an attitude of humility. 'I feel at fault here, Maurice.' Maurice shook his head but Berrington went on. 'I hired Jeannie Ferrami. Of course, I had no idea that she would devise this method of work—but all the same it's my responsibility, and I think I have to get you out of it.'

'What do you propose?'

'I can't ask you not to release that press statement. I don't have the right. You can't put one research project above the welfare of the entire university, I realize that.' He looked up.

Maurice hesitated. For a split second Berrington wondered fearfully if he suspected he was being manoeuvred into a corner. But if the thought crossed his mind it did not linger. 'I appreciate your saying that, Berry. But what will you do about Jeannie?'

Berrington relaxed. It seemed he had done it. 'I guess she's my problem,' he said. 'Leave her to me.'

CHAPTER TWENTY-TWO

STEVE DROPPED off to sleep in the early hours of Wednesday morning.

The jail was quiet, Porky was snoring, and Steve had not slept for forty-two hours. He tried to stay awake, rehearsing his bail application speech to the judge for tomorrow, but he kept slipping into a waking dream in which the judge smiled benignly on him and said, *Bail is granted, let this man go free,* and he walked out of the court into the sunny street. Sitting on the floor of the cell in his usual position, with his back to the wall, he caught himself nodding off, and jerked awake several times, but finally nature conquered will-power.

He was in a profound sleep when he was shocked awake by a painful blow to his ribs. He gasped and opened his eyes. Porky had kicked him and was now bending over him, eyes wide with craziness, screaming: 'You stole my dope, motherfucker! Where d'you stash it, where? Give it up right now or you're a dead man!'

Steve reacted without thinking. He came up off the floor like a spring uncoiling, his right arm outstretched rigid, and poked two fingers into Porky's eyes. Porky yelled in pain and stepped backwards. Steve followed, trying to push his fingers right through Porky's brain to the back of his head. Somewhere in the distance, he could hear a voice that sounded a lot like his own, screaming abuse.

Porky took another step back and sat down hard on the toilet, covering his eyes with his hands.

Steve put both hands behind Porky's neck, pulled his head forward, and kneed him in the face. Blood spurted from Porky's mouth. Steve grabbed him by the shirt, yanked him off the toilet seat and dropped him on the floor. He was about to kick him, when sanity began to return. He hesitated, staring down at Porky bleeding on the floor, and the red mist of rage cleared. 'Oh, no,' he said. 'What have I done?'

The gate of the cell flew open and two cops burst in, brandishing nightsticks.

Steve held up his hands in front of him.

'Just calm down,' said one of the cops.

'I'm calm, now,' Steve said.

The cops handcuffed him and took him out of the cell. One punched him in the stomach, hard. He doubled over, gasping. 'That's just in case you were thinking of starting any more trouble,' the cop said.

He heard the sound of the cell door crashing shut and the voice of Spike the turnkey in his habitual humorous mood. 'You need medical attention, Porky?' Spike said. ''Cause there's a veterinarian on East Baltimore Street.' He cackled at his own joke.

Steve straightened up, recovering from the punch. It still hurt but he could breathe. He looked through the bars at Porky. He was sitting upright, rubbing his eyes.

Through bleeding lips he replied to Spike. 'Fuck you, asshole.'

Steve was relieved: Porky was not badly hurt.

Spike said: 'It was time to pull you out of there anyway, college boy. These gentlemen have come to take you to court.' He consulted a sheet of paper. 'Let's see, who else is for the Northern District Court? Mr Robert Sandilands, known as Sniff . . .' He got three other men out of cells and chained them all together with Steve. Then the two cops took them to the parking garage and put them on a bus.

Steve hoped he would never have to go back to that place.

It was still dark outside. Steve guessed it must be around six a.m. Courts did not start work until nine or ten o'clock in the morning, so he would have a long wait. They drove through the city for fifteen or twenty minutes then entered a garage door in a court building. They got off the bus and went down into the basement.

There were eight barred pens around a central open area. Each pen had a bench and a toilet, but they were larger than the cells at police headquarters, and all four prisoners were put in a pen that already had six men in it. Their chains were removed and dumped on a table in the middle of the room. There were several turnkeys, presided over by a tall black woman with a sergeant's uniform and a mean expression.

Over the next hour another thirty or more prisoners arrived. They were accommodated twelve to a pen. There were shouts and whistles when a small group of women were brought in. They were put in a pen at the far end of the room.

After that nothing much happened for several hours. Breakfast was brought, but Steve once again refused food: he could not get used to the idea of eating in the toilet. Some prisoners talked noisily, most remained sullen and quiet. Many looked hung over. The banter between prisoners and guards was not quite as foul as it had been in the last place, and Steve wondered idly if that was because there was a woman in charge.

Jails were nothing like what they showed on TV, he reflected. Television shows and movies made prisons seem like low-grade hotels: they never showed the unscreened toilets, the verbal abuse, or the beatings given to those who misbehaved.

Today might be his last day in jail. If he had believed in God he would have prayed with all his heart.

He figured it was about midday when they began taking prisoners out of the cells.

Steve was in the second batch. They were handcuffed again and ten men were chained together. Then they went up to the court.

The courtroom was like a Methodist chapel. The walls were painted green up to a black line at waist level and then cream above that. There was a green carpet on the floor and nine rows of blond wood benches like pews.

In the back row sat Steve's mother and father.

He gasped with shock.

Dad wore his colonel's uniform, with his hat under

his arm. He sat straight-backed, as if standing at attention. He had Celtic colouring, blue eyes and dark hair and the shadow of a heavy beard on his clean-shaven cheeks. His expression was rigidly blank, taut with suppressed emotion. Mom sat beside him, small and plump, her pretty round face puffy with crying.

Steve wished he could fall through the floor. He would have gone back to Porky's cell willingly to escape this moment. He stopped walking, holding up the entire line of prisoners, and stared in dumb agony at his parents, until the turnkey gave him a shove and he stumbled forward to the front bench.

A woman clerk sat at the front of the court, facing the prisoners. A male turnkey guarded the door. The only other official present was a bespectacled black man of about forty wearing a suit coat, tie, and blue jeans. He asked the names of the prisoners and checked them against a list.

Steve looked back over his shoulder. There was no one on the public benches except for his parents. He was grateful he had family that cared enough to show up: none of the other prisoners did. All the same he would have preferred to go through this humiliation unwitnessed.

His father stood up and came forward. The man in blue jeans spoke officiously to him. 'Yes, sir?'

'I'm Steven Logan's father, I'd like to speak to him,' Dad said in an authoritative voice. 'May I know who you are?'

'David Purdy, I'm the pre-trial investigator, I called you this morning.'

So that was how Mom and Dad found out, Steve realized. He should have guessed. The court commissioner had told him an investigator would check his details. The simplest way to do that would be to call his parents. He winced at the thought of that phone call. What had the investigator said? *I need to check the address of Steven Logan, who is in custody in Baltimore, accused of rape. Are you his mother?*

Dad shook the man's hand and said: 'How do you do, Mr Purdy.' But Steve could tell Dad hated him.

Purdy said: 'You can speak to your son, go ahead, no problem.'

Dad nodded curtly. He edged along the bench behind the prisoners and sat directly behind Steve. He put his hand on Steve's shoulder and squeezed gently. Tears came to Steve's eyes. 'Dad, I didn't do this,' he said.

'I know, Steve,' his father said.

His simple faith was too much for Steve, and he started to cry. Once he began he could not stop. He was weak with hunger and lack of sleep. All the strain and misery of the last two days overwhelmed him, and tears flowed freely. He kept swallowing and dabbing at his face with his manacled hands.

After a while Dad said: 'We wanted to get you a lawyer but there wasn't time—we only just made it here.'

Steve nodded. He would be his own lawyer if he could just get himself under control.

Two girls were brought in by a woman turnkey. They were not handcuffed. They sat down and giggled. They looked about eighteen.

'How the hell did this happen, anyway?' Dad said to Steve.

Trying to answer the question helped Steve stop crying. 'I must look like the guy who did it,' he said. He sniffed and swallowed. 'The victim picked me out at a line-up. And I was in the neighbourhood at the time, I told the police that. The DNA test will clear me, but it takes three days. I'm hoping I'll get bail today.'

'Tell the judge we're here,' Dad said. 'It will probably help.'

Steve felt like a child, being comforted by his father. It brought back a bittersweet memory of the day he got his first bicycle. It must have been his fifth birthday. The bike was the kind with a pair of stabilizing wheels at the back to prevent it falling over. Their house had a large garden with two steps leading down to a patio. 'Ride around the lawn and steer clear of the steps,' Dad had said; but the first thing little Stevie did was try to ride his bicycle down the steps. He crashed, damaging the bike and himself; and he fully expected his father to get mad at him for disobeying a direct order. Dad had picked him up, bathed his wounds gently, and fixed the bike, and although Stevie waited for the explosion, it did not come. Dad never even said, *I told you so.* No matter what happened, Steve's parents were always on his side.

The judge came in.

She was an attractive white woman of about fifty, very small and neat. She wore a black robe and carried a can of Diet Coke which she put on the desk when she sat down.

Steve tried to read her face. Was she cruel or benign? In a good mood or a foul temper? A warm-hearted, liberal-minded woman with a soul, or an obsessive martinet who secretly wished she could send them all to the electric chair? He stared at her blue eyes, her sharp nose, her grey-streaked dark hair. Did she have a husband with a beer gut, a grown son she worried about, an adored grandchild with whom she rolled around on the carpet? Or did she live alone in an expensive apartment full of stark modern furniture with sharp corners? His law lectures had told him the theoretical reasons for granting or refusing bail, but now they seemed almost irrelevant. All that really mattered was whether this woman was kindly or not.

She looked at the row of prisoners and said: 'Good afternoon. This is your bail review.' Her voice was low but clear, her diction precise. Everything about her seemed exact and tidy—except for that Coke can, a touch of humanity that gave Steve hope.

'Have you all received your statement of charges?' They all had. She went on to recite a script about what their rights were and how to get a lawyer.

After that was done, she said: 'When named, please raise your right hand. Ian Thompson.' A prisoner raised his hand. She read out the charges and the penalties he faced. Ian Thompson had apparently burglarized three houses in the swanky Roland Park neighbourhood. A young Hispanic man with his arm in a sling, he showed no interest in his fate and appeared bored by the whole process.

As she told him he was entitled to a preliminary

hearing and a jury trial, Steve waited eagerly to see if he would get bail.

The pre-trial investigator stood up. Speaking very fast, he said that Thompson had lived at his address for one year and had a wife and a baby, but no job. He also had a heroin habit and a criminal record. Steve would not have released such a man onto the streets.

However, the judge set his bail at twenty-five thousand dollars. Steve felt encouraged. He knew that the accused normally had to put up only ten per cent of the bail in cash, so Thompson would be free if he could find twenty-five hundred dollars. That seemed lenient.

One of the girls was next. She had been in a fight with another girl and was charged with assault. The pre-trial investigator told the judge that she lived with her parents and worked at the checkout of a nearby supermarket. She was obviously a good risk, and the judge gave her bail in her own recognizance, which meant she did not have to put up any money at all.

That was another soft decision, and Steve's spirits rose a notch.

The defendant was also ordered not to go to the address of the girl she had fought with. That reminded Steve that a judge could attach conditions to the bail. Perhaps he should volunteer to stay away from Lisa Hoxton. He had no idea where she lived or what she looked like, but he was ready to say anything that might help get him out of jail.

The next defendant was a middle-aged white man who had exposed his penis to women shoppers in the feminine hygiene section of a Rite-Aid drugstore. He had a long record of similar offences. He lived alone but had been at the same address for five years. To Steve's surprise and dismay, the judge refused bail. The man was small and thin: Steve felt he was a harmless nutcase. But perhaps this judge, as a woman, was particularly tough on sex crimes.

She looked at her sheet and said: 'Steven Charles Logan.'

Steve raised his hand. *Please let me out of here, please.*

'You are charged with rape in the first degree, which carries a possible penalty of life imprisonment.'

Behind him, Steve heard his mother gasp.

The judge went on to read out the other charges and penalties, then the pre-trial investigator stood up. He recited Steve's age, address and occupation, and said that he had no criminal record and no addictions. Steve thought he sounded like a model citizen by comparison with most of the other defendants. Surely she had to take note of that?

When Purdy had finished, Steve said: 'May I speak, Your Honour?'

'Yes, but remember that it may not be in your interest to tell me anything about the crime.'

He stood up. 'I'm innocent, Your Honour, but it seems I may bear a resemblance to the rapist, so if you grant me bail I'll promise not to approach the victim, if you want to make that a condition of bail.'

'I certainly would.'

He wanted to plead with her for his freedom, but all

the eloquent speeches he had composed in his cell now vanished from his mind, and he could think of nothing to say. Feeling frustrated, he sat down.

Behind him, his father stood up. 'Your Honour, I'm Steven's father, Colonel Charles Logan. I'd be glad to answer any questions you may want to ask me.'

She gave him a frosty look. 'That won't be necessary.'

Steve wondered why she seemed to resent his father's intervention. Maybe she was just making it clear she was not impressed by his military rank. Perhaps she wanted to say, *Everyone is equal in my court, regardless of how respectable and middle-class they might be.*

Dad sat down again.

The judge looked at Steve. 'Mr Logan, was the woman known to you before the alleged crime took place?'

'I've never met her,' Steve said.

'Had you ever *seen* her before?'

Steve guessed she was wondering whether he had been stalking Lisa Hoxton for some time before attacking her. He replied: 'I can't tell, I don't know what she looks like.'

The judge seemed to reflect on that for a few seconds. Steve felt as if he were hanging on to a ledge by his fingertips. Just a word from her would rescue him. But if she refused him bail it would be like falling into the abyss.

At last she spoke: 'Bail is granted in the sum of two hundred thousand dollars.'

Relief washed over Steve like a tidal wave, and his whole body relaxed. 'Thank God for that,' he murmured.

'You will not approach Lisa Hoxton nor go to 1321 Vine Avenue.'

Steve felt Dad grasp his shoulder again. He reached up with his manacled hands and touched his father's bony fingers.

It would be another hour or two before he was free, he knew; but he did not mind too much, now that he was sure of freedom. He would eat six Big Macs and sleep the clock around. He wanted a hot bath and clean clothes and his wristwatch back. He wanted to bask in the company of people who did not say 'motherfucker' in every sentence.

And he realized, somewhat to his surprise, that what he wanted most of all was to call Jeannie Ferrami.

CHAPTER TWENTY-THREE

JEANNIE WAS in a bilious mood as she returned to her office. Maurice Obell was a coward. An aggressive newspaper reporter had made some inaccurate insinuations, that was all, yet the man had crumbled. And Berrington was too weak to defend her effectively.

Her computer search engine was her greatest achievement. She had started to develop it when she realized that her research into criminality would never get far without a new means of finding subjects for study. She had taken three years over it. It was her one truly outstanding achievement, not counting tennis championships. If she had a particular intellectual talent, it was for that kind of logical puzzle. Although she studied the psychology of unpredictable, irrational human beings, she did it by manipulating masses of data on hundreds and thousands of individuals: the work was statistical and mathematical. If her search engine was no good, she felt, she herself would be worthless. She might as well give up and become a stewardess, like Penny Watermeadow.

She was surprised to see Annette Bigelow waiting outside her door. Annette was a graduate student whose work Jeannie supervised as part of her teaching duties. Now she recalled that last week Annette had submitted her proposal for the year's work, and they had an appointment this morning to discuss it. Jeannie decided to cancel the meeting: she had more important things to do. Then she saw the eager expression on the young woman's face, and recalled how crucial these meetings were when you were a student; and she forced herself to smile and say: 'I'm sorry to keep you waiting. Let's get started right away.'

Fortunately she had read the proposal carefully and made notes. Annette was planning to trawl through existing data on twins to see if she could find correlations in the areas of political opinions and moral attitudes. It was an interesting notion and her plan was scientifically sound. Jeannie suggested some minor improvements and gave her the go-ahead.

As Annette was leaving, Ted Ransome put his head around the door. 'You look as if you're about to cut someone's balls off,' he said.

'Not yours, though,' Jeannie smiled. 'Come in and have a cup of coffee.'

'Handsome' Ransome was her favourite man in the department. An associate professor who studied the psychology of perception, he was happily married with two small children. Jeannie knew he found her attractive, but he did not do anything about it. There was a pleasant frisson of sexual tension between them that never threatened to become a problem.

She switched on the coffee maker beside her desk and told him about the *New York Times* and Maurice

Obell. 'But here's the big question,' she finished. 'Who tipped off the *Times*?'

'It has to be Sophie,' he said.

Sophie Chapple was the only other woman on the faculty of the psychology department. Although she was close to fifty and a full professor, she saw Jeannie as some kind of rival and had behaved jealously from the beginning of the semester, complaining about everything from Jeannie's miniskirts to the way she parked her car.

'Would she do a thing like that?' Jeannie said.

'Like a shot.'

'I guess you're right.' Jeannie never ceased to marvel at the pettiness of top scientists. She had once seen a revered mathematician punch the most brilliant physicist in America for jumping the queue in the cafeteria. 'Maybe I'll ask her.'

He raised his eyebrows. 'She'll lie.'

'But she'll look guilty.'

'There'll be a row.'

'There's already a row.'

The phone rang. Jeannie picked it up and gestured to Ted to pour the coffee. 'Hello.'

'Naomi Freelander here.'

Jeannie hesitated. 'I'm not sure I should talk to you.'

'I believe you've stopped using medical databases for your research.'

'No.'

'What do you mean, "No"?'

'I mean I haven't stopped. Your phone calls have

started some discussions, but no decisions have been made.'

'I have a fax here from the university president's office. In it, the university apologizes to people whose privacy has been invaded, and assures them that the programme has been discontinued.'

Jeannie was aghast. 'They sent out that release?'

'You didn't know?'

'I saw a draft and I didn't agree to it.'

'It seems like they've cancelled your programme without telling you.'

'They can't.'

'What do you mean?'

'I have a contract with this university. They can't just do whatever the hell they like.'

'Are you telling me you're going to continue in defiance of the university authorities?'

'Defiance doesn't come into it. They don't have the power to command me.' Jeannie caught Ted's eye. He lifted a hand and moved it from side to side in a negative gesture. He was right, Jeannie realized: this was not the way to talk to the press. She changed her tack. 'Look,' she said in a reasonable voice, 'you yourself said that the invasion of privacy is *potential*, in this case.'

'Yes . . .'

'And you have completely failed to find anyone who is willing to complain about my programme. Yet you have no qualms about getting this research project cancelled.'

'I don't judge, I report.'

'Do you know what my research is about? I'm trying to find out what makes people criminals. I'm the first person to think of a really promising way to study this problem. If things work out right, what I discover could make America a better place for your grandchildren to grow up in.'

'I don't have any grandchildren.'

'Is that your excuse?'

'I don't need excuses—'

'Perhaps not, but wouldn't you do better to find a case of invasion of privacy that someone really cares about? Wouldn't that make an even better story for the newspaper?'

'I'll be the judge of that.'

Jeannie sighed. She had done her best. Gritting her teeth, she tried to end the conversation on a friendly note. 'Well, good luck with it.'

'I appreciate your cooperation, Dr Ferrami.'

'Goodbye.' Jeannie hung up and said: 'You bitch.'

Ted handed her a mug of coffee. 'I gather they've announced that your programme is cancelled.'

'I can't understand it. Berrington said we'd talk about what to do.'

Ted lowered his voice. 'You don't know Berry as well as I do. Take it from me, he's a snake. I wouldn't trust him out of my sight.'

'Perhaps it was a mistake,' Jeannie said, clutching at straws. 'Maybe Dr Obell's secretary sent the release out in error.'

'Possibly,' Ted said. 'But my money's on the snake theory.'

'Do you think I should call the *Times* and say my phone was answered by an impostor?'

He laughed. 'I think you should go along to Berry's office and ask him if he meant for the release to go out before he talked to you.'

'Good idea.' She swallowed her coffee and stood up.

He went to the door. 'Good luck. I'm rooting for you.'

'Thanks.' She thought of kissing his cheek and decided not to.

She walked along the corridor and up a flight of stairs to Berrington's office. His door was locked. She went to the office of the secretary who serviced all the professors. 'Hi, Julie, where's Berry?'

'He left for the day, but he asked me to fix an appointment for you tomorrow.'

Damn. The bastard was avoiding her. Ted's theory was right. 'What time tomorrow?'

'Nine thirty?'

'I'll be here.'

She went down to her floor and stepped into the lab. Lisa was at the bench, checking the concentration of Steven's and Dennis's DNA that she had in the test tubes. She had mixed two microlitres of each sample with two millilitres of fluorescent dye. The dye glowed in contact with DNA, and the quantity of DNA was shown by how much it glowed, measured by a DNA fluorometer, with a dial giving the result in nanograms of DNA per microlitre of sample.

'How are you?' Jeannie asked.

'I'm fine.'

Jeannie looked hard at Lisa's face. She was still in denial, that was obvious. Her expression was impassive, as she concentrated on her work, but the strain showed underneath. 'Did you talk to your mother yet?' Lisa's parents lived in Pittsburgh.

'I don't want to worry her.'

'It's what she's there for. Call her.'

'Maybe tonight.'

Jeannie told the story of the *New York Times* reporter while Lisa worked. She mixed the DNA samples with an enzyme called a restriction endonuclease. These enzymes destroyed foreign DNA that might get into the body. They did so by cutting the long molecule of DNA into thousands of shorter fragments. What made them so useful to genetic engineers was that an endonuclease always cut the DNA at the same specific point. So the fragments from two blood samples could be compared. If they matched, the blood came from the same individual or from identical twins. If the fragments were different, they must come from different individuals.

It was like cutting an inch of tape from a cassette of an opera. Take a fragment cut five minutes from the start of two different tapes: if the music on both pieces of tape is a duet that goes *Se a caso Madama*, they both come from *The Marriage of Figaro*. To guard against the possibility that two completely different operas might have the same sequence of notes at just that point, it was necessary to compare several fragments, not just one.

The process of fragmentation took several hours and could not be hurried: if the DNA was not completely fragmented, the test would not work.

Lisa was shocked by the story Jeannie told, but she was not quite as sympathetic as Jeannie expected. Perhaps that was because she had suffered a devastating trauma just three days earlier, and Jeannie's crisis seemed minor by comparison. 'If you have to drop your project,' Lisa said, 'what would you study instead?'

'I've no idea,' Jeannie replied. 'I can't imagine dropping this.' Lisa simply did not empathize with the yearning to understand that drove a scientist, Jeannie realized. To Lisa, a technician, one research project was much the same as another.

Jeannie returned to her office and called the Bella Vista Sunset Home. With all that was going on in her own life she had been lax about talking to her mother. 'May I speak to Mrs Ferrami, please,' she said.

The reply was abrupt. 'They're having lunch.'

Jeannie hesitated. 'Okay. Would you please tell her that her daughter Jeannie called, and I'll try again later.'

'Yeah.'

Jeannie had the feeling that the woman was not writing this down. 'That's J-E-A-N-N-I-E,' she said. 'Her daughter.'

'Yeah, okay.'

'Thank you, I appreciate it.'

'Sure.'

Jeannie hung up. She had to get Mom out of there. She still had not done anything about getting weekend teaching work.

She checked her watch: it was just after noon. She picked up her mouse and looked at her screen, but it seemed pointless to work when her project might be cancelled. Feeling angry and helpless, she decided to quit for the day.

She turned off her computer, locked her office and left the building. She still had her red Mercedes. She got in and stroked the steering wheel with a pleasant sense of familiarity.

She tried to cheer herself up. She had a father, that was a rare privilege. Maybe she should spend time with him, enjoy the novelty. They could drive down to the harbour front and walk around together. She could buy him a new sport coat in Brooks Brothers. She did not have the money, but she would charge it. What the hell, life was short.

Feeling better, she drove home and parked outside her house. 'Daddy, I'm home,' she called as she went up the stairs. When she entered the living room she sensed something wrong. After a moment she noticed the TV had been moved. Maybe he had taken it into the bedroom to watch. She looked in the next room: he was not there. She returned to the living room. 'Oh, no,' she said. Her VCR was gone, too. 'Daddy, you didn't!' Her stereo had disappeared and the computer was gone from her desk. 'No,' she said. 'No, I don't believe it!' She ran back to her bedroom and opened her jewellery box. The one-carat diamond nose stud Will Temple had given her had gone.

The phone rang and she picked it up automatically.

'It's Steve Logan,' the voice said. 'How are you?'

'This is the most terrible day of my life,' she said, and she began to cry.

CHAPTER TWENTY-FOUR

STEVE LOGAN hung up the phone.

He had showered and shaved and dressed in clean clothes, and he was full of his mother's lasagne. He had told his parents every detail of his ordeal, moment by moment. They had insisted on getting legal advice, even though he told them the charges were sure to be dropped as soon as the DNA test results came through, and he was going to see a lawyer first thing tomorrow. He had slept all the way from Baltimore to Washington in the back of his father's Lincoln Mark VIII, and although that hardly made up for the one and a half nights he had stayed awake, nevertheless he felt fine.

And he wanted to see Jeannie.

He had felt that way before he called her. Now that he knew how much trouble she was in, he was even more eager. He wanted to put his arms around her and tell her everything would be all right.

He also felt there had to be a connection between her problems and his. Everything went wrong for both of them, it seemed to Steve, from the moment she introduced him to her boss and Berrington freaked.

He wanted to know more about the mystery of his

origins. He had not told his parents that part. It was too bizarre and troubling. But he needed to talk to Jeannie about it.

He picked up the phone again to call her right back, then he changed his mind. She would say she did not want company. Depressed people usually felt that way, even when they really needed a shoulder to cry on. Maybe he should just show up on her doorstep and say, *Hey, let's try to cheer each other up.*

He went into the kitchen. Mom was scrubbing the lasagne dish with a wire brush. Dad had gone to his office for an hour. Steve began to load crockery into the dishwasher. 'Mom,' he said, 'this is going to sound a little strange to you, but . . .'

'You're going to see a girl,' she said.

He smiled. 'How did you know?'

'I'm your mother, I'm telepathic. What's her name?'

'Jeannie Ferrami. *Doctor* Ferrami.'

'I'm a Jewish mother now? I'm supposed to be impressed that she's a doctor?'

'She's a scientist, not a physician.'

'If she already has her doctorate, she must be older than you.'

'Twenty-nine.'

'Hm. What's she like?'

'Well, she's kind of striking, you know, she's tall, and very fit—she's a hell of a tennis player—with a lot of dark hair, and dark eyes, and a pierced nostril with this very delicate thin silver ring, and she's, like, forceful, she says what she wants, in a direct way, but she laughs a lot, too, I made her laugh a couple of times, but mainly she's just this . . .' He sought for a word. '. . . She's just this *presence*, when she's around you simply can't look anywhere else . . .' He tailed off.

For a moment his mother just stared at him, then she said: 'Oh, boy—you've got it bad.'

'Well, not necessarily . . .' He stopped himself. 'Yeah, you're right. I'm crazy about her.'

'Does she feel the same?'

'Not yet.'

His mother smiled fondly. 'Go on, go see her. I hope she deserves you.'

He kissed her. 'How did you get to be such a good person?'

'Practice,' she said.

Steve's car was parked outside: they had picked it up from the Jones Falls campus and his mother had driven it back to Washington. Now he got on I-95 and drove back to Baltimore.

Jeannie was ready for some tender loving care. She had told him, when he called her, how her father had robbed her and the university president had betrayed her. She needed someone to cherish her, and that was a job he was qualified to do.

As he drove he pictured her sitting next to him on a couch, laughing, and saying things like, *I'm so glad you came over, You've made me feel much better, Why don't we just take off all our clothes and get into bed?*

He stopped at a strip mall in the Mount Washington neighbourhood and bought a seafood pizza, a ten-dollar bottle of chardonnay, a container of Ben & Jerry's ice cream—Rainforest Crunch flavor—and ten yellow carnations. The front page of the *Wall Street Journal* caught his eye with a headline about Threeplex Inc. That was the company that funded Jeannie's research into twins, he recalled. It seemed they were about to be taken over by Landsmann, a German conglomerate. He bought the paper.

His delightful fantasies were clouded by the worrying thought that she might have gone out since he talked to her. Or she might be in, but not answering the door. Or she might have visitors.

He was pleased to see a red Mercedes 280C parked near her house: she must be in. Then he realized she might have gone out on foot. Or in a taxi. Or a friend's car.

She had an entry phone. He pressed the bell and stared at the speaker, willing it to make a noise. Nothing happened. He rang again. There was a crackling noise. His heart leaped. An irritable voice said: 'Who is it?'

'It's Steve Logan. I came to cheer you up.'

There was a long pause. 'Steve, I don't feel like having visitors.'

'At least let me give you these flowers.'

She did not reply. She was scared, he thought, and he felt bitterly disappointed. She had said she believed he was innocent, but that was when he was safely behind bars. Now that he was on her doorstep and she was alone, it was not so easy. 'You haven't changed your mind about me, have you?' he said. 'You still believe I'm innocent? If not, I'll just go away.'

The buzzer sounded and the door opened.

She was a woman who could not resist a challenge, he thought.

He stepped into a tiny lobby with two more doors. One stood open and led to a flight of stairs. At the top stood Jeannie, in a bright green T-shirt.

'I guess you'd better come up,' she said.

It was not the most enthusiastic of welcomes, but he smiled and went up the stairs, carrying his gifts in a paper sack. She showed him into a little living room with a kitchen nook. She liked black and white with splashes of vivid colour, he noted. She had a black-upholstered couch with orange cushions, an electric-blue clock on a white-painted wall, bright yellow lampshades and a white kitchen counter with red coffee mugs.

He put his sack on the kitchen counter. 'Look,' he said. 'You need something to eat, to make you feel better.' He took out the pizza. 'And a glass of wine to ease the tension. Then, when you're ready to give yourself a special treat, you can eat this ice cream right out of the carton, don't even put it in a dish. And after the food and drink is all gone you'll still have the flowers. See?'

She stared at him as if he were a man from Mars.

He added: 'And anyway, I figured you needed someone to come over here and tell you that you're a wonderful, special person.'

Her eyes filled with tears. 'Fuck you!' she said. 'I never cry!'

He put his hands on her shoulders. It was the first

time he had touched her. Tentatively, he drew her to him. She did not resist. Hardly able to believe his luck, he put his arms around her. She was nearly as tall as he. She rested her head on his shoulder, and her body shook with sobs. He stroked her hair. It was soft and heavy. He got a hard-on like a fire hose, and he eased away from her a fraction, hoping she would not notice. 'It's going to be all right,' he said. 'You'll work things out.'

She remained slumped in his arms for a long, delicious moment. He felt the warmth of her body and inhaled her scent. He wondered whether to kiss her. He hesitated, afraid that if he rushed her she would reject him. Then the moment passed and she moved away.

She wiped her nose on the hem of her baggy T-shirt, giving him a sexy glimpse of a flat, suntanned stomach. 'Thanks,' she said. 'I needed a shoulder to cry on.'

He felt let down by her matter-of-fact tone. For him it had been a moment of intense feeling; for her, no more than a release of tension. 'All part of the service,' he said facetiously, then wished he had kept quiet.

She opened a cupboard and took out plates. 'I feel better already,' she said. 'Let's eat.'

He perched on a stool at her kitchen counter. She cut the pizza and took the cork out of the wine. He enjoyed watching her move around her home, closing a drawer with her hip, squinting at a wineglass to see if it was clean, picking up a corkscrew with her long, capable fingers. He remembered the first girl he ever fell in love with. Her name was Bonnie, and she was seven, the same age as he; and he had stared at her strawberry-blond ringlets and green eyes and thought what a miracle it was that someone so perfect could exist in the playground of Spillar Road Grade School. For some time he had entertained the notion that she might actually be an angel.

He did not think Jeannie was an angel, but there was a fluid physical grace about her that gave him the same awestruck sensation.

'You're resilient,' she commented. 'Last time I saw you, you looked awful. It was only twenty-four hours ago, but you seem completely recovered.'

'I got off lightly. I have a sore place where Detective Allaston banged my head on the wall, and a big bruise where Porky Butcher kicked me in the ribs at five o'clock this morning, but I'll be okay, so long as I never have to go back inside that jail.' He put the thought out of his mind. He was not going back: the DNA test would eliminate him as a suspect.

He looked at her bookshelf. She had a lot of nonfiction, biographies of Darwin and Einstein and Francis Bacon; some women novelists he had not read, Erica Jong and Joyce Carol Oates; five or six Edith Whartons; some modern classics. 'Hey, you have my all-time favourite novel!' he said.

'Let me guess: *To Kill a Mockingbird*.'

He was astonished. 'How did you know?'

'Come on. The hero is a lawyer who defies social prejudice to defend an innocent man. Isn't that your dream? Besides, I didn't think you'd pick *The Women's Room*.'

He shook his head in resignation. 'You know so much about me. It's unnerving.'

'What do you think is my favourite book?'

'Is this a test?'

'You bet.'

'Oh . . . uh, *Middlemarch*.'

'Why?'

'It has a strong, independent-minded heroine.'

'But she doesn't *do* anything! Anyway, the book I'm thinking of isn't a novel. Guess again.'

He shook his head. 'A nonfiction book.' Then inspiration struck. 'I know. The story of a brilliant, elegant scientific discovery that explained something crucial about human life. I bet it's *The Double Helix*.'

'Hey, very good!'

They started to eat. The pizza was still warm. Jeannie was thoughtfully silent for a while, then she said: 'I really messed up today. I can see it now. I needed to keep the whole crisis low-key. I should have kept saying, *Well, maybe, we can discuss that, let's not make any hasty decisions.* Instead I defied the university, then made it worse by telling the press.'

'You strike me as an uncompromising person,' he said.

She nodded. 'There's *uncompromising*, and then there's *dumb*.'

He showed her the *Wall Street Journal*. 'This may explain why your department is oversensitive about bad publicity at the moment. Your sponsor is about to be taken over.'

She looked at the first paragraph. 'A hundred and

eighty million dollars, wow.' She read on while chewing a slice of pizza. When she finished the article she shook her head. 'Your theory is interesting, but I don't buy it.'

'Why not?'

'It was Maurice Obell who seemed to be against me, not Berrington. Although Berrington can be sneaky, they say. Anyway, I'm not that important. I represent such a tiny fraction of the research Threeplex sponsors. Even if my work really did invade people's privacy, that wouldn't be enough of a scandal to threaten a multi-million-dollar takeover.'

Steve wiped his fingers on a paper napkin and picked up a framed photograph of a woman with a baby. The woman looked a bit like Jeannie with straight hair. 'Your sister?' he guessed.

'Yes. Patty. She has three kids now—all boys.'

'I don't have any brothers or sisters,' he said. Then he remembered. 'Unless you count Dennis Pinker.' Jeannie's face changed, and he said: 'You're looking at me like a specimen.'

'I'm sorry. Want to try the ice cream?'

'You bet.'

She put the tub on the table and got out two spoons. That pleased him. Eating out of the same container was one step closer to kissing. She ate with relish. He wondered if she made love with the same kind of greedy enthusiasm.

He swallowed a spoonful of Rainforest Crunch and said: 'I'm so glad you believe in me. The cops sure don't.'

'If you're a rapist, my whole theory falls to pieces.'

'Even so, not many women would have let me in tonight. Especially believing I have the same genes as Dennis Pinker.'

'I hesitated,' she said. 'But you proved me right.'

'How?'

She gestured to indicate the remains of their dinner. 'If Dennis Pinker is attracted to a woman, he pulls a knife and orders her to take off her panties. You bring pizza.'

Steve laughed.

'It may sound funny,' Jeannie said, 'but it's a world of difference.'

'There's something you ought to know about me,' Steve said. 'A secret.'

She put down her spoon. 'What?'

'I almost killed someone once.'

'How?'

He told her the story of the fight with Tip Hendricks. 'That's why I'm so bothered by this stuff about my origins,' he said. 'I can't tell you how disturbing it is to be told that Mom and Dad may not be my parents. What if my real father is a killer?'

Jeannie shook her head. 'You were in a schoolboy fight that got out of hand. That doesn't make you a psychopath. And what about the other guy? Tip?'

'Someone else killed him a couple of years later. By then he was dealing dope. He got into an argument with his supplier, and the guy shot him through the head.'

'He's the psychopath, I figure,' Jeannie said. 'That's what happens to them. They can't stay out of trouble. A big strong kid like you might clash with the law once, but you survive the incident and go on to lead a normal life. Whereas Dennis will be in and out of jail until someone kills him.'

'How old are you, Jeannie?'

'You didn't like me calling you a big strong kid.'

'I'm twenty-two.'

'I'm twenty-nine. It's a big difference.'

'Do I seem like a kid to you?'

'Listen, I don't know, a man of thirty probably wouldn't drive here from Washington just to bring me pizza. It was kind of impulsive.'

'Are you sorry I did it?'

'No.' She touched his hand. 'I'm real glad.'

He still did not know where he was with her. But she had cried on his shoulder. You don't use a kid for that, he thought.

'When will you know about my genes?' he said.

She looked at her watch. 'The blotting is probably done. Lisa will make the film in the morning.'

'You mean the test is completed?'

'Just about.'

'Can't we look at the results now? I can't wait to find out if I have the same DNA as Dennis Pinker.'

'I guess we could,' Jeannie said. 'I'm pretty curious myself.'

'Then what are we waiting for?'

CHAPTER TWENTY-FIVE

BERRINGTON JONES had a plastic card that would open any door in Nut House.

No one else knew. Even the other full professors fondly imagined their rooms were private. They knew the office cleaners had master keys. So did the campus security guards. But it never occurred to faculty that it could not be very difficult to get hold of a key that was even given to cleaners.

All the same, Berrington had never used his master key. Snooping was undignified: not his style. Pete Watlingson probably had photos of naked boys in his desk drawer, Ted Ransome undoubtedly stashed a little marijuana somewhere, Sophie Chapple might keep a vibrator for those long, lonely afternoons, but Berrington did not want to know about it. The master key was only for emergencies.

This was an emergency.

The university had ordered Jeannie to stop using her computer search program, and they had announced to the world that it had been discontinued, but how could he be sure it was true? He could not see the electronic messages fly along the phone lines from one terminal to another. Throughout the day the thought had nagged him that she might already be searching another database. And there was no telling what she might find.

So he had returned to his office and now sat at his desk, as the warm dusk gathered over the red brick of the campus buildings, tapping a plastic card against his computer mouse and getting ready to do something that went against all his instincts.

His dignity was precious. He had developed it early. As the smallest boy in the class, without a father to tell him how to deal with bullies, his mother too worried about making ends meet to concern herself with his happiness, he had slowly created an air of superiority, an aloofness that protected him. At Harvard he had furtively studied a classmate from a rich old-money family, taking in the details of his leather belts and linen handkerchiefs, his tweed suits and cashmere scarves; learning how he unfolded his napkin and held chairs for ladies; marvelling at the mixture of ease and deference with which he treated the professors, the superficial charm and underlying coldness of his relations with his social inferiors. By the time Berrington began work on his Master's degree he was widely assumed to be a Brahmin himself.

And the cloak of dignity was difficult to take off. Some professors could remove their jackets and join in a game of touch football with a group of undergraduates, but not Berrington. The students never told him jokes or invited him to their parties; but nor did they cheek him or talk during his lectures or question his grades.

In a sense his whole life since the creation of Threeplex had been a deception, but he had carried it off with boldness and panache. However, there was no stylish way to sneak into someone else's room and search it.

He checked his watch. The lab would be closed now. Most of his colleagues had left, heading for their suburban homes or for the bar of the Faculty Club. This was as good a moment as any. There was no time when the building was guaranteed to be empty: scientists worked whenever the mood took them. If he were seen, he would have to brazen it out.

He left his office, went down the stairs, and walked along the corridor to Jeannie's door. There was no one around. He swiped the card through the card reader and her door opened. He stepped inside, switched on the lights, and closed the door behind him.

It was the smallest office in the building. In fact it had been a storeroom, but Sophie Chapple had maliciously insisted it become Jeannie's office, on the spurious grounds that a bigger room was needed to store the boxes of printed questionnaires the department used. It was a narrow room with a small window. However, Jeannie had livened it up with two wooden chairs painted bright red, a spindly palm in a pot, and a reproduction of a Picasso etching, a bullfight in vivid shades of yellow and orange.

He picked up the framed picture on her desk. It was a black-and-white photograph of a good-looking man with sideburns and a wide tie, and a young woman with a determined expression: Jeannie's parents in the seventies, he guessed. Otherwise her desk was completely clear. Tidy girl.

He sat down and switched on her computer. While it was booting up he went through her drawers. The top one contained ballpoints and scratch pads. In another he found a box of tampons and a pair of pantyhose in an unopened packet. Berrington hated pantyhose. He cherished adolescent memories of garter belts and stockings with seams. Pantyhose were unhealthy, too, like nylon jockey shorts. If President Proust made him surgeon-general, he planned to put a health warning on all pantyhose. The next drawer contained a hand mirror and a brush with some of Jeannie's long dark hair caught in its bristles; the last a pocket dictionary and a paperback book called *A Thousand Acres.* No secrets so far.

Her menu came up on screen. He picked up her mouse and clicked on *Calendar.* Her appointments were predictable: lectures and classes, laboratory time, tennis games, dates for drinks and movies. She was going to Oriole Park at Camden Yards to watch the ball game on Saturday; Ted Ransome and his wife were having her over to brunch on Sunday; her car was due to be serviced on Monday. There was no entry that said *Scan medical files of Acme Insurance.* Her to-do list was equally mundane: *Buy vitamins, call Ghita, Lisa birthday gift, check modem.*

He exited the diary and began to look through her files. She had masses of statistics on spreadsheets. Her word-processing files were smaller: some correspondence, designs for questionnaires, a draft of an article.

Using the Find feature, he searched her entire WP directory for the word *database.* It came up several times in the article and again in file copies of three outgoing letters, but none of the references told him where she planned to use her search engine next. 'Come on,' he said aloud, 'there has to be something, for God's sake.'

She had a filing cabinet but there was not much in it: she had been here only a few weeks. After a year or two it would be stuffed full of completed questionnaires, the raw data of psychological research. Now she had a few incoming letters in one file, departmental memos in another, photocopies of articles in a third.

In an otherwise empty cupboard he found, face down, a framed picture of Jeannie with a tall, bearded man, both of them on bicycles beside a lake. Berrington inferred a love affair that had ended.

He now felt even more worried. This was the room of an organized person, the type who planned ahead. She filed her incoming letters and kept copies of everything she sent out. There ought to be evidence here of what she was going to do next. She had no reason to be secretive about it: until today there had been no suggestion that she had anything to be ashamed of. She must be planning another database sweep. The only possible explanation for the absence of clues was that she had made the arrangements by phone or in person, perhaps with someone who was a close friend. And if that were the case he might not be able to find out anything about it by searching her room.

He heard a footstep in the corridor outside, and

tensed. There was a click as a card was passed through the card reader. Berrington stared helplessly at the door. There was nothing he could do: he was caught red-handed, sitting at her desk, with her computer on. He could not pretend to have wandered in here by accident.

The door opened. He expected to see Jeannie, but in fact it was a security guard.

The man knew him. 'Oh, hi, Professor,' the guard said. 'I saw the light on so I thought I'd check: Dr Ferrami usually keeps her door open when she's here.'

Berrington struggled not to blush. 'That's quite all right,' he said. *Never apologize, never explain.* 'I'll be sure to close the door when I'm through here.'

'Great.'

The guard stood silent, waiting for an explanation. Berrington clamped his jaw shut. Eventually the man said: 'Well, good night, Professor.'

'Good night.'

The guard left.

Berrington relaxed. *No problem.*

He checked that her modem was switched on, then clicked on America Online and accessed her mailbox. Her terminal was programmed to give her password automatically. She had three pieces of mail. He downloaded them all. The first was a notice about increased prices for using the Internet. The second came from the University of Minnesota and read:

> I'll be in Baltimore on Friday and would like to have a drink with you for old times' sake. Love, Will.

Berrington wondered if Will was the bearded guy in the bike picture. He binned it and opened the third letter.

It electrified him.

> You'll be relieved to know that I'm running your scan on our fingerprint file tonight. Call me. Ghita.

It was from the FBI.

'Son of a bitch,' Berrington whispered. 'This will kill us.'

CHAPTER TWENTY-SIX

BERRINGTON WAS afraid to talk on the phone about Jeannie and the FBI fingerprint file. So many telephone calls were monitored by intelligence agencies. Nowadays the surveillance was done by computers programmed to listen for key words and phrases. If someone said *plutonium* or *heroin* or *kill the president*, the computer would tape the conversation and alert a human listener. The last thing Berrington needed was some CIA eavesdropper wondering why Senator Proust was so interested in FBI fingerprint files.

So he got in his silver Lincoln Town Car and drove at ninety miles an hour on the Baltimore–Washington Parkway. He often broke the speed limit. In fact he was impatient with all kinds of rules. It was a contradiction in him, he recognized that. He hated peace marchers and drug takers, homosexuals and feminists and rock musicians and all nonconformists who flouted American traditions. Yet at the same time he resented anyone who tried to tell him where to park his car or how much to pay his employees or how many fire extinguishers to put in his laboratory.

As he drove, he wondered about Jim Proust's contacts in the intelligence community. Were they just a bunch of old soldiers who sat around telling stories about how they had blackmailed anti-war protesters and assassinated South American presidents? Or were they still at the cutting edge? Did they still help one another, like the Mafia, and regard the return of a favour as an almost religious obligation? Or were those days over? It was a long time since Jim had left the CIA: even he might not know.

It was late, but Jim was waiting for Berrington at his office in the Capitol building. 'What the hell has happened that you couldn't tell me on the phone?' he said.

'She's about to run her computer program on the FBI's fingerprint file.'

Jim went pale. 'Will it work?'

'It worked on dental records, why wouldn't it work on fingerprints?'

'Jesus H. Christ,' Jim said feelingly.

'How many prints do they have on file?'

'More than twenty million sets, as I recall. They can't be all criminals. Are there that many criminals in America?'

'I don't know, maybe they have prints of dead people too. Focus, Jim, for Christ's sake. Can you stop this happening?'

'Who's her contact at the Bureau?'

Berrington handed him the printout he had made of Jeannie's E-mail. As Jim studied it, Berrington looked around. On the walls of his office, Jim had photographs of himself with every American president after Kennedy. There was a uniformed Captain Proust saluting Lyndon Johnson; Major Proust, still with a full head of straight blond hair, shaking hands with Dick Nixon; Colonel Proust glaring balefully at Jimmy Carter; General Proust sharing a joke with Ronald Reagan, both of them laughing fit to bust; Proust in a business suit, deputy director of the CIA, deep in conversation with a frowning George Bush; and Senator Proust, now bald and wearing spectacles, wagging a finger at Bill Clinton. He was also pictured dancing with Margaret Thatcher, playing golf with Bob Dole and horse riding with Ross Perot. Berrington had a few such photos, but Jim had a whole damn gallery. Who was he trying to impress? Himself, probably. Constantly seeing himself with the most powerful people in the world told Jim he was important.

'I never heard of anyone called Ghita Sumra,' Jim said. 'She can't be high up.'

'Who *do* you know at the FBI?' Berrington said impatiently.

'Have you ever met the Creanes, David and Hilary?'

Berrington shook his head.

'He's an assistant director, she's a recovering alcoholic. They're both about fifty. Ten years ago, when I was running the CIA, David worked for me in the Diplomatic Directorate, keeping tabs on all the foreign embassies and their espionage sections. I liked him. Anyway, one afternoon Hilary got drunk and went out in her Honda Civic and killed a six-year-old kid, a black girl, on Beulah Road out in Springfield. She drove on, stopped at a shopping mall, and called Dave at Langley. He went over there in his Thunderbird, picked her up and took her home, then reported the Honda stolen.'

'But something went wrong.'

'There was a witness to the accident who was sure the car had been driven by a middle-aged white woman, and a stubborn detective who knew that not many women steal cars. The witness positively identified Hilary, and she broke down and confessed.'

'What happened?'

'I went to the District Attorney. He wanted to put them both in jail. I swore it was an important matter of national security and persuaded him to drop the prosecution. Hilary started going to AA and she hasn't had a drink since.'

'And Dave moved over to the Bureau and did well.'

'And boy, does he owe me.'

'Can he stop this Ghita woman?'

'He's one of nine assistant directors reporting to the deputy director. He doesn't run the fingerprint division, but he's a powerful guy.'

'But can he do it?'

'I don't know! I'll ask, okay? If it can be done, he'll do it for me.'

'Okay, Jim,' Berrington said. 'Pick up the damn phone and ask him.'

CHAPTER TWENTY-SEVEN

JEANNIE SWITCHED on the lights in the psychology lab and Steve followed her in. 'The genetic language has four letters,' she said. 'A, C, G and T.'

'Why those four?'

'Adenine, cytosine, guanine and thymine. They're the chemical compounds attached to the long central strands of the DNA molecule. They form words and sentences, such as *Put five toes on each foot.*'

'But everyone's DNA must say *Put five toes on each foot.*'

'Good point. Your DNA is very similar to mine and everyone else's in the world. We even have a lot in common with the animals, because they're made of the same proteins as we are.'

'So how do you tell the difference between Dennis's DNA and mine?'

'Between the words there are bits that don't mean anything, they're just gibberish. They're like spaces in a sentence. They're called oligonucleotides, but everyone calls them oligos. In the space between *five* and *toes*, there might be an oligo that reads TATAGAGACCCC, repeated.'

'Everyone has TATAGAGACCCC?'

'Yes, but the number of repeats varies. Where you have thirty one TATAGAGACCCC oligos between *five* and *toes*, I might have two hundred and eighty-seven. It doesn't matter how many you have, because the oligo doesn't mean anything.'

'How do you compare my oligos with Dennis's?'

She showed him a rectangular plate about the size and shape of a book. 'We cover this plate with a gel, make slots all across the top, and drop samples of your DNA and Dennis's into the slots. Then we put the plate in here.' On the bench was a small glass tank. 'We pass an electric current through the gel for a couple of hours. This causes the fragments of DNA to ooze through the gel in straight lines. But small fragments move faster than big ones. So your fragment, with thirty-one oligos, will finish up ahead of mine with two hundred and eighty-seven.'

'How can you see how far they've moved?'

'We use chemicals called probes. They attach themselves to specific oligos. Suppose we have an oligo that attracts TATAGAGACCCC.' She showed him a piece of rag like a dishcloth. 'We take a nylon membrane soaked in a probe solution and lay it on the gel so it blots up the fragments. Probes are also luminous, so they'll mark a photographic film.' She looked in another tank. 'I see Lisa has already laid the nylon on the film.' She peered down at it. 'I think the pattern has been formed. All we need to do is fix the film.'

Steve tried to see the image on the film as she washed it in a bowl of some chemical then rinsed it under a tap. His history was written on that page. But all he could see was a ladder-like pattern on the clear plastic. Finally she shook it dry then pegged it in front of a light-box.

Steve peered at it. The film was streaked, from top to bottom, with straight lines, about a quarter of an inch wide, like grey tracks. The tracks were numbered along the bottom of the film, 1 to 18. Within the tracks were neat black marks like hyphens. It meant nothing to him.

Jeannie said: 'The black marks show you how far along the tracks your fragments travelled.'

'But there are two black marks in each track.'

'That's because you have two strands of DNA, one from your father and one from your mother.'

'Of course. The double helix.'

'Right. And your parents had different oligos.' She consulted a sheet of notes then looked up. 'Are you sure you're ready for this—one way or the other?'

'Sure.'

'Okay.' She looked down again. 'Track three is your blood.'

There were two marks about an inch apart, halfway down the film.

'Track four is a control. It's probably my blood, or Lisa's. The marks should be in a completely different position.'

'They are.' The two marks were very close together, right at the bottom of the film near the numbers.

'Track five is Dennis Pinker. Are the marks in the same position as yours, or different?'

'The same,' Steve said. 'They match exactly.'

She looked at him. 'Steve,' she said, 'you're twins.'

He did not want to believe it. 'Is there any chance of a mistake?'

'Sure,' she said. 'There's a one-in-a-hundred chance that two unrelated individuals could have a fragment the same on both maternal and paternal DNA. We normally test four different fragments, using different oligos and different probes. That reduces the chance of a mistake to one in a hundred million. Lisa will do three more: they take half a day each. But I know what they're going to say. And so do you, don't you?'

'I guess I do,' Steve sighed. 'I'd better start believing this. Where the hell did I come from?'

Jeannie looked thoughtful. 'Something you said has been on my mind: *I don't have any brothers or sisters.* From what you've said about your parents, they seem like the kind of people who might want a house full of kids, three or four.'

'You're right,' Steve said. 'But Mom had trouble conceiving. She was thirty-three, and she had been married to Dad for ten years, when I came along. She wrote a book about it: *What to Do When You Can't Get Pregnant.* It was her first bestseller. She bought a summer cabin in Virginia with the money.'

'Charlotte Pinker was thirty-nine when Dennis was born. I bet they had subfertility problems too. I wonder if that's significant.'

'How could it be?'

'I don't know. Did your mother have any kind of special treatment?'

'I never read the book. Shall I call her?'

'Would you?'

'It's time I told them about this mystery, anyway.'

Jeannie pointed to a desk. 'Use Lisa's phone.'

He dialled his home. His mother answered. 'Hi, Mom.'

'Was she pleased to see you?'

'Not at first. But I'm still with her.'

'So she doesn't hate you.'

Steve looked at Jeannie. 'She doesn't hate me, Mom, but she thinks I'm too young.'

'Is she listening?'

'Yes, and I think I'm embarrassing her, which is a first. Mom, we're in the laboratory, and we have kind of a puzzle. My DNA appears to be the same as that of another subject she's studying, a guy called Dennis Pinker.'

'It can't be the same—you'd have to be identical twins.'

'And that would only be possible if I'd been adopted.'

'Steve, you weren't adopted, if that's what you're thinking. And you weren't one of twins. God knows how I would have coped with two of you.'

'Did you have any kind of special fertility treatment before I was born?'

'Yes, I did. The doctor recommended me to a place in Philadelphia that a number of officers' wives had been to. It was called the Aventine Clinic. I had hormone treatment.'

Steve repeated that to Jeannie, and she scribbled a note on a pad of Post-Its.

Mom went on: 'The treatment worked, and there you are, the fruit of all that effort, sitting in Baltimore pestering a beautiful woman seven years your senior when you should be here in DC taking care of your white-haired old mother.'

Steve laughed. 'Thanks, Mom.'

'Hey, Steve?'

'Still here.'

'Don't be late. You have to see a lawyer in the morning. Let's get you out of this legal mess before you start worrying about your DNA.'

'I won't be late. Bye.' He hung up.

Jeannie said: 'I'm going to call Charlotte Pinker right away. I hope she's not already asleep.' She flicked through Lisa's Rolodex, then picked up the phone and dialled. After a moment she spoke. 'Hi, Mrs Pinker, this is Dr Ferrami from Jones Falls University. I'm fine, thank you, how are you? I hope you won't mind my asking you one more question. Well, that's very kind and understanding of you. Yes . . . Before you got pregnant with Dennis, did you have any kind of fertility treatment?' There was a long pause, then Jeannie's face lit up with excitement. 'In Philadelphia? Yes, I've heard of it. Hormone treatment. That's very interesting, that helps me. Thank you again. Goodbye.' She cradled the handset. 'Bingo,' she said. 'Charlotte went to the same clinic.'

'That's fantastic,' Steve said. 'But what does it mean?'

'I have no idea,' Jeannie said. She picked up the phone again and tapped four-eleven. 'How do I get

Philadelphia information? Thanks.' She dialled again. 'The Aventine Clinic.' There was a pause. She looked at Steve and said: 'It probably closed years ago.'

He watched her, mesmerized. Her face was alight with enthusiasm as her mind raced ahead. She looked ravishing. He wished he could do more to help her.

Suddenly she picked up a pencil and scribbled a number. 'Thank you!' she said into the phone. She hung up. 'It's still there!'

Steve was riveted. The mystery of his genes might be resolved. 'Records,' he said. 'The clinic must have records. There might be clues there.'

'I need to go there,' Jeannie said. She frowned thoughtfully. 'I have a release signed by Charlotte Pinker—we ask everyone we interview to sign one—and it gives us permission to look at any medical records. Could you get your mother to sign one tonight and fax it to me at JFU?'

'Sure.'

She dialled again, punching the numbers feverishly. 'Good evening, is that the Aventine Clinic? Do you have a night manager on duty? Thank you.'

There was a long pause. She tapped her pencil impatiently. Steve watched adoringly. As far as he was concerned, this could go on all night.

'Good evening, Mr Ringwood, this is Dr Ferrami from the psychology department at Jones Falls University. Two of my research subjects attended your clinic twenty-three years ago and it would be helpful to me to look at their records. I have releases from them which I can fax to you in advance . . . That's very helpful. Would tomorrow be too soon? Shall we say two p.m.? You've been very kind. I'll do that. Thank you. Goodbye.'

'Fertility clinic,' Steve said thoughtfully. 'Didn't I read, in that *Wall Street Journal* piece, that Threeplex owns fertility clinics?'

Jeannie stared at him, open mouthed. 'Oh, my God,' she said in a low voice. 'Of course it does.'

'I wonder if there's any connection?'

'I just bet there is,' said Jeannie.

'If there is, then . . .'

'Then Berrington Jones may know a lot more about you and Dennis than he's letting on.'

CHAPTER TWENTY-EIGHT

IT HAD BEEN a pig of a day, but it had ended all right, Berrington thought as he stepped out of the shower.

He looked at himself in the mirror. He was in great shape for fifty-nine: lean, upright, with faintly tanned skin and an almost flat stomach. His pubic hair was dark, but that was because he dyed it to get rid of the embarrassing grey. It was important to him to be able to take off his clothes in front of a woman without turning out the light.

He had begun the day by thinking he had Jeannie Ferrami over a barrel, but she had proved tougher than he expected. I won't underestimate her again, he thought.

On his way back from Washington he had dropped by Preston Barck's house to brief him on the latest development. As always, Preston had been even more worried and pessimistic than the situation warranted. Affected by Preston's mood, Berrington had driven home under a cloud of gloom. But when he walked into the house the phone had been ringing, and Jim, speaking in an improvised code, had confirmed that David Creane would stop the FBI cooperating with

Jeannie. He had promised to make the necessary phone calls tonight.

Berrington towelled himself dry and put on blue cotton pyjamas and a blue-and-white striped bathrobe. Marianne, the housekeeper, had the evening off, but there was a casserole in the refrigerator: chicken *provençale*, according to the note she had left in careful, childish handwriting. He put it in the oven and poured a small glass of Springbank malt whisky. As he took the first sip, the phone rang.

It was his ex-wife, Vivvie. 'The *Wall Street Journal* says you're going to be rich,' she said.

He pictured her, a slender blonde of sixty years, sitting on the terrace of her California house, watching the sun go down over the Pacific Ocean. 'I suppose you want to come back to me.'

'I thought about it, Berry. I thought about it very seriously for at least ten seconds. Then I realized a hundred and eighty million dollars wasn't enough.'

That made him laugh.

'Seriously, Berry, I'm pleased for you.'

He knew she was sincere. She had plenty of money of her own. After leaving him she had gone into the real estate business in Santa Barbara and had done well. 'Thank you.'

'What are you going to do with the money? Leave it to the boy?'

Their son was studying to be a certified public accountant. 'He won't need it, he'll make a fortune as an accountant. I might give some of the money to Jim Proust. He's going to run for president.'

'What'll you get in return? Do you want to be the US ambassador in Paris?'

'No, but I'd consider surgeon-general.'

'Hey, Berry, you're serious about this. But I guess you shouldn't say too much on the phone.'

'True.'

'I gotta go, my date just rang the doorbell. See you sooner, Montezuma.' It was an old family joke.

He gave her the response. 'In a flash, succotash.' He cradled the phone.

He found it a little depressing that Vivvie was going out for the evening with a date—he had no idea who it might be—while he was sitting at home alone with his whisky. Apart from the death of his father, Vivvie's leaving him was the great sadness of Berrington's life. He did not blame her for going: he had been hopelessly unfaithful. But he had loved her, and he still missed her, thirteen years after the divorce. The fact that he was at fault only made him sadder. Joshing with her on the phone reminded him of how much fun they had had together in the good times.

He turned on the TV and watched *Prime Time Live* while his dinner was warming. The kitchen filled with the fragrance of the herbs Marianne used. She was a great cook. Perhaps it was because Martinique had been a French colony.

Just as he was taking the casserole out of the oven, the phone rang again. This time it was Preston Barck. He sounded shaken. 'I just heard from Dick Minsky in Philadelphia,' he said. 'Jeannie Ferrami has made an appointment to go to the Aventine Clinic tomorrow.'

Berrington sat down heavily. 'Christ on a pony,' he said. 'How the hell did she get on to the clinic?'

'I don't know. Dick wasn't there, the night manager took the call. But apparently she said some of her research subjects had treatment years ago and she wanted to check their medical records. Promised to fax over her releases and said she'd be there at two p.m. Thank God Dick happened to call in about something else and the night manager mentioned it.'

Dick Minsky had been one of the first people Threeplex hired, back in the seventies. He had been the mail room boy then: now he was general manager of the clinics. He had never been a member of the inner circle—only Jim, Preston and Berrington could ever belong to that club—but he knew that the company's past held secrets. Discretion was automatic with him.

'What did you tell Dick to do?'

'Cancel the appointment, of course. If she shows up anyway, turn her away. Tell her she can't see the records.'

Berrington shook his head. 'Not good enough.'

'Why?'

'It will just make her more curious. She'll try to find some other way to get at the files.'

'Like how?'

Berrington sighed. Preston could be unimaginative. 'Well, if I were her, I'd call Landsmann, get Michael Madigan's secretary on the phone, and say he ought to look at the Aventine Clinic's records from twenty-three years ago before he closes the takeover deal. That would get him asking questions, wouldn't it?'

'Well, what do you suggest?' Preston said tetchily.

'I think we're going to have to shred all the record cards from the seventies.'

There was a moment of silence. 'Berry, those records are unique. Scientifically, they're priceless—'

'You think I don't know that?' Berrington snapped.

'There must be another way.'

Berrington sighed. He felt as bad as Preston did about it. He had fondly imagined that one day, many years in the future, someone would write the story of their pioneering experiments, and their boldness and scientific brilliance would be revealed to the world. It broke his heart to see the historical evidence wiped out in this guilty and underhand way. But it was inevitable now. 'While the records exist, they're a threat to us. They have to be destroyed. And it had better be done right away.'

'What'll we tell the staff?'

'Shit, I don't know, Preston, make something up, for Christ's sake. New corporate document management strategy. So long as they start shredding first thing in the morning I don't care what you tell them.'

'I guess you're right. Okay, I'll get back to Dick right away. Will you call Jim and bring him up to date?'

'Sure.'

'Bye.'

Berrington dialled Jim Proust's home number. His wife, a wispy woman with a downtrodden air, answered the phone and put Jim on. 'I'm in bed, Berry, what the hell is it now?'

The three of them were getting very snappy with one another.

Berrington told Jim what Preston had reported and the action they had decided on.

'Good move,' Jim said. 'But it's not enough. There are other ways this Ferrami woman could come at us.'

Berrington felt a spasm of irritation. Nothing was ever enough for Jim. No matter what you proposed, Jim would always want tougher action, more extreme measures. Then he suppressed his annoyance. Jim was making sense this time, he reflected. Jeannie had proved to be a real bloodhound, unwavering in her pursuit of the scent. One setback would not make her give up. 'I agree,' he said to Jim. 'And Steve Logan is out of jail, I heard earlier today, so she's not entirely alone. We have to deal with her long-term.'

'She has to be scared off.'

'Jim, for Christ's sake—'

'I know this brings out the wimp in you, Berry, but it has to be done.'

'Forget it.'

'Look—'

'I have a better idea, Jim, if you'll listen for a minute.'

'Okay, I'm listening.'

'I'm going to have her fired.'

Jim thought about it for a while. 'I don't know—will that do it?'

'Sure. Look, she imagines she's stumbled on a biological anomaly. It's the kind of thing that could make a young scientist's career. She has no idea of what's underneath all this: she believes the university is just afraid of bad publicity. If she loses her job, she'll have no facilities to pursue her investigation, and no reason to stick to it. Besides, she'll be too busy looking for another job. I happen to know she needs money.'

'Maybe you're right.'

Berrington was suspicious. Jim was agreeing too readily. 'You're not planning to do something on your own, are you?' he said.

Jim evaded the question. 'Can you do that, can you get her fired?'

'Sure.'

'But you told me Tuesday that it's a university, not the fucking army.'

'That's true, you can't just yell at people and they do what you told them. But I've been in the academic world for most of the last forty years. I know how to work the machinery. When it's really necessary, I can get rid of an assistant professor without breaking a sweat.'

'Okay.'

Berrington frowned. 'We're together on this, right, Jim?'

'Right.'

'Okay. Sleep well.

'Goodnight.'

Berrington hung up the phone. His chicken *provençale* was cold. He dumped it in the trash and went to bed.

He lay awake for a long time, thinking about Jeannie Ferrami. At two a.m. he got up and took a Dalmane. Then, at last, he went to sleep.

CHAPTER TWENTY-NINE

IT WAS A hot night in Philadelphia. In the tenement building, all the doors and windows were open: none of the rooms had air-conditioning. The sounds of the street floated up to apartment 5A on the top floor: car horns, laughter, snatches of music. On a cheap pine desk, scratched and marked with old cigarette burns, a phone was ringing.

He picked it up.

A voice like a bark said: 'This is Jim.'

'Hey, Uncle Jim, how are you?'

'I'm worried about you.'

'How so?'

'I know what happened on Sunday night.'

He hesitated, not sure how to reply. 'They've arrested someone for that.'

'But his girlfriend thinks he's innocent.'

'So?'

'She's coming to Philadelphia tomorrow.'

'What for?'

'I'm not sure. But I think she's a danger.'

'Shit.'

'You may want to do something about her.'

'Such as?'

'It's up to you.'

'How would I find her?'

'Do you know the Aventine Clinic? It's in your neighbourhood.'

'Sure, it's on Chestnut, I pass it every day.'

'She'll be there at two p.m.'

'How will I know her?'

'Tall, dark hair, pierced nostril, about thirty.'

'That could be a lot of women.'

'She'll probably be driving an old red Mercedes.'

'That narrows it down.'

'Now, bear in mind, the other guy is out on bail.'

He frowned. 'So what?'

'So, if she should meet with an accident, after she's been seen with you . . .'

'I get it. They'll assume it was him.'

'You always were quick-thinking, my boy.'

He laughed. 'And you always were mean-thinking, Uncle.'

'One more thing.'

'I'm listening.'

'She's beautiful. So enjoy.'

'Bye, Uncle Jim. And thanks.'

THURSDAY

CHAPTER THIRTY

JEANNIE HAD the Thunderbird dream again.

The first part of the dream was something that really happened, when she was nine and her sister was six, and their father was—briefly—living with them. He was flush with money at the time (and it was not until years later that Jeannie realized he must have got it from a successful robbery). He brought home a new Ford Thunderbird with a turquoise paint job and matching turquoise upholstery, the most beautiful car imaginable to a nine-year-old girl. They all went for a ride, Jeannie and Patty sitting in the front on the bench seat between Daddy and Mom. As they were cruising along the George Washington Memorial Parkway, Daddy put Jeannie on his lap and let her take the wheel.

In real life, she had steered the car into the fast lane and got a fright when a car that was trying to pass honked loudly and Daddy jerked the wheel and brought the Thunderbird back on track. But in the dream Daddy was no longer there, she was driving without help, and Mom and Patty sat quite unperturbed beside her even though they *knew* she couldn't see over the dashboard, and she just gripped the wheel tighter and tighter and tighter, waiting for the crash, while the other cars honked the doorbell at her louder and louder.

She woke up with her fingernails digging into the palms of her hands and the insistent chime of her doorbell in her ears. It was six a.m. She lay still for a moment, savouring the relief that washed over her from the realization that it was only a dream. Then she jumped out of bed and went to the entry phone. 'Hello?'

'It's Ghita, wake up and let me in.'

Ghita lived in Baltimore and worked at FBI headquarters in Washington. She must be on her way to the office for an early start, Jeannie thought. She pressed the button that opened the door.

Jeannie pulled on an oversize T-shirt that reached almost to her knees: it was decent enough for a girlfriend. Ghita came up the stairs, the picture of a fast-rising corporate executive in a navy linen suit, black hair cut in a bob, stud earrings, large lightweight spectacles, *New York Times* under her arm. 'What the hell is going on?' Ghita said without preamble.

Jeannie said: 'I don't know, I just woke up.' This was going to be bad news, she could tell.

'My boss called me at home late last night and told me to have nothing more to do with you.'

'No!' She needed the FBI results to show that her method worked, despite the puzzle of Steven and Dennis. 'Damn! Did he say why?'

'Claimed your methods infringed people's privacy.'

'Unusual for the FBI to worry about a little thing like that.'

'It seems the *New York Times* feels the same way.'

Ghita showed Jeannie the newspaper. On the front page was an article headed:

> **Gene Research Ethics:**
> **Doubts, Fears and a Squabble**

Jeannie was afraid the 'squabble' was a reference to her own situation, and she was right.

> Jean Ferrami is a determined young woman. Against the wishes of her scientific colleagues and the president of Jones Falls University in Baltimore, Md., she stubbornly insists on continuing to scan medical records, looking for twins.
>
> 'I've got a contract,' she says. 'They can't give me orders.' And doubts about the ethics of her work will not shake her resolve.

Jeannie had a sick feeling in the pit of her stomach. 'My God, this is awful,' she said.

The report then moved on to another topic, research on human embryos; and Jeannie had to turn to page 19 before she found another reference to herself.

> A new headache for college authorities has been created by the case of Dr. Jean Ferrami of the psychology department at Jones Falls. Although the university president, Dr. Maurice Obell, and leading psychologist Prof. Berrington Jones both agree her work is unethical, she refuses to stop—and there may be nothing they can do to compel her.

Jeannie read to the end, but the newspaper did not report her insistence that her work was ethically blameless. The focus was entirely on the drama of her defiance.

It was shocking and painful to be attacked this way. She felt hurt and outraged at the same time, the way she had when a thief had knocked her flying and snatched her billfold in a supermarket in Minneapolis years ago. Even though she knew the reporter was malicious and unscrupulous, she was ashamed, as if she had really done wrong. And she felt exposed, held up to the scorn of the nation.

'I may have trouble finding *anyone* who will let me scan a database now,' she said despondently. 'Do you want some coffee? I need something to cheer me up. Not many days start as badly as this.'

'I'm sorry, Jeannie, but I'm in trouble too, for getting the Bureau involved.'

As Jeannie started the coffee machine, she was struck by a thought. 'This article is unfair, but if your boss spoke to you last night, it can't have been the newspaper that prompted his call.'

'Maybe he knew the article was coming.'

'I wonder who tipped him off?'

'He didn't say exactly, but he told me he had had a phone call from Capitol Hill.'

Jeannie frowned. 'It sounds as if this is political. Why the hell would a congressman or senator be interested enough in what I'm doing to tell the FBI not to work with me?'

'Maybe it was just a friendly warning from someone who knew about the article.'

Jeannie shook her head. 'The article doesn't mention the Bureau. Nobody else knows I'm working on FBI files. I didn't even tell Berrington.'

'I'll try to find out who the call came from.'

Jeannie looked in her freezer. 'Have you had breakfast? I have cinnamon buns.'

'No, thanks.'

'I guess I'm not hungry either.' She closed the refrigerator door. She felt despairing. Was there nothing she could do? 'Ghita, I don't suppose you could run my scan without your boss's knowledge?'

She did not have much hope that Ghita would agree. But the answer surprised her. Ghita frowned and said: 'Didn't you get my E-mail yesterday?'

'I left early. What did it say?'

'That I was going to run your scan last night.'

'And did you?'

'Yes. That's why I've come to see you. I did it last night, before he called me.'

Suddenly Jeannie was hopeful again. 'What? And you have the results?'

'I sent them to you by E-mail.'

Jeannie was thrilled. 'But that's great! Did you look? Were there many twins?'

'Quite a lot, twenty or thirty pairs.'

'That's great! That means the system works!'

'But I told my boss I hadn't run the scan. I was scared and I lied.'

Jeannie frowned. 'That's awkward. I mean, what if he finds out, at some time in the future?'

'Exactly. Jeannie, you have to destroy that list.'

'What?'

'If he ever finds out about it, I'm finished.'

'But I can't destroy it! Not if it proves me right!'

Ghita's face set in determined lines. 'You have to.'

'This is awful,' Jeannie said miserably. 'How can I destroy something that might save me?'

'I got into this by doing you a favour,' Ghita said, wagging a finger. 'You have to get me out of it!'

Jeannie did not see that it was entirely her fault. With a touch of acerbity she said: 'I didn't tell you to lie to your boss.'

That angered Ghita. 'I was scared!'

'Wait a minute,' Jeannie said. 'Let's stay cool.' She poured coffee into mugs and gave Ghita one. 'Suppose you go into work today and tell your boss there was a misunderstanding. You gave instructions that the sweep should be cancelled, but you later found it had already been carried out and the results E-mailed.'

Ghita took her coffee but did not drink it. She seemed close to tears. 'Can you imagine working for the FBI? I'm up against the most macho men in middle America. They're looking for any excuse to say that women can't hack it.'

'But you won't get fired.'

'You got me over a barrel.'

It was true, there was nothing Ghita could say to force Jeannie. But Jeannie said: 'Come on, it's not that way.'

Ghita did not soften. 'Yes, it is that way. I'm asking you to destroy that list.'

'I can't.'

'Then there's nothing more to say.' Ghita went to the door.

'Don't leave like this,' Jeannie said. 'We've been friends for too long.'

Ghita went.

'Shit,' Jeannie said. 'Shit.'

The street door slammed.

Did I just lose one of my oldest friends? Jeannie thought.

Ghita had let her down. Jeannie understood the reasons: there was a lot of pressure on a young woman trying to make a career. All the same, it was Jeannie who was under attack, not Ghita. Ghita's friendship had not survived the test of a crisis.

Jeannie wondered if other friends would go the same way.

Feeling miserable, she took a quick shower and began to throw on her clothes. Then she made herself stop and think. She was going into battle: she had better dress for it. She took off her black jeans and red T-shirt and started again. She washed and blow-dried her hair. She made up her face carefully: foundation, powder, mascara and lipstick. She dressed in a black suit with a dove-grey blouse, sheer stockings and patent-leather shoes with a heel. She changed her nose ring for a plain stud.

She studied herself in a full-length mirror. She felt dangerous and she looked formidable. 'Kill, Jeannie, kill,' she murmured. Then she went out.

CHAPTER THIRTY-ONE

JEANNIE THOUGHT about Steve Logan as she drove to JFU. She had called him a big strong kid, but in fact he was more mature than some men ever got to be. She had cried on his shoulder, so she must trust him at some deep level. She had liked the way he smelled, sort of like tobacco before it is lit. Despite her distress she could not help noticing his erection, although he had tried not to let her feel it. It was flattering that he should get so excited just hugging her, and she smiled as she recalled the scene. It was a pity he was not ten or fifteen years older.

Steve reminded her of her first love, Bobby Springfield. She was thirteen, he was fifteen. She knew almost nothing about love and sex, but he was equally ignorant, and they had embarked on a voyage of discovery together. She blushed as she remembered the things they had done in the back row of the Moviedrome on Saturday nights. The exciting thing about Bobby, as with Steve, was a sense of passion constrained. Bobby had wanted her so badly, and had been so inflamed by stroking her nipples or touching her panties, that she had felt enormously powerful. For a while she had abused that power, getting him all hot and bothered just to prove she could do it. But she soon realized, even at the age of thirteen, that that was a foolish game. Still she never lost the sense of risk, of delight in playing with a chained giant. And she felt that with Steve.

He was the only good thing on her horizon. She was in bad trouble. She could not resign from her post here at JFU now. After the *New York Times* had made her famous for defying her bosses, she would find it hard to get another scientific job. If I were a professor, I wouldn't hire someone who caused this kind of trouble, she thought.

But it was too late for her to take a more cautious stance. Her only hope was to press on stubbornly, using the FBI data, and produce scientific results so convincing that people would look again at her methodology and debate its ethics seriously.

It was nine o'clock when she pulled into her parking space. As she locked the car and walked into Nut House she had an acid feeling in her stomach: too much tension and no food.

As soon as she stepped into her office, she knew someone had been there.

It was not the cleaners. She was familiar with the changes they made: the chairs shifted an inch or two, cup rings swabbed, the wastebasket on the wrong side of the desk. This was different. Someone had sat at her computer. The keyboard was at the wrong angle: the intruder had unconsciously shifted it to his or her habitual position. The mouse had been left in the middle of the pad, whereas she always tucked it neatly up against the edge of the keyboard. Looking around, she noticed a cupboard door open a crack and a corner of paper sticking out of the edge of a filing cabinet.

The room had been searched.

At least, she reflected, it had been done amateurishly. It was not like the CIA was after her. All the same it made her deeply uneasy, and she had butterflies in her stomach as she sat down and turned on her PC. Who had been here? A member of the faculty? A student? A bribed security guard? Some outsider? And why?

An envelope had been slipped under her door. It contained a release, signed by Lorraine Logan and faxed to Nut House by Steve. She took Charlotte Pinker's release out of a file and put both in her briefcase. She would fax them to the Aventine Clinic.

She sat at her desk and retrieved her E-mail. There was only one message: the results of the FBI scan. 'Hallelujah,' she breathed.

She downloaded the list of names and addresses with profound relief. She was vindicated: the scan had in fact found pairs. She could hardly wait to check them out and see whether there were any more anomalies like Steve and Dennis.

Ghita had sent her an earlier E-mail message, saying she was going to run the scan, Jeannie recalled. What had happened to that? She wondered if it had been downloaded by last night's snooper. That could explain the panicky late-night call to Ghita's boss.

She was about to look at the names on the list when the phone rang. It was the university president. 'Maurice Obell here. I think we had better discuss this report in the *New York Times*, don't you?'

Jeannie's stomach tightened. Here we go, she thought apprehensively. It begins. 'Of course,' she said. 'What time would suit you?'

'I was hoping you might step into my office right away.'

'I'll be there in five minutes.'

She copied the FBI results onto a floppy disk then exited from the Internet. She took the disk out of her computer and picked up a pen. She thought for a moment, then wrote on the label SHOPPING.LST. No doubt it was an unnecessary precaution, but it made her feel better.

She slipped the floppy into the box containing her back-up files and went out.

The day was already heating up. As she crossed the campus she asked herself what she wanted out of this meeting with Obell. Her only objective was to be allowed to continue with her research. She needed to be tough and make it clear she was not to be bullied; but ideally she would soothe the anger of the university authorities and de-escalate the conflict.

She was glad she had worn the black suit, even though she was sweating in it: it made her look older and more authoritative. Her high heels clacked on the flagstones as she approached Hillside Hall. She was ushered straight into the president's lavish office.

Berrington Jones was sitting there, a copy of the *New York Times* in his hand. She smiled at him, glad to have an ally. He nodded rather coolly and said: 'Good morning, Jeannie.'

Maurice Obell was in his wheelchair behind his big desk. With his usual abrupt manner he said: 'The university simply cannot tolerate this, Dr Ferrami.'

He did not ask her to sit, but she was not going to be carpeted like a schoolgirl, so she selected a chair, moved it, sat down and crossed her legs. 'It was a pity you told the press you had cancelled my project before checking whether you had the legal right so to do,' she said as coolly as she could. 'I fully agree with you that it made the college look foolish.'

He bridled. 'It was not I who made us look foolish.'

That was enough being tough, she decided; now was the moment to tell him they were both on the same side. She uncrossed her legs. 'Of course not,' she said. 'The truth is we were both a little hasty, and the press took advantage of us.'

Berrington put in: 'The damage is done, now—there's no point in apologizing.'

'I wasn't apologizing,' she snapped. She turned back to Obell and smiled. 'However, I do think we should stop bickering.'

Once again Berrington answered her. 'It's too late for that,' he said.

'I'm sure it's not,' she said. She wondered why Berrington had said that. He ought to want a reconciliation: it was not in his interests to be inflammatory. She kept her eyes and her smile on the president. 'We're rational people. We must be able to find a compromise that would allow me to continue my work and yet preserve the university's dignity.'

Obell clearly liked that idea, although he frowned and said: 'I don't quite see how . . .'

'This is all a waste of time,' Berrington said impatiently.

It was the third time he had made a quarrelsome interjection. Jeannie choked back another waspish rejoinder. Why was he being like this? Did he *want* her to stop doing her research and get into trouble with the university and be discredited? It began to seem that way. Was it *Berrington* who had sneaked into her room and downloaded her E-mail and warned off the FBI? Could it even be he who had tipped off the *New York Times* in the first place and started this whole row? She was so stunned by the perverse logic of this notion that she fell silent.

'We have already decided the university's course of action,' Berrington said.

She realized she had mistaken the power structure in the room. Berrington was the boss here, not Obell. Berrington was the conduit for Threeplex's research millions, which Obell needed. Berrington had nothing to fear from Obell; rather the reverse. She had been watching the monkey instead of the organ-grinder.

Berrington had now dropped the pretence that the university president was in charge. 'We didn't call you in here to ask your opinion,' he said.

'Then why did you call me in?' Jeannie asked.

'To fire you,' he replied.

She was stunned. She had expected the threat of dismissal, but not the thing itself. She could hardly take it in. 'What do you mean?' she said stupidly.

'I mean you're fired,' Berrington said. He smoothed his eyebrows with the tip of his right index finger, a sign that he was pleased with himself.

Jeannie felt as if she had been punched. I can't be fired, she thought. I've only been here a few weeks. I was getting on so well, working so hard. I thought they all liked me, except Sophie Chapple. How did this happen so fast?

She tried to collect her thoughts. 'You can't fire me,' she said.

'We just did.'

'No.' As she got over the initial shock, she began to feel angry and defiant. 'You're not tribal chieftains here. There's a procedure.' Universities usually could not fire faculty without some kind of hearing. It was mentioned in her contract, but she had never checked the details. Suddenly it was vitally important to her.

Maurice Obell supplied the information. 'There will be a hearing before the discipline committee of the university senate, of course,' he said. 'Normally, four weeks' notice is required; but in view of the bad publicity surrounding this case I, as president, have invoked the emergency procedure, and the hearing will be held tomorrow morning.'

Jeannie was bewildered by how fast they had acted. The discipline committee? Emergency procedure? Tomorrow morning? This was not a discussion. It was more like being arrested. She half expected Obell to read out her rights.

He did something similar. He pushed a folder across his desk. 'In there you will find the procedural rules of the committee. You may be represented by a lawyer or other advocate provided you notify the chair of the committee in advance.'

Jeannie at last managed a sensible question. 'Who's the chair?'

'Jack Budgen,' said Obell.

Berrington looked up sharply. 'Is that already settled?'

'The chair is appointed annually,' Obell said. 'Jack took over at the start of the semester.'

'I didn't know that.' Berrington looked annoyed, and Jeannie knew why. Jack Budgen was her tennis partner. That was encouraging: he ought to be fair to her. All was not lost. She would have a chance to defend herself, and her research methods, in front of a group of academics. There would be a serious discussion, not the glib superficialities of the *New York Times.*

And she had the results of her FBI sweep. She began to see how she would defend herself. She would show the committee the FBI data. With luck there would be one or two pairs who did not know they were twins. That would be impressive. Then she would explain the precautions she took to protect individuals' privacy . . .

'I think that's all,' said Maurice Obell.

Jeannie was being dismissed. She stood up. 'What a pity it's come to this,' she said.

Berrington said quickly: 'You brought it to this.'

He was like an argumentative child. She did not have the patience for pointless wrangling. She gave him a disdainful look and left the room.

As she crossed the campus she reflected ruefully that she had completely failed to achieve her aims. She had wanted a negotiated settlement, and she had got a gladiatorial contest. But Berrington and Obell had made their decision before she walked into the room. The meeting had been a formality.

She returned to Nut House. As she approached her room she noticed with irritation that the cleaners had left a black plastic garbage bag right outside her office. She would call them immediately. But when she tried to open her door it seemed to be jammed. She swiped her card through the card reader several times but the door did not open. She was about to walk to reception and call maintenance when a dreadful thought occurred to her.

She looked inside the black bag. It was not full of waste paper and styrofoam coffee cups. The first thing she saw was her canvas Land's End briefcase. Also in the sack was the Kleenex box from her drawer, a paperback copy of *A Thousand Acres* by Jane Smiley, two framed photographs and her hairbrush.

They had cleared out her desk and locked her out of her room.

She was devastated. This was a worse blow than what had happened in Maurice Obell's office. That was just words. This made her feel cut off from a huge part of her life. This is my *room*, she thought; how can they shut me out? 'You fucking creeps,' she said aloud.

It must have been done by security while she was in Obell's office. Of course they had not warned her: that would have given her the chance to take anything she really needed. Once again she had been surprised by their ruthlessness.

It was like an amputation. They had taken away her science, her work. She did not know what to do with herself, where to go. For eleven years she had been a scientist—as an undergraduate, graduate student, doctoral student, postdoctoral, and assistant professor. Now, suddenly, she was nothing.

As her spirits sank from despondency to black despair, she remembered the disk with the FBI data. She rummaged through the contents of the plastic sack, but there were no floppy disks. Her results, the backbone of her defence, were locked inside the room.

She pounded futilely on the door with her fist. A passing student who took her statistics class gave her a startled look and said: 'Can I help you, Professor?'

She recalled his name. 'Hi, Ben. You could kick down this goddamn door.'

He studied the door, looking dubious.

'I didn't mean it,' she said. 'I'm fine, thanks.'

He shrugged and walked on.

There was no point standing and staring at the locked door. She picked up the plastic bag and walked into the lab. Lisa was at her desk, keying data into a computer. 'I've been fired,' Jeannie said.

Lisa stared at her. '*What?*'

'They locked me out of my office and dumped my stuff in this fucking garbage bag.'

'I don't believe it!'

Jeannie took her briefcase out of the bag and extracted the *New York Times.* 'It's on account of this.'

Lisa read the first two paragraphs and said: 'But this is bullshit.'

Jeannie sat down. 'I know. So why is Berrington pretending to take it seriously?'

'You think he's pretending?'

'I'm sure of it. He's too smart to let himself be rattled by this kind of crap. He has some other agenda.' Jeannie drummed her feet on the floor, helpless with frustration. 'He's ready to do anything, he's really going out on a limb with this . . . there must be something big at stake for him.' Perhaps she would find the answer in the medical records of the Aventine Clinic in Philadelphia. She checked her watch. She was due there at two p.m.: she had to leave soon.

Lisa still could not take in the news. 'They can't just *fire* you,' she said indignantly.

'There's a disciplinary hearing tomorrow morning.'

'My God, they're serious.'

'They sure are.'

'Is there anything I can do?'

There was, but Jeannie was afraid to ask. She looked appraisingly at Lisa. Lisa was wearing a high-neck blouse with a loose sweater over it, despite the hot weather: she was covering up her body, a reaction to the rape, no doubt. She still looked solemn, like someone recently bereaved.

Would her friendship prove as fragile as Ghita's? Jeannie was terrified of the answer. If Lisa let her down who would she have left? But she had to put her to the test, even though this was the worst possible time. 'You could try to get into my office,' she said hesitantly. 'The results from the FBI are in there.'

Lisa did not answer right away. 'Did they change your lock, or something?'

'It's easier than that. They alter the code electronically so that your card no longer works. I won't be able to get into the building after hours either, I'll bet.'

'It's hard to take this in, it's happened so quickly.'

Jeannie hated pressuring Lisa to take risks. She racked her brains for a let-out. 'Maybe I could get in myself. A cleaner might let me in, but my guess is that the lock will no longer respond to their cards either. If I'm not using the room it won't need cleaning anyway. But security must be able to get in.'

'They won't help you. They'll know you've been locked out deliberately.'

'That's true,' Jeannie said. 'They might let you in, though. You could say you needed something from my room.'

Lisa looked thoughtful.

'I hate to ask you,' Jeannie said.

Then Lisa's expression changed. 'Hell, yes,' she said at last. 'Of course I'll try it.'

Jeannie felt choked up. 'Thanks,' she said. She bit her lip. 'You're a friend.' She reached across the desk and squeezed Lisa's hand.

Lisa was embarrassed by Jeannie's emotion. 'Where in your room is the FBI list?' she said practically.

'The information is on a floppy disk labelled SHOPPING.LST, in a box of floppies in my desk drawer.'

'Got it.' Lisa frowned. 'I can't understand why they're so against you.'

'It all started with Steve Logan,' Jeannie said. 'Ever since Berrington saw him here there has been trouble. But I think I may be on the way to understanding why.' She stood up.

'What are you going to do now?' said Lisa.

'I'm going to Philadelphia.'

CHAPTER THIRTY-TWO

BERRINGTON STARED out of the window of his office. No one was using the tennis court this morning. His imagination pictured Jeannie there. He had seen her on the first or second day of the semester, racing across the court in her short skirt, brown legs pumping, white shoes flashing . . . He had fallen for her then. He frowned, wondering why he had been so struck by her athleticism. Seeing women play sports was not a special turn-on for him. He never watched *American Gladiators,* unlike Professor Gormley in Egyptology, who had every show on videotapes and reran them, according to rumour, late at night in his den at home. But when Jeannie played tennis she achieved a special grace. It was like watching a lion break into a sprint in a nature film: the muscles flowed beneath the skin, the hair flew in the slipstream, and the body moved, stopped, turned and moved again with astonishing, supernatural suddenness. It was mesmerizing to watch and he had been captivated. Now she was threatening everything he had worked for all his life, yet he still wished he could watch her play tennis one more time.

It was maddening that he could not simply dismiss her, even though her salary was essentially paid by him.

Jones Falls University was her employer, and Threeplex had already given them the money. A college could not fire faculty the way a restaurant could fire an incompetent waiter. That was why he had to go through this rigmarole.

'The hell with her,' he said aloud, and he went back to his desk.

This morning's interview had proceeded smoothly, until the revelation about Jack Budgen. Berrington had got Maurice good and riled in advance, and had neatly prevented any rapprochement. But it was bad news that the chair of the discipline committee was to be Jeannie's tennis partner. Berrington had not checked this out in advance: he had assumed he would have some influence over the choice of chair, and he had been dismayed to learn that the appointment was a done thing.

There was a grave danger Jack would see Jeannie's side of the story.

He scratched his head worriedly. Berrington never socialized with his academic colleagues—he preferred the more glamorous company of political and media types. But he knew Jack Budgen's background. Jack had retired from professional tennis at the age of thirty and returned to college to get his doctorate. Already too old to begin a career in chemistry, his subject, he had become an administrator. Running the university's complex of libraries and balancing the conflicting demands of rival departments required a tactful and obliging nature, and Jack did it well.

How could Jack be swayed? He was not a devious man: quite the reverse—his easygoing nature went along with a kind of naivety. He would be offended if Berrington openly lobbied him, or blatantly offered some kind of bribe. But it might be possible to influence him discreetly.

Berrington himself had accepted a bribe once. He still felt knots in his guts whenever he thought of it. It had happened early in his career, before he became a full professor. A woman undergraduate had been caught cheating—paying another student to write her term paper. Her name was Judy Gilmore and she was really cute. She ought to have been expelled from the university, but the head of the department had the power to impose a lesser punishment. Judy had come to Berrington's office to 'talk about the problem'. She had crossed and uncrossed her legs, and gazed mournfully into his eyes, and bent forward so that he could look down the front of her shirt and glimpse a lacy brassiere. He had been sympathetic and had promised to intercede for her. She cried and thanked him, then took his hand, then kissed him on the lips, and finally she unzipped his fly.

She never suggested a deal. She did not offer him sex before he agreed to help her, and after they had screwed on the floor she calmly dressed and combed her hair and kissed him and left. But the next day he had persuaded the department head to let her off with a warning.

He had taken the bribe because he had been able to tell himself it was not a bribe. Judy asked him for help, he agreed, she fell for his charms, and they made love. As time went by he came to see this as pure sophistry.

The offer of sex had been implicit in her manner, and when he promised her what she asked she had wisely sealed the bargain. He liked to think of himself as a principled man, and he had done something absolutely shameful.

Bribing someone was almost as bad as taking a bribe. All the same, he would bribe Jack Budgen if he could. The thought made him grimace in disgust, but it had to be done. He was desperate.

He would do it the way Judy had: by giving Jack the opportunity to kid himself about it.

Berrington thought for a few minutes more, then he picked up the phone and called Jack.

'Thanks for sending me a copy of your memo about the biophysics library extension,' he began.

There was a startled pause. 'Oh, yes. That was a while ago—but I'm glad you found time to read it.'

Berrington had barely glanced at the document. 'I think your proposal has a lot of merit. I'm just calling to say that I'll back you when it comes before the appropriations board.'

'Thank you. I appreciate that.'

'In fact I might be able to persuade Threeplex to put up part of the funding.'

Jack seized on that idea eagerly. 'We could call it the Threeplex Biophysics Library.'

'Good idea. I'll speak to them about it.' Berrington wanted Jack to bring up the subject of Jeannie. Maybe they could get to her via tennis. 'How was your summer?' he said. 'Did you get to Wimbledon?'

'Not this year. Too much work.'

'That's too bad.' With trepidation, he pretended he was about to hang up. 'Talk to you later.'

As he had hoped, Jack forestalled him. 'Uh, Berry, what do you think about this crap in the newspapers? About Jeannie?'

Berrington concealed his relief and spoke dismissively. 'Oh, that—tempest in a teapot.'

'I've been trying to call her but she's not in her office.'

'Don't worry about Threeplex,' Berrington said, although Jack had not mentioned the company. 'They're relaxed about the whole thing. Fortunately, Maurice Obell has acted quickly and decisively.'

'You mean the disciplinary hearing.'

'I imagine that will be a formality. She's embarrassing the university, she's refused to stop, and she's gone to the press. I doubt she'll even trouble to defend herself. I've told the people at Threeplex that we have the situation under control. At present there's no threat to the college's relationship with them.'

'That's good.'

'Of course, if the committee should take Jeannie's side against Maurice, for some reason, we'd be in trouble. But I don't think that's very likely—do you?' Berrington held his breath.

'You know I'm chair of the committee?'

Jack had evaded the question. *Damn you.* 'Yes, and I'm very pleased there's such a cool head in charge of the proceedings.' He mentioned a shaven-headed professor of philosophy. 'If Malcolm Barnet had been chair, God knows what might have happened.'

Jack laughed. 'The senate has more sense. They wouldn't put Malcolm in charge of the parking committee—he'd try to use it as an instrument of social change.'

'But with you in charge I assume the committee will support the president.'

Once again Jack's reply was tantalizingly ambivalent. 'Not all the committee members are predictable.'

You bastard, are you doing this to torment me? 'But the chair is not a loose cannon, I'm sure of that.' Berrington wiped a droplet of sweat from his forehead.

There was a pause. 'Berry, it would be wrong for me to prejudge the issue . . .'

The hell with you!

'. . . But I think I can say that Threeplex need not worry about this.'

At last! 'Thank you, Jack. I appreciate it.'

'Strictly between the two of us, of course.'

'Naturally.'

'Then I'll see you tomorrow.'

'Bye.' Berrington hung up. *Jesus, that was hard!*

Did Jack really not know he had just been bribed? Did he kid himself about it? Or did he understand perfectly well, but simply pretend not to?

It did not matter, so long as he steered the committee the right way.

That might not be the end of it, of course. The committee's decision had to be ratified by a meeting of the full senate. At some point Jeannie might hire a hotshot lawyer and start to sue the university for all kinds of compensation. The case could drag on for years. But her investigations would be halted, and that was all that mattered.

However, the committee's decision was not yet in the bag. If things went wrong tomorrow morning, Jeannie could be back at her desk by midday, hot on the trail of Genetico's guilty secrets. Berrington shuddered: God forbid. He pulled a scratch pad to him and wrote down the names of the committee members.

Jack Budgen—Library
Tenniel Biddenham—History of Art
Milton Powers—Mathematics
Mark Trader—Anthropology
Jane Edelsborough—Physics

Biddenham, Powers and Trader were conventional men, long-standing professors whose careers were bound up with Jones Falls and its continued prestige and prosperity. They could be relied upon to support the university president, Berrington felt sure. The dark horse was the woman, Jane Edelsborough.

He would deal with her next.

CHAPTER THIRTY-THREE

DRIVING TO Philadelphia on I-95, Jeannie found herself thinking about Steve Logan again.

She had kissed him goodbye last night, in the visitors' parking lot on the Jones Falls campus. She found herself regretting that the kiss had been so fleeting. His lips were full and dry, his skin warm. She quite liked the idea of doing it again.

Why was she prejudiced against him because of his age? What was so great about older men? Will Temple, aged thirty-nine, had dropped her for an empty-headed heiress. So much for maturity.

She pressed the Seek button on her radio, looking for a good station, and got Nirvana playing 'Come as You Are'. Whenever she thought about dating a man her own age, or younger, she got a scared feeling, a bit like the frisson of danger that went with a Nirvana track. Older men were reassuring, they knew what to do.

Is this me? she thought. Jeannie Ferrami, the woman who does as she pleases and tells the world to go screw? I need reassurance? Get out of here!

It was true, though. Perhaps it was because of her

father. After him, she never wanted another irresponsible man in her life. On the other hand, her father was living proof that older men could be just as irresponsible as young.

She guessed Daddy was sleeping in cheap hotels somewhere in Baltimore. When he had drunk and gambled whatever money he got for her computer and her TV—which would not take him long—he would either steal something else or throw himself on the mercy of his other daughter, Patty. Jeannie hated him for stealing her stuff. However, the incident had served to bring out the best in Steve Logan. He had been a prince. What the hell, she thought; when next I see Steve Logan I'm going to kiss him again, and this time I'll kiss him good.

She became tense as she threaded the Mercedes through the crowded centre of Philadelphia. This could be the big breakthrough. She might be about to find the solution to the puzzle of Steve and Dennis.

The Aventine Clinic was in University City, west of the Shuylkill River, a neighbourhood of college buildings and student apartments. The clinic itself was a pleasant low-rise fifties building surrounded by trees. Jeannie parked at a meter on the street and went inside.

There were four people in the waiting area: a young couple, the woman looking strained and the man nervous, plus two other women of about Jeannie's age, all sitting in a square of low couches, looking at magazines. A chirpy receptionist asked Jeannie to take a seat, and she picked up a glossy brochure about Threeplex, Inc. She held it open on her lap without reading it: instead she stared at the soothingly meaningless abstract art on the lobby walls and tapped her feet impatiently on the carpeted floor.

She hated hospitals. She had only once been a patient. At the age of twenty-three she had had an abortion. The father was an aspiring film director. She stopped taking the contraceptive pill because they split up, but he came back after a few days, there was a loving reconciliation, and they had unprotected sex and she got pregnant. The operation proceeded without complications, but Jeannie cried for days, and she lost all affection for the film director, even though he was supportive throughout.

He had just made his first Hollywood movie, an action picture. Jeannie had gone alone to see it at the Charles Cinema in Baltimore. The only touch of humanity in an otherwise mechanical story of men shooting at one another was when the hero's girlfriend became depressed after an abortion and threw him out. The man, a police detective, had been bewildered and heartbroken. Jeannie had cried.

The memory still hurt. She stood up and paced the floor. A minute later a man emerged from the back of the lobby and said: 'Dr Ferrami!' in a loud voice. He was an anxiously jolly man of about fifty, with a bald pate and a monkish fringe of ginger hair. 'Hello, hello, good to meet you,' he said with unwarranted enthusiasm.

Jeannie shook his hand. 'Last night I spoke to a Mr Ringwood.'

'Yes, yes! I'm a colleague of his, my name's Dick

Minsky. How do you do?' Dick had a nervous tic that made him blink violently every few seconds: Jeannie felt sorry for him.

He led her up a staircase. 'What's led to your enquiry, may I ask?'

'A medical mystery,' she explained. 'The two women have sons who appear to be identical twins, yet they seem to be unrelated. The only connection I've been able to find is that both women were treated here before getting pregnant.'

'Is that so?' he said as if he were not really listening. Jeannie was surprised: she had expected him to be intrigued.

They entered a corner office. 'All our records can be accessed by computer, provided you have the right code,' he said. He sat at a screen. 'Now, the patients we're interested in are . . .?'

'Charlotte Pinker and Lorraine Logan.'

'This won't take a minute.' He began to key in the names.

Jeannie contained her impatience. These records might reveal nothing at all. She looked around the room. It was too grand an office for a mere filing clerk. Dick must be more than just a 'colleague' of Mr Ringwood's, she thought. 'What's your role here at the clinic, Dick?' she said.

'I'm the general manager.'

She raised her eyebrows, but he did not look up from the keyboard. Why was her enquiry being dealt with by such a senior person? she wondered, and a sense of unease crept into her mood like a wisp of smoke.

He frowned. 'That's odd. The computer says we have no record of either name.'

Jeannie's unease gelled. I'm about to be lied to, she thought. The prospect of a solution to the puzzle receded into the far distance again. A sense of anti-climax washed over her and depressed her.

He spun his screen around so that she could see it. 'Do I have the correct spellings?'

'Yes.'

'When do you think these patients attended the clinic?'

'Approximately twenty-three years ago.'

He looked at her. 'Oh, dear,' he said, and he blinked hard. 'Then I'm afraid you've made a wasted journey.'

'Why?'

'We don't keep records from that far back. It's our corporate document management strategy.'

Jeannie narrowed her eyes at him. 'You throw away old records?'

'We shred the cards, yes, after twenty years, unless of course the patient has been readmitted, in which case the record is transferred to the computer.'

It was a sickening disappointment, and a waste of precious hours that she needed to prepare her defence for tomorrow. She said bitterly: 'How strange that Mr Ringwood didn't tell me this when I talked to him last night.'

'He really should have. Perhaps you didn't mention the dates.'

'I'm quite sure I told him the two women were treated here twenty-three years ago.' Jeannie remembered adding a year to Steve's age to get the right period.

'Then it's hard to understand.'

Somehow Jeannie was not completely surprised at the way this had turned out. Dick Minsky, with his exaggerated friendliness and nervous blink, was the caricature of a man with a guilty conscience.

He turned his screen back to its original position. Seeming regretful, he said: 'I'm afraid there's no more I can do for you.'

'Could we talk to Mr Ringwood, and ask him why he didn't tell me about the cards being shredded?'

'I'm afraid Peter's off sick today.'

'What a remarkable coincidence.'

He tried to look offended, but the result was a parody. 'I hope you're not implying that we're trying to keep something from you.'

'Why would I think that?'

'I have no idea.' He stood up. 'And now, I'm afraid, I've run out of time.'

Jeannie got up and preceded him to the door. He followed her down the stairs to the lobby. 'Good day to you,' he said stiffly.

'Goodbye,' she said.

Outside the door she hesitated. She felt combative. She was tempted to do something provocative, to show them they could not manipulate her totally. She decided to snoop around a bit.

The parking lot was full of doctors' cars, late-model Cadillacs and BMWs. She strolled around one side of the building. A black man with a white beard was sweeping up litter with a noisy blower. There was nothing remarkable or even interesting there. She came up against a blank wall and retraced her steps.

Through the glass door at the front she saw Dick Minsky, still in the lobby, talking to the chirpy secretary. He watched anxiously as Jeannie walked by.

Circling the building in the other direction, she came to the garbage dump. Three men wearing heavy-weight gloves were loading trash onto a truck. This was stupid, Jeannie decided. She was acting like the detective in a hard-boiled mystery. She was about to turn back when something struck her. The men were lifting huge brown plastic sacks of trash effortlessly, as if they weighed very little. What would a clinic be throwing away that was bulky but light?

Shredded paper?

She heard Dick Minsky's voice. He sounded scared. 'Would you please leave now, Dr Ferrami?'

She turned. He was coming around the corner of the building, accompanied by a man in the police-style uniform used by security guards.

She walked quickly to a stack of sacks.

Dick Minsky shouted: 'Hey!'

The garbage men stared at her but she ignored them. She ripped a hole in one sack, reached inside, and pulled out a handful of the contents.

She was holding a sheaf of strips of thin brown card. When she looked closely at the strips she could see they had been written on, some in pen and some with a typewriter. These were shredded hospital record cards.

There could be only one reason why so many sacks were being taken away today.

They had destroyed their records *this morning*—only hours after she had called.

She dropped the shreds on the ground and walked away. One of the garbage men indignantly shouted at her, but she ignored him.

Now there was no doubt.

She stood in front of Dick Minsky, hands on hips. He had been lying to her, and that was why he was a nervous wreck. 'You've got a shameful secret here, haven't you?' she yelled. 'Something you're trying to hide by destroying these records?'

He was completely terrified. 'Of course not,' he managed. 'And, by the way, the suggestion is offensive.'

'Of course it is,' she said. Her temper got the better of her. She pointed at him with the rolled-up Threeplex brochure she was still carrying. 'But this investigation is very important to me, and you'd better believe that anyone who *lies* to me about it is going to be fucked over, but good, before I'm finished.'

'Please leave,' he said.

The security guard took her by the left elbow.

'I'm leaving,' she said. 'No need to hold me.'

He did not release her. 'This way, please,' he said.

He was a middle-aged man with grey hair and a pot belly. In this mood Jeannie was not going to be mauled by him. With her right hand she grasped the arm he was holding her with. The muscles of his upper arm were flabby. 'Let go, please,' she said, and she squeezed. Her hands were strong and her grip was more powerful than most men's. The guard tried to retain his grasp on her elbow but the pain was too much for him, and after a moment he released her. 'Thank you,' she said.

She walked away.

She felt better. She had been right to think there was a clue in this clinic. Their efforts to keep her from learning anything were the best possible confirmation that they had a guilty secret. The solution to the mystery was connected with this place. But where did that get her?

She went to her car but did not get in. It was two thirty and she had had no lunch. She was too excited to eat much but she needed a cup of coffee. Across the street was a café next to a gospel hall. It looked cheap and clean. She crossed the road and went inside.

Her threat to Dick Minsky had been empty: there was nothing she could do to harm him. She had achieved nothing by getting mad at him. In fact she had tipped her hand, making it clear that she knew she was being lied to. Now they were on their guard.

The café was quiet but for a few students finishing lunch. She ordered coffee and a salad. While she was waiting, she opened the brochure she had picked up in the lobby of the clinic. She read:

> *The Aventine Clinic was founded in 1972 by Threeplex, Inc., as a pioneering center for research and development of human* in vitro *fertilization—the creation of what the newspapers call 'test-tube babies.'*

And suddenly it was all clear.

CHAPTER THIRTY-FOUR

JANE EDELSBOROUGH was a widow in her early fifties. A statuesque but untidy woman, she normally dressed in loose ethnic clothes and sandals. She had a commanding intellect, but no one would have guessed it to look at her. Berrington found such people baffling. If you were clever, he thought, why disguise yourself as an idiot by dressing badly? Yet universities were full of such people—in fact he was exceptional in taking care over his appearance.

Today he was looking especially natty in a navy linen jacket and matching vest with lightweight houndstooth-check pants. He inspected his image in the mirror behind the door before leaving his office on his way to see Jane.

He headed for the Student Union. Faculty rarely ate there—Berrington had never entered the place—but Jane had gone there for a late lunch, according to the chatty secretary in Physics.

The lobby of the union was full of kids in shorts standing in line to get money out of the bank teller machines. He stepped into the cafeteria and looked around. She was in a far corner, reading a journal and eating French fries with her fingers.

The place was a food court, such as Berrington had seen in airports and shopping malls, with a Pizza Hut, an ice-cream counter and a Burger King as well as a regular cafeteria. Berrington picked up a tray and went into the cafeteria section. Inside a glass-fronted case were a few tired sandwiches and some doleful cakes. He shuddered: in normal circumstances he would drive to the next state rather than eat here.

This was going to be difficult. Jane was not his kind of woman. That made it even more likely that she would lean the wrong way at the discipline hearing. He had to make a friend of her in a short time. It would call for all his powers of charm.

He bought a piece of cheesecake and a cup of coffee and carried them to Jane's table. He felt jittery, but he forced himself to look and sound relaxed. 'Jane,' he said. 'This is a pleasant surprise. May I join you?'

'Sure,' she said amiably, putting her journal aside. She took off her glasses, revealing deep brown eyes with wrinkles of amusement at the corners, but she looked a mess: her long grey hair was tied in some kind of colourless rag and she wore a shapeless grey-green blouse with sweat marks at the armpits. 'I don't think I've ever seen you in here,' she said.

'I've never been here. But at our age it's important not to get set in our ways—don't you agree?'

'I'm younger than you,' she said mildly. 'Although I guess no one would think so.'

'Sure they would.' He took a bite of his cheesecake. The base was as tough as cardboard and the filling tasted like lemon-flavoured shaving-cream. He swallowed with an effort. 'What do you think of Jack Budgen's proposed Biophysics Library?'

'Is that why you came to see me?'

'I didn't come here to see you, I came to try the food, and I wish I hadn't. It's awful. How can you eat here?'

She dug a spoon into some kind of dessert. 'I don't notice what I eat, Berry, I think about my particle accelerator. Tell me about the new library.'

Berrington had been like her, obsessed by work, once upon a time. He had never allowed himself to look like a hobo on account of it, but nevertheless as a young scientist he had lived for the thrill of discovery. However, his life had taken a different direction. His books were popularizations of other people's work: he had not written an original paper in fifteen or twenty years. For a moment he wondered whether he might have been happier if he had made a different choice. Slovenly Jane, eating cheap food while she ruminated over problems in nuclear physics, had an air of calm and contentment that Berrington had never known.

And he was not managing to charm her. She was too wise. Perhaps he should flatter her intellectually. 'I just think you should have a bigger input. You're the senior physicist on campus, one of the most distinguished scientists JFU has—you ought to be involved in this library.'

'Is it even going to happen?'

'I think Threeplex is going to finance it.'

'Well, that's a piece of good news. But what's your interest?'

'Thirty years ago I made my name when I started

asking which human characteristics are inherited and which are learned. Because of my work, and the work of others like me, we now know that a human being's genetic inheritance is more important than his upbringing and environment in determining a whole range of psychological traits.'

'Nature, not nurture.'

'Exactly. I proved that a human being *is* his DNA. The young generation is interested in how this process works. What is the mechanism by which a combination of chemicals gives me blue eyes and another combination gives you eyes which are a deep, dark shade of brown, almost chocolate-coloured, I guess.'

'Berry!' she said with a wry smile. 'If I were a thirty-year-old secretary with perky breasts I might imagine you were flirting with me.'

That was better, he thought. She had softened at last. 'Perky?' he said, grinning. He deliberately looked at her bust, then back up at her face. 'I believe you're as perky as you feel.'

She laughed, but he could tell she was pleased. At last he was getting somewhere with her. Then she said: 'I have to go.'

Damn. He could not keep control of this interaction. He had to get her attention in a hurry. He stood up to leave with her. 'There will probably be a committee to oversee the creation of the new library,' he said as they walked out of the cafeteria. 'I'd like your opinion on who should be on it.'

'Gosh, I'll need to think about that. Right now I have to give a lecture on antimatter.'

Goddamn it, I'm losing her, Berrington thought.

Then she said: 'Can we talk again?'

Berrington grasped at a straw. 'How about over dinner?'

She looked startled. 'All right,' she said after a moment.

'Tonight?'

A bemused look came over her face. 'Why not?'

That would give him another chance, at least. Relieved, he said: 'I'll pick you up at eight.'

'Okay.' She gave him her address and he made a note in a pocket pad.

'What kind of food do you like?' he said. 'Oh, don't answer that, I remember, you think about your particle accelerator.' They emerged into the hot sun. He squeezed her arm lightly. 'See you tonight.'

'Berry,' she said. 'You're not *after* something, are you?'

He winked at her. 'What have you got?'

She laughed and walked away.

CHAPTER THIRTY-FIVE

TEST-TUBE BABIES. *In vitro* fertilization. That was the link. Jeannie saw it all.

Charlotte Pinker and Lorraine Logan had both been treated for subfertility at the Aventine Clinic. The clinic had pioneered *in vitro* fertilization: the process by which sperm from the father and an egg from the mother are brought together in the laboratory, and the resulting embryo is then implanted in the woman's womb.

Identical twins occur when an embryo splits in half, in the womb, and becomes two individuals. That might have happened in the test tube. Then the twins from the test tube could have been implanted in two different women. That was how identical twins could be born to two unrelated mothers. Bingo.

The waitress brought Jeannie's salad but she was too excited to eat it.

Test-tube babies were no more than a theory in the early seventies, she was sure. But Threeplex had obviously been years ahead in its research.

Both Lorraine and Charlotte said they had been given hormone therapy. It seemed the clinic had lied to them about their treatment.

That was bad enough, but as Jeannie thought

through the implications she realized something worse. The embryo that split might have been the biological child of Lorraine and Charles, or of Charlotte and the Major—but not both. One of them had been implanted with another couple's child.

Jeannie's heart filled with horror and loathing as she realized they could *both* have been given the babies of total strangers.

She wondered why Threeplex had deceived its patients in this appalling way. The technique was untried: perhaps they needed human guinea pigs. Maybe they had applied for permission and had been refused. Or they could have had some other reason for secrecy.

Whatever their motive for lying to the women, Jeannie now understood why her investigation scared Threeplex so badly. Impregnating a woman with an alien embryo, without her knowledge, was about as unethical as could be imagined. It was no wonder they were desperate to cover it up. If Lorraine Logan ever found out what had been done to her, there would be hell to pay.

She took a sip of coffee. The drive to Philadelphia had not been wasted after all. She did not yet have all the answers but she had solved the central puzzle. It was deeply satisfying.

Looking up, she was astonished to see Steve walk in.

She blinked and stared. He was wearing khakis and a blue button-down, and as he came in he closed the door behind him with his heel.

She smiled broadly and stood up to greet him. 'Steve!' she said delightedly. Remembering her resolution, she threw her arms around him and kissed him on the lips. He smelled different today, less tobacco and more spice. He hugged her to him and kissed her back. She heard the voice of an older woman saying: 'My God, I remember when I felt like that,' and several people laughed.

She released him. 'Sit here. Do you want something to eat? Share my salad. What are you doing here? I can't believe it. You must have followed me. No, no, you knew the name of the clinic and you decided to meet me.'

'I just felt like talking to you.' He smoothed his eyebrows with the tip of his index finger. Something about the action bothered her—*Who else have I seen do that?*—but she pushed it to the back of her mind.

'You go in for big surprises.'

Suddenly he seemed edgy. 'I do?'

'You like to show up unexpectedly, don't you?'

'I guess so.'

She smiled at him. 'You're a little strange today. What's on your mind?'

'Listen, you got me all hot and bothered,' he said. 'Can we get out of here?'

'Sure.' She put a five-dollar bill on the table and stood up.

'Where's your car?' she said as they stepped outside.

'Let's take yours.'

They got into the red Mercedes. She fastened her seat belt, but he did not. As soon as she pulled away he edged close to her on the bench seat, lifted her hair, and started kissing her neck. She liked it, but she felt embarrassed, and she said: 'I think we may be a little too old to do this in a car.'

'Okay,' he said. He stopped and turned to face forward, but he left his arm draped around her shoulders. She was heading east on Chestnut. As they came to the bridge he said: 'Take the expressway—there's something I want to show you.' Following the signs, she turned right onto Shuylkill Avenue and pulled up at a stop light.

The hand over her shoulder dropped lower and he started fondling her breast. She felt her nipple stiffen in response to his touch, but all the same she felt uncomfortable. It was strangely like being felt up on a subway train. She said: 'Steve, I like you, but you're going a little too fast for me.'

He made no reply, but his fingers found her nipple and pinched it hard.

'Ow!' she said. 'That hurt! For Pete's sake, what's got into you?' She shoved him away with her right hand. The light went green and she drove down the on-ramp for the Shuylkill Expressway.

'I don't know where I am with you,' he complained. 'First you kiss me like a nymphomaniac, then you freeze.'

And I imagined this boy was mature! 'Listen, a girl kisses you because she wants to kiss you. It's not a licence for you to do anything the hell you want to her. And you should *never* hurt.' She eased onto the southbound two-lane of the expressway.

'Some girls like to be hurt,' he said, putting a hand on her knee.

She moved his hand. 'What do you want to show me, anyway?' she said, trying to distract him.

'This,' he said, taking her right hand. A moment later she felt his naked penis, stiff and hot.

'Jesus Christ!' She snatched her hand away. Boy, had she misjudged this one! 'Put it away, Steve, and stop acting like a goddamned adolescent!'

The next thing she knew, something struck her a mighty blow on the side of the face.

She screamed and jerked sideways. An air-horn blared as her car swung across the next lane of the expressway in front of a Mack truck. The bones of her face burned with agony and she tasted blood. Fighting to ignore the pain, she regained control of the car.

She realized with astonishment that he had punched her.

No one had ever done that.

'You son of a bitch!' she screamed.

'Now give me a hand job,' he said. 'Otherwise I'll beat the shit out of you.'

'Fuck you!' she yelled.

Out of the corner of her eye she saw him draw back his fist for another blow.

Without thinking, she trod on the brake.

He was thrown forward and his punch missed her. His head banged the windshield. Tyres screeched in protest as a white stretch limousine swerved to avoid the Mercedes.

As he recovered his balance, she released the brake.

The car coasted forward. If she stopped in the fast lane of the expressway for a few seconds, she thought, he would be so terrified he would plead with her to drive on. She trod on the brake once more, throwing him forward again.

This time he recovered more quickly. The car came to a halt. Cars and trucks swerved around it, horns blaring. Jeannie was terrified: at any moment another vehicle could slam into the back of the Mercedes. But her plan did not work: he seemed to have no fear. He put his hand up her skirt, grasped the waist of her pantyhose, and pulled. There was a tearing sound as her tights ripped open.

She tried to push him away but he was all over her. Surely he would not try to rape her right there on the expressway? In despair she opened her door but she could not get out because she had her seat belt fastened. She tried to undo it but she could not get at the buckle because of Steve.

To her left, traffic was joining the expressway from another ramp, coming directly into the fast lane at sixty miles an hour and flashing by. Was there not a single driver who would stop and help a woman who was being attacked?

As she struggled to push him away, her foot came off the brake and the car crept forward. Maybe she could keep him off balance, she thought. She had control of the car, it was her only advantage. In desperation she put her foot on the accelerator pedal and floored it.

The car took off with a lurch. Brakes squealed as a Greyhound bus narrowly missed her fender. Steve was thrown back in his seat and distracted briefly, but a few seconds later his hands were all over her again, pulling her breasts out of her brassiere and thrusting inside her panties as she tried to drive. She was frantic. He did not seem to care if he killed both of them. What the hell could she do to stop him?

She swung the car hard across to the left, throwing him up against the passenger door. She almost hit a garbage truck, and for a cliffhanging instant she looked into the petrified face of the driver, an elderly man with a grey moustache; then she swung the wheel the other way and the Mercedes lurched out of danger.

Steve grabbed her again. She braked hard, then floored the accelerator, but he laughed as he was thrown around, just as if he were on a joyride at a carnival; and then he came back at her.

She hit him with her right elbow and her fist but she could not put any power into the blows while she was at the wheel, and she succeeded only in distracting him for a few more seconds.

How long could this go on? Were there no cop cars in this town?

Over his shoulder she saw that she was passing an off-ramp. There was an ancient sky-blue Cadillac on her nearside a few yards behind her. At the last moment she swung the steering wheel. Her tyres screeched, the Mercedes went up on two wheels, and Steve fell against her helplessly. The blue Cadillac swerved to avoid her, there was a fanfare of outraged car horns, then she heard the thud of cars crashing and the xylophone sound of breaking glass. Her nearside wheels came down again and hit the tarmac with a bone-shuddering thump. She was on the ramp. The car fishtailed, threatening to hit the concrete parapet on either side, but she got it straight.

She accelerated down a long off-ramp. As soon as the car was stable, Steve thrust his hand between her legs and attempted to get his fingers inside her panties. She wriggled, trying to stop him. She glanced at his face. He was smiling, his eyes wide, panting and sweating with sexual excitement. He was having fun. This was *crazy.*

There were no cars ahead or behind her. The ramp ended in a stop light which was green. To her left was a cemetery. She saw a sign pointing right that read *Civic Center Blvd* and she swung that way, hoping to see a busy town hall with crowds of people on the sidewalk. To her dismay the street was a bleak desert of disused halls and concrete plazas. Ahead of her, a light turned red. If she stopped, she was done for.

Steve got his hand inside her panties and said: 'Stop the car!' Like her, he had realized that if he raped her here there was a good chance no one would interfere.

He was hurting her now, pinching and thrusting with his fingers, but worse than the pain was the fear of what was to come. She accelerated wildly toward the red light.

An ambulance came from the left, swinging in front of her. She braked hard and swerved to miss it, thinking crazily, *If I crash now, at least help is at hand.*

Suddenly Steve withdrew his hands from her body. She had a moment of blessed relief. Then he grabbed the transmission lever and pushed it into neutral. The car suddenly lost momentum. She yanked it back into drive and floored the pedal, passing the ambulance.

How long can this go on? Jeannie thought. She had to get to a neighbourhood where there were some people before the car stopped or crashed. But Philadelphia had turned into a moonscape.

He grabbed the steering wheel and tried to pull the car over on to the sidewalk. Jeannie jerked it back quickly. The rear wheels skidded and the ambulance honked indignantly.

He tried again. This time he was cleverer. He knocked the transmission into neutral with his left hand and grabbed the wheel with his right. The car slowed down and mounted the kerb.

Jeannie took both hands off the wheel, put them on Steve's chest and shoved him away with all her might. Her strength surprised him and he was flung backwards. She put the car in drive and stamped on the accelerator pedal. The car rocketed forward yet again, but Jeannie knew that she could not fight him off much longer. Any second now he would succeed in stopping the car, and she would be trapped in here with him. He recovered his balance as she turned into a left-hand bend. He got both hands on the steering wheel, and she thought, *This is the end, I can't do any more.* Then the car rounded the bend and the cityscape changed abruptly.

There was a busy street, a hospital with people standing outside, a line of taxicabs, and a sidewalk stall selling Chinese food. 'Yes!' Jeannie shouted triumphantly. She stamped on the brake. Steve jerked the wheel and she pulled it back. Fishtailing, the car screeched to a halt in the middle of the road. A dozen cab drivers at the food stand turned to look.

Steve opened his door, got out and ran.

'Thank God,' Jeannie breathed.

A moment later he had disappeared.

Jeannie sat there, panting. He was gone. The nightmare was over.

One of the drivers came over and put his head inside the passenger door. Hastily Jeannie rearranged her clothing. 'Are you okay, lady?' he said.

'I guess so,' she replied breathlessly.

'What the heck was that all about?'

She shook her head. 'I sure wish I knew,' she said.

CHAPTER THIRTY-SIX

STEVE SAT on a low wall near Jeannie's house, waiting for her. It was hot, but he took advantage of the shade of a big maple tree. She lived in an old working-class neighbourhood of traditional row houses. Teenagers from a nearby school were walking home, laughing and quarrelling and eating candy. It was not long since he had been like that: eight or nine years.

But now he was worried and desperate. This afternoon his lawyer had talked to Sergeant Delaware of the Sex Crimes Unit in Baltimore. She had told him she had the results of the DNA test. The DNA from traces of sperm in Lisa Hoxton's vagina exactly matched the DNA in Steve's blood.

He was devastated. He had been sure the DNA test would end this agony.

He could tell that his lawyer no longer believed in his innocence. Mom and Dad did, but they were baffled: they both knew enough to realize that DNA testing was extremely reliable.

In his worst moments he wondered if he had some kind of split personality. Maybe there was another Steve who took over and raped women and gave him his body back afterwards. That way he would not know what he had done. He recalled, ominously, that there were a few seconds of his fight with Tip Hendricks that he had never been able to bring to mind. And he had been ready to drive his fingers into Porky Butcher's brain. Was it his alter ego who did these things? He did not really believe it. There had to be another explanation.

The ray of hope was the mystery surrounding him and Dennis Pinker. Dennis had the same DNA as Steve. Something was wrong here. And the only person who could figure it out was Jeannie Ferrami.

The kids disappeared into their homes, and the sun dipped behind the row of houses on the other side of the street. Towards six o'clock the red Mercedes eased into a parking slot fifty yards away. Jeannie got out. At first she did not see Steve. She opened the trunk and took out a large black plastic garbage bag. Then she locked the car and came along the sidewalk towards him. She was dressed formally, in a black skirted suit, but she looked dishevelled, and there was a weariness in her walk that touched his heart. He wondered what had happened to give her this battle-worn look. She was still gorgeous, though, and he watched her with longing in his heart.

As she got near him he stood up, smiling, and took a step towards her.

She glanced at him, met his eye and recognized him. A look of horror came over her face.

She opened her mouth and screamed.

He stopped dead. Aghast, he said: 'Jeannie, what is it?'

'Get away from me!' she yelled. 'Don't you touch me! I'm calling the cops right now!'

Nonplussed, Steve held his hands up in a defensive gesture. 'Sure, sure, anything you say. I'm not touching you, okay? What the hell has gotten into you?'

A neighbour came out of the front door Jeannie shared. He must be the occupant of the apartment beneath hers, Steve figured. He was an old black man wearing a check shirt and a tie. 'Is everything all right, Jeannie?' he said. 'I thought I heard someone cry out.'

'It was me, Mr Oliver,' she said in a shaky voice. 'This jerk attacked me in my car in Philadelphia this afternoon.'

'Attacked you?' Steve said incredulously. 'I wouldn't do that!'

'You bastard, you did it two hours ago.'

Steve was stung. He was sick of being accused of brutality. 'Fuck you, I haven't been to Philadelphia for years.'

Mr Oliver intervened. 'This young gentleman been sitting on that wall for nigh on two hours, Jeannie. He ain't been to no Philadelphia this afternoon.'

Jean looked indignant and seemed ready to accuse her good-natured neighbour of lying.

Steve noticed that she was wearing no stockings: her bare legs looked odd with such a formal outfit. One side of her face was slightly swollen and reddish. His fury evaporated. *Someone* had attacked her. He yearned to put his arms around her and comfort her. It made her fear of him even more distressing. 'He hurt you,' he said. 'The bastard.'

Her face changed. The look of terror went. She spoke to the neighbour. 'He got here two hours ago?'

The man shrugged. 'Hour and forty, maybe fifty minutes.'

'You're sure?'

'Jeannie, if he was in Philadelphia two hours ago he must have come here on the Concorde.'

She looked at Steve. 'It must have been Dennis.'

He walked towards her. She did not step back. He reached out and touched her swollen cheek with his fingertips. 'Poor Jeannie,' he said.

'I thought it was you,' she said, and tears came to her eyes.

He folded her in his arms. Slowly he felt her body lose its stiffness, and she leaned on him trustingly. He stroked her head and twined his fingers in the heavy waves of her dark hair. He closed his eyes, thinking how lean and strong her body was. I'll bet Dennis has some bruises too, he thought. I hope so.

Mr Oliver coughed. 'Would you youngsters like a cup of coffee?'

Jeannie detached herself from Steve. 'No, thanks,' she said. 'I just want to get out of these clothes.'

Tension was written on her face, but she looked even more bewitching. I'm falling in love with this woman, he thought. It's not just that I want to sleep with her—though it's that too. I want her to be my friend. I want to watch TV with her, and go to the supermarket with her, and give her NyQuil on a spoon when she has a cold. I want to see how she brushes her teeth and pulls on her jeans and butters her toast. I want her to ask me does the orange lipstick suit her and should she buy razors and what time will I be home.

He wondered if he had the nerve to tell her that.

She crossed the row porch to her door. Steve hesitated. He wanted to follow her, but he needed an invitation.

She turned on the doorstep. 'Come on,' she said.

He followed her up the stairs and entered the living room behind her. She dropped the black plastic bag on the rug. She went into the kitchen nook and kicked off her shoes, then, to his astonishment, she dropped them in the kitchen bin. 'I'll never wear these goddamn clothes again,' she said angrily. She took off her jacket and threw that away. Then, as Steve stared in disbelief, she unbuttoned her blouse and took it off and put that in the bin too.

She was wearing a plain black cotton brassiere. Surely, Steve thought, she was not going to take that off right in front of him. But she reached behind her back, unfastened it, and tossed it into the trash. She had firm, shallow breasts with prominent brown nipples. There was a faint red mark on her shoulder where the strap had been too tight. Steve's throat went dry.

She unzipped her skirt and let it fall to the floor. She wore simple black bikini panties. Steve gazed at her open-mouthed. Her body was perfect: the strong shoulders, the neat breasts, the flat belly, and the long, sculptured legs. She pushed her panties down, swept them up in a bundle with the skirt, and shoved the bundle into the bin. Her pubic hair was a dense mass of black curls.

She looked blankly at Steve for a moment, almost as if she were not sure what he was doing there. Then she said: 'I have to take a shower.' Naked, she walked past him. He looked hungrily at her back, drinking in the details of her shoulder blades, her narrow waist, the swelling curves of her hips, and the muscles of her legs. She was so lovely it hurt.

She left the room. A moment later he heard water running.

'Jesus,' he breathed. He sat on her black couch. What did it mean? Was that some kind of test? What was she trying to say to him?

He smiled. What a wonderful body, so slim and strong and perfectly proportioned. No matter what else happened, he would never forget the way she looked.

She showered for a long time. He realized that in the drama of her accusation he had not told her his mystifying news. At last the water stopped. A minute later she returned to the room in a big fuchsia-pink towelling robe, wet hair plastered to her head. She sat on the couch beside him and said: 'Did I dream it, or did I just strip off in front of you?'

'No dream,' he said. 'You dumped your clothes in the trash.'

'My God, I don't know what came over me.'

'You don't have anything to apologize for. I'm glad you trust me so much. I can't tell you what that means to me.'

'You must think I'm out of my mind.'

'No, but I think you're probably shocked after what happened to you in Philadelphia.'

'Maybe that's it. I just remember feeling I had to get rid of the clothes I was wearing when it happened.'

'This may be the moment to open that bottle of vodka you keep in the freezer.'

She shook her head. 'What I really want is some jasmine tea.'

'Let me make it.' He got up and went behind the kitchen counter. 'Why are you carrying a garbage bag around?'

'I was fired today. They put all my personal stuff in that bag and locked me out of my room.'

'What?' He was incredulous. 'How come?'

'There was an article in the *New York Times* today saying that my use of databases violates people's privacy. But I think Berrington Jones was just using that as an excuse to get rid of me.'

He burned with indignation. He wanted to protest, to spring to her defence, to save her from this malicious persecution. 'Can they dismiss you just like that?'

'No, there's a hearing tomorrow morning in the front of the discipline committee of the university senate.'

'You and I are both having an unbelievably bad week.' He was going to tell her about the DNA test when she picked up the phone.

'I need the number of Greenwood Penitentiary, it's near Richmond, Virginia.' As Steve filled the kettle, she scribbled a number and dialled again. 'May I speak to Warden Temoigne? My name is Dr Ferrami. Yes, I'll hold. Thank you . . . Good evening, Warden, how are you? I'm fine. This may sound like a silly question, but is Dennis Pinker still in jail? You're sure? You saw him with your own eyes? Thank you. And you take care of yourself, too. Bye.' She looked up at Steve. 'Dennis is still in jail. The warden spoke to him an hour ago.'

Steve put a spoonful of jasmine tea into the pot and found two cups. 'Jeannie, the cops have the result of their DNA test.'

She went very still. 'And . . .?'

'The DNA from Lisa's vagina matches the DNA from my blood.'

In a bemused voice she said: 'Are you thinking what I'm thinking?'

'Someone who looks like me and has my DNA raped Lisa Hoxton on Sunday. The same guy attacked you in Philadelphia today. *And it wasn't Dennis Pinker.*'

Their eyes locked, and Jeannie said: 'There are three of you.'

'Jesus Christ.' He felt despairing. 'But this is even more unlikely. The cops will never believe it. How could something like this happen?'

'Wait,' she said excitedly. 'You don't know what I discovered this afternoon, before I ran into your double. I have the explanation.'

'Dear God, let this be true.'

She looked concerned. 'Steve, you're going to find it shocking.'

'I don't care, I just want to understand.'

She reached into the black plastic garbage bag and retrieved a canvas briefcase. 'Look at this.' She took out a glossy brochure folded open to the first page. She handed it to Steve and he read the opening paragraph:

The Aventine Clinic was founded in 1972 by Threeplex, Inc., as a pioneering center for research and development of human in vitro *fertilization—the creation of what the newspapers call 'test-tube babies.'*

Steve said: 'You think Dennis and I are test-tube babies?'

'Yes.'

He had a strange, nauseous feeling in the pit of his stomach. 'That's weird. But what does it explain?'

'Identical twins could be conceived in the laboratory and then implanted in the wombs of different women.'

Steve's sick feeling got worse. 'But did the sperm and egg come from Mom and Dad—or from the Pinkers?'

'I don't know.'

'So the Pinkers could be my real parents. God.'

'There's another possibility.'

Steve could see from the worried look on Jeannie's face that she was afraid this would shock him too. His mind leaped ahead and he guessed what she was going to say. 'Maybe the sperm and egg didn't come from my parents *or* the Pinkers. I could be the child of total strangers.'

She did not reply, but her solemn look told him he was right.

He felt disoriented. It was like a dream in which he suddenly found himself falling through the air. 'It's hard to take in,' he said. The kettle switched itself off. For something to do with his hands, Steve poured boiling water into the teapot. 'I've never much resembled either Mom or Dad. Do I look like one of the Pinkers?'

'No.'

'Then it's most probably strangers.'

'Steve, none of this takes away the fact that your Mom and Dad loved you and raised you and would still give their lives for you.'

With a shaky hand he poured tea into two cups. He gave one to Jeannie and sat beside her on the couch. 'How does all this explain the third twin?'

'If there were twins in the test tube, there could have been triplets. It's the same process: one of the embryos split again. It happens in nature, so I guess it can happen in the laboratory.'

Steve still felt as if he were spinning through the air, but now he began to get another sensation: relief. It was a bizarre story that Jeannie told, but at least it provided a rational explanation of why he had been accused of two brutal crimes.

'Do Mom and Dad know any of this?'

'I don't believe they do. Your mother and Charlotte Pinker told me they went into the clinic for hormone treatment. *In vitro* fertilization was not practised in those days. Threeplex must have been years ahead of everyone else with the technique. And I think they tried it without telling their patients what they were doing.'

'No wonder Threeplex is scared,' Steve said. 'Now I understand why Berrington is so desperate to discredit you.'

'Yeah. What they did was *really* unethical. It makes invasion of privacy look petty.'

'It wasn't just unethical. It could ruin Threeplex, financially.'

She looked excited. 'That would explain a lot. But how could it ruin them?'

'It's a tort—a civil wrong. We covered this last year in law school.' In the back of his mind he was thinking, *Why the hell am I talking to her about torts—I want to tell her how much I love her.* 'If Threeplex offered a woman hormone treatment, then deliberately impregnated her with someone else's foetus without telling her, that's a breach of implied contract by fraud.'

'But it happened so long ago. Isn't there a statute of limitations?'

'Yes, but it runs from the time of *discovery* of the fraud.'

'I still don't see how it would ruin the company.'

'This is an ideal case for punitive damages. That means the money is not just to compensate the victim, say for the cost of bringing up someone else's child. It's also to punish the people who did it, and make sure they and others are scared to commit the same wrong again.'

'How much?'

'Threeplex knowingly abused a woman's body for their own secret purposes—I'm sure any lawyer worth his salt would ask for a hundred million dollars.'

'According to that piece in the *Wall Street Journal* yesterday, the entire company is only worth a hundred and eighty million.'

'So they would be ruined.'

'It might take years to come to trial.'

'But don't you see? Just the *threat* would sabotage the takeover!'

'How so?'

'The danger that Threeplex may have to pay a fortune in damages reduces the value of the shares. The takeover would at least be postponed until Landsmann could assess the amount of the liability.'

'Wow. So it's not just their reputations that are on the line. They could lose all that money, too.'

'Exactly.' Steve's mind came back to his own problems. 'None of this helps me,' he said, suddenly feeling gloomy again. 'I need to be able to prove your theory of the third twin. The only way of doing that is to find him.' A thought struck him. 'Could your computer search engine be used? Do you see what I mean?'

'Sure.'

He grew excited. 'If one search threw up me and Dennis, another search might throw up me and the third, or Dennis and the third, or all three of us.'

'Yes.'

She was not as thrilled as she ought to be. 'Can you do it?'

'After this bad publicity I'm going to have trouble getting anyone to let me use their database.'

'Damn!'

'But there is one possibility. I've already run a sweep of the FBI fingerprint file.'

Steve's spirits rocketed again. 'Dennis is sure to be on their files. If the third one has ever had his prints taken the sweep will have picked him up! This is great!'

'But the results are on a floppy disk in my office.'

'Oh, no! And you've been locked out!'

'Yes.'

'Hell, I'll bust down the door, let's go there now, what are we waiting for?'

'You could end up back in jail. And there may be an easier way.'

With an effort Steve calmed down. 'You're right. There has to be another way of getting that disk.'

Jeannie picked up the phone. 'I asked Lisa Hoxton to try to get into my office. Let's see if she succeeded.' She dialled a number. 'Hey, Lisa, how are you . . . Me? Not too good. Listen, this is going to sound incredible to you.' She summarized what she had found out. 'I know it's hard to believe, but I can prove it if I can get my hands on that floppy disk . . . You couldn't get into my room? Shit.' Jeannie's face fell. 'Well, thanks for trying. I know you took a chance. I really appreciate it. Yeah. Bye.'

She hung up and said: 'Lisa tried to persuade a security guard to let her in. She almost succeeded, then he checked with his superior and almost got fired.'

'What do we try next?'

'If I get my job back tomorrow morning at the hearing I can just walk into my office.'

'Who's your lawyer?'

'I don't have a lawyer, I've never needed one.'

'You can bet the college will have the most expensive lawyer in town.'

'Shit. I can't afford a lawyer.'

Steve hardly dared to say what was in his mind. 'Well . . . I'm a lawyer.'

She looked speculatively at him.

'I've only done a year of law school, but in our advocacy exercises I scored highest in my class.' He was thrilled by the idea of defending her against the might of Jones Falls University. But would she think him too young and inexperienced? He tried to read her mind and failed. She kept looking at him. He stared right back, gazing into her dark eyes. I could do this indefinitely, he thought.

Then she leaned over and kissed him on the lips, lightly and fleetingly. 'Hell, Steve, you're the real thing,' she said.

It was a very quick kiss but it was electric. He felt great. He was not sure what she meant by *the real thing* but it must be good.

He would have to justify her faith in him. He began to worry about the hearing. 'Do you have any idea of the rules of the committee, the procedure for the hearing?'

She reached into her canvas briefcase and handed him a cardboard folder.

He scanned the contents. The rules were a mixture of college tradition and modern legal jargon. Offences for which faculty could be dismissed included blasphemy and sodomy, but the one that seemed most relevant to Jeannie was traditional: bringing the university into infamy and disrepute.

The discipline committee did not in fact have the final say: it merely made a recommendation to the senate, the governing body of the university. That was worth knowing. If Jeannie lost tomorrow, the senate might serve as a court of appeal.

'Do you have a copy of your contract?' Steve asked.

'Sure.' Jeannie went to a small desk in the corner and opened a file drawer. 'Here it is.'

Steve read it quickly. In clause 12 she agreed to be bound by the decisions of the university's senate. That would make it difficult for her to legally challenge the final decision.

He returned to the discipline committee rules. 'It says you have to notify the chair in advance if you wish to be represented by a lawyer or other person,' he said.

'I'll call Jack Budgen right away,' Jeannie said. 'It's eight o'clock—he'll be at home.' She picked up the phone.

'Wait,' Steve said. 'Let's think about the conversation first.'

'You're so right. You're thinking strategically, and I'm not.'

Steve felt pleased. The first piece of advice he had given as her lawyer had been good. 'This man holds your fate in his hands. What's he like?'

'He's chief librarian, and my tennis opponent.'

'The guy you were playing on Sunday?'

'Yes. An administrator rather than an academic. A good tactical player, but my guess is he never had the killer instinct to make it to the top in tennis.'

'Okay, so he has a somewhat competitive relationship with you.'

'I guess so.'

'Now, what impression do we want to give him?' He ticked points on his fingers. 'One: we want to appear upbeat and confident of success. You're looking forward eagerly to the hearing. You're innocent, you're glad of the opportunity to prove it, and you have faith that the committee will see the truth of the matter, under Budgen's wise direction.'

'Okay.'

'Two: You're the underdog. You're a weak, helpless girl—'

'Are you kidding?'

He grinned. 'Scratch that. You're a very junior academic and you're up against Berrington and Obell, two wily old operators who are used to getting their own way at JFU. Hell, you can't even afford a real lawyer. Is Budgen Jewish?'

'I don't know. He might be.'

'I hope so. Minorities are more likely to turn against the establishment. Three: the story of why Berrington is persecuting you like this has to come out. It's a shocking story, but it must be told.'

'How does it help me to say that?'

'It plants the idea that Berrington might have something to hide.'

'Good. Anything else?'

'I don't think so.'

Jeannie dialled the number and handed him the phone.

Steve took it with trepidation. This was the first call he had ever made as someone's lawyer. *Pray God I don't screw up.*

As he listened to the ringing tone, he tried to recall how Jack Budgen played tennis. Steve had been concentrating on Jeannie, of course, but he remembered a fit, bald man of about fifty, playing a well-paced, wily game. Budgen had defeated Jeannie even though she was younger and stronger. Steve vowed not to underestimate him.

The phone was answered in a quiet, cultured voice. 'Hello?'

'Professor Budgen, my name is Steven Logan.'

There was a short pause. 'Do I know you, Mr Logan?'

'No, sir. I'm calling you in your capacity as chair of the discipline committee of Jones Falls University, to let you know that I'll be accompanying Dr Ferrami tomorrow. She's looking forward to the hearing and she's eager to lay these charges to rest.'

Budgen's tone was cool. 'Are you a lawyer?'

Steve found his breath coming fast, as if he had been running, and he made an effort to stay calm. 'I'm at law school. Dr Ferrami can't afford a lawyer. However, I'm going to do my best to help her present her case clearly, and if I go wrong I'll have to throw myself on your mercy.' He paused, giving Budgen the chance to make a friendly remark or even just a sympathetic grunt; but there was a cold silence. Steve ploughed on. 'May I ask who will be representing the college?'

'I understand they've hired Henry Quinn, from Harvey Horrocks Quinn.'

Steve was awestruck. It was one of the oldest firms in Washington. He tried to sound relaxed. 'A deeply respectable Wasp law firm,' he remarked with a small chuckle.

'Indeed?'

Steve's charm was not working on this man. It was time to sound tough. 'One thing I should perhaps mention. We must now tell the true story of why Berrington Jones has acted against Dr Ferrami in this way. We will not accept any cancellation of the hearing, on any terms. That would leave a cloud over her head. The truth must come out, I'm afraid.'

'I know of no proposal to cancel the hearing.'

Of course not. There was no such proposal. Steve carried on with his bravado. 'But if there should be one, please be advised that it would be unacceptable to Dr Ferrami.' He decided to wind this up before he got himself in too deep. 'Professor, I thank you for your courtesy and I look forward to seeing you in the morning.'

'Goodbye.'

Steve hung up. 'Wow, what an iceberg.'

Jeannie looked puzzled. 'He's not normally like that. Maybe he was just being formal.'

Steve was pretty sure Budgen had already made up his mind and was hostile to Jeannie, but he did not tell her that. 'Anyway, I got our three points across. And I discovered that JFU has hired Henry Quinn.'

'Is he good?'

He was legendary. It made Steve go cold to think he was going to go up against Henry Quinn. But he did not want to depress Jeannie. 'Quinn used to be very good, but he may be past his prime.'

She accepted that. 'What should we do now?'

Steve looked at her. The pink bathrobe had gaped

open at the front, and he could see one neat breast nestling in the folds of soft towelling. 'We should go over the questions you'll be asked at the hearing,' he said regretfully. 'We've got a lot of work to do tonight.'

CHAPTER THIRTY-SEVEN

JANE EDELSBOROUGH looked a lot better naked than she did dressed.

She lay on a pale pink sheet, lit by the flame of a scented candle. Her clear, soft skin was more attractive than the muddy earth colours she always wore. The loose clothes she favoured tended to hide her body: she was something of an amazon, with a deep bosom and broad hips. She was heavy, but it suited her.

Lying on the bed, she smiled languidly at Berrington as he pulled on his blue boxer shorts. 'Wow, that was better than I expected,' she said.

Berrington felt the same, although he was not crass enough to say so. Jane knew things that he normally had to teach to the younger women he usually took to bed. He wondered idly where she had learned to be such a good lay. She had been married once: her husband, a cigarette smoker, had died of lung cancer ten years ago. They must have had a great sex life together.

He had enjoyed it so much that he had not needed his usual fantasy, in which he had just made love to a famous beauty, Cindy Crawford or Bridget Fonda or Princess Diana, and she was lying beside him, murmuring in his ear, *Thank you, Berry, that was the best it's ever been for me, you're so great, thank you.*

'I feel so guilty,' Jane said. 'I haven't done anything this wicked for a long time.'

'Wicked?' he said, tying his shoelaces. 'I don't see why. You're free, white and twenty-one, as we used to say.' He noticed her wince: the phrase *free, white and twenty-one* was now politically incorrect. 'You're single, anyway,' he added hastily.

'Oh, it's not the fucking that was wicked,' she said languorously. 'It's just that I know you only did it because I'm on the committee for tomorrow's hearing.'

He froze in the act of putting on his striped necktie.

She went on: 'I'm supposed to think you saw me across the student cafeteria and became entranced by my sexual magnetism?' She smiled ruefully at him. 'I don't have any sexual magnetism, Berry, not for someone as superficial as you. You had to have an ulterior motive and it took me about five seconds to figure out what it could be.'

Berrington felt a fool. He did not know what to say.

'Now in your case, you *do* have sexual magnetism. Buckets. You've got charm and a nice body, you dress well and you smell good. Most of all, anyone can see that you really like women. You may manipulate them and exploit them, but you love them too. You are the perfect one-night stand, and I thank you.'

With that she pulled the sheet over her naked body, rolled on to her side and closed her eyes.

Berrington finished dressing as quickly as he could.

Before he left, he sat on the edge of the bed. She

opened her eyes. He said: 'Will you support me, tomorrow?'

She sat upright and kissed him fondly. 'I'll have to listen to the evidence before I make up my mind,' she said.

He ground his teeth. 'It's terribly important to me, more than you know.'

She nodded sympathetically, but her reply was implacable. 'I guess it's just as important to Jeannie Ferrami.'

He squeezed her left breast, soft and heavy. 'But who is more important to you—Jeannie or me?'

'I know what it's like to be a young woman academic in a male-dominated university. I'll never forget that.'

'Shit.' He took his hand away.

'You could stay the night, you know. Then we could do it again in the morning.'

He stood up. 'I've got too much on my mind.'

She closed her eyes. 'That's too bad.'

He went out.

His car was parked in the driveway of her suburban house, next to her Jaguar. That Jaguar should have been a warning to me, he thought; a sign that there is more to her than meets the eye. He had been used, but he had enjoyed it. He wondered if women sometimes felt that way after he seduced them.

As he drove home he worried about tomorrow's hearing. He had the four men on the committee on his side, but he had failed to win a promise of support from Jane. Was there anything else he could do? At this late stage there did not seem to be.

When he got home there was a message from Jim Proust on his answering machine. Not more bad news, please, he thought. He sat at the desk in his den and dialled Jim's home. 'This is Berry.'

'The FBI fucked up,' Jim said without preamble.

Berrington's spirits sank farther. 'Tell me.'

'They were told to cancel that search, but the order didn't get through in time.'

'Goddamn.'

'The results were sent to her by E-mail.'

He felt afraid. 'Who was on the list?'

'We don't know. The Bureau didn't keep a copy.'

This was insupportable. 'We have to know!'

'Maybe you can find out. The list could be in her office.'

'She's locked out of her office.' Berrington was struck by a hopeful thought. 'She might not have retrieved her mail.' His mood lifted a little.

'Can you do that?'

'Sure.' Berrington looked at his gold Rolex. 'I'll go in to the college right now.'

'Call me as soon as you know.'

'You bet.'

He got back in his car and drove to Jones Falls University. The campus was dark and deserted. He parked outside Nut House and went in. He felt less embarrassed about sneaking into Jeannie's office the second time. What the hell, there was too much at stake for him to worry about his dignity.

He turned on her computer and accessed her mailbox. She had one piece of mail. *Please, God, let this be the*

FBI list. He downloaded it. To his disappointment, it was another message from her friend at the University of Minnesota:

> Did you get my E-mail yesterday? I'll be in Baltimore tomorrow and would really like to see you again, even if only for a few minutes. Please call me. Love, Will.

She had not got yesterday's message, because Berrington had downloaded it then erased it. She would not get this one, either. But where was the FBI list? She must have downloaded it yesterday morning, before security locked her out.

Where had she saved it? Berrington searched her hard disk for the words *FBI, F.B.I.* with dots, and *Federal Bureau of Investigation.* He found nothing. He searched through a box of diskettes in her drawer, but they were just back-ups of the files on her computer. 'This woman even keeps a back-up copy of her goddamn shopping list,' he muttered.

He used Jeannie's phone to call Jim again. 'Nothing,' he said abruptly.

'We have to know who is on that list!' Jim barked.

Berrington said sarcastically: 'What shall I do, Jim—kidnap and torture her?'

'She must have the list, right?'

'It's not in her mailbox, so she must have downloaded it.'

'So if it's not in her office, she must have it at home.'

'Logical.' Berrington saw where he was heading.

'Can you have her place . . .' He was reluctant to say *searched by the FBI* on the phone. 'Can you have it checked out?'

'I guess so. David Creane failed to deliver, so I guess he still owes me a favour. I'll call him.'

'Tomorrow morning would be a good time. The hearing is at ten, she'll be there for a couple of hours.'

'Gotcha. I'll get it done. But what if she keeps it in her goddamn handbag? What do we do then?'

'I don't know. Goodnight, Jim.'

'Night.'

After hanging up, Berrington sat there for a while, looking at the narrow room enlivened by Jeannie's bright, bold colours. If things went wrong tomorrow, she could be back at this desk by lunchtime, with her FBI list, charging ahead with her investigation, all set to ruin three good men.

It must not happen, he thought desperately; it must not happen.

FRIDAY

CHAPTER THIRTY-EIGHT

JEANNIE WOKE up in her compact white-walled living room, on her black couch, in Steve's arms, wearing only her fuchsia-pink towelling bathrobe.

How did I get here?

They had spent half the night rehearsing for today's hearing. Jeannie's heart lurched: her fate was to be decided this morning.

But how come I'm lying in his lap?

Around three o'clock she had yawned and closed her eyes for a moment.

And then . . .?

She must have fallen asleep.

At some point he had gone into the bedroom and taken the blue-and-red striped quilt off the bed and tucked it around her, for she was snug beneath it.

But Steve could not be responsible for the way she was lying, with her head on his thigh and her arm around his waist. She must have done that herself, in her sleep. It was a bit embarrassing: her face was very close to his crotch. She wondered what he thought of her. Her behaviour had been very off the wall. Undressing in front of him then falling asleep on him: she was behaving as you would with a long-time lover.

Well, I've got an excuse for acting weird: I've had a weird week.

She had been ill-treated by patrolman McHenty, robbed by her father, accused by the *New York Times*, threatened with a knife by Dennis Pinker, fired by the college and attacked in her car. She felt damaged.

Her face throbbed gently where she had been punched yesterday, but the injuries were not merely physical. The attack had bruised her psyche, too. When she recalled the fight in the car, her anger returned and she wanted to get the man by the throat. Even when she was not remembering, she felt a low background hum of unhappiness, as if her life was somehow of less value because of the attack.

It was surprising she could trust any man; astonishing that she could fall asleep on a couch with one who looked exactly like her attackers. But now she could be even more sure of Steve. Neither of the others could have spent the night like this, alone with a girl, without forcing himself on her.

She frowned. Steve had done something in the night, she recalled vaguely; something nice. Yes: she had a dreamy memory of big hands rhythmically caressing her hair, it seemed for a long time, while she dozed, as comfortable as a stroked cat.

She smiled and stirred, and he spoke immediately. 'Are you awake?'

She yawned and stretched. 'I'm sorry I fell asleep on you. Are you okay?'

'The blood supply to my left leg was cut off at about five a.m., but once I got used to that I was fine.'

She sat upright so that she could see him better. His clothes were creased, his hair was mussed and he had a growth of fair stubble, but he looked good enough to eat. 'Did you sleep?'

He shook his head. 'I was enjoying myself too much, watching you.'

'Don't say I snore.'

'You don't snore. You dribble a little, that's all.' He dabbed at a damp spot on his pants.

'Oh, gross!' She stood up. The bright blue clock on the wall caught her eye: it was eight thirty. 'We don't have much time,' she said in alarm. 'The hearing starts at ten.'

'You shower while I make coffee,' Steve said generously.

She stared at him. He was unreal. 'Did you come from Santa Claus?'

He laughed. 'According to your theory, I come from a test tube.' Then his face went solemn again. 'What the hell, who knows.'

Her mood darkened along with his. She went into the bedroom, dropped her clothes on the floor, and got into the shower. As she washed her hair she brooded over how hard she had struggled over the last ten years: the contest for scholarships, the intensive tennis training combined with long hours of study; the peevish nitpicking of her doctoral supervisor. She had worked like a robot to get where she was today, all because she wanted to be a scientist and help the human race understand itself better. And now Berrington Jones was about to throw it all away.

The shower made her feel better. As she was towelling her hair, the phone rang. She picked up the bedside extension. 'Yeah.'

'Jeannie, it's Patty.'

'Hi, Sis, what's happening?'

'Daddy showed up.'

Jeannie sat on the bed. 'How is he?'

'Broke, but healthy.'

'He came to me first,' Jeannie said. 'He arrived on Monday. Tuesday he got a little ticked off because I didn't cook him dinner. Wednesday he took off, with my computer and my TV and my stereo. He must have already spent or gambled whatever he got for them.'

Patty gasped. 'Oh, Jeannie, that's awful!'

'Ain't it just. So lock up your valuables.'

'To steal from his own family! Oh, God, if Zip finds out he'll throw him out.'

'Patty, I have even worse problems. I may be fired from my job today.'

'Jeannie, why?'

'I don't have time to explain now, but I'll call you later.'

'Okay.'

'Have you talked to Mom?'

'Every day.'

'Oh, good, that makes me feel better. I talked to her once, then the next time I called she was at lunch.'

'The people who answer the phone are really unhelpful. We have to get Mom out of there soon.'

She'll be there a lot longer if I get fired today. 'I'll talk to you later.'

'Good luck!'

Jeannie hung up. She noticed there was a steaming mug of coffee on the bedside table. She shook her head in amazement. It was only a cup of coffee, but what astonished her was the way Steve knew what she needed. It seemed to come naturally to him to be supportive. And he didn't want anything in return. In her experience, on the rare occasions when a man put a woman's needs ahead of his own, he expected her to act like a geisha for a month in gratitude.

Steve was different. *If I'd known men came in this version, I would have ordered one years ago.*

She had done everything alone, all her adult life. Her father had never been around to support her. Mom had always been strong, but in the end her strength had become almost as much a problem as Daddy's weakness. Mom had plans for Jeannie and she was not willing to give them up. She wanted Jeannie to be a hairdresser. She had even got Jeannie a job, two weeks before her sixteenth birthday, washing hair and sweeping the floor at the Salon Alexis in Adams-Morgan. Jeannie's desire to be a scientist was utterly incomprehensible to her. 'You could be a qualified stylist before the other girls have graduated college!' Mom had said. She never understood why Jeannie threw a tantrum and refused even to take a look at the salon.

She was not alone today. She had Steve to support her. It did not matter to her that he was not qualified—a hotshot Washington lawyer was not necessarily the best choice to impress five professors. The important thing was that he would be there.

She put on her bathrobe and called to him. 'You want the shower?'

'Sure.' He came into the bedroom. 'I wish I had a clean shirt.'

'I don't have a man's shirt—wait a minute, I do.' She had remembered the white Ralph Lauren button-down Lisa had borrowed after the fire. It belonged to someone in the math department. Jeannie had sent it to the laundry and now it was in the closet, wrapped in cellophane. She gave it to Steve.

'My size, seventeen thirty-six,' he said. 'Perfect.'

'Don't ask me where it came from, it's a long story,' she said. 'I think I have a tie here somewhere, too.' She opened a drawer and took out a blue silk spotted tie she sometimes wore with a white blouse, for a snappy mannish look. 'Here.'

'Thanks.' He went into the tiny bathroom.

She felt a twinge of disappointment. She had been looking forward to seeing him take off his shirt. Men, she thought; the creeps expose themselves without being asked, the hunks are as shy as nuns.

'Can I borrow your razor?' he called.

'Sure, be my guest.' *Memo to self: do sex with this guy before he becomes too much like a brother.*

She looked for her best black suit and remembered she had thrown it in the trash yesterday. 'Damn fool,' she muttered to herself. She could probably retrieve it, but it would be creased and stained. She had a longline electric-blue jacket: she could wear that with a white T-shirt and black pants. It was a bit too bright, but it would serve.

She sat at her mirror and did her make-up. Steve came out of the bathroom, looking handsomely formal in the shirt and tie. 'There are some cinnamon buns in the freezer,' she said. 'You could defrost them in the microwave if you're hungry.'

'Great,' he said. 'You want something?'

'I'm too tense to eat. I could drink another cup of coffee, though.'

He brought the coffee while she was finishing her make-up. She drank it quickly and put on her clothes. When she went into the living room, he was sitting at the kitchen counter. 'Did you find the buns?'

'Sure.'

'What happened to them?'

'You said you weren't hungry, so I ate them all.'

'All four?'

'Uh . . . in fact there were two packets.'

'You ate *eight* cinnamon buns?'

He looked embarrassed. 'I get hungry.'

She laughed. 'Let's go.'

As she turned away he grabbed her arm. 'One minute.'

'What?'

'Jeannie, it's fun being friends and I really like just hanging out with you, you know, but you have to understand this isn't all I want.'

'I do know that.'

'I'm falling in love with you.'

She looked into his eyes. He was very sincere. 'I'm getting kind of attached to you, too,' she said lightly.

'I want to make love to you, and I want it so bad it hurts.'

I could listen to this kind of talk all day, she thought. 'Listen,' she said, 'if you fuck like you eat, I'm yours.'

His face fell, and she realized she had said the wrong thing.

'I'm sorry,' she said. 'I didn't mean to make a joke of it.'

He gave a never-mind shrug.

She took his hand. 'Listen. First we're going to save me. Then we're going to save you. Then we'll have some fun.'

He squeezed her hand. 'Okay.'

They went outside. 'Let's drive together,' she said. 'I'll bring you back to your car later.'

They got into her Mercedes. The car radio came on as she started the engine. Easing into the traffic on 41st Street she heard the newsreader mention Threeplex, and she turned up the volume. 'Senator Jim Proust, a former director of the CIA, is expected to confirm today he will seek the Republican nomination in next year's presidential election. His campaign promise: ten per cent income tax, paid for by the abolition of welfare. Campaign finance will not be a problem, commentators say, as he stands to make sixty million dollars from an agreed takeover of his medical research company, Threeplex. In sports, the Philadelphia Rams—'

Jeannie switched off. 'What do you think of that?'

Steve shook his head in dismay. 'The stakes keep getting higher,' he said. 'If we break the true story of Threeplex, and the takeover bid is cancelled, Jim Proust won't be able to pay for a presidential campaign. And Proust is a serious bad guy: a spook, ex-CIA, against gun control, everything. You're standing in the way of some dangerous people, Jeannie.'

She gritted her teeth. 'That makes them all the more worth fighting against. I was raised on welfare, Steve. If Proust becomes president, girls like me will always be hairdressers.'

CHAPTER THIRTY-NINE

THERE WAS a small demonstration outside Hillside Hall, the administrative office building of Jones Falls University. Thirty or forty students, mostly women, stood in a cluster in front of the steps. It was a quiet, disciplined protest. Getting closer, Steve read a banner:

Reinstate Ferrami Now!

It seemed like a good omen to Steve. 'They're supporting you,' he said to Jeannie.

She looked closer, and a flush of pleasure spread across her face. 'So they are. My God, someone loves me after all.'

Another placard read:

U
can't do
this to
JF

A cheer went up when they spotted Jeannie. She went over to them, smiling. Steve followed, proud of her. Not every professor would get such spontaneous support from students. She shook hands with the men and kissed the women. Steve noticed a pretty blonde woman staring at him.

Jeannie hugged an older woman in the crowd. 'Sophie!' she said. 'What can I say?'

'Good luck in there,' the woman said.

Jeannie detached herself from the crowd, beaming, and they walked toward the building. He said: 'Well, *they* think you should keep your job.'

'I can't tell you how much that means to me,' she said. 'That older woman is Sophie Chapple, a professor in the psychology department. I thought she hated me. I can't believe she's standing up for me.'

'Who was the pretty girl at the front?'

Jeannie gave him a curious look. 'You don't recognize her?'

'I'm pretty sure I've never seen her before, but she couldn't take her eyes off me.' Then he guessed. 'Oh, my God, it must be the victim.'

'Lisa Hoxton.'

'No wonder she stared.' He could not help glancing back. She was a pretty, lively looking girl, small and rather plump. His double had attacked her and thrown her to the floor and forced her to have sex. A small knot of disgust twisted inside Steve. She was just an ordinary young woman, and now she had a nightmare memory that would haunt her all her life.

The administrative building was a grand old house. Jeannie led him across the marbled hall and through a door marked Old Dining Room into a gloomy chamber in the baronial style: high ceiling, narrow Gothic windows and thick-legged oak furniture. A long table stood in front of a carved stone fireplace.

Four men and a middle-aged woman sat along one side of the table. Steve recognized the bald man in the middle as Jeannie's tennis opponent, Jack Budgen. This was the committee, he presumed: the group that held Jeannie's fate in its hands. He took a deep breath.

Leaning over the table, he shook Jack Budgen's hand and said: 'Good morning, Dr Budgen. I'm Steven Logan. We spoke yesterday.' Some instinct took over and he found himself exuding a relaxed confidence that was the opposite of what he felt. He shook hands with each of the committee members, and they told him their names.

Two more men sat on the near side of the table, at the far end. The little guy in the navy vested suit was Berrington Jones, whom Steve had met last Monday. The thin, sandy-haired man in a charcoal double-breasted pinstripe had to be Henry Quinn. Steve shook hands with both.

Quinn looked superciliously at him and said: 'What are your legal qualifications, young man?'

Steve gave him a friendly smile and spoke in a low voice that no one else could hear. 'Go fuck yourself, Henry.'

Quinn flinched as if he had been struck, and Steve thought: That will be the last time the old bastard condescends to me.

He held a chair for Jeannie and they both sat down.

'Well, perhaps we should begin,' Jack said. 'These

proceedings are informal. I believe everyone has received a copy of the rubric, so we know the rules. The charge is laid by Professor Berrington Jones, who proposes that Dr Jean Ferrami be dismissed because she has brought Jones Falls University into disrepute.'

As Budgen spoke, Steve watched the committee members, looking eagerly for signs of sympathy. He was not reassured. Only the woman, Jane Edelsborough, would look at Jeannie: the others did not meet her eye. Four against, one in favour, at the start, he thought. It was not good.

Jack said: 'Berrington is represented by Mr Quinn.'

Quinn got to his feet and opened his briefcase. Steve noticed that his fingers were stained yellow from cigarettes. He took out a sheaf of blow-up photocopies of the *New York Times* piece about Jeannie and handed one to every person in the room. The result was that the table was covered with pieces of paper saying GENE RESEARCH ETHICS: DOUBTS, FEARS AND A SQUABBLE. It was a powerful visual reminder of the trouble Jeannie had caused. Steve wished he had brought some papers to give out, so that he could have covered up Quinn's.

This simple, effective opening move by Quinn intimidated Steve. How could he possibly compete with a man who had probably thirty years of courtroom experience? I can't win this, he thought in a sudden panic.

Quinn began to speak. His voice was dry and precise, with no trace of a local accent. He spoke slowly and pedantically. Steve hoped that might be a mistake with this jury of intellectuals who did not need things spelt out for them in words of one syllable. Quinn summarized the history of the discipline committee and explained its position in the university government. He defined 'disrepute' and produced a copy of Jeannie's employment contract. Steve began to feel better as Quinn droned on.

At last he wound up his preamble and started to question Berrington. He began by asking when Berrington had first heard about Jeannie's computer search program.

'Last Monday afternoon,' Berrington replied. He recounted the conversation he and Jeannie had had. His story tallied with what Jeannie had told Steve.

Then Berrington said: 'As soon as I clearly understood her technique, I told her that in my opinion what she was doing was illegal.'

Jeannie burst out: '*What?*'

Quinn ignored her and asked Berrington: 'And what was her reaction?'

'She became very angry—'

'You damn liar!' Jeannie said.

Berrington flushed at this accusation.

Jack Budgen intervened. 'Please, no interruptions,' he said.

Steve kept an eye on the committee. They had all looked at Jeannie: they could hardly help it. He put a hand on her arm, as if restraining her.

'He's telling barefaced lies!' she protested.

'What did you expect?' Steve said in a low voice. 'He's playing hardball.'

'I'm sorry,' she whispered.

'Don't be,' he said in her ear. 'Keep it up. They could see your anger was genuine.'

Berrington went on: 'She became petulant, just as she is now. She told me she could do what she liked, she had a contract.'

One of the men on the committee, Tenniel Biddenham, frowned darkly, obviously disliking the idea of a junior member of faculty quoting her contract to her professor. Berrington was clever, Steve realized. He knew how to take a point scored against him and turn it to his advantage.

Quinn asked Berrington: 'What did you do?'

'Well, I realized I might be wrong. I'm not a lawyer. So I decided to get legal advice. If my fears were confirmed, I could show her independent proof. But if it turned out that what she was doing was harmless, I could drop the matter without a confrontation.'

'And did you take advice?'

'As things turned out, I was overtaken by events. Before I had a chance to see a lawyer, the *New York Times* got on the case.'

Jeannie whispered: 'Bullshit.'

'Are you sure?' Steve asked her.

'Positive.'

He made a note.

'Tell us what happened on Wednesday, please,' Quinn said to Berrington.

'My worst fears came true. The university president, Maurice Obell, summoned me to his office and asked me to explain why he was getting aggressive phone calls from the press about the research in my department. We drafted a press announcement as a basis for discussion and called in Dr Ferrami.'

'Jesus Christ!' muttered Jeannie.

Berrington went on: 'She refused to talk about the press release. Once again she blew her top, insisted she could do what she liked, and stormed out.'

Steve looked an enquiry at Jeannie. She said in a low voice: 'A clever lie. They presented me with the press announcement as a fait accompli.'

Steve nodded, but he decided not to take up this point in cross-examination. The committee would probably feel Jeannie should not have stormed out anyway.

'The reporter told us she had a deadline of noon that day,' Berrington continued smoothly. 'Dr Obell felt the university had to say something decisive, and I must say I agreed with him one hundred per cent.'

'And did your announcement have the effect you hoped for?'

'No. It was a total failure. But that was because it was completely undermined by Dr Ferrami. She told the reporter that she intended to ignore us and there was nothing we could do about it.'

'Did anyone outside the university comment on the story?'

'They certainly did.'

Something about the way Berrington answered that question rang a warning bell in Steve's head and he made a note.

'I got a phone call from Preston Barck, the president of Threeplex, which is an important donor to the university, and in particular funds the entire twins research programme,' Berrington continued. 'He was naturally concerned about the way his money was being spent. The article made it look as if the university authorities were impotent. Preston said to me, "Who's running the damn school, anyway?" It was very embarrassing.'

'Was that your principal concern? The embarrassment of having been defied by a junior member of the faculty?'

'Certainly not. The main problem was the damage to Jones Falls that would be caused by Dr Ferrami's work.'

Nice move, Steve thought. In their hearts all the committee members would hate to be defied by an assistant professor, and Berrington had drawn their sympathy. But Quinn had moved quickly to put the whole complaint on a more high-minded level, so that they could tell themselves that by firing Jeannie they would be protecting the university, not just punishing a disobedient subordinate.

Berrington said: 'A university should be sensitive to privacy issues. Donors give us money, and students compete for places here, because this is one of the nation's most venerable educational institutions. The suggestion that we are careless with people's civil rights is very damaging.'

It was a quietly eloquent formulation, and all the panel would approve. Steve nodded to show that he agreed too, hoping they would notice and conclude that this was not the question at issue.

Quinn asked Berrington: 'So how many options faced you at that point?'

'Exactly one. We had to show that we did not sanction invasion of privacy by university researchers. We also needed to demonstrate that we had the authority to enforce our own rules. The way to do that was to fire Dr Ferrami. There was no alternative.'

'Thank you, Professor,' said Quinn, and he sat down.

Steve felt pessimistic. Quinn was every bit as skilful as expected. Berrington had been dreadfully plausible. He had presented a picture of a reasonable, concerned human being doing his best to deal with a hot-tempered, careless subordinate. It was the more credible for having a lacing of reality: Jeannie *was* quick-tempered.

But it was not the truth. That was all Steve had going for him. Jeannie was in the right. He just had to prove it.

Jack Budgen said: 'Have you any questions, Mr Logan?'

'I sure do,' said Steve. He paused for a moment, collecting his thoughts.

This was his fantasy. He was not in a courtroom, and he was not even a real lawyer, but he was defending an underdog against the injustice of a mighty institution. The odds were against him but truth was on his side. It was what he dreamed about.

He stood up and looked hard at Berrington. If Jeannie's theory was right, the man had to feel strange in this situation. It must be like Dr Frankenstein being questioned by his monster. Steve wanted to play on that a little, to shake Berrington's composure, before starting on the material questions.

'You know me, don't you, Professor?' Steve said.

Berrington looked unnerved. 'Ah . . . I believe we met on Monday, yes.'

'And you know all about me.'

'I . . . don't quite follow you.'

'I underwent a day of tests in your laboratory, so you have a great deal of information on me.'

'I see what you mean, yes.'

Berrington looked thoroughly discomfited.

Steve moved behind Jeannie's chair, so that they would all have to look at her. It was much harder to think evil of someone who returned your gaze with an open, fearless expression.

'Professor, let me begin with the first claim you made, that you intended to seek legal advice after your conversation with Dr Ferrami on Monday.'

'Yes.'

'You didn't actually see a lawyer.'

'No, I was overtaken by events.'

'You didn't make an appointment to see a lawyer.'

'There wasn't time—'

'In the two days between your conversation with Dr Ferrami and your conversation with Dr Obell about the *New York Times*, you didn't even ask your secretary to make an appointment with a lawyer.'

'No.'

'Nor did you ask around, or speak to any of your colleagues, to find out the name of someone suitable.'

'No.'

'In fact you're quite unable to substantiate this claim.'

Berrington smiled confidently. 'However, I have a reputation as an honest man.'

'Dr Ferrami recalls the conversation very vividly.'

'Good.'

'She says you made no mention of legal problems or privacy worries, your only concern was whether the search engine worked.'

'Perhaps she's forgotten.'

'Or perhaps you've misremembered.' Steve felt he had won that point, and he changed tack abruptly. 'Did the *New York Times* reporter, Ms Freelander, say how she heard about Dr Ferrami's work?'

'If she did, Dr Obell never mentioned it to me.'

'So you didn't ask.'

'No.'

'Did it occur to you to *wonder* how she knew?'

'I guess I assumed that reporters have their sources.'

'Since Dr Ferrami hasn't published anything about this project, the source must have been an individual.'

Berrington hesitated and looked to Quinn for guidance. Quinn stood up. 'Sir,' he said, addressing Jack Budgen. 'The witness shouldn't be called upon to speculate.'

Budgen nodded.

Steve said: 'But this is an informal hearing—we don't have to be constrained by rigid courtroom procedure.'

Jane Edelsborough spoke for the first time. 'The questions seem interesting and relevant to me, Jack.'

Berrington threw her a black look, and she made a little shrug of apology. It was an intimate exchange, and

Steve wondered what the relationship was between those two.

Budgen waited, perhaps hoping another committee member would offer a contrary view so that he could make the decision as chair; but no one else spoke. 'All right,' he said after a pause. 'Proceed, Mr Logan.'

Steve could hardly believe he had won their first procedural dispute. The professors did not like a fancy lawyer telling them what was or was not a legitimate line of questioning. His throat was dry with tension. He poured water from a carafe into a glass with a shaky hand.

He took a sip then turned again to Berrington and said: 'Ms Freelander knew more than just the general nature of Dr Ferrami's work, didn't she?'

'Yes.'

'She knew exactly how Dr Ferrami searched for raised-apart twins by scanning databases. This is a new technique, developed by her, known only to you and a few other colleagues in the psychology department.'

'If you say so.'

'It looks as if her information came from within the department, doesn't it?'

'Maybe.'

'What motive could a colleague possibly have for creating bad publicity about Dr Ferrami and her work?'

'I really couldn't say.'

'But it seems like the doing of a malicious, perhaps jealous, rival—wouldn't you say?'

'Perhaps.'

Steve nodded in satisfaction. He felt he was getting into the swing of this, developing a rhythm. He began to feel that maybe he *could* win, after all.

Don't get complacent, he told himself. Scoring points is not the same as winning the case.

'Let me turn to the second claim you made. When Mr Quinn asked you if people outside the university had commented on the newspaper story, you replied: "They certainly did." Do you want to stick by that assertion?'

'Yes.'

'Exactly how many phone calls did you receive from donors, other than the one from Preston Barck?'

'Well, I spoke with Herb Abrahams—'

Steve could tell he was dissembling. 'Pardon me for interrupting you, Professor.' Berrington looked surprised but he stopped speaking. 'Did Mr Abrahams call you, or vice versa?'

'Uh, I believe I called Herb.'

'We'll come to that in a moment. First, just tell us how many important donors called *you* to express their concern about the *New York Times* allegations.'

Berrington looked rattled. 'I'm not sure anyone called me specifically about that.'

'How many calls did you receive from potential students?'

'None.'

'Did anyone at all call you to talk about the article?'

'I guess not.'

'Did you receive any mail on the subject?'

'Not yet.'

'It doesn't appear to have caused *much* of a fuss, then.'

'I don't think you can draw that conclusion.'

It was a feeble response, and Steve paused to let that sink in. Berrington appeared embarrassed. The committee were alert, following every cut and thrust. Steve looked at Jeannie. Her face was alight with hope.

He resumed. 'Let's talk about the one phone call you did receive, from Preston Barck, the president of Threeplex. You made it sound as if he was simply a donor concerned about the way his money is being used, but he's more than that, isn't he? When did you first meet him?'

'When I was at Harvard, forty years ago.'

'He must be one of your oldest friends.'

'Yes.'

'And in later years I believe you and he set up Threeplex together.'

'Yes.'

'So he's also your business partner.'

'Yes.'

'The company is in the process of being taken over by Landsmann, the German pharmaceuticals conglomerate.'

'Yes.

'No doubt Mr Barck will make a lot of money out of the takeover.'

'No doubt.'

'How much?'

'I think that's confidential.'

Steve decided not to press him on the amount. His reluctance to disclose the figure was damaging enough.

'Another friend of yours stands to make a killing: Senator Proust. According to the news today, he's going to use his payout to finance a presidential election campaign.'

'I didn't watch the news this morning.'

'But Jim Proust is a friend of yours, isn't he? You must have known he was thinking of running for president.'

'I believe everyone knew he was *thinking* of it.'

'Are you going to make money from the takeover?'

'Yes.'

Steve moved away from Jeannie and towards Berrington, so that all eyes would be on Berrington. 'So you're a shareholder, not just a consultant.'

'It's common enough to be both.'

'Professor, how much will you make from this takeover?'

'I think that's private.'

Steve was not going to let him get away with it this time. 'At any rate, the price being paid for the company is one hundred and eighty million dollars, according to the *Wall Street Journal*.'

'Yes.'

Steve repeated the amount. 'One hundred and eighty million dollars.' He paused long enough to create a pregnant silence. It was the kind of money that professors never saw, and he wanted to give the committee members the feeling that Berrington was not one of them at all, but a being of a different kind altogether. 'You are one of three people who will share one hundred and eighty million dollars.'

Berrington nodded.

'So you had a lot to be nervous about when you learned of the *New York Times* article. Your friend Preston is selling his company, your friend Jim is running for president, and you're about to make a fortune. Are you sure it was the reputation of Jones Falls that was on your mind when you fired Dr Ferrami? Or was it all your other worries? Let's be frank, Professor—you panicked.'

'I most certainly—'

'You read a hostile newspaper article, you envisioned the takeover melting away, and you reacted hastily. You let the *New York Times* scare you.'

'It takes more than the *New York Times* to scare me, young man. I acted quickly and decisively, but not hastily.'

'You made no attempt to discover the source of the newspaper's information.'

'No.'

'How many days did you spend investigating the truth, or otherwise, of the allegations?'

'It didn't take long—'

'Hours rather than days?'

'Yes—'

'Or was it in fact *less than an hour* before you had approved a press release saying that Dr Ferrami's programme was cancelled?'

'I'm quite sure it was more than an hour.'

Steve shrugged emphatically. 'Let us be generous and say it was two hours. Was that long enough?' He turned and gestured towards Jeannie, so that they would look at her. 'After two hours you decided to jettison a young scientist's entire research programme?' The pain was visible on Jeannie's face. Steve felt an agonizing pang of pity for her. But he had to play on her emotion, for her own good. He twisted the knife in the wound. 'After two hours you knew enough to make a decision to destroy the work of years? Enough to end a promising career? Enough to ruin a woman's life?'

'I asked her to defend herself,' Berrington said indignantly. 'She lost her temper and walked out of the room!'

Steve hesitated, then decided to take a theatrical risk. 'She walked out of the room!' he said in mock amazement. 'She walked out of the room! You showed her a press release announcing the cancellation of her programme. No investigation of the source of the newspaper story, no appraisal of the validity of the allegations, no time for discussion, no due process of any kind—you simply declared to this young scientist that her entire life was ruined—and all she did was *walk out of the room*?' Berrington opened his mouth to speak but Steve overrode him. 'When I think of the injustice, the illegality, the sheer *foolishness* of what you did on Wednesday morning, Professor, I cannot imagine how Dr Ferrami summoned the restraint and self-discipline to confine herself to such a simple, eloquent protest.' He walked back to his seat in silence, then turned to the committee and said: 'No more questions.'

Jeannie's eyes were lowered, but she squeezed his arm. He leaned over and whispered: 'How are you?'

'I'm okay.'

He patted her hand. He wanted to say, *I think we've won it,* but that would have been tempting fate.

Henry Quinn stood up. He seemed unperturbed. He should have looked more worried after Steve made mincemeat of his client. But no doubt it was part of his skill to remain unruffled no matter how badly his case was going.

Quinn said: 'Professor, if the university had not discontinued Dr Ferrami's research programme, and had not fired her, would that have made any difference to the takeover of Threeplex by Landsmann?'

'None at all,' Berrington replied.

'Thank you. No more questions.'

That was pretty effective, Steve thought sourly. It kind of punctured his whole cross-examination. He tried not to let Jeannie see the disappointment on his face.

It was Jeannie's turn, and Steve stood up and led her through her evidence. She was calm and clear as she described her research programme and explained the importance of finding raised-apart twins who were criminals. She detailed the precautions she took to ensure that no one's medical details became known before they had signed a release.

He expected Quinn to cross-examine her, and try to show that there was a minuscule chance that confidential information would be revealed by accident. Steve and Jeannie had rehearsed this last night, with him playing the role of prosecution lawyer. But to his surprise Quinn did not have any questions. Was he afraid she would defend herself too ably? Or was he confident he had the verdict sewn up?

Quinn summed up first. He repeated much of Berrington's evidence, once again being more tedious than Steve thought wise. His concluding speech was short enough, however. 'This is a crisis that should never have happened,' he said. 'The university authorities behaved judiciously throughout. It was Dr Ferrami's impetuousness and intransigence that caused all the drama. Of course she has a contract, and that contract governs her relations with her employer. But senior faculty are, after all, required to supervise junior faculty; and junior faculty, if they have any sense at all, will listen to wise counsel from those older and more experienced than they. Dr Ferrami's stubborn defiance turned a problem into a crisis, and the only solution to the crisis is for her to leave the university.' He sat down.

It was time for Steve's speech. He had been rehearsing it all night. He stood up.

'What is Jones Falls University for?'

He paused for dramatic effect.

'The answer may be expressed in one word: knowledge. If we wanted a nutshell definition of the role of the university in American society, we might say its function is to *seek* knowledge and to *spread* knowledge.'

He looked at each of the committee, inviting their agreement. Jane Edelsborough nodded. The others were impassive.

He resumed: 'Now and again, that function comes

under attack. There are always people who want to hide the truth, for one reason or another: political motives, religious prejudice . . .' He looked at Berrington. '. . . or commercial advantage. I think everyone here would agree that the school's intellectual independence is crucial to its reputation. That independence has to be balanced against other obligations, obviously, such as the need to respect the civil rights of individuals. However, a vigorous defence of the university's right to pursue knowledge would enhance its reputation among all thinking people.'

He waved a hand to indicate the university. 'Jones Falls is important to everyone here. The reputation of an academic may rise and fall with that of the institution where he or she works. I ask you to think about the effect your verdict will have on the reputation of JFU as a free, independent academic institution. Will the university be cowed by the intellectually shallow assault of a daily newspaper? Will a programme of scientific research be cancelled for the sake of a commercial takeover bid? I hope not. I hope the committee will bolster JFU's reputation by showing that what matters here is one simple value: truth.' He looked at them, letting his words sink in. He could not tell, from their expressions, whether his speech had touched them or not. After a moment he sat down.

'Thank you,' said Jack Budgen. 'Would everyone except committee members step outside while we deliberate, please?'

Steve held the door for Jeannie and followed her into the hallway. They left the building and stood in the shade of a tree. Jeannie was pale with tension. 'What do you think?' she said.

'We have to win,' he said. 'We're right.'

'What am I going to do if we lose?' she said. 'Move to Nebraska? Get a job as a schoolteacher? Become a stewardess, like Penny Watermeadow?'

'Who's Penny Watermeadow?'

Before she could answer him, she saw something over his shoulder that made her hesitate. Steve turned around and saw Henry Quinn, smoking a cigarette. 'You were very sharp in there,' Quinn said. 'I hope you won't think me condescending if I say I enjoyed matching wits with you.'

Jeannie made a disgusted noise and turned away.

Steve was able to be more detached. Lawyers were supposed to be like this, friendly with their opponents outside the courtroom. Besides, one day he might find himself asking Quinn for a job. 'Thank you,' he said politely.

'You certainly had the best of the arguments,' Quinn went on, surprising Steve by his frankness. 'On the other hand, in a case like this people vote their self-interest, and all those committee members are senior professors. They'll find it hard to support a youngster against someone of their own group, regardless of the arguments.'

'They are all intellectuals,' Steve said. 'They're committed to rationality.'

Quinn nodded. 'You might be right,' he said. He gave Steve a speculative look then said: 'Have you any idea what this is *really* about?'

'What do you mean?' Steve said cautiously.

'Berrington is obviously terrified of *something*, and it isn't bad publicity. I wondered if you and Dr Ferrami might know what.'

'I believe we do,' Steve said. 'But we can't prove it, yet.'

'Keep trying,' Quinn said. He dropped his cigarette and trod on it. 'God forbid that Jim Proust should be president.' He turned away.

What about that, Steve thought; a closet liberal.

Jack Budgen appeared in the entrance and made a summoning gesture. Steve took Jeannie's arm and they went back in.

He studied the faces of the committee. Jack Budgen met his eye. Jane Edelsborough gave him a little smile.

That was a good sign. His hopes soared.

They all sat down.

Jack Budgen shuffled his papers unnecessarily. 'We thank both parties for enabling this hearing to be conducted with dignity.' He paused solemnly. 'Our decision is unanimous. We recommend to the senate of this university that Dr Jean Ferrami be dismissed. Thank you.'

Jeannie buried her head in her hands.

CHAPTER FORTY

WHEN AT last Jeannie was alone, she threw herself on her bed and cried.

She cried for a long time. She pounded her pillows, shouted at the wall, and uttered the filthiest words she knew; then she buried her face in the quilt and cried some more. Her sheets were wet with tears and streaked black with mascara.

After a while she got up and washed her face and put coffee on. 'It's not like you've got cancer,' she said to herself. 'Come on, shape up.' But it was hard. She was not going to die, okay, but she had lost everything she lived for.

She thought of herself at twenty-one. She had graduated *summa cum laude* and won the Mayfair Lites Challenge in the same year. She saw herself on the court, holding the cup high in the traditional gesture of triumph. The world had been at her feet. When she looked back she felt as if a different person had held up that trophy.

She sat on the couch drinking coffee. Her father, that old bastard, had stolen her TV, so she could not even watch dumb soap operas to take her mind off her misery. She would have pigged out on chocolate if she had any. She thought of booze but decided it would make her more depressed. Shopping? She would probably burst into tears in the fitting room, and anyway she was now even more broke than before.

At around two o'clock the phone rang.

Jeannie ignored it.

However, the caller was persistent, and she got fed up with listening to the ring, so in the end she picked it up.

It was Steve. After the hearing he had gone back to Washington for a meeting with his lawyer. 'I'm at the law office now,' he said. 'We want you to take legal action against Jones Falls for recovery of your FBI list. My family will pay the costs. They think it will be worth it for the chance of finding the third twin.'

Jeannie said: 'I don't give a shit about the third twin.'

There was a pause, then he said: 'It's important to me.'

She sighed. *With all my troubles, I'm supposed to worry about Steve?* Then she caught herself. *He worried about me, didn't he?* She felt ashamed. 'Steve, forgive me,' she said. 'I'm feeling sorry for myself. Of course I'll help you. What do I have to do?'

'Nothing. The lawyer will go to court, provided you give your permission.'

She began to think again. 'Isn't it a little dangerous? I mean, I presume JFU will have to be notified of our application. Then Berrington will know where the list is. And he'll get to it before we do.'

'Damn, you're right. Let me tell him that.'

A moment later another voice came on the phone.

'Dr Ferrami, this is Runciman Brewer, we're on a conference link with Steve now. Where exactly is this data?'

'In my desk drawer, on a floppy disk marked SHOPPING.LST.'

'We can apply for access to your room without specifying what we're looking for.'

'Then I think they might just wipe everything off my computer and all my disks.'

'I just don't have a better idea.'

Steve said: 'What we need is a burglar.'

Jeannie said: 'Oh, my God.'

'What?'

Daddy.

The lawyer said: 'What is it, Dr Ferrami?'

'Can you hold off on this court application?' Jeannie said.

'Yes. We probably couldn't get rolling before Monday, anyway. Why?'

'I just had an idea. Let me see if I can work it out. If not, we'll go down the legal road next week. Steve?'

'Still here.'

'Call me later.'

'You bet.'

Jeannie hung up.

Daddy could get into her office.

He was at Patty's house now. He was broke, so he wasn't going anywhere. And he owed her. Oh, boy, did he owe her.

If she could find the third twin Steve would be cleared. And if she could prove to the world what

Berrington and his friends had done in the seventies, maybe she would get her job back.

Could she ask her father to do this? It was against the law. He could end up in jail if things went wrong. He took that risk constantly, of course; but this time it would be her fault.

She told herself they would not get caught.

The doorbell rang. She lifted the handset. 'Yes.'

'Jeannie?'

It was a familiar voice. 'Yes,' she said. 'Who's this?'

'Will Temple.'

'*Will?*'

'I sent you two E-mails, didn't you get them?'

What the hell was Will Temple doing here? 'Come in,' she said, and she pressed the button.

He came up the stairs wearing tan chinos and a navy blue polo shirt. His hair was shorter, and although he still had the fair beard she had loved so much, instead of growing wild and bushy it was now a neatly trimmed goatee. The heiress had tidied him up.

She could not bring herself to let him kiss her cheek: he had hurt her too badly. She put out her hand to shake. 'This is a surprise,' she said. 'I haven't been able to retrieve my E-mail for a couple of days.'

'I'm attending a conference in Washington,' he said. 'I rented a car and drove out here.'

'Want some coffee?'

'Sure.'

'Have a seat.' She put fresh coffee on.

He looked around. 'Nice apartment.'

'Thanks.'

'Different.'

'You mean different from our old place.' The living room of their apartment in Minneapolis had been a big, untidy space full of overstuffed couches and bicycle wheels and tennis rackets and guitars. This room was pristine by comparison. 'I guess I reacted against all that clutter.'

'You seemed to like it at the time.'

'I did. Things change.'

He nodded and changed the subject. 'I read about you in the *New York Times*. That article was bullshit.'

'It's done for me, though. I was fired today.'

'No!'

She poured coffee and sat opposite him and told him the story of the hearing. When she had finished he said: 'This guy Steve—are you serious about him?'

'I don't know. I have an open mind.'

'You're not dating?'

'No, but he wants to, and I really like him. How about you? Are you still with Georgina Tinkerton Ross?'

'No.' He shook his head regretfully. 'Jeannie, what I really came here to do is tell you that breaking up with you was the greatest mistake of my life.'

Jeannie was touched by how sad he looked. Part of her was pleased that he regretted losing her, but she did not wish him unhappy.

'You were the best thing that ever happened to me,' he said. 'You're strong, but you're good. And you're smart: I have to have someone smart. We were right for each other. We loved each other.'

'I was very hurt at the time,' she said. 'But I got over it.'

'I'm not sure I did.'

She gave him an appraising look. He was a big man, not cute like Steve but attractive in a more rugged way. She prodded her libido, like a doctor touching a bruise, but there was no response, no trace left of the overwhelming physical desire she had once felt for Will's strong body.

He had come to ask her to go back to him, that was clear now. And she knew what her answer was. She did not want him any more. He was about a week too late.

It would be kinder not to put him through the humiliation of asking and being rejected. She stood up. 'Will, I have something important to do and I have to run. I wish I'd got your messages, then we could have spent more time together.'

He read the subtext and looked sadder. 'Too bad,' he said. He stood up.

She held out her hand to shake. 'Thanks for dropping by.'

He pulled her to him to kiss her. She offered her cheek. He kissed it softly, then released her. 'I wish I could rewrite our script,' he said. 'I'd give it a happier ending.'

'Goodbye, Will.'

'Goodbye, Jeannie.'

She watched him walk down the stairs and out the door.

Her phone rang.

She picked it up. 'Hello?'

'Getting fired is not the worst thing that can happen to you.'

It was a man, his voice slightly muffled as if he was speaking through something to disguise it.

Jeannie said: 'Who is this?'

'Stop nosing into things that don't concern you.'

Who the hell was this? 'What things?'

'The one you met in Philadelphia was supposed to kill you.'

Jeannie stopped breathing. Suddenly she was very scared.

The voice went on: 'He got carried away and messed up. But he could visit you again.'

Jeannie whispered: 'Oh, God . . .'

'Be warned.'

There was a click then the dial tone. He had hung up.

Jeannie cradled the handset and stood staring at the phone.

No one had ever threatened to kill her. It was horrifying to know another human being wanted to end her life. She felt paralysed. *What are you supposed to do?*

She sat on her couch, struggling to regain her strength of will. She felt like giving up. She was too bruised and battered to carry on fighting these powerful, shadowy enemies. They were too strong. They could get her fired, have her attacked, search her office, steal her E-mail; they seemed to be able to do anything. Perhaps they really could kill her.

It was so unfair. What right did they have? She was a good scientist, and they had ruined her career. They were willing to see Steve sent to jail for the rape of Lisa. They were threatening to kill her. She began to feel angry. Who did they think they were? She was not going to have her life ruined by these arrogant creeps who thought they could manipulate everything for their own benefit and to hell with everyone else. The more she thought about it, the angrier she got. I won't let them win, she thought. I have the power to hurt them—I must have, or they wouldn't feel the need to warn me off and threaten to kill me. I'm going to use that power. I don't care what happens to me so long as I can mess things up for them. I'm smart, and I'm determined, and I'm Jeannie Fucking Ferrami, so look out, you bastards, here I come.

CHAPTER FORTY-ONE

JEANNIE'S FATHER was sitting on the couch in Patty's untidy living room, with a cup of coffee in his lap, watching *General Hospital* and eating a slice of carrot cake.

When she walked in and saw him, Jeannie lost it. 'How could you do it?' she screamed. 'How could you rob your own daughter?'

He jumped to his feet, spilling his coffee and dropping his cake.

Patty followed Jeannie in. 'Please, don't make a scene,' she said. 'Zip will be home soon.'

Daddy said: 'I'm sorry, Jeannie, I'm ashamed.'

Patty got down on her knees and started mopping the spilled coffee with a clutch of Kleenex. On the screen, a handsome doctor in surgeon's coveralls was kissing a pretty woman.

'You know I'm broke,' Jeannie yelled. 'You know I'm trying to raise enough money to pay for a decent nursing home for my mother—your wife! And still you could steal my fucking TV!'

'You shouldn't swear—'

'Jesus, give me strength.'

'I'm sorry.'

Jeannie said: 'I don't get it. I just don't get it.'

Patty said: 'Leave him alone, Jeannie.'

'But I have to know. How could you do such a thing?'

'All right, I'll tell you,' Daddy said with a sudden access of force that surprised her. 'I'll tell you why I did it. Because I've lost my goddamn nerve.' Tears came to his eyes. 'I robbed my own daughter because I'm too old and scared to rob anyone else, so now you know the truth.'

He was so pathetic that Jeannie's anger evaporated in a moment. 'Oh, Daddy, I'm sorry,' she said. 'Sit down, I'll get the Dustbuster.'

She picked up the overturned cup and took it into the kitchen. She came back with the Dustbuster and hoovered up the cake crumbs. Patty finished mopping up the coffee.

'I don't deserve you girls, I know that,' Daddy said as he sat down again.

Patty said: 'I'll get you another cup of coffee.'

The TV surgeon said, *Let's go away together, just the two of us, somewhere wonderful*, and the woman said, *But what about your wife?* and the doctor looked sulky. Jeannie turned the set off and sat beside her father.

'What do you mean, you've lost your nerve?' she asked, curious. 'What happened?'

He sighed. 'When I got out of jail I cased a building in Georgetown. It was a small business, an architecture partnership that had just re-equipped the entire staff with fifteen or twenty personal computers and some other stuff, printers and fax machines. The guy who supplied the equipment to the company tipped me off:

he was going to buy it from me and sell it back to them when they got the insurance money. I would have got ten thousand dollars.'

Patty said: 'I don't want my boys to hear this.' She checked they were not in the hallway, and closed the door.

Jeannie said to Daddy: 'So what went wrong?'

'I reversed the van up to the back of the building, disarmed the burglar alarm and opened the loading-bay door. Then I started to think about what would happen if a cop came along. I never used to give a damn, in the old days, but I guess it's ten years since I did something like that. Anyway, I was so scared I started to shake. I went inside, unplugged one computer, carried it out, put it in the van and drove away. Next day I came to your place.'

'And robbed me.'

'I never intended to, honey. I thought you'd help me get on my feet and find a legitimate job of some kind. Then, when you were out, the old feeling came over me. I'm sitting there, I'm looking at the stereo and thinking I could get a couple hundred bucks for that, and maybe a hundred for the TV, and I just did it. After I sold it all I wanted to kill myself, I swear.'

'But you didn't.'

Patty said: 'Jeannie!'

Daddy said: 'I had a few drinks and got into a poker game and by the morning I was broke again.'

'So you came to see Patty.'

'I won't do it to you, Patty. I won't do it to anyone again. I'm going to go straight.'

'You better!' Patty said.

'I have to, I got no choice.'

Jeannie said: 'But not yet.'

They both looked at her. Patty said nervously: 'Jeannie, what are you talking about?'

'You have to do one more job,' Jeannie said to Daddy. 'For me. A burglary. Tonight.'

CHAPTER FORTY-TWO

IT WAS getting dark as they entered the Jones Falls campus. 'Pity we don't have a more anonymous car,' her father said as Jeannie drove the red Mercedes into the student parking lot. 'A Ford Taurus is good, or a Buick Regal. You see fifty of those a day, nobody remembers them.'

He got out of the car, carrying a battered tan leather briefcase. In his checked shirt and rumpled pants, with untidy hair and worn shoes, he looked just like a professor.

Jeannie felt strange. She had known for years that her daddy was a thief, but she herself had never done anything more illegal than driving at seventy miles an hour. Now she was about to break into a building. It felt like crossing an important line. She did not think she was doing wrong but, all the same, her self-image was shaken. She had always thought of herself as a law-abiding citizen. Criminals, including her father, had always seemed to belong to another species. Now she was joining them.

Most of the students and faculty had gone home, but there were still a few people walking around: professors working late, students going to social events, janitors locking up and security guards patrolling. Jeannie hoped she would not see anyone she knew.

She was wound up tight like a guitar string, ready to snap. She was afraid for her father more than herself. If they were caught it would be deeply humiliating for her, but that was all: the courts did not send you to jail for breaking into your own office and stealing one floppy disk. But Daddy, with his record, would go down for years. He would be an old man when he came out.

The street lamps and exterior building lights were beginning to come on. Jeannie and her father walked past the tennis court, where two women were playing under floodlights. Jeannie remembered Steve speaking to her after the game last Sunday. She had given him the brush-off automatically, he had looked so confident and pleased with himself. How wrong she had been in her first judgement of him.

She nodded towards the Ruth W. Acorn Psychology Building. 'That's the place,' she said. 'Everyone calls it Nut House.'

'Keep walking at the same speed,' he said. 'How do you get in that front door?'

'A plastic card, same as my office door. But my card doesn't work any more. I might be able to borrow one.'

'No need. I hate accomplices. How do we get around the back?'

'I'll show you.' A footpath across a lawn led past the far side of Nut House towards the visitors' parking lot. Jeannie followed it, then turned off to a paved yard at the back of the building. Her father ran a professional eye over the rear elevation. 'What's that door?' he said, pointing.

'I think it's a fire door.'

He nodded. 'It probably has a crossbar at waist level, the kind that opens the door if you push against it.'

'I believe it does. Is that where we're going to get in?'

'Yes.'

Jeannie remembered a sign on the inside of it that read THIS DOOR IS ALARMED. 'You'll set off an alarm,' she said.

'No, I won't,' he replied. He looked around. 'Do many people come around the back here?'

'No. Especially at night.'

'Okay. Let's go to work.' He put his briefcase on the ground, opened it, and took out a small black plastic box with a dial. Pressing a button, he ran the box all around the door frame, watching the dial. The needle jumped in the top right-hand corner. He gave a grunt of satisfaction.

He returned the box to the briefcase and took out another similar instrument, plus a roll of electrician's tape. He taped the instrument to the top right-hand corner of the door and threw a switch. There was a low hum. 'That should confuse the burglar alarm,' he said.

He took out a long piece of wire that had once been a laundry shirt hanger. He bent it carefully into a twisted shape then inserted the hooked end into the crack of the door. He wiggled it for a few seconds, then pulled.

The door came open.

The alarm did not sound.

He picked up his briefcase and stepped inside.

'Wait,' Jeannie said. 'This isn't right. Close the door and let's go home.'

'Hey, come on, don't be scared.'

'I can't do this to you. If you're caught, you'll be in jail until you're seventy years old.'

'Jeannie, I *want* to do this. I've been a rotten father to you for so long. This is my chance to help you for a change. It's important to me. Come on, please.'

Jeannie stepped inside.

He closed the door. 'Lead the way.'

She ran up the fire stairs to the second floor and hurried along the corridor to her office. He was right behind her. She pointed to the door.

He took yet another electronic instrument out of his briefcase. This one had a metal plate the size of a charge card attached to it by wires. He inserted the plate into the card reader and switched on the instrument. 'It tries every possible combination,' he said.

She was amazed by how easily he had entered a building that had such up-to-date security.

'You know something?' he said. 'I ain't scared!'

'Jesus, I am,' Jeannie said.

'No, seriously, I got my nerve back, maybe because you're with me.' He grinned. 'Hey, we could be a team.'

She shook her head. 'Forget it. I couldn't stand the tension.'

It occurred to her that Berrington might have come in here and carried away her computer and all her disks. It would be dreadful if she had taken this awful risk for nothing. 'How long will this take?' she said impatiently.

'Any second now.'

A moment later the door gently swung open.

'Won't you step inside?' he said proudly.

She went in and turned on the light. Her computer was still on the desk. Jeannie opened the drawer. There was her box of back-up disks. She flipped through them frenziedly. SHOPPING.LST was there. She picked it up. 'Thank God,' she said.

Now that she had the disk in her hand she could not wait to read the information on it. Desperate though she was to get out of Nut House, she was tempted to look at the file right here and now. She did not have a computer at home: Daddy had sold it. To read the disk she would have to borrow a PC. That would take time and explanations.

She decided to take a chance.

She switched on the computer on her desk and waited for it to boot up.

'What are you doing?' Daddy said.

'I want to read the file.'

'Can't you do that at home?'

'I don't have a computer at home, Daddy. It was stolen.'

He missed the irony. 'Hurry up, then.' He went to the window and looked out.

The screen flickered and she clicked on WP. She slid the floppy into the disk drive and switched on her printer.

The alarms went off all at once.

Jeannie thought her heart had stopped. The noise was deafening. 'What happened?' she yelled.

Her father was white with fear. 'That damn emitter must have failed, or maybe someone took it off the door,' he yelled. 'We're finished, Jeannie, run!'

She wanted to snatch the disk out of the computer and bolt, but she forced herself to think coolly. If she were caught now and the disk taken from her, she would have lost everything. She had to look at the list while she could. She grabbed her father's arm. 'Just a few more seconds!'

He glanced out of the window. 'Damn, that looks like a security man!'

'I just have to print this! Wait for me!'

He was shaking. 'I can't, Jeannie, I can't! I'm sorry!' He snatched up his briefcase and ran.

Jeannie felt pity for him but she could not stop now. She retrieved the A-drive directory, highlighted the FBI file, and clicked on Print.

Nothing happened. Her printer was still warming up. She cursed.

She went to the window. Two security guards were entering the front of the building.

She closed her office door.

She stared at her inkjet printer. 'Come on, come *on*.'

At last it ticked and whirred and sucked up a sheet from the paper tray.

She sprung the floppy out of the disk drive and slipped it into the pocket of her electric-blue jacket.

The printer regurgitated four sheets of paper then stopped.

Heart pounding, Jeannie snatched up the pages and scanned the lines of print.

There were thirty or forty pairs of names. Most were male, but this was not surprising: almost all crimes were committed by men. In some cases the address was a prison. The list was exactly what she had hoped for. But now she wanted something special. She looked for either *Steven Logan* or *Dennis Pinker.*

Both were there.

And they were linked with a third: *Wayne Stattner.*

'Yes!' Jeannie shouted exultantly.

There was an address in New York City and a 212 phone number.

She stared at the name. *Wayne Stattner.* This was the man who had raped Lisa right here in the gym and attacked Jeannie in Philadelphia. 'You bastard,' she whispered vengefully. 'We're going to get you.'

First she had to escape with the information. She stuffed the papers into her pocket, switched out the lights and opened the door.

She heard voices in the corridor, raised against the noise of the alarm which was still wailing. She was too late. Carefully, she closed the door again. Her legs felt weak, and she leaned on the door, listening.

She heard a man's voice shout: 'I'm sure there was a light on in one of these.'

Another voice replied: 'We better check each one.'

Jeannie glanced around her little room in the dim light from the street lamps outside. There was nowhere to hide.

She opened the door a crack. She could not see or

hear anything. She poked her head out. At the far end of the corridor light streamed out of an open door. She waited and watched. The guards came out, killed the light, closed the door and went into the next room, which was the laboratory. It would take them a minute or two to search that. Could she slip past the door unseen and make it to the stairwell?

Jeannie stepped out into the corridor and closed the door behind her with a shaky hand.

She walked along the corridor. By an effort of will she restrained herself from breaking into a run.

She passed the lab door. She could not resist the temptation to glance inside. Both guards had their backs to her: one was looking inside a stationery closet and the other was staring curiously at a row of DNA test films on a light box. They did not see her.

Almost there.

She walked on to the end of the corridor and opened the swing door.

As she was about to step through, a voice called out: 'Hey! You! Stop!'

Every nerve strained to make a run for it, but she controlled herself. She let the door swing closed, turned, and smiled.

Two guards ran along the corridor towards her. They were both men in their late fifties, probably retired cops.

Her throat was tight and she had trouble breathing. 'Good evening,' she said. 'How can I help you gentlemen?' The sound of the alarm covered the tremor in her voice.

'An alarm has gone off in the building,' said one.

It was a stupid thing to say, but she let it pass. 'Do you think there's an intruder?'

'There may be. Have you seen or heard anything unusual, Professor?'

The guards assumed she was a member of faculty: that was good. 'As a matter of fact, I thought I heard breaking glass. It seemed to come from the floor above, although I couldn't be sure.'

The two guards looked at one another. 'We'll check it out,' said one.

The other was less suggestible. 'May I ask what you have in your pocket?'

'Some papers.'

'Obviously. May I see them?'

Jeannie was not going to hand them over to anyone: they were too precious. Improvising, she pretended to agree then change her mind. 'Sure,' she said, taking them out. Then she folded them and put them back in. 'On second thoughts, no, you can't. They're personal.'

'I have to insist. In our training we're told that papers can be as valuable as anything else in a place like this.'

'I'm afraid I'm not going to let you read my private correspondence just because an alarm goes off in a college building.'

'In that case, I must ask you to come with me to our security office and speak to my supervisor.'

'All right,' she said. 'I'll meet you outside.' She backed quickly through the swing door and went light-footed down the stairs.

The guards came running after her. 'Wait!'

She let them catch up with her in the ground-floor lobby. One took her arm while the other opened the door. They stepped outside.

'No need to hold me,' she said.

'I prefer to,' he said. He was panting from the effort of chasing her down the stairs.

She had been here before. She grasped the wrist of the hand that was holding her and squeezed hard. The guard said 'Ow!' and released her.

Jeannie ran.

'Hey! You bitch, stop!' They gave chase.

They had no chance. She was twenty-five years younger and as fit as a racehorse. Her fear left her as she got farther away from the two men. She ran like the wind, laughing. They chased her for a few yards then gave up. She looked back and saw them both bent over, panting.

She ran all the way to the parking lot.

Her father was waiting beside her car. She unlocked it and they both got in. She tore out of the parking lot with her lights off.

'I'm sorry, Jeannie,' he said. 'I thought even if I couldn't do it for myself, maybe I could do it for you. But it's no use. I've lost it. I'll never rob again.'

'That's good news!' she said. 'And I got what I wanted!'

'I wish I could be a good father to you. I guess it's too late to start.'

She drove out of the campus into the street and turned on her headlights. 'It's not too late, Daddy. Really it's not.'

'Maybe. I tried for you, anyway, didn't I?'

'You tried, and you succeeded! You got me in! I couldn't have done it alone.'

'Yeah, I guess you're right.'

She drove home fast. She was anxious to check the phone number on the printout. If it was out of date she had a problem. And she wanted to hear Wayne Stattner's voice.

As soon as they got inside her apartment she picked up the phone and called the number.

A man answered. 'Hello?'

She could not tell anything from one word. She said: 'May I speak to Wayne Stattner, please?'

'Yeah, Wayne speaking, who's this?'

It sounded just like Steve's voice. *You son of a bitch, why did you rip my tights?* She suppressed her resentment and said: 'Mr Stattner, I'm with a market research company that has chosen you to receive a very special offer—'

'Fuck off and die,' Wayne said, and he hung up.

'It's him,' Jeannie said to her father. 'He even sounds like Steve, except Steve is politer.'

She had briefly explained the scenario to her father. He grasped the broad outlines although he found it somewhat bewildering. 'What are you going to do next?'

'Call the cops.' She dialled the Sex Crimes Unit and asked for Sergeant Delaware.

Daddy shook his head in amazement. 'This is hard for me to get used to: the idea of working with the police. I sure hope this sergeant is different from every other detective I've ever met.'

'I believe she probably is.'

She did not expect to find Mish at her desk—it was nine o'clock. She planned to ask them to get an urgent message to her. But by good luck Mish was still in the building. 'Catching up with my paperwork,' she explained. 'What's up?'

'Steve Logan and Dennis Pinker are not twins.'

'But I thought—'

'They're triplets.'

There was a long pause. When Mish spoke again, her tone was guarded. 'How do you know?'

'You remember I told you how I found Steve and Dennis—by searching a dental database for pairs of similar records?'

'Yes.'

'This week I searched the FBI's fingerprint file for similar fingerprints. The program gave me Steve, Dennis and a third man in a group.'

'They have the same fingerprints?'

'Not exactly the same. Similar. But I just called the third man. His voice is like Steve's. I'll bet my life they look alike. Mish, you have to believe me.'

'Do you have an address?'

'Yeah. In New York.'

'Give.'

'There's a condition.'

Mish's voice hardened. 'Jeannie, this is the police. You don't make conditions, you just answer the goddamn questions, now give me the address.'

'I have to satisfy myself. I want to see him.'

'Do you want to go to jail, that's the question for you

right now, because if not you better give me that address.'

'I want us both to go see him together. Tomorrow.'

There was a pause. 'I ought to throw you in the slammer for abetting a felon.'

'We could catch the first plane to New York in the morning.'

'Okay.'

SATURDAY

CHAPTER FORTY-THREE

THEY CAUGHT the USAir flight to New York at six forty in the morning.

Jeannie was full of hope. This might be the end of the nightmare for Steve. She had called him last night to bring him up to date and he had been ecstatic. He had wanted to come to New York with them but Jeannie knew Mish would not allow it. She had promised to call him as soon as she had more news.

Mish was maintaining a kind of tolerant scepticism. She found it hard to believe Jeannie's story but she had to check it out.

Jeannie's data did not reveal why Wayne Stattner's fingerprints were on file with the FBI, but Mish had checked overnight, and she told Jeannie the story as they took off from Baltimore-Washington International Airport. Four years ago, the distraught parents of a missing fourteen-year-old girl had tracked her down to Stattner's New York apartment. They accused him of kidnap. He denied it, saying the girl had not been coerced. The girl herself said she was in love with him. Wayne was only nineteen at the time, so in the end there had been no prosecution.

The story suggested that Stattner needed to dominate

women, but to Jeannie it did not quite fit in with the psychology of a rapist. However, Mish said there were no strict rules.

Jeannie had not told Mish about the man who attacked her in Philadelphia. She knew Mish would not take her word for it that the man was not Steve. Mish would want to question Steve herself and Steve did not need that. In consequence she also had to keep quiet about the man who had called yesterday and threatened her life. She had not told anyone about that, not even Steve: she did not want to add to his worries.

Jeannie wanted to like Mish, but there was always a tension between them. Mish as a cop expected people to do what she told them, and Jeannie hated that in a person. To try to get closer to her, Jeannie asked her how she came to be a cop.

'I used to be a secretary, and I got a job with the FBI,' she replied. 'I was there ten years. I began to think I could do the job better than the agent I worked for. So I applied for police training. Went to the academy, became a patrol officer, then volunteered for undercover work with the drugs squad. That was scary, but I proved I was tough.'

For a moment Jeannie felt alienated from her companion. She smoked a little weed herself now and again, and she resented people who wanted to throw her in jail for it.

'Then I moved to the Child Abuse Unit,' Mish went on. 'I didn't last long there. Nobody does. It's important work, but a person can only see so much of that stuff. You'd go crazy. So finally I came to Sex Crimes.'

'Doesn't sound much of an improvement.'

'At least the victims are adults. And after a couple of years they made me a sergeant and put me in charge of the unit.'

'I think all rape detectives should be women,' Jeannie said.

'I'm not sure I agree.'

Jeannie was surprised. 'Don't you think victims would talk more easily to a woman?'

'Elderly victims, perhaps; women over seventy, say.'

Jeannie shuddered at the thought of frail old women being raped.

Mish went on: 'But, frankly, most victims will tell their story to a lamppost.'

'Men always think the woman asked for it.'

'But the report of rape must be challenged at some point, if there's going to be a fair trial. And when it comes to that kind of interrogation, women can be more brutal than men, especially to other women.'

Jeannie found that hard to believe, and she wondered whether Mish was simply defending her male colleagues to an outsider.

When they ran out of things to talk about, Jeannie fell into a reverie, wondering what the future held for her. She could not get used to the idea that she might not continue to be a scientist for the rest of her life. In her dream of the future she was a famous old woman, grey-haired and cantankerous but world-renowned for her work, and students were told, *We did not understand human criminal behaviour until the publication of Jean*

Ferrami's revolutionary book in the year 2000. But now that would not happen. She needed a new fantasy.

They arrived at LaGuardia a few minutes after eight o'clock and took a battered yellow New York taxi into the city. The cab had busted springs, and it bounced and rattled across Queens and through the Midtown Tunnel into Manhattan. Jeannie would have been uncomfortable in a Cadillac: she was on her way to see the man who had attacked her in her car, and her stomach felt like a cauldron of hot acid.

Wayne Stattner's address turned out to be a downtown loft building just south of Houston Street. It was a sunny Saturday morning and already there were young people on the streets, shopping for bagels and drinking cappuccino in the sidewalk cafés and looking in the windows of art galleries.

A detective from the First Precinct was waiting for them, double-parked outside the building in a tan Ford Escort with a dented rear door. He shook hands and grumpily introduced himself as Herb Reitz. Jeannie guessed that babysitting out-of-town detectives was a chore.

Mish said: 'We appreciate your coming out on a Saturday to help us.' She gave him a warm, flirtatious smile.

He mellowed a little. 'No problem.'

'Any time you need help in Baltimore I want you to call me personally.'

'I sure will.'

Jeannie wanted to say, *For Christ's sake let's get on with it!*

They went into the building and took a slow freight elevator to the top. 'One apartment on each floor,' Herb said. 'This is an affluent suspect. What did he do?'

'Rape,' Mish said.

The elevator stopped. The door opened directly on to another door, so that they could not get out until the apartment door was opened. Mish rang a bell. There was a long silence. Herb held open the elevator doors. Jeannie prayed Wayne would not have gone out of town for the weekend: she could not stand the anticlimax. Mish rang again and kept her finger on the button.

At last a voice came from within. 'Who the fuck is it?'

It was him. The voice made Jeannie go cold with horror.

Herb said: 'The police, that's who the fuck it is. Now open the door.'

The tone changed. 'Please hold your ID up to the glass panel in front of you.'

Herb showed his detective's shield to the panel.

'Okay, just a minute.'

This is it, Jeannie thought. Now I'm going to see him.

The door was opened by a tousled, barefoot young man in a faded black towelling bathrobe.

Jeannie stared at him, feeling disoriented.

He was Steve's double—except that he had black hair.

Herb said: 'Wayne Stattner?'

'Yes.'

He must have dyed it, she thought. He must have dyed it yesterday, or Thursday night.

'I'm Detective Herb Reitz from the First Precinct.'

'I'm always keen to cooperate with the police, Herb,' said Wayne. He glanced at Mish and Jeannie. Jeannie saw no flicker of recognition in his face. 'Won't you all come in?'

They stepped inside. The windowless lobby was painted black with three red doors. In a corner stood a human skeleton of the type used in medical schools, but this one was gagged with a red scarf and had steel police handcuffs on its bony wrists.

Wayne led them through one of the red doors into a big, high-ceilinged loft. Black velvet curtains were drawn across the windows, and the place was lit by low lamps. On one wall was a full-size Nazi flag. A collection of whips stood in an umbrella stand, displayed under a spotlight. A large oil painting of a crucifixion rested on an artist's easel: looking closer, Jeannie saw that the naked figure being crucified was not Christ but a voluptuous woman with long blond hair. She shuddered with disgust.

This was the home of a sadist: that could not have been more obvious if he had put a sign out.

Herb was staring around in amazement. 'What do you do for a living, Mr Stattner?'

'I own two nightclubs here in New York. Frankly, that's why I'm so keen to cooperate with the police. I have to keep my hands spotlessly clean, for business purposes.'

Herb clicked his fingers. 'Of course, Wayne Stattner. I read about you in *New York* magazine. *Manhattan's Young Millionaires.* I should have recognized the name.'

'Won't you sit down?'

Jeannie headed for a seat then saw it was an electric chair of the type used for executions. She did a double take, grimaced and sat elsewhere.

Herb said: 'This is Sergeant Michelle Delaware of the Baltimore City Police.'

'Baltimore?' said Wayne, showing surprise. Jeannie was watching his face for signs of fear, but he seemed to be a good actor. 'They have crime in Baltimore?' he said sarcastically.

Jeannie said: 'Your hair's dyed, isn't it?'

Mish flashed her a look of annoyance: Jeannie was supposed to observe, not interrogate the suspect.

However, Wayne did not mind the question. 'Smart of you to notice.'

I was right, Jeannie thought jubilantly. It is him. She looked at his hands and remembered them tearing her clothes. You've had it, you bastard, she thought.

'When did you dye it?' she asked.

'When I was fifteen,' he said.

Liar.

'Black has been fashionable ever since I can remember.'

Your hair was fair on Thursday, when you pushed your big hands up my skirt, and on Sunday, when you raped my friend Lisa in the gym at JFU.

But why was he lying? Did he know they had a fair-haired suspect?

He said: 'What's this all about? Is my hair colour a *clue*? I love mysteries.'

'We won't keep you long,' Mish said briskly. 'We

need to know where you were last Sunday evening at eight o'clock.'

Jeannie wondered if he would have an alibi. It would be so easy for him to claim he had been playing cards with some lowlife types, then pay them to back him up, or say he had been in bed with a hooker who would perjure herself for a fix.

But he surprised her. 'That's easy,' he said. 'I was in California.'

'Can anyone corroborate that?'

He laughed. 'About a hundred million people, I guess.'

Jeannie was beginning to get a bad feeling about this. He couldn't have a real alibi. He *had* to be the rapist.

Mish said: 'What do you mean?'

'I was at the Emmies.'

Jeannie remembered that the Emmy awards dinner had been showing on TV in Lisa's hospital room. How could Wayne have been at the ceremony? He could hardly have got to the airport in the time it took Jeannie to reach the hospital.

'I didn't win anything, of course,' he added. 'I'm not in that business. But Salina Jones did, and she's an old friend.'

He glanced at the oil painting, and Jeannie realized that the woman in the picture resembled the actress who played Babe, the daughter of grouchy Brian in the restaurant sitcom *Too Many Cooks.* She must have posed.

Wayne said: 'Salina won best actress in a comedy, and I kissed her on both cheeks as she came off the stage with her trophy in her hand. It was a beautiful moment, caught for ever by the television cameras and beamed instantly to the world. I have it on video. And there's a photo in this week's *People* magazine.'

He pointed to a magazine lying on the carpet.

With a sinking heart, Jeannie picked it up. There was a picture of Wayne, looking incredibly dashing in a tuxedo, kissing Salina as she grasped her Emmy statuette.

His hair was black.

The caption read *New York nightclub impresario Wayne Stattner congratulates old flame Salina Jones on her Emmy for* Too Many Cooks *in Hollywood Sunday night.*

It was about as impregnable as an alibi could be.

How was this possible?

Mish said: 'Well, Mr Stattner, we don't need to take up any more of your time.'

'What did you think I might have done?'

'We're investigating a rape that took place in Baltimore on Sunday night.'

'Not me,' Wayne said.

Mish glanced at the crucifixion and he followed her gaze. 'All my victims are volunteers,' he said, and he gave her a long, suggestive look.

She flushed dark and turned away.

Jeannie was desolate. All her hopes were dashed. But her brain was still working, and as they got up to leave she said: 'May I ask you something?'

'Sure,' said Wayne, ever obliging.

'Do you have any brothers or sisters?'

'I'm an only child.'

'Around the time you were born, your father was in the military, am I right?'

'Yes, he was a helicopter pilot instructor at Fort Bragg. How did you know?'

'Do you happen to know if your mother had difficulty conceiving?'

'These are funny questions for a cop.'

Mish said: 'Dr Ferrami is a scientist at Jones Falls University. Her research is closely connected with the case I'm working on.'

Jeannie said: 'Did your mother ever say anything about having fertility treatment?'

'Not to me.'

'Would you mind if I asked her?'

'She's dead.'

'I'm sorry to hear that. How about your father?'

He shrugged. 'You could call him.'

'I'd like to.'

'He lives in Miami. I'll give you the number.'

Jeannie handed him a pen. He scribbled a number on a page of *People* magazine and tore off the corner.

They went to the door. Herb said: 'Thank you for your cooperation, Mr Stattner.'

'Any time.'

As they went down in the lift, Jeannie said disconsolately: 'Do you believe his alibi?'

'I'll check it out,' Mish said. 'But it feels solid.'

Jeannie shook her head. 'I can't believe he's innocent.'

'He's guilty as hell, honey—but not of this one.'

CHAPTER FORTY-FOUR

STEVE WAS waiting by the phone. He sat in the big kitchen of his parents' home in Georgetown, watching his mother making meat loaf, waiting for Jeannie to call. He wondered if Wayne Stattner really was his double. He wondered if Jeannie and Sergeant Delaware would find him at his New York address. He wondered if Wayne would confess to raping Lisa Hoxton.

Mom was chopping onions. She had been dazed and astonished when first told what had been done to her at the Aventine Clinic in December 1972. She had not really believed it, but had accepted it provisionally, as it were for the sake of argument, while they spoke to the lawyer. Last night Steve had sat up late with Mom and Dad, talking over their strange history. Mom had got angry then: the notion of doctors experimenting on patients without permission was just the kind of thing to make her mad. In her column she talked a lot about women's right to control their own bodies.

Surprisingly, Dad was calmer. Steve would have expected a man to have a stronger reaction to the cuckoo aspect of the whole story. But Dad had been tirelessly rational, going over Jeannie's logic, speculating about other possible explanations for the phenomenon of the triplets, concluding in the end that she was probably right. However, reacting calmly was part of Dad's code. It did not necessarily tell you how he was feeling underneath. Right now he was out in the yard, placidly watering a flower bed, but inside he might be boiling.

Mom started frying onions, and the smell made Steve's mouth water. 'Meat loaf with mashed potatoes and ketchup,' he said. 'One of the great meals.'

She smiled. 'When you were five years old you wanted it every day.'

'I remember. In that little kitchen in Hoover Tower.'

'Do you remember that?'

'Just. I remember moving out, and how strange it felt having a house instead of an apartment.'

'That was about the time I started to make money from my first book, *What to Do When You Can't Get Pregnant.*' She sighed. 'If the truth about how I got pregnant ever comes out, that book is going to look pretty silly.'

'I hope all the people who bought it don't ask for their money back.'

She put minced beef into the frying pan with the onions and wiped her hands. 'I've been thinking about this stuff all night, and you know something? I'm glad they did that to me in the Aventine Clinic.'

'Why? Last night you were mad.'

'And in a way I'm still mad, about being used like a laboratory chimpanzee. But I realized one simple thing:

if they hadn't experimented on me, I wouldn't have you. Beside that, nothing else matters.'

'You don't mind that I'm not really yours?'

She put her arm around him. 'You're mine, Steve. Nothing can change that.'

The phone rang and Steve snatched it up. 'Hello?'

'This is Jeannie.'

'What happened?' Steve said breathlessly. 'Was he there?'

'Yes, and he's your double, except he dyes his hair black.'

'My God—there *are* three of us.'

'Yes. Wayne's mother is dead, but I just spoke with his father, in Florida, and he confirmed that she was treated at the Aventine Clinic.'

It was good news, but she sounded dispirited, and Steve's elation was checked. 'You don't seem as pleased as you ought to be.'

'He has an alibi for Sunday.'

'Shit.' His hopes sank again. 'How can he? What sort of an alibi?'

'Watertight. He was at the Emmies in Los Angeles. There are photographs.'

'He's in the movie business?'

'Nightclub owner. He's a minor celebrity.'

Steve could see why she was so down. Her discovery of Wayne had been brilliant—but it had got them no farther forward. But he was mystified as well as downcast. 'Then who raped Lisa?'

'Do you remember what Sherlock Holmes says?

"When you have eliminated the impossible, what remains—no matter how improbable—must be the truth." Or maybe it was Hercule Poirot.'

His heart went cold. Surely she did not believe *he* had raped Lisa? '*What's* the truth?'

'There are four twins.'

'*Quadruplets?* Jeannie, this is getting crazy.'

'Not quadruplets. I can't believe this embryo divided into four by *accident.* It had to be deliberate, part of the experiment.'

'Is that possible?'

'It is nowadays. You've heard of cloning. Back in the seventies it was just an idea. But Threeplex seems to have been years ahead of the rest of the field—perhaps because they were working in secret and could experiment on humans.'

'You're saying I'm a clone.'

'You have to be. I'm sorry, Steve. I keep giving you shattering news. It's a good thing you have the parents you have.'

'Yeah. What's he like, Wayne?'

'Creepy. He has a painting that shows Salina Jones being crucified naked. I couldn't wait to get out of his apartment.'

Steve was silent. *One of my clones is a murderer, the other is a sadist, and the hypothetical fourth is a rapist. Where does that leave me?*

Jeannie said: 'The clone idea also explains why you all have different birthdays. The embryos were kept in the laboratory for varying periods before being implanted in the women's wombs.'

Why did this happen to me? Why couldn't I be like everyone else?

'They're closing the flight, I have to go.'

'I want to see you. I'll drive to Baltimore.'

'Okay. Bye.'

Steve hung up the phone. 'You got that,' he said to his mother.

'Yeah. He looks just like you, but he's got an alibi, so she thinks there must be four of you, and you're clones.'

'If we're clones, I must be like them.'

'No. You're different, because you're mine.'

'But I'm not.' He saw the spasm of pain pass across his mother's face, but he was hurting too. 'I'm the child of two complete strangers selected by research scientists employed by Threeplex. That's my ancestry.'

'You must be different from the others, you *behave* differently.'

'But does that prove that my nature is different from theirs? Or just that I've learned to hide it, like a domesticated animal? Did you make me what I am? Or did Threeplex?'

'I don't know, my son,' said Mom. 'I just don't know.'

CHAPTER FORTY-FIVE

JEANNIE TOOK a shower and washed her hair, then made up her eyes carefully. She decided not to use lipstick or blush. She dressed in a V-neck purple sweater and skin-tight grey leggings, with no underwear or shoes. She put in her favourite nose jewel, a small sapphire in a silver mount. In the mirror she looked like sex on a stick. 'Off to church, young lady?' she said aloud. Then she winked at herself and went into the living room.

Her father had gone again. He preferred to be at Patty's where he had his three grandchildren to keep him amused. Patty had come to pick him up while Jeannie was in New York.

She had nothing to do but wait for Steve. She tried not to think of the day's great disappointment. She had had enough. She felt hungry: she had kept going on coffee all day. She wondered whether to eat now or hang on until he got here. She smiled as she remembered his eating eight cinnamon buns for breakfast. Was that only yesterday? It seemed a week ago.

Suddenly she realized she did not have any food in the refrigerator. How awful if he arrived hungry and she could not feed him! She hurriedly pulled on a pair of Doc Marten boots and ran outside. She drove to the 7-Eleven on the corner of Falls Road and 36th Street and bought eggs, Canadian bacon, milk, a loaf of seven-grain bread, ready-washed salad, Dos Equis beer, Ben & Jerry's Rainforest Crunch flavour ice cream, and four more packets of frozen cinnamon buns.

While she was standing at the checkout she realized he might arrive while she was out. He might even go away again! She ran out of the store with her arms full and drove home like a maniac, imagining him waiting impatiently on the doorstep.

There was no one outside her house and no sign of his rusty Datsun. She went inside and put the food in the refrigerator. She took the eggs out of the carton and put them in the egg tray, undid the six-pack of beer, and loaded the coffee machine ready to start. Then she had nothing to do again.

It occurred to her that she was behaving uncharacteristically. She had never before worried about whether a man might be hungry. Her normal attitude, even with Will Temple, had been that if he's hungry he'll fix himself something to eat, and if the refrigerator is empty he'll go to the store, and if the store is closed he'll get drive-through. But now she was suffering an attack of domesticity. Steve was having a bigger impact on her than other men, even though she had only known him a few days—

The doorbell sounded like an explosion.

Jeannie leaped up, heart pounding, and spoke into the entryphone. 'Yes?'

'Jeannie? It's Steve.'

She touched the button that unlocked the door. She stood still for a moment, feeling foolish. She was acting like a teenage girl. She watched Steve come up the stairs in a grey T-shirt and loose-fitting blue jeans. His face showed the pain and disappointment of the last twenty-four hours. She threw her arms around him and embraced him. His strong body felt tense and strained.

She led him into the living room. He sat on the sofa and she switched on the coffee machine. She felt very close to him. They had not done the usual things, dated and gone to restaurants and watched movies together, the way Jeannie had previously got to know a man. Instead they had fought battles side by side and puzzled over mysteries together and been persecuted by half-hidden enemies. It had made them friends very quickly.

'Want some coffee?'

He shook his head. 'I'd rather hold hands.'

She sat beside him on the couch and took his hand. He leaned towards her. She turned up her face and he kissed her lips. It was their first real kiss. She squeezed his hand hard and parted her lips. The taste of his mouth made her think of wood smoke. For a moment her passion was derailed as she asked herself if she had brushed her teeth; then she remembered that she had, and she relaxed again. He touched her breasts through the soft wool of her sweater, his big hands surprisingly gentle. She did the same to him, rubbing the palms of her hands across his chest.

It got serious very quickly.

He pulled away to look at her. He stared into her face as if he wanted to burn her features into his memory. With his fingertips he touched her eyebrows, her cheekbones, the tip of her nose, and her lips, as gently as if he was afraid of breaking something. He shook his head from side to side slightly, as if he could not believe what he saw.

In his gaze she saw profound longing. This man yearned for her with all his being. It turned her on. Her passion blew up like a sudden wind from the south, hot and tempestuous. She felt the sensation of melting in her loins that she had not had for a year and a half. She wanted everything all at once, his body on top of her and his tongue in her mouth and his hands everywhere.

She held his head and pulled his face to her and kissed him again, this time with her mouth open wide. She leaned backwards on the couch until he was half lying on her, his weight crushing her chest. Eventually she pushed him away, panting, and said: 'Bedroom.'

She untangled herself from him and went into the bedroom ahead of him. She pulled her sweater over her head and threw it on the floor. He came into the room and closed the door behind him with his heel. Seeing her undressing, he took off his T-shirt with one swift movement.

They all do that, she thought; *they all close the door with their heel.*

He pulled off his shoes, unbuckled his belt, and took off his blue jeans. His body was perfect, broad shoulders and a muscular chest and narrow hips in white jockey shorts.

But which one is he?

He moved towards her and she took two steps back.

The man on the phone said: 'He could visit you again.'

He frowned. 'What's the matter?'

She was suddenly scared. 'I can't do this,' she said.

He took a deep breath and blew hard. 'Wow,' he said. He looked away. 'Wow.'

She crossed her arms on her chest, covering her breasts. 'I don't know who you are.'

Comprehension dawned. 'Oh, my God.' He sat on the bed with his back to her, and his big shoulders slumped dispiritedly. But it could have been an act. 'You think I'm the one you met in Philadelphia.'

'I thought he was Steve.'

'But why would he pretend to be me?'

'It doesn't matter.'

'He wouldn't just do it in the hope of a sly fuck,' he said. 'My doubles have peculiar ways of getting their kicks, but this isn't one of them. If he wanted to fuck you he'd pull a knife on you, or rip your stockings, or set fire to the building, wouldn't he?'

'I got a phone call,' Jeannie said shakily. 'Anonymous. He said: *The one you met in Philadelphia was supposed to kill you. He got carried away and messed up. But he could visit you again.* That's why you have to leave, now.' She snatched her sweater up off the floor and pulled it on hastily. It did not make her feel any safer.

There was sympathy in his gaze. 'Poor Jeannie,' he said. 'The bastards have scared you good. I'm sorry.' He stood up and pulled on his jeans.

Suddenly she felt sure she was wrong. The Philadelphia clone, the rapist, would never start dressing again in this situation. He would throw her on the bed and tear off her clothes and try to take her by force. This man was different. This was Steve. She felt an almost irresistible desire to fling her arms around him and make love to him. 'Steve . . .'

He smiled. 'That's me.'

But was this the aim of his act? When he had won her confidence, and they were naked in bed, and he was lying on top of her, would he change and reveal his true nature, the nature that loved to see women in fear and pain? She shuddered with dread.

It was no good. She averted her eyes. 'You'd better go,' she said.

'You could question me,' he said.

'All right. Where did I first meet Steve?'

'At the tennis court.'

It was the right answer. 'But both Steve and the rapist were at JFU that day.'

'Ask me something else.'

'How many cinnamon buns did Steve eat on Friday morning?'

He grinned. 'Eight, I'm ashamed to say.'

She shook her head despairingly. 'This place could be bugged. They've searched my office and downloaded my E-mail, they could be listening to us now. It's no good. I don't know Steve Logan that well, and what I do know, others might know too.'

'I guess you're right,' he said, putting his T-shirt back on.

He sat on the bed and put on his shoes. She went into the living room, not wanting to stand in the bedroom and watch him dress. Was this a terrible mistake? Or was it the smartest move she had ever made? She felt a bereft ache in her loins: she had wanted so badly to make love to Steve. Yet the thought that she might have found herself in bed with someone like Wayne Stattner made her shaky with fear.

He came in, fully dressed. She looked into his eyes, searching for something there, some sign that would assuage her doubts, but she did not find it. *I don't know who you are, I just don't know!*

He read her mind. 'It's no use, I can tell. Trust is trust, and when it's gone, it's gone.' He let his resentment show for a moment. 'What a downer, what a motherfucking downer.'

His anger scared her. She was strong, but he was stronger. She wanted him out of the apartment, and fast.

He sensed her urgency. 'Okay, I'm leaving,' he said. He went to the door. 'You realize *he* wouldn't leave.'

She nodded.

He said what she was thinking. 'But until I really leave, you can't be sure. And if I leave and come right back, that doesn't count either. For you to know it's me, I have to *really* go away.'

'Yes.' She was sure now that this was Steve, but her doubts would return unless he really went away.

'We need a secret code, so you know it's me.'

'Okay.'

'I'll think of something.'

'Okay.'

'Goodbye,' he said. 'I won't try to kiss you.'

He went down the stairs. 'Call me,' he shouted.

She stood still, frozen to the spot, until she heard the slam of the street door.

She bit her lip. She felt like crying. She went to the kitchen counter and poured coffee into a mug. She raised the mug to her lips but it slipped through her fingers and fell to the floor, where it smashed on the tiles. 'Fuck,' she said.

Her legs went weak, and she slumped on the couch. She had felt in terrible danger. Now she knew the danger had been imaginary, but she still felt profoundly grateful that it had passed. Her body felt swollen with unfulfilled desire. She touched her crotch: her leggings were damp. 'Soon,' she breathed. 'Soon.' She thought about how it would be the next time they met, how she would embrace him and kiss him and apologize, and how tenderly he would forgive her; and as she envisioned it she touched herself with her fingertips, and after a few moments a spasm of pleasure went through her.

Then she slept for a while.

CHAPTER FORTY-SIX

It was the humiliation that got to Berrington.

He kept defeating Jeannie Ferrami, but he was never able to feel good about it. She had forced him to go sneaking around like a petty thief. He had surreptitiously leaked a story to a newspaper, crept into her room and searched her desk drawers, and now he was watching her house. But fear compelled him. His world seemed about to fall around him. He was desperate.

He would never have thought he would be doing this a few weeks from his sixtieth birthday: sitting in his car, parked at the kerb, watching someone else's front door like a grubby private eye. What would his mother think? She was still alive, a slim, well-dressed woman of eighty-four, living in a small town in Maine, writing witty letters to the local newspaper and determinedly hanging on to her post as chief flower-arranger for the Episcopalian church. She would shudder with shame to know what her son had been reduced to.

God forbid he should be seen by anyone he knew. He was careful not to meet the eyes of passers-by. His car was unfortunately conspicuous. He thought of it as a discreetly elegant automobile, but there were not many silver Lincoln Town Cars parked along this street:

ageing Japanese compacts and lovingly preserved Pontiac Firebirds were the local favourites. Berrington himself was not the kind of person to fade into the background, with his distinctive grey hair. For a while he had held a street map open in front of him, resting on the steering wheel, for camouflage, but this was a friendly neighbourhood, and two people had tapped on the window and offered to give him directions, so he had to put the map away. He consoled himself with the thought that anyone who lived in such a low-rent area could not possibly be important.

He now had no idea what Jeannie was up to. The FBI had failed to find that list in her apartment. Berrington had to assume the worst: the list had led her to another clone. If that were so, disaster was not far away. Berrington, Jim and Preston were staring close up at public exposure, disgrace and ruin.

It was Jim who had suggested that Berrington watch Jeannie's house. 'We have to know what she's up to, who comes and goes,' Jim had said, and Berrington had reluctantly agreed. He had got here early, and nothing had happened until around midday when Jeannie was dropped off by a black woman he recognized as one of the detectives investigating the rape. She had interviewed him briefly on Monday. He had found her attractive. He managed to remember her name: Sergeant Delaware.

He called Proust from the pay phone in the McDonald's on the corner, and Proust promised to get his FBI friend to find out whom they had been to see. Berrington imagined the FBI man saying, *Sergeant Delaware made contact today with a suspect we have under surveillance, for security reasons I can't reveal any more than that, but it would be helpful to us to know exactly what she did this morning and what case she was working on.*

An hour or so later Jeannie had left in a rush, looking heartbreakingly sexy in a purple sweater. Berrington had not followed her car: despite his fear, he could no bring himself to do something so undignified. But she had come back a few minutes later carrying a couple of brown paper sacks from a grocery store. The next arrival was one of the clones, presumably Steve Logan.

He had not stayed long. If I'd been in his shoes, Berrington thought, with Jeannie dressed like that, I would have stayed there all night and most of Sunday.

He checked the car's clock for the twentieth time and decided to call Jim again. He might have heard from the FBI by now.

Berrington left his car and walked to the corner. The smell of French fries made him hungry but he did not like to eat hamburgers out of styrofoam containers. He got a cup of black coffee and went to the pay phone.

'They went to New York,' Jim told him.

It was as Berrington had feared. 'Wayne Stattner,' he said.

'Yup.'

'Shit. What did they do?'

'Asked him to account for his movements last Sunday, and like that. He was at the Emmies. Had his picture in *People* magazine. End of story.'

'Any indication what Jeannie might be planning to do next?'

'No. What's happening there?'

'Not a lot. I can see her door from here. She did some shopping, Steve Logan came and went, nothing. Maybe they've run out of ideas.'

'And maybe not. All we know is that your scheme of firing her didn't shut her up.'

'All right, Jim, don't rub it in. Wait—she's coming out.' She had changed her clothes: she was wearing white jeans and a royal blue sleeveless blouse that showed her strong arms.

'Follow her,' Jim said.

'The hell with that. She's getting into her car.'

'Berry, we have to know where she goes.'

'I'm not a cop, goddamn it!'

A little girl on her way to the ladies' room with her mother said: 'That man shouted, Mommy.'

'Hush, darling,' her mother said.

Berrington lowered his voice. 'She's pulling away.'

'Get in your damn car!'

'Fuck you, Jim.'

'Follow her!' Jim hung up.

Berrington cradled the phone.

Jeannie's red Mercedes went by and turned south on Falls Road.

Berrington ran to his car.

CHAPTER FORTY-SEVEN

JEANNIE STUDIED Steve's father. Charles was dark haired, with the shadow of a heavy beard on his jaw. His expression was dour and his manner rigidly precise. Although it was Saturday and he had been gardening, he wore neatly pressed dark pants and a short-sleeved shirt with a collar. He did not look like Steve in any way. The only thing Steve might have got from him was a taste for conservative clothes. Most of Jeannie's students wore ripped denim and black leather, but Steve favoured khakis and button-downs.

Steve had not yet come home, and Charles speculated that he might have dropped by his law school library to read up on rape trials. Steve's mother was lying down. Charles made fresh lemonade, and he and Jeannie went out on the patio of the Georgetown house and sat on lawn chairs.

Jeannie had woken up from her doze with a brilliant idea in the forefront of her mind. She had thought of a way to find the fourth clone. But she would need Charles's help. And she was not sure he would be willing to do what she had to ask him.

Charles passed her a tall, cold glass, then took one

himself and sat down. 'May I call you by your first name?' he said.

'Please do.'

'And I hope you'll do the same.'

'Sure.'

They sipped their lemonade, then he said: 'Jeannie—what is this all about?'

She put down her glass. 'I think it's an experiment,' she said. 'Berrington and Proust were both in the military until shortly before they set up Threeplex. I suspect the company was originally a cover for a military project.'

'I've been a soldier all my adult life, and I'm ready to believe almost anything crazy of the army. But what interest could they have in women's fertility problems?'

'Think of this. Steve and his doubles are tall, strong, fit and handsome. They're also very smart, although their propensity to violence gets in the way of their achievements. But Steve and Dennis have IQ scores off the scale, and I suspect the other two would be the same: Wayne is already a millionaire at the age of twenty-two, and the fourth one has at least been clever enough to totally evade detection.'

'Where does that get you?'

'I don't know. I wonder if the army was trying to breed the perfect soldier.'

It was no more than an idle speculation, and she said it casually, but it electrified Charles. 'Oh, my God,' he said, and an expression of shocked comprehension spread over his face. 'I think I remember hearing about this.'

'What do you mean?'

'There was a rumour, back in the seventies, that went all around the military. The Russians had a breeding programme, people said. They were making perfect soldiers, perfect athletes, perfect chess players, everything. Some people said we should be doing the same. Others said we already were.'

'So that's it!' Jeannie felt that at last she was beginning to understand. 'They picked a healthy, aggressive, intelligent, blond-haired man and woman and got them to donate the sperm and egg that went together to form the embryo. But what they were really interested in was the possibility of *duplicating* the perfect soldier once they had created him. The crucial part of the experiment was the multiple division of the embryo and the implanting into the host mothers. And it worked.' She frowned. 'I wonder what happened next.'

'I can answer that,' Charles said. 'Watergate. All those crazy secret schemes were cancelled after that.'

'But Threeplex went legitimate, like the Mafia. And because they really did find out how to make test-tube babies, the company was profitable. The profits financed the research into genetic engineering that they've been doing ever since. I suspect that my own project is probably part of their grand scheme.'

'Which is what?'

'A breed of perfect Americans: intelligent, aggressive, and blond. A master race.' She shrugged. 'It's an old idea, but it's possible now, with modern genetics.'

'So why would they sell the company? It doesn't make sense.'

'Maybe it does,' Jeannie said thoughtfully. 'When they got the takeover bid, perhaps they saw it as an opportunity to move into high gear. The money will finance Proust's run at the presidency. If they get into the White House they can do all the research they want—*and* put their ideas into practice.'

Charles nodded. 'There's a piece about Proust's ideas in today's *Washington Post.* I don't think I want to live in his kind of world. If we're all aggressive, obedient solders, who's going to write the poems and play the blues and go on anti-war protest marches?'

Jeannie raised her eyebrows. It was a surprising thought to come from a career soldier. 'There's more to it than that,' she said. 'Human variation has a purpose. There's a reason we're born different from both our parents. Evolution is a trial-and-error business. You can't prevent nature's failed experiments without eliminating the successes too.'

Charles sighed. 'And all this means I'm not Steve's father.'

'Don't say that.'

He opened his billfold and took out a photo. 'I have to tell you something, Jeannie. I never suspected any of this stuff about clones, but I've often looked at Steve and wondered if there was anything at all of me in him.'

'Can't you see it?' she said.

'A resemblance?'

'No physical resemblance. But Steve has a profound sense of duty. None of the other clones could give a darn about duty. He got it from you!'

Charles still looked grim. 'There's bad in him. I know it.'

She touched his arm. 'Listen to me. Steve was what I call a wild child—disobedient, impulsive, fearless, bursting with energy—wasn't he?'

Charles smiled ruefully. 'That's the truth.'

'So were Dennis Pinker and Wayne Stattner. Such children are almost impossible to raise right. That's why Dennis is a murderer and Wayne a sadist. But *Steve isn't like them*—and you're the reason why. Only the most patient, understanding and dedicated of parents can bring up such children to be normal human beings. But Steve *is* normal.'

'I pray you're right.' Charles opened his billfold to replace the photo.

Jeannie forestalled him. 'May I see it?'

'Sure.'

Jeannie studied the picture. It had been taken quite recently. Steve was wearing a blue checked shirt and his hair was a little too long. He was grinning shyly at the camera. 'I don't have a photo of him,' Jeannie said regretfully as she handed it back.

'Have that one.'

'I couldn't. You keep it next to your heart.'

'I have a million photos of Steve. I'll put another one in my billfold.'

'Thanks, I really appreciate it.'

'You seem very fond of him.'

'I love him, Charles.'

'You do?'

Jeannie nodded. 'When I think he might be sent to

jail for this rape, I want to offer to go instead of him.'

Charles gave a wry smile. 'So do I.'

'That's love, isn't it?'

'Sure is.'

Jeannie felt self-conscious. She had not meant to say all this to Steve's father. She had not really known it herself: it had just come out, and then she realized it was true.

He said: 'How does Steve feel about you?'

She smiled: 'I could be modest . . .'

'Don't bother.'

'He's crazy for me.'

'That doesn't surprise me. Not just because you're beautiful, though you are. You're strong, too: that's obvious. He needs someone strong—especially with this accusation over his head.'

Jeannie gave him a calculating look. It was time to ask him. 'There is something you could do, you know.'

'Tell me what it is.'

Jeannie had rehearsed this speech in the car all the way to Washington. 'If I could search another database, I might find the real rapist. But after the publicity in the *New York Times*, no government agency or insurance company is going to take the risk of working with me. Unless . . .'

'What?'

Jeannie leaned forward in her lawn chair. 'Threeplex experimented on soldiers' wives who were referred to them by army hospitals. Therefore most or all of the clones were probably born in army hospitals.'

He nodded slowly.

'The babies must have had army medical records, twenty-two years ago. Those records may still exist.'

'I'm sure they do. The army never throws anything away.'

Jeannie's hopes rose a notch. But there was another problem. 'That long ago, they would have been paper files. Might they have been transferred to computer?'

'I'm sure they have. It's the only way to store everything.'

'Then it is possible,' Jeannie said, controlling her excitement.

He looked thoughtful.

She gave him a hard stare. 'Charles, can you get me access?'

'What, exactly, do you need to do?'

'I have to load my program into the computer then let it search all the files.'

'How long does it take?'

'No way of knowing. That depends on the size of the database and the power of the computer.'

'Does it interfere with normal data retrieval?'

'It could slow it down.'

He frowned.

'Will you do it?' Jeannie said impatiently.

'If we're caught, it's the end of my career.'

'Will you?'

'Hell, yes.'

CHAPTER FORTY-EIGHT

STEVE WAS thrilled to see Jeannie sitting on the patio drinking lemonade and talking earnestly to his father as if they were old friends. This is what I want, he thought; I want Jeannie in my life. Then I can deal with anything.

He crossed the lawn from the garage, smiling, and kissed her lips softly. 'You two look like conspirators,' he said.

Jeannie explained what they were planning, and Steve allowed himself to feel hopeful again.

Dad said to Jeannie: 'I'm not computer-literate. I'll need help loading your program.'

'I'll come with you.'

'I'll bet you don't have your passport here.'

'I sure don't.'

'I can't get you into the Data Center without identification.'

'I could go home and get it.'

'I'll come with you,' Steve said. 'I have my passport upstairs. I'm sure I could load the program.'

Dad looked a query at Jeannie.

She nodded. 'The process is simple. If there are any

glitches you can call me from the Data Center and I'll talk you through it.'

'Okay.'

Dad went into the kitchen and brought out the phone. He dialled a number. 'Don, this is Charlie. Who won the golf? . . . I knew you could do it. But I'll beat you next week, you watch. Listen, I need a favour, kind of unusual. I want to check my son's medical records from way back when . . . Yeah, he's got some kind of rare condition, not life-threatening but serious, and there may be a clue in his early history. Would you arrange security clearance for me to go into the Command Data Center?'

There was a long pause. Steve could not read his father's face. At last he said: 'Thanks, Don, I really appreciate it.'

Steve punched the air and said: 'Yes!'

Dad put a finger to his lips then went on speaking into the phone. 'Steve will be with me. We'll be there in fifteen or twenty minutes, if that's all right . . . Thanks again.' He hung up.

Steve ran up to his room and came back with his passport.

Jeannie had the disks in a small plastic box. She handed them to Steve. 'Put the one marked No. 1 in the disk drive and the instructions will come up on the screen.'

He looked at his father. 'Ready?'

'Let's go.'

'Good luck,' Jeannie said.

They got in the Lincoln Mark VIII and drove to the

Pentagon. They parked in the biggest parking lot in the world. In the Midwest there were *towns* smaller than the Pentagon parking lot. They went up a flight of steps to a second-floor entrance.

When he was thirteen Steve had been taken on a visitor's tour of the place by a tall young man with an impossibly short haircut. The building consisted of five concentric rings linked by ten corridors like the spokes of a wheel. There were five floors and no elevators. He had lost his sense of direction within seconds. The main thing he remembered was that in the middle of the central courtyard was a building called Ground Zero which was a hotdog stand.

Now his father led the way past a closed barber shop, a restaurant and a Metro entrance to a security checkpoint. Steve showed his passport and was signed in as a visitor and given a pass to stick to his shirt front.

There were relatively few people here on a Saturday evening, and the corridors were deserted but for a few late workers, mostly in uniform, and one or two of the golf carts used for transporting bulky objects and VIPs. Last time he was here Steve had been reassured by the monolithic might of the building: it was all there to protect him. Now he felt differently. Somewhere in this maze of rings and corridors a plot had been hatched, the plot that had created him and his doppelgängers. This bureaucratic haystack existed to hide the truth he sought, and the men and women in crisp army, navy and air force uniforms were now his foes.

They went along a corridor, up a staircase and around a ring to another security point. This one took longer. Steve's full name and address had to be keyed in and they waited a minute or two for the computer to clear him. For the first time in his life he felt that a security check was aimed at him, he was the one they were looking for. He felt furtive and guilty, although he had done nothing wrong. It was a weird sensation. Criminals must feel like this all the time, he thought. And spies, and smugglers, and unfaithful husbands.

They passed on, turned several more corners and came to a pair of glass doors. Beyond the doors, a dozen or so young soldiers were sitting in front of computer screens, keying in data, or feeding paper documents into optical character recognition machines. A guard outside the door checked Steve's passport yet again, then let them in.

The room was carpeted and quiet, windowless and softly lit, with the characterless atmosphere of purified air. The operation was being run by a colonel, a grey-haired man with a pencil-line moustache. He did not know Steve's father but he was expecting them. His tone was brisk as he directed them to the terminal they would use: perhaps he regarded their visit as a nuisance.

Dad told him: 'We need to search the medical records of babies born in military hospitals around twenty-two years ago.'

'Those records are not held here.'

Steve's heart sank. Surely they could not be defeated that easily?

'Where are they held?'

'In St Louis.'

'Can't you access them from here?'

'You need priority clearance to use the data link. You don't have that.'

'I didn't anticipate this problem, Colonel,' Dad said testily. 'Do you want me to call General Krohner again? He may not thank us for bothering him unnecessarily on a Saturday night, but I will if you insist.'

The colonel weighed a minor breach of rules against the risk of irritating a general. 'I guess that'll be okay. The line isn't being used, and we need to test it sometime this weekend.'

'Thank you.'

The colonel called over a woman in lieutenant's uniform and introduced her as Caroline Gambol. She was about fifty, overweight and corseted, with the manner of a headmistress. Dad repeated what he had told the colonel.

Lieutenant Gambol said: 'Are you aware that those records are governed by the Privacy Act, sir?'

'Yes, and we have authorization.'

She sat at the terminal and touched the keyboard. After a few minutes she said: 'What kind of search do you want to run?'

'We have our own search program.'

'Yes, sir. I'll be glad to load that for you.'

Dad looked at Steve. Steve shrugged and handed the woman the floppy disks.

As she was loading the program she looked curiously at Steve. 'Who wrote this software?'

'A professor at Jones Falls.'

'It's very clever,' she said. 'I've never seen anything quite like it.' She looked at the colonel, who was watching over her shoulder. 'Have you, sir?'

He shook his head.

'It's loaded. Shall I run the search?'

'Go ahead.'

Lieutenant Gambol pressed Enter.

CHAPTER FORTY-NINE

A HUNCH MADE Berrington follow Colonel Logan's black Lincoln Mark VIII when it emerged from the driveway of the Georgetown house. He was not sure whether Jeannie was in the car: he could see only the colonel and Steve in the front, but it was a coupé, and she might have been in the back.

He was glad to have something to do. The combination of inactivity and pressing anxiety was wearying. His back ached and his legs were stiff. He wished he could give it all up and go. He might be sitting in a restaurant with a good bottle of wine, or at home listening to a CD of Mahler's Ninth Symphony, or undressing Pippa Harpenden. But then he thought of the rewards that the takeover would bring. First there would be the money: sixty million dollars was his share. Then the chance of political power, with Jim Proust in the White House and himself as surgeon-general. Finally, if they succeeded, a new and different America for the twenty-first century, America as it used to be, strong and brave and pure. And so he gritted his teeth and persisted with this grubby exercise in snooping.

For a while he found it relatively easy to track Logan through the slow-moving Washington traffic. He stayed two cars behind, like in the gumshoe movies. The Mark VIII was elegant, he thought idly. Maybe he should trade in his Town Car. The sedan had presence, but it was middle-aged: the coupé was more dashing. He wondered how much he would get trading in the Town Car. Then he remembered that by Monday night he would be rich. He could buy a Ferrari, if he wanted to look dashing.

Then the Mark VIII went through a light and around a corner, the light turned red, the car in front of Berrington stopped, and he lost sight of Logan's car. He cursed and leaned on his horn. He had been wool-gathering. He shook his head to clear it. The tedium of surveillance was sapping his concentration. When the light turned green again he screeched around the corner and accelerated hard.

A few moments later he saw the black coupé waiting at a light, and he breathed easier.

They drove around the Lincoln Memorial then crossed the Potomac by Arlington Bridge. Were they heading for National Airport? They took Washington Boulevard, and Berrington realized their destination must be the Pentagon.

He followed them down the off-ramp into the Pentagon's immense parking lot. He found a slot in the next lane, turned off his engine, and watched. Steve and his father got out of the car and headed for the building.

He checked the Mark VIII. There was no one left inside. Jeannie must have stayed behind at the house in Georgetown. What were Steve and his father up to? And Jeannie?

He walked twenty or thirty yards behind them. He hated this. He dreaded being spotted. What would he say if they confronted him? It would be unbearably humiliating.

Thankfully, neither of them looked back. They went up a flight of steps and entered the building. He stayed with them until they passed through a security barrier and he had to turn back.

He found a pay phone and called Jim Proust. 'I'm at the Pentagon. I followed Jeannie to the Logan house, then trailed Steve Logan and his father here. I'm worried, Jim.'

'The colonel works at the Pentagon, doesn't he?'

'Yeah.'

'It could be innocent.'

'But why would he go to his office on a Saturday evening?'

'For a poker game in the general's office, if I remember my army days.'

'You don't take your kid to a poker game, no matter what age he is.'

'What's at the Pentagon that could harm us?'

'Records.'

'No,' Jim said. 'The army has no record of what we did. I'm sure of that.'

'We have to know what they're doing. Isn't there some way you can find out?'

'I guess. If I don't have friends at the Pentagon, I don't have them anywhere. I'll make some calls. Stay in touch.'

Berrington hung up and stood staring at the phone.

The frustration was maddening. Everything he had worked for all his life was imperilled, and what was he doing? Following people around like a grubby private eye. But there was nothing else he *could* do. Seething with helpless impatience, he turned around and went back to his car to wait.

CHAPTER FIFTY

STEVE WAITED in a fever of anticipation. If this worked, it would tell him who raped Lisa Hoxton, and then he would have a chance of proving his innocence. But what if it went wrong? The search might not work, or medical records might have been lost or wiped from the database. Computers were always giving you dumb messages: *Not found* or *Out of memory* or *General protection fault.*

The terminal made a doorbell sound. Steve looked at the screen. The search had finished. On the screen was a list of names and addresses in pairs. Jeannie's program had worked. But were the clones on the list?

He controlled his eagerness. The first priority was to make a copy of the list.

He found a box of new diskettes in a drawer and slid one into the disk drive. He copied the list onto the disk, ejected it and slid it into the back pocket of his jeans.

Only then did he begin to study the names.

He did not recognize any of them. He scrolled down: there seemed to be several pages. It would be easier to scan a piece of paper. He called Lieutenant Gambol. 'Can I print from this terminal?'

'Sure,' she said. 'You can use that laser printer.' She came over and showed him how.

Steve stood over the laser printer, watching avidly as the pages came out. He was hoping to see his own name listed alongside three others: Dennis Pinker, Wayne Stattner, and the man who raped Lisa Hoxton. His father watched over his shoulder.

The first page contained only pairs, no groups of three or four.

The name *Steven Logan* appeared halfway down the second page. Dad spotted it at the same time. 'There you are,' he said with suppressed excitement.

But there was something wrong. There were too many names grouped together. Along with *Steven Logan, Dennis Pinker* and *Wayne Stattner* were *Henry Irwin King, Per Ericson, Murray Claud, Harvey John Jones* and *George Dassault.* Steve's elation turned to bafflement.

Dad frowned. 'Who are they all?'

Steve counted. 'There are eight names.'

'Eight?' Dad said. 'Eight?'

Then Steve saw it. 'That's how many Threeplex made,' he said. 'Eight of us.'

'Eight clones!' Dad said in amazement. 'What the hell did they think they were doing?'

'I wonder how the search found them,' Steve said. He looked at the last sheet out of the printer. At the foot it said *Common characteristic: Electrocardiogram.*

'That's right, I remember,' Dad said. 'You had an electrocardiogram when you were a week old, I never knew why.'

'We all did. And identical twins have similar hearts.'

'I still can't believe it,' Dad said. 'There are eight boys in the world exactly like you.'

'Look at these addresses,' Steve said. 'All army bases.'

'Most of those people won't be at the same address now. Doesn't the program pull out any other information?'

'No. That's how come it doesn't invade people's privacy.'

'So how does she track them down?'

'I asked her that. At the university they have every phone book on CD-ROM. If that fails they use driving licence registries, credit reference agencies and other sources.'

'The heck with privacy,' Dad said. 'I'm going to pull these people's full medical histories, see if we get any clues.'

'I could use a cup of coffee,' Steve said. 'Is there any around?'

'No beverages are allowed in the Data Center. Spilled liquids play havoc with computers. There's a little rest area with a coffee maker and a Coke machine around the corner.'

'I'll be right back.' He left the Data Center with a nod to the guard at the door. The rest area had a couple of tables and a few chairs, and machines selling soda and candy. He ate two Snickers bars and drank a cup of coffee then headed back to the Data Center.

He stopped outside the glass doors. Several new people were inside, including a general and two armed military policemen. The general was arguing with Dad, and the colonel with the pencil-line moustache seemed to be speaking at the same time. Their body language made Steve wary. Something bad was happening. He stepped into the room and stood by the door. Instinct told him not to draw attention to himself.

He heard the general say: 'I have my orders, Colonel Logan, and you're under arrest.'

Steve went cold.

How had this happened? It was not just that they had discovered Dad was peeking at people's medical records. That might be a serious matter but it was hardly an arresting offence. There was more to this. Somehow Threeplex had arranged it.

What should he do?

Dad was saying angrily: 'You don't have the right!'

The general shouted back at him: 'Don't lecture me about my goddamn *rights*, Colonel.'

There was no point in Steve joining in the argument. He had the floppy disk with the list of names right in his pocket. Dad was in trouble, but he could look after himself. Steve should just get out of there with the information.

He turned and went out through the glass doors.

He walked briskly, trying to look as if he knew where he was going. He felt like a fugitive. He struggled to remember how he had got here through the maze. He turned a couple of corners and walked through a security checkpoint.

'Just a minute, sir!' the guard said.

Steve stopped and turned, heart racing. 'Yes?' he said, trying to sound like a busy person impatient to get on with his work.

'I need to log you out on the computer. May I see your identification?'

'Of course.' Steve handed over his passport.

The guard checked his picture then keyed his name into the computer. 'Thank you, sir,' he said, handing back the passport.

Steve walked away along the corridor. One more checkpoint and he was out.

Behind him he heard the voice of Caroline Gambol. 'Mr Logan! One moment, please!'

He glanced back over his shoulder. She was running along the corridor behind him, red-faced and puffing.

'Oh, shit,' he said.

He darted around a corner and found a staircase. He ran down the steps to the next floor. He had the names that could clear him of the rape charge: he was not going to let anyone stop him getting out of here with the information, not even the US Army.

To leave the building he needed to get to ring E, the outermost. He hurried along a spoke corridor, passing ring C. A golf cart loaded with cleaning materials went by in the opposite direction. When he was halfway to ring D he heard Lieutenant Gambol's voice again. 'Mr Logan!' She was still following him. She shouted down the long, wide corridor. 'The general wishes to speak with you!' A man in air force uniform glanced curiously through an office door. Fortunately there were relatively few people around on a Saturday evening. Steve found a staircase and went up. That ought to slow the podgy lieutenant.

On the next floor he hurried along the corridor to

ring D, followed the ring around two corners, then went down again. There was no further sign of Lieutenant Gambol. He had shaken her off, he thought with relief.

He was pretty sure he was on the exit level. He went clockwise around ring D to the next corridor. It looked familiar: this was the way he had come in. He followed the corridor outwards and came to the security checkpoint where he had entered. He was almost free.

Then he saw Lieutenant Gambol.

She was standing at the checkpoint with the guard, flushed and breathless.

Steve cursed. He had not shaken her off after all. She had simply got to the exit ahead of him.

He decided to brazen it out.

He walked up to the guard and took off his visitor's badge.

'You can keep that on,' Lieutenant Gambol said. 'The general would like to speak with you.'

Steve put the badge down on the counter. Masking his fear with a show of confidence, he said: 'I'm afraid I don't have time. Goodbye, Lieutenant, and thank you for your cooperation.'

'I must insist,' she said.

Steve pretended to be impatient. 'You're not in a position to insist,' he said. 'I'm a civilian: you can't command me. I've done nothing wrong, so you can't arrest me. I'm not carrying any military property, as you can see.' He hoped the floppy disk in his back pocket was not visible. 'It would be illegal of you to attempt to detain me.'

She spoke to the guard, a man of about thirty who was three or four inches shorter than Steve. 'Don't let him leave,' she said.

Steve smiled at the guard. 'If you touch me, soldier, it will be assault. I'll be justified in punching you out, and believe me, I'll do it.'

Lieutenant Gambol looked around for reinforcements, but the only people in sight were two cleaners and an electrician working on a light fitting.

Steve walked toward the entrance.

Lieutenant Gambol cried: 'Stop him!'

Behind him he heard the guard shout: 'Stop, or I'll shoot!'

Steve turned. The guard had drawn a pistol and was pointing it at him.

The cleaners and the electrician froze, watching.

The guard's hands were shaking as he pointed the gun at Steve.

Steve felt his muscles seize up as he stared down the barrel. With an effort he shook off his paralysis. A Pentagon guard would not fire at an unarmed civilian, he was sure. 'You won't shoot me,' he said. 'It would be murder.'

He turned and walked to the door.

It was the longest walk of his life. The distance was only three or four yards but it felt as if it took years. The skin of his back seemed to burn with anticipation.

As he put his hand on the door, a shot rang out.

Someone screamed.

The thought flashed through Steve's mind, *He fired over my head*, but he did not look back. He flew through the door and ran down the long flight of steps. Night had fallen while he was inside, and the parking lot was lit by street lamps. He heard shouting behind him, then another shot. He reached the bottom of the stairway and veered off the footpath into the bushes.

He emerged onto a road and kept running. He came to a row of bus stops. He slowed to a walk. A bus was pulling up at one of the stops. Two soldiers got off and a woman civilian got on. Steve boarded right behind her.

The bus pulled away.

The bus drove out of the parking lot and onto the expressway, leaving the Pentagon behind.

CHAPTER FIFTY-ONE

In a couple of hours Jeannie had come to like Lorraine Logan enormously.

She was much heavier than she seemed in the photograph that appeared at the top of her lonely-hearts column in the newspapers. She smiled a lot, causing her chubby face to crease up. To take Jeannie's mind and her own off their worries, she talked of the problems people wrote to her about: domineering in-laws, violent husbands, impotent boyfriends, bosses with wandering hands, daughters who took drugs. Whatever the subject, Lorraine managed to say something that made Jeannie think, *Of course—how come I never saw it that way before?*

They sat on the patio as the day cooled, waiting anxiously for Steve and his father to return. Jeannie told Lorraine about the rape of Lisa. 'She'll try for as long as she can to act as if it never happened,' Lorraine said.

'Yes, that's exactly how she is now.'

'That phase can last six months. But sooner or later she'll realize she has to stop denying what happened and come to terms with it. That stage often begins when the woman tries to resume normal sex and finds she doesn't feel the way she used to. That's when they write to me.'

'What do you advise?'

'Counselling. There isn't an easy solution. Rape damages a woman's soul, and it has to be mended.'

'The detective recommended counselling.'

Lorraine raised her eyebrows. 'He's a pretty smart cop.'

Jeannie smiled. 'She.'

Lorraine laughed. 'We reprove men for making sexist assumptions. I beg you, don't tell anyone what I just did.'

'I promise.'

There was a short silence, then Lorraine said: 'Steve loves you.'

Jeannie nodded. 'Yeah, I think he really does.'

'A mother can tell.'

'So he's been in love before.'

'You don't miss a trick, do you?' Lorraine smiled. 'Yes, he has. But only once.'

'Tell me about her—if you think he wouldn't mind.'

'Okay. Her name was Fanny Gallaher. She had green eyes and wavy dark-red hair. She was vivacious and careless and she was the only girl in high school who *wasn't* interested in Steve. He pursued her, and she resisted him, for months. But he won her in the end, and they dated for about a year.'

'Do you think they slept together?'

'I know they did. They used to spend nights together here. I don't believe in forcing kids to make out in parking lots.'

'What about her parents?'

'I talked to Fanny's mother. She felt the same way about it.'

'I lost my virginity in the alley behind a punk rock club at the age of fourteen. It was such a depressing experience that I didn't have sexual intercourse again until I was twenty-one. I wish my mother had been more like you.'

'I don't think it really matters whether parents are strict or lenient, as long as they're consistent. Kids can live with more or less any set of rules so long as they know what they are. It's arbitrary tyranny that gets them mixed up.'

'Why did Steve and Fanny break up?'

'He had a problem . . . He should probably tell you about it himself.'

'Are you talking about the fight with Tip Hendricks?'

Lorraine raised her eyebrows. 'He told you! My goodness, he *really* trusts you.'

They heard a car outside. Lorraine got up and went to the corner of the house to look out into the street. 'Steve's come home in a taxicab,' she said in a puzzled tone.

Jeannie stood up. 'How does he look?'

Before Lorraine could answer, he appeared on the patio. 'Where's your father?' she asked him.

'Dad got arrested.'

Jeannie said: 'Oh, God. Why?'

'I'm not sure. I think the Threeplex people somehow found out, or guessed, what we were up to, and pulled some strings. They sent two military police to grab him. But I got away.'

Lorraine said suspiciously: 'Stevie, there's something you aren't telling me.'

'A guard fired two shots.'

Lorraine gave a small scream.

'I think he was aiming over my head. Anyway, I'm fine.'

Jeannie's mouth went dry. The thought of bullets being fired at Steve horrified her. He might have died!

'The sweep worked, though.' Steve took a diskette from his back pocket. 'Here's the list. And wait till you hear what's on it.'

Jeannie swallowed hard. 'What?'

'There aren't four clones.'

'How come?'

'There are eight.'

Jeannie's jaw dropped. 'Eight of you?'

'We found eight identical electrocardiograms.'

Threeplex had split the embryo seven times, and implanted eight unknowing women with the children of strangers. The arrogance was unbelievable.

But Jeannie's suspicion had been proved. This was what Berrington was so desperate to conceal. When this news was made public, Threeplex would be disgraced and Jeannie would be vindicated.

And Steve would be cleared.

'You did it!' she said. She hugged him. Then a snag occurred to her. 'But which of the eight committed the rape?'

'We'll have to find out,' Steve said. 'And that won't be easy. The addresses we have are the places where their parents lived at the time they were born. They're almost certainly out of date.'

'We can try to track them down. That's Lisa's specialty.' Jeannie stood up. 'I'd better get back to Baltimore. This is going to take most of the night.'

'I'll come with you.'

'What about your father? You have to get him out of the hands of the military police.'

Lorraine said: 'You're needed here, Steve. I'm going to call our lawyer right now—I have his home number—but you'll have to tell him what happened.'

'All right,' he said reluctantly.

'I should call Lisa before I leave, so she can get ready,' Jeannie said. The phone was on the patio table. 'May I?'

'Of course.'

She dialled Lisa's number. The phone rang four times, then there was the characteristic pause of an answering machine kicking in. 'Damn,' Jeannie said as she listened to Lisa's message. When it finished she said: 'Lisa, please call me. I'm leaving Washington now, I'll be home around ten. Something really important has happened.' She hung up.

Steve said: 'I'll walk you to your car.'

She said goodbye to Lorraine, who hugged her warmly.

Outside, Steve handed her the diskette. 'Take care of that,' he said. 'There's no copy, and we won't get another chance.'

She put it in her bag. 'Don't worry. It's my future, too.' She kissed him hard.

'Oh boy,' he said after a while. 'Could we do a lot of this, quite soon?'

'Yes. But don't endanger yourself meanwhile. I don't want to lose you. Be careful.'

He smiled. 'I love it that you're worried about me. It's almost worth it.'

She kissed him again, softly this time. 'I'll call you.'

She got in the car and pulled away.

She drove fast and got home in under an hour.

She was disappointed to find there was no message from Lisa on her machine. She worried that maybe Lisa was asleep, or watching TV and not listening to her messages. *Don't panic, think.* She ran out again and drove to Lisa's place, an apartment building in Charles Village. She rang the entry phone at the street door but there was no answer. Where the hell had Lisa gone? She did not have a boyfriend to take her out on a Saturday night. *Please God she hasn't gone to see her mother in Pittsburgh.*

Lisa lived in 12B. Jeannie rang the bell of 12A. Again there was no reply. Maybe the damn system was not working. Seething with frustration, she tried 12C.

A grouchy male voice said: 'Yeah, who is it?'

'I'm sorry to trouble you, but I'm a friend of Lisa Hoxton next door to you and I need to reach her really urgently. Would you happen to know where she is?'

The voice replied: 'Where do you think you are, lady—Hicksville, USA? I don't even know what my neighbour *looks* like.' *Click.*

'Where are you from, New York?' she said angrily to the unheeding loudspeaker.

She went home, driving as if she were in a race, and called Lisa's answering machine again. 'Lisa, please call me *the second* you get in, *no matter what time of night.* I'll be waiting by the phone.'

After that there was no more she could do. Without Lisa she could not even get into Nut House.

She took a shower and wrapped herself in her pink bathrobe. She felt hungry and microwaved a frozen cinnamon bun, but eating nauseated her, so she threw it away and drank coffee with milk in it. She wished she had a TV to distract her.

She got out the picture Charles had given her of Steve. She would have to get a frame for it. She stuck it to the refrigerator door with a fridge magnet.

That started her looking at her photograph albums. She smiled to see Daddy in a brown chalk-stripe suit with broad lapels and flared pants, standing beside the turquoise Thunderbird. There were several pages of Jeannie in tennis whites, triumphantly holding a series of silver cups and shields. Here was Mom pushing Patty in an old-fashioned stroller, there was Will Temple in a cowboy hat, cutting up and making Jeannie laugh—

The phone rang.

She leaped up, dropping the album on the floor, and snatched up the handset. 'Lisa?'

'Hi, Jeannie, what's the big emergency?'

She collapsed on the couch, weak with gratitude. 'Thank God! I called you hours ago, where have you been?'

'I went to a movie with Catherine and Bill. Is that a crime?'

'I'm sorry, I have no right to cross-examine you—'

'It's okay. I'm your friend. You can get ratty with me. I'll do it to you one day.'

Jeannie laughed. 'Thanks. Listen, I have a list of five names of people who might be Steve's double.' She was deliberately understating the case: the truth was too hard to swallow in one lump. 'I need to track them down tonight. Will you help me?'

There was a pause. 'Jeannie, I almost got into serious trouble when I tried to get into your room. I could have got myself and the security guard fired. I want to help you, but I need this job.'

Jeannie felt coldly fearful. *No, you can't let me down, not when I'm this close.* 'Please.'

'I'm scared.'

Fear was replaced by fierce determination. *Hell, I'm not going to let you get away with this.* 'Lisa, it's almost Sunday.' *I don't like doing this to you, but I have to.* 'A week ago I walked into a burning building to look for you.'

'I know, I know.'

'I was scared then.'

There was a long silence. 'You're right,' Lisa said at last. 'Okay, I'll do it.'

Jeannie suppressed a victory whoop. 'How soon can you get there?'

'Fifteen minutes.'

'I'll meet you outside.'

Jeannie hung up. She ran into the bedroom,

dropped her robe on the floor, and pulled on black jeans and a turquoise T-shirt. She threw on a black Levi jacket and ran downstairs.

She left the house at midnight.

SUNDAY

CHAPTER FIFTY-TWO

SHE REACHED the university before Lisa. She parked in the visitors' lot, not wanting her distinctive car to be seen outside Nut House, then walked across the dark, deserted campus. While she waited impatiently outside the front of the building she wished she had stopped off to buy something to eat. She had had nothing all day. She thought wistfully of a cheeseburger with French fries, a slice of pizza with pepperoni, apple pie with vanilla ice cream, or even a big garlicky Caesar salad. At last Lisa drove up in her smart white Honda.

She got out of the car and took Jeannie by the hands. 'I feel ashamed,' she said. 'You shouldn't have had to remind me what a friend you've been to me.'

'I understand, though,' Jeannie said.

'I'm sorry.'

Jeannie hugged her.

They went inside and turned on the lights in the lab. Jeannie started the coffee machine while Lisa booted up her computer. It felt weird to be in the lab in the middle of the night. The antiseptic white decor, the bright lights, and the silent machines all around made her think of a morgue.

She thought they would probably get a visit from security sooner or later. After Jeannie's break-in they would be keeping an eye on Nut House, and they would see the lights. But it was not unusual for scientists to work odd hours in the lab, and there would be no trouble, unless a guard happened to recognize Jeannie from last night. 'If a security guard comes to check on us, I'm going to hide in the stationery cupboard,' she said to Lisa. 'Just in case the guard is someone who knows I'm not supposed to be here.'

'I hope we get enough warning of his approach,' Lisa said nervously.

'We should arrange some kind of alarm.' Jeannie was eager to get on with searching for the clones, but she contained her impatience: this would be a sensible precaution. She looked around the lab thoughtfully, and her eye fell upon a small flower arrangement on Lisa's desk. 'How much do you love that glass vase?' she said.

Lisa shrugged. 'I got it in Kmart. I can get another.'

Jeannie dumped the flowers and emptied the water into a sink. She took from a shelf a copy of *Identical Twins Reared Apart* by Susan L. Farber. She went to the end of the corridor where a pair of swing doors gave on to the staircase. She pulled the doors a little inwards and used the book to wedge them there, then she balanced the vase on the top edge of the doors, straddling the gap. There was no way anyone could come in without causing the vase to fall and smash.

Watching her, Lisa said: 'What'll I say if they ask me why I did that?'

'You didn't want anyone to sneak up on you,' Jeannie replied.

Lisa nodded, satisfied. 'God knows I have reason enough to be paranoid.'

'Let's get going,' Jeannie said.

They went back into the lab, leaving the door open to be sure they would hear the glass breaking. Jeannie put her precious floppy disk into Lisa's computer and printed the Pentagon results. There were the names of the eight babies whose electrocardiograms were as similar as if they had all come from one person. Eight tiny hearts beating exactly the same way. Somehow Berrington had arranged for the army hospitals to give these babies this test. No doubt copies had been sent to the Aventine Clinic, where they had remained until they were shredded on Thursday. But Berrington had forgotten, or perhaps never realized, that the army would keep the original graphs.

'Let's start with Henry King,' she suggested. 'Full name Henry Irwin King.'

On her desk Lisa had two CD-ROM drives, one on top of the other. She took two CDs from her desk drawer and put one in each drive. 'We have every residential phone in the United States on those two discs,' she said. 'And we have software that enables us to search both discs at the same time.'

A Windows screen appeared on the monitor. 'People don't always put their full name in the phone book, unfortunately,' she said. 'Let's just see how many H. Kings there are in the USA.' She typed

H* King

and clicked on *Count.* After a moment a *Count* window appeared with the number 1,129.

Jeannie was discouraged. 'It will take all night to call that many numbers!'

'Wait, we may be able to do better.' Lisa typed

Henry I. King OR Henry Irwin King

and clicked on the *Retrieve* icon, a picture of a dog. After a moment a list appeared on the screen. 'We have three Henry Irwin Kings and seventeen Henry I. Kings. What's his last known address?'

Jeannie consulted her printout. 'Fort Devens, Massachusetts.'

'Okay, we have one Henry Irwin King in Amherst and four Henry I. Kings in Boston.'

'Let's call them.'

'You do realize it's one o'clock in the morning.'

'I can't wait until tomorrow.'

'People won't talk to you at this time of night.'

'Sure they will,' Jeannie said. It was bravado. She knew she would have trouble. She just was not prepared to wait until morning. This was too important. 'I'll say I'm from the police, tracking down a serial killer.'

'That has to be against the law.'

'Give me the Amherst number.'

Lisa highlighted the listing and pressed F2. There was a rapid series of beeps from the computer's modem. Jeannie picked up the phone.

She heard seven rings, then a sleepy voice answered: 'Yes?'

'This is Detective Susan Farber of the Amherst Police Department,' she said. She half-expected him to say, *The hell it is,* but he made no response, and she went on briskly: 'We're sorry to call you in the middle of the night but it's an urgent police matter. Am I speaking to Henry Irwin King?'

'Yes—what's happened?'

It sounded like the voice of a middle-aged man, but Jeannie persisted just to be sure. 'This is just a routine inquiry.'

That was a mistake. 'Routine?' he said tetchily. 'At this time of night?'

Improvising hastily, she said: 'We're investigating a serious crime and we need to eliminate you as a suspect, sir. Could you tell me your date and place of birth?'

'I was born in Greenfield, Massachusetts, on the fourth of May, nineteen forty-five. Okay?'

'You don't have a son of the same name, do you?'

'No, I have three daughters. Can I go back to sleep now?'

'We don't need to trouble you any further. Thank you for cooperating with the police, and have a good night's rest.' She hung up and looked triumphantly at Lisa. 'See? He talked to me. He didn't like it, but he talked.'

Lisa laughed. 'Dr Ferrami, you have a talent to deceive.'

Jeannie grinned. 'All it takes is chutzpah. Let's do

the Henry I. Kings. I'll call the first two, you take the last two.'

Only one of them could use the automatic dialling feature. Jeannie found a scratch pad and a ballpoint and scribbled the two numbers, then she picked up a phone and dialled manually. A male voice answered and she went into her spiel. 'This is Detective Susan Farber of the Boston city police—'

'What the fuck are you doing calling me at this time of night?' the man burst out. 'Do you know who I am?'

'I assume you're Henry King—'

'Assume you just lost your fucking job, you dumb cunt,' he raged. 'Susan who did you say?'

'I just need to check on your date of birth, Mr King—'

'Put me on to your lieutenant right away.'

'Mr King—'

'Do as I say!'

'Goddamn gorilla,' Jeannie said, and she hung up. She felt quite shaky. 'I hope it's not going to be a night of conversations like that.'

Lisa had already hung up. 'Mine was Jamaican, and had the accent to prove it,' she said. 'I gather yours was unpleasant.'

'Very.'

'We could stop now, and carry on in the morning.'

Jeannie was not going to be defeated by one rude man. 'Hell, no,' she said. 'I can take a little verbal abuse.'

'Whatever you say.'

'He sounded a lot older than twenty-two, so we can forget him. Let's try the other two.'

Bracing herself, she dialled again.

Her third Henry King had not yet gone to bed: there was music in the background and other voices in the room. 'Yeah, who's this?' he said.

He sounded about the right age, and Jeannie felt hopeful. She did her impersonation of a cop again, but he was suspicious. 'How do I know you're the police?'

He sounded just like Steve, and Jeannie's heart missed a beat. This could be one of the clones. But how should she deal with his suspicions? She decided to brazen it out. 'Would you like to call me back here at police headquarters?' she offered recklessly.

There was a pause. 'No, forget it,' he said.

Jeannie breathed again.

'I'm Henry King,' he said. 'They call me Hank. What do you want?'

'Could I first check your date and place of birth?'

'I was born in Fort Devens exactly twenty-two years ago. It's my birthday, as a matter of fact, well it was yesterday, Saturday.'

It was him! Jeannie had found one clone already. Next she had to establish whether he was in Baltimore last Sunday. She tried to keep the excitement out of her voice as she said: 'Could you tell me when you last travelled outside the state?'

'Let me see, that was August, I went to New York.'

Jeannie's instincts said he was telling the truth, but

she continued to question him. 'What were you doing last Sunday?'

'I was working.'

'What work do you do?'

'Well, I'm a graduate student at MIT, but I have a Sunday job tending bar at the Blue Note Café in Cambridge.'

Jeannie scribbled a note. 'And that's where you were last Sunday?'

'Yep. Served at least a hundred people.'

'Thank you, Mr King.' If this was true, he was not the one who had raped Lisa. 'Would you just give me that phone number so I can confirm your alibi?'

'I don't recall the number, but it's in the book. What am I supposed to have done?'

'We're investigating a case of arson.'

'I'm glad I have an alibi.'

She found it unnerving to hear Steve's voice and know she was listening to a stranger. She wished she could see Henry King, to check the visual resemblance. Reluctantly she drew the conversation to a close. 'Thank you again, sir. Good night.' She hung up and blew out her cheeks, drained by the effort of deception. 'Whew!'

Lisa had been listening. 'You found him?'

'Yes, he was born in Fort Devens and he's twenty-two today. He's the Henry King we're looking for, sure enough.'

'Good work!'

'But he seems to have an alibi. He says he was working at a bar in Cambridge.' She looked at her scratch pad. 'The Blue Note.'

'Shall we check it out?' Lisa's hunting instinct had been aroused and she was keen.

Jeannie nodded. 'It's late, but I guess a bar should still be open, especially on a Saturday night. Can you get the number from your CD-ROM?'

'We only have residential numbers. Business listings are another set of discs.'

Jeannie called information, got the number and dialled it. The phone was answered right away.

'This is Detective Susan Farber of the Boston police. Let me speak to the manager, please.'

'This is the manager, what's wrong?' The man had a Hispanic accent and he sounded worried.

'Do you have an employee named Henry King?'

'Hank, yeah, what he do now?'

It sounded as if Henry King had been in trouble with the law before. 'Maybe nothing. When did you last see him?'

'Today, I mean yesterday, Saturday, he was working the day shift.'

'And before that?'

'Lemme see, last Sunday, he worked the four-to-midnight.'

'Would you swear to that if necessary, sir?'

'Sure, why not? Whoever got killed, Hank didn't do it.'

'Thank you for your cooperation, sir.'

'Hey, no problem.' The manager seemed relieved that was all she wanted. If I were a real cop, Jeannie thought, I'd guess he had a guilty conscience. 'Call me any time.' He hung up.

Jeannie said disappointedly: 'Alibi stands up.'

'Don't be downhearted,' Lisa said. 'We've done very well to eliminate him so quickly—especially as it's such a common name. Let's try Per Ericson. There won't be so many of them.'

The Pentagon list said Per Ericson had been born in Fort Rucker, but twenty-two years later there were no Per Ericsons in Alabama. Lisa tried

P* Erics?on

in case it should be spelled with a double *s*, then she tried

P* Erics$n

to include the spellings *Ericsen* and *Ericsan*, but the computer found nothing.

'Try Philadelphia,' Jeannie suggested. 'That's where he attacked me.'

There were three in Philadelphia. The first turned out to be a Peder, the second was a frail elderly voice on an answering machine, and the third was a woman, Petra. Jeannie and Lisa began to work their way through all the P. Ericsons in the USA, thirty-three listings.

Lisa's second P. Ericson was bad-tempered and abusive, and she was white faced as she hung up the phone, but she drank a cup of coffee then carried on determinedly.

Each call was a small drama. Jeannie had to summon up the nerve to pretend to be a cop. It was agony wondering if the voice answering the phone would be the man who had said, *Now give me a hand job, otherwise I'll beat the shit out of you.* Then there was the strain of maintaining her impersonation of a police detective against the scepticism or rudeness of the people who answered the phone. And most calls ended in disappointment.

As Jeannie was hanging up from her sixth fruitless call, she heard Lisa say: 'Oh, I'm terribly sorry. Our information must be out of date. Please forgive this intrusion, Mrs Ericson. Goodbye.' She hung up, looking crushed. 'He's the one, all right,' she said solemnly. 'But he died last winter. That was his mother. She burst into tears when I asked for him.'

She wondered momentarily what Per Ericson had been like. Was he a psychopath, like Dennis, or was he like Steve? 'How did he die?'

'He was a ski champion, apparently, and he broke his neck trying something risky.'

A daredevil, without fear. 'That sounds like our man.'

It had not occurred to Jeannie that not all eight might be alive. Now she realized that there must have been more than eight implants. Even nowadays, when the technique was well established, many implants failed to 'take'. And it was also likely that some of the mothers had miscarried. Threeplex might have experimented on fifteen or twenty women, or even more.

'It's hard making these calls,' Lisa said.

'Do you want to take a break?'

'No.' Lisa shook herself. 'We're doing well. We've

eliminated two of the five and it's not yet three a.m. Who's next?'

'George Dassault.'

Jeannie was beginning to believe they would find the rapist, but they were not so lucky with the next name. There were only seven George Dassaults in the USA, but three of them did not answer their phones. None had any connection with either Baltimore or Philadelphia—one was in Buffalo, one in Sacramento and one in Houston—but that did not prove anything. There was nothing they could do but move on. Lisa printed the list of phone numbers so they could try again later.

There was another snag. 'I guess there's no guarantee that the man we're after is on the CD-ROM,' Jeannie said.

'That's true. He might not have a phone. Or his number could be unlisted.'

'He could be listed under a nickname, Spike Dassault or Flip Jones.'

Lisa giggled. 'He could have become a rap singer and changed his name to Icey Creamo Creamy.'

'He could be a wrestler called Iron Billy.'

'He could be writing westerns under the name Buck Remington.'

'Or pornography as Heidi Whiplash.'

'Dick Swiftly.'

'Henrietta Pussy.'

Their laughter was abruptly cut off by the crash of breaking glass. Jeannie shot off her stool and darted into the stationery cupboard. She closed the door behind her and stood in the dark, listening.

She heard Lisa say nervously: 'Who is it?'

'Security,' came a man's voice. 'Did you put that glass there?'

'Yes.'

'May I ask why?'

'So nobody could sneak up on me. I get nervous working here late.'

'Well, I ain't gonna sweep it up. I ain't a cleaner.'

'Okay, just leave it.'

'Are you on your own, miss?'

'Yes.'

'I'll just look around.'

'Be my guest.'

Jeannie took hold of the door handle with both hands. If he tried to open it, she would prevent him.

She heard him walking around the lab. 'What kind of work are you doing, anyway?' His voice was very close.

Lisa was farther away. 'I'd love to talk, but I just don't have time, I'm really busy.'

If she wasn't busy, buster, she wouldn't be here in the middle of the goddamn night, so why don't you just butt out and leave her be?

'Okay, no problem.' His voice was right outside the door. 'What's in here?'

Jeannie grasped the handle firmly and pulled upwards, ready to resist pressure.

'That's where we keep the radioactive virus chromosomes,' Lisa said. 'It's probably quite safe though, you can go in if it's not locked.'

Jeannie suppressed a hysterical laugh. There was no such thing as a radioactive virus chromosome.

'I guess I'll skip it,' the guard said. Jeannie was about to relax her grip on the door handle when she felt sudden pressure. She pulled upwards with all her might. 'It's locked, anyway,' he said.

There was a pause. When next he spoke his voice was distant, and Jeannie relaxed. 'If you get lonely, come on over to the guardhouse. I'll make you a cup of coffee.'

'Thanks,' Lisa said.

Jeannie's tension began to ease, but she cautiously stayed where she was, waiting for the All Clear. After a couple of minutes Lisa opened the door. 'He's left the building,' she said.

They went back to the phones.

Murray Claud was another unusual name, and they tracked him down quickly. It was Jeannie who made the call. Murray Claud senior told her, in a voice full of bitterness and bewilderment, that his son had been jailed in Athens, three years ago, after a knife fight in a taverna, and would not be released until January at the earliest. 'That boy could have been anything,' he said. 'Astronaut. Nobel prizewinner. Movie star. President of the United States. He has brains, charm and good looks. And he threw it away. Just threw it all away.'

She understood the father's pain. He thought he was responsible. She was sorely tempted to tell him the truth, but she was unprepared, and anyway there was no time. She promised herself she would call him again, one day, and give him what consolation she could. Then she hung up.

They left Harvey Jones until last because they knew he would be the hardest.

Jeannie was daunted to find there were almost a million Joneses in America, and H. was a common initial. His middle name was John. He had been born at Walter Reed Hospital in Washington, DC, so Jeannie and Lisa began by calling every Harvey Jones, every H. J. Jones, and every H. Jones in the Washington phone book. They did not find one who had been born approximately twenty-two years ago at Walter Reed; but worse, they accumulated a long list of maybes: people who did not answer their phones.

Once again Jeannie began to doubt whether this would work. They had three unresolved George Dassaults and now twenty or thirty H. Joneses. Her approach was theoretically sound, but if people did not answer their phones she could not question them. Her eyes were getting bleary and she was feeling jumpy from too much coffee and no sleep.

At four a.m. she and Lisa began on the Philadelphia Joneses.

At four thirty Jeannie found him.

She thought it was going to be another maybe. The phone rang four times, then there was the characteristic pause and click of an answering machine. But the voice on the machine was eerily familiar. 'You've reached Harvey Jones's place,' the message said, and the hairs on the back of her neck stood up. It was like listening to Steve: the pitch of the voice, the diction, and the phrasing were all Steve's. 'I can't come to the phone right now, so please leave a message after the long tone.'

Jeannie hung up and checked the address. It was an apartment on Spruce Street, in University City, not far from the Aventine Clinic. She noticed her hands were shaking. It was because she wanted to get him by the throat.

'I've found him,' she said to Lisa.

'Oh, my God.'

'It's a machine, but it's his voice, and he lives in Philadelphia, near where I was attacked.'

'Let me listen.' Lisa called the number. As she heard the message her pink cheeks turned white. 'It's him,' she said. She hung up. 'I can hear him now. *Take off those pretty panties,* he said. Oh, God.'

Jeannie picked up the phone and called police headquarters.

CHAPTER FIFTY-THREE

BERRINGTON JONES did not sleep on Saturday night.

He remained in the Pentagon parking lot, watching Colonel Logan's black Lincoln Mark VIII, until midnight, when he called Proust and learned that Logan had been arrested but Steve had escaped, presumably by subway or bus as he had not taken his father's car.

'What were they doing in the Pentagon?' he asked Jim.

'They were in the Command Data Center. I'm in the process of finding out exactly what they were up to. See if you can track down the boy, or the Ferrami girl.'

Berrington no longer objected to doing surveillance. The situation was desperate. This was no time to stand on his dignity: if he failed to stop Jeannie, he would have no dignity left anyway.

When he returned to the Logan house it was dark and deserted, and Jeannie's red Mercedes had gone. He waited there for an hour but no one arrived. Assuming she had returned home, he drove back to Baltimore and cruised up and down her street, but the car was not there either.

It was getting light when at last he pulled up outside

his house in Roland Park. He went inside and called Jim, but there was no reply from his home or his office. Berrington lay on the bed in his clothes, with his eyes shut, but although he was exhausted he stayed awake, worrying.

At seven o'clock he got up and called again, but he still could not reach Jim. He took a shower, shaved, and dressed in black cotton chinos and a striped polo shirt. He squeezed a big glass of orange juice and drank it standing in the kitchen. He looked at the Sunday edition of the Baltimore *Sun* but the headlines meant nothing to him, it was as if they were written in Finnish.

Proust called at eight.

Jim had spent half the night at the Pentagon with a friend who was a general, questioning the Data Center personnel under the pretext of investigating a security breach. The general, a buddy from Jim's CIA days, knew only that Logan was trying to expose an undercover operation from the seventies and Jim wanted to prevent him.

Colonel Logan, who was still under arrest, would not say anything except *I want a lawyer.* However, the results of Jeannie's sweep were on the computer terminal Steve had been using, so Jim had been able to find out what they had discovered. 'I guess you must have ordered electrocardiograms on all the babies,' Jim said.

Berrington had forgotten, but now it came back. 'Yes, we did.'

'Logan found them.'

'All of them?'

'All eight.'

It was the worst possible news. The electrocardiograms, like those of identical twins, were as similar as if they had been taken from one person on different days. Steve and his father, and presumably Jeannie, must now know that Steve was one of eight clones.

'Hell,' Berrington said. 'We've kept this secret for twenty-two years, and now this damn girl has found it out.'

'I told you we should have made her vanish.'

Jim was at his most offensive when under pressure. After a sleepless night Berrington had no patience. 'If you say *I told you so* I'll blow your goddamn head off, I swear to God.'

'All right, all right!'

'Does Preston know?'

'Yes. He says we're finished, but he always says that.'

'This time he could be right.'

Jim's voice took on its parade-ground tone. 'You may be ready to wimp out, Berry, but I'm not,' he grated. 'All we have to do is keep the lid on this until the press conference tomorrow. If we can manage that, the takeover will go through.'

'But what happens after that?'

'After that we'll have a hundred and eighty million dollars, and that buys a lot of silence.'

Berrington wanted to believe him. 'You're such a smartass, what do you think we should do next?'

'We have to find out how much they know. No one is sure whether Steven Logan had a copy of the list of names and addresses in his pocket when he got away. The woman lieutenant in the Data Center swears he did not, but her word isn't enough for me. Now, the addresses he has are twenty-two years old. But here's my question. With just the names, can Jeannie Ferrami track them down?'

'The answer is yes,' Berrington said. 'We're experts at that in the psychology department. We have to do it all the time, track down identical twins. If she got that list last night she could have found some of them by now.'

'I was afraid of that. Is there any way we can check?'

'I guess I could call them and find out if they've heard from her.'

'You'd have to be discreet.'

'You aggravate me, Jim. Sometimes you act like you're the only guy in America with half a fucking brain. Of course I'll be discreet. I'll get back to you.' He hung up with a bang.

The names of the clones and their phone numbers, written in a simple code, were in his Wizard. He took it out of his desk drawer and turned it on.

He had kept track of them over the years. He felt more paternal towards them than either Preston or Jim. In the early days he had written occasional letters from the Aventine Clinic, asking for information under the pretext of follow-up studies on the hormone treatment. Later, when that became implausible, he had employed a variety of subterfuges, such as pretending to be a real-estate broker and calling to ask if the family was thinking of selling the house, or whether the parents were interested in buying a book that listed scholarships available to the children of former military personnel. He had watched with ever-increasing dismay as most of them progressed from bright but disobedient children to fearless delinquent teenagers to brilliant, unstable adults. They were the unlucky byproducts of a historic experiment. He had never regretted the experiment, but he felt guilty about the boys. He had cried when Per Ericson killed himself doing somersaults on a ski slope in Vail.

He looked at the list while he dreamed up a pretext for calling today. Then he picked up the phone and dialled Murray Claud's father. The phone rang and rang but no one answered. Eventually Berrington figured this was the day he went to visit his son in jail.

He called George Dassault next. This time he was luckier. The phone was answered by a familiar young voice. 'Yeah, who's this?'

Berrington said: 'This is Bell Telephone, sir, and we're checking up on fraudulent phone calls. Have you received any odd or unusual calls in the last twenty-four hours?'

'Nope, can't say I have. But I've been out of town since Friday, so I wasn't here to answer the phone anyway.'

'Thank you for cooperating with our survey, sir. Goodbye.'

Jeannie might have George's name, but she had not reached him. That was inconclusive.

Berrington tried Hank King in Boston next.

'Yeah, who's this?'

It was astonishing, Berrington reflected, that they all answered the phone in the same charmless way. There could not be a gene for phone manners. But twins research was full of such phenomena. 'This is A. T. & T.,' Berrington said. 'We're doing a survey of fraudulent phone use and we'd like to know whether you have received any strange or suspicious calls in the last twenty-four hours.'

Hank's voice was slurred. 'Jeez, I've been partying so hard I wouldn't remember.' Berrington rolled up his eyes. It was Hank's birthday yesterday, of course. He was sure to be drunk or drugged or both. 'No, wait a minute! There was something. I remember. It was the middle of the fucking night. She said she was with the Boston police.'

'She?' That could have been Jeannie, Berrington thought with a premonition of bad news.

'Yeah, it was a woman.'

'Did she give her name? That would enable us to check her bona fides.'

'Sure she did, but I can't remember. Sarah or Carol or Margaret or—Susan, that was it, Detective Susan Farber.'

That settled it. Susan Farber was the author of *Identical Twins Reared Apart*, the only book on the subject. Jeannie had used the first name that came into her head. That meant she had the list of clones. Berrington was appalled. Grimly, he pressed on with his questions. 'What did she say, sir?'

'She asked my date and place of birth.'

That would establish that she was talking to the right Henry King.

'I thought it was, like, a little weird,' Hank went on. 'Was it some kind of scam?'

Berrington invented something on the spur of the moment. 'She was prospecting for leads for an insurance company. It's illegal, but they do it. A. T. & T. is sorry you were bothered, Mr King, and we thank you for cooperating with our investigation.'

'Sure.'

Berrington hung up, feeling completely desolate. Jeannie had the names. It was only a matter of time before she tracked them all down.

Berrington was in the deepest trouble of his life.

CHAPTER FIFTY-FOUR

MISH DELAWARE refused point-blank to drive to Philadelphia and interview Harvey Jones. 'We did that yesterday, honey,' she said when Jeannie finally got her on the phone at seven thirty a.m. 'Today's my granddaughter's first birthday. I have a life, you know?'

'But you *know* I'm right!' Jeannie protested. 'I was right about Wayne Stattner—he *was* a double for Steve.'

'Except for his hair. And he had an alibi.'

'But what are you going to do?'

'I'm going to call the Philadelphia police and talk to someone on the Sex Crimes Unit there and ask them to go see him. I'll fax them the E-FIT picture. They'll check whether Harvey Jones resembles the picture and ask him if he can account for his movements last Sunday afternoon. If the answers are *Yes* and *No*, we got a suspect.'

Jeannie banged the phone down in a fury. After all she had been through! After she had stayed up all night tracking down the clones!

She sure as hell was not going to sit around waiting for the police to do something. She decided she would go to Philadelphia and check Harvey out. She would not accost him or even speak to him. But she could park outside his home and see if he came out. Failing that she could speak to his neighbours and show them the picture of Steve that Charles had given her. One way or another she would establish that he *was* Steve's double.

She got to Philadelphia around ten thirty. In University City there were smartly dressed black families congregating outside the gospel churches and idle teenagers smoking on the stoops of the ageing houses, but the students were still in bed, their presence betrayed only by rusty Toyotas and sagging Chevrolets with stickers hailing college sports teams and local radio stations.

Harvey Jones's building was a huge, ramshackle Victorian house divided into apartments. Jeannie found a parking slot across the street and watched the front door for a while.

At eleven o'clock she went in.

The building was hanging on grimly to the vestiges of respectability. A threadbare runner climbed the stairs wearily, and there were dusty plastic flowers in cheap vases on the window ledges. Neat paper notices, written in the cursive hand of an elderly woman, asked tenants to shut their doors quietly, put out their garbage in securely closed plastic sacks, and not let children play in the hallways.

He lives here, Jeannie thought, and her skin crawled. *I wonder if he's here now.*

Harvey's address was 5B, which had to be the top floor. She knocked on the first door on the ground floor. A bleary-eyed man with long hair and a tangled beard came to the door barefoot. She showed him the photo. He shook his head and slammed the door. She remembered the resident in Lisa's building who had said to her, *Where do you think you are, lady—Hicksville, USA? I don't even know what my neighbour* looks *like.*

She clenched her teeth and walked up four flights to the top of the house. There was a card in a little metal frame attached to the door of 5B, saying simply *Jones.* The door had no other features.

Jeannie stood outside, listening. All she could hear was the frightened beating of her heart. No sound came from inside. He probably was not there.

She rapped on the door of 5A. A moment later the door opened and an elderly white man came out. He was wearing a chalk-stripe suit that had once been dashing, and his hair was so ginger it had to be dyed. He seemed friendly. 'Hi,' he said.

'Hi. Is your neighbour home?'

'No.'

Jeannie was relieved and disappointed at the same time. She took out the photo of Steve that Charles had given her. 'Does he look like this?'

The neighbour took the photo from her and squinted at it. 'Yeah, that's him.'

I was right! Vindicated again! My computer search engine works.

'Gorgeous, ain't he?'

The neighbour was gay, Jeannie guessed. An elegant old gay man. She smiled. 'I think so too. Any idea where he might be this morning?'

'He goes away most Sundays. Leaves around ten, comes back after supper.'

'Did he go away last Sunday?'

'Yes, young lady, I believe he did.'

He's the right one, he has to be.

'Do you know where he goes?'

'No.'

I do, though. He goes to Baltimore.

The man went on: 'He doesn't talk much. In fact he doesn't talk at all. You a detective?'

'No, although I feel like one.'

'What's he done?'

Jeannie hesitated, then thought, *Why not tell the truth?* 'I think he's a rapist,' she said.

The man was not surprised. 'I could believe that. He's peculiar. I've seen girls leave here sobbing. Twice, that's happened.'

'I wish I could look inside.' She might find something that would link him with the rape.

He gave her a sly look. 'I have a key.'

'You do?'

'The previous occupant gave it to me. We were friendly. I never returned it after he left. And this guy didn't change the locks when he moved in. Figures he's too big and strong to be robbed, I guess.'

'Would you let me in?'

He hesitated. 'I'm curious to look inside myself. But what if he comes back while we're in there? He's kind of large—I'd hate to have him mad at me.'

The thought scared Jeannie, too, but her curiosity was even stronger. 'I'll take the risk if you will,' she said.

'Wait there. I'll be right back.'

What would she find inside? A temple of sadism like Wayne Stattner's home? A gruesome slum full of half-finished takeaway meals and dirty laundry? The excessive neatness of an obsessional personality?

The neighbour reappeared. 'I'm Maldwyn, by the way.'

'I'm Jeannie.'

'My real name is Bert, actually, but that's so unglamorous, don't you think? I've always called myself Maldwyn.' He turned a key in the door of 5B and went in.

Jeannie followed.

It was a typical student apartment, a bedsitting room with a kitchen nook and a small bathroom. It was furnished with an assortment of junk: a pine dresser, a painted table, three mismatched chairs, a sagging sofa and a big old TV set. It had not been cleaned for a while, and the bed was unmade. It was disappointingly typical.

Jeannie closed the apartment door behind her.

Maldwyn said: 'Don't touch anything, just look—I don't want him to suspect I came in here.'

Jeannie asked herself what she expected to find. A plan of the gymnasium building, the pool machine room marked *Rape her here*? He had not taken Lisa's underwear as a grotesque souvenir. Perhaps he had stalked her and photographed her for weeks before he pounced. He might have a little collection of pilfered items: a lipstick, a restaurant check, the discarded wrapping from a candy bar, junk mail with her address on it.

As she looked around, she began to see Harvey's personality in the details. On one wall was a centrefold, torn from a men's magazine, showing a naked woman with shaved pubic hair and a ring through the flesh of her labia. It made Jeannie shudder.

She inspected the bookcase. She saw the Marquis de Sade's *One Hundred Days of Sodom* and a series of X-rated videotapes with titles like *Pain* and *Extreme.* There were also some textbooks on economics and business: Harvey seemed to be doing an MBA.

'Can I look at his clothes?' she said. She did not want to offend Maldwyn.

'Sure, why not?'

She opened his drawers and closets. Harvey's clothes were like Steve's, somewhat conservative for his age: chinos and polo shirts, tweed sport coats and button-downs, Oxford shoes and loafers. The refrigerator was empty but for two six-packs of beer and a bottle of milk: Harvey ate out. Under the bed was a sports bag containing a squash racket and a dirty towel.

Jeannie was disappointed. This was where the monster lived, but it was not a palace of perversion, just a grubby room with some nasty pornography in it.

'I'm done,' she said to Maldwyn. 'I'm not sure what I was looking for, but it's not here.'

Then she saw it.

Hanging on a hook behind the apartment door was a red baseball cap.

Jeannie's spirits soared. *I was right, and I found the bastard, and here's the proof!* She looked closer. The word SECURITY was printed on the front in white letters. She could not resist the temptation to do a triumphant war dance around Harvey Jones's apartment.

'Found something, huh?'

'The creep was wearing that hat when he raped my friend. Let's get out of here.'

They left the apartment, closing the door. Jeannie shook hands with Maldwyn. 'I can't thank you enough. This is really important.'

'What are you going to do now?' he asked.

'Go back to Baltimore and call the police,' she said.

Driving home on I-95, she thought about Harvey Jones. Why did he go to Baltimore on Sundays? To see a girlfriend? Perhaps, but the likeliest explanation was that his parents lived there. A lot of students took their laundry home at weekends. He was probably in the city now, eating his mother's pot roast or watching a football game on TV with his father. Would he assault another girl on his way home?

How many Jones families were there in Baltimore: a thousand? She knew one of them, of course: her former boss, Professor Berrington Jones—

Oh, my God. Jones.

She was so shocked she had to pull over on the interstate.

Harvey Jones could be Berrington's son.

She suddenly remembered the little gesture Harvey had made, in the coffee shop in Philadelphia where she had met him. He had smoothed his eyebrows with the tip of his index finger. It had bothered her at the time, because she knew she had seen it before. She could not recall who else did it, and she had thought vaguely that it must have been Steve or Dennis, for the clones did have identical gestures. But now she remembered. *It was Berrington.* Berrington smoothed his eyebrows with the tip of his index finger. There was something about the action that irritated Jeannie, something annoyingly smug, or perhaps vain. This was not a gesture that all the clones had in common, like closing the door with their heel when they came into a room. Harvey had learned it from his father, as an expression of self-satisfaction.

Harvey was probably at Berrington's house right now.

CHAPTER FIFTY-FIVE

Preston Barck and Jim Proust arrived at Berrington's house around midday and sat in the den drinking beer. None of them had slept much and they looked and felt wasted. Marianne, the housekeeper, was preparing Sunday lunch, and the fragrant smell of her cooking wafted in from the kitchen, but nothing could raise the spirits of the three partners.

'Jeannie has talked to Hank King, and to Per Ericson's mother,' Berrington said despondently. 'I wasn't able to check any others but she'll track them all down before long.'

Jim said: 'Let's be realistic: exactly what can she do by this time tomorrow?'

Preston Barck was suicidal. 'I'll tell you what I'd do in her place,' he said. 'I'd want to make a highly public demonstration of what I'd found, so if I could get hold of two or three of the boys I'd take them to New York and go on *Good Morning America.* Television loves twins.'

'God forbid,' Berrington said.

A car drew up outside. Jim looked out of the window and said: 'Rusty old Datsun.'

Preston said: 'I'm beginning to like Jim's original idea. Make them all vanish.'

'I won't have any killing!' Berrington shouted.

'Don't yell, Berry,' Jim said with surprising mildness. 'To tell you the truth, I guess I was bragging a bit when I talked about making people vanish. Maybe there was a time when I had the power to order people killed, but I really don't any more. I've asked some favours of old friends in the last few days; and although they've come through, I've realized there are limits.'

Berrington thought, *Thank God for that.*

'But I have another idea,' Jim said.

The other two stared at him.

'We approach each of the eight families discreetly. We confess that mistakes were made at the clinic in its early days. We say that no harm was done but we want to avoid sensational publicity. We offer them a million dollars each in compensation. We make it payable over ten years, and tell them the payments stop if they talk—to anyone: the press, Jeannie Ferrami, scientists, anyone.'

Berrington nodded slowly. 'My God, it might just work. Who's going to say no to a million dollars?'

Preston said: 'Lorraine Logan. She wants to prove her son's innocence.'

'That's right. She wouldn't do it for ten million.'

'Everyone has their price,' Jim said, regaining some of his characteristic bluster. 'Anyway, there isn't much she can do without the cooperation of one or two of the others.'

Preston was nodding. Berrington, too, found he had new hope. There might be a way to shut the Logans up. But there was a more serious snag. 'What if Jeannie goes public in the next twenty-four hours?' he said. 'Landsmann would probably postpone the takeover while they investigate the allegations. And then we won't have any millions of dollars to throw around.'

Jim said: 'We *have* to know what her intentions are: how much she's discovered already and what she plans to do about it.'

'I don't see any way to do that,' Berrington said.

'I do,' said Jim. 'We know one person who could easily win her confidence and find out exactly what's on her mind.'

Berrington felt anger rise inside him. 'I know what you're thinking—'

'Here he comes now,' Jim said.

There was a footstep in the hall, and Berrington's son came in.

'Hi, Dad!' he said. 'Hey, Uncle Jim, Uncle Preston, how are you?'

Berrington looked at him with a mixture of pride and sorrow. The boy looked adorable in navy blue corduroy pants and a sky-blue cotton sweater. He picked up my dress sense, anyway, Berrington thought. He said: 'We have to talk, Harvey.'

Jim stood up. 'Want a beer, kid?'

'Sure,' Harvey said.

Jim had an annoying tendency to encourage Harvey in bad habits. 'Forget the beer,' Berrington snapped. 'Jim, why don't you and Preston go into the drawing room and let us two talk.' The drawing room was a stiffly formal space that Berrington never used.

Preston and Jim left. Berrington got up and hugged

Harvey. 'I love you, son,' he said. 'Even though you're wicked.'

'Am I wicked?'

'What you did to that poor girl in the basement of the gym was one of the most wicked things a man can do.'

Harvey shrugged.

Dear God, I failed to instil in him any sense of right and wrong, Berrington thought. But it was too late now for such regrets. 'Sit down and listen for a minute,' he said.

Harvey sat.

'Your mother and I tried for years to have a baby but there were problems,' he said. 'At the time, Preston was working on *in vitro* fertilization, where the sperm and the egg are brought together in the laboratory and then the embryo is implanted in the womb.'

'Are you saying I was a test-tube baby?'

'This is secret. You must never tell anyone, all your life. Not even your mother.'

'She doesn't *know*?' Harvey said in astonishment.

'There's more to it than that. Preston took one live embryo and split it, forming twins.'

'That's the guy who's been arrested for the rape?'

'He split it more than once.'

Harvey nodded. All of them had the same quick intelligence. 'How many?' he said.

'Eight.'

'Wow. And I guess the sperm didn't come from you.'

'No.'

'Who?'

'An army lieutenant from Fort Bragg: tall, strong, fit, intelligent, aggressive, and good-looking.'

'And the mother?'

'A civilian typist from West Point, similarly well favoured.'

A wounded grin twisted the boy's handsome face. 'My real parents.'

Berrington winced. 'No, they're not,' he said. 'You grew in your mother's belly. She gave birth to you, and believe me it hurt. We watched you take your first unsteady steps, and struggle to manoeuvre a spoonful of mashed potato into your mouth, and lisp your first words.'

Watching his son's face, Berrington could not tell whether Harvey believed him or not.

'Hell, we loved you more and more as you became less lovable. Every damn year the same reports from school: *He is very aggressive, he has not yet learned to share, he hits other children, he has difficulty with team games, he disrupts the class, he must learn to respect members of the opposite sex.* Every time you got expelled from a school we trudged around begging and pleading to get you into another one. We tried cajoling you, beating you, withdrawing privileges. We took you to three different child psychologists. You made our lives miserable.'

'Are you saying I ruined the marriage?'

'No, son, I did that all on my own. What I'm trying to tell you is that I love you *whatever you do,* just like any other parent.'

Harvey was still troubled. 'Why are you telling me now?'

'Steve Logan, one of your doubles, was a subject for study in my department. I had a hell of a shock when I saw him, as you may imagine. Then the police arrested him for the rape of Lisa Hoxton. But one of the professors, Jeannie Ferrami, got suspicious. To cut a long story short, she's tracked you down. She wants to prove Steve Logan's innocence. And she probably wants to expose the whole story of the clones and ruin me.'

'She's the woman I met in Philadelphia.'

Berrington was mystified. 'You've met her?'

'Uncle Jim called me and told me to give her a scare.'

Berrington was enraged. 'The son of a bitch, I'm going to tear his fucking head off his shoulders—'

'Calm down, Dad, nothing happened. I went for a ride in her car. She's cute, in her way.'

Berrington controlled himself with an effort. 'Your Uncle Jim has always been irresponsible in his attitude to you. He likes your wildness, no doubt because he's such an uptight asshole himself.'

'I like him.'

'Let's talk about what we have to do. We need to know Jeannie Ferrami's intentions, especially over the next twenty-four hours. You need to know whether she has any evidence that links you to Lisa Hoxton. We can't think of any way to get to her—but one.'

Harvey nodded. 'You want me to go talk to her, pretending to be Steve Logan.'

'Yes.'

He grinned. 'Sounds fun.'

Berrington groaned. 'Don't do anything foolish, please. Just talk to her.'

'Want me to go right away?'

'Yes, please. I hate to ask you to do this—but it's for you as much as for me.'

'Relax, Dad—what could happen?'

'Maybe I worry too much. I guess there's no great danger in going to a girl's apartment.'

'What if the real Steve is there?'

'Check the cars in the street. He has a Datsun like yours, that's another reason the police were so sure he was the perpetrator.'

'No kidding!'

'You're like identical twins, you make the same choices. If his car is there, don't go in. Call me, and we'll try to think of some way to get him out.'

'Suppose he walked there?'

'He lives in Washington.'

'Okay.' Harvey stood up. 'What's the girl's address?'

'She lives in Hampden.' Berrington scribbled the street address on a card and handed it over. 'Be careful, okay?'

'Sure. See you sooner, Montezuma.'

Berrington forced a smile. 'In a flash, succotash.'

CHAPTER FIFTY-SIX

HARVEY CRUISED up and down Jeannie's street, looking for a car just like his own. There were lots of elderly automobiles but no rusty light-coloured Datsuns. Steve Logan was not around.

He pulled into a slot near her house and turned off the engine. He sat thinking for a moment. He would need his wits about him. He was glad he had not drunk that beer Uncle Jim had offered him.

He knew she would take him for Steve, because she had done so once before, in Philadelphia. The two of them were identical in appearance. But conversation would be more tricky. She would make references to all sorts of things he was supposed to know about. He would have to answer without betraying his ignorance. He had to keep her confidence long enough to find out what evidence she had against him and what she planned to do with her knowledge. It would be very easy to make a slip and betray himself.

But even while he thought soberly about the daunting challenge of impersonating Steve, he could hardly contain his excitement at the prospect of seeing her again. What he had done in her car had been the most thrilling sexual encounter he had ever had. It was even better than being in the women's locker room when they were all panicking. He got aroused every time he thought about ripping her clothes while the car swerved all over the expressway.

He knew he should concentrate on his task now. He must not think of her face contorted in fear and her strong legs writhing. He ought to get the information from her and leave. But all his life he had never been able to do the sensible thing.

*

Jeannie called police headquarters as soon as she got home. She knew Mish would not be there, but she left a message asking her to call urgently. 'Didn't you leave an urgent message for her earlier today?' she was asked.

'Yes, but this is another one, just as important.'

'I'll do my best to pass it on,' the voice said sceptically.

Next she called Steve's house, but there was no reply. She guessed he and Lorraine were with their lawyer, trying to get Charles freed, and he would call when he could.

She was disappointed: she wanted to tell someone the good news.

The thrill of having found Harvey's apartment wore off and she felt depressed. Her thoughts returned to the danger that faced her of a future with no money, no job and no way to help her mother.

To cheer herself up she made brunch. She scrambled three eggs and grilled the bacon she had bought yesterday for Steve, and ate it with toast and coffee. As she was putting the dishes in the dishwasher, the doorbell rang.

She lifted the handset. 'Hello?'

'Jeannie? It's Steve.'

'Come on in!' she said happily.

He was wearing a cotton sweater the colour of his eyes, and he looked good enough to eat. She kissed him and hugged him hard, letting him feel her breasts against his chest. His hand slid down her back to her ass and pressed her to him. Today he smelled different again: he had used some kind of aftershave with a herbal fragrance. He tasted different, too, sort of like he had been drinking tea.

After a while she broke away. 'Let's not go too fast,' she panted. She wanted to savour this. 'Come in and sit down. I have so much to tell you!'

He sat on the couch and she went to the refrigerator. 'Wine, beer, coffee?'

'Wine sounds good.'

'Do you think it will be okay?'

*

What the hell did she mean by that? *Do you think it will be okay?* 'I don't know,' he said.

'How long ago did we open it?'

Okay, they shared a bottle of wine but didn't finish it, so she replaced the cork and put the bottle in the refrigerator, and now she's wondering whether it has oxidized. But she wants me to decide. 'Let's see, what day was it?'

'It was Wednesday, that's four days.'

He could not even see whether it was red or white. *Shit.* 'Hell, just pour a glass and we'll try it.'

'What a smart idea.' She poured some wine into a glass and handed it to him. He tasted it. 'It's drinkable,' he said.

She leaned over the back of the sofa. 'Let me taste.' She kissed his lips. 'Open your mouth,' she said. 'I want to taste the wine.' He chuckled and did as she said. She put the tip of her tongue into his mouth. *My God, this woman is sexy.* 'You're right,' she said. 'It's drinkable.' Laughing, she filled his glass and poured some for herself.

He was beginning to enjoy himself. 'Put some music on,' he suggested.

'On what?'

He had no idea what she was talking about. *Oh, Christ, I've made a slip.* He looked around the apartment: no stereo. *Dumb.*

She said: 'Daddy stole my stereo, remember? I don't have anything to play music on. Wait a minute, I do.' She went into the next room—bedroom, presumably—and came back with one of those waterproof radios for hanging in the shower. 'It's a silly thing, Mom gave it to me one Christmas, before she started to go crazy.'

Daddy stole her stereo, Mom's crazy—what the hell kind of a family does she come from?

'The sound is terrible, but it's all I've got.' She turned it on. 'I keep it tuned to 92Q.'

'Twenty jams in a row,' he said automatically.

'How do you know about that?'

Oh, shit, Steve wouldn't know Baltimore radio stations. 'I picked it up in the car on the way here.'

'What sort of music do you like?'

I have no idea what Steve likes, but I guess you don't either, so the truth will do. 'I'm into gangsta rap—Snoop Doggy Dog, Ice Cube, that kind of stuff.'

'Oh, fuck, you make me feel middle-aged.'

'What do you like?'

'The Ramones, the Sex Pistols, the Damned. I mean, when I was a kid, like *really* a kid, punk was it, you know? My mom would listen to all this cheesy music from the sixties that never did anything for me, then, when I was about eleven, suddenly, bang! Talking Heads. Remember "Psycho Killer"?'

'I sure don't!'

'Okay, your mother was right, I'm too old for you.' She sat beside him. She put her head on his shoulder and slipped her hand under the sky-blue sweater. She rubbed his chest, brushing his nipples with her fingertips. It felt good. 'I'm so glad you're here,' she said.

He wanted to touch her nipples too, but he had more important things to do. With a huge effort of will he said: 'We need to talk seriously.'

'You're right.' She sat up and took a sip of the wine. 'You first. Is your father still under arrest?'

Jesus, what do I say to that? 'No, you first,' he said. 'You said you had so much to tell me.'

'Okay. Number one, I know who raped Lisa. His name is Harvey Jones and he lives in Philadelphia.'

Christ Almighty! Harvey struggled to keep his

expression impassive. *Thank God I came here.* 'Is there proof he did it?'

'I went to his apartment. The neighbour let me in with a duplicate key.'

That fucking old homo, I'll break his scraggy neck.

'I found the baseball cap he was wearing last Sunday. It was hanging on a hook behind the door.'

Jesus! I should have thrown it away. But I never thought anyone would track me down! 'You've done amazingly well,' he said. *Steve would be thrilled by this news, it lets him off the hook.* 'I don't know how to thank you.'

'I'll think of something,' she said with a sexy grin.

Can I get back to Philadelphia in time to get rid of that hat before the police get there? 'You've told the police all this, have you?'

'No. I've left a message for Mish but she hasn't called yet.'

Hallelujah! I still have a chance.

Jeannie went on: 'Don't worry. He has no idea we're on to him. But you haven't heard the best part. Who else do we know called Jones?'

Do I say 'Berrington'? Would Steve think of that? 'It's a common name . . .'

'Berrington, of course! I think Harvey has been brought up as Berrington's son!'

I'm supposed to be amazed. 'Incredible!' he said. *What the hell do I do next? Maybe Dad would have some ideas. I have to tell him about all this. I need an excuse to make a phone call.*

She took his hand. 'Hey, look at your nails!'

Oh, fuck, what now? 'What about them?'

'They grow so fast! When you came out of jail, they were all jagged and broken. Now they look great!'

'I always heal fast.'

*

She turned his hand over and licked his palm.

'You're hot today,' he said.

'Oh, God, I've come on too strong, haven't I?' She had been told this by other men. Steve had been kind of reticent ever since he came in, and now she understood why. 'I know what you're saying. All last week I was pushing you away, and now you feel like I'm about to eat you for supper.'

He nodded. 'Yeah, sort of.'

'That's just the way I am. Once I decide for a guy, that's it.' She bounced up out of the couch. 'Okay, I'm backing off.' She went into the kitchen nook and took out an omelette pan. It was so heavy she needed both hands to lift it. 'I bought food for you yesterday. Are you hungry?' The pan was dusty—she did not cook much—so she wiped it with a dishcloth. 'Want some eggs?'

'Not really. So tell me, were you a punk?'

She put down the pan. 'Yeah, for a while. Ripped clothes, green hair.'

'Drugs?'

'I used to do speed at school whenever I had the money.'

'Which parts of your body did you pierce?'

She suddenly remembered the centrefold on Harvey Jones's wall, of the shaved woman with a ring through the lips of her cunt, and she shuddered. 'Only my nose,' she said. 'I gave up punk for tennis when I was fifteen.'

'I knew a girl who had a nipple ring.'

Jeannie felt jealous. 'Did you sleep with her?'

'Sure.'

'Bastard.'

'Hey, did you think I was a virgin?'

'Don't ask me to be rational!'

He held up his hands in a defensive gesture. 'Okay, I won't.'

'You still haven't told me what happened to your dad. Did you get him released?'

'Why don't I phone home and get the latest news?'

*

If she heard him dialling a seven-digit number, she would know he was making a local call, whereas his father had mentioned that Steve Logan lived in Washington, DC. He held the cradle down with a finger while he tapped three random digits, to represent an area code, then he released it and dialled his father's home.

Dad answered, and Harvey said: 'Hi, Mom.' He gripped the handset hard, hoping his father would not say, *Who is this, you must have the wrong number.*

But his father got it immediately. 'You're with Jeannie?'

Well done, Dad. 'Yes. I called to find out whether Dad got out of jail yet.'

'Colonel Logan is still under arrest, but he's not in jail. The military police have him.'

'That's too bad, I was hoping he might have been released by now.'

Hesitantly, Dad said: 'Can you tell me . . . anything?'

Harvey was constantly tempted to glance at Jeannie and check whether she was buying his act. But he knew such a glance would give him a guilty air, so he forced himself to stare at the wall. 'Jeannie has worked wonders, Mom. She's discovered the real rapist.' He tried hard to put a pleased tone into his voice. 'His name's Harvey Jones. We're just waiting for the detective to return her call so she can break the news.'

'Jesus! That's terrible!'

'Yeah, isn't it great!' *Don't sound so ironic, you fool!*

'At least we're forewarned. Can you stop her talking to the police?'

'I think I have to.'

'What about Threeplex? Does she have any plans to publicize what she's found out about us?'

'I don't know yet.' *Let me get off the phone before I say anything to give myself away.*

'Make sure you find out. That's important too.'

All right! 'Okay. Well, I hope Dad gets out soon. Call me here if you get any news, okay?'

'Is it safe?'

'Just ask for Steve.' He laughed, as if he had made a joke.

'Jeannie might recognize my voice. But I could get Preston to make the call.'

'Exactly.'

'Okay.'

'Bye.' Harvey hung up.

Jeannie said: 'I ought to call police headquarters again. Maybe they didn't understand how urgent this is.' She picked up the phone.

He realized he was going to have to kill her.

'Kiss me again first,' he said.

*

She slid into his arms, leaning against the kitchen counter. She opened her mouth to his kiss. He stroked her side. 'Nice sweater,' he murmured, then he grasped her breast with his big hand.

Her nipple stiffened in response, but somehow she did not feel as good as she expected to. She tried to relax and enjoy the moment she had been looking forward to. He slipped his hands under her sweater, and she arched her back slightly as he held both her breasts. As always, she suffered a moment of embarrassment, fearful that he would be disappointed with them. Every man she had ever slept with had loved her breasts, but she still harboured the notion that they were too small. Like the others, Steve showed no sign of dissatisfaction. He pushed up her sweater, bent his head to her chest, and started sucking her nipples.

She looked down at him. The first time a boy did this to her she thought it was absurd, a reversion to childhood. But she soon came to like it, and even enjoyed doing it to a man. Now, however, nothing was working. Her body responded, but some doubt nagged at the back of her mind and she could not concentrate on pleasure. She was annoyed with herself. *I messed every-*

thing up yesterday, being paranoid, I'm not going to do it again today.

He sensed her unease. Straightening up, he said: 'You're not comfortable. Let's sit on the couch.' Taking her agreement for granted, he sat down. She followed. He smoothed his eyebrows with the tip of his index finger and reached for her.

She flinched away.

'What?' he said.

No! It can't be!

'You . . . you . . . did that thing, with your eyebrow.'

'What thing?'

She sprang up from the couch. 'You creep!' she screamed. 'How dare you!'

'What the fuck is going on?' he said, but the pretence was thin: she could tell from his face that he knew exactly what was happening.

'Get out of my place!' she screamed.

He tried to keep up the façade. 'First you're all over me, then you pull this!'

'I know who you are, you bastard, you're Harvey!'

He gave up his act. 'How did you know?'

'You touched your eyebrow with your fingertip, just like Berrington.'

'Well, what does it matter?' he said, standing up. 'If we're so alike, you could pretend I'm Steve.'

'Get the fuck out of here!'

He touched the front of his pants, showing her his erection. 'Now that we've got this far, I'm not leaving here with blue balls.'

Oh, Jesus, I'm in bad trouble now. This guy is an animal. 'Keep away from me!'

He stepped towards her, smiling. 'I'm going to take off those tight jeans and see what's underneath.'

She remembered Mish saying that rapists enjoy the victim's fear. 'I'm not afraid of you,' she said, trying to make her voice calm. 'But if you touch me, I swear I'll kill you.'

He moved dreadfully quickly. In a flash he grabbed her, lifted her and threw her on the floor.

The phone rang.

She screamed: 'Help! Mr Oliver! Help!'

Harvey snatched up the dishcloth from the kitchen counter and stuffed it roughly into her mouth, bruising her lips. She gagged and began to cough. He held her wrists so that she could not use her hands to pull the cloth out of her mouth. She tried to push it out with her tongue but she could not, it was too big. Had Mr Oliver heard her scream? He was old and he turned up the volume of his TV very loud.

The phone kept on ringing.

Harvey grabbed the waist of her jeans. She wriggled away from him. He slapped her face so hard she saw stars. While she was dazed, he let go of her wrists and pulled off her jeans and her panties. 'Wow, what a hairy one,' he said.

Jeannie snatched the cloth out of her mouth and screamed: 'Help me, help!'

Harvey covered her mouth with his big hand, muffling her yells, and fell on her, knocking the wind out of her. For a few moments she was helpless, struggling to breathe. His knuckles bruised her thighs as he fumbled one-handed with his fly. Then he was pushing against her, looking for the way in. She wriggled desperately, trying to throw him off, but he was too heavy.

The phone was still ringing. Then the doorbell rang too.

Harvey did not stop.

Jeannie opened her mouth. Harvey's fingers slid between her teeth. She bit down hard, as hard as she could, thinking that she did not care if she broke her teeth on his bones. Warm blood spurted into her mouth and she heard him cry out in anguish as he jerked his hand away.

The doorbell rang again, long and insistently.

Jeannie spat out Harvey's blood and yelled again. 'Help!' she screamed. 'Help, help, help!'

There was a loud bang from downstairs, then another, then a crash and the sound of wood splintering.

Harvey scrambled to his feet, clutching his wounded hand.

Jeannie rolled over, stood up, and took three steps away from him.

The door flew open. Harvey swung around, turning his back on Jeannie.

Steve burst in.

Steve and Harvey stared at one another in astonishment for a frozen moment.

They were exactly the same. What would happen if they fought? They were equal in height, weight, strength and fitness. A fight could go on for ever.

On impulse, Jeannie picked up the omelette pan with both hands. Imagining that she was hitting a cross-court ground shot with her famous double-handed backhand, she shifted her weight to her front foot, locked her wrists and swung the heavy pan with all her might.

She hit the back of Harvey's head right on the sweet spot.

There was a sickening thud. Harvey's legs seemed to go soft. He sank to his knees, swaying.

As if she had run to the net for the volley, Jeannie lifted the pan high with her right hand and brought it down as hard as she could on top of his head.

His eyes rolled up and he went limp and crashed to the floor.

Steve said: 'Boy, am I glad you didn't hit the wrong twin.'

Jeannie started to shake. She dropped the pan and sat on a kitchen stool. Steve put his arms around her. 'It's over,' he said.

'No, it's not,' she replied. 'It's only just begun.'

The phone was still ringing.

CHAPTER FIFTY-SEVEN

'YOU LAID him out, the bastard,' Steve said. 'Who is he?'

'This is Harvey Jones,' Jeannie answered. 'And he's Berrington Jones's son.'

Steve was amazed. 'Berrington brought up one of the eight as his son? Well, I'll be damned.'

Jeannie stared at the unconscious figure on the floor. 'What are we going to do?'

'For a start, why don't we answer the phone?'

Automatically, Jeannie picked it up. It was Lisa. 'It almost happened to me,' Jeannie said without preamble.

'Oh, no!'

'The same guy.'

'I can't believe it! Shall I come right over?'

'Thanks, I'd like that.'

Jeannie hung up. She ached all over from having been thrown to the floor, and her mouth hurt where he had forced the gag in. She could still taste Harvey's blood. She poured a glass of water, rinsed her mouth, and spat into the kitchen sink. Then she said: 'We're in a dangerous place, Steve. The people we're up against have powerful friends.'

'I know.'

'They might try to kill us.'

'Tell me about it.'

The notion made it hard for Jeannie to think. I must not become paralysed by fear, she thought. 'Do you think if I promise never to tell what I know, they might leave me alone?'

Steve considered that for a moment, then he said: 'No, I don't.'

'Nor do I. So I've got no choice but to fight.'

There was a footstep on the stairs and Mr Oliver put his head around the door. 'What the heck happened here?' he said. He looked from the unconscious Harvey on the floor to Steve and back again. 'Well, I'll be.'

Steve picked up Jeannie's black Levi's and handed them to her, and she slipped them on quickly, covering her nakedness. If Mr Oliver noticed, he was too tactful to say anything. Pointing at Harvey he said: 'This must be that guy in Philadelphia. No wonder you thought it was your boyfriend. They got to be twins!'

Steve said: 'I'm going to tie him up before he comes round. Do you have any cord, Jeannie?'

Mr Oliver said: 'I have some electric cable. I'll get my tool box.' He went out.

Jeannie hugged Steve gratefully. She felt as if she had awakened from a nightmare. 'I thought he was you,' she said. 'It was just like yesterday, but this time I wasn't being paranoid, I was right.'

'We said we should make up a code, then we didn't get around to it.'

'Let's do it now. When you approached me on the

tennis court last Sunday, you said, *I play a little tennis myself.*'

'And you modestly said, *If you only play a* little *tennis, you're probably not in my league.*'

'That's the code. If one of us says the first line, the other has to say the second.'

'Done.'

Mr Oliver came back with his tool box. He rolled Harvey over and started to tie his hands in front, binding the palms flat against one another but leaving the pinkie fingers free.

Steve said: 'Why not tie his hands behind his back?'

Mr Oliver looked bashful. 'If you'll excuse me for mentioning it, this way he can hold his own dick when he has to take a piss. I learned that in Europe during the war.' He started to bind Harvey's feet. 'This guy won't cause you no more trouble. Now what are you planning to do about the front door?'

Jeannie looked at Steve, who said: 'I bust it pretty bad.'

'I'd better call a carpenter,' Jeannie said.

Mr Oliver said: 'I got some loose timber in the yard. I could fix it so we can lock the door tonight. Then we could get someone to make a good job of it tomorrow.'

Jeannie felt profoundly grateful to him. 'Thank you, that's so kind.'

'Don't mention it. This is the most interesting thing that's happened to me since World War Two.'

'I'll help you,' Steve offered.

Mr Oliver shook his head. 'You two have a lot to discuss, I can see that. Like whether you're going to call the cops on this guy you have trussed up on your carpet.' Without waiting for an answer he picked up his tool box and went downstairs.

Jeannie collected her thoughts. 'Tomorrow, Threeplex will be sold for a hundred and eighty million dollars and Proust will be on the presidential trail. Meanwhile I've got no job and my reputation is shot. I'll never work as a scientist again. But I could turn both situations around, with what I know.'

'How are you going to do that?'

'Well . . . I could issue a press release about the experiments.'

'Wouldn't you need some kind of proof?'

'You and Harvey together make pretty dramatic evidence. Especially if we could get you on TV together.'

'Yeah—on *Sixty Minutes* or something. I like that.' His face fell again. 'But Harvey wouldn't cooperate.'

'They can film him tied up. Then we call the cops, and they can film that too.'

Steve nodded. 'The trouble is, you probably have to act before Landsmann and Threeplex finalize the takeover. Once they have the money, they may be able to ride out any bad publicity we generate. But I don't see how you can get on TV in the next few hours. And their press conference is tomorrow morning, according to the *Wall Street Journal*.'

'Maybe we should hold our own press conference.'

Steve snapped his fingers. 'I've got it! We gatecrash *their* press conference.'

'Hell, yes. Then maybe the people from Landsmann

will decide not to sign the papers, and the takeover will be cancelled.'

'And Berrington won't make all those millions of dollars.'

'And Jim Proust won't run for president.'

'We must be crazy,' Steve said. 'These are some of the most powerful people in America, and we're talking about spoiling their party.'

The sound of hammering came from below as Mr Oliver began to mend the door. Jeannie said: 'They hate black people, you know. All this bullshit about good genes and second-rate Americans is just code. They're white supremacists all dressed up with modern science. They want to make Mr Oliver a second-class citizen. The hell with them, I'm not going to stand by and watch.'

'We need a plan,' Steve said practically.

'Okay, here goes,' Jeannie said. 'First we have to find out where the Threeplex press conference is being held.'

'Probably a Baltimore hotel.'

'We'll call them all, if necessary.'

'We should probably take a room in the hotel.'

'Good idea. Then I sneak into the press conference somehow, and stand up in the middle of it and make a speech to the assembled media.'

'They'll shut you up.'

'I should have a press release ready to give out. But then you'll come in with Harvey. Twins are so photogenic, all the cameras will be on you.'

Steve frowned. 'What do you prove by having me and Harvey there?'

'Because you're identical you'll have the kind of dramatic impact that should cause the press to start asking questions. It won't take them long to check that you have different mothers. Once they learn that, they'll know there's a mystery to be uncovered, just as I did. And you know how they investigate presidential candidates.'

'Three would be better than two, though,' Steve said. 'Do you think we could get one of the others there?'

'We could try. We could invite them all and hope that at least one will show up.'

On the floor, Harvey opened his eyes and groaned.

Jeannie had almost forgotten about him. Looking at him now, she hoped his head hurt. Then she felt guilty about being so vengeful. 'After the way I hit him, he probably should see a doctor.'

Harvey came round fast. 'Untie me, you fucking bitch,' he said.

'Forget the doctor,' Jeannie said.

'Untie me now, or I swear I'll slash your tits with a razor as soon as I'm free.'

Jeannie stuffed the dishcloth in his mouth. 'Shut up, Harvey,' she said.

Steve said pensively: 'It's going to be interesting trying to sneak him into a hotel tied up.'

Lisa's voice came from downstairs, greeting Mr Oliver. A moment later she came in, wearing blue jeans and heavy Doc Marten boots. She looked at Steve and Harvey and said: 'My God, it's true.'

Steve stood up. 'I'm the one you picked out of the line-up,' he said. 'But he's the one who attacked you.'

Jeannie explained: 'Harvey tried to do to me what he did to you. Steve came by just in time and broke the door down.'

Lisa went over to where Harvey lay. She stared at him for a long moment, then thoughtfully drew back her foot and kicked him in the ribs as hard as she could with a Doc Marten toecap. He groaned and writhed in pain.

She did it again. 'Boy,' she said, shaking her head, 'that feels good.'

Jeannie swiftly brought Lisa up to date with the day's developments. 'A lot happened while I was sleeping,' Lisa said in amazement.

Steve said: 'You've been at JFU a year, Lisa—I'm surprised you never met Berrington's son.'

'Berrington never socializes with academic colleagues,' she said. 'He's too much of a celebrity. It's quite possible *nobody* at JFU has ever met Harvey.'

Jeannie outlined the plan for disrupting the press conference. 'We were just saying we could feel more confident if one of the other clones was going to be there.'

'Well, Per Ericson is dead, and Dennis Pinker and Murray Claud are in jail, but that still leaves three possibilities: Henry King in Boston, Wayne Stattner in New York, and George Dassault—he could be in Buffalo, Sacramento or Houston, we don't know which, but we could try them all again. I kept all the phone numbers.'

'So did I,' Jeannie said.

Steve said: 'Could they get here on time?'

'We could check flights on CompuServe,' Lisa said. 'Where's your computer, Jeannie?'

'Stolen.'

'I have my Powerbook in the trunk, I'll get it.'

While she was out, Jeannie said: 'We're going to have to think very hard about how to persuade these guys to fly to Baltimore at short notice. And we'll have to offer to pay their fares. I'm not sure my credit card will stand it.'

'I have an American Express card my mom gave me for emergencies. I know she'll consider this an emergency.'

'What a great mom,' Jeannie said enviously.

'That's the truth.'

Lisa came back in and plugged her computer into Jeannie's modem line.

'Wait a minute,' Jeannie said. 'Let's get organized.'

CHAPTER FIFTY-EIGHT

JEANNIE WROTE the press release, Lisa accessed WorldSpan Travelshopper and checked flights, and Steve got the Yellow Pages and started calling all the major hotels to say: 'Do you have a press conference scheduled tomorrow for Threeplex, Inc., or Landsmann?'

After six tries it occurred to him that the press conference did not have to take place in a hotel. It could be held in a restaurant, or a more exotic location such as on board a ship; or they might have a big enough room at Threeplex headquarters, just north of the city. But on his seventh call a helpful desk clerk said: 'Yes, that's in the Regency Room at noon, sir.'

'Great!' Steve said. Jeannie looked an enquiry at him, and Steve grinned and made a thumbs-up sign. 'Could I reserve a room for tonight, please?'

'I'll connect you with reservations, please hold on for one moment.'

He booked a room, paying with his mother's American Express card. As he hung up, Lisa said: 'There are three flights that would get Henry King here on time, all USAir. They leave at six twenty, seven forty and nine forty-five. Seats are available on all of them.'

'Book a seat on the nine forty-five,' Jeannie said.

Steve passed Lisa the credit card and she tapped in the details.

Jeannie said: 'I still don't know how to persuade him to come.'

'Did you say he's a student, working in a bar?' Steve said.

'Yeah.'

'He needs money. Let me try something. What's his number?'

Jeannie gave it to him. 'He's called Hank,' she said.

Steve called the number. No one answered the phone. He shook his head disappointedly. 'Nobody home,' he said.

Jeannie looked downcast for a moment, then she snapped her fingers. 'Maybe he's working at that bar.' She gave Steve the number and he dialled it.

The phone was answered by a man with a Hispanic accent. 'The Blue Note.'

'May I speak to Hank?'

'He's supposed to be working, you know?' the man said irritably.

Steve grinned at Jeannie and mouthed, *He's there!* 'It's very important, I won't keep him long.'

A minute later a voice just like Steve's own came down the line. 'Yeah, who's this?'

'Hi, Hank, my name is Steve Logan, and we have something in common.'

'Are you selling something?'

'Your mother and mine both received treatment at a

place called the Aventine Clinic before we were born. You can check that with her.'

'Yeah, so?'

'To cut a long story short, I'm suing the clinic for ten million dollars and I'd like you to join in the suit with me.'

There was a thoughtful pause. 'I don't know if you're for real or not, buddy, but either way I don't have the money for a lawsuit.'

'I'll pay all the legal costs. I don't want your money.'

'So why are you calling me?'

'Because my case would be strengthened by having you on board.'

'You better write me with the details—'

'That's the problem. I need you to be here in Baltimore, at the Stouffer Hotel, tomorrow at noon. I'm holding a press conference ahead of my lawsuit and I want you to appear.'

'Who wants to go to Baltimore? Like, it's not Honolulu.'

Get serious, asshole. 'You have a reservation on the USAir flight out of Logan at nine forty-five. Your ticket is paid for, you can check with the airline. Just pick it up at the airport.'

'You're offering to split ten million dollars with me?'

'Oh, no. You get your own ten million.'

'What are you suing them for?'

'Breach of implied contract by fraud.'

'I'm a business student, isn't there a statute of limitations on that? Anything that happened twenty-three years ago—'

'There is a statute of limitations, but it runs from the time of discovery of the fraud. Which in this case was last week.'

In the background, a Hispanic voice shouted: 'Hey, Hank, you got about a hundred customers waiting!'

Hank said into the phone: 'You're beginning to sound a little more convincing.'

'Does that mean you'll come?'

'Hell, no. It means I'll think about it after I get off work tonight. Now I have to serve drinks.'

'You can reach me at the hotel,' Steve said, but he was too late: Hank had hung up.

Jeannie and Lisa were staring at him.

He shrugged. 'I don't know,' he said frustratedly. 'I don't know if I convinced him or not.'

Lisa said: 'We'll just have to wait and see if he shows up.'

'What does Wayne Stattner do for a living?'

'He owns nightclubs. He probably already has ten million dollars.'

'Then we'll have to pique his curiosity. Do you have a number?'

'No.'

Steve called information.

'If he's a celebrity he might not be listed.'

'There may be an office number.' He got through and gave the name. A few moments later he got the number. He called it, and got an answering machine. 'Hi, Wayne, my name is Steve Logan and you may notice that my voice sounds exactly like yours. That's because, believe it or not, we are identical. I'm six foot two, a hundred and ninety pounds, and I look exactly like you except for hair colour. Some other things we probably have in common: I'm allergic to macadamia nuts, I have no nails on my little toes, and when I'm thinking I scratch the back of my left hand with the fingers of my right. Now here's the kicker: we're not twins. There are several of us. One committed a crime at Jones Falls University last Sunday—that's why you got a visit from the Baltimore police yesterday. And we're meeting tomorrow at the Stouffer Hotel in Baltimore at noon. This is weird, Wayne, but I swear to you it's all true. Call me or Dr Jean Ferrami at the hotel, or just show up. It will be interesting.' He hung up and looked at Jeannie. 'What do you think?'

She shrugged. 'He's a man who can afford to follow his whims. He may be intrigued. And a nightclub owner probably doesn't have anything pressing to do on a Monday morning. On the other hand, I wouldn't take a plane on the strength of a phone message like that.'

The phone rang and Steve picked it up automatically. 'Hello?'

'Can I speak to Steve?' The voice was unfamiliar.

'This is Steve.'

'This is Uncle Preston. I'm putting your Dad on.'

Steve did not have an Uncle Preston. He frowned, mystified. A moment later another voice came on the line. 'Is anyone with you, is she listening?'

Suddenly Steve understood. Mystification gave way to shock. He could not think what to do. 'Hold on a moment,' he said. He covered the mouthpiece with his hand. 'I think this is Berrington Jones!' he said to

Jeannie. 'And he thinks I'm Harvey. What the hell do I do?'

Jeannie spread her hands in a gesture of bewilderment. 'Improvise,' she said.

'Gee, thanks.' Steve put the phone to his ear. 'Uh, yeah, this is Steve,' he said.

'What's going on? You've been there hours!'

'I guess so . . .'

'Have you found out what Jeannie's planning to do?'

'Uh . . . yes, I have.'

'Then get back here and tell us!'

'Okay.'

'You're not trapped in any way, are you?'

'No.'

'I suppose you've been fucking her.'

'You could say that.'

'Get your goddamn pants on and come home! We're all in bad trouble!'

'Okay.'

'Now, when you hang up, you're going to say it was someone who works for your parents' lawyer, calling to say you're needed in DC as soon as possible. That's your cover story, and it gives you a reason to hurry. Okay?'

'Okay. I'll be there as fast as I can.'

Berrington hung up and Steve did likewise.

Steve's shoulders slumped with relief. 'I think I fooled him.'

Jeannie said: 'What did he say?'

'It was very interesting. It seems Harvey was sent here

to find out what your intentions are. They're worried about what you might do with the knowledge you have.'

'*They?* Who?'

'Berrington and someone called Uncle Preston.'

'Preston Barck, president of Threeplex. So why did they call?'

'Impatience. Berrington got fed up with waiting. I guess he and his cronies are waiting to find out so they can figure out how to respond. He told me to pretend I have to go to Washington to see the lawyer, then get back to his house as fast as I can.'

Jeannie looked worried. 'This is very bad. When Harvey doesn't show up, Berrington will know something's wrong. The Threeplex people will be forewarned. There's no telling what they might do: move the press conference to another location, step up security so we can't get in, even cancel the event altogether and sign the papers in a lawyer's office.'

Steve frowned, staring at the floor. He had an idea but he hesitated to propose it. Finally he said: 'Then Harvey must go home.'

Jeannie shook her head. 'He's been lying there on the floor listening to us. He'll tell them everything.'

'Not if I go in his place.'

Jeannie and Lisa stared at him, aghast.

He had not worked it out, he was thinking aloud. 'I'll go to Berrington's home and pretend to be Harvey. I'll reassure them.'

'Steve, it's so hazardous. You don't know anything about their life. You wouldn't even know where the bathroom was.'

'If Harvey could fool you, I guess I could fool Berrington.' Steve tried to sound more confident than he felt.

'Harvey didn't fool me. I found him out.'

'He fooled you for a while.'

'Less than an hour. You'd have to stay there longer.'

'Not much. Harvey normally returns to Baltimore on Sunday evening, we know that. I'll be back here by midnight.'

'But Berrington is Harvey's *father*. It's impossible.'

He knew she was right. 'Do you have a better idea?'

Jeannie thought for a long moment, then she said: 'No.'

CHAPTER FIFTY-NINE

STEVE PUT on Harvey's blue corduroy pants and light blue sweater and drove Harvey's Datsun to Roland Park. It was dark by the time he reached Berrington's house. He parked behind a silver-grey Lincoln Town Car and sat for a moment, summoning his courage.

He had to get this right. If he was found out, Jeannie was finished. But he had nothing to go on, no information to work with. He would have to be alert to every hint, sensitive to expectations, relaxed about errors. He wished he was an actor.

What mood is Harvey in? he asked himself. *He's been summoned rather peremptorily by his father. He might have been enjoying himself with Jeannie. I think he's in a bad mood.*

He sighed. He could not postpone the dread moment any longer. He got out of the car and went to the front door.

There were several keys on Harvey's key ring. He peered at the lock on Berrington's front door. He thought he could make out the word *Yale*. He looked for a Yale key. Before he could find one, Berrington opened the door. 'What are you standing there for?' he said irritably. 'Get in here.'

Steve stepped inside.

'Go in the den,' Berrington said.

Where the fuck is the den? Steve fought down a wave of panic. The house was a standard suburban ranch-style split-level built in the seventies. To his left, through an arch, he could see a living room with formal furniture and no one in it. Straight ahead was a passage with several doors off it which, he guessed, led to bedrooms. On his right were two closed doors. One of them was probably the den—but which?

'Go in the den,' Berrington repeated, as if he might not have heard the first time.

Steve picked a door at random.

He had chosen the wrong door. This was a bathroom.

Berrington looked at him with an irritated frown.

Steve hesitated for a moment, then remembered he was supposed to be in a bad temper. 'I can take a piss first, can't I?' he snapped. Without waiting for an answer he went in and closed the door.

It was a guest bathroom, with just a toilet and a handbasin. He leaned on the edge of the basin and looked in the mirror. 'You have to be crazy,' he said to his reflection.

He flushed the toilet, washed his hands and went out.

He could hear male voices from farther inside the house. He opened the door next to the bathroom: this was the den. He stepped inside, closed the door behind him and took a swift look around. There was a desk, a wood file cabinet, lots of bookshelves, a TV and some couches. On the desk was a photograph of an attractive blonde woman of about forty, wearing clothes that looked about twenty years out of date, holding a baby. *Berrington's ex-wife? My 'mother'?* He opened the desk drawers one after the other, glancing inside, then he looked in the file cabinet. There was a bottle of Springbank malt whisky and some crystal glasses in the bottom drawer, almost as if they were meant to be concealed. Perhaps it was a whim of Berrington's. As he closed the drawer, the room door opened and Berrington came in, followed by two men. Steve recognized Senator Proust, whose large bald head and big nose were familiar from the TV news. He presumed the quiet, black-haired man was 'Uncle' Preston Barck, the president of Threeplex.

He remembered to be bad-tempered. 'You needn't have dragged me back here in such a goddamn hurry.'

Berrington adopted a conciliatory tone. 'We just finished supper,' he said. 'You want something? Marianne can make up a tray.'

Steve's stomach was knotted with tension, but Harvey would surely have wanted supper, and Steve needed to appear as natural as possible, so he pretended to soften and said: 'Sure, I'll have something.'

Berrington shouted: 'Marianne!' After a moment a pretty, nervous-looking black girl appeared at the door. 'Bring Harvey some supper on a tray,' Berrington said.

'Right away, monsieur,' she said quietly.

Steve watched her go, noting that she went through

the living room on her way to the kitchen. Presumably the dining room was also that way, unless they ate in the kitchen.

Proust leaned forward and said: 'Well, my boy, what did you learn?'

Steve had invented a fictional plan of action for Jeannie. 'I guess you can relax, for the moment at least,' he said. 'Jeannie Ferrami intends to take legal action against Jones Falls University for wrongful dismissal. She thinks she will be able to cite the existence of the clones during that proceeding. Until then she has no plans for publicity. She has an appointment with a lawyer on Wednesday.'

The three older men looked relieved. Proust said: 'A wrongful dismissal suit. That will take at least a year. We have plenty of time to do what we need to do.'

Fooled you, you malevolent old bastards.

Berrington said: 'What about the Lisa Hoxton case?'

'She knows who I am, and she thinks I did it, but she has no proof. She will probably accuse me, but I believe it will be seen as a wild accusation by a vengeful former employee.'

He nodded. 'That's good, but you still need a lawyer. You know what we'll do. You'll stay here tonight—it's too late to drive back to Philadelphia anyway.'

I don't want to spend the night here! 'I don't know . . .'

'You'll come to the press conference with me in the morning, and right afterwards we'll go see Henry Quinn.'

It's too risky!

Don't panic, think.

If I stayed here, I would know exactly what these three creeps are up to at any moment. That's worth a degree of risk. I guess nothing much can happen while I'm asleep. I could sneak a call to Jeannie, to let her know what's going on. He made a split-second decision. 'Okay,' he said.

Proust said: 'Well, we've been sitting here worrying ourselves to death for nothing.'

Barck was not quite so quick to accept the good news. He said suspiciously: 'It didn't *occur* to the girl to try and sabotage the takeover of Threeplex?'

'She's smart, but I don't think she's business-minded,' Steve said.

Proust winked and said: 'What's she like in the sack, eh?'

'Feisty,' Steve said with a grin, and Proust roared with laughter.

Marianne came in with a tray: sliced chicken, a salad with onions, bread and a Budweiser. Steve smiled at her. 'Thank you,' he said. 'This looks great.'

She gave him a startled look, and Steve realized Harvey probably did not say thank you very often. He caught the eye of Preston Barck, who was frowning. *Careful, careful! Don't spoil it now, you've got them where you want them, all you have to do is get through the next hour or so until bedtime.*

He started to eat. Barck said: 'Do you remember me taking you to the Plaza Hotel in New York for lunch when you were ten years old?'

Steve was about to say *Yes* when he caught the trace of a puzzled frown on Berrington's face. *Is this a test? Is Barck suspicious?* 'The Plaza?' he said with a frown.

Either way, he could give only one answer. 'Gee, Uncle Preston, I don't remember that.'

'Maybe it was my sister's boy,' Barck said.

Whew.

Berrington got up. 'All that beer is making me piss like a horse,' he said. He went out.

'I need a Scotch,' Proust said.

Steve said: 'Try the bottom drawer of the file cabinet. That's where Dad usually keeps it.'

Proust went to the cabinet and opened the drawer. 'Well done, boy!' he said. He took out the bottle and some glasses.

'I've known about that hiding place since I was twelve years old,' Steve said. 'That was when I started stealing it.'

Proust roared with laughter. Steve stole a glance at Barck. The wary look had gone from his face, and he was smiling.

CHAPTER SIXTY

Mr Oliver produced an enormous pistol he had kept from World War Two. 'Took it off a German prisoner,' he said. 'Coloured soldiers weren't generally allowed to carry firearms in those days.' He sat on Jeannie's couch, pointing the gun at Harvey.

Lisa was on the phone, trying to find George Dassault.

Jeannie said: 'I'm going to check myself into the hotel and reconnoitre.' She put a few things into a suitcase and drove to the Stouffer Hotel, thinking about how they would get Harvey to a room without attracting the attention of hotel security.

The Stouffer had an underground garage: that was a good start. She left her car there and took the elevator. It went only to the lobby, not to the rooms, she observed. To get to the rooms you had to take another elevator. But all elevators were grouped together in a passageway off the main lobby, not visible from the reception desk, and it would take only a few seconds to cross the passage from the garage elevator to the room elevator. Would they be carrying Harvey, or dragging him, or would he be cooperative and walk? She found it difficult to envisage.

She checked in, went to her room, put down her case, then left immediately and drove back to her apartment.

'I reached George Dassault!' Lisa said excitedly as soon as she walked in.

'That's great! Where?'

'I found his mother in Buffalo, and she gave me his number in New York. He's an actor in a play off-off-off Broadway.'

'Will he come tomorrow?'

'Yes. "I'll do anything for publicity," he said. I fixed up his flight and I said I'd meet him at the airport.'

'That's wonderful!'

'We'll have three clones: it will look incredible on TV.'

'If we can get Harvey into the hotel.' Jeannie turned to Mr Oliver. 'We can avoid the hotel doorman by driving into the underground garage. The garage elevator goes only as far as the ground floor of the hotel. You have to get out there and get another elevator to the rooms. But the elevator bank is kind of concealed.'

Mr Oliver said dubiously: 'All the same, we're going to have to keep him quiet for a good five, maybe ten minutes while we get him from the car to the room. And what if some of the hotel guests see him all tied up? They might ask questions, or call security.'

Jeannie looked at Harvey, lying bound and gagged on the floor. He was watching them and listening. 'I've been thinking about this, and I have some ideas,' Jeannie said. 'Can you retie his feet so he can walk, but not very fast?'

'Sure.'

While Mr Oliver was doing that, Jeannie went into her bedroom. From her closet she took a colourful sarong she had bought for the beach, a big wraparound shawl, a handkerchief and a Nancy Reagan mask she had been given at a party and had forgotten to throw away.

Mr Oliver was getting Harvey to his feet. As soon as he was upright, Harvey took a swing at Mr Oliver with his bound hands. Jeannie gasped and Lisa screamed. But Mr Oliver seemed to have been expecting it. He dodged the blow easily, then hit Harvey in the stomach with the butt of the gun. Harvey grunted and bent double, and Mr Oliver hit him with the gun butt again, this time on his head. Harvey sank to his knees. Mr Oliver hauled him up again. Now he seemed docile.

'I want to dress him up,' Jeannie said.

'You go ahead,' Mr Oliver said. 'I'll just stand by and hurt him now and again to keep him cooperative.'

Nervously, Jeannie wrapped the sarong around Harvey's waist and tied it like a skirt. Her hands were unsteady: she hated being this close to him. The skirt was long, and covered Harvey's ankles, concealing the length of electrical cable that hobbled him. She draped the shawl over his shoulders and fastened it with a safety pin to the bonds on his wrists, so that he looked as if he were clutching the corners of the shawl like an old lady. Next she rolled the handkerchief and tied it across his open mouth, securing it with a knot behind his neck, so that the dishcloth could not fall out. Finally she put on the Nancy Reagan mask to hide the gag. 'He's been to a costume party, dressed as Nancy Reagan, and he's drunk,' she said.

'That's pretty good,' Mr Oliver said.

The phone rang. Jeannie picked it up. 'Hello?'

'This is Mish Delaware.'

Jeannie had forgotten about her. It was fourteen or fifteen hours since she had been desperate to contact her. 'Hi,' she said.

'You were right. Harvey Jones did it.'

'How do you know?'

'The Philadelphia police were quick off the mark. They went to his apartment. He wasn't there, but a neighbour let them in. They found the hat and realized it was the one in the description.'

'That's great!'

'I'm ready to arrest him, but I don't know where he is. Do you?'

Jeannie looked at him, dressed like a six-foot-two Nancy Reagan. 'No idea,' she said. 'But I can tell you where he'll be at noon tomorrow.'

'Go on.'

'Regency Room, Stouffer Hotel, at a press conference.'

'Thanks.'

'Mish, do me a favour?'

'What?'

'Don't arrest him until the press conference is over. It's really important to me that he's there.'

She hesitated, then said: 'Okay.'

'Thanks. I appreciate it.' Jeannie hung up. 'Okay, let's get him in the car.'

Mr Oliver said: 'You go ahead and open the doors. I'll bring him.'

Jeannie picked up her keys and ran downstairs into the street. Night had fallen, but there was bright starlight as well as the shadowy illumination of the street lights. She looked along the street. A young couple in ripped jeans were strolling in the opposite direction, hand in hand. On the other side of the road, a man in a straw hat was walking a yellow Labrador. They would all be able to see clearly what was going on. Would they look? Would they care?

Jeannie unlocked her car and opened the door.

Harvey and Mr Oliver came out of the house, very close together, Mr Oliver pushing his prisoner forward, Harvey stumbling. Lisa followed them, closing the door of the house.

For an instant, the scene struck Jeannie as absurd. Hysterical laughter bubbled up into her throat. She put her fist in her mouth to silence it.

Harvey reached the car and Mr Oliver gave a final shove. Harvey half fell into the back seat.

Jeannie's moment of hilarity passed. She looked again at the other people in the street. The man in the straw hat was watching his dog urinate on the tyre of a Subaru. The young couple had not turned around.

So far, so good.

'I'll get in the back with him,' Mr Oliver said.

'Okay.'

Lisa got in the front passenger seat and Jeannie drove.

Downtown was quiet on Sunday night. She entered

the parking garage beneath the hotel and parked as close as possible to the elevator shaft, to minimize the distance they had to drag Harvey. The garage was not deserted. They had to wait in the car while a dressed-up couple got out of a Lexus and went up to the hotel. Then, when there was no one to see, they got out of the car.

Jeannie took a wrench from her trunk, showed it to Harvey, then tucked it into the pocket of her blue jeans. Mr Oliver had his wartime pistol in his waistband, concealed by the tail of his shirt. They pulled Harvey out of the car. Jeannie expected him to turn violent at any moment, but he walked peaceably to the elevator.

It took a long time to arrive.

When it came they bundled him in and Jeannie pressed the button for the lobby.

As they went up, Mr Oliver punched Harvey in the stomach again.

Jeannie was shocked: there had been no provocation.

Harvey groaned and doubled over just the doors were opening. Two men waiting for the elevator stared at Harvey. Mr Oliver led him stumbling out, saying: 'Excuse me, gentlemen, this young man has had one drink too many.' They got out of the way smartly.

Another elevator stood waiting. They got Harvey into it and Jeannie pressed the button for the eighth floor. She sighed with relief as the doors closed.

They rode to their floor without incident. Harvey was recovering from Mr Oliver's punch, but they were almost at their destination. Jeannie led the way to the room she had taken. As they got there she saw with dismay that the door was open, and hanging on the doorknob was a card saying *Room being serviced.* The maid must be turning down the bed, or something. Jeannie groaned.

Suddenly Harvey began to thrash around, making noises of protest in his throat, swinging wildly with his bound hands. Mr Oliver tried to hit him but he dodged and took three steps along the corridor.

Jeannie stooped in front of him, grabbed the cord binding his ankles with both hands, and heaved. Harvey stumbled. Jeannie tugged again, this time with no effect. *God, he's heavy.* He raised his hands to strike her. She braced herself and pulled with all her might. His feet flew from under him and he went down with a crash.

'My goodness, what in Heaven's name is going on?' said a prim voice. The maid, a black woman of about sixty in an immaculate uniform, had stepped out of the room.

Mr Oliver knelt at Harvey's head and lifted his shoulders. 'This young man been partying too hard,' he said. 'Threw up all over the hood of my limousine.'

I get it, he's our driver, just for the maid's benefit.

'Partying?' said the maid. 'Look more like fighting to me.'

Speaking to Jeannie, Mr Oliver said: 'Could you lift his feet, mam?'

Jeannie did so.

They lifted Harvey. He wriggled. Mr Oliver appeared to drop him, but put his knee in the way so that Harvey fell on it and was winded.

'Be careful, you'll hurt him!' the maid said.

'Once more, mam,' Mr Oliver said.

They picked him up and carried him into the room. They dumped him on the nearer of the two beds.

The maid followed them in. 'I hope he ain't going to throw up in here.'

Mr Oliver smiled at her. 'Now how come I've never seen you around here before? I have an eye for a pretty girl but I don't recall noticing you.'

'Don't be fresh,' she said, but she was smiling. 'I ain't no girl.'

'I'm seventy-one, and you can't be a day over forty-five.'

'I'm fifty-nine, too old to listen to your jive.'

He took her arm and gently led her out of the room, saying: 'Hey, I'm almost through with these folks. Do you want to go for a ride in my limousine?'

'With puke all over it? No way!' She cackled.

'I could get it cleaned up.'

'I have a husband waiting for me at home, and if he could hear you talking now there'd be worse than puke on your hood, Mr Limo.'

'Oh-oh.' Mr Oliver put up his hands in a defensive gesture. 'I never meant no harm.' Miming fear, he backed into the room and closed the door.

Jeannie fell into a chair. 'God Almighty, we did it,' she said.

CHAPTER SIXTY-ONE

As soon as Steve had finished eating he stood up and said: 'I need to turn in.' He wanted to retire to Harvey's room as soon as possible. When he was alone he would be safe from discovery.

The party broke up. Proust swallowed the rest of his whisky, and Berrington walked the two guests to their cars.

Steve saw an opportunity to call Jeannie and tell her what was going on. He snatched up the phone and called information. They took a long time to answer. *Come on, come on!* At last he got through and asked for the number of the hotel. He misdialled the first time and got some restaurant. Frantically, he dialled again and at last reached the hotel. 'I'd like to speak to Dr Jean Ferrami,' he said.

Berrington came back into the den just as Steve heard her voice. 'Hello?'

'Hi, Linda, this is Harvey,' he said.

'Steve, is that you?'

'Yeah, I've decided to stay over at my Dad's place, it's a little late for a long drive.'

'For God's sake, Steve, are you okay?'

'Some business to take care of, but nothing I can't handle. How was your day, honey?'

'We've got him into the hotel room. It wasn't easy, but we did it. Lisa contacted George Dassault. He promised to come, so we should have three, at least.'

'Good. I'm going to bed now. I'm still hoping to see you tomorrow, honey, okay?'

'Hey, good luck.'

'You too. Good night.'

Berrington winked. 'Hot babe?'

'Warm.'

Berrington took out some pills and washed one down with whisky. Catching Steve's glance at the bottle, he explained: 'Dalmane. I need something to help me sleep, after all this.'

'Good night, Dad.'

Berrington put his arm around Steve's shoulders. 'Good night, son,' he said. 'Don't worry, we'll come through all right.'

He really loves his rotten son, Steve thought; and for a moment he felt irrationally guilty for deceiving a fond father.

Then he realized he did not know where his bedroom was.

He left the den and took a few steps along the passage that he guessed led to the bedrooms. He had no idea which door led to Harvey's room. Looking back, he saw that Berrington could not watch him from the den. Quickly, he opened the nearest door, trying desperately to do so silently.

It led to a full bathroom, with shower and tub.

He closed it gently.

Next to it was a closet full of towels and linen.

He tried the door opposite. It opened into a big bedroom with a double bed and lots of closets. A pinstriped suit in a dry-cleaner's bag hung from a doorknob. He did not think Harvey had a pinstriped suit. He was about to close the door softly when he was shocked to hear Berrington's voice, right behind him. 'You need something from my room?'

He gave a guilty start. For a moment he was struck dumb. *What the hell can I say?* Then words came to him. 'I don't have anything to sleep in.'

'Since when have you taken to wearing pyjamas?' Berrington's voice could have been suspicious or merely puzzled: Steve could not tell.

Improvising wildly, he said: 'I thought you might have an oversize T-shirt.'

'Nothing that will fit those shoulders, my boy,' Berrington said, and to Steve's relief he laughed.

Steve shrugged. 'It doesn't matter.' He moved on.

At the end of the passage were two doors, on opposite sides: Harvey's room, and the maid's, presumably.

But which is which?

Steve loitered, hoping that Berrington would disappear into his own room before Steve had to make the choice.

When he reached the end of the passage he glanced back. Berrington was watching him.

'Night, Dad,' he said.

'Goodnight.'

Left or right? No way to tell. Pick one at random.

Steve opened the door on his right.

Rugby shirt on the back of a chair, Snoop Doggy Dog CD on the bed, *Playboy* on the desk.

A boy's room. Thank God.

He stepped inside and closed the door behind him with his heel.

He slumped against the door, weak with relief.

After a moment he undressed and got into bed, feeling very weird in Harvey's bed in Harvey's room in Harvey's father's home. He turned out the light and lay awake, listening to the sounds of the strange house. For a while he heard footsteps, doors closing and taps running, then the place was quiet.

He dozed lightly and woke suddenly. *There's someone else in the room.*

He caught a distinctive smell of some flowery perfume mixed with garlic and spices, then he saw the outline of Marianne's small form cross the window.

Before he could say anything she was getting into bed with him.

He whispered: 'Hey!'

'I'm going to blow you just the way you like,' she said, but he could hear fear in her voice.

'No,' he said, pushing her away as she burrowed under the bedclothes toward his groin. She was naked.

'Please don't hurt me tonight, please, 'Arvey,' she said. She had a French accent.

Steve figured it out. Marianne was an immigrant, and Harvey had her so terrified she not only did anything he asked but also anticipated his demands.

How did he get away with beating the poor girl, when his father was in the next room? Didn't she make a noise? Then Steve remembered the sleeping pill. Berrington slept so heavily that Marianne's cries did not wake him.

'I'm not going to hurt you, Marianne,' he said. 'Relax.'

She started kissing his face. 'Be nice, please be nice, I'll do everything you like, but don't hurt me.'

'Marianne,' he said sternly. 'Be still.'

She froze.

He put his arm around her thin shoulders. Her skin was soft and warm. 'Just lie there a moment and calm down,' he said, stroking her back. 'Nobody is going to hurt you any more, I promise.'

She was tense, expecting blows, but gradually she relaxed. She moved closer to him.

He had an erection, he could not help it. He knew he could make love to her easily. Lying there, holding her small, trembling body, he was powerfully tempted. No one would ever know. How delightful it would be to stroke her and arouse her. She would be so surprised and pleased to be loved gently and considerately. They would kiss and touch all night.

He sighed. But it would be wrong. She was not a volunteer. Insecurity and fear had brought her to this bed, not desire. *Yes, Steve, you can fuck her—and you will be exploiting a frightened immigrant who believes she has no choice. And that would be contemptible. You would despise a man who could do that.*

'Do you feel better now?' he said.

'Yes . . .'

'Then go back to your own bed.'

She touched his face, then kissed his mouth softly. He kept his lips firmly shut but patted her hair in a friendly way.

She stared at him in the half dark. 'You're not him, are you,' she said.

'No,' Steve said. 'I'm not him.'

A moment later she was gone.

He still had an erection.

Why am I not him? Because of the way I was brought up? Hell, no.

I could have fucked her. I could be Harvey. I'm not him because I choose *not to be. My parents didn't make that decision just now: I did. Thanks for your help, Mom and Dad, but it was me, not you, who sent her back to her room.*

Berrington didn't create me, and you didn't create me.

I did.

MONDAY

CHAPTER SIXTY-TWO

STEVE WOKE up with a start.

Where am I?

Someone was shaking his shoulder, a man in striped pyjamas. It was Berrington Jones. He suffered a moment of disorientation, then everything came back to him.

'Dress smart for the press conference, please,' Berrington said. 'In the closet you'll find a shirt you left here a couple of weeks ago. Marianne laundered it. Come to my room and pick out a tie to borrow.' He went out.

Berrington talked to his son as if to a difficult, disobedient child, Steve reflected as he got out of bed. The unspoken sentence *Don't argue, just do it* was attached to every utterance. But his abrupt manner made conversation easier for Steve. He could get away with monosyllabic responses that did not risk betraying his ignorance.

It was eight a.m. Wearing his undershorts, he went along the passage to the bathroom. He took a shower, then shaved with a disposable razor he found in the bathroom cabinet. He moved slowly, postponing the moment when he would have to put himself at risk by conversing with Berrington.

Wrapping a towel around his waist, he went to Berrington's room, in accordance with his orders. Berrington was not there. Steve opened the closet. Berrington's ties were cheesy: stripes and small dots and foulards, all in shiny silk, nothing up to date. He picked one with broad horizontal stripes. He needed underwear, too. He looked at Berrington's boxer shorts. Although he was much taller than Berrington, they had the same waist size. He took a plain blue pair.

When he was dressed he braced himself for another ordeal of deception. Just a few more hours and it would be all over. He had to allay Berrington's suspicions until a few minutes after noon, when Jeannie would interrupt the press conference.

He took a deep breath and went out.

He followed the smell of frying bacon to the kitchen. Marianne was at the stove. She stared wide-eyed at Steve. Steve had a momentary panic: if Berrington noticed her expression he might ask her what was wrong—and the poor girl was so terrified she would probably tell him. But Berrington was watching CNN on a small TV set and he was not the type to take an interest in the help.

Steve sat down and Marianne poured him coffee and juice. He gave her a reassuring smile to calm her down.

Berrington held up a hand for silence—unnecessarily, for Steve had no intention of making small talk—and the anchor read an item about the takeover of Threeplex. 'Michael Madigan, CEO of Landsmann North America, said last night that the disclosure phase had been satisfactorily completed, and the deal will be signed in public at a press conference in Baltimore today. Shares in Landsmann rose fifty pfennigs on the Frankfurt exchange in early trading this morning. General Motors third-quarter figures—'

There was a ring at the doorbell and Berrington hit the mute button. He looked out of the kitchen window and said: 'There's a police car outside.'

Steve was struck by a terrible thought. If Jeannie had reached Mish Delaware and told her what she had learned about Harvey, the police could have decided to arrest Harvey. And Steve was going to have trouble denying that he was Harvey Jones, when he was wearing Harvey's clothes and sitting in Harvey's father's kitchen eating blueberry muffins made by Harvey's father's cook.

He did not want to go back to jail.

But that was not the worst of it. If he should be arrested now, he would miss the press conference. If none of the other clones showed up, Jeannie would only have Harvey. And one twin did not prove anything.

Berrington got up to go to the door.

Steve said: 'What if they're after me?'

Marianne looked as if she was going to die.

Berrington said: 'I'll tell them you're not here.' He left the room.

Steve could not hear the conversation on the doorstep. He sat frozen to his seat, neither eating nor drinking. Marianne stood like a statue at the stove, with a kitchen spatula in her hand.

Eventually Berrington came back in. 'Three of our

neighbours were robbed last night,' he said. 'I guess we got lucky.'

*

Through the night Jeannie and Mr Oliver had taken shifts, one guarding Harvey while the other lay down, but neither of them got much rest. Only Harvey slept, snoring behind his gag.

In the morning they took turns in the bathroom. Jeannie dressed in the clothes she had brought in her suitcase, a white blouse and black skirt, so that she could be taken for a waitress.

They ordered breakfast from room service. They could not let the waiter into the room, for then he would see Harvey trussed up on the bed, so Mr Oliver signed the check at the door, saying: 'My wife's undressed, I'll take the trolley from here.'

He let Harvey drink a glass of orange juice, holding it to his mouth while Jeannie stood behind him ready to hit him with her wrench if he tried anything.

Jeannie waited anxiously for Steve to call. What had happened to him? He had spent the night at Berrington's house. Was he keeping up the pretence?

Lisa arrived at nine o'clock with a pile of copies of the press release, then left for the airport, to meet George Dassault and any other clones who might show. None of the three had called.

Steve called at nine thirty. 'I have to be quick,' he said. 'Berrington's in the bathroom. Everything's all right, I'm coming to the press conference with him.'

'He doesn't suspect anything?'

'No—although I've had some tense moments. How's my double?'

'Subdued.'

'Gotta go.'

'Steve?'

'Make it fast!'

'I love you.' She hung up. *I shouldn't have said that, a girl is supposed to play hard to get. Well, to hell with it.*

At ten she went on a scouting expedition to check out the Regency Room. It was a corner room with a little lobby and a door to an anteroom. A publicist was already there, assembling a backdrop with the Threeplex logo for the benefit of the TV cameras.

Jeannie took a swift look around then returned to her room.

Lisa called from the airport. 'Bad news,' she said. 'The New York flight is late.'

'Oh, Christ!' Jeannie said. 'Any sign of the others, Wayne or Hank?'

'No.'

'How late is George's plane?'

'It's expected at eleven thirty.'

'You might still get here.'

'If I drive like the wind.'

*

At eleven o'clock Berrington emerged from his bedroom pulling on his suit coat. He was wearing a blue chalk-stripe with a vest over a white shirt with French cuffs, old-fashioned but effective. 'Let's get going,' he said.

Steve put on Harvey's tweed sport coat. It fitted perfectly, of course, and it looked a lot like one Steve himself owned.

They went outside. They were both overdressed for this weather. They got into the silver Lincoln and turned on the air-conditioning. Berrington drove fast, heading down town. To Steve's relief he did not talk much on the journey. He parked in the hotel garage.

'Threeplex hired a public-relations outfit to run this event,' he said as they went up in the elevator. 'Our in-house publicity department has never handled anything this big.'

As they headed for the Regency Room, a smartly coiffed woman in a black suit intercepted them. 'I'm Caren Beamish from Total Communications,' she said brightly. 'Would you like to come to the VIP room?' She showed them into a small room where snacks and drinks were laid out.

Steve was mildly bothered: he would have liked to take a look at the layout of the conference room. But perhaps it made no difference. As long as Berrington continued to believe he was Harvey right up until the appearance of Jeannie, nothing else mattered.

There were six or seven people in the VIP room already, including Proust and Barck. With Proust was a muscular young man in a black suit who looked like a bodyguard. Berrington introduced Steve to Michael Madigan, the head of Landsmann's North American operations.

Berrington nervously gulped a glass of white wine.

Steve could have used a martini—he had much more reason to be scared than Berrington—but he had to keep his wits about him and he could not afford to relax for an instant. He looked at the watch he had taken from Harvey's wrist. It was five to twelve. *Just a few more minutes. And when this is over,* then *I'll have a martini.*

Caren Beamish clapped her hands for attention and said: 'Gentlemen, are we ready?' There were muttered replies and nods. 'Then everyone but the platform party should take their seats now, please.'

That's it. I've succeeded. It's over.

Berrington turned to Steve and said: 'See you sooner, Montezuma.' He looked expectant.

'Sure,' Steve said.

Berrington grinned. 'What do you mean, *sure*? Give me the rest of it!'

Steve went cold. He had no idea what Berrington was talking about. It seemed to be a catchphrase, like *See you later, alligator,* but a private one. Obviously there was a reply, but it wasn't *In a while, crocodile.* What the hell could it be? Steve cursed inwardly. The press conference was about to open—he needed to keep up the pretence for just a few more seconds!

Berrington frowned in puzzlement, staring at him.

Steve felt perspiration break out on his forehead.

'You can't have forgotten it,' Berrington said, and Steve saw suspicion dawn in his eyes.

'Of course I haven't,' Steve replied quickly—too quickly, for then he realized that he had committed himself.

Senator Proust was listening now. Berrington said: 'So give me the rest of it.' Steve saw him cut his eyes to Proust's bodyguard, and the man tensed visibly.

In desperation, Steve said: 'In an hour, Eisenhower.'

There was a moment's silence.

Then Berrington said: 'That's a good one!' and laughed.

Steve relaxed. That must be the game: you had to make up a new response every time. He thanked his stars. To hide his relief, he turned away.

'Showtime, everybody,' said the publicist.

'This way,' Proust said to Steve. 'You don't want to walk out onto the stage.' He opened a door and Steve stepped through.

He found himself in a bathroom. Turning around, he said: 'No, this is—'

Proust's bodyguard was right behind him. Before Steve knew what was happening, the man had him in a painful half nelson. 'Make a noise and I'll break your fucking arms,' he said.

*

Berrington stepped into the bathroom behind the bodyguard. Jim Proust followed him and closed the door.

The bodyguard held the boy tightly.

Berrington's blood was boiling. 'You young punk,' he hissed. 'Which one are you? Steve Logan, I suppose.'

The boy tried to keep up the pretence. 'Dad, what are you doing?'

'Forget it, the game's up—now where is my son?'

The boy did not answer.

Jim said: 'Berry, what the hell is going on?'

Berrington tried to calm down. 'This isn't Harvey,' he said to Jim. 'This is one of the others, probably the Logan boy. He must have been impersonating Harvey since yesterday evening. Harvey himself must be locked away somewhere.'

Jim paled. 'That means that what he told us about Jeannie Ferrami's intentions was a blind!'

Berrington nodded grimly. 'She's probably planning some kind of protest at the press conference.'

Proust said: 'Shit, not in front of all the cameras!'

'That's what I'd do in her place—wouldn't you?'

Proust thought for a moment. 'Will Madigan keep his nerve?'

Berrington shook his head. 'I couldn't say. He'd look pretty foolish, cancelling the takeover at the last minute. On the other hand, he'd look even more foolish paying a hundred and eighty million dollars for a company that's about to be sued for every penny it's got. He could go either way.'

'Then we've got to find Jeannie Ferrami and stop her!'

'She might have checked into the hotel.' Berrington snatched up the phone beside the toilet. 'This is Professor Jones at the Threeplex press conference in the Regency Room,' he said in his most authoritative voice. 'We're waiting for Dr Ferrami—what room is she in?'

'I'm sorry, we're not allowed to give out room numbers, sir.' Berrington was about to explode when she added: 'Would you like me to connect you?'

'Yes, sure.' He heard the ringing tone. After a wait, it was answered by a man who sounded elderly. Improvising, Berrington said: 'Your laundry is ready, Mr Blenkinsop.'

'I didn't give out no laundry.'

'Oh, I'm sorry, sir—what room are you in?' He held his breath.

'Eight twenty-one.'

'I wanted eight twelve. My apologies.'

'No problem.'

Berrington hung up. 'They're in room eight twenty-one,' he said excitedly. 'I bet Harvey's there.'

Proust said: 'The press conference is about to start.'

'We may be too late.' Berrington hesitated, torn. He did not want to delay the announcement by a single second, but he needed to forestall whatever Jeannie was planning. After a moment he said to Jim: 'Why don't you go on stage with Madigan and Preston? I'll do my best to find Harvey and stop Jeannie Ferrami.'

'Okay.'

Berrington looked at Steve. 'I'd be happier if I could take your security man with me. But we can't let Steve loose.'

The bodyguard said: 'No problem, sir. I can handcuff him to a pipe.'

'Great. Do it.'

Berrington and Proust returned to the VIP room. Madigan looked curiously at them. 'Something wrong, gentlemen?'

Proust said: 'A minor security question, Mike. Berrington is going to handle it while we go ahead with our announcement.'

Madigan was not quite satisfied. 'Security?'

Berrington said: 'A woman I fired last week, Jean Ferrami, is in the hotel. She may pull some kind of stunt. I'm going to head her off at the pass.'

That was enough for him. 'Okay, let's get on with it.'

Madigan, Barck and Proust went into the conference room. The bodyguard came out of the bathroom. Berrington and he hurried out into the corridor and pressed the button to summon the elevator. Berrington was apprehensive and worried. He was not a man of action—never had been. The kind of combat he was used to took place on college committees. He hoped he was not about to get in a fistfight.

They went to the eighth floor and ran to room eight twenty-one. Berrington rapped on the door. A man's voice called: 'Who is it?'

Berrington said: 'Housekeeping.'

'We're okay, thank you, sir.'

'I need to check your bathroom, please.'

'Come back later.'

'There's a problem, sir.'

'I'm busy right now. Come back in an hour.'

Berrington looked at the bodyguard. 'Can you kick this door down?'

The man looked pleased. Then he looked over Berrington's shoulder and hesitated. Following the direction of his glance, Berrington saw an elderly couple with shopping bags emerge from the elevator.

They walked slowly along the corridor towards eight twenty-one. Berrington waited while they passed. They stopped outside eight thirty. The husband put down his shopping, searched for his key, fumbled it into the lock, and opened the door. At last the couple disappeared into the room.

The bodyguard kicked the door.

The door frame cracked and splintered, but the door held. There was the sound of rapid footsteps from inside.

He kicked it again, and it flew open.

He rushed inside and Berrington followed.

They were brought up short by the sight of an elderly black man pointing a huge antiquated pistol at them.

'Stick up your hands, shut that door, get in here and lie face down, or I'll shoot you both dead,' the man said. 'After the way you bust in here, ain't no jury in Baltimore going to convict me for killing you.'

Berrington raised his hands.

Suddenly a figure catapulted off the bed. Berrington just had time to see that it was Harvey, with his wrists tied together and some kind of gag over his mouth. The old man swung the gun towards him. Berrington was terrified that his son was about to be shot. He cried out: 'No!'

The old man moved a fraction of a second too late. Harvey's bound arms knocked the pistol out of his hands. The bodyguard leaped for it and snatched it up from the carpet. Standing up, he pointed it at the old man.

Berrington breathed again.

The old man slowly raised his arms in the air.

The bodyguard picked up the room phone. 'Hotel security to room eight twenty-one,' he said. 'There's a guest here with a gun.'

Berrington looked around the room. There was no sign of Jeannie.

*

Jeannie emerged from the elevator, wearing her white blouse and black skirt and carrying a tray of tea she had ordered from room service. Her heart was beating like a bass drum. Walking at a brisk, waitressy pace, she entered the Regency Room.

In the little lobby, two women with checklists sat behind tables. A hotel security guard stood near, chatting to them. Presumably no one was supposed to get in without an invitation, but Jeannie was betting they would not question a waitress with a tray. She forced herself to smile at the guard as she headed for the inner door.

'Hey!' he said.

She turned at the door.

'They have plenty of coffee and beverages in there.'

'This is jasmine tea, a special request.'

'Who for?'

She thought fast. 'Senator Proust.' She prayed he was there.

'Okay, go ahead.'

She smiled again, opened the door and walked into the conference room.

At the far end, three men in suits were sitting behind

a table on a raised dais. In front of them was a pile of legal documents. One of the men was making a formal speech. The audience consisted of about forty people with notebooks, miniature cassette tape recorders and hand-held television cameras.

Jeannie walked to the front. Standing beside the dais was a woman in a black suit and designer spectacles. She wore a badge saying

CAREN BEAMISH
Total Communications!

She was the publicist Jeannie had seen earlier, assembling the backdrop. She looked curiously at Jeannie but did not try to stop her, assuming—as Jeannie had intended—that someone had ordered something from room service.

The men on the dais had name cards in front of them. She recognized Senator Proust on the right. On the left was Preston Barck. The one in the middle, who was speaking, was Michael Madigan. 'Threeplex is not just an exciting biotechnology company,' he was saying in a boring tone.

Jeannie smiled and put down the tray in front of him. He looked mildly surprised and stopped in his speech for a moment.

Jeannie turned to the audience. 'I have a very special announcement,' she said.

*

Steve was sitting on the bathroom floor with his left hand handcuffed to the waste pipe of the bathroom washbasin, feeling angry and desperate. Berrington had found him out a few seconds before his time ran out. Now he was searching for Jeannie and might ruin the entire plan if he found her. Steve had to get away to warn her.

The pipe was attached at its top end to the drain of the basin. It turned in an S-bend then disappeared into the wall. Contorting his body, Steve got his foot on the pipe, drew it back, and kicked. The entire sanitary fitting shuddered. He kicked again. The mortar around the pipe where it entered the wall began to crumble. He kicked several more times. The mortar fell away, but the pipe was strong.

Frustrated, he peered up to where the pipe joined the washbasin. Maybe that join was weaker. He grasped the pipe with both hands and shook it frenziedly. Once again everything trembled but nothing broke.

He looked at the S-bend. There was a knurled collar around the pipe just above the bend. Plumbers unscrewed it when they had to clean out the bend, he knew, but they used a tool. He got his left hand to the collar, gripped it as hard as he could, and tried to turn it. His fingers slipped and he grazed his knuckles painfully.

He tapped the underside of the sink. It was made of some kind of artificial marble, quite strong. He looked again at the place where the pipe connected with the drain. If he could break that seal, he might be able to pull the pipe out. Then he could easily slip the handcuff over the end and be free.

He changed his position, drew back his foot and started kicking again.

*

Jeannie said: 'Twenty-three years ago, Threeplex carried out illegal and irresponsible experiments on eight unsuspecting American women.' Her breath was coming fast and she struggled to speak normally and project her voice. 'All the women were wives of army officers.' She searched the audience for Steve but could not see him. Where the hell was he? He was supposed to be here—he was the proof!

Caren Beamish said in a shaky voice: 'This is a private function, please leave immediately.'

Jeannie ignored her. 'The women went to Threeplex's clinic in Philadelphia to have hormone treatment for subfertility.' She let her anger show. 'Without permission they were impregnated with embryos from total strangers.'

There was a buzz of comment from the assembled journalists. They were interested, Jeannie could tell.

She raised her voice: 'Preston Barck, supposedly a responsible scientist, was so obsessed with his pioneering work in cloning that he divided an embryo seven times, producing eight identical embryos, and implanted them in eight unsuspecting women.'

Jeannie spotted Mish Delaware sitting at the back, watching with an expression of faint amusement. But

Berrington was not in the room. That was surprising—and worrying.

On the platform, Preston Barck stood up and spoke. 'Ladies and gentlemen, I apologize for this. We were warned there might be a disturbance.'

Jeannie ploughed on. 'This outrage has been kept secret for twenty-three years. The three perpetrators—Preston Barck, Senator Proust and Professor Berrington Jones—have been prepared to go to any lengths to cover it up, as I know from bitter experience.'

Caren Beamish was speaking into a hotel phone. Jeannie heard her say: 'Get some goddamn security in here right away, please.'

Under the tray, Jeannie had been carrying a sheaf of copies of the press release that she had written and Lisa had photocopied. 'All the details are in this handout,' she said, and she began to pass them around as she carried on speaking. 'Those eight alien embryos grew and were born, and seven of them are alive today. You'll know them, because they all look alike.'

She could tell from the journalists' expressions that she had them where she wanted them. A glance at the platform showed Proust with a face like thunder and Preston Barck looking as if he wanted to die.

About now, Mr Oliver was supposed to walk in with Harvey, so that everyone could see he looked just like Steve, and possibly George Dassault as well. But there was no sign of any of them. *Don't leave it too late!*

Jeannie carried on speaking. 'You would think they were identical twins—and in fact they have identical

DNA—but they were born to eight different mothers. I study twins, and the puzzle of the twins who had different mothers was what first started me investigating this shameful story.'

The door at the back of the room burst open. Jeannie looked up, hoping to see one of the clones. But it was Berrington who rushed in. Breathlessly, as if he had been running, Berrington said: 'Ladies and gentlemen, this lady is suffering from a nervous breakdown and has lately been dismissed from her job. She was a researcher on a project funded by Threeplex and bears the company a grudge. Hotel security has just arrested an accomplice of hers on another floor. Please bear with us while they escort this person from the building, then our press conference can resume.'

Jeannie was knocked for a loop. Where were Mr Oliver and Harvey? And what had happened to Steve? Her speech and her handout meant nothing without evidence. She had only a few seconds left. Something had gone terribly wrong. Berrington had somehow foiled her plan.

A uniformed security guard strode into the room and spoke to Berrington.

In desperation, Jeannie turned to Michael Madigan. He had a frosty look on his face, and she guessed he was the kind of man who hated interruptions to his smoothly organized routine. All the same she tried. 'I see you have the legal papers in front of you, Mr Madigan,' she said. 'Don't you think you should check out this story before you sign? Just suppose I'm right—imagine how much money those eight women could sue you for!'

Madigan said mildly: 'I'm not in the habit of making business decisions based on tipoffs from nutcases.'

The journalists laughed, and Berrington began to look more confident. The security guard approached Jeannie.

She said to the audience: 'I was hoping to show you two or three of the clones, by way of proof. But . . . they haven't showed up.'

The reporters laughed again, and Jeannie realized she had become a joke. It was all over, and she had lost.

The guard took her firmly by the arm and pushed her towards the door. She could have fought him off, but there was no point.

She passed Berrington and saw him smile. She felt tears come to her eyes, but she swallowed them and held her head high. To hell with you all, she thought; one day you'll find out I was right.

Behind her, she heard Caren Beamish say: 'Mr Madigan, if you would care to resume your remarks?'

As Jeannie and the guard reached the door it opened and Lisa came in.

Jeannie gasped when she saw that right behind her was one of the clones.

It must be George Dassault. He had come! But one was not enough—she needed two to make her point. If only Steve would show up, or Mr Oliver with Harvey!

Then, with blinding joy, she saw a second clone walk in. It must be Henry King. She shook off the security guard. 'Look!' she yelled. 'Look here!'

As she spoke, a third clone walked in. The black hair told her it was Wayne Stattner.

'See!' Jeannie yelled. 'Here they are! They're identical!'

All the cameras swung away from the platform and pointed at the newcomers. Lights flashed as photographers began to snap the incident.

'I told you!' Jeannie said triumphantly to the journalists. 'Now ask them about their parents. They're not triplets—their mothers have never met! Ask them. Go on, ask them!'

She realized she was sounding too excited, and she made an effort to calm down, but it was difficult, she felt so happy. Several reporters leaped up and approached the three clones, eager to question them. The guard took Jeannie's arm again, but she was now at the centre of a crowd and could not move anyway.

In the background she heard Berrington raise his voice over the buzz of the reporters. 'Ladies and gentlemen, if we could have your attention, please!' He began by sounding angry but soon became petulant. 'We *would* like to continue with the press conference!' It was no good. The pack had scented a real story, and they had lost interest in speeches.

Out of the corner of her eye, Jeannie saw Senator Proust slip quietly out of the room.

A young man thrust a microphone at her and said: 'How did you find out about these experiments?'

Jeannie said into the microphone: 'My name is Dr Jean Ferrami and I'm a scientist at Jones Falls University, in the psychology department. In the course of my work I came across this group of people who seem to be identical twins but aren't related. I investigated.

Berrington Jones attempted to have me fired to prevent my finding out the truth. Despite that, I discovered the clones were the result of a military experiment conducted by Threeplex.' She looked around the room.

Where was Steve?

*

Steve gave one more kick, and the waste pipe sprang away from the underside of the washbasin in a shower of mortar and marble chips. Heaving on the pipe, he pulled it away from the sink and slipped the handcuff through the gap. Freed, he got to his feet.

He put his left hand in his pocket to conceal the handcuff that dangled from his wrist, then he left the bathroom.

The VIP room was empty.

Not sure what he might find in the conference room, he stepped out into the corridor.

Next to the VIP room was a door marked *Regency Room*. Farther along the corridor, waiting for the elevator, was one of his doubles.

Who was it? The man was rubbing his wrists, as if they were sore; and he had a red mark across both cheeks that looked as if it might have been made by a tight gag. This was Harvey, who had spent the night tied up.

He looked up and caught Steve's eye.

They stared at one another for a long moment. It was like looking into a mirror. Steve tried to see beyond Harvey's appearance, read his face and look into his heart, and see the cancer that made him evil. But he could not. All he saw was a man just like himself, who had walked down the same road and taken a different turning.

He tore his eyes away from Harvey and went into the Regency Room.

It was pandemonium. Jeannie and Lisa were in the centre of a crowd of cameramen. He saw one, no two, *three* clones with them. He pushed through to her. 'Jeannie!' he said.

She looked up at him, her face blank.

'It's Steve!' he said.

Mish Delaware was beside her.

Steve said to Mish: 'If you're looking for Harvey he's outside, waiting for the elevator.'

Mish said to Jeannie: 'Can you tell which one this is?'

'Sure.' Jeannie looked at him and said: 'I play a little tennis myself.'

He grinned. 'If you only play a *little* tennis, you're probably not in my league.'

'Thank God!' she said. She threw her arms around him. He smiled and bent to her face, and they kissed.

The cameras swung around to them, a sea of flash-guns glittered, and that was the picture on the front page of newspapers all over the world the following morning.

NEXT JUNE

CHAPTER SIXTY-THREE

FOREST LAWNS was like a genteel old-fashioned hotel. It had flowered wallpaper, and china knick-nacks in glass cases, and occasional tables with spindly legs. It smelled of pot-pourri, not disinfectant, and the staff called Jeannie's mother *Mrs Ferrami,* not *Maria* or *dear.* Mom had a little suite, with a small parlour where visitors could sit and have tea.

'This is my husband, Mom,' Jeannie said, and Steve gave his most charming smile and shook her hand.

'What a nice-looking boy,' Mom said. 'What work do you do, Steve?'

'I'm studying law.'

'Law. That's a good career.'

She had flashes of rationality interspersed with longer periods of confusion.

Jeannie said: 'Daddy came to our wedding.'

'How is your father?'

'He's good. He's too old to rob people any more, so he protects them instead. He started his own security firm. It's doing well.'

'I haven't seen him for twenty years.'

'Yes, you have, Mom. He visits you. But you forget.' Jeannie changed the subject. 'You look well.' Her mother was wearing a pretty cotton shirtwaist with a candy stripe. Her hair was permed and her nails were manicured. 'Do you like it here? It's better than Bella Vista, don't you think?'

Mom began to look worried. 'How are we going to pay for it, Jeannie? I don't have any money.'

'I have a new job, Mom. I can afford it.'

'What job is that?'

Jeannie knew she would not understand, but she told her anyway. 'I'm Director of Genetics Research for a big company called Landsmann.' Michael Madigan had offered her the job after someone explained her search engine to him. The salary was three times what she had been making at Jones Falls. Even more exciting was the work, which was at the leading edge of genetics research.

'That's nice,' Mom said. 'Oh! Before I forget—there was a picture of you in the newspaper. I saved it.' She delved into her handbag and brought out a folded clipping. She straightened it out and gave it to Jeannie.

Jeannie had seen it before, but she studied it as if it was new to her. It showed her at the congressional inquiry into the experiments at the Aventine Clinic. The inquiry had not yet produced its report, but there was not much doubt what it would say. The questioning of Jim Proust, televised nationwide, had been a public humiliation such as had never been seen before. Proust had blustered and shouted and lied, and with every word his guilt had become plainer. When it was over he had resigned as a senator.

Berrington Jones had not been allowed to resign but

had been dismissed from Jones Falls by the discipline committee. Jeannie had heard he had moved to California, where he was living on a small allowance from his ex-wife.

Preston Barck had resigned as president of Threeplex, which had been liquidated to pay agreed compensation to the eight mothers of the clones. A small sum had been set aside to pay for counselling to help each of the clones deal with their troubled history.

And Harvey Jones was serving five years for arson and rape.

Mom said: 'The paper says you had to *testify*. You weren't in any kind of trouble, were you?'

Jeannie exchanged a smile with Steve. 'For a week, back in September, I was kind of in trouble, Mom. But it worked out all right in the end.'

'That's good.'

Jeannie stood up. 'We have to go now. It's our honeymoon. We have a plane to catch.'

'Where are you going?'

'A little resort in the Caribbean. People say it's the most beautiful place in the whole world.'

Steve shook Mom's hand, and Jeannie kissed her goodbye.

'Have a good rest, honey,' Mom said as they left. 'You deserve it.'

ACKNOWLEDGEMENTS

I am deeply grateful to the following people for their kind help with the research for *The Third Twin:*

In the Baltimore City Police: Lieutenant Frederic Tabor, Lieutenant Larry Leeson, Sergeant Sue Young, Detective Alexis Russell, Detective Aaron Stewart, Detective Andrea Nolan, Detective Leonard Douglas;

In the Baltimore County Police: Sergeant David Moxley and Detective Karen Gentry;

Court Commissioner Cheryl Alston, Judge Barbara Baer Waxman, Assistant State's Attorney Mark Cohen;

Carole Kimmell, RN, at Mercy Hospital; Professor Trish VanZandt and her colleagues at Johns Hopkins University; Ms Bonnie Ariano, Executive Director of the Sexual Assault & Domestic Violence Center in Baltimore;

At the University of Minnesota: Professor Thomas Bouchard, Professor Matthew McGue, Professor David Lykken;

At the Pentagon: Lieutenant-Colonel Letwich, Captain Regenor;

At Fort Detrick in Frederick, Md: Ms Eileen Mitchell, Mr Chuck Dasey, Colonel David Franz;

Peter D. Martin of the Metropolitan Police Forensic

Science Laboratory; Ruth and Norman Glick; computer experts Wade Chambers, Rob Cook and Alan Gold; and especially professional researcher Dan Starer, of Research for Writers, New York City, who put me in touch with most of the above people.

I am also grateful to my editors Suzanne Baboneau, Marjorie Chapman and Ann Patty; to friends and family who read drafts of the book and made comments, including Barbara Follett, Emanuele Follett, Katya Follett, Jann Turner, Kim Turner, John Evans, George Brennan and Ken Burrows; to agents Amy Berkower, Bob Bookman and—most of all—my oldest collaborator and sharpest critic, Al Zuckerman.

PAPER MONEY

Introduction

This book was written in 1976, immediately before *Eye of the Needle*, and I think it is the best of my unsuccessful books. It was published under the pseudonym Zachary Stone, as was *The Modigliani Scandal*, because the books are similar: they lack a central character, but feature several groups of characters whose stories are linked and share a common climax.

In *Paper Money* the links are less fortuitous, for the book is supposed to show how crime, high finance, and journalism are corruptly interconnected. The ending is rather sombre by comparison with *The Modigliani Scandal* – in fact it is almost a tragedy. However, it is the differences and similarities between *Paper Money* and *Eye of the Needle* that are most instructive. (Readers who want the cake, not the recipe, should skip this and go straight to Chapter One.) The plot of *Paper Money* is the cleverest I have ever devised, and the small sales of the book convinced me that clever plots satisfy authors more than readers. The plot of *Eye of the Needle* is of course very simple – in fact it can be written down in three paragraphs, as indeed I did write it when I first thought of it. *Eye of the Needle* has only three or four main characters whereas *Paper Money* has a dozen or so. Yet with its complex plot and large cast, *Paper Money* is only half the length of *Eye of the Needle.* As a writer I have always had to struggle against a tendency to underwrite, and in *Paper Money* you see me struggling in vain. Consequently the many characters are painted in brisk, bold brushstrokes, and the book lacks the feeling of detailed personal involvement with the private lives of the characters that readers demand of a best seller.

One of the strengths of the book is its form. The action takes place during a single day in the life of a London evening newspaper (I worked for such a newspaper in 1973 and 1974) and each chapter chronicles one hour of that day in three or four scenes describing both what happens at the news desk and what happens in the stories the paper is covering (or missing). *Eye of the Needle* has an even more rigid structure, although nobody to my knowledge has ever noticed it: there are six parts, each with six chapters (except for the last part, which has seven), the first chapter in each part dealing with the spy, the second with the spy catchers, and so on until the sixth, which always tells of the international military consequences of what has gone before. Readers do not notice such things – and why should they? – but still I suspect that regularity, and even symmetry, contribute to what they perceive as a well-told story.

The other feature *Paper Money* shares with *Eye of*

the Needle is a wealth of good minor characters – tarts, thieves, half-witted children, working-class wives, and lonely old men. In subsequent books I have not done this, for it only diverts from the main characters and their story; yet I often wonder whether I am being too clever.

Today I am not as sure as I was in 1976 of the links between crime, high finance, and journalism; but I think this book is true to life in another way. It presents a detailed picture of the London that I knew in the seventies, with its policemen and crooks, bankers and call girls, reporters and politicians, its shops and slums, its roads and its river. I loved it, and I hope you will too.

Six a.m.

Chapter One

It was the luckiest night of Tim Fitzpeterson's life.

He thought this the moment he opened his eyes and saw the girl, in bed beside him, still sleeping. He did not move, for fear of waking her; but he looked at her, almost furtively, in the cold light of the London dawn. She slept flat on her back, with the absolute relaxation of small children. Tim was reminded of his own Adrienne when she was little. He put the unwelcome thought out of his mind.

The girl beside him had red hair, fitting her small head like a cap, showing her tiny ears. All her features were small: nose, chin, cheekbones, dainty teeth. Once, in the night, he had covered her face with his broad, clumsy hands, pressing his fingers gently into the hollows of her eyes and her cheeks, opening her soft lips with his thumbs, as if his skin could feel her beauty like the heat from a fire.

Her left arm lay limply outside the coverlet, which was pushed down to reveal narrow, delicate shoulders and one shallow breast, its nipple soft in slumber.

They lay apart, not quite touching, although he could feel the warmth of her thigh close to his. He looked away from her, up at the ceiling, and for a moment he let the sheer joy of remembered fornication wash over him like a physical thrill; then he got up.

He stood beside the bed and looked back at her. She was undisturbed. The candid morning light made her no less lovely, despite tousled hair and the untidy remains of what had been elaborate make-up. Daybreak was less kind to Tim Fitzpeterson, he knew. That was why he tried not to wake her: he wanted to look in a mirror before she saw him.

He went naked, padding across the dull green living room carpet to the bathroom. In the space of a few moments he saw the place as if for the first time, and found it hopelessly unexciting. The carpet was matched by an even duller green sofa, with fading flowered cushions. There was a plain wooden desk, of the kind to be found in a million offices; an elderly black-and-white television set; a filing cabinet; and a bookshelf of legal and economic textbooks plus several volumes of *Hansard*. He had once thought it so dashing to have a London pied-à-terre.

The bathroom had a full-length mirror – bought not by Tim, but by his wife, in the days before she had totally retired from town life. He looked in it while he waited for the bath to fill, wondering what there was about this middle-aged body that could drive a beautiful girl of – what, twenty-five? – into a frenzy of lust. He was healthy, but not fit; not in the sense with which that word is used to describe men who do exercises and visit gymnasia. He was short, and his naturally broad frame was thickened by a little superfluous fat, particularly on the chest, waist, and buttocks. His physique was okay, for a man of forty-one, but it was nothing to excite even the most physical of women.

The mirror became obscured by steam, and Tim got into the bath. He rested his head and closed his eyes. It occurred to him that he had had less than two hours of sleep, yet he felt quite fresh. His upbringing would have him believe that pain and discomfort, if not actual illness, were the consequences of late nights, dancing, adultery, and strong drink. All those sins together ought to bring down the wrath of God.

No: the wages of sin were sheer delight. He began to soap himself languidly. It had started at one of those appalling dinners: grapefruit cocktail, overdone steak and *bombe* no *surprise* for three hundred members of a useless organization. Tim's speech had been just another exposition of the Government's current strategy, emotionally weighted to appeal to the particular sympathies of the audience. Afterwards he had agreed to go somewhere else for a drink with one of his colleagues – a brilliant young economist – and two faintly interesting people from the audience.

The venue turned out to be a nightclub which would normally have been beyond Tim's means; but someone else had paid the entrance. Once inside, he began to enjoy himself, so much so that he bought a bottle of champagne with his credit card. More people had joined their group: a film company executive

Tim had vaguely heard of; a playwright he hadn't; a left-wing economist who shook hands with a wry smile and avoided shop talk; and the girls.

The champagne and the floor show inflamed him slightly. In the old days, he would at this point have taken Julia home and made love to her roughly – she liked that, just occasionally. But now she no longer came to town, and he no longer went to nightclubs; not normally.

The girls had not been introduced. Tim started to talk to the nearest, a flat-chested redhead in a long dress of some pale colour. She looked like a model, and said she was an actress. He expected that he would find her boring, and that she would reciprocate. That was when he got the first intimation that tonight would be special: she seemed to find him fascinating.

Their close conversation gradually isolated them from the rest of the party, until someone suggested another club. Tim immediately said he would go home. The redhead caught his arm and asked him not to; and Tim, who was being gallant to a beautiful woman for the first time in twenty years, instantly agreed to go along.

He wondered, as he got out of the bath, what they had talked about for so long. The work of a Junior Minister in the Department of Energy was hardly cocktail-party conversation: when it was not technical, it was highly confidential. Perhaps they had discussed politics. Had he told wry anecdotes about senior politicians, in the deadpan tone which was his only way of being humorous? He could not remember. All he could recall was the way she had sat, with every part of her body angled devotedly towards him: head, shoulders, knees, feet; a physical attitude that was at once intimate and teasing.

He wiped steam off the shaving mirror and rubbed his chin speculatively, sizing up the task. He had very dark hair, and his beard, if he were to grow it, would be thick. The rest of his face was, to say the least, ordinary. The chin was receding, the nose sharply pointed with twin white marks either side of the bridge where spectacles had rested for thirty-five years, the mouth not small but a little grim, the ears too large, the forehead intellectually high. No character could be read there. It was a face trained to conceal thoughts, instead of displaying emotion.

He switched on the shaver and grimaced to bring all of his left cheek into view. He was not even ugly. Some girls had a thing about ugly men, he had heard – he was in no position to verify such generalizations about women – but Tim Fitzpeterson did not even fit into that dubiously fortunate category.

But perhaps it was time to think again about the categories he fitted into. The second club they had visited had been the kind of place he would never knowingly have entered. He was no music-lover, and if he had liked it his taste would not have included the blaring, insistent row which drowned conversation in The Black Hole. Nevertheless, he had danced to it – the jerky, exhibitionist dancing that seemed to be *de rigueur* there. He enjoyed it, and thought he acquitted himself well enough; there were no amused glances from the other patrons, as he feared there might be. Perhaps that was because many of them were his age.

The disc jockey, a bearded young man in a T-shirt improbably printed with the words 'Harvard Business School', capriciously played a slow ballad, sung by an American with a heavy cold. They were on the small dance floor at the time. The girl came close to him and wound her arms around him. Then he knew she meant it; and he had to decide whether he was equally serious. With her hot, lithe body clinging to him as closely as a wet towel, he made up his mind very quickly. He bent his head – she was slightly shorter than he – and murmured into her ear: 'Come and have a drink at my flat.'

He kissed her in the taxi – *there* was something he had not done for many years! The kiss was so luscious, like a kiss in a dream, that he touched her breasts, wonderfully small and hard under the loose gown; and after that they found it difficult to restrain themselves until they reached home.

The token drink was forgotten. We must have got into bed in less than a minute, Tim thought smugly. He finished shaving and looked around for cologne. There was an old bottle in the wall cabinet.

He went back to the bedroom. She was still asleep. He found his dressing gown and cigarettes and sat in the upright chair by the window. I was pretty terrific in bed, he thought. He knew he was kidding himself:

she had been the activist, the creative one. On her initiative they had done things which Tim could not suggest to Julia after fifteen years in the same bed.

Yes, Julia. He gazed unseeing from the first-floor window, across the narrow street to the red-brick Victorian school, its meagre playground painted with the fading yellow lines of a netball court. He still felt the same about Julia: if he had loved her before, he loved her now. This girl was different. But wasn't that what fools always told themselves before embarking on an affair?

Let's not be hasty, he told himself. For her this might be a one-night stand. He could not assume she would want to see him again. Yet he wanted to decide where his aims lay before asking her what the options were: government had taught him to brief himself before meetings.

He had a formula for the approach to complex issues. First, what have I got to lose?

Julia, again: plump, intelligent, contented; her horizons contracting inexorably with every year of motherhood. There had been a time when he lived for her: he bought the clothes she liked, he read novels because she was interested in novels, and his political successes pleased him all the more because they pleased her. But the centre of gravity of his life had shifted. Now Julia held sway only over trivia. She wanted to live in Hampshire, and it did not matter to him, so they lived there. She wanted him to wear check jackets, but Westminster chic demanded sober suits, so he wore dark, faintly patterned greys and navy blues.

When he analysed his feelings, he found there was not a lot to tie him to Julia. A little sentiment, perhaps; a nostalgic picture of her, with her hair in a pony-tail, doing the jive in a tapered skirt. Was that love or something? He doubted it.

The girls? That was something else. Katie, Penny and Adrienne: only Katie was old enough to understand love and marriage. They did not see much of him, but he took the view that a little father-love goes a long way, and is a great deal better than no father at all. There was no room for debate there: his opinion was fixed.

And there was his career. A divorce might not harm a Junior Minister, but it could ruin a man higher up. There had never been a divorced Prime Minister. Tim Fitzpeterson wanted that job.

So there was a lot to lose – in fact, all he held dear. He turned his gaze from the window to the bed. The girl had rolled onto her side, facing away. She was right to have her hair short – it emphasized the slender neck and pretty shoulders. Her back tapered sharply to a small waist, then disappeared beneath a crumpled sheet. Her skin was faintly tanned.

There was so much to gain. 'Joy' was a word Tim had little use for, but it entered his thoughts now. If he had known joy before, he could not remember when. Satisfaction, yes: in the writing of a sound, comprehensive report; in the winning of one of those countless small battles in committees and in the House of Commons; in a book that was correct or a wine that was right. But the savagely chemical pleasure he had with this girl was new.

There; those were the pros and cons. The formula said, now add them up and see which is greater. But this time the formula would not work. Tim had acquaintances who said it never did. Perhaps they were right. It might be a mistake to think that reasons could be counted like pound notes: he was reminded, curiously, of a phrase from a college philosophy lecture, 'the bewitchment of our intelligence by means of language'. Which is longer – an aeroplane or a one-act play? Which do I prefer – satisfaction or joy? His thinking was getting woolly. He made a disgusted noise, then looked quickly at the bed to see whether he had disturbed her. She slept on. Good.

Out in the street, a grey Rolls-Royce pulled up at the kerb a hundred yards away. Nobody got out. Tim looked more closely, and saw the driver open a newspaper. A chauffeur, perhaps, picking someone up at six-thirty? A businessman who had travelled overnight and arrived too early? Tim could not read the number plate. But he could see that the driver was a big man; big enough to make the interior of the car seem as cramped as a Mini.

He turned his mind back to his dilemma. What do we do in politics, he thought, when we face two forceful but conflicting demands? The answer came immediately: we choose a course of action which, really or apparently, meets both needs. The parallel was obvious. He would stay married to Julia and have an affair with this girl. It seemed a very political solution, and it pleased him.

He lit another cigarette and thought about the future. It was a pleasant pastime. There would be many more nights here at the flat; the occasional weekend in a small hotel in the country; perhaps even a fortnight in the sun, on some discreet little beach in North Africa or the West Indies. She would be sensational in a bikini.

Other hopes paled beside these. He was tempted by the thought that his early life had been wasted; but he knew the idea to be extravagant. Not wasted, then; but it was as if he had spent his youth working out long-division sums and never discovered differential calculus.

He decided to talk to her about the problem and his solution. She would say it could not be done, and he would tell her that making compromises work was his special talent.

How should he begin? 'Darling, I want to do this again, often.' That seemed all right. What would she say? 'So would I,' or: 'Call me at this number,' or: 'Sorry, Timmy, I'm a one-night girl.'

No, not that; it wasn't possible. Last night had been good for her, too. He was special for her. She had said so.

He stood up and put out his cigarette. I'll go over to the bed, he thought; and I'll pull the blankets off her gently, and look at her nakedness for a few moments; then I'll lie beside her, and kiss her belly, and her thighs, and her breasts, until she wakes; and then I'll make love to her again.

He looked away from her and out of the window, savouring the anticipation. The Rolls was still there, like a grey slug in the gutter. For some reason it bothered him. He put it out of his mind, and went over to wake the girl.

Chapter Two

Felix Laski did not have much money, despite the fact that he was very rich. His wealth took the form of shares, land, buildings, and occasionally more nebulous assets like half a film script or one third of an invention for making instant potato chips. Newspapers were fond of saying that if all his riches were turned into cash, he would have so many millions of pounds; and Laski was equally fond of pointing out that to turn his riches into cash would be close to impossible.

He walked from Waterloo railway station to the City, because he believed that laziness caused heart attacks in men of his age. This concern with his health was foolish, for he was as fit a fifty-year-old as could be found within the Square Mile. Just short of six feet tall, with a chest like the stern of a battleship, he was about as vulnerable to cardiac arrest as a young ox.

He cut a striking figure, walking across Blackfriars Bridge in the brittle sunshine of the early morning. His clothes were expensive, from the blue silk shirt to the handmade shoes; by City standards he was a dandy. This was because every man in the village where Laski had been born wore cotton dungarees and a cloth cap; now good clothes gave him a buzz by reminding him of what he had left behind.

The clothes were part of his image, which was that of a buccaneer. His deals usually involved risk, or opportunism, or both; and he took care that from the outside they looked sharper than they were. A reputation for having the magic touch was worth more than a merchant bank.

It was the image that had seduced Peters. Laski thought about Peters as he walked briskly past St Paul's Cathedral towards their rendezvous. A small, narrow-minded man, his expertise was in the movement of cash: not credit, but physical funds, paper money. He worked for the Bank of England, the ultimate source of legal tender. His job was to arrange for the creation and destruction of notes and coins. He did not make policy – that was done at a higher level, perhaps in the Cabinet – but he knew how many fivers Barclays Bank needed before they did.

Laski had first met him at the cocktail-party opening of an office block built by a discount house. Laski went to such affairs for no reason other than to meet people like Peters, who might one day come in useful. Five years later, Peters became useful. Laski phoned him at the Bank, and asked him to recommend a numismatist to advise on a fictitious purchase of old coins. Peters announced that he was a collector, in a small way, and that he would look at them himself, if Laski wished. Splendid, Laski said, and rushed out to get the coins. Peters advised him to buy. Suddenly, they were friends.

(The purchase became the foundation of a collection which was now worth double what Laski had paid for it. That was incidental to his purpose, but he was inordinately proud of it.)

It turned out that Peters was an early riser, partly because he liked it, but also because money was moved around in the mornings, and so the bulk of his work needed to be done before nine o'clock. Laski learned that it was Peters' custom to drink coffee in a particular café at around six-thirty each day, and he began to join him, at first occasionally, and then regularly. Laski pretended to be an early riser himself, and joined in Peters' praise of the quiet streets and the crisp morning air. In truth he liked to get up late, but he was prepared to make a lot of sacrifices if there was half a chance of this far-fetched scheme coming off.

He turned in to the café, breathing hard. At his age, even a fit man was entitled to blow after a long walk. The place smelled of coffee and fresh bread. The walls were hung with plastic tomatoes and water-colours of the proprietor's home town in Italy. Behind the counter, a woman in overalls and a long-haired youth were making mountains of sandwiches ready for the hundreds of people who would snatch a bite at their desks this lunch-time. A radio was on somewhere, but it was not loud. Peters was already there, at a window seat.

Laski bought coffee and a *leberwurst* sandwich and sat down opposite Peters, who was eating doughnuts

– he seemed to be one of those people who never put on weight. Laski said: 'It's going to be a fine day.' His voice was deep and resonant, like an actor's, with just a trace of some East European accent.

Peters said: 'Beautiful. And I shall be in my garden by four-thirty.'

Laski sipped coffee and looked at the other man. Peters had very short hair and a small moustache, and his face looked pinched. He had not yet started work, and he was already looking forward to going home; Laski thought that tragic. He felt a momentary pang of compassion for Peters and all the other little men for whom work was a means instead of an end.

'I like my work,' Peters said, as if reading Laski's mind.

Laski covered his surprise. 'But you like your garden better.'

'In this weather, yes. Do you have a garden . . . Felix?'

'My housekeeper tends the window boxes. I'm not a man of hobbies.' Laski reflected on Peters' hesitant use of his Christian name. The man was slightly awe-struck, he decided. Good.

'No time, I suppose. You must work very hard.'

'So people tell me. It's just that I prefer to spend the hours between six p.m. and midnight making fifty thousand dollars than watching actors pretend to kill each other on television.'

Peters laughed. 'The most imaginative brain in the City turns out to have no imagination.'

'I don't follow that.'

'You don't read novels or go to the cinema, either, do you?'

'No.'

'You see? You've got a blind spot – you can't empathize with fiction. It's true of many of the most enterprising businessmen. The incapacity seems to go with heightened acumen, like a blind man's hypersensitive hearing.'

Laski frowned. Being analysed put him at a disadvantage. 'Maybe,' he said.

Peters seemed to sense his discomfort. 'I'm fascinated by the careers of great entrepreneurs,' he said.

'So am I,' Laski said. 'I'm all in favour of pinching other people's brainwaves.'

'What was your first coup, Felix?'

Laski relaxed. This was more familiar territory. 'I suppose it was Woolwich Chemicals,' he said. 'That was a small pharmaceuticals manufacturer. After the war they set up a small chain of High Street chemists' shops, with the object of guaranteeing their markets. The trouble was, they knew all about chemistry and nothing about retailing, and the shops ate up most of the profits made by the factory.

'I was working for a stockbroker at the time, and I'd made a little money playing the market. I went to my boss and offered him a half-share in the profits if he would finance the deal. We bought the company, and immediately sold the factory to ICI for almost as much as we paid for the shares. Then we closed the shops and sold them one by one – they were all in prime sites.'

'I'll never understand this sort of thing,' Peters said. 'If the factory and the shops were worth so much, why were the shares cheap?'

'Because the enterprise was losing money. They hadn't paid a dividend for years. The management didn't have the guts to cash in their chips, so to speak. We did. Everything in business is courage.' He started to eat his sandwich.

'It's fascinating,' Peters said. He looked at his watch. 'I must go.'

'Big day?' Laski said lightly.

'Today's one of *the* days – and that always means headaches.'

'Did you solve that problem?'

'Which?'

'Routes.' Laski lowered his voice a fraction. 'Your security people wanted you to send the convoy a different way each time.'

'No.' Peters was embarrassed: it had been indiscreet of him to tell Laski about that dilemma. 'There is really only one sensible way to get there. However . . .' He stood up.

Laski smiled and kept his voice casual. 'So today's big shipment goes by the old direct route.'

Peters put a finger to his lips. 'Security,' he said.

'Sure.'

Peters picked up his raincoat. 'Good-bye.'

'I'll see you tomorrow,' Laski said, smiling broadly.

Chapter Three

Arthur Cole climbed the steps from the station, his breath rattling unhealthily in his chest. A gust of warm air came up from the bowels of the Underground, wrapped itself snugly around him, and blew away. He shivered slightly as he emerged into the street.

The sunshine took him by surprise – it had hardly been dawn when he boarded the train. The air was chilled and sweet. Later it would become poisonous enough to knock out a policeman on point duty. Cole remembered the first time that had happened: the story had been an *Evening Post* exclusive.

He walked slowly until his breathing eased. Twenty-five years in newspapers have ruined my health, he thought. In truth, any industry would have done the same, for he was prone to worry and to drink, and his chest was weak; but it comforted him to blame his profession.

Anyway, he had given up smoking. He had been a non-smoker for – he looked at his watch – one hundred and twenty-eight minutes, unless he counted the night, in which case it was eight hours. He had already passed several moments of risk: immediately after the alarm clock went off at four-thirty (he usually smoked one on the WC); driving away from his house, at the moment when he got into top gear and turned on the radio ready for the five o'clock news; accelerating down the first fast stretch of the A12 as his large Ford hit its stride; and waiting on a cold, open-air tube station in East London for the earliest train of the day.

The BBC's five o'clock bulletin had not cheered him. It had had all his attention as he drove, for the route was so familiar that he negotiated the bends and roundabouts automatically, from memory. The lead story came from Westminster: the latest industrial relations bill had been passed by Parliament, but the majority had been narrow. Cole had caught the story the previous night on television. That meant the morning papers would certainly have it, which in turn meant that the *Post* could do nothing with it unless there were developments later in the day.

There was a story about the Retail Price Index. The source would be official government statistics, which would have been embargoed until midnight: again, the mornings would have it.

It was no surprise to learn that the car workers' strike was still on – it would hardly have been settled overnight.

Test cricket in Australia solved the sports editor's problem, but the score was not sufficiently sensational for the front page.

Cole began to worry.

He entered the *Evening Post* building and took the lift. The newsroom occupied the entire first floor. It was a huge, I-shaped open-plan office. Cole entered at the foot of the I. To his left were the typewriters and telephones of the copytakers, who would type out stories dictated over the phone; to the right, the filing cabinets and bookshelves of specialist writers – political, industrial, crime, defence, and more. Cole walked up the stem of the I, through rows of desks belonging to ordinary common-or-garden reporters, to the long news desk which divided the room in two. Behind it was the U-shaped sub-editors' table, and beyond that, in the crosspiece of the I, was the sports department – a semi-independent kingdom, with its own editor, reporters, and subs. Cole occasionally showed curious relatives around the place; he always told them: 'It's supposed to work like a production line. Usually it's more like a bun fight.' It was an exaggeration, but it always got a laugh.

The room was brightly lit, and empty. As deputy news editor, Cole had a section of the news desk to himself. He opened a drawer and took out a coin, then walked to the vending machine in Sport and punched buttons for instant tea with milk and sugar. A teleprinter chattered to life, breaking the silence.

As Cole walked back to his desk with his paper cup, the far door bumped open. A short, grey-haired figure came in, wearing a bulky parka and cycle clips. Cole waved and called: 'Morning, George.'

Paper Money

'Hello, Arthur. Cold enough for you?' George began to take off his coat. The body inside it was small and thin. Despite his age, George's title was Head Lad: he was chief of the office's team of messengers. He lived in Potters Bar and cycled to work. Arthur thought that an astonishing feat.

Arthur put down his tea, shrugged out of his raincoat, turned on the radio, and sat down. The radio began to murmur. He sipped tea and gazed straight ahead. The newsroom was scruffy – chairs were scattered randomly, newspapers and sheets of copy paper littered the desks, and redecoration had been postponed in last year's economy drive – but the scene was too familiar to register. Cole's mind was on the first edition, which would be on the streets in three hours.

Today's paper would have sixteen pages. Fourteen of the first edition's pages already existed as semicylindrical metal plates on the press downstairs. They contained advertising, features, television programmes, and news written in such a way that its age would – it was hoped – be overlooked by the reader. That left the back page for the sports editor and the front page for Arthur Cole.

Parliament, a strike, and inflation – they were all yesterday stories. There was not much he could do with them. Any of them could be dressed up with a today intro, like 'Cabinet Ministers today held an inquest on the Government's narrow escape . . .' There was one of those for every situation. Yesterday's disaster became today's news story with 'Dawn today revealed the full horror . . .' Yesterday's murder benefited from 'Detectives today searched London for the man who . . .' Arthur's problem had given birth to scores of clichés. In a civilized society, he thought, when there was no news there would be no newspapers. It was an old thought, and he brushed it out of his mind impatiently.

Everyone accepted that the first edition was rubbish three days out of six. But that gave no comfort, because it was the reason Arthur Cole had the job of producing that edition. He had been deputy news editor for five years. Twice during that period the news editor's chair had fallen vacant, and both times a younger man than Cole had been promoted. Someone had decided that the number two job was the limit of his capabilities. He disagreed.

The only way he could demonstrate his talent was by turning out an excellent first edition. Unfortunately, how good the edition was depended largely upon luck. Cole's strategy was to aim for a paper which was consistently slightly better than the opposition's first edition. He thought he was succeeding: whether anyone upstairs had noticed, he had no idea; and he would not let himself worry about it.

George came up behind him and dumped a pile of newspapers on his desk. 'Young Stephen's reported sick again,' he grumbled.

Arthur smiled. 'What is it – a hangover or a runny nose?'

'Remember what they used to tell us? "If you can walk, you can work." Not this lot.'

Arthur nodded.

'Am I right?' George said.

'You're right.' The two of them had been Lads together on the *Post*. Arthur had got his NUJ card after the war. George, who had not been called up, had remained a messenger.

George said: 'We were keen. We *wanted* to work.'

Arthur picked up the top newspaper from the pile. This was not the first time George had complained about his staff, nor the first time Arthur had commiserated with him. But Arthur knew what was wrong with the Lads of today. Thirty years ago, a smart Lad could become a reporter; nowadays, that road was closed. The new system had a double impact: bright youngsters stayed at school instead of becoming messengers; and those who did become messengers knew they had no prospects, so they did as little work as they could get away with. But Arthur could not say this to George, because it would call attention to the fact that Arthur had done so much better than his old colleague. So he agreed that the youth of today were rotten.

George seemed disposed to persist with his grouse. Arthur cut him off by saying: 'Anything on the overnight wire?'

'I'll get it. Only I've got to do all the papers myself—'

'I'd better see the wire copy first.' Arthur turned away. He hated to pull rank. He had never learned to do it naturally, perhaps because he took no pleasure in it. He looked at the *Morning Star*: they had led with the industry bill.

It was unlikely that there would be any national news on the teletype yet; it was too early. But foreign news came in sporadically during the night, and more often than not it included one story which could be the splash, in a pinch. Most nights there was a major fire, a multiple murder, a riot, or a coup somewhere in the world. The *Post* was a London paper and did not like to lead with foreign news unless it was sensational; but it might be better than 'Cabinet Ministers today held an inquest . . .'

George dumped a sheet of paper several feet long on his desk. Not cutting the sheet into individual stories was his way of showing displeasure. He probably wanted Arthur to complain, so that he could point out how much work there was for him to do with the early Lad off sick. Arthur fumbled in his desk for scissors, and began to read.

He went through a political story from Washington, a Test Match report, and a Middle East roundup. He was halfway through a minor Hollywood divorce when the phone rang. He picked it up and said: 'Newsdesk.'

'I've got an item for your gossip column.' It was a man's voice, with a broad Cockney accent.

Cole was instantly sceptical. This was not the voice

of a man who would have inside information on the love lives of the aristocracy. He said: 'Good. Would you like to tell me your name?'

'Never mind about that. Do you know who Tim Fitzpeterson is?'

'Of course.'

'Well, he's making a fool of himself with a redhead. She must be twenty years younger than him. Do you want his phone number?'

'Please.' Cole wrote it down. He was interested now. If a Minister's marriage had broken up, it would make a good story, not just a gossip item. 'Who's the girl?' he said.

'Calls herself an actress. Truth is, she's a brass. Just give him a ring right away, and ask him about Dizi Disney.' The line went dead.

Cole frowned. This was a little odd: most tipsters wanted money, especially for news of this kind. He shrugged. It was worth checking out. He would give it to a reporter later on.

Then he changed his mind. Innumerable stories had been lost for ever by being put aside for a few minutes. Fitzpeterson might leave for the House, or his Whitehall office. And the informant had said: 'Give him a ring right away.'

Cole read the number off his notebook and dialled.

Seven a.m.

Chapter Four

'Have you ever watched yourself doing it in the mirror?' she had asked; and when Tim admitted he had not, she insisted they try it. They were standing in front of the full-length glass in the bathroom when the phone rang. The noise made Tim jump, and she said: 'Ouch! Careful.'

He wanted to ignore it, but the intrusion of the outside world took away his desire. He left her, and went into the bedroom. The phone was on a chair underneath a pile of her clothes. He found it and lifted the receiver. 'Yes?'

'Mr Fitzpeterson?' It was the voice of a middle-aged man with a London accent. He sounded slightly asthmatic.

'Yes. Who is that?'

'*Evening Post*, sir. I'm sorry to call you so early. I have to ask you whether it's true you're getting divorced.'

Tim sat down heavily. For a moment he was unable to speak.

'Are you there, sir?'

'Who the devil told you that?'

'The informant mentioned a woman called Dizi Disney. Do you know her?'

'I've never heard of her.' Tim was regaining his composure. 'Don't wake me up in the morning with idle rumours.' He put the phone down.

The girl came into the bedroom. 'You look quite white,' she said. 'Who was it?'

'What's your name?' he snapped.

'Dizi Disney.'

'Jesus Christ.' His hands were trembling. He clenched his fists and stood up. 'The papers have got hold of a whisper that I'm getting divorced!'

'They must hear that sort of thing about famous people all the time.'

'They mentioned your name!' He slammed one fist into the palm of his other hand. 'How could they find out so quickly? What am I going to do?'

She turned her back on him and put her panties on.

He stared out of the window. The grey Rolls was still there, but now it was empty. He wondered where the driver had gone. The stray thought annoyed him. He tried to assess the situation coolly. Someone had seen him leave a club with the girl, and phoned the information to a reporter. The informant had built the incident up for dramatic effect. But Tim was sure no one had seen them enter the flat together.

'Listen,' he said. 'Last night you said you weren't feeling well. I took you out of the club and got a taxi. The cab dropped me off then took you home. All right?'

'Whatever you say,' she said uninterestedly.

Her attitude infuriated him. 'For God's sake, this involves you!'

'I think my part in it is over.'

'What does that mean?'

There was a knock at the door.

Tim said: 'Oh, Jesus, no.'

The girl zipped up her dress. 'I'll go.'

'Don't be such a damn fool.' He grabbed her arm. 'You mustn't be seen here, don't you understand? Stay here in the bedroom. I'll open the door. If I have to ask them in, just keep quiet until they go.'

He put on his underwear shorts and struggled into his dressing gown as he crossed the living room. There was a tiny hall, and a front door with a peephole. Tim swung the flap aside and put an eye to the glass.

The man outside looked vaguely familiar. He had the face of a boxer. Broad-shouldered and well built, he would have been a heavyweight. He wore a grey coat with a velvet collar. Tim put his age at late twenties. He did not look like a newspaper reporter.

Tim unbolted the door and opened it. 'What is it?' he said.

Without speaking, the man pushed Tim aside, stepped in, and closed the door behind him. He walked into the living room.

Tim took a deep breath and tried not to panic. He followed the man. 'I'm going to call the police,' he said.

The man sat down. He called: 'Are you in there, Dizi?'

The girl came to the bedroom door.

The man said: 'Make us a cup of tea, girl.'

'Do you know him?' Tim asked her incredulously.

She ignored him and went into the kitchen.

The man laughed. 'Know me? She works for me.'

Tim sat down. 'What is this all about?' he said weakly.

'All in good time.' The man looked around. 'I can't say you've got a nice place here, because you haven't. I expected you to have something a bit flash, know what I mean? By the way, in case you haven't recognized me, I'm Tony Cox.' He stuck out his hand. Tim ignored it. Cox said: 'Please yourself.'

Tim was remembering – the face and the name were familiar. He thought Cox was a fairly wealthy businessman, but he could not recall what his business was. He thought he had seen the man's picture in a newspaper – something to do with raising money for boys' clubs in the East End.

Cox jerked his head towards the kitchen. 'Did you enjoy her?'

'For God's sake,' Tim said.

The girl came in, carrying two mugs on a tray. Cox asked her: 'Did he enjoy it?'

'What do you think?' she said sourly.

Cox took out his wallet and counted out some notes. 'Here you are,' he said to her. 'You done a good job. Now you can fuck off.'

She took the money and put it in a handbag. She said: 'You know, Tone, I think the thing I like most about you is your beautiful manners.' She went out without looking at Tim.

Tim thought: I've made the biggest mistake of my life.

As the girl left, the door slammed.

Cox winked. 'She's a good girl.'

'She's the lowest form of human life,' Tim spat.

'Now, don't be like that. She's just a good actress. She might have got into films if I hadn't of found her first.'

'I presume you're a ponce.'

Anger flashed in Cox's eyes, but he controlled it. 'You'll regret that little joke,' he said mildly. 'All you need to know about me and Dizi is that she does what I tell her to. If I say "Keep your mouth shut," she does. And if I say "Tell the nice man from the *News of the World* how Mr Fitzpeterson seduced you," she will. Know what I mean?'

Tim said: 'I suppose it was you who contacted the *Evening Post*.'

'Don't worry! Without confirmation, they can't do a thing. And only three people can confirm the story: you, Dizi, and me. You're not going to say anything, Dizi's got no will of her own, and I can keep a secret.'

Tim lit a cigarette. He was finding his confidence again. Cox was just a working-class hoodlum, despite his velvet collar and his grey Rolls-Royce. Tim had the feeling he could handle the man. He said: 'If this is blackmail, you're on to a loser. I haven't any money.'

'Quite warm in here, isn't it?' Cox stood up and took his coat off. 'Well,' he resumed, 'if you haven't got money, we'll have to think of something else you can give me.'

Tim frowned. He was lost again.

Cox continued: 'In the last few months, half a dozen or so companies have put in bids for drilling rights in a new oil field called Shield, right?'

Tim was astonished. Surely this crook could not be connected with any of those respectable companies? He said: 'Yes, but it's too late for me to influence the result – the decision has been made. It will be announced this afternoon.'

'Don't jump to conclusions. I know it's too late to change it. But you can tell me who's won the licence.'

Tim stared. Was that all he wanted? It was too good to be true! He said: 'What possible use could you have for that sort of information?'

'None, really. I'm going to trade it for another piece of information. I've got a deal going with this gent, see. He doesn't know how I get my inside dope, and he doesn't know what I do with the stuff he tells me. That way he keeps his nose clean. Know what I mean? Now, then: who gets the licence?'

It was so easy, Tim thought. Two words, and the nightmare would be over. A breach of confidence like this could ruin his career: but then, if he did not do it, his career was finished anyway.

Cox said: 'If you're not sure what to do, just think of the headlines. "The Minister and the Actress. He wouldn't make an honest woman of me, showgirl weeps." Remember poor old Tony Lambton?'

'Shut up,' Tim said. 'It's Hamilton Holdings.'

Cox smiled. 'My friend will be pleased,' he said. 'Where's the phone?'

Tim jerked a thumb. 'Bedroom,' he said wearily.

Cox went into the room, and Tim closed his eyes. How naïve he had been, to think that a young girl like Dizi could fall head over heels in love with someone like him. He was a patsy in some elaborate scheme which was much bigger than petty blackmail.

He could hear Cox speaking. 'Laski? It's me. Hamilton Holdings. You got that? Announcement this afternoon. Now, what about your end?' There was a pause. 'Today? Terrific. You've made my day, pal. And the route?' Another pause. 'What do you mean, you *think* it's the usual? You're supposed – okay, okay. So long.'

Tim knew of Laski – he was an ageing City whiz kid – but he was emotionally too exhausted to feel appropriately astonished. He could believe anything of anyone now.

Cox came back in. Tim stood up. Cox said: 'Well, a successful little morning, one way and another. And don't feel too bad about it. After all, it was the best night's nooky you'll ever have.'

'Are you going to leave now, please?' Tim said.

'Well, there is one more little matter to discuss. Give us your dressing gown.'

'Why?'

'I'll show you. Come on.'

Tim was too battered to argue. He slipped the robe off his shoulders and handed it over. He stood in his shorts, waiting.

Cox threw the garment to one side. 'I want you to remember that word "ponce",' he said. Then he punched Tim in the stomach.

Tim turned away and doubled over in agony. Cox reached out, grabbed his genitals in one huge hand, and squeezed. Tim tried to scream, but he had no breath. His mouth gaped in a soundless howl as he tried desperately to suck air.

Cox let go and kicked him. Tim toppled to the floor. He curled up there, and his eyes flooded with tears. He had no pride, no dignity left. He said: 'Please don't hurt me any more.'

Tony Cox smiled and put his coat on. 'Not just yet,' he said. Then he went away.

Chapter Five

The Hon. Derek Hamilton woke up with a pain. He lay in bed with his eyes shut while he traced the discomfort to his abdomen, examined it, and graded it bad but not incapacitating. Then he recalled last night's dinner. Asparagus mousse was harmless; he had refused seafood pancakes; his steak had been well done; he had taken cheese in preference to apple tart. A light white wine, coffee with cream, brandy—

Brandy. Damn, he should stick to port.

He knew how the day would go. He would do without breakfast, and by mid-morning the hunger would be as bad as the ulcer pain, so he would eat something. By lunch-time the hunger would be back and the ulcer would be worse. During the afternoon some trivial thing would irritate him beyond all reason, he would yell at his staff, and his stomach would ball into a knot of pain which made him incapable of thinking at all. He would go home and take too many pain killers. He would sleep, wake with a headache, eat dinner, take sleeping pills, and go to bed.

At least he could look forward to bedtime.

He rolled over, yanked open the drawer of the

bedside table, found a tablet, and put it in his mouth. Then he sat up and picked up his cup of tea. He sipped, swallowed, and said: 'Good morning, dear.'

'Morning.' Ellen Hamilton sat on the edge of the twin bed, wearing a silk robe, perching her cup on one slender knee. She had brushed her hair already. Her nightwear was as elegant as the rest of her large wardrobe, despite the fact that only he ever saw it, and he was not interested. That did not matter, he surmised: it was not that she wanted men to desire her – only that she should be able to think of herself as desirable.

He finished his tea and swung his legs to the floor. His ulcer protested at the sudden movement, and he winced with pain.

Ellen said: 'Again?'

He nodded. 'Brandy last night. Ought to know better.'

Her face was expressionless. 'I suppose it has nothing to do with yesterday's half-year results.'

He heaved himself to his feet and walked slowly across the expanse of oyster-coloured carpet to the bathroom. The face he saw in the mirror was round and red, balding, with rolls of fat under the jaw. He examined his morning beard, pulling the loose skin this way and that to make the bristles stand up. He began to shave. He had done this every day for the last forty years, and still he found it tiresome.

Yes, the half-year results were bad. Hamilton Holdings was in trouble.

Paper Money

When he had inherited Hamilton Printing from his father it had been efficient, successful, and profitable. Jasper Hamilton had been a printer – fascinated by typefaces, keen on the new technology, loving the oily smell of the presses. His son was a businessman. He had taken the flow of profits from the works and diverted it into more businesses – wine importing, retailing, publishing, paper mills, commercial radio. This had achieved its primary purpose of turning income into wealth and thereby avoiding tax. Instead of Bibles and paperbacks and posters, he had concerned himself with liquidity and yields. He had bought up companies and started new enterprises, building an empire.

The continuing success of the original business disguised the flimsiness of the superstructure for a long time. But when the printing complex weakened, Hamilton discovered that most of his other businesses were marginal; that he had underestimated the capital investment needed to nurse them to maturity; and that some of them were very long-term indeed. He sold forty-nine per cent of his equity in each of the companies, then transferred his stock to a holding company and sold forty-nine per cent of that. He raised more money, and negotiated an overdraft running into seven figures. The borrowing kept the organization alive, but the interest – rising fast through the decade – ate up what little profit there was.

Meanwhile, Derek Hamilton cultivated an ulcer.

The rescue programme had been inaugurated almost a year ago. Credit had been tightened in an attempt to reduce the overdraft; costs had been cut by every means possible from cancellation of advertising campaigns to utilization of print-roll off-cuts for stationery. Hamilton was running a tight ship now; but inflation and the economic slump ran faster. The six-month results had been expected to show the world that Hamilton Holdings had turned the corner. Instead they demonstrated further decline.

He patted his face dry with a warm towel, splashed on cologne, and returned to the bedroom. Ellen was dressed, sitting in front of the mirror, making up her face. She always managed to dress and undress while her husband was out of the bedroom: it occurred to him that he had not seen her naked for years. He wondered why. Had she run to seed, the fifty-five-year-old skin wrinkling and the once-firm flesh sagging? Would nakedness destroy the illusion of desirability? Perhaps; but he suspected something more complex. It was obscurely connected with the way his own body had aged, he thought, as he climbed into his cavernous underpants. She was always decently clad; therefore he never lusted after her; therefore she never had to reveal how undesirable *she* found *him*. Such a combination of deviousness and sensitivity would be characteristic.

She said: 'What are you going to do?'

The question caught him off balance. He thought at first that she must know what he was thinking, and be referring to that; then he realized she was continuing the conversation about the business. He fastened his braces, wondering what to tell her. 'I'm not sure,' he said eventually.

She peered closely into the mirror, doing something to her eyelashes. 'Sometimes I wonder what you want out of life.'

He stared at her. Her upbringing had taught her to be indirect and never to ask personal questions, for seriousness and emotion spoiled parties and caused ladies to faint. It would have cost her considerable effort to enquire about the purpose of someone's existence.

He sat on the edge of his bed and spoke to her back. 'I must cut out brandy, that's all.'

'I'm sure you know it has nothing to do with what you eat and drink.' She applied lipstick, contorting her mouth to spread it evenly. 'It began nine years ago, and your father died ten years ago.'

'I've got printing ink in my blood.' The response came formally, like a catechism. The conversation would have seemed dislocated to an eavesdropper, but they knew its logic. There was a code: the death of his father meant his assumption of control of the business; his ulcer meant his business problems.

She said: 'You *haven't* got ink in your veins. Your father had, but *you* can't stand the smell of the old works.'

'I inherited a strong business, and I want to bequeath to my sons an even stronger one. Isn't that what people of our class are supposed to do with their lives?'

'Our sons aren't interested in what we leave them. Michael is building his own business from scratch, and all Andrew wants to do is vaccinate the whole of the African continent against chicken pox.'

He could not tell how serious she was now. The things she was doing to her face made her expression unreadable. No doubt it was deliberate. Almost everything she did was deliberate.

He said: 'I have a duty. I employ more than two thousand people, and many more jobs are directly dependent upon the health of my companies.'

'I think you've done your duty. You kept the firm going during a time of crisis – not everyone managed that. You've sacrificed your health to it; and you've given it ten years of your life, and . . . God knows what else.' Her voice dropped on the final phrase, as if at the last minute she regretted saying it.

'Should I give it my pride as well?' he said. He carried on dressing, tying a tight little knot in his tie. 'I've turned a jobbing printer's into one of the thousand biggest companies in the country. My business is worth five times what my father's was. I put it together, and I have to make it work.'

'You have to do better than your father.'

'Is that such a poor ambition?'

'Yes!' Her sudden vehemence was a shock. 'You should want good health, and long life, and – and my happiness.'

'If the company was prosperous, perhaps I could sell it. As things are, I wouldn't get its asset value.' He looked at his watch. 'I must go down.'

He descended the broad staircase. A portrait of his father dominated the hall. People often thought it was Derek at fifty. In fact it was Jasper at sixty-five. The phone on the hall stand shrilled as he passed. He ignored it: he did not take calls in the morning.

He went into the small dining room – the large one was reserved for parties, which were rare these days. The circular table was laid with silver cutlery. An elderly woman in an apron brought in half a grapefruit in a bone china dish.

'Not today, Mrs Tremlett,' he told her. 'Just a cup of tea, please.' He picked up the *Financial Times*.

The woman hesitated, then put the dish down in Ellen's place. Hamilton glanced up. 'Just take it away, will you?' he said irritably. 'Serve Mrs Hamilton's breakfast when Mrs Hamilton comes down, and not before, please.'

'Very good,' Mrs Tremlett murmured. She took the grapefruit away.

When Ellen came in she picked up the argument where they had left it. 'I don't think it matters whether you get five million or five hundred thousand for the company. Either way we'd be better off than we are now. Since we don't live comfortably, I fail to see the point of being comfortably off.'

He put down the paper and looked at her. She was wearing an original tailored suit in a cream-coloured fabric, with a printed silk blouse and handmade shoes. He said: 'You have a pleasant home, with a small staff. You've friends here, and a social life in town when you care to take advantage of it. This morning you're wearing several hundred pounds' worth of clothes, and you'll probably go no farther than the village. Sometimes I wonder what *you* want out of life.'

She blushed – a rare event. 'I'll tell you,' she began.

There was a knock at the door, and a good-looking man came in, wearing an overcoat and carrying a cap. 'Good morning, sir, madam,' he said. 'If we're to catch the seven forty-five, sir . . .'

Hamilton said: 'All right, Pritchard. Just wait in the hall.'

'Very good, sir. May I ask if you'll be using the car today, madam?'

Hamilton looked at Ellen. She kept her eyes on her dish as she said: 'I expect so, yes.'

Pritchard nodded and went out.

Hamilton said: 'You were about to tell me what you want out of life.'

'I don't think it's a breakfast-table subject, especially when you're rushing to catch a train.'

'Very well.' He stood up. 'Enjoy your drive. Don't go too fast.'

'What?'

'Drive carefully.'

'Oh. Oh, Pritchard drives me.'

He bent to kiss her cheek, but she turned her face to him and kissed his lips. When he pulled away, her face was flushed. She held his arm and said: 'I want you, Derek.'

He stared at her.

'I want us to spend a long, contented retirement together,' she went on, speaking hurriedly. 'I want you to relax, and eat the right food, and grow healthy and slim again. I want the man who came courting in an open-top Riley, and the man who came back from the war with medals and married me, and the man who held my hand when I bore my children. I want to love *you.*'

He stood nonplussed. She had never been like this with him, never. He felt hopelessly incapable of dealing with it. He did not know what to say, what to do, where to look. He said: 'I . . . must catch the train.'

She regained her composure quickly. 'Yes. You must hurry.'

He looked at her a moment longer, but she would not meet his eyes. He said: 'Um . . . good-bye.'

She nodded dumbly.

He went out. He put on his hat in the hall, then let Pritchard open the front door for him. The dark-blue Mercedes stood on the gravel drive, gleaming in the sunshine. Pritchard must wash it every morning before I get up, Hamilton thought.

The conversation with Ellen had been most peculiar, he decided, as they drove to the railway station. Through the window he watched the play of sunlight on the already-browning leaves, and ran over the key scenes in his mind. *I want to love you*, she had said, with the emphasis on *you*. Talking of the things he had sacrificed for the business, she had said *and God knows what else*.

I want to love you, not someone else. Was that what she meant? Had he lost the fidelity of his wife, as well as his health? Perhaps she simply wanted him to think she might be having an affair. That was more like Ellen. She dealt in subtleties. Cries for help were not her style.

After the six-month results, he needed domestic problems like a creditors' meeting.

There was something else. She had blushed when Pritchard asked if she would be using the car; then, hastily, she had said *Pritchard drives me*.

Hamilton said: 'Where do you take Mrs Hamilton, Pritchard?'

'She drives herself, sir. I make myself useful around the house – there's always plenty—'

'Yes, all right,' Hamilton interrupted. 'This isn't a time-and-motion study. I was only curious.'

'Sir.'

His ulcer stabbed him. Tea, he thought: I should drink milk in the morning.

Chapter Six

Herbert Chieseman switched on the light, silenced the alarm clock, turned up the volume of the radio which had been playing all night, and pressed the rewind button of the reel-to-reel tape recorder. Then he got out of bed.

He put the kettle on, and stared out of the studio apartment window while he waited for the seven-hour tape to return to the start. The morning was clear and bright. The sun would be strong later, but now it was chilly. He put on trousers and a sweater over the underwear he had worn in bed, and stepped into carpet slippers.

His home was a single large room in a north London Victorian house which was past its best. The furniture, the Ascot heater, and the old gas cooker belonged to the landlord. The radio was Herbert's. His rent included the use of a communal bathroom and – most important – exclusive use of the attic.

The radio dominated the room. It was a powerful VHF receiver, made from parts he had carefully selected in half a dozen shops along Tottenham Court Road. The aerial was in the roof loft. The tape deck was also homemade.

He poured tea into a cup, added condensed milk from a tin, and sat at his work table. Apart from the electronic equipment, the table bore only a telephone, a ruled exercise book, and a ballpoint pen. He opened the book at a clean page and wrote the date at the top in a large, cursive script. Then he reduced the volume of the radio and began to play the night's tape at high speed. Each time a high-pitched squeal indicated that there was speech on the recording, he slowed the reel with his finger until he could distinguish the words.

'... car proceed to Holloway Road, the bottom end, to assist PC ...'

'... Ludlow Road, West Five, a Mrs Shaftesbury – sounds like a domestic, Twenty-One ...'

'... Inspector says if that Chinese is still open he'll have chicken fried rice with chips ...'

'... Holloway Road get a move on, that PC's in trouble ...'

Herbert stopped the tape and made a note.

'... reported burglary of a house – that's near Wimbledon Common, Jack ...'

'... Eighteen, do you read ...'

'... any cars Lee area free to assist Fire Brigade at twenty-two Feather Street ...'

Herbert made another note.

'... Eighteen, do you read ...'

'... I don't know, give her an aspirin ...'

'... assault with a knife, not serious ...'

'... where the hell have you been, Eighteen ...'

Herbert's attention strayed to the photograph on

the mantelpiece above the boarded-in fireplace. The picture was flattering: Herbert had known this, twenty years ago, when she had given it to him; but now he had forgotten. Oddly, he did not think of her as she really had been, any more. When he remembered her he visualized a woman with flawless skin and hand-tinted cheeks, posing before a faded panorama in a photographer's studio.

'. . . theft of one colour television and damage to a plate-glass window . . .'

He had been the first among his circle of friends to 'lose the wife', as they would put it. Two or three of them had suffered the tragedy since: one had become a cheerful drunkard, another had married a widow. Herbert had buried his head in his hobby, radio. He began listening to police broadcasts during the day when he did not feel well enough to go to work, which was quite often.

'. . . Grey Avenue, Golders Green, reported assault . . .'

One day, after hearing the police talk about a bank raid, he had telephoned the *Evening Post*. A reporter had thanked him for the information and taken his name and address. The raid had been a big one – a quarter of a million pounds – and the story was on the front page of the *Post* that evening. Herbert had been proud to have given them the tip-off, and told the story in three pubs that night. Then he forgot about it. Three months later he got a cheque for fifty pounds from the newspaper. With the cheque was a statement which read: 'Two shot in £250,000 raid' and gave the date of the robbery.

'... leave it out, Charlie, if she won't make a complaint, forget it ...'

The following day Herbert had stayed at home and phoned the *Post* every time he picked something up on the police wavelength. That afternoon he got a call from a man who said he was deputy news editor, who explained just what the paper wanted from people like Herbert. He was told not to report an assault unless a gun was used or someone was killed; not to bother with burglaries unless the address was in Belgravia, Chelsea, or Kensington; not to report robberies except when weapons were used or very large amounts of cash stolen.

'... proceed to twenty-three, Narrow Road, and wait ...'

He got the idea quickly, because he was not stupid, and the *Post*'s news values were far from subtle. Soon he realized he was earning slightly more on his 'sick' days than when he went to work. What was more, he preferred listening to the radio to making boxes for cameras. So he gave in his notice, and became what the newspaper called an earwig.

'... better give me that description now ...'

After he had been working full-time on the radio for a few weeks the deputy news editor came to his house – it was before he moved to the studio apartment – to talk to him. The newspaperman said Herbert's work was very useful to the paper, and how would he like to work for them exclusively? That would mean Herbert would phone tips only to the *Post*, and not to other papers. But he would get a weekly retainer to make up for the loss of income. Herbert did not say that he never had phoned any other papers. He accepted the offer graciously.

'. . . sit tight and we'll get you some assistance in a few minutes . . .'

Over the years he had improved both his equipment and his understanding of what the newspaper wanted. He learned that they were grateful for more or less anything early in the morning, but as the day wore on they became more choosy, until by about three p.m. nothing less than murder in the street or large-scale robbery with violence interested them. He also discovered that the paper, like the police, was a lot less interested in a crime done to a coloured man in a coloured area. Herbert thought this quite reasonable, since he, as an *Evening Post* reader, was not much interested in what the wogs did to each other in their own parts of London; and he surmised, correctly, that the reason the *Post* was not interested was simply that people like Herbert who bought the *Post* weren't interested. And he learned to read between the lines of police jargon: knew when an assault was trivial or a complaint domestic; heard the note of urgency in the operations-room sergeant's voice when a call for assistance was desperate; discovered how to switch his mind off when they decided to read out great lists of stolen-car numbers over the air.

The speeded-up sound of his own alarm clock came out of the big speaker, and he turned the deck off. He increased the volume on the radio, then dialled the *Post*'s number. He sipped his tea while he waited for an answer.

'*Post*, g'morning.' It was a man's voice.

'Copytakers, please,' Herbert said. There was another pause.

'Copy.'

'Hello. Chieseman here, timing at oh seven fifty-nine.'

There was a clatter of typewriters in the background. 'Hello, Bertie. Anything doing?'

'Seems to have been a quiet night,' Herbert said.

Eight a.m.

Chapter Seven

Tony Cox stood in a phone booth on the corner of Quill Street, Bethnal Green, with the receiver to his ear. He was perspiring inside the warm coat with the velvet collar. In his hand he held the end of a chain which was attached to the collar of the dog outside. The dog was sweating, too.

The phone at the other end of the line was answered, and Tony pressed a coin into the slot.

A voice said: 'Yes?' in the tone of one who is not really accustomed to these new-fangled telephones.

Tony spoke curtly. 'It's today. Get it together.' He hung up without giving his name or waiting for an answer.

He strode off along the narrow pavement, pulling the dog behind him. It was a pedigree boxer with a trim, powerful body, and Tony continually had to yank at the chain to make it keep pace. The dog was strong, but its master was a great deal stronger.

The doors of the old terraced houses gave directly on to the street. Tony stopped at the one outside which was parked the grey Rolls-Royce. He pushed the house door open. It was never locked, for the occupants had no fear of thieves.

There was a smell of cooking in the little house. Pulling the dog behind him, Tony went into the kitchen and sat on a chair. He unhooked the chain from the dog's collar and sent it away with a hefty slap on the rump. He stood up and took off his coat.

A kettle was warming on the gas cooker, and there was sliced bacon on a piece of greaseproof paper. Tony opened a drawer and took out a kitchen knife with a ten-inch blade. He tested the edge with his thumb, decided it needed sharpening, and went out into the yard.

There was an old grinding wheel in the lean-to shed. Tony sat beside it on a wooden stool and worked the treadle, the way he had seen the old man do it years ago. It made Tony feel good to do things the way his father had. He pictured him: a tall man, and handsome, with wavy hair and glittering eyes, making sparks with the grinder while his children shrieked with laughter. He had been a stallholder in a street market, selling china and saucepans, calling his wares in that strong, carrying voice. He used to make a performance of pretending to needle the grocer next to him, shouting: 'There y'are, I just sold a pot for half a nicker. How many spuds d'you sell afore you take ten bob?' He could spot a strange woman yards away, and would use his good looks shamelessly. 'I tell you what, darling—' this to a middle-aged woman in a hairnet '—we don't get many beautiful young girls down this end of the market, so I'm going to sell you this at a loss and hope you'll come back.

Look at it – solid copper bottom, if you'll pardon the word, and it's my last one; I've made my profit on the rest, so you can have it for two quid, half what I paid for it, just because you made an old man's heart beat faster, and take it quick afore I change my mind.'

Tony had been shocked by the speed at which the old man changed after the one lung went. His hair turned white, the cheeks sank between the bones, and the fine voice went high and whining. The stall was rightfully Tony's, but by then he had his own sources of income, so he had let it go to young Harry, his dumb brother, who had married a beautiful Whitechapel girl with the patience to learn how to talk with her hands. It took guts for a dumb man to run a market stall, writing on a blackboard when he needed to speak to the customers, and keeping in his pocket a plain postcard bearing the word THANKS in capital letters to flash when a sale was made. But he ran it well, and Tony lent him the money to move into a proper shop and hire a manager, and he made a success of that, too. Guts – they ran in the family.

The kitchen knife was sharp enough. He tested it and cut his thumb. Holding it to his lips, he went into the kitchen.

His mother was there. Lillian Cox was short and a little overweight – her son had inherited the tendency to plumpness without the shortness – and she had much more energy than the average sixty-three-year-old. She said: 'I'm doing you a bit of fried bread.'

'Lovely.' He put the knife down and found a

bandage. 'Take care with that knife – I done it a bit too sharp.'

She fussed over his cut, then, making him hold it under the cold tap and count to one hundred, then putting on antiseptic cream, and gauze, and finally a roll of bandage held with a safety pin. He stood still and let her do what she wished.

She said: 'Ah, but you're a good boy to sharpen the knives for me. Where you been so early, anyhow?'

'Took the dog up the park. And I had to ring someone up.'

She made a disgusted noise. 'I don't know what's wrong with the phone in the parlour, I'm sure.'

He leaned over the cooker to sniff the frying bacon. 'You know how it is, Mum. The Old Bill listen to that one.'

She put a teapot in his hand. 'Go in there and pour the tea out, then.'

He took the pot into the living room and put it down on a mat. The square table was laid with an embroidered cloth, cutlery for two, salt and pepper and sauce bottles.

Tony sat nearest the fireplace, where the old man used to sit. From there he reached into the sideboard and took out two cups and two saucers. He pictured the old man again, overseeing mealtimes with the back of his hand and a good deal of rhyming slang. 'Get your chalks off the Cain,' he would bark if they put their arms on the table. The only thing Tony held against him was the way he treated Mum. Being so handsome and that, he had a few women on the side, and at times he would spend his money buying them gin instead of bringing it home. Those times, Tony and his brother would go up the Smithfield market, stealing scraps from under the tables to sell to the soap factory for a few coppers. And he never went in the Army – but then, a lot of wide boys went on the trot in wartime.

'What are you going to do – go back to sleep, or pour that tea out?' Lillian put a plate in front of Tony and sat down opposite him. 'Never mind, I'll do it now.'

Tony picked up his cutlery, holding his knife like a pencil, and began to eat. There were sausages, two fried eggs, a mess of canned tomatoes, and several slices of fried bread. He took a mouthful before reaching for the brown sauce. He was hungry after his morning's exertions.

His mother passed him his tea. She said: 'I don't know, we was never afraid to use the phone when your father was alive, God rest his soul. He was careful to stay out of the way of the Old Bill.'

Tony thought they had had no phone in his father's day, but he let that pass. He said: 'Yeah. He was so careful, he died a pauper.'

'But an honest one.'

'Was he?'

'You know bloody well he was, and never let me hear you say no different.'

'I don't like you to swear, Mum.'

'You shouldn't provoke me.'

Tony ate silently and finished quickly. He emptied his teacup and began to unwrap a cigar.

His mother picked up his cup. 'More tea?'

He looked at his watch. 'No, thanks. I've got a couple of things to do.' He set fire to the cigar and stood up. 'That's set me up lovely, that breakfast.'

She narrowed her eyes. 'Are you having a tickle?'

This annoyed him. He blew smoke into the air. 'Who needs to know?'

'It's your life. Go on, then, I'll see you later. Mind you look after yourself.'

He looked at her a moment longer. Although she gave in to him, she was a strong woman. She had led the family since the old man went: mending marriages, borrowing from one son to lend to another, giving advice, using her disapproval as a powerful sanction. She had resisted all efforts to move her from Quill Street to a nice little bungalow in Bournemouth, suspecting – rightly – that the old house and its memories were a potent symbol of her authority. Once, there had been queenly arrogance in her high-bridged nose and pointed chin; now, she was regal but resigned, like an abdicated monarch; knowing she was wise to release the reins of power, but regretting it all the same. Tony realized that this was why she needed him: he was king now, and having him to live with her kept her close to the throne. He loved her for needing him. No one else needed him.

She stood up. 'Well, are you going?'

'Yes.' He realized he had been lost in thought. He put an arm around her shoulders and squeezed briefly. He never kissed her. 'Ta-ta, Mum.' He picked up his coat, patted the dog, and went out.

The interior of the Rolls was hot. He pressed the button that lowered the window before settling himself in the leather seat and pulling away.

He took pleasure in the car as he threaded it through the narrow East End streets. Its shameless luxury, in contrast with the mean streets and undignified old houses, told the story of Tony Cox's life. People looked at the car – housewives, paperboys, working men, villains – and said to each other: 'There's Tony Cox. He did well.'

He flicked cigar ash through the open window. He *had* done well. He had bought his first car for six pounds when he was sixteen years old. The blank Ministry of Transport certificate had cost him thirty shillings on the black market. He filled in the blanks and resold the car for eighty pounds.

Before long he had a used car lot which he gradually turned into a legitimate business. Then he sold it, with the stock, for five thousand pounds, and went into the long firm racket.

He used the five thousand to open a bank account, giving as a reference the name of the man who had bought the car lot. He told the bank manager his real name, but gave a false address – the same false address he had given the purchaser of the car business.

He took a lease on a warehouse, paying three

months' rent in advance. He bought small quantities of radio, television, and hi-fi equipment from manufacturers and resold it to shops in London. He paid suppliers on the dot, and his bank account was busy. Within a couple of months he was making a small loss, and had a reputation for credit-worthiness.

At that point he made a series of very large orders. Small manufacturers to whom he had promptly paid a couple of bills of five hundred pounds each were glad to supply him with three or four thousand pounds' worth of goods on the same credit terms: he looked like becoming a good customer.

With a warehouse full of expensive electronic gadgetry for which he had paid nothing, he held a sale. Record players, colour television sets, digital clocks, tape decks, amplifiers, and radios went for knock-down prices, sometimes as little as half their retail value. In two days the warehouse was empty and Tony Cox had three thousand pounds in cash in two suitcases. He locked the warehouse and went home.

He shivered in the front seat of the warm car as he remembered. He would never take risks like those again. Suppose one of the suppliers had got wind of the sale? Suppose the bank manager had seen Tony in a pub a few days later?

He still did the occasional long firm, but these days he used front men, who took long holidays in Spain as soon as the axe fell. And *nobody* saw Tony's face.

However, his business interests had diversified. He owned property in Central London which he let to young ladies at extremely high rents; he ran night-clubs; he even managed a couple of pop groups. Some of his projects were legitimate, some criminal; some were a mixture, and others were on the nebulous borderline between the two, where the law is unsure of itself but respectable businessmen with reputations to worry about fear to tread.

The Old Bill knew about him, of course. There were so many grasses about nowadays that nobody could become a respected villain without his name going into a file at Scotland Yard. But getting evidence was the problem, especially with a few detectives around who were prepared to warn Tony in advance of a raid. The money he spent in that direction was never skimped. Every August there were three or four police families in Benidorm on Tony's money.

Not that he trusted them. They were useful, but they were all telling themselves that one day they would repay their debt of loyalty by turning him in. A bent copper was still, ultimately, a copper. So all transactions were cash; no books were kept, except in Tony's head; all jobs were done by his cronies on verbal instructions.

Increasingly, he played even safer by simply acting as a banker. A draftsman would get some inside information and dream up a plan; then he would recruit a villain to organize the equipment and manpower. The two of them would then come to Tony and tell him the plan. If he liked it, he would lend them the money for bribes, guns, motor cars, explosives, and anything else they needed. When they had done the job they would repay the loan five or six times over out of the proceeds.

Today's job was not so simple. He was draftsman as well as banker for this one. It meant he had to be extra careful.

He stopped the car in a back street and got out. Here the houses were larger – they had been built for foremen and craftsmen rather than dockers and labourers – but they were no more sound than the hovels of Quill Street. The concrete facings were cracking, the wooden window frames were rotten, and the front gardens were smaller than the boot of Tony's car. Only about half of them were lived in: the rest were warehouses, offices, or shops.

The door Tony knocked on bore the sign 'Billiards and Snooker' with most of the 'and' missing. It was opened immediately and he stepped inside.

He shook hands with Walter Burden then followed him upstairs. A road accident had left Walter with a limp and a stammer, depriving him of his job as a docker. Tony had given him the managership of the billiards hall, knowing that the gesture – which cost Tony nothing – would be rewarded by increased respect among East Enders and undying loyalty on Walter's part.

Walter said: 'Want a cup of tea, Tony?'

'No, thanks, Walter, I just had my breakfast.' He looked around the first-floor hall with a proprietorial air. The tables were covered, the linoleum floor swept, the cues racked neatly. 'You keep the place nice.'

'Only doing my job, Tone. You looked after me, see.'

'Yeah.' Cox went to the window and looked down on the street. A blue Morris 1100 was parked a few yards away on the opposite side of the road. There were two people in it. Tony felt curiously satisfied: he had been right to take this precaution. 'Where's the phone, Walter?'

'In the office.' Walter opened a door, ushered Tony in, and closed it, staying outside.

The office was tidy and clean. Tony sat at the desk and dialled a number.

A voice said: 'Yeah?'

'Pick me up,' Tony said.

'Five minutes.'

Tony hung up. His cigar had gone out. When things made him nervous, he let his smoke go out. He relit it with a gold Dunhill, then went out.

He showed himself at the window again. 'All right, mate, I'm off,' he said to Walter. 'If one of the young detective-constables in the blue car takes it into his head to knock on the door, don't answer it. I'll be about half an hour.'

'Don't w-worry. You can rely on me, you know that.' Walter nodded his head like a bird.

'Yeah, I know.' Tony touched the old man's shoulder briefly, then went to the back of the hall. He opened the door and trotted rapidly down the fire escape.

He picked his way around a rusting baby carriage, a sodden mattress, and three fifths of an old car. Weeds sprouted stubbornly in the cracked concrete of the yard. A grubby cat scampered out of his way. His Italian shoes got dirty.

A gate led from the yard to a narrow lane. Tony walked to the end of the lane. As he got there, a small red Fiat with three men in it drew up at the kerb. Tony got in and sat in the empty seat in the back. The car pulled away immediately.

The driver was Jacko, Tony's first lieutenant. Beside Jacko was Deaf Willie, who knew more about explosives now than he had twenty years ago when he lost his left eardrum. In the back with Tony was Peter 'Jesse' James, whose two obsessions were firearms and girls with fat bottoms. They were good men; all permanent members of Tony's firm.

Tony said: 'How's the boy, Willie?

Deaf Willie turned his good ear towards Tony. 'What?'

'I said, how's young Billy?'

'Eighteen today,' Willie said. 'He's the same, Tone. He'll never be able to look after hisself. The social worker told us to think about putting him in a home.'

Tony tutted sympathetically. He went out of his way to be kind to Deaf Willie's half-witted son; mental illness frightened him. 'You don't want to do that.'

Willie said: 'I said to the wife, what does a social

worker know? This one's a girl of about twenty. Been to college. Still, she don't push herself.'

Jacko broke in impatiently. 'We're all set, Tony. The lads are there, the motors are ready.'

'Good.' Tony looked at Jesse James. 'Shooters?'

'Got a couple of shotguns and an Uzi.'

'A what?'

Jesse grinned proudly. 'It's a nine-millimetre machine pistol. Israeli.'

'Stroll on,' Tony muttered.

Jacko said: 'Here we are.'

Tony took a cloth cap from his pocket and fixed it on his head. 'You've put the lads indoors, have you?'

'Yes,' Jacko said.

'I don't mind them knowing it's a Tony Cox job, but I don't want them to be able to say they saw me.'

'I know.'

The car pulled into a scrap yard. It was a remarkably tidy yard. The shells of cars were piled three high in orderly lines, and component parts were stacked neatly round about: pillars of tyres, a pyramid of rear axles, a cube of cylinder blocks.

Near the gateway were a crane and a long car transporter. Farther in, a plain blue Ford van with double rear wheels stood next to the yard's heavy-duty oxy-acetylene cutting gear.

The car stopped and Tony got out. He was pleased. He liked things neat. The other three stood around, waiting for him to do something. Jacko lit a cigarette.

Tony said: 'Did you fix the owner of the yard?'

Jacko nodded. 'He made sure the crane, the transporter, and the cutting gear were here. But he doesn't know what they're for, and we've tied him up, just for the sake of appearances.' He started to cough.

Tony took the cigarette out of Jacko's mouth and dropped it in the mud. 'Those things make you cough,' he said. He took a cigar from his pocket. 'Smoke this and die old.'

Tony walked back towards the yard gate. The three men followed. Tony trod gingerly around potholes and swampy patches, past a stack of thousands of lead-acid accumulators, between mounds of drive shafts and gearboxes, to the crane. It was a smallish model, on caterpillar tracks, capable of lifting a car, a van, or a light truck. He unbuttoned his overcoat and climbed the ladder to the high cab.

He sat in the operator's seat. The all-round windows enabled him to see the whole of the yard. It was triangular in plan. One side was a railway viaduct, its brick arches filled in by storerooms. A high wall on the adjacent side separated the yard from a playground and a bomb site. The road ran along the front of the yard, curving slightly as it followed the bend of the river a few yards beyond. It was a wide road, but little used.

In the lee of the viaduct was a hut made of old wooden doors supporting a tar-paper roof. The men would be in there, huddled around an electric fire, drinking tea and smoking nervously.

Everything was right. Tony felt elation rise in his

belly as instinct told him it would work. He climbed out of the crane.

He deliberately kept his voice low, steady and casual. 'This van doesn't always go the same route. There are lots of ways from the City to Loughton. But this place is on most of the routes, right? They got to pass here unless they want to go via Birmingham or Watford. Now, they do go daft ways occasionally. Today might be one of those days. So, if it doesn't come off, just give the lads a bonus and send them home until next time.'

Jacko said: 'They all know the score.'

'Good. Anything else?'

The three men were silent.

Tony gave his final instructions. 'Everybody wears a mask. Everybody wears gloves. Nobody speaks.' He looked to each man in turn for acknowledgement. Then he said: 'Okay, take me back.'

There was no conversation as the red Fiat wound its way through the little streets to the lane behind the billiard hall.

Tony got out, then leaned on the front passenger door and spoke through the open window. 'It's a good plan, and if you do right, it will work. There's a couple of wrinkles you don't know about – safeguards, inside men. Keep calm, do good, and we'll have it away.' He paused. 'And don't shoot nobody with that bleeding tommy-gun, for fuck's sake.'

He walked up the lane and entered the billiard hall by the back door. Walter was playing billiards at one of the tables. He straightened up when he heard the door.

'All right, Tone?'

Tony went to the window. 'Did pally stay put?' He could see the blue Morris in the same place.

'Yes. They've been smoking theirself to death.'

It was fortunate, Tony thought, that the law did not have enough manpower to watch him at night as well as in the day. The nine-to-five surveillance was quite useful, for it permitted him to establish alibis without seriously restricting his activities. One of these days they would start following him twenty-four hours a day. But he would have plenty of advance notice of that.

Walter jerked a thumb at the table. 'Fancy a break?'

'No.' Tony left the window. 'I got a busy day.' He went down the stairs, and Walter hobbled after him.

'Ta-ta, Walter,' he said as he went out into the street.

'So long, Tony,' Walter said. 'God bless you, boy.'

Chapter Eight

The newsroom came to life suddenly. At eight o'clock it had been as still as a morgue, the quietness broken only by inanimate sounds like the stuttering of the teleprinter and the rustle of the newspapers Cole was reading. Now three copytakers were pounding the keys, a Lad was whistling a pop song, and a photographer in a leather coat was arguing with a sub-editor about a football match. The reporters were drifting in. Most of them had an early-morning routine, Cole had observed: one bought tea, another lit a cigarette, another turned to page three of the *Sun* to look at the nude; each using an habitual crutch to help him start the day.

Cole believed in letting people sit down for a few minutes before setting them to work: it made for an atmosphere of order and cool-headedness. His news editor, Cliff Poulson, had a different approach. Poulson, with his froglike green eyes and Yorkshire accent, liked to say: 'Don't take your coat off, lad.' His delight in snap decisions, his perpetual hurry, and his brittle air of bonhomie created a frenetic atmosphere. Poulson was a speed freak. Cole did not reckon a story had ever missed an edition because someone took a minute out to think about it.

Kevin Hart had been here for five minutes now. He was reading the *Mirror*, with one hip perched on the edge of a desk, the trousers of his striped suit falling gracefully. Cole called out to him. 'Give the Yard a ring, please, Kevin.' The young man picked up a telephone.

The Bertie Chieseman tips were on his desk: a thick wad of copy. Cole looked around. Most of the reporters were in. It was time to get them working. He sorted through the tips, impaling some on a sharp metal spike, handing others to reporters with brief instructions. 'Anna, a PC got into trouble in the Holloway Road – ring the nearest nick and find out what it was all about. If it's drunks, forget it. Joe, this fire in the East End – check with the Brigade. A burglary in Chelsea, Phillip. Look up the address in Kelly's Directory in case anyone famous lives there. Barney – "Police pursued and arrested an Irishman after calling at a house in Queenstown Street, Camden." Ring the Yard and ask them if it's anything to do with the IRA.'

An internal phone beeped and he lifted it. 'Arthur Cole.'

'What have you got for me, Arthur?'

Cole recognized the voice of the picture editor. He said: 'At the moment, it looks as though the splash will be last night's vote in the Commons.'

'But that was on the television yesterday!'

'Did you call to ask me things or tell me things?'

'I suppose I'd better have somebody at Downing Street for a today picture of the Prime Minister. Anything else?'

'Nothing that isn't in the morning papers.'

'Thank you, Arthur.'

Cole hung up. It was poor, to be leading on a yesterday story. He was doing his best to update it – two reporters were ringing around for reactions. They were getting backbench MPs to shoot off their mouths, but no Ministers.

A middle-aged reporter with a pipe called out: 'Mrs Poulson just rang. Cliff won't be in today. He's got Delhi belly.'

Cole groaned. 'How did he catch that in Orpington?'

'Curry supper.'

'Okay.' That was clever, Cole thought. It looked like being the dullest day for news in the month, and Poulson was off sick. With the assistant news editor on holiday, Cole was on his own.

Kevin Hart approached the desk. 'Nothing from the Yard,' he said. 'It's been quiet all night.'

Cole looked up. Hart was about twenty-three and very tall, with curly fair hair which he wore long. Cole suppressed a spasm of irritation. 'That is ridiculous,' he said. 'Scotland Yard never has a completely quiet night. What's the matter with that Press Bureau?'

'We ought to do a story – "London's first crime-free night for a thousand years," ' Hart said with a grin.

His levity annoyed Cole. 'Never be satisfied with that kind of reply from the Yard,' he said coldly.

Hart flushed. It embarrassed him to be lectured like a cub reporter. 'I'll ring them back, shall I?'

'No,' said Cole, seeing that he had made his point. 'I want you to do a story. You know this new oil field in the North Sea?'

Hart nodded. 'It's called Shield.'

'Yes. Later on the Energy Minister is going to announce who has got the licence to develop it. Do a holding piece to run until we get the announcement. Background, what the licence will mean to the people who are bidding, how the Minister makes up his mind. This afternoon we can sling your piece out and leave a hole in the paper for the real news.'

'Okay.' Hart turned away and made for the library. He knew he was being given a dumb job as a kind of punishment, but he took his medicine gracefully, Cole thought. He stared at the boy's back for a moment. He got on Cole's nerves, with his long hair and his suits. He had rather too much self-confidence – but then, reporters needed a lot of cheek.

Cole stood up and went to the sub-editors' table. The deputy chief sub had in front of him the wire service story about the passing of the Industry Bill and the new stuff Cole's reporters had come up with. Cole looked over his shoulder. On a scratch pad he had written:

REBEL MPs TOLD
'JOIN THE LIBS'

The man scratched his beard and looked up. 'What do you think?'

'It looks like a story about Women's Lib,' Cole said. 'I hate it.'

'So do I.' The sub tore the sheet off the pad, crumpled it, and tossed it in a metal bin. 'What else is new?'

'Nothing. I've only just given out the tips.'

The bearded man nodded and glanced reflexively at the clock hanging from the ceiling in front. 'Let's hope we get something decent for the second.'

Cole leaned over him and wrote on the pad:

REBEL MPs TOLD
'JOIN LIBERALS'

He said: 'It makes more sense, but it's the same count.'

The sub grinned. 'Want a job?'

Cole went back to his desk. Annela Sims came up and said: 'The Holloway Road incident came to nothing. A bunch of rowdies, no arrests.'

Cole said: 'Okay.'

Joe Barnard put down the phone and called: 'There's not a lot to this fire, Arthur. Nobody hurt.'

'How many people living there?' Cole said automatically.

'Two adults, three children.'

'So, it's a family of five escaped death. Write it.'

Phillip Jones said: 'The burgled flat seems to belong to Nicholas Crost, quite a well-known violinist.'

'Good,' Cole said. 'Ring Chelsea nick and find out what was taken.'

'I did already,' Phillip grinned. 'There's a Stradivarius missing.'

Cole smiled. 'Good boy. Write it, then get down there and see if you can interview the heartbroken maestro.'

The phone rang, and Cole picked it up.

Although he would not have admitted it, he was thoroughly enjoying himself.

Nine a.m.

Chapter Nine

Tim Fitzpeterson was dry of tears, but the weeping had not helped. He lay on the bed, his face buried in the damp pillow. To move was agony. He tried not to think at all, his mind turning away thoughts like an innkeeper with a full house. At one point his brain switched off completely, and he dozed for a few moments, but the escape from pain and despair was brief, and he woke up again.

He did not rise from the bed because there was nothing he wanted to do, nowhere he could go, nobody he felt he could face. All he could do was think about the promise of joy that had been so false. Cox had been right when he said so coarsely, 'It was the best night's nooky you'll ever have.' Tim could not quite banish the flashing memories of her slim, writhing body; but now they had a dreadfully bitter taste. She had shown him Paradise then slammed the door. She, of course, had been faking ecstasy; but there had been nothing simulated about Tim's own pleasure. A few hours ago he had been contemplating a new life, enhanced by the kind of sexual love he had forgotten existed. Now it was hard to see any point at all in tomorrow.

He could hear the noise of the children in the playground outside, shouting and shrieking and quarrelling; and he envied them the utter triviality of their lives. He pictured himself as a schoolboy, in a black blazer and short grey trousers, walking three miles of Dorset country lanes to get to the one-class primary school. He was the brightest pupil they had ever had, which was not saying much. But they taught him arithmetic and got him a place at the grammar school, and that was all he needed.

He had flourished in the grammar school, he remembered. He had been the leader of the gang, the one who organized playground games and classroom rebellions. Until he got his glasses.

There: he had been trying to remember when in his life he had felt despair like this; and now he knew. It had been the first day he wore his glasses to school. The members of his gang had been at first dismayed, then amused, then scornful. By playtime he was being followed by a crowd chanting 'Four-eyes'. After lunch he tried to organize a football match, but John Willcott said: 'It's not your game.' Tim put his spectacles in their case and punched Willcott's head; but Willcott was big, and Tim, who normally dominated by force of personality, was no fighter. Tim ended up staunching a bloody nose in the cloakroom while Willcott picked teams.

He tried to make a comeback during History, by flicking inky paper pellets at Willcott under the nose of Miss Percival, known as Old Percy. But the normally indulgent Percy decided to have a clampdown that day, and Tim was sent to the headmaster for six of the best. On the way home he had another fight, lost again, and tore his blazer; his mother took the money for a new one out of the nest egg Tim was saving to buy a crystal radio kit, setting him back six months. It was the blackest day of young Tim's life, and his leadership qualities remained stifled until he went to college and joined the Party.

A lost fight, a torn blazer, and six of the best: he could wish for problems like that now. A whistle blew in the playground outside the flat, and the noise of the children ceased abruptly. I could end my troubles that quickly, Tim thought; and the idea appealed.

What was I living for yesterday? he wondered. Good work, my reputation, a successful government; none of these things seemed to matter today. The school whistle meant it was past nine o'clock. Tim should have been chairing a committee meeting to discuss the productivity of different kinds of power station. How could I ever have been interested in anything so meaningless? He thought of his pet project, a forecast of the energy needs of British industry through to the year 2000. He could summon no enthusiasm for it. He thought of his daughters, and dreaded the idea of facing them. Everything turned to ashes in his mouth. What did it matter who would win the next election? Britain's fortunes were determined by forces outside its leaders' control. He had always known it was a game, but he no longer wanted the prizes.

There was nobody he could talk to, nobody. He imagined the conversation with his wife: 'Darling, I've been foolish and disloyal. I was seduced by a whore, a beautiful, supple girl, and blackmailed . . .' Julia would freeze on him. He could see her face, taking on a rigid look of distaste as she withdrew from emotional contact. He would reach out to her with his hand, and she would say: 'Don't touch me.' No, he could not tell Julia; not until he was sure his own wounds had healed – and he did not think he could survive that long.

Anyone else? Cabinet colleagues would say: 'Good God, Tim, old chap – I'm terribly sorry . . .' and immediately begin to map out a fallback position for the time when it got out. They would take care not to be associated with anything he sponsored, not to be seen with him too often; might even make a morality speech to establish Puritan credentials. He did not hate them for what he knew they would do: his prognosis was based on what *he* would do in that situation.

His agent had come close to being a friend, once or twice. But the man was young; he could not know how much depended upon fidelity in a twenty-year-old marriage; he would cynically recommend a thorough cover-up and overlook the damage already done to a man's soul.

His sister, then? An ordinary woman, married to a carpenter, she had always envied Tim a little. She would wallow in it. Tim could not contemplate that.

His father was dead, his mother senile. Was he that short of friends? What had he done with his life, to be left with no one who would love him right or wrong? Perhaps it was that that kind of commitment was two-way, and he had been careful to see that there was nobody he wouldn't be able to abandon if they became a liability.

There was no support to be had. Only his own resources were available. What do we do, he thought wearily, when we lose the election by a landslide? Regroup, draw up the scenario for the years of opposition, start hacking away at the foundations, use our anger and our disappointment as fuel for the fight. He looked inside himself for courage, and hatred, and bitterness, to enable him to deny the victory to Tony Cox; and found only cowardice and spite. At other times he had lost battles and suffered humiliation, but he was a man, and men had the strength to struggle on, didn't they?

His strength had always come from a certain image of himself: a civilized man, steadfast, trustworthy, loyal, and courageous; able to win with pride and lose with grace. Tony Cox had shown him a new picture; naïve enough to be seduced by an empty-headed girl; weak enough to betray his trust at the first threat of blackmail; frightened enough to crawl on the floor and beg for mercy.

He screwed up his eyes tightly, but still the image invaded his mind. It would be with him for the rest of his life.

But that need not be long.

At last he moved. He sat on the edge of the bed, then stood up. There was blood, his blood, on the sheet, a disgraceful reminder. The sun had moved around the sky, and now shone brightly through the window. Tim would have liked to close the window, but the effort was too much. He hobbled out of the bedroom, and went through the living room into the kitchen. The kettle and the teapot were where *she* had left them after making tea. She had spilled a few leaves carelessly over the Formica counter top, and she had not bothered to put the bottle of milk back into the little fridge.

The first-aid kit was in a high, locked cupboard, where small children could not reach. Tim pulled a stool across the Marley-tiled floor and stood on it. The key was on top of the cupboard. He unlocked the door and took down an old biscuit tin with a picture of Durham Cathedral on the lid.

He got off the stool and put the tin down. Inside he found bandages, a roll of bandage, scissors, antiseptic cream, gripe water for babies, a displaced tube of Ambre Solaire, and a large, full bottle of sleeping tablets. He took out the tablets and replaced the lid. Then he found a glass in another cupboard.

He kept *not* doing things: not putting the milk away, not clearing up the spilled tea leaves, not replacing the first-aid tin, not closing the door of the crockery cupboard. There was no need, he had to keep reminding himself.

He took the glass and the tablets into the living room and put them on his desk. The desk was bare except for a telephone: he always cleared it when he finished working.

He opened the cupboard beneath the television set. Here was the drink he had planned to offer her. There was whisky, gin, dry sherry, a good brandy, and an untouched bottle of *eau de vie prunes* that someone had brought back from the Dordogne. Tim chose the gin, although he did not like it.

He poured some into the glass on the desk, then sat down in the upright chair.

He did not have the will to wait, perhaps years, for the revenge which would restore his self-respect. However, right now he could not harm Cox without doing worse damage to himself. Exposing Cox would expose Tim.

But the dead feel no pain.

He could destroy Cox, and then die.

In the circumstances it seemed the only thing to do.

Chapter Ten

Derek Hamilton was met at Waterloo Station by another chauffeur, this time in a Jaguar. The Chairman's Rolls-Royce had gone in the economy drive: sadly, the unions had not appreciated the gesture. The chauffeur touched his cap and held the door, and Hamilton got in without speaking.

As the car pulled away he made a decision. He would not go straight to the office. He said: 'Take me to Nathaniel Fett – do you know where it is?'

The chauffeur said: 'Yes, sir.'

They crossed Waterloo Bridge and turned into Aldwych, heading for the City. Hamilton and Fett had both gone to Westminster School: Nathaniel Fett senior had known that his son would not suffer for his Jewishness there, and Lord Hamilton had believed that the school would not turn his son into an upper-class twit – his Lordship's phrase.

The two boys had superficially similar backgrounds. Both had wealthy, dynamic fathers and beautiful mothers; both were from intellectual households where politicians came to dinner; both grew up surrounded by good paintings and unlimited books. Yet, as the friendship grew, and the two young men went to Oxford – Fett to Balliol, Hamilton to Magdalen – the Hamilton house had suffered by the comparison. Derek came to see his own father's intellect as shallow. Old man Fett would tolerantly discuss abstract painting, communism, and be-bop jazz, then tear them to pieces with surgical accuracy. Lord Hamilton held the same conservative views, but expressed them in the thundering clichés of a House of Lords speech.

Derek smiled to himself in the back of the car. He had been too hard on his father; perhaps sons always were. Few men had known more about political skirmishing: the old man's cleverness had given him real power, whereas Nathaniel's father had been too wise ever to wield real influence in affairs of state.

Nathaniel had inherited that wisdom and made a career of it. The stockbroking firm which had been owned by six generations of firstborn sons named Nathaniel Fett had been changed, by the seventh, into a merchant bank. People had always gone to Nathaniel for advice, even at school. Now he advised on mergers, share issues, and take-overs.

The car pulled up. Hamilton said: 'Wait for me, please.'

The offices of Nathaniel Fett were not impressive – the firm had no need to prove itself rich. There was a small nameplate outside a street door near the Bank of England. The entrance was flanked by a sandwich shop on one side and a tobacconist's on the other. A casual observer might have taken it for a small, and none-too-prosperous, insurance or shipping company; but he would not have known how far the premises to either side were occupied by the one firm.

The inside was comfortable, rather than opulent, with air conditioning, concealed lighting, and carpets which had aged well and stopped short of the walls. The same casual observer might have thought that the paintings hanging on the walls were expensive. He would have been right and wrong: they were expensive, but they were not hanging on the walls. They were set into the brickwork behind armoured glass – only the false frames actually hung on top of the wallpaper.

Hamilton was shown straight in to Fett's ground-floor office. Nathaniel was sitting in a club chair reading the *Financial Times*. He stood up to shake hands.

Hamilton said: 'I've never seen you sitting at that desk. Is it just for decoration?'

'Sit down, Derek. Tea, coffee, sherry?'

'A glass of milk, please.'

'If you would, Valerie.' Fett nodded to his secretary and she went out. 'The desk – no, I never use it. Everything I write is dictated; nothing I read is too heavy to hold in my hands; why should I sit at a desk like a clerk in Dickens?'

'So it is for decoration.'

'It's been here longer than I. Too big to get out through the door and too valuable to chop up. I think they built the place around it.'

Hamilton smiled. Valerie brought in his milk and

went out again. He sipped and studied his friend. Fett and his office matched: both were small but not dwarfish, dark but not gloomy, relaxed without being frivolous. The man had heavy-rimmed glasses and brilliantined hair. He wore a club tie, a mark of social acceptability: it was the only Jewish thing about him, Hamilton thought wryly.

He put his glass down and said: 'Were you reading about me?'

'Just skimming. A predictable reaction. Ten years ago, results like that from a company like Hamilton would have made waves from audio shares to zinc prices. Today, it's just another conglomerate in trouble. There's a word for it: recession.'

Hamilton sighed. 'Why do we do it, Nathaniel?'

'I beg your pardon?' Fett was startled.

He shrugged. 'Why do we overwork, lose sleep, risk fortunes?'

'And get ulcers.' Fett smiled, but a subtle change had come over his demeanour. His eyes narrowed behind the pebble-lensed spectacles, and he smoothed the bristly hair at the back of his head in a gesture Hamilton recognized to be defensive. Fett was retreating into his role as a careful adviser, a friendly counsel with an objective viewpoint. But his reply was measuredly casual. 'To make money. What else?'

Hamilton shook his head. His friend always had to be beckoned twice before stepping into deeper water. 'Sixth-form economics,' he said derisively. 'I would have made more profit if I'd sold my inheritance and put it into the Post Office. Most people who own large businesses could live very comfortably for the rest of their lives by doing that. Why do we conserve our fortunes, and try to enlarge them? Is it greed, or power, or adventure? Are we all compulsive gamblers?'

Fett said: 'I suppose Ellen has been saying this kind of thing to you.'

Hamilton laughed. 'You're right, but it pains me that you think I'm incapable of such ponderings on my own.'

'Oh, I don't doubt you mean it. It's just that Ellen has a way of saying what you are thinking. All the same, you wouldn't be repeating these things to me if they hadn't struck a chord.' He paused. 'Derek, be careful not to lose Ellen.'

They stared at one another for a moment, then they both looked away. There was silence. They had reached the limit of intimacy permitted by their friendship.

Eventually Fett said: 'We might get a cheeky bid in the next few days.'

Hamilton was surprised. 'Why?'

'Someone might think he can pick you up at a bargain price while you're depressed and panicked by the interim results.'

'What would your advice be, then?' Hamilton asked thoughtfully.

'It depends on the offer. But I'd probably say "Wait." We should know today whether you've won the oil-field licence.'

'Shield.'

'Yes. Win that, and your shares will strengthen.'

'We're still a poor prospect for profits.'

'But ideal material for an asset stripper.'

'Interesting,' Hamilton mused. 'A gambler would make the bid today, before the Minister's announcement. An opportunist would do it tomorrow, if we win the licence. A genuine investor would wait until next week.'

'And a wise man would say no to all of them.'

Hamilton smiled. 'Money isn't everything, Nathaniel.'

'Good lord!'

'Is that so heretical?'

'Not at all.' Fett was amused, and his eyes sparkled behind the spectacles. 'I've known it for years. What surprises me is that *you* should say it.'

'It surprises me, too.' Hamilton paused. 'A matter of curiosity: do you think we'll get the licence?'

'Can't say.' Suddenly the broker's face was unreadable again. 'Depends whether the Minister believes it should go to an already-profitable company as a bonus, or to an ailing one as a lifebelt.'

'Hm. Neither, I suspect. Remember, we only head the syndicate: it's the total package that counts. The Hamilton section, in control, provides City contacts and management expertise. We'll *raise* the development money, rather than supply it out of our own pocket. Others in the team offer engineering skills, oil experience, marketing facilities, and so on.'

'So you've a good chance.'

Hamilton smiled again. 'Socrates.'

'Why?'

'He always made people answer their own questions.' Hamilton lifted his heavy frame out of the chair. 'I must go.'

Fett walked to the door with him. 'Derek, about Ellen – I hope you don't mind my saying . . .'

'No.' They shook hands. 'I value your judgement.'

Fett nodded, and opened the door. 'Whatever you do, don't panic.'

'Okey-dokey.' As he went out, Hamilton realized that he had not used *that* expression for thirty years.

Chapter Eleven

Two motor-cycle police parked their machines either side of the rear entrance to the bank. One of them produced an identity card and held it flat against the small window beside the door. The man inside read the card carefully, then picked up a red telephone and spoke into it.

A black van without markings drove between the motor-cycles and stopped with its nose to the door. The side windows of its cab were fitted with wire mesh internally, and the two men inside wore police-type uniforms with crash helmets and transparent visors. The body of the van had no windows, despite the fact that there was a third man in there.

Two more police bikes drew up behind the van, completing the convoy.

The steel door to the building lifted smoothly and noiselessly, and the van pulled in. It was in a short tunnel, brightly lit by fluorescent tubes. Its way was blocked by another door identical with the first. The van stopped and the door behind closed. The police motor-cyclists remained in the street.

The van driver wound his window down and spoke

through the wire mesh into a microphone on a stand. 'Morning,' he said cheerfully.

There was a large plate-glass window in one wall of the tunnel. Behind the window, which was bulletproof, a bright-eyed man in shirtsleeves spoke into another microphone. His amplified words resonated in the confined space. 'Code word, please.'

The driver, whose name was Ron Biggins, said: 'Obadiah.' The Controller who had set up today's run was a deacon in a Baptist church.

The shirtsleeved man pressed a large red button in the white-painted wall behind him, and the second steel door slid upward. Ron Biggins muttered: 'Miserable sod,' and eased the van forward. Again the steel door closed behind it.

It was now in a windowless room in the bowels of the building. Most of the floor space was occupied by a turntable. The room was otherwise empty. Ron steered carefully onto the marked tracks and switched off his engine. The turntable jerked, and the van moved slowly through 180 degrees then stopped.

The rear doors were now opposite the lift in the far wall. As Ron watched in his wing mirror, the lift doors parted and a bespectacled man in a black jacket and striped trousers emerged. He carried a key, holding it out in front of him as if it were a torch or a gun. He unlocked the van's rear doors, then they were opened from the inside. The third guard got out.

Two more men came out of the lift, carrying between them a formidable metal box the size of a suitcase. They loaded it into the van and went back for more.

Ron looked around. The room was bare, apart from its two entrances, three parallel lines of fluorescent lights, and a vent for the air conditioning. It was small, and not quite rectangular. Ron guessed that few of the people who worked at the bank would know it was there at all. The lift presumably went only to the vault, and the steel door to the street had no apparent connection with the main entrance around the corner.

The guard who had been inside, Stephen Younger, came around to the left-hand side of the van; and Ron's co-driver, Max Fitch, lowered his window. Stephen said: 'Big one today.'

'Makes no difference to us,' Ron said sourly. He looked back at his mirror. The loading was finished.

Stephen said to Max: 'The gaffer here likes Westerns.'

'Yeah?' Max was interested. He had not been here before, and the clerk in striped trousers did not look like a John Wayne fan. 'How do you know?' he asked.

'Watch. Here he comes.'

The clerk came to Ron's window and said: 'Move 'em out!'

Max spluttered and tried to cover his laughter. Stephen went around to the back of the van and got in. The clerk locked him in.

The three bank employees disappeared into the lift. Nothing happened for two or three minutes; then the steel door lifted. Ron fired the engine and drove into the tunnel. They waited for the inner door to close and the outer one to open. Just before they pulled away, Max said into the microphone: 'So long, Laughing Boy.'

The van emerged into the street.

The motor-cycle escort was ready. They took up their positions, two in front and two behind, and the convoy headed east.

At a large road junction in East London, the van turned onto the A11. It was watched by a large man in a grey coat with a velvet collar, who immediately went into a phone booth.

Max Fitch said: 'Guess who I just saw.'

'No idea.'

'Tony Cox.'

Ron's expression was blank. 'Who's he when he's at home?'

'Used to be a boxer. Good, he was. I saw him knock out Kid Vittorio at Bethnal Green Baths, it must be ten years ago. Hell of a boy.'

Max really wanted to be a detective, but he had failed the police force intelligence test and gone into security. He read a great deal of crime fiction, and consequently laboured under the delusion that the CID's most potent weapon was logical deduction. At home he did things like finding a lipstick-smeared cigarette butt in the ashtray and announcing grandly that he had reason to believe that Mrs Ashford from next door had been in the house.

He shifted restlessly in his seat. 'Them cases are

what they keep old notes in, aren't they?'

'Yes,' Ron said.

'So we must be going to the destruction plant in Essex,' Max said proudly. 'Right, Ron?'

Ron was staring at the outriders in front of the van and frowning. As the senior member of the team, he was the only one who got told where they were going. But he was not thinking of the route, or the job, or even Tony Cox the ex-boxer. He was trying to figure out why his eldest daughter had fallen in love with a hippie.

Chapter Twelve

Felix Laski's office in Poultry did not display his name anywhere. It was an old building, standing shoulder-to-shoulder with two others of different design. Had he been able to get planning permission to knock it down and build a skyscraper, he could have made millions. Instead it stood as an example of the way his wealth was locked up. But he reckoned that, in the long term, sheer pressure would blow the lid off planning restrictions; and he was a patient man where business was concerned.

Almost all of the building was sublet. Most of the tenants were minor foreign banks who needed an address near Threadneedle Street, and their names were well displayed. People tended to assume that Laski had interests in the banks, and he encouraged this error in every way short of outright lying. Besides, he did own one of the banks.

The furnishings inside were adequate but cheap: solid old typewriters, shop-soiled filing cabinets, secondhand desks, and the threadbare minimum of carpet. Like every successful man in middle age, Laski liked to explain his achievement in aphorisms: a favourite was 'I never spend money. I invest.' It was truer than most dicta of its kind. His one home, a small mansion in Kent, had been rising in value since he bought it shortly after the war; his meals were often expense-account affairs with business prospects; and even the paintings he owned – kept in a safe, not hung on walls – had been bought because his art dealer said they would appreciate. To him, money was like the toy bank notes in Monopoly: he wanted it, not for what it could buy, but because it was needed to play the game.

Still, his lifestyle was not uncomfortable. A primary-school teacher, or the wife of an agricultural labourer, would have thought he lived in unpardonable luxury.

The room he used as his own office was small. There was a desk bearing three telephones, a swivel chair behind it, two more chairs for callers, and a long, upholstered couch against the wall. The bookshelf beside the wall safe held scores of weighty volumes on taxation and company law. It was a room without a personality: no photographs of loved ones on the desk, no pictures on the walls, no foolish plastic pen holder given by a well-meaning grandchild, no ashtray brought home from Clovelly or stolen from the Hilton.

Laski's secretary was an efficient, overweight girl who wore her skirts too short. He often told people: 'When they were giving out sex appeal, Carol was elsewhere getting extra rations of brains.' That was a good joke, an English joke, the kind directors told each other in the executive canteen. Carol had arrived at nine twenty-five to find her boss's 'out' tray full of work which had not been there last night. Laski liked to do things like that: it impressed the staff and helped to counteract envy. Carol had not touched the papers until she had made him coffee. He liked that, too.

He was sitting on the couch, hidden behind *The Times*, with the coffee near him on the arm of the chair, when Ellen Hamilton came in.

She closed the door silently and tiptoed across the carpet, so that he did not see her until she pushed the newspaper down and looked at him over it. The sudden rustle made him jump with shock.

She said: 'Mr Laski.'

He said: 'Mrs Hamilton!'

She lifted her skirt to her waist and said: 'Kiss me good morning.'

Under the skirt she wore old-fashioned stockings with no panties. Laski leaned forward and rubbed his face in the crisp, sweet-smelling pubic hair. His heart beat a little faster, and he felt delightfully wicked, the way he had the first time he kissed a woman's vulva.

He sat back and looked up at her. 'What I like about you is the way you manage to make sex seem dirty,' he said. He folded the newspaper and dropped it to the floor.

She lowered her skirt and said: 'Sometimes I just get the hots.'

He smiled knowingly, and let his eyes roam her

body. She was about fifty, and very slender, with small, pointed breasts. Her ageing complexion was saved by a deep suntan which she nourished all winter under an ultraviolet lamp. Her hair was black, straight, and well cut; and the grey hairs which appeared from time to time were swiftly obliterated in an expensive Knightsbridge salon. She wore a cream-coloured outfit: very elegant, very expensive, and very English. He ran his hand up the inside of her thigh, under the perfectly tailored skirt. With intimate insolence his fingers probed between her buttocks. He wondered whether anyone would believe that the demure wife of the Hon. Derek Hamilton went around with no panties on just so that Felix Laski could feel her arse any time he wanted to.

She wriggled pleasurably, then moved slightly away and sat down beside him on the couch where, during the last few months, she had fulfilled some of his weirdest sexual fantasies.

He had intended Mrs Hamilton to be a minor character in his grand scenario, but she had turned out to be a very enjoyable bonus.

He had met her at a garden party. The hosts were friends of the Hamiltons', not of his; but he got an invitation by pretending a financial fancy for the host's company, a light-engineering group. It was a hot day in July. The women wore summer dresses and the men, linen jackets; Laski had a white suit. With his tall, distinguished figure and faintly foreign looks, he cut quite a dash, and he knew it.

There was croquet for the older guests, tennis for the young people, and a pool for the children. The hosts provided endless champagne and strawberries with cream. Laski had done his homework on the host – even his pretences were thorough – and he knew they could hardly afford it. Yet he had been invited reluctantly, and only because he had more or less asked. Why should a couple who were short of money give a pointless party for people they did not need? English society baffled him. Oh, he knew its rules, and understood their logic; but he would never know why people played the game.

The psychology of middle-aged women was something he understood much more profoundly. He took Ellen Hamilton's hand with just a hint of a bow, and saw a twinkle in her eye. That, and the fact that her husband was gross while she remained beautiful, was enough to tell him that she would respond to flirtation. A woman like her was sure to spend a great deal of time wondering whether she could still excite a man's lust. She might also be wondering whether she would ever know sexual pleasure again.

Laski proceeded to play the European charmer like an outrageous old ham. He fetched chairs for her, summoned waiters to top up her glass, and touched her discreetly but frequently: her hand, her arm, her shoulders, her hip. There was no point in subtlety, he felt: if she wanted to be seduced, he might as well give the message of his availability as clearly as possible; and if she did not want to be seduced, nothing he could do would change her mind.

When she had finished her strawberries – he ate none: to refuse mouth-watering food was a mark of class – he began to guide her away from the house. They moved from group to group, lingering where the conversation interested them, passing on quickly from social gossip. She introduced him to several people, and he was able to introduce her to two stock-brokers he knew slightly. They watched the children splashing around, and Laski said in her ear: 'Did you bring your bikini?' She giggled. They sat in the shade of a mature oak and looked at the tennis players, who were boringly professional. They walked along a gravel path which wound through a small landscaped wood; and when they were out of sight, he took her face in his hands and kissed her. She opened her mouth to him, and ran her hands up inside his jacket, and dug her fingers into his chest with a force that surprised him; then she pulled away and looked furtively up and down the path.

Quickly he said: 'Have dinner with me? Soon?'

'Soon,' she said.

Then they walked back to the party and split up. She left without saying good-bye to him. The next day he took a suite at a hotel in Park Lane, and there he gave her dinner and champagne, then he took her to bed. It was in the bedroom that he discovered how wrong he had been about her. He expected her to be hungry, but easily satisfied. Instead, he found that her sexual tastes were at least as bizarre as his own. Over the next few weeks they did everything that two people can do to one another, and when they ran out of ideas Laski made a phone call and another woman arrived to open up a whole new series of permutations. Ellen did everything with the delighted thoroughness of a child in a fairground where all the rides are suddenly free.

He looked at her, sitting beside him on the couch in his office, as he remembered; and he felt suffused with a sentiment which he thought people would probably call love.

He said to her: 'What do *you* like about *me*?'

'What an egocentric question!'

'I told you what I like about you. Come on, satisfy my ego. What is it?'

She looked down at his lap. 'I give you three guesses.'

He laughed. 'Would you like coffee?'

'No, thank you. I'm going shopping. I just came in for a quick feel.'

'You're a shameless old baggage.'

'What a funny thing to say.'

'How is Derek?'

'Another funny thing to say. He's depressed. Why do you ask?'

Laski shrugged. 'The man interests me. How could he possess a prize like Ellen Hamilton, then let her slip through his fingers?'

She looked away. 'Talk about something else.'

'All right. Are you happy?'

She smiled again. 'Yes. I only hope it will last.'

'Why shouldn't it?' he said lightly.

'I don't know. I meet you, and I fuck like . . . like . . .'

'Like a bunny.'

'What?'

'Fuck like a bunny. This is the correct English expression.'

She opened her mouth and laughed. 'You old fool. I love you when you're being all Prussian and correct. I know you only do it to amuse me.'

'So: we meet, and we fuck like bunnies, and you don't think it can last.'

'You can't deny the whole thing has an air of impermanence.'

'Would you have it otherwise?' he asked carefully.

'I don't know.'

It was the only answer she could give, he realized. She added: 'Would you?'

He chose his words. 'This is the first time I have had occasion to reflect upon the permanence or otherwise of our relationship.'

'Stop talking like the Chairman's Annual Report.'

'If you will stop talking like the heroine of a romantic novelette. Speaking of Chairmen's Reports, I suppose that is what Derek is depressed about.'

'Yes. He thinks it's his ulcer that makes him feel bad, but I know better.'

'Would he sell the company, do you think?'

'I wish he would.' She looked at Laski sharply. 'Would you buy it?'

'I might.'

She stared at him for a long moment. He knew that she was evaluating what he had said, weighing possibilities, considering his motives. She was a clever woman.

She decided to let it pass. 'I must go,' she said. 'I want to be home for lunch.'

They stood up. He kissed her mouth, and ran his hands all over her body with sensual familiarity. She put a finger into his mouth, and he sucked it.

'Goodbye,' she said.

'I'll call you,' Laski told her.

Then she was gone. Laski went to the bookcase and stared unseeingly at the spine of *The Directory of Directors*. She had said, *I only hope it will last*, and he needed to think about that. She had a way of saying things that made him think. She was a subtle woman. What did she want, then – marriage? She had said she did not know what she wanted, and although she could hardly have said anything else, he had a feeling she was sincere. So, what do I want? he thought. Do I want to marry her?

He sat down behind his desk. He had a lot to do. He pressed the intercom and spoke to Carol. 'Ring the Department of Energy for me, and find out exactly when – I mean what *time* – they plan to announce the name of the company that won the licence for the Shield oil field.'

'Certainly,' she said.

'Then ring Fett and Co. for me. I want Nathaniel Fett, the boss.'

'Right.'

He flipped the switch up. He thought again: do I want to marry Ellen Hamilton?

Suddenly he knew the answer, and it astonished him.

Ten a.m.

Chapter Thirteen

The editor of the *Evening Post* was under the illusion that he belonged to the ruling class. The son of a railway clerk, he had climbed the social ladder very fast in the twenty years since he left school. When he needed reassurance, he would remind himself that he was a director of Evening Post Ltd, and an opinion former; and that his income placed him in the top nine per cent of heads of households. It did not occur to him that he would never have become an opinion former were it not that his opinions coincided exactly with those of the newspaper's proprietor; nor that his directorship was in the proprietor's gift; nor that the ruling class is defined by wealth, rather than income. And he had no idea that his ready-to-wear suit by Cardin, his shaky plum-in-the-mouth accent, and his four-bedroom executive home in Chislehurst marked him plainly, in the jaundiced eyes of cynics like Arthur Cole, as a poor boy made good: more plainly than if he had worn a cloth cap and cycle clips.

Cole arrived in the editor's office on the dot of ten o'clock, with his tie straightened, his thoughts marshalled, and his list typed out. He realized instantly that that was an error. He should have burst in two minutes late in his shirtsleeves, to give the impression he had reluctantly torn himself away from the hot seat in the newsroom powerhouse for the purpose of giving less essential personnel a quick rundown on what was going on in really important departments. But then, he always thought of these things too late: he was no good at office politics. It would be interesting to watch how other executives made their entrance into the morning conference.

The editor's office was trendy. The desk was white and the easy chairs came from Habitat. Vertical venetian blinds shaded the blue carpet from sunlight, and the aluminium-and-melamine bookcases had smoked-glass doors. On a side table were copies of all the morning papers, and a pile of yesterday's editions of the *Evening Post*.

He sat behind the white desk, smoking a thin cigar and reading the *Mirror*. The sight made Cole yearn for a cigarette. He popped a peppermint into his mouth as a substitute.

The others came in in a bunch: the picture editor, in a tight-fitting shirt, with shoulder-length hair many women would envy; the sports editor, in a tweed jacket and lilac shirt; the features editor, with a pipe and a permanent slight grin; and the circulation manager, a young man in an immaculate grey suit who had started out selling encyclopedias and risen to this lofty height in only five years. The dramatic last-minute entrance was made by the chief sub-editor, the paper's designer; a short man with close-cropped hair, wearing braces. There was a pencil behind his ear.

When they were all seated, the editor tossed the *Mirror* onto the side table and pulled his chair closer to his desk. He said: 'No first edition yet?'

'No.' The chief sub looked at his watch. 'We lost eight minutes because of a web break.'

The editor switched his gaze to the circulation manager. 'How does that affect you?'

He, too, was looking at his watch. 'If it's only eight minutes, and if you can catch up by the next edition, we can wear it.'

The editor said: 'We seem to have a web break every bloody day.'

'It's this bog-paper we're printing on,' the chief sub said.

'Well, we have to live with it until we start to make a profit again.' The editor picked up the list of news stories Cole had put on his desk. 'There's nothing here to start a circulation boom, Arthur.'

'It's a quiet morning. With luck we'll have a Cabinet crisis by midday.'

'And they're two-a-penny with this bloody government.' The editor continued to read the list. 'I like this Stradivarius story.'

Cole ran down the list, speaking briefly about each item. When he had finished, the editor said: 'And not a splash among 'em. I don't like to lead all day on politics. We're supposed to cover "every facet of the Londoner's day", to quote our own advertising. I don't suppose we can make this Strad a million-pound violin?'

'It's a nice idea,' Cole said. 'But I don't suppose it's worth that much. Still, we'll try it on.'

The chief sub said: 'If it won't work in sterling, try the million-*dollar* violin. Better still, the million-dollar fiddle.'

'Good thinking,' the editor said. 'Let's have a library picture of a similar fiddle, and interviews with three top violinists about how they would feel if they lost their favourite instrument.' He paused. 'I want to go big on the oil-field licence, too. People are interested in this North Sea oil – it's supposed to be our economic salvation.'

Cole said: 'The announcement is due at twelve-thirty. We're getting a holding piece meanwhile.'

'Careful what you say. Our own parent company is one of the contenders, in case you didn't know. Remember that an oil well isn't instant riches – it means several years of heavy investment first.'

'Sure,' Cole nodded.

The circulation manager turned to the chief sub. 'Let's have street placards on the violin story, and this fire in the East End—'

The door opened noisily, and the circulation manager stopped speaking. They all looked up to see Kevin Hart standing in the doorway, looking flushed and excited. Cole groaned inwardly.

Hart said: 'I'm sorry to interrupt, but I think this is the big one.'

'What is it?' the editor said mildly.

'I just took a phone call from Timothy Fitzpeterson, a Junior Minister in the—'

'I know who he is,' the editor said. 'What did he say?'

'He claims he's being blackmailed by two people called Laski and Cox. He sounded pretty far gone. He—'

The editor interrupted again. 'Do you know his voice?'

The young reporter looked flustered. He had obviously been expecting instant panic, not a cross-examination. 'I've never spoken to Fitzpeterson before,' he said.

Cole put in: 'I had a fairly nasty anonymous tip about him this morning. I checked it out – he denied it.'

The editor grimaced. 'It stinks,' he said. The chief sub nodded agreement. Hart looked crestfallen.

Cole said: 'All right, Kevin, we'll discuss it when I come out.'

Hart went out and closed the door.

'Excitable fellow,' the editor commented.

Cole said: 'He's not stupid, but he's got a lot to learn.'

'So teach him,' the editor said. 'Now, what's lined up on the picture desk?'

Chapter Fourteen

Ron Biggins was thinking about his daughter. In this, he was at fault: he should have been thinking about the van he was driving, and its cargo of several hundred thousand pounds' worth of paper money – soiled, torn, folded, scribbled-on, and fit only for the Bank of England's destruction plant in Loughton, Essex. But perhaps his distraction was forgivable: for a man's daughter is more important than paper money; and when she is his only daughter, she is a queen; and when she is his only *child*, well, she just about fills his life.

After all, Ron thought, a man spends his life bringing her up, in the hope that when she comes of age he can hand her over to a steady, reliable type who will look after her the way her father did. Not some drunken, dirty, longaired, pot-smoking, unemployed *fucking layabout—*

'What?' said Max Fitch.

Ron snapped back into the present. 'Did I speak?'

'You were muttering,' Max told him. 'You got something on your mind?'

'I just might have, son,' Ron said. I just might have

murder on my mind, he thought, but he knew he did not mean it. He accelerated slightly to keep the regulation distance between the van and the motor cyclists. He had nearly taken the young swine by the throat, though, when he had said, 'Me and Judy thought we might live together, like, for a while, see how it goes, see?' It had been as casual as if he were proposing to take her to a matineé. The man was twenty-two years of age, five years older than Judy – thank God she was still a minor, obliged to obey her father. The boyfriend – his name was Lou – had sat in the parlour, looking nervous, in a nondescript shirt, grubby jeans held up with an elaborate leather belt like some medieval instrument of torture, and open sandals which showed his filthy dirty feet. When Ron asked what he did for a living, he said he was an unemployed poet, and Ron suspected the lad was taking the mickey.

After the remark about living together, Ron threw him out. The rows had been going on ever since. First, he had explained to Judy that she must not live with Lou because she ought to save herself for her husband; whereupon she laughed in his face and said she had already slept with him at least a dozen times, when she was supposed to be spending the night with a girlfriend in Finchley. He said he supposed she was going to say she was in the pudding club; and she said he should not be so stupid, she had been on the pill since her sixteenth birthday, when her mother had taken her up to the family planning clinic. That was when Ron came near to hitting his wife for the first time in twenty years of marriage.

Ron got a pal in the police force to check out Louis Thurley, aged twenty-two, unemployed, of Barracks Road, Harringey. The Criminal Records Office had turned up two convictions: one for possession of cannabis resin at the Reading pop festival, and one for stealing food from Tesco's in Muswell Hill. That information should have finished it. It did convince Ron's wife, but Judy just said that she knew all about both incidents. Pot shouldn't be an offence, she declared, and as far as the theft was concerned, Ron and his friends had simply sat on the supermarket floor eating pork pies off the shelf until they got arrested. They had done it because they believed food should be free, and because they were hungry and broke. She seemed to think their attitude was totally reasonable.

Unable to make her see sense, Ron had finally forbidden her to go out in the evening. She had taken it calmly. She would do as he said, and in four months' time, when she was eighteen, she would move into Lou's studio apartment with his three mates and the girl they all shared.

Ron was defeated. He had been obsessed by the problem for eight days, and still he could see no way to rescue his daughter from a life of misery – for that was what it meant, without a shadow of doubt. Ron had seen it happen. A young girl marries a wrong 'un. She goes out to work while he sits at home watching the racing on television. He does a bit of villainy from time to time to keep himself in beer and smokes. She has a few babies, he gets nicked and goes inside for a stretch, and suddenly the poor girl is trying to bring up a family on the Assistance with no husband.

He would give his life for Judy – he *had* given her eighteen years of it – and all she wanted to do was throw away everything Ron stood for and spit in his eye. He would have wept, if he could remember how.

He could not get it out of his mind, so he was still thinking about it at 10:16 a.m. this day. That was why he did not notice the ambush sooner. But his lack of concentration made little difference to what happened in the next few seconds.

He turned under a railway arch into a long, curving road which had the river on its left-hand side and a scrap yard on the right. It was a mild, clear day, and so, as he followed the gentle bend, he had no difficulty in seeing the large car transporter, piled high with battered and crushed vehicles, reversing with difficulty into the scrap yard gate.

At first it looked as though the truck would be out of the way by the time the convoy reached it. But the driver obviously did not have the angle of approach quite right, for he pulled forward again, completely blocking the road.

The two motor cycles in front braked to a halt, and Ron drew the van up behind them. One cyclist heaved his machine onto its stand and jumped up on the footplate of the cab to shout at the driver. The truck's engine was revving noisily, and black smoke poured from its exhaust in clouds.

'Report an unscheduled stop,' Ron said. 'Let's work the routine like the book says.'

Max picked up the radio microphone. 'Mobile to Obadiah Control.'

Ron was looking at the truck. It carried an odd assortment of vehicles. There was an elderly green van with 'Coopers Family Butcher' painted on the side; a crumpled Ford Anglia with no wheels; two Volkswagen Beetles piled one on top of the other; and, on the upper rack, a large white Australian Ford with a coachline and a new-looking Triumph. The whole thing looked a bit unsteady, especially the two Beetles in a rusty embrace, like a pair of copulating insects Ron looked back at the cab: the motor cyclist was making signs at the driver to get out of the convoy's way.

Max repeated: 'Mobile to Obadiah Control. Come in, please.'

We must be quite low, Ron thought, this close to the river. Maybe reception is bad. He looked again at the cars on the transporter, and realized that they were not roped down. That really was dangerous. How far had the transporter travelled with its load of unsecured scrap?

Suddenly he understood. 'Give the Mayday!' he yelled.

Max stared at him. 'What?'

Something hit the roof of the van with a clang. The

truck driver jumped out of his cab onto the motor cyclist. Several men in stocking masks swarmed over the scrap yard wall. Ron glanced in his wing mirror and saw the two motor cyclists behind the van being knocked from their machines.

The van lurched and then, incomprehensibly, seemed to rise in the air. Ron looked to his right and saw the arm of a crane reaching over the wall to his roof. He snatched the microphone from a bemused Max as one of the masked men ran towards the van. The man lobbed something small and black, like a cricket ball, at the windshield.

The next second passed slowly, in a series of pictures, like a film seen frame by frozen frame: a crash helmet flying through the air; a wooden club landing on someone's head; Max grabbing the gear stick as the van tilted; Ron's own thumb pressing the talk button on the microphone as he said 'Obadiah Mayd—'; the small bomb that looked like a cricket ball hitting the windshield and exploding, sending toughened glass fragments into the air in a shower; and then the physical blow as the shock wave hit and the quiet darkness of unconsciousness.

Sergeant Wilkinson heard the call sign 'Obadiah' from the currency shipment, but he ignored it. It had been a busy morning, with three major traffic hold-ups, a cross-London chase after a hit-and-run driver, two serious accidents, a warehouse fire, and an impromptu demonstration in Downing Street by a group of anarchists. When the call came in he was taking a cup of instant coffee and a ham roll from a young West Indian girl and saying: 'What does your husband think about you coming to work with no bra?'

The girl, who had a large bust, said: 'He doesn't notice,' and giggled.

Constable Jones, on the other side of the console, said: 'There you are, Dave, take the hint.'

Wilkinson said: 'What are you doing tonight?'

She laughed, knowing he was not serious. 'Working,' she said.

The radio said: 'Mobile to Obadiah Control. Come in, please.'

Wilkinson said: 'Another job? What?'

'I'm a go-go dancer in a pub.'

'Topless?'

'You'll have to come along and see, won't you?' the girl said, and she pushed her trolley on.

The radio said: 'Mayd—' then there was a muffled bang, like a burst of static, or an explosion.

The grin faded rapidly from Wilkinson's young face. He flicked a switch and spoke into the microphone. 'Obadiah Control, come in, Mobile.'

There was no reply. Wilkinson called to his supervisor, putting a note of urgency into his voice. 'Guvnor!'

Inspector 'Harry' Harrison came across to Wilkinson's position. A tall man, he had been running his hands through his thinning hair, and now he looked more distraught than he was. He said: 'Everything under control, Sergeant?'

'I think I caught a Mayday from Obadiah, guv.'

Harrison snapped: 'What do you mean, *think*?'

Wilkinson had not made sergeant by admitting his mistakes. He said: 'Distorted message, sir.'

Harrison picked up the mike. 'Obadiah Control to Mobile, do you read? Over.' He waited, then repeated the message. There was no reply. He said to Wilkinson: 'A distorted message, then they go off the air. We've got to treat it as a hijack. That's all I need.' He had the air of a man to whom Fate has been not merely unjust but positively vindictive.

Wilkinson said: 'I didn't get a location.'

They both turned to look at the giant map of London on the wall.

Wilkinson said: 'They took the river route. Last time they checked in was at Aldgate. Traffic's normal, so they must be somewhere like, say, Dagenham.'

'Great,' Harrison said sarcastically. He thought for a moment. 'Put out an all-cars alert. Then detach three from East London patrols and send them on a search. Alert Essex, and make sure those idle sods know how much bloody money is in that van. All right, on your bike.'

Wilkinson began to make the calls. Harrison stood behind him for a few moments, deep in thought. 'We should get a call before too long – someone must have seen it happen,' he muttered. He thought a bit more. 'But then, if chummy is clever enough to knock the radio out before the boys can call in, he's clever enough to do the job somewhere quiet.' There was a longer pause. Finally Harrison said: 'Personally, I don't think we stand a sodding chance.'

It was going like a dream, Jacko thought. The currency van had been hoisted over the wall and gently set down beside the cutting gear. The four police motor cycles had been tossed aboard the transporter, which had then reversed into the yard. The riders now lay in a neat line, each of them handcuffed hand and foot, and the yard gates were shut.

Two of the boys, wearing goggles over their stocking masks, made a man-sized hole in the side of the currency van while another plain blue van was backed up. A large rectangle of steel fell away, and a uniformed guard jumped out with his hands above his head. Jesse handcuffed him and made him lie down beside the police escort.

The cutting gear was wheeled away rapidly, and two more men got into the currency van and began to pass the chests out. They were put straight into the second van.

Jacko cast an eye over the prisoners. They had all been bashed about a bit, but not seriously. All were conscious. Jacko was perspiring under the mask, but he dare not take it off.

There was a shout from the cabin of the crane, where one of the boys was keeping watch. Jacko looked up. At the same time, he heard the sound of a siren.

He looked around. It couldn't be true! The whole idea was that they should knock the guards out before they had time to radio for help. He cursed. The men were looking to him for guidance.

The transporter had backed behind a pile of tyres, so the white motor cycles could not be seen. The two vans and the crane looked innocent enough. Jacko shouted: 'Everybody get under cover!' Then he remembered the prisoners. No time to drag them out of the way. His eye lit upon a tarpaulin. He pulled it over the five bodies, then dived behind a skip.

The siren came nearer. The car was travelling very fast. He heard the squeal of tyres as it swung under the railway arch, then the scream of the engine as the car touched seventy in third before changing up. The sound got louder, then suddenly the pitch of the siren dropped and the noise began to recede. Jacko breathed a sigh of relief, then heard the second siren. He yelled: 'Stay down!'

The second car passed, and he heard a third. There was the same squeal under the arch, the same third-gear burst after the corner – but this time the car slowed outside the gate.

Everything seemed very quiet. Jacko's face was unbearably hot under the nylon. He felt he was going to suffocate. He heard a sound like policeman's boots scraping on the gate. One of them must be climbing up to have a look over. Suddenly Jacko remembered that there were two more guards in the cab of the van. He hoped to Christ they didn't come round just now.

What was the copper up to? He hadn't climbed right over, but he hadn't fallen back, either. If they came in for a good look, it would all be up. No, don't panic, he thought, ten of us can see to a carful of wollies. But it would take time, and they might have left one in the car, who could radio for reinforcements—

Jacko could almost feel all that money slipping through his fingers. He wanted to risk a peep around the side of the skip, but he told himself there was no point: he would know when they left by the sound of the car.

What were they doing?

He looked again at the currency van. Jesus, one of the blokes was moving. Jacko hefted his shotgun. It was going to come to a fight. He whispered: 'Oh, bollocks.'

There was a noise from the van – a hoarse yell. Jacko scrambled to his feet and stepped around the skip with his gun ready.

There was nobody there.

Then he heard the car pull away with a screech of tyres. Its siren started up again and faded into the distance.

Deaf Willie emerged from behind the rusty shell of a Mercedes taxi. Together, they went towards the van. Willie said: 'Jolly good fun, ain't it?'

'Yes,' Jacko said sourly. 'Better than watching the

bloody television.' They looked inside the van. The driver was groaning, but he did not look badly hurt. 'Out you come, Grandad,' Jacko said through the broken window. 'Tea break's over.'

The voice had a calming effect on Ron Biggins. Until then he had been dazed and panicky. He did not seem to be hearing properly, there was a pain in his head, and when he put his hand up to his face he touched something sticky.

The sight of a man in a stocking mask was curiously bracing. It was all very clear. An extremely efficient raid – in fact, Ron was somewhat awed by the smoothness of the operation. They had known the route, and the timing, of the currency van's trip. He began to feel angry. No doubt a percentage of the haul would find its way into the secret bank account of a corrupt detective. Like most police and security workers, he hated bent coppers even more than villains.

The man who had called him Grandad opened the door, reaching through the shattered glass of the side window to operate the internal lock. Ron got out. The movement hurt him.

The man was young – Ron could distinguish long hair underneath the stocking. He wore jeans and carried a shotgun. He gave Ron a contemptuous push and said: 'Hands out, neatly together, Pop. You can go to hospital in a minute.'

The pain in Ron's head seemed to grow with his

anger. He fought down an urge to kick out at something, and made himself remember how he was supposed to behave during a raid: *Don't resist, cooperate with them, give them the money. We're insured for it, your own life is more valuable to us, don't be a hero.*

He began to breathe hard. In his concussed mind he confused the young man holding the shotgun with the corrupt detective and with Lou Thurley, panting and groaning on top of innocent, virginal Judy, in some verminous bed at a dingy studio apartment; and suddenly he realized that it was this man who had messed up his, Ron's, life, and that maybe a hero was what he needed to be to win back the respect of his only child; and that no-goods like this corrupt detective wearing a stocking mask in bed with Judy and carrying a shotgun was the kind who always messed it up for good people like Ron Biggins; so he took two steps forward and punched the astonished young man's nose, and the man stumbled and pulled both triggers of his gun, shooting not Ron, but another masked man beside him, who screamed blood and fell down; and Ron stared, horrified, at the blood until the first man hit him over the head very hard with the metal barrel of the gun, and Ron passed out again.

Jacko knelt beside Deaf Willie and pulled the shreds of stocking away from the older man's face. Willie's face was a dreadful mess, and Jacko went pale. Jacko and his like usually inflicted wounds upon their victims and one another with blunt instruments; consequently Jacko had never seen gunshot wounds before. And since in-house training in first aid was not one of the perks in Tony Cox's management training scheme, Jacko did not really know what to do. But he was capable of quick thinking.

He looked up. The others were standing around, staring. Jacko yelled: 'Get on with it, you dozy bastards!' They jumped.

He bent closer to Willie and said: 'Can you hear me, mate?'

Willie's face twisted, but he was unable to speak.

Jesse knelt on Willie's other side. 'We got to get him to hospital,' he said.

Jacko was ahead of him. 'I need a hot car,' he said. He pointed to a blue Volvo parked nearby. 'Whose is that?'

'It belongs to the owner of the yard,' Jesse said.

'Perfect. Help me get Willie in there.'

Jacko took his shoulders and Jesse his legs. They carried him to the car, whimpering, and put him on the backseat. The keys were in the ignition.

One of the men called from the currency truck: 'All done, Jacko.'

Jacko would have struck the man for using his name, but he was preoccupied. He said to Jesse: 'Know where you're going?'

'Yes, but you're supposed to come with me.'

'Never mind. I'll get Willie to hospital somehow, and meet you at the farm. Tell Tony what happened.

Now, drive *slow*, don't shoot the lights, pull up at zebra crossings, do it like it was a bleeding driving test, okay?'

'Yes,' Jesse said. He ran back to the getaway van and tested the rear doors. They were locked. He stripped the brown paper off the number plates – its purpose had been to stop the guards getting the number; Tony Cox thought of everything – and got behind the wheel.

Jacko started the Volvo. Someone opened the yard gate. The rest of the men were already getting into their own cars and peeling off their gloves and masks. Jesse pulled out in the van and turned right. Jacko followed him out and went the opposite way.

As he accelerated down the street, he glanced at his watch: ten twenty-seven. The whole thing had taken eleven minutes. Tony was right: he had said they would be away and clear in the time it takes a squad car to get from Vine Street nick to the Isle of Dogs. It had been a beautiful job, except for poor Deaf Willie. Jacko hoped he would live to spend his share.

He was approaching the hospital. He had figured out the way he would play it, but he needed Willie to be out of sight. He said: 'Will? Can you get on the floor?' There was no response. Jacko glanced back. Willie's eyes were such a mess that words like 'open' and 'shut' no longer applied. But the poor sod must be unconscious. Jacko reached behind and pulled the body off the seat onto the floor. It fell with a painful bump.

He steered into the hospital grounds and parked in

the car park. He got out of the car and followed signs for Casualty. Just inside the entrance he found a pay phone. He opened the directory and found the number of the hospital.

He dialled, thumbed a coin into the slot, and asked for Casualty. A phone on a desk near where he stood buzzed twice, and the sister picked it up.

She said: 'One moment, please,' and laid the receiver on the desk. She was a plump woman in her forties wearing a crisply starched uniform and a harassed air. She wrote a few words in a book, then picked the phone up again.

'Casualty, can I help you?'

Jacko spoke quietly, watching the sister's face. 'There is a man with shotgun wounds in the back of a blue Volvo car in your car park.'

The portly nurse paled. 'You mean here?'

Jacko was angry. 'Yes, you dozy old cow, in your own hospital. Now get off your bum and go and get him!' He was tempted to slam the phone down, but he stopped himself and pressed the cradle instead: if he could see the sister, then she could see him. He held the dead phone to his ear while she put hers down, got to her feet, summoned a nurse, and went out into the car park.

Jacko went farther into the hospital and left by another exit. He looked across from the main gate and saw a stretcher being carried across the car park. He had done all he could for Willie.

Now he needed another car.

Chapter Fifteen

Felix Laski liked the office of Nathaniel Fett. It was a comfortable room with unobtrusive decor, a good place in which to do business. It had none of the gimmicks Laski used in his own office to give him advantage, like a desk by the window so that his own face was in shadow, or the low, unsteady visitors' chairs, or the priceless bone china coffee cups which people were terrified of dropping. Fett's office had the atmosphere of a club for company chairmen: no doubt it was deliberate. Laski noticed two things as he shook Fett's long, narrow hand: first, that there was a large, apparently little-used desk; and second, that Fett wore a club tie. The tie was a curious choice for a Jew, he reflected; then, on second thoughts, he decided it was not curious at all. Fett wore it for the same reason Laski wore a beautifully tailored Savile Row pinstriped suit: as a badge which said I, too, am an Englishman. So, Laski thought; even after six generations of banking Fetts, Nathaniel is still a little insecure. It was a piece of information which could be used.

Fett said: 'Sit down, Laski. Would you like coffee?'

'I drink coffee all day. It's bad for the heart. No, thank you.'

'A drink?'

Laski shook his head. Refusing hospitality was one of his ways of putting a host at a disadvantage. He said: 'I knew your father quite well, until he retired. His death was a loss. This is said of so many people, but in his case it is true.'

'Thank you.' Fett sat back in a club chair opposite Laski and crossed his legs. His eyes were inscrutable behind the thick glasses. 'It was ten years ago,' he added.

'So long? He was much older than I, of course, but he knew that, like his ancestors, I came from Warsaw.'

Fett nodded. 'The first Nathaniel Fett crossed Europe with a bag of gold and a donkey.'

'I did the same journey on a stolen Nazi motor cycle and a suitcase full of worthless Reichsmarks.'

'Yet your rise was so much more meteoric.'

It was a put-down, Laski realized: Fett was saying *We may be jumped-up Polish Jews, but we're not half as jumped-up as you.* The stockbroker was Laski's match at this game; and with those spectacles to hide his expression he did not need the light behind him. Laski smiled. 'You're like your father. One never knew what he was thinking.'

'You haven't yet given me anything to think about.'

'Ah.' So the small talk is over, Laski thought. 'I'm sorry my phone call was a little mysterious. It was good of you to see me at short notice.'

'You said you had a seven-figure proposal to put to one of my clients: how could I *not* see you? Would you like a cigar?' Fett got up and proffered a box from a side table.

Laski said: 'Thank you.' He lingered a little too long over his choice; then, as his hand descended to take a cigar, he said: 'I want to buy Hamilton Holdings from Derek Hamilton.'

The timing was perfect, but Fett showed no flicker of surprise. Laski had hoped he might drop the box. But, of course, Fett had known Laski would choose that moment to drop the bombshell; had created the moment for just that purpose.

He closed the box and gave Laski a light without speaking. He sat down again and crossed his legs. 'Hamilton Holdings, for seven figures.'

'Exactly one million pounds. When a man sells his life's work, he is entitled to a nice round figure.'

'Oh, I see the psychology of your approach,' Fett said lightly. 'This is not entirely unexpected.'

'What?'

'I don't mean we expected *you*. We expected somebody. The time is ripe.'

'The bid is substantially more than the value of the shares at current prices.'

'The margin is about right,' Fett said.

Laski spread his hands, palms upwards, in a gesture of appeal. 'Let's not fence,' he said. 'It's a high offer.'

'But less than what the shares will be worth if Derek's syndicate gets the oil well.'

'Which brings me to my only condition. The offer depends upon the deal being done this morning.'

Fett looked at his watch. 'It's almost eleven. Do you really think this could be done – even assuming Derek's interested – in one hour?'

Laski tapped his briefcase. 'I have all the necessary documents drawn up.'

'We could hardly read them—'

'I also have a letter of intent containing heads of agreement. That will satisfy me.'

'I should have guessed you would be prepared.' Fett considered for a moment. 'Of course, if Derek *doesn't* get the oil well, the shares will probably go down a bit.'

'I am a gambler,' Laski smiled.

Fett continued: 'In which case, you will sell off the company's assets and close down the unprofitable branches.'

'Not at all,' Laski lied. 'I think it could be profitable in its present form with new top management.'

'You're probably right. Well, it's a sensible offer; one that I'm obliged to put to the client.'

'Don't play hard to get. Think of the commission on a million pounds.'

'Yes,' Fett said coldly. 'I'll ring Derek.' He picked up a phone from a coffee table and said: 'Derek Hamilton, please.'

Laski puffed at his cigar and concealed his anxiety.

'Derek, it's Nathaniel. I've got Felix Laski with me. He's made an offer.' There was a pause. 'Yes, we did, didn't we? One million in round figures. You would . . . all right. We'll be here. What? Ah . . . I see.'

He gave a faintly embarrassed laugh. 'Ten minutes.' He put the phone down. 'Well, Laski, he's coming over. Let's read those documents of yours while we're waiting.'

Laski could not resist saying: 'He's interested, then.'

'He could be.'

'He said something else, didn't he?'

Fett gave the embarrassed little laugh again. 'I suppose there's no harm in telling you. He said that if he gives you the company by midday, he wants the money in his hand by noon.'

Eleven a.m.

Chapter Sixteen

Kevin Hart found the address the news desk had given him and parked on a yellow line. His car was a two-year-old Rover with a V8 engine, for he was a bachelor, and the *Evening Post* paid Fleet Street salaries, so he was a good deal wealthier than most men aged twenty-two. He knew this, and he took pleasure in it; and he was not old enough discreetly to conceal that pleasure, which was why men like Arthur Cole disliked him.

Arthur had been very ratty when he came out of the editor's conference. He had sat behind the news desk, given out a batch of assignments in the usual way, then called Kevin and told him to come around to his side of the desk and sit down: a sure sign that he was about to be given what the reporters called a bollocking.

Arthur had surprised him by talking, not about the way he had barged into the conference, but about the story. He had asked: 'What was the voice like?'

Kevin said: 'Middle-aged man, Home Counties accent. He was choosing his words. Maybe too carefully – he might have been drunk, or distressed.'

'That's not the voice I heard this morning,' Arthur mused. 'Mine was younger, and Cockney. What did yours say?'

Kevin read from his shorthand. 'I am Tim Fitz-peterson, and I am being blackmailed by two people called Laski and Cox. I want you to crucify the bastards when I'm gone.'

Arthur shook his head in disbelief. 'That all?'

'Well, I asked what they were blackmailing him with, and he said, "God, you're all the same," and put the phone down on me.' Kevin paused, expecting a rebuke. 'Was that the wrong question?'

Arthur shrugged. 'It was, but I can't think of a right one.' He picked up the phone and dialled, then handed the receiver to Kevin. 'Ask him if he's phoned us in the last half hour.'

Kevin listened for a moment, then cradled the handset. 'Busy signal.'

'No help.' Arthur patted his pockets, looking for cigarettes.

'You're giving it up,' said Kevin, recognizing the symptoms.

'So I am.' Arthur began to chew his nails. 'You see, the blackmailer's biggest hold over a politician is the threat to go to the newspapers. Therefore, the blackmailers wouldn't ring us and give us the story. That would be throwing away their trump card. By the same token, since the papers are what the victim fears, he wouldn't ring us and say he was being blackmailed.' With the air of one who comes to a final conclusion, he finished: 'That's why I think the whole thing is a hoax.'

Kevin took it for a dismissal. He stood up. 'I'll get back to the oil story.'

'No,' Arthur said. 'We've got to check it out. You'd better go round there and knock on his door.'

'Oh, good.'

'But next time you think of interrupting an editor's conference, sit down and count to one hundred first.'

Kevin could not suppress a grin. 'Sure.'

But the more he thought about it, the less chance he gave the story of standing up. In the car he had tried to recall what he knew of Tim Fitzpeterson. The man was a low-profile moderate. He had a degree in economics, and was reputed to be clever, but he just did not seem to be sufficiently lively or imaginative a person to provide blackmailers with any raw material. Kevin recalled a photograph of Fitzpeterson and family – a plain wife and three awkward girls – on a Spanish beach. The politician had worn a dreadful pair of khaki shorts.

At first sight, the building outside which Kevin now stood seemed an unlikely love nest. It was a dirty grey thirties block in a Westminster back street. Had it not been so close to Parliament, it would have become a slum by now. As he entered, Kevin saw that the landlords had upgraded the place with a lift and a hall porter: no doubt they called the flats 'luxury service apartments'.

It would be impossible, he thought, to keep a wife

and three children here; or, at least, a man like Fitzpeterson would think it impossible. It followed that the flat was a pied-à-terre, so Fitzpeterson might have homosexual orgies or pot parties here after all.

Stop speculating, he told himself; you'll know in a minute.

There was no avoiding the hall porter. His cubbyhole faced the single lift across a narrow lobby. A cadaverous man with a sunken, white face, he looked for all the world as if he were chained to the desk and never allowed to see the light of day. As Kevin approached, the man put down a book called *How to Make Your Second Million* and removed his glasses.

Kevin pointed to the book. 'I'd like to know how to make my first.'

'Nine,' said the porter in a patiently bored voice.

'What?'

'You're the ninth person to say that.'

'Oh. Sorry.'

'Then you ask why I'm reading it, and I say a resident lent it to me, and you say you'd like to make friends with that resident. Now that we've got all that out of the way, what can I do for you?'

Kevin knew how to deal with smart alecks. Pander, pander, he told himself. Aloud, he said: 'What number's Mr Fitzpeterson in?'

'I'll ring him for you.' The porter reached for the house phone.

'Just a minute.' Kevin brought out his wallet and

selected two notes. 'I'd like to surprise him.' He winked, and laid the money on the counter.

The man took the money and said loudly: 'Certainly, sir, as you're his brother. Five C.'

'Thanks.' Kevin crossed to the lift and pressed the button. The conspiratorial wink had done the trick more than the bribe, he guessed. He got into the lift, pressed the button for the fifth floor, then held the doors open. The porter was reaching for the house phone. Kevin said: 'A surprise. Remember?' The porter picked up his book without replying.

The lift creaked upwards Kevin felt a familiar, physical sensation of anticipation. He always did just before knocking on a door for a story. The feeling was not unpleasant, but it was invariably mixed with a trace of worry that he might not score.

The top-floor landing was graced with a token square of thin nylon carpet and a few fading watercolours, tasteless but inoffensive. There were four flats, each with a bell, a letter-box and a peephole. Kevin found 5C, took a deep breath, and rang the bell.

There was no answer. After a while he rang again, then put his ear to the door to listen. He could hear nothing. The tension drained out of him, leaving him a little depressed.

Wondering what to do, he walked across the landing to the tiny window and looked out. There was a school across the road. A class of girls played netball in the playground. From where he was, Kevin could not tell whether they were old enough for him to lust after.

He went back to Fitzpeterson's door and leaned on the bell. The noise of the lift arriving startled him. If it was a neighbour, maybe he could ask—

The sight of a tall young policeman emerging from the lift shocked him. He felt guilty. But, to his surprise, the constable saluted him.

'You must be the gentleman's brother,' the policeman said.

Kevin thought fast. 'Who told you that?' he said.

'The porter.'

Kevin came at him fast with another question. 'And why are you here?'

'Just checking he's all right. He didn't turn up for a meeting this morning, and his phone's off the hook. They ought to have bodyguards, you know, but they won't, these Ministers.' He looked at the door. 'No answer?'

'No.'

'Any reason you know of he might have been . . . well, ill? Upset? Called away?'

Kevin said: 'Well, he rang me up this morning and sounded distressed. That's why I came.' It was a very dangerous game he was playing, he knew; but he had not lied yet, and anyway it was too late to back out.

The policeman said: 'Perhaps we should get the key from the porter.'

Kevin did not want that. He said: 'I wonder if we should break the door down. My God, if he's ill in there . . .'

The policeman was young and inexperienced, and

the prospect of breaking a door down seemed to appeal to him. He said: 'It could be as bad as that, you think?'

'Who knows? For the sake of a door . . . the Fitzpetersons are not a *poor* family.'

'No, sir.' He needed no more encouragement. He put his shoulder to the door experimentally. 'One good shove . . .'

Kevin stood close to him, and the two men hit the door simultaneously. They made more noise than impact. Kevin said: 'It's not like this in the movies,' then bit his tongue – the remark was inappropriately flippant.

The policeman seemed not to notice. He said: 'Once more.'

This time they both put all their weight into it. The doorpost splintered and the female half of the lock came free, falling to the floor as the door flew open.

Kevin let the policeman go in first. As he followed him into the hall, the man said: 'No smell of gas.'

'All-electric flats,' Kevin said, guessing.

There were three doors off the tiny hall. The first led into a small bathroom, where Kevin glimpsed a row of toothbrushes and a full-length mirror. The second stood open, revealing a kitchen which looked as if it might have been searched recently. They went through the third door, and saw Fitzpeterson immediately.

He sat in an upright chair at his desk, his head in

his arms, as if he had fallen asleep over his work. But there was no work on his desk: just the phone, a glass, and an empty bottle. The bottle was small, and made of brown glass, with a white cap and a white label bearing handwriting – the kind of bottle chemists use to dispense sleeping pills.

For all his youth, the policeman acted commendably fast. He said: 'Mr Fitzpeterson, sir!' very loudly; and without pause crossed the room and thrust his hand inside the dressing gown to feel the prone man's heart. Kevin stood very still for a moment. At last the policeman said: 'Still alive.'

The young constable seemed to take command. He waved Kevin towards Fitzpeterson. 'Talk to him!' he said. Then he took a radio from his breast pocket and spoke into it.

Kevin took the politician's shoulder. The body felt curiously dead under the dressing gown. 'Wake up! Wake up!' he said.

The policeman finished on the radio and joined him. 'Ambulance any minute,' he said. 'Let's walk him.'

They took an arm each and tried to make the unconscious man walk. Kevin said: 'Is this what you're supposed to do?'

'I bloody well hope so.'

'Wish I'd paid attention at my first-aid classes.'

'You and me both.'

Kevin was itching to get to a phone. He could see the headline: I SAVE MINISTER'S LIFE. He was not a callous young man, but he had long known that the story which made his name would probably be a tragedy for someone else. Now that it had happened he wanted to use it before it slipped through his fingers. He wished the ambulance would hurry.

There was no reaction from Fitzpeterson to the walking treatment. The policeman said: 'Talk to him. Tell him who you are.'

This was getting a bit near the bone. Kevin swallowed hard and said: 'Tim, Tim! It's me.'

'Tell him your name.'

Kevin was saved by an ambulance in the street. He shouted over the noise of the siren: 'Let's get him onto the landing, ready.'

They dragged the limp body out through the door. As they waited by the lift, the policeman felt Fitzpeterson's heart again. 'Struth, I can't feel nothing,' he said.

The lift arrived, and two ambulance men emerged. The elder took a quick look and said: 'Overdose?'

'Yes,' the policeman said.

'No stretcher, then, Bill. Keep him standing.'

The policeman said to Kevin: 'Do you want to go with him?'

It was the last thing Kevin wanted to do. 'I should stay here and use the phone,' he said.

The ambulance men were in the elevator, supporting Fitzpeterson between them. 'We're off,' the elder said, and pressed the button.

The policeman got out his radio again, and Kevin

went back into the flat. The phone was on the desk, but he did not want the copper listening in. Maybe there was an extension in the bedroom.

He went through. There was a grey Trimphone on a little chipboard bedside unit. He dialled the *Post*.

'Copy, please . . . Kevin Hart here. Government Minister Tim Fitzpeterson was rushed to hospital today after attempting to commit suicide point paragraph. I discovered the comatose body of the Energy Ministry's oil supremo after he had told me comma in a hysterical phone call comma that he was being blackmailed point par. The Minister . . .' Kevin tailed off.

'You still there?' the copytaker demanded.

Kevin was silent. He had just noticed the blood on the crumpled sheets beside him, and he felt ill.

Chapter Seventeen

What do I get out of my work? Derek Hamilton had been asking himself this question all morning, while the drugs wore off and the pain of his ulcer became sharper and more frequent. Like the pain, the question surfaced at moments of stress. Hamilton had begun badly, in a meeting with a finance director who had proposed a schedule of expenditure cuts amounting to a fifty-per-cent shutdown of the entire operation. The plan was no good – it would have helped cash flow and destroyed profitability – but Hamilton could see no alternatives, and the dilemma had made him angry. He had yelled at the accountant: 'I ask you for solutions and you tell me to close up the bloody shop!' Such behaviour towards senior management was quite intolerable, he knew. The man would certainly resign, and might not be dissuaded. Then his secretary, an elegant unflappable married woman who spoke three languages, had bothered him with a list of trivia, and he had shouted at her, too. Being what she was, she probably thought it part of her job to take that kind of maltreatment, but that was no excuse, he thought.

And each time he cursed himself, and his staff, and

his ulcer, he found himself wondering: What am I doing here?

He ran over possible answers as the car took him the short distance between his office and Nathaniel Fett's. Money as an incentive could not be dismissed quite as easily as he sometimes pretended. It was true that he and Ellen could live comfortably on his capital, or even the interest on his capital. But his dreams went beyond a comfortable life. Real success in business would mean a million-pound yacht, and a villa in Cannes, and a grouse moor of his own, and the chance to buy the Picassos he liked instead of just looking at reproductions in glossy books. Such were his dreams: or such they had been – it was now probably too late. Hamilton Holdings would not make sensational profits in his lifetime.

As a young man he had wanted power and prestige, he supposed. In that he had failed. There was no prestige in being chairman of an ailing company, no matter how big; and his power was rendered worthless by the strictures of the accountants.

He was not sure what people meant when they talked about job satisfaction. It was an odd expression, calling to mind a picture of a craftsman making a table from a piece of wood, or a farmer leading a herd of plump lambs to market. Business was not like that: even if one were moderately successful, there would always be new frustrations. And for Hamilton there was nothing other than business. Even if he had wanted to, he had not the ability to make tables or breed sheep, write textbooks or design office blocks.

He thought again about his sons. Ellen had been right: neither of them was counting on the inheritance. If asked for their counsel, they would certainly say: 'It's yours – spend it!' Nevertheless, it went against his instincts to dispose of the business which had made his family rich. Perhaps, he thought, I should disobey my instinct – following it has not made me happy.

For the first time he wondered what he would do if he did not have to go to the office. He had no interest in village life. Walking to the pub with a dog on a lead, like his neighbour Colonel Quinton, would bore Hamilton. Newspapers would hold no interest – he only read the business pages now, and if he had no business even they would be dull. He was fond of his garden, but he could not see himself spending all day digging weeds and forking in fertilizer.

What were the things we used to do, when we were young? It seemed, in retrospect, that Ellen and he had spent an awful lot of time doing absolutely nothing. They had gone for long drives in his two-seater, sometimes meeting friends for a picnic. Why? Why get in a car, go a long way, eat sandwiches and come back? They had gone to shows and to restaurants, but that was in the evening. Yet there had always seemed to be too few free days for them to spend together.

Well, it might be time for him and Ellen to start rediscovering each other. And a million pounds would buy some of his dreams. They could have a villa –

perhaps not in Cannes, but somewhere in the Sud. He could buy a yacht big enough for the Mediterranean and small enough for him to drive himself. The grouse moor was out of the question, but there might be enough left for one or two decent paintings.

This Laski fellow was buying a headache. However, headaches seemed to be his speciality. Hamilton knew a little about him. The man had no background, no education, no family; but he had brains and cash, and in hard times those things counted for more than good breeding. Perhaps Laski and Hamilton Holdings deserved each other.

It was an odd thing Hamilton had said to Nathaniel Fett: 'Tell Laski that if I sell him my company by midday, I want the money in my hand by noon.' How eccentric, to ask for cash on the nail like the proprietor of a Glasgow liquor store. But he knew why he had done it. The effect had been to take the decision out of his hands: if Laski could produce the money, the deal would be done; if not, not. Incapable of making up his mind, Hamilton had tossed a ha'penny.

Suddenly he hoped fervently that Laski would be able to raise the cash. Derek Hamilton wanted never to go back to the office.

The car drew up outside Fett's place, and he got out.

Chapter Eighteen

The beauty of being an earwig, Bertie Chieseman had found, was that you could do almost anything while you were listening to the police radio. And the tragedy of it, from his point of view, was that there was nothing much he wanted to do.

Already this morning he had swept the carpet – a process of raising dust only for it to fall again soon afterwards – while the airwaves were filled with uninteresting messages about traffic in the Old Kent Road. He had also shaved at the sink in the corner, using a safety razor and hot water from the Ascot; and fried a single rasher of bacon on the cooker in the same room for his breakfast. He ate very little.

He had called the *Evening Post* only once since his first report at eight o'clock: to tip them off about an ambulance call to a block of flats in Westminster. The name of the patient had not been mentioned over the air, but Bertie had surmised from the address that it might, just possibly, be someone important. It was up to the news desk to phone ambulance headquarters and ask the name; and if headquarters had been told, they would pass the information on. Often the ambulance men did not make their report until the patient was in the hospital. Bertie occasionally talked to reporters, and he always asked them questions about how they used the information he gave them, and turned it into stories. He was quite well informed about the mechanics of journalism.

Apart from that and the traffic, there had been only shoplifting, petty vandalism, a couple of accidents, a small demonstration in Downing Street, and one mystery.

The mystery was in East London, but that was about all Bertie knew. He had heard an all-cars alert, but the subsequent message had been uninformative: the cars were asked to look out for a plain blue van with a certain registration number. It might simply have been hijacked with a cargo of cigarettes, or it might be driven by someone the police wanted to question, or it might have been in a robbery. The word 'Obadiah' had been used; Bertie did not know why. Immediately after the alert, three cars had been detached from regular patrol to search for the van. That meant very little.

The fuss might be over nothing at all – perhaps even some Flying Squad inspector's runaway wife; Bertie had known it to happen. On the other hand, it could be big. He was waiting for more information.

The landlady came up while he was cleaning his frying pan with warm water and a rag. He dried his hands on his sweater and got out the rent book. Mrs Keeney, in an apron and curlers, stared in awe at the radio equipment, although she saw it every week.

Bertie gave her the money and she signed the book. Then she handed him a letter.

'I don't know why you don't have some nice music on,' she said.

He smiled. He had not told her what he used the radio for, as it was against the law to listen to police radio. 'I'm not very musical,' he said.

She shook her head resignedly, and went out. Bertie opened the letter. It was his monthly cheque from the *Evening Post*. He had had a good spell: the cheque was for five hundred pounds. Bertie paid no tax. He found it difficult to spend all his money. The job compelled him to live fairly simply. He spent every evening in pubs, and on Sundays he went out in the car, his one luxury, a bright new Ford Capri. He went to all sorts of places, like a tourist: he had been to Canterbury Cathedral, Windsor Castle, Beaulieu, St Albans, Bath, Oxford; he visited safari parks, stately homes, ancient monuments, historic towns, racetracks and funfairs with equal enjoyment. He had never had so much money in his life. There was enough to buy everything he wanted, and a little left over to save.

He put the cheque in a drawer and finished cleaning the frying pan. As he was putting it away the radio crackled, and a sixth sense told him to listen carefully.

'That's right, blue Bedford six-wheeler. Alpha Charlie London two oh three Mother. Has it what? Distinguishing marks? Yes, if you look inside you'll notice it has a most unusual feature – six large boxes of used notes.'

Bertie frowned. The radio operator at headquarters was being funny, obviously; but what he said implied that the missing van was carrying a large sum of money. That sort of van did not go missing accidentally. It must have been hijacked.

Bertie sat down at his table and picked up the phone.

Chapter Nineteen

Felix Laski and Nathaniel Fett stood up when Derek Hamilton entered the room. Laski, the would-be buyer, and Hamilton, the vendor, shook hands briefly, like boxers before a fight. Laski realized with a shock that he and Hamilton were wearing identical suits: dark blue with a pinstripe. They even had the same six-button double-breasted jacket without vents. But Hamilton's gross body took away any elegance the style had. On him, the most beautiful suit would look like a length of cloth wrapped around a jelly. Laski knew, without looking in a mirror, that his own suit appeared to be much more expensive.

He told himself not to feel superior. The wrong attitude could ruin a negotiation. He said: 'Nice to see you again, Hamilton.'

Hamilton nodded. 'How do you do, Mr Laski.' The chair squeaked as he sat down.

The use of 'Mr' did not escape Laski. Hamilton would only employ the unadorned surname with his equals.

Laski crossed his legs and waited for Fett, the broker, to open the proceedings. He studied Hamilton out of the corner of his eye. The man might have been handsome in his youth, he decided: he had a high forehead, a straight nose, and bright blue eyes. Right now he looked relaxed, with his hands folded in his lap. Laski thought: He had made up his mind already.

Fett said: 'For the record, Derek owns five hundred and ten thousand shares in Hamilton Holdings, Limited, a public company. Another four hundred and ninety thousand are owned by various parties, and there are no unissued shares. Mr Laski, you offer to buy those five hundred and ten thousand shares for the sum of one million pounds, on condition the deed of sale is dated today and signed at twelve noon.'

'Or that a letter to that intent is so dated and signed.'

'Quite so.'

Laski tuned out as Fett continued to enunciate formalities in a dry monotone. He was thinking that Hamilton probably deserved to lose his wife. A woman as vivacious and highly sexed as Ellen was entitled to a full-blooded love life: her husband had no right to let himself run to seed.

Here I am, he thought, stealing the man's wife and taking away his life's work, and still he can make me squirm by calling me Mister.

'As I see it,' Fett was concluding, 'the deal can be done just as Mr Laski has outlined it. The documents are satisfactory. There remains only the larger question of whether, and under what conditions, Derek will sell.' He sat back with the air of one who has completed a ritual.

Hamilton looked at Laski. 'What are your plans for the group?' he asked.

Laski suppressed a sigh. There was no point to any kind of cross-examination. He was quite free to tell Hamilton a pack of lies. He did just that. 'The first step would be a large capital injection,' he said. 'Then an improvement in management services, a shake-out at top level in the operating companies, and some streamlining in low-performance sectors.' Nothing could have been farther from the truth, but if Hamilton wanted to read the script from the top, Laski was happy to go along with it.

'You've chosen a crucial moment at which to make your offer.'

'Not really,' Laski said. 'The oil well, if it happens, will be a bonus. What I'm buying is a fundamentally sound group which is going through a bad patch. I shall make it profitable without meddling with its infrastructure. That happens to be my particular talent.' He smiled self-consciously. 'Despite my reputation, I'm interested in running real industries, not trading in equities.'

He caught a hostile glance from Fett: the broker knew he was lying. 'So why the twelve o'clock deadline?'

'I think the price of Hamilton shares will go up unreasonably if you get the licence. This could be my last chance for some time of buying at a sensible price.'

'Fair enough,' Hamilton said, taking the initiative away from Fett. 'But I, too, have set a deadline. How do you feel about that?'

'Quite happy,' Laski lied. In truth he was desperately worried. Hamilton's wish to see the money 'in his hand' at the time the deal was signed, was unexpected. Laski had planned to pay a deposit today and the balance when final contracts were exchanged. But although Hamilton's stipulation was eccentric, it was perfectly reasonable. Once the letter had been signed Laski was able to trade in the shares, either selling them or using them to raise a loan. What he planned was to use the shares – at their oil-inflated price – to raise the money to pay for the original purchase.

But he had fallen into the pit he had dug. He had tempted Hamilton with a fast deal, and the old man had gone for it too well. Laski did not know what he was going to do, for he did not have a million pounds – he would have been scraping the barrel for the one-hundred-thousand deposit. But he did know what he was *not* going to do: he would not let this deal slip through his fingers.

'Quite happy,' he repeated.

Fett said: 'Derek, perhaps now is the time you and I should have a few minutes together—'

'I don't think so,' Hamilton interrupted. 'Unless you plan to tell me that this deal is riddled with pitfalls?'

'Not at all.'

'In that case –' Hamilton turned to Laski ' – I accept.'

Laski stood up and shook Hamilton's hand. The

fat man was mildly embarrassed by the gesture, but it was one Laski believed in. Men like Hamilton could always find escape clauses in a contract, but they could not bear to renege on a handshake.

Laski said: 'The funds are in the Cotton Bank of Jamaica – London branch, of course. I imagine this presents no problem.' He drew a cheque-book from his pocket.

Fett frowned. It was a very small bank, but perfectly respectable. He would have preferred a cheque drawn on a clearing bank, but he could hardly object at this stage without seeming obstructive: Laski knew he would feel like this.

Laski wrote the cheque and handed it to Hamilton. 'It's not often a man pockets a million pounds,' he said.

Hamilton seemed to become jovial. He smiled: 'It's not often a man spends it.'

Laski said: 'When I was ten years old our rooster died, and I went with my father to market to buy a new one. It cost the equivalent of . . . oh, three pounds. But my family had saved for a year to accumulate that money. More heart searching went into the purchase of that rooster than any financial deal I have ever done, this one included.' He smiled, knowing they were uneasy to hear this story, and not caring. 'A million pounds is nothing, but a rooster can save a whole family from starvation.'

Hamilton mumbled: 'Very true.'

Laski reverted to his normal image. 'Let me call the

bank to warn them that this cheque is on its way.'

'Surely.' Fett took him to the door and pointed. 'That room is empty. Valerie will give you a line.'

'Thank you. When I return, we can sign the letters.' Laski went into the little room and picked up the phone. When he heard the dialling tone, he looked out of the room to make sure Valerie was not listening. She was at the filing cabinet. Laski dialled.

'Cotton Bank of Jamaica.'

'Laski here. Give me Jones.'

There was a pause.

'Good morning, Mr Laski.'

'Jones, I've just signed a cheque for a million pounds.'

At first there was no reply. Then Jones said: 'Jesus. You haven't got it.'

'All the same, you will clear the cheque.'

'But what about Threadneedle Street?' The banker's voice was rising in pitch. 'We don't have enough cash on deposit at the bank!'

'We'll cross that bridge when we come to it.'

'Mr Laski. This bank cannot authorize one million pounds to be transferred from its account at the Bank of England to another account at the Bank of England, because this bank does not have one million pounds on deposit at the Bank of England. I don't think I can make the situation plainer.'

'Jones, who owns the Cotton Bank of Jamaica?'

Jones drew in his breath loudly. 'You do, sir.'

'Quite.' Laski put the phone down.

Twelve Noon

Chapter Twenty

Peter 'Jesse' James was perspiring. The midday sun was unseasonably strong, and the wide glass windscreen of the van magnified its heat, so that the rays burned his naked, meaty forearms and scorched the legs of his trousers. He was awful hot.

As well as that, he was terrified.

Jacko had told him to drive slowly. The advice was superfluous. A mile from the scrap yard he had run into heavy traffic; and it had been bumper-to-bumper since then, across half of south London. He could not have hurried if he had wanted to.

He had both of the van's sliding side doors open, but this did not help. There was no wind when the vehicle was stationary, and all he got when he moved was a light breeze of warm exhaust smoke.

Jesse believed driving ought to be an adventure. He had been in love with cars since he stole his first motor – a Zephyr-Zodiac with customized fins – at the age of twelve. He liked to race away from traffic lights, double-declutch on bends, and scare the hell out of Sunday drivers. When another motorist dared to sound his horn, Jesse would yell curses and shake his fist, and fantasize about shooting the bastard through the head. In his own car he kept a pistol in the glove compartment. It had never been used.

But driving was no fun when you had a fortune in stolen money in the back. You had to accelerate gradually and brake evenly, give the old slowing-down signal when you pulled up, refrain from overtaking, and give way to pedestrians at road junctions. It occurred to him that there was such a thing as suspiciously good behaviour: an intelligent copper, seeing a youngish bloke in a van poodling along like an old dear on a driving test, might well smell a rat.

He came to yet another junction on the interminable South Circular Road. The light turned from green to amber. Jesse's instinct was to push his foot to the floor and race the signal. He gave a weary sigh, flapped his arm out of the window like a fool, and came to a careful stop.

He should try not to worry – nervous people made mistakes. He ought to forget the money, think about something else. He had driven thousands of miles through the exasperating traffic of London without ever being stopped by the law: why should today be different? Even the Old Bill couldn't *smell* hot money.

The lights changed and he pulled forward. The road narrowed into a shopping centre where delivery trucks lined the kerb and a series of pedestrian crossings slowed the flow of cars. The narrow pavements were thronged with shoppers and obstructed by several hawkers flogging substandard costume jewellery and ironing-board covers.

The women were wearing summery clothes – there was something to be said for the hot weather. Jesse started to watch the tight T-shirts, the delightfully loose-fitting frocks and the bare knees as he crawled forward a few yards at a time. He liked girls with big bottoms, and he scanned the crowds for a suitable specimen to undress with his eyes.

He spotted her a good fifty yards away. She was wearing a blue nylon sweater and tight white trousers. She probably thought she was overweight, but Jesse would have told her otherwise. She had a nice, old-fashioned bra which made her tits look like torpedoes; and her high-waisted slacks flared out over big hips. Jesse peered at her, hoping to see her tits wobble. They did.

What he would like to do, was to stand behind her, and pull her trousers down slowly, then—

The car in front moved forward twenty yards, and Jesse followed it. It was a brand-new Marina with a vinyl roof. Maybe he would get one with his share of the takings. The line of cars stopped again. Jesse pulled the handbrake and looked for the plump girl.

He did not pick her up until the traffic was moving off again. As he let the clutch in he saw her, looking in the window of a shoe shop, her back to him. The trousers were so tight that he could see the hem of her panties, two diagonal lines pointing to the fork of her thighs. He loved it when you could see their panties under the trousers: it turned him on almost as much as a bare bum. Then I'd slide her panties down, he thought, and—

There was a crash of steel on steel. The van stopped with a bump, throwing Jesse forward against the steering wheel. The doors slid shut with a double bang. He knew, before he looked, what he had done; and the taste of fear made him feel sick.

The Marina in front had stopped sooner than it needed to, and Jesse, wrapped up in the plump girl with the tight trousers, had gone straight into its back.

He got out of the van. The driver of the saloon car was already inspecting the damage. He looked up at Jesse, his face red with anger. 'You mad bastard,' he spat. 'What are you – blind, or stupid?' He had a Lancashire accent.

Jesse ignored him and looked at the bumpers of the two vehicles, folded together in a steel kiss. He made an effort to keep calm. 'Sorry, pal. My fault.'

'Sorry! You people should be banned from the ruddy road.'

Jesse stared at the man. He was short and portly, and wore a suit. His round face was a picture of righteous indignation. He had the quick aggressiveness of small people, and their characteristic backward tilt of the head. Jesse hated him instantly. He looked like a sergeant-major. Jesse would have liked to punch his face; or better, shoot him through the forehead.

'We all make mistakes,' he said with forced amiability. 'Let's just give each other our names and everything, and get on. It's only a little bump. Don't make a national disaster of it.'

It was the wrong thing to say. The short man became even redder. 'You're not getting off that lightly,' he said.

The traffic in front had moved on, and drivers behind were getting impatient. Several of them sounded their horns. One man got out of his car.

The Marina driver was writing the number of the van in a little notebook. That type of man always does have a little notebook and pencil in his jacket pocket, Jesse thought.

He closed the book. 'This is bloody careless driving. I'm going to ring the police.'

The driver from behind said: 'How about moving this little lot out the way, so the rest of us can get on?'

Jesse sensed an ally. 'Nothing I'd rather do, mate, but this fellow wants to call in Kojak on the case.'

The portly man wagged a finger. 'I know your type – drive like a hooligan and let the insurance pay. I'm having you up, Sonny Jim.'

Jesse took a step forward, clenching his fists; then stopped himself. He was getting panicky. 'The police have got enough to do,' he pleaded.

The other man's eyes narrowed. He had seen Jesse's fear. 'We'll let them decide whether they've got better things to do.' He looked around, and spotted a phone booth. 'You stop here.' He turned away.

Jesse grabbed his shoulder. He was scared now. He said: 'This is nothing to do with the police!'

The man turned and knocked Jesse's hand away. 'Get off, you young punk—'

Jesse seized him by the lapels and pulled him onto his toes. 'I'll give you punk . . .' Suddenly he became conscious of the crowd that had gathered, looking on with interest. There were about a dozen people. He stared at them. They were mostly housewives with shopping bags. The girl with the tight trousers was at the front. He realized he was doing all the wrong things.

He decided to get out of it.

He let the aggrieved man go and got into the van. The man stared at him disbelievingly.

Jesse restarted the stalled engine and backed up. There was a wrenching sound as the vehicles parted. He could see that the Marina's bumper hung loose, and its rear-light cluster was smashed. Fifty quid to put right, and a tenner if you do the work yourself, he thought wildly.

The portly man moved in front of the van and stood there like Neptune, waving an officious finger. 'You stay right here!' he shouted. The crowd was growing as the row became more spectacular. There was a lull in the oncoming traffic, and the cars behind began to pull out past the accident.

Jesse found first gear and revved the engine. The man stood his ground. Jesse engaged the clutch with a jerk, and the van shot forward.

Too late, the portly man dived towards the kerb. Jesse heard a dull thud from the nearside wing as he swung out. A car behind braked with a squeal of tyres. Jesse changed up and tore away without looking back.

The street seemed narrow and oppressive, traplike, as he hurtled along, ignoring pedestrian crossings, swerving and braking. He tried desperately to think. He had screwed it all up. The whole tickle had gone beautifully, and Jesse James had pranged the getaway motor. A vanload of paper money blown on a fifty-nicker crunch. Arseholes.

Stay cool, he told himself. It wasn't a blowout until he was locked up. There was still time, if only he could *think*.

He slowed the van and turned off the main road. There was no point in attracting attention again. He threaded his way through a series of back streets while he figured it out.

What would happen now? A bystander would phone the police, especially as he had knocked down the portly man. The van's number was in the little notebook; besides, somebody in the crowd would have noted it too. It would be reported as a hit-and-run, and the number would go out over the air to patrol cars. Anything from three minutes to fifteen to get that far. Another five minutes, and they would broadcast a description of Jesse. What was he wearing? Blue trousers and an orange shirt. Arseholes.

What would Tony Cox say, if he were here to be asked? Jesse recalled the guvnor's fleshy face and heard his voice. *Tell yourself what the problem is, right?*

Jesse said aloud: 'The police have got my number and description.'

Think what you'd have to do to solve the problem.

'What the hell can I do, Tone? Change my number plate and my appearance?'

Then do it, right?

Jesse frowned. Tony's analytical thinking only went so far. Where the hell could he get number plates, and how could he fit them?

Of course, it was easy.

He found his way to a main road and drove along until he came to a garage. He pulled on to the forecourt. Quad stamps, he thought: jolly good show. There was a repair shop behind the pumps. A tanker was discharging on the far side.

The attendant approached, cleaning his spectacles on an oily rag. 'Five quids' worth,' Jesse said. 'Where's the khasi?'

'Round the side.'

Jesse followed the jerked thumb. A rough concrete path led alongside the garage. He found a broken door marked 'Gents' and went past it.

Behind the garage was a small patch of waste ground where newish cars in for repair jostled with rusty doors, buckled wings, and discarded machinery. Jesse could not see what he was looking for.

The back entrance to the repair shop gaped open beside him, big enough to drive a bus through. There was no point in being furtive. He walked in.

It took a moment to adjust to the gloom after the

sunlight outside. The air smelled of engine oil and ozone. A Mini was on a ramp at head height, its entrails hanging down obscenely. The front end of an articulated truck was wired up to a Krypton tester. A Jaguar on chocks had its wheels off. There was no one about. He looked at his wristwatch: they would be having their dinner. He looked around.

He spotted the things he needed.

A pair of red-and-white trade plates stood on an oil drum in a corner. He crossed the floor and picked them up. He looked around again, and stole two more things: clean overalls hanging on a peg in the brick wall, and a length of dirty string off the floor.

A voice said: 'Looking for something, brother?'

Jesse jerked around, his heart in his mouth. A black mechanic in a grimy overall stood on the far side of the shop, leaning on the gleaming white wing of the Jaguar, his mouth full of food. His Afro haircut shifted as he chewed. Jesse tried to cover the trade plates with the overalls. 'The khasi,' he said. 'Want to change my clothes.' He held his breath.

The mechanic pointed. 'Outside,' he said. He swallowed, and took another bite out of a Scotch egg.

'Thanks.' Jesse hurried out.

'Any time,' the mechanic called after him. Jesse realized the man had an Irish accent. Irish spades? That was a new one.

The pump attendant was waiting beside the van. Jesse climbed in and threw the overalls and their contents over the seat into the back. The attendant looked curiously at the bundle. Jesse said: 'My overalls were hanging out the back door. It must be filthy. How much?'

'We generally charge a fiver for five quids' worth. I didn't notice it.'

'Nor did I, for fifty bleeding miles. I did say five quids' worth, didn't I?'

'That's what you said. No charge for the bog.'

Jesse gave him a five-pound note and pulled away rapidly.

He was a little off his route now, which was good. The area was quieter than the places he had travelled through earlier. There were oldish detached houses on either side, set back from the road. Horse-chestnut trees lined the pavements. He saw a Green Line bus stop.

He needed a quiet lane in which to perform the switch. He checked his watch again. It must be fifteen minutes since the accident. There was no time left for finesse.

He took the next turning. The street was called Brook Avenue. All the houses were semis. He needed somewhere less exposed, for Christ's sake! He could not switch plates in full view of sixty nosy housewives.

He took another turn, and another – and found a service road behind a little row of shops. He pulled in and stopped. There were garages and garbage cans, and the back doors through which goods were delivered to the stores. It was the best he could hope for.

He climbed over the seat into the back of the van. It was very hot. He sat on one of the money chests and pulled the overalls up his legs. Jesus, he was nearly there: give me a couple more minutes, he thought – it was almost a prayer.

He stood up, bending over, and shrugged into the garment. If I'd blown it, Tony would have slit my throat, he thought. He shuddered. Tony Cox was a hard bastard. He had a bit of a kink about punishment.

Jesse zipped up the overalls. He knew about eyewitness descriptions. The police would by now be looking for a very big, vicious-looking character with desperate eyes, wearing an orange shirt and jeans. Anyone actually looking at Jesse would just see a mechanic.

He picked up the trade plates. The string had gone – he must have dropped it. He looked around the floor. Damn, there was *always* a piece of rope floating around on the floor of a van! He opened the toolbox and found a length of oily string tied around the jack.

He got out and went to the front of the van. He worked carefully, afraid to botch the job by hurrying. He tied the red-and-white trade plate over the original number plate, just as garages usually did when taking a commercial vehicle for a road test. He stood back and examined his work. It looked fine.

He went to the rear of the van and repeated the job on the back plate. It was done. He breathed more easily.

'Changing the plates, then?'

Jesse jumped and turned. His heart sank. The voice belonged to a policeman.

For Jesse it was the last straw. He could think of no more wrinkles, no more plausible lies, no more ruses. His instincts deserted him. He did not have a single thing to say.

The copper walked towards him. He was quite young, with ginger sideburns and a freckled nose. 'Trouble?'

Jesse was amazed to see him smile. A ray of hope penetrated his petrified brain. He found his tongue. 'Plates worked loose,' he said. 'Just tightened them up.'

The copper nodded. 'I used to drive one of these,' he said conversationally. 'Easier than driving a car. Lovely jobs.'

It crossed Jesse's mind that the man might be playing a sadistic cat-and-mouse game, knowing perfectly well that Jesse was the driver of the hit-and-run van, but pretending ignorance so as to shock him at the last minute.

'Easy when they're running right,' he said. The sweat on his face felt cold.

'Well, you've done it now. On your way, you're blocking the road.'

Like a sleepwalker, Jesse climbed into the cab and started the engine. Where was the copper's car? Did he have his radio switched off? Had the overalls and the trade plates fooled him?

If he were to walk around to the front of the van

and see the dent made by the bumper of the Marina—

Jesse eased his foot off the clutch and drove slowly along the service road. He stopped at the end and looked both ways. In his wing mirror, he saw the policeman at the far end getting into a patrol car.

Jesse pulled into the road and the patrol car was lost from view. He wiped his brow. He was trembling.

'Gawd, stone the crows,' he breathed.

Chapter Twenty-One

Evan Jones was drinking whisky before lunch for the first time in his life. There was a reason. He had a Code, and he had broken it – also for the first time. He was explaining this to his friend, Arny Matthews, but he was not doing too well, for he was unused to whisky, and the first double was already reaching his brain.

'It's my upbringing, see,' he said in his musical Welsh accent. 'Strict chapel. We lived by the Book. Now, a man can exchange one Code for another, but he can't shake the habit of obedience. See?'

'I see,' said Arny, who did not see at all. Evan was manager of the London branch of the Cotton Bank of Jamaica, and Arny was a senior actuary at Fire and General Marine Insurance, and they lived in adjoining mock-Tudor houses in Woking, Surrey. Their friendship was shallow, but permanent.

'Bankers have a Code,' Evan continued. 'Do you know, it caused quite a stir when I told my parents I wanted to be a banker. In South Wales the grammar-school boys are expected to become teachers, or ministers, or Coal Board clerks, or trade union officials – but not bankers.'

'My mother didn't even know what an actuary was,' said Arny sympathetically, missing the point.

'I'm not talking about the principles of good banking – the law of the least risk, the collateral to more-than-cover the loan, higher interest for longer term – I don't mean all that.'

'No.' Arny now had no idea what Evan did mean. But he sensed that Evan was going to be indiscreet, and like everyone in the City he enjoyed the indiscretions of others. 'Have another?' He picked up the glasses.

Evan nodded assent, and watched Arny go to the bar. The two of them often met in the lounge of Pollard's before catching the train home together. Evan liked the plush seats, and the quiet, and the faintly servile barmen. He had no time for the newer kind of pub that was springing up in the Square Mile: trendy, crowded cellars with loud music for the long-haired whiz kids in their three-piece suits and gaudy ties, drinking lager in pints or Continental aperitifs.

'I'm talking about integrity,' Evan resumed when Arny came back. 'A banker can be a fool, and survive, if he's straight; but if he hasn't got integrity . . .'

'Absolutely.'

'Now, take Felix Laski. There's a man totally without integrity.'

'This is the man who's taken you over.'

'To my everlasting regret, yes. Shall I tell you how he got control?'

Arny leaned forward in his seat, holding a cigarette halfway to his lips. 'Okay.'

'We had a customer called South Middlesex Properties. They were tied up with a discounting outfit we knew, and we wanted an outlet for a lot of long-term money. The loan was too big for the property company, really, but the collateral was vast. To cut a long story short, they defaulted on the loan.'

'But you had the property,' Arny said. 'Surely the title deeds were in your vault.'

'Worthless. What we had were copies – and so did several other creditors.'

'Straightforward fraud.'

'Indeed, although somehow they managed to make it look like mere incompetence. However, we were in a hole. Laski bailed us out in exchange for a majority holding.'

'Shrewd.'

'Shrewder than you think, Arny. Laski practically controlled South Middlesex Properties. Mind you, he wasn't a director. But he had shares, and he was employed by them as a consultant, and the management was weak . . .'

'So he bought into the Cotton Bank with the money he'd borrowed and defaulted on.'

'Looks like it, doesn't it?'

Arny shook his head. 'I find that very hard to credit.'

'You wouldn't if you knew the bugger.' Two men in solicitors' stripes sat at the next table with half-pints of beer, and Evan lowered his voice. 'A man totally without integrity,' he repeated.

'What a stroke to pull.' There was a note of admiration in Arny's voice. 'You could have gone to the newspapers – if it's true.'

'Who the hell would publish it, other than *Private Eye*? But it's true, boy. There is no depth to which that man will not sink.' He took a large swallow of whisky. 'You know what he's done today?'

'It couldn't be worse than the South Middlesex deal,' Arny goaded him.

'Couldn't it? Ha!' Evan's face was slightly flushed now, and the glass trembled in his hand. He spoke slowly and deliberately. 'He has instructed me – instructed, mind you – to clear a rubber cheque for a million pounds.' He set down his glass with a flourish.

'But what about Threadneedle Street?'

'My exact words to him!' The two solicitors looked around, and Evan realized he had shouted. He spoke more quietly. 'My *very* words. You'll never believe what he said. He said: "Who owns the Cotton Bank of Jamaica?" Then he put the phone down on me.'

'So what did you do?'

Evan shrugged. 'When the payee phoned up, I said the cheque was good.'

Arny whistled. 'What *you* say makes no difference. It's the Bank of England who have to make the transfer. And when they discover that you haven't got a million—'

'I told him all that.' Evan realized he was close to tears, and felt ashamed. 'I have never, in thirty years of banking, since I started behind the counter of Barclays Bank in Cardiff, passed a rubber cheque. Until today.' He emptied his glass and stared at it gloomily. 'Have another?'

'No. You shouldn't, either. Will you resign?'

'Must do.' He shook his head from side to side. 'Thirty years. Come on, have another.'

'No,' Arny said firmly. 'You should go home.' He stood up and took Evan's elbow.

'All right.'

The two men walked out of the wine bar and into the street. The sun was high and hot. Lunch-hour queues were beginning to form at cafés and sandwich shops. A couple of pretty secretaries walked by eating ice-cream cones.

Arny said: 'Lovely weather, for the time of year.'

'Beautiful,' Evan said lugubriously.

Arny stepped off the kerb and hailed a taxi. The black cab swerved across and pulled up with a squeal.

Evan said: 'Where are you going?'

'Not me. You.' Arny opened the door and said to the driver: 'Waterloo Station.'

Evan stumbled in and sat down on the back seat.

'Go home before you get too drunk to walk,' Arny said. He shut the door.

Evan opened the window. 'Thanks,' he said.

'Home's the best place.'

Evan nodded. 'I wish I knew what I'm going to tell Myfanwy.'

*

Arny watched the cab disappear, then walked towards his office, thinking about his friend. Evan was finished as a banker. A reputation for honesty was made slowly and lost quickly in the City. Evan would lose his as surely as if he had tried to pick the pocket of the Chancellor of the Exchequer. He might get a decent pension out of it, but he would never get another job.

Arny was secure, if hard up: quite the opposite of Evan's plight. He earned a respectable salary, but he had borrowed money to build an extension to his lounge, and he was having difficulty with the payments. He could see a way to earn out of Evan's misfortune. It felt disloyal. However, he reasoned, Evan could suffer no more.

He went into a phone booth and dialled a number. The pips went and he thumbed in a coin. '*Evening Post*?'

'Which department?'

'City Editor.'

There was a pause, then a new voice said: 'City desk.'

'Mervyn?'

'Speaking.'

'This is Arnold Matthews.'

'Hello, Arny. What goes on?'

Arny took a deep breath. 'The Cotton Bank of Jamaica is in trouble.'

Chapter Twenty-Two

Doreen, the wife of Deaf Willie, sat stiffly upright in the front of Jacko's car, clutching a handbag in her lap. Her face was pale, and her lips were twisted into a strange expression compounded of fury and dread. She was a large-boned woman, very tall with broad hips, and tending to plumpness because of Willie's liking for chips. She was also poorly dressed, and this was because of Willie's liking for brown ale. She stared straight ahead, and spoke to Jacko out of the side of her mouth.

'Who've took him up the hospital, then?'

'I don't know, Doreen,' Jacko lied. 'Perhaps it was a job, and they didn't want to let on who, you know. All I know is, I get a phone call, Deaf Willie's up the hospital, tell his missus, bang.' He made a slamming-the-phone-down gesture.

'Liar,' Doreen said evenly.

Jacko fell silent.

In the back of the car, Willie's son, Billy, stared vacantly out of the window. With his long, awkward body he was cramped in the small space. Normally he enjoyed travelling in cars, but today his mother was very tense, and he knew something bad had happened. Just what it was, he was not sure: things were confusing. Ma seemed to be cross with Jacko, but Jacko was a friend. Jacko had said that Dad was up the hospital, but not that he was ill; and indeed, how could he be? For he had been well when he left the house early this morning.

The hospital was a large brick building, faintly Gothic, which had once been the residence of the Mayor of Southwark. Several flat-roofed extensions had been built in the grounds, and tarmacadamed car parks had obliterated the rest of the lawns.

Jacko stopped near the entrance to Casualty. No one spoke as they got out of the car and walked across to the door. They passed an ambulance man with a pipe in his mouth, leaning against an anti-smoking poster on the side of his vehicle.

They went from the heat of the car park into the cool of the hospital. The familiar antiseptic smell caused a nauseous surge of fear in Doreen's stomach. Green plastic chairs were ranged around the walls, and a desk was placed centrally, opposite the entrance. Doreen noticed a small boy nursing a glass cut, a young man with his arm in an improvised sling, and a girl with her head in her hands. Somewhere nearby a woman moaned. Doreen felt panicky.

The West Indian nurse at the desk was speaking into a telephone. They waited for her to finish, then Doreen said: 'Have you had a William Johnson brought in here this morning?'

The nurse did not look at her. 'Just a minute,

please.' She made a note on a scribbling pad, then glanced up as an ambulance arrived outside. She said: 'Would you sit down, please?' She came around the desk and walked past them to the door.

Jacko moved away, as if to sit down, and Doreen snatched at his sleeve. 'Stay here!' she commanded. 'I'm not waiting bloody hours – I'm stopping here until she tells me.'

They watched as a stretcher was brought in. The prone figure was wrapped in a bloody blanket. The nurse escorted the bearers through a pair of swing doors.

A plump white woman in sister's uniform arrived through another door, and Doreen waylaid her. 'Why can't I find out whether my husband's here?' she said shrilly.

The sister stopped, and took the three of them in at a glance. The black nurse came back in.

Doreen said: 'I asked her and she wouldn't tell me.'

The sister said: 'Nurse, why were these people not attended to?'

'I thought the road-accident case with two severed limbs looked sicker than this lady.'

'You did the right thing, but there's no need for witticism.' The plump sister turned to Doreen. 'What is your husband's name?'

'William Johnson.'

The sister looked in a register. 'That name isn't here.' She paused. 'But we do have an unidentified patient. Male, white, medium build, middle-aged, with gunshot wounds to the head.'

Jacko said: 'That's him.'

Doreen said: 'Oh, my God!'

The sister picked up the phone. 'You'd better see him, to find out whether he is your husband.' She dialled a single number and waited for a moment. 'Oh, Doctor, this is Sister Rowe in Casualty. I have a woman here who may be the wife of the gunshot patient. Yes. I will . . . we'll meet you there.' She hung up and said: 'Please follow me.'

Doreen fought back despair as they trod the linoleum corridor floors through the hospital. She had dreaded this ever since the day, fifteen or more years ago, when she had discovered she had married a villain. She had always suspected it; Willie had told her he was in business, and she asked no more questions because in the days when they were courting a girl who wanted a husband learned not to come on strong. But it was never easy to keep secrets in marriage. There had been a knock at the door, when little Billy was still in nappies, and Willie had looked out of the front window and seen a copper. Before answering the door he said to Doreen: 'Last night, there was a poker game here: me, and Scotch Harry, and Tom Webster, and old Gordon. It started at ten, and went on till four in the morning.' Doreen, who had been up half the night in an empty house, trying to get Billy to sleep, had nodded dumbly; and when the Old Bill asked her, she said what Willie had told her to say. Since then she had worried.

When it's only a suspicion, you can tell yourself not to worry; but when you *know* your husband is out there somewhere breaking into a factory or a shop or even a bank, you can't help wondering if he'll ever come home.

She was not sure why she was so full of rage and fear. She did not love Willie, not in any familiar sense of the word. He was a pretty lousy husband: always out at night, bad with money, and a poor lover. The marriage had varied from tolerable to miserable. Doreen had two miscarriages, then Billy; after that they stopped trying. They stuck together because of Billy, and she did not suppose they were the only couple to do *that*. Not that Willie shouldered much of the burden of bringing up a handicapped child, but it seemed to make him just guilty enough to stay married. The boy loved his father.

No, Willie, I don't love you, she thought. But I want you and I need you; I like to have you there in bed, and sitting next to me watching television, and doing your pools at the table; and if *that* was called love, I'd say I love you.

They had stopped walking, and the sister was speaking. 'I'll call you in when Doctor's ready,' she said. She disappeared into a ward, closing the door behind her.

Doreen stared hard at the blank, cream-painted wall, trying not to wonder what was behind it. She had done this once before, after the Componiparts payroll job. But then it had been different: they had come to the house saying 'Willie's up the hospital, but he's all right – just stunned.' He had put too much gelignite on the safe door, and had lost all hearing in one ear. She had gone to the hospital – a different one – and waited; but she had known he was okay.

After that job she had tried, for the first and only time, to make him go straight. He had seemed willing, until he got out of hospital and was faced with the prospect of actually doing something about it. He sat around the house for a few days, then when he ran out of money he did another job. Later he let it slip that Tony Cox had taken him on the firm. He was proud, and Doreen was furious.

She hated Tony Cox ever afterwards. Tony knew it, too. He had been at their home, once, eating a plate of chips and talking to Willie about boxing, when suddenly he looked up at Doreen and said: 'What you got against me, girl?'

Willie looked worried and said: 'Go easy, Tone.'

Doreen tossed her head and said: 'You're a villain.'

Tony laughed at that, showing a mouthful of half-chewed chips. Then he said: 'So's your husband – didn't you know?' After that they went back to talking about boxing.

Doreen never had quick answers for clever people like Tony, so she said no more. Her opinion made no difference to anything, anyway. It would never occur to Willie that the fact that she disliked someone was a reason for not bringing him to the house. It was Willie's house, even if Doreen had to pay the rent out of her income from the mail-order catalogue every other week.

It was a Tony Cox job that Willie had been on today. Doreen had got that from Jacko's wife – Willie wouldn't tell her. If Willie dies, she thought, I swear to God I'll swing for that Tony Cox. Oh, God, let him be all right—

The door opened and the sister put her head out. 'Would you like to come in, please?'

Doreen went first. A short, dark-skinned doctor with thick black hair stood near the door. She ignored him and went straight to the bedside.

At first she was confused. The figure on the high, metal-framed bed was covered to the neck in a sheet, and from the chin to the top of the head in bandages. She had been expecting to see a face, and know instantly whether it was Willie. For a moment she did not know what to do. Then she knelt down and gently pulled back the sheet.

The doctor said: 'Mrs Johnson, is this your husband?'

She said: 'Oh, God, Willie, what have they done?' Her head fell slowly forward until her brow rested on her husband's bare shoulder.

Distantly, she heard Jacko say: 'That's him. William Johnson.' He went on to give Willie's age and address. Doreen became aware that Billy was standing close to her. After a few moments the boy put his hand on her shoulder. His presence forced her to deny grief, or at least postpone it. She composed her features and stood up.

The doctor looked grave. 'Your husband will live,' he said.

She put her arm around her son. 'What have they done to him?'

'Shotgun pellets. Close range.'

She was gripping Billy's shoulder very hard. She was *not* going to cry. 'But he'll be all right?'

'I said he'll live, Mrs Johnson. But we may not be able to save his eyesight.'

'What?'

'He's going to be blind.'

Doreen shut her eyes tight and screamed: 'No!'

They were all around her, very quickly; they had been expecting hysterics. She fought them off. She saw Jacko's face in front of her, and she shouted: 'Tony Cox done this, you bastard!' She hit Jacko. 'You bastard!'

She heard Billy sob, and she calmed down immediately. She turned to the boy and pulled him to her, hugging him. He was several inches taller than she. 'There, there, Billy,' she murmured. 'Your Dad's alive, be glad of that.'

The doctor said: 'You should go home, now. We have a phone number where we can reach you . . .'

'I'll take her,' Jacko said. 'It's my phone, but I live close.'

Doreen detached herself from Billy and went to

the door. The sister opened it. Two policemen stood outside.

Jacko said: 'What's this, then?' He sounded outraged.

The doctor said: 'We are obliged to inform the police in cases like this.'

Doreen saw that one of the police was a woman. She was seized with the urge to blurt out the fact that Willie had been shot on a Tony Cox job: that would screw Tony. But she had acquired the habit of deceiving the police during fifteen years of marriage to a thief. And she knew, as soon as the thought crossed her mind, that Willie would never forgive her for squealing.

She could not tell the police. But, suddenly, she knew who she could tell.

She said: 'I want to make a phone call.'

One p.m.

Chapter Twenty-Three

Kevin Hart ran up the stairs and entered the newsroom of the *Evening Post*. A Lad in a Brutus shirt and platform shoes walked past him, carrying a pile of newspapers: the one o'clock edition. Kevin snatched one off the top and sat down at a desk.

His story was on the front page.

The headline was: GOVT. OIL BOSS COLLAPSES. Kevin stared for a moment at the delightful words 'By Kevin Hart.' Then he read on.

> Junior Minister Mr Tim Fitzpeterson was found unconscious at his Westminster flat today.
>
> An empty bottle of pills was found beside him.
>
> Mr Fitzpeterson, a Department of Energy Minister responsible for oil policy, was rushed to the hospital in an ambulance.
>
> I called at his flat to interview him at the same time as PC Ron Bowler, who had been sent to check after the Minister failed to appear at a committee meeting.
>
> We found Mr Fitzpeterson slumped at his desk. An ambulance was called immediately.

A Department of Energy spokesman said: 'It appears that Mr Fitzpeterson took an accidental overdose. A full enquiry is to be made.'

Tim Fitzpeterson is 41. He has a wife and three daughters.

A hospital spokesman said later: 'He is off the critical list.'

Kevin read the whole thing through again, hardly able to believe what he was reading. The story he had dictated over the phone had been rewritten beyond recognition. He felt empty and bitter. This was to have been his moment of glory, and some spineless sub-editor had soured it.

What about the anonymous tip that Fitzpeterson had a girlfriend? What about the call from the man himself, claiming he was being blackmailed? Newspapers were supposed to tell the truth, weren't they?

His anger grew. He had not entered the business to become a mindless hack. Exaggeration was one thing – he was quite prepared to turn a drunken brawl into a gang war for the sake of a story on a slow day – but suppression of important facts, especially concerning politicians, was not part of the game.

If a reporter couldn't insist on the truth, who the hell could?

He stood up, folded the newspaper, and walked across to the news desk.

Arthur Cole was putting a phone down. He looked up at Kevin.

Kevin thrust the paper under his nose. 'What's this, Arthur? We've got a blackmailed politician committing suicide, and the *Evening Post* says it's an accidental overdose.'

Cole looked past him. 'Barney,' he called. 'Here a minute.'

Kevin said: 'What's going on, Arthur?'

Cole looked at him. 'Oh, fuck off, Kevin,' he said.

Kevin stared at him.

Cole said to the reporter called Barney: 'Ring Essex police and find out whether they've been alerted to look for the getaway van.'

Kevin turned away, dumbfounded. He had been ready for discussion, argument, even a row; but not for such a casual dismissal. He sat down again, on the far side of the room, with his back to the news desk, staring blindly at the paper. Was this what provincial diehards had known when they warned him about Fleet Street? Was this what the nutcase lefties at college had meant when they said the Press was a whore?

It's not as if I'm a lousy idealist, he thought. I'll defend our prurience and our sensationalism, and I'll say with the best of them that the people get the papers they deserve. But I'm not a total cynic, not yet, for God's sake. I believe we're here to discover the truth, and then to print it.

He began to wonder whether he really wanted to be a journalist. It was dull most of the time. There was the occasional high, when something went right, a story turned good and you got a by-line; or when a big story broke, and six or seven of you got on to the phones at once in a race with the opposition and with each other – something like that was going on now, a currency raid, but Kevin was out of it. But nine tenths of your time was spent waiting: waiting for detectives to come out of police stations, waiting for juries to return verdicts, waiting for celebrities to arrive, waiting just for a story to break.

Kevin had thought that Fleet Street would be different from the Midlands evening paper he had joined when he left university. He had been content, as a trainee reporter, to interview dim, self-important councilmen, to publish the exaggerated complaints of council house tenants, and to write stories about amateur dramatics, lost dogs, and waves of petty vandalism. He had occasionally done things he was quite proud of: a series about the problems of the town's immigrants; a controversial feature on how the Town Hall wasted money; coverage of a lengthy and complex planning inquiry. The move to Fleet Street, he had fondly imagined, would mean doing the important stories on a national level and dropping the trivia entirely. He had found instead that all the serious topics – politics, economics, industry, the arts – were handled by specialists; and that the line for those specialist jobs was a long line of bright, talented people just like Kevin Hart.

He needed a way to shine – something which would make the *Post*'s executives notice him and say: 'Young Hart is good – are we making the most of him?'

One good break could do it: a hot tip, an exclusive interview, a spectacular piece of initiative.

He had thought he had found that something today, and he had been wrong. Now he wondered whether it would ever happen.

He stood up and went to the Gents'. What else can I do? he thought. I could always go into computers, or advertising, or public relations, or retail management. But I want to leave newspapers as a success, not a failure.

While he was washing his hands, Arthur Cole came in. The older man spoke to Kevin over his shoulder. To Kevin's astonishment, he said: 'Sorry about that, Kevin. You know how it gets on that news desk sometimes.'

Kevin pulled down a length of towel. He was not sure what to say.

Cole moved across to the washbasin. 'No hard feelings?'

'I'm not offended,' Kevin said. 'I don't mind you swearing. I wouldn't care if you called me the biggest bastard on earth.' He hesitated. This was not what he wanted to say. He stared in the mirror for a moment, then took the plunge. 'But when my story appears in the paper without half of the facts, I start to wonder if I ought to become a computer programmer.'

Cole filled the basin with cold water and splashed some on his face. He fumbled for the towel and wiped himself dry. 'You ought to know this, but I'll tell you anyway,' he began. 'The story we put in the paper consisted of what we *know*, and only what we know. We *know* Fitzpeterson was found unconscious and rushed to hospital, and we *know* there was an empty bottle beside him, because you saw all that. You were in the right place at the right time, which, incidentally, is an important talent for a reporter to have. Now, what else do we know? We know we got an anonymous tip that the man had spent the night with a whore; and that someone phoned up claiming to be Fitzpeterson and saying he was being blackmailed by Laski and Cox. Now, if we print those two facts, we cannot but imply that they are connected with the overdose; indeed, that he took the overdose because he was being blackmailed over the whore.'

Kevin said: 'But that implication is *so* obvious that surely we're deceiving people if we don't print it!'

'And what if the calls were hoaxes, the tablets were indigestion pills, and the man's in a diabetic coma? And we've ruined his career?'

'Isn't that a bit unlikely?'

'You bet. Kevin, I'm ninety per cent sure that the truth is the way your original story read. But we're not here to print our suspicions. Now, let's get back to work.'

Kevin followed Arthur through the door and across the newsroom. He felt like the heroine in the movie who says: 'I'm so confused, I don't know *what* to do!' He was half inclined to think that Arthur was right; but he also felt that things should not be that way.

A phone rang at an unattended desk, and Kevin picked it up. 'Newsroom.'

'Are you a reporter?' It was a woman's voice.

'Yes, madam. My name is Kevin Hart. How can I help you?'

'My husband's been shot and I want justice.'

Kevin sighed. A domestic shooting meant a court case, which in turn meant there was no way the paper could do much of a story. He guessed that the woman was going to tell him who had shot her husband and ask him to print it. But it was juries who decided who shot whom, not newspapers. Kevin said: 'Tell me your name, please?'

'Doreen Johnson, five Yew Street, east one. My Willie was shot on this currency job.' The woman's voice cracked. 'He's been blinded.' She started to shout. 'It was a Tony Cox job, so just print that!' The line went dead.

Kevin put the phone down slowly, trying to take it in.

This was turning out to be one hell of a day for phone calls.

He picked up his notebook and went to the news desk.

Arthur said: 'Got something?'

'Don't know,' Kevin told him. 'A woman phoned up. Gave me her name and address. She said her husband was on the currency raid, that he was shot in the face and blinded, and that it was a Tony Cox job.'

Arthur stared. 'Cox?' he said. '*Cox*?'

Someone called: 'Arthur!'

Kevin looked up, annoyed at the interruption. The voice belonged to Mervyn Glazier, the paper's City editor, a stocky young man in battered suede shoes and a sweat-stained shirt.

Glazier came nearer and said: 'I may have a story for your pages this afternoon. Possible collapse of a bank. It's called the Cotton Bank of Jamaica, and it's owned by a man called Felix Laski.'

Arthur and Kevin stared at one another.

Arthur said: 'Laski? *Laski*?'

Kevin said: 'Jesus Christ.'

Arthur frowned, scratched his head, and said wonderingly: 'What the hell is going on?'

Chapter Twenty-Four

The blue Morris was still tailing Tony Cox. He spotted it in the car park of the pub when he came out. He hoped they would not play silly buggers and breathalyse him: he had drunk three pints of lager with his smoked-salmon sandwiches.

The detectives pulled out of the exit a few seconds behind the Rolls. Tony was not concerned. He had lost them once today, and he could do it again. The simplest way would have been to find a fast stretch of road and put his foot down. However, he would prefer that they did not know they had lost him, just like this morning.

It would not be difficult.

He crossed the river and entered the West End. As he picked his way through the traffic he wondered about the Old Bill's motives in following him around. It was partly a simple case of making a nuisance of themselves, he was sure. What did the briefs call it? Harassment. They figured that if they tailed him long enough he would get impatient or careless and do something stupid. But that was only the justification: the real motive probably lay in Scotland Yard politics. Perhaps the Assistant Commissioner (Crime) had threatened to take the Tony Cox firm away from CI and give it to the Flying Squad, so CI had laid on the surveillance in order to be able to say they were doing something.

So long as they did not get all serious about it, Tony did not mind. They had got serious once, a few years ago. At that time Tony's firm had been under the eagle eye of the CID at West End Central. Tony had had a close understanding with the detective-inspector working on his case. One week the DI had refused his usual money, and warned Tony that the game was over. The only way Tony had been able to square it had been to sacrifice some of his soldiers. He and the DI had set up five middle-management villains on extortion charges. The five had gone to jail, the Press had praised the CID for breaking the gang's hold on London, and business had gone on as usual. Sadly, that DI later went down himself, for planting cannabis on a student: a sorry end to a promising career, Tony felt.

He pulled into a multistorey car park in Soho. He paused at the entry, spending a long time taking his ticket from the machine, and watched the blue Morris in his mirrors. One of the detectives jumped out of the car and ran across the road to cover the pedestrian exit. The other found a parking space on a meter a few yards away – a position from which he could see cars coming out of the building. Tony nodded, satisfied.

He drove up to the first floor and stopped the Rolls

beside the office. Inside he found a young man he did not know.

He said: 'I'm Tony Cox. I want you to park mine and get me one of your long-stay motors – one that's not likely to be picked up today.'

The man frowned. He had frizzy, untidy hair and oil-stained jeans with frayed bottoms. He said: 'I can't do that, mate.'

Tony tapped his foot impatiently. 'I don't like saying things twice, son. *I'm Tony Cox.*'

The young man laughed. He stood up, putting down a comic, and said: 'I don't care who you are, you—'

Tony hit him in the stomach. His large fist landed with a soft thump. It was like punching a feather pillow. The attendant doubled over, moaning and gasping for air.

'I'm short of time, boy,' Tony said.

The office door opened. 'What's going on?' An older man in a baseball cap entered. 'Oh, it's you, Tony. Having trouble?'

'Where have you been – smoking in the bog?' Tony said harshly. 'I want a car that can't be traced to me, and I'm in a hurry.'

'No problem,' the older man said. He took a bunch of keys from a hook on the asbestos wall. 'Got a nice Granada, in here for a fortnight. Three-litre automatic, a nice bronze colour—'

'I don't give a toss what colour it is.' Tony took the keys.

'Over there.' The man pointed. 'I'll park yours.'

Tony went out of the office and got into the Granada. He put on the safety belt and pulled away. He paused beside his own car, which the man in the cap was now sitting in.

'What's your name?' Tony said.

'I'm Davy Brewster, Tony.'

'All right, Davy Brewster.' Tony reached for his wallet and took out two ten-pound notes. 'Make sure the kid keeps his mouth shut, okay?'

'No problem. Thanks very much.' Davy took the money.

Tony pulled away. As he drove, he put on sunglasses and his cloth cap. When he emerged into the street, the blue Morris was away to his right. He put his right elbow on the window ledge, covering his face, and steered with his left hand. The second detective, on Tony's left, had his back to the road so that he could see the pedestrian exit. The man was pretending to look in the window of a religious bookshop.

Tony looked in his mirror as he accelerated away. Neither of them had seen him.

'Easy,' Tony said aloud. He drove south.

The car was quite pleasant, with automatic gears and power-assisted steering. It had a tape deck. Tony sorted through the cassettes, found a Beatles album, and put it on. Then he lit a cigar.

In less than an hour he would be at the farm, counting the money.

Felix Laski had been well worth cultivating, Tony

thought. They had met in the restaurant of one of Tony's clubs. The Cox casinos served the best food in London. They had to. Tony's motto was: if you serve peanuts, you get monkeys for customers. He wanted rich people in his gambling clubs, not yobboes asking for draft bitter and five penn'orth of chips. He did not like fancy food himself, but on the night he met Laski he was eating a vast, rare T-bone steak at a table near the financier's.

The chef was pinched from Prunier's. Tony did not know what he did to the steaks, but the result was sensational. The tall, elegant man at the next table had caught his eye: a fine-looking man for his age. He was with a young girl whom Tony instantly marked as a tart.

Tony had finished his steak, and was tucking into a mountain of trifle, when the accident happened. The waiter was serving Laski with cannelloni, and somehow a half-full bottle of claret got knocked over. The tart squealed and jumped out of the way, and a few drops of wine spattered Laski's brilliant white shirt.

Tony acted immediately. He stood up, dropping his napkin on the table, and summoned three waiters and the maître d'hôtel. He spoke first to the waiter who had caused the mess. 'Go and get changed. Pick up your cards on Friday.' He turned to the others. 'Bernardo, a cloth. Giulio, another bottle of wine. Monsieur Charles, another table, and no bill for this gentleman.' Finally he spoke to the diners. 'I'm the proprietor, Tony Cox. Please have your dinner on the house, with my apologies, and I hope you'll have the most expensive dishes on the menu, beginning with a bottle of Dom Perignon.'

Laski spoke then. 'These things can't be helped.' His voice was deep and faintly accented. 'But it is nice to have such a generous, old-fashioned apology.' He smiled.

'It missed my dress,' the tart said. Her accent confirmed Tony's guess about her profession: she came from the same part of London as he did.

The maître d'hôtel said: 'M'sieur Cox, the house is full. There is no other table.'

Tony pointed to his own table. 'What's wrong with that one? Clear it, quickly.'

'Please don't,' Laski said. 'We wouldn't like to deprive you.'

'I insist.'

'Then, please join us.'

Tony looked at them both. The tart obviously didn't like the idea. Was the gent just being polite, or did he mean it? Well, Tony had almost finished, so if it didn't work out he could leave the table quite soon.

'I don't want to intrude—'

'You won't be,' Laski said. 'And you can tell me how to win at roulette.'

'Right-oh,' Tony said.

He stayed with them all evening. He and Laski got on famously, and it was made clear early on that what the girl thought did not count. Tony told stories of villainy in the world of gambling clubs, and Laski matched him, anecdote for anecdote, with tales of Stock Exchange sharp practice. It transpired that Laski was not a gambler, but that he liked to bring people to the club. When they went into the casino he bought fifty pounds' worth of chips and gave them all to the girl. The evening ended when Laski, by now quite drunk, said: 'I suppose I should take her home and screw her.'

After that they met several times – never by arrangement – in the club, and always ended up getting drunk together. After a while Tony let the other man know that he was gay, and Laski did nothing about it, from which Tony concluded that the financier was a tolerant heterosexual.

It pleased Tony to know that he could befriend someone of Laski's class. The scene in the restaurant was the easiest bit, and it was well rehearsed: the grand gestures, the posture of command, the heavy courtesy, and a conscious moderating of his accent. But to maintain the acquaintance with someone as brainy, as rich, and as used to moving in near-aristocratic circles as Laski was, seemed quite an achievement.

It was Laski who made the first move towards a deeper relationship. They had been bragging-drunk in the early hours of a Sunday morning, and Laski had been talking about the power of money. 'Given enough money,' he said, 'I can find out anything in the City – right down to the combination of the lock on the vault in the Bank of England.'

Tony said: 'Sex is better.'

'What do you mean?'

'Sex is a better weapon. I can find out anything in London, using sex.'

'Now that I doubt,' said Laski, whose sexual urges were well under control.

Tony shrugged. 'All right. Challenge me.'

That was when Laski made his move. 'The development licence for the Shield oil field. Find out who's got it – before the government makes the announcement.'

Tony saw the gleam in the financier's eye, and guessed that the whole conversation had been planned. 'Why don't you ask me something difficult?' he countered. 'Politicians and civil servants are much too easy.'

'It will do,' Laski smiled.

'Okay. But I've got to challenge you, too.'

Laski's eyes narrowed. 'Go on.'

Tony said the first thing that came into his head. 'Find out the schedule for deliveries of used notes to the currency destruction plant of the Bank of England.'

'It won't even cost me money,' Laski said confidently.

And that was how it had started. Tony grinned as he drove the Ford through south London. He did not know how Laski had managed to keep his half of the bargain; but Tony's side had been a doddle. Who has the information we want? The Minister. What's he like? The next thing to a virgin – a faithful husband. Is he getting his oats from the wife? Not much. Will he fall for the oldest trick in the game? Like a dream.

The tape ended, and he turned it over. He wondered how much money had been in the currency van – a hundred grand? Maybe even a quarter of a million. Much more than that would be embarrassing. You couldn't walk into Barclays Bank with sacks full of used fivers without arousing suspicion. About a hundred and fifty grand would be ideal. Five gees for each of the boys, a few more for expenses, and about fifty thousand surreptitiously added to the takings of various legitimate businesses tonight. Gambling clubs were very useful for concealing illicit income.

The boys knew what to do with five grand. Pay off a few debts, buy a secondhand car, put a few hundred in each of two or three bank accounts, give the wife a new coat, lend the mother-in-law a couple of bob, spend a night in the pub, and bang, it was all gone. But give them twenty thousand and they started to get silly ideas. When unemployed labourers and freelance odd-job men were heard to talk about villas in the South of France, the law began to get suspicious.

Tony grinned at himself. I should worry about having too much money, he thought. Problems of success are the kind I like. Don't count your chicks before you've laid them, Jacko sometimes said. The van might be full of worn-out halfpennies for melting down.

Now *that* would be a chuckle.

He was nearly there. He started to whistle.

Chapter Twenty-Five

Felix Laski sat in his office, watching a television screen and tearing a buff envelope into narrow strips. The closed-circuit TV was the modern equivalent of the tickertape; and Laski felt like the worried broker in an old movie about the 1929 crash. The set continuously screened market news and price movements in equities, commodities, and currency. There had been no mention of the oil licence. Hamilton shares had dropped five points on yesterday, and trading was moderate.

He finished demolishing the envelope and dropped the scraps into a metal waste-paper basket. The oil licence should have been announced an hour ago.

He picked up the blue phone and dialled 123. 'At the third stroke, the time will be one forty-seven, and fifty seconds.' The announcement was more than an hour late. He dialled the Department of Energy and asked for the Press Office. A woman told him: 'The Secretary of State has been delayed. The Press conference will begin as soon as he arrives, and the announcement will be made immediately he opens the conference.'

The hell with your delays, Laski thought: I've got a fortune riding on this.

He pressed the intercom. 'Carol?' There was no reply. He bellowed: 'Carol!'

The girl poked her head around the door. 'I'm sorry, I was at the filing cabinet.'

'Get me some coffee.'

'Certainly.'

He took from his 'in' tray a file headed: Precision Tubing – Sales Report, 1st Quarter. It was a piece of routine espionage on a firm he was thinking of taking over. He had a theory that capital equipment tended to do well when a slump was bottoming out. But does Precision have the capacity for expansion? he wondered.

He looked at the first page of the report, winced at the sales director's indigestible prose, and tossed the file aside. When he took a gamble and lost, he could accept it with equanimity. What threw him was something going wrong for unknown reasons. He knew he would not be able to concentrate on anything until the Shield business was settled.

He fingered the sharp crease of his trousers, and thought about Tony Cox. He had taken to the young hoodlum, despite his obvious homosexuality, because he sensed what the English called a kindred spirit. Like Laski, Cox had come from poverty to wealth on determination, opportunism, and ruthlessness. Also like Laski, he tried in small ways to take the edge off his lower-class manners: Laski was doing it better, but only because he had been practising longer. Cox wanted to be like Laski, and he would make it – by the time he was in his fifties, he would be a distinguished, grey-haired City gent.

Laski realized he did not have a single sound reason for trusting Cox. There was his instinct, of course, which told him the young man was honest with people he knew: but the Tony Coxes of this world were practised deceivers. Had he simply invented the whole thing about Tim Fitzpeterson?

The television set screened the Hamilton Holdings price again: it was down another point. Laski wished they wouldn't use that damn computer typeface, all horizontal and vertical lines: it strained his eyes. He began to calculate what he stood to lose if Hamilton did not get the licence.

If he could sell the 510,000 shares right now, he would have lost only a few thousand pounds. But it would not be possible to dump the lot at the market value. And the price was still slipping. Say a loss of twenty thousand at the outside. And a psychological setback – damage to his reputation as a winner.

Was there anything else at risk? What Cox planned to do with the information Laski had supplied was certain to be criminal. However, since Laski did not actually know about it, he could not be convicted of conspiracy.

There was still Britain's Official Secrets Act – mild by East European standards, but a formidable piece of legislation. It was illegal to approach a civil servant and get from him confidential data. Proving that Laski had done that would be difficult, but not impossible.

He had asked Peters whether he had a big day ahead, and Peters had said: 'One of *the* days.' Then Laski had said to Cox: 'It's today.' Well, if Cox and Peters could be persuaded to testify, then Laski would be convicted. But Peters did not even know he had given away a secret, and nobody would think of asking him. Suppose Cox was arrested? The British police had ways of squeezing information out of people, even if they did not use baseball bats. Cox might say he got the information from Laski, then they would check Laski's movements on the day, and they might discover he had taken coffee with Peters . . .

It was a pretty distant possibility. Laski was more worried about finishing off the Hamilton deal.

The phone rang. Laski answered: 'Yes?'

'It's Threadneedle Street – Mr Ley,' Carol said.

Laski tutted. 'It's probably about the Cotton Bank. Put him on to Jones.'

'He's been through to the Cotton Bank, and Mr Jones has gone home.'

'Gone home? All right, I'll take it.'

He heard Carol say: 'I have Mr Laski for you now.'

'Laski?' The voice was high-pitched, the accent an aristocratic drawl.

'Yes.'

'Ley here, Bank of England.'

'How are you?'

'Good afternoon. Now look here, old chap—' Laski rolled his eyes at this phrase '—you've made out rather a large cheque to Fett and Company.'

Laski paled. 'My God, have they presented it already?'

'Yes, well, I rather gathered the ink was still wet. Now the thing is, it's drawn on the Cotton Bank, as you obviously know, and the poor little Cotton Bank can't cover it. Do you follow me?'

'Of course I follow you.' The bloody man was talking as if to a child. Nothing annoyed Laski more. 'Clearly, my instructions as to the arrangements for providing these funds have not been followed. However, perhaps I can plead that my staff might well have thought they had a little time to spare.'

'Mmm. It's nice, really, to have the funds ready before you sign the damn thing, you know, just to be safe, don't you think?'

Laski thought fast. Damn, this need not have happened if the announcement had been made on time. And where the devil was Jones? 'You may have guessed that the cheque is payment for a controlling interest in Hamilton Holdings. I should think those shares would stand as security—'

'Oh, dear me, no,' Ley interrupted. 'That really wouldn't do. The Bank of England is not in business to finance speculation on the stock market.'

Maybe not, Laski thought; but if the announcement had been made, and you knew that Hamilton Holdings now had an oil well, you wouldn't be making this fuss. It occurred to him that perhaps they did know, and Hamilton had not got the oil well; hence the phone call. He felt angry. 'Look, you're a bank,' he said. 'I'll pay you the rate for twenty-four-hour money—'

'The Bank is not accustomed to being in the money market.'

Laski raised his voice. 'You know damn well I can cover that cheque with ease, given a little time! If you return it, my reputation is gone. Are you going to ruin me for the sake of a lousy million overnight and a foolish tradition?'

Ley's voice went very cold. 'Mr Laski, our traditions exist specifically for the purpose of ruining people who sign cheques they cannot honour. If this draft cannot be cleared today, I shall ask the payee to re-present. That means, in effect, that you have an hour and a half in which to make a cash deposit of one million pounds at Threadneedle Street. Good day.'

'Damn you,' Laski said, but the line was dead. He cradled the receiver, cracking the plastic of the phone. His mind raced. There had to be a way of raising a million instantly . . . didn't there?

His coffee had arrived while he was on the phone. He had not noticed Carol come in. He sipped it, and made a face.

'Carol!' he shouted.

She opened the door. 'Yes?'

Red-faced and trembling, he threw the delicate china cup into the metal waste-paper basket, where it shattered noisily. He bellowed: 'The bloody coffee is cold!'

The girl turned around and fled.

Two p.m.

Chapter Twenty-six

Two p.m.

[illegible]

He went [illegible]

remember [illegible]

[illegible]

Chapter Twenty-Six

Young Billy Johnson was looking for Tony Cox, but he kept forgetting this.

He had got out of the house quite fast after they all returned from the hospital. His mother was doing a lot of screaming, there were a few policemen hanging around, and Jacko had been carted off to the station to help with inquiries. The neighbours and relatives who kept dropping in added to the confusion. Billy liked quiet.

Nobody seemed disposed to get his lunch or pay him any attention, so he ate a packet of ginger biscuits and went out the back way, telling Mrs Glebe from three doors down that he was going up to his auntie's to watch her colour television.

He had been getting things sorted out as he walked. Walking helped him to think. When he found himself baffled, he could look at the cars and the shops and the people for a while, to rest his mind.

He went towards his auntie's at first, until he remembered that he did not really want to go there; he had only said that to stop Mrs Glebe from making trouble. Then he had to think where he *was* going. He stopped, looking in the window of a record shop, painstakingly reading the names on the gaudy sleeves, and trying to match them to songs he had heard on the radio. He had a record player, but he never had any money to buy records, and his parents' taste did not suit him. Ma liked soppy songs, Pa liked brass bands, and Billy liked rock-and-roll. The only other person he knew who liked rock-and-roll was Tony Cox—

That was it. He was looking for Tony Cox.

He headed in what he thought was roughly the direction for Bethnal Green. He knew the East End very well – every street, every shop, all the bomb sites, patches of waste ground, canals and parks – but he knew it in bits. He passed a demolition site, and remembered that Granny Parker had lived there, and had sat stubbornly in her front room while the old houses on either side had been torn down, until she had caught pneumonia and died, relieving the London Borough of Tower Hamlets of the problem of what to do about her. Billy had followed the story with interest: it was like something on the television. Yes, he knew every particle of the East London landscape; but he could not connect them together in his mind. He knew Commercial Road and he knew Mile End Road, but he did not know that they met at Aldgate. Despite this, he could almost always find his way home, even if sometimes it took longer than he expected; and if he really got lost the Old Bill would run him back to the house in a squad car. All the coppers knew his pa.

By the time he got to Wapping, he had forgotten his destination again; but he thought he was probably going to see the ships. He got in through a hole in a fence: the same hole he had used with Snowy White and Tubby Toms that day when they caught a rat and the others told Billy to take it home to his Ma, because she would be pleased and cook it for tea. She had not been pleased, of course: she jumped in the air and dropped a bag of sugar and screamed, and later she cried and said they shouldn't make fun of Billy. People often played tricks on him, but he did not mind, because it was nice to have pals.

He wandered around for a while. He had the feeling that there used to be more ships here, in the days when he was little. Today he could see only one. It was a big one, quite low in the water, with a name on the side which he could not read. The men were running a pipe from the ship to a warehouse.

He stood watching for a while, then asked one of the men: 'What's in it?'

The man, who wore a cloth cap and a waistcoat, looked at him. 'Wine, mate.'

Billy was surprised. 'In the ship? All wine? Full?'

'Yes, mate. Château Morocco, vintage about last Thursday.' All the men laughed at this, but Billy did not understand it. He laughed all the same. The men worked on for a while, then the one he had spoken to said: 'What are you doing here, anyway?'

Billy thought for a moment, then said: 'I've forgot.'

The man looked hard at him, and mumbled something to one of the others. Billy heard part of the reply: '—might fall in the bleeding drink.' The first man went inside the warehouse.

After a while, a docks' policeman came along. He said to the men: 'Is this the lad?' They nodded, and the copper addressed Billy. 'Are you lost?'

'No,' Billy said.

'Where are you going?'

Billy was about to say he was not going anywhere, but that seemed the wrong answer. Suddenly he remembered. 'Bethnal Green.'

'All right, come with me and I'll set you on the right road.'

Always willing to take the line of least resistance, Billy walked alongside the copper to the dock gate.

'Where do you live, then?' the man asked.

'Yew Street.'

'Does your mother know where you are?'

Billy decided that the policeman was another Mrs Glebe, and that a lie was called for. 'Yes. I'm going up my auntie's.'

'Sure you know the way?'

'Yes.'

They were at the gate. The copper looked at him speculatively, then made up his mind. 'All right, then, off you go. Don't wander around the docks no more – you're safer to stop outside.'

'Thanks,' Billy said. When in doubt, he thanked people. He walked off.

It was getting easier to remember. Pa was up the

hospital. He was going to be blind, and it was Tony Cox's fault. Billy knew one blind man – well, two, if you counted Squint Thatcher, who was blind only when he went up West with his accordion. But really blind, there was only Hopcraft, who lived alone in a smelly house on the Isle of Dogs and carried a white stick. Would Pa have to wear sunglasses and walk very slowly, tapping the kerb with a stick? The thought upset Billy.

People usually thought he was incapable of getting upset, because he never shed tears. That was how they found out he was different, when he was a baby: he used to hurt himself and not cry. Ma sometimes said: 'He do feel things, but he don't never show it.'

Pa used to say that Ma got upset often enough for two, anyway.

When really awful things happened, like the rat joke that Snowy and Tubby played, Billy found he got all boiled up inside, and he *wanted* to do something drastic, like scream, but it just never happened.

He had killed the rat, and that had helped. He had held it with one hand, and with the other banged it on the head with a brick until it stopped wriggling.

He would do something like that to Tony Cox.

It occurred to him that Tony was bigger than a rat – indeed, bigger than Billy. That baffled him, so he put it out of his mind.

He stopped at the end of a street. The corner house had a shop downstairs – one of the old shops, where they sold lots of things. Billy knew the owner's daughter, a pretty girl with long hair called Sharon. A couple of years ago she let him feel her tits, but then she ran away from him and would not speak to him any more. For days afterwards he had thought of nothing else but the small round mounds under her blouse, and the way he felt when he touched them. Eventually he had realized that the experience was one of those nice things that never happen twice.

He went into the shop. Sharon's mother was behind the counter, wearing candy-striped nylon overalls. She did not recognize Billy.

He smiled and said: 'Hello.'

'Can I help you?' She was uneasy.

Billy said: 'How's Sharon?'

'Fine, thanks. She's out at the moment. Do you know her?'

'Yes.' Billy looked around the shop, at the assortment of food, hardware, books, fancy goods, tobacco, and confectionery. He wanted to say, She let me feel her tits once, but he knew that would not be right. 'I used to play with her.'

It seemed to be the answer the woman wanted: she looked relieved. She smiled, and Billy saw that her teeth were brown-stained, like his father's. She said: 'Can I serve you with something?'

There was a clatter of shoes on stairs, and Sharon came into the shop from the door behind the counter. Billy was surprised: she looked much older. Her hair was short, and her tits were quite big, wobbling under a T-shirt. She had long legs in tight jeans. She called: 'Bye, Mum.' She was rushing out.

Billy said: 'Hello, Sharon!'

She stopped and stared at him. Recognition flickered in her face. 'Oh, hi, Billy. Can't stop.' Then she was gone.

Her mother looked embarrassed. 'I'm sorry – I forgot she was upstairs still—'

'It's all right. I forget a lot of things.'

'Well, can I serve you with something?' the woman repeated.

'I want a knife.'

It had popped into Billy's head from nowhere, but he knew straight away that it was right. There was no point in banging a strong man like Tony Cox on the head with a stone – he would just hit you back. So you had to knife him in the back, like an Indian.

'For yourself, or your mother?'

'Me.'

'What's it for?'

Billy knew he shouldn't tell her that. He frowned, and said: 'Cutting things. String, and that.'

'Oh.' The woman reached into the window display, and pulled out a knife in a sheath, like Boy Scouts had.

Billy took all the money out of his trouser pocket. Money was something he was not good about – he always let the shopkeeper take however much was needed.

Sharon's mother looked and said: 'But you've only got eight pence.'

'Is it enough?'

She sighed. 'No, I'm sorry.'

'Well, can I have some bubblegum, then?'

The woman put the knife back in the window and took a packet of gum from a shelf. 'Six pence.'

Billy offered his handful of money, and the woman took some coins.

'Thanks,' Billy said. He went out into the street and opened the packet. He liked to put it all in his mouth at once. He walked on, chewing with enjoyment. For the moment, he had forgotten where he was going.

He stopped to watch some men digging a hole in the pavement. The tops of their heads were level with Billy's feet. He saw, with interest, that the wall of the trench changed colour as it went down. First there was the pavement, then some black stuff like tar, then loose brown earth, then wet clay. In the bottom lay a pipe made of clean new concrete. Why did they put pipes under the pavement? Billy had no idea. He leaned over and said: 'Why are you putting a pipe under the pavement?'

A workman looked up at him and said: 'We're hiding it from the Russians.'

'Oh.' Billy nodded, as if he understood. After a moment he moved on.

He felt hungry, but there was something he had to do before he went home for lunch. Lunch? He had eaten a packet of biscuits because Pa was up the hospital. That had something to do with why he was here in Bethnal Green, but he could not quite make the connection.

He turned a corner, looked at the road name on a sign tacked high up on a wall, and saw that he was in Quill Street. Now he remembered. This was where Tony Cox lived – at number nineteen. He would knock on the door—

No. He didn't know why, but he felt sure he ought to creep in by the back door. There was a lane behind the terrace. Billy walked along it until he came to the back of Tony's house.

All the taste was gone from his bubblegum, so he took it out of his mouth and threw it away before quietly unlatching the back gate and walking stealthily in.

Chapter Twenty-Seven

Tony Cox drove slowly along the rutted mud track, out of consideration for his own comfort rather than for the owner of the 'borrowed' car. The lane, which had no name, led from a B-road to a farmhouse with a barn. The barn, the empty, dilapidated house, and the acre of infertile land surrounding them, were owned by a company called Land Development Ltd; which was in turn owned by a compulsive gambler who owed Tony Cox a lot of money. The barn was occasionally used to store job lots of fire-damaged goods bought at rock-bottom prices, so it was not unusual for a van and a car to draw up in the farmyard.

The five-bar gate at the end of the lane was open, and Tony drove in. There was no sign of the blue van, but Jesse was leaning against the farmhouse wall, smoking a cigarette. He came across to open the car door for Tony.

'It haven't gone smooth, Tony,' he said immediately.

Tony got out of the car. 'Is the money here?'

'In the van.' Jesse jerked his head toward the barn. 'But it never went smooth.'

'Let's get inside – it's too hot out here.' Tony heaved

the barn door open and stepped in. Jesse followed him. A quantity of packing cases occupied one third of the floor area. Tony read the labels on a couple: they contained surplus Forces uniforms and coats. The blue van stood opposite the door. Tony noticed that trade plates had been tied over the original number plates with string.

'What have you been playing at?' he asked incredulously.

'Oh, blimey, Tony, wait till you hear what I've had to do.'

'Well bloody tell me then!'

'Well, I had a prang, see – nothing much, just a little bump. But the geezer gets out of his car and wants to call the police. So I pisses off, don't I. But he stands in the way and I hits him.'

Tony cursed softly.

Now fear showed in Jesse's face. 'Well, I knew the law would be looking for me, didn't I. So I stops at this garage, goes round the back to the khasi, and nicks a set of trade plates and these overalls.' He nodded eagerly, as if to lend his own approval to his actions. 'Then I come on here.'

Tony stared at him in amazement, then burst out laughing. 'You mad bastard!' he chuckled.

Jesse looked relieved. 'I done the best thing for it, though, didn't I?'

Tony's laughter subsided. 'You mad bastard,' he repeated. 'Here you are, with a fortune in hot money in the van, and you stop—' his chest heaved, and he wheezed with renewed laughter'—you stop at a garage and nick a pair of overalls!'

Jesse smiled too, not from amusement but out of the pleasure of a fear removed. Then he became serious again. 'There is proper bad news, though.'

'Gorblimey, what else?'

'The van driver tried to be a hero.'

'You never killed him?' Tony said anxiously.

'No, just knocked him on the head. But Jacko's shooter went off in the fracas—' he pronounced it frackarse '—and Deaf Willie got hit. In the boat race. He's bad, Tone.'

'Oh, balls.' Tony sat down suddenly on an old three-legged stool. 'Oh, poor old Willie. Did they take him up the hospital, did they?'

Jesse nodded. 'That's why Jacko's not here. He's took him. Whether he got there alive . . .'

'That bad?'

Jesse nodded.

'Oh, balls.' He was silent for a while. 'He don't get no luck, Deaf Willie. The one ear's gone already, and his boy's a mental case, and his wife looks like Henry Cooper – and now this.' He clicked his tongue in sorrow. 'We'll give him a double share, but it won't mend his head.' He got up.

Jesse opened the van, relieved that he had managed to convey the bad news without suffering Tony's wrath.

Tony rubbed his hands together. 'Right, let's have a look at what we got.'

There were nine grey steel chests in the back of the van. They looked like squat metal suitcases, each with handles at both ends, each secured by a double lock. They were heavy. The two men unloaded them, one by one, and lined them up in the centre of the barn. Tony looked at them greedily. His expression showed an almost sensual pleasure. He said: 'It's like Ali Baba and the forty bloody thieves, mate.'

Jesse was taking plastic explosive, wires and detonators out of a duffle bag in a corner of the barn. 'I wish Willie was here to do the bang-bangs.'

Tony said: 'I wish he was here, full stop.'

Jesse prepared to blow open the chests. He stuck the jellylike explosive all around the locks, attached detonators and wires, and connected each tiny bomb to the plunger-type trigger.

Watching him, Tony said: 'You seem to know what you're doing.'

'I've seen Willie do it often enough.' He grinned. 'Maybe I can become the firm's peterman—'

'Willie ain't dead,' Tony interrupted gruffly. 'Not so far as we know.'

Jesse picked up the trigger and, trailing wires, took it outside. Tony followed him.

Tony said: 'Drive the van outside, in case of the petrol going up, know what I mean?'

'There's no danger—'

'You've never done a peter before, and I'm not taking the risk.'

'Okay.' Jesse closed the rear doors and backed the

van into the farmyard. Then he opened the bonnet and used crocodile clips to connect the trigger with the van's battery.

He said: 'Hold your breath,' and pressed the plunger.

There was a muffled bang.

The two men went back inside. The chests stood in line with their tops hanging open at odd, twisted angles.

'You done a good job,' Tony said.

The chests were neatly and tightly packed. The bundles of notes were stacked twenty across, ten wide, and five deep: one thousand bundles per chest. Each bundle contained one hundred notes. That made one hundred thousand notes per chest.

The first six chests contained ten-shilling notes, obsolete and worthless.

Tony said: 'Jesus H. Christ.'

The next contained oncers, but it was not quite full. Tony counted eight hundred bundles. The last chest but one also contained one-pound notes, and it was full. Tony said: 'That's better. Just about right.'

The last chest was packed solid with tenners.

Tony muttered: 'Gawd help us.'

Jesse's eyes were wide. 'How much is it, Tony?'

'One million, one hundred and eighty thousand pounds sterling, my son.'

Jesse gave a whoop of delight. 'We're rich! We're lousy with it!'

Tony's face was sombre. 'I suppose we could burn all the tenners.'

'What are you talking about?' Jesse looked at him as if he were mad. 'What do you mean, burn them? You going potty?'

Tony turned around and gripped Jesse's arm, squeezing hard. 'Listen. If you go into the Rose and Crown, ask for a half of bitter and a meat pie, and pay with a tenner; and if you do that every day for a week; what will they all think?'

'They'll think I've had a tickle. You're hurting my arm, Tone.'

'And how long would it take for one of those dirty little snouts in there to get round the nick and spill it? Five minutes?' He let go. 'It's too much, Jess. Your trouble is, you don't think. This much money, you've got to keep it somewhere – and if it's kept somewhere, the Old Bill can find it.'

Jesse found this point of view too radical to digest. 'But you can't throw money away.'

'You're not listening to me, are you? They've got Deaf Willie, right? Their driver will connect Willie with the raid, right? And they know Willie's on my firm, so they know we done the job, right? You bet your life they'll be up your place tonight, slitting the mattresses and digging up the potato patch. Now, five grand in oncers might be your life savings, but fifty grand in tenners gotta be incriminating, right?'

'I never thought of it that way,' Jesse said.

'The word for it is overkill.'

'I suppose you can't put that much money in the Abbey National. Anybody can have a good night at the dogs, but if you got too much, it proves you've had a tickle, see?' Jesse was explaining it back to Tony, as if to demonstrate that he understood. 'That's it, ain't it?'

'Yes.' Tony had lost interest in the lecture. He was trying to think of a foolproof way of disposing of hot money in large quantity.

'And you can't walk into Barclays Bank with over a million nicker and ask to open a savings account, can you?'

'You're getting it,' Tony said sarcastically. Suddenly he looked sharply at Jesse. 'Ah, but who *can* walk into the bank with a pile of money and not arouse suspicion?'

Jesse was lost. 'Well, nobody can.'

'You reckon?' Tony pointed to the packing cases of surplus Forces clothes. 'Open a couple of those boxes. I want you dressed as a Royal Navy seaman. I've just had a bloody clever idea.'

Chapter Twenty-Eight

An editor's conference in the afternoon was rare. The editor sometimes said: 'The mornings are fun, the afternoons are work.' Up until lunch-time, his efforts were expended in the production of a newspaper. By two o'clock it was too late to do anything significant: the content of the paper was more or less determined, most of the day's editions had been printed and distributed, and the editor turned his brain to what he called administrative sludge. But he had to be around, in case something came up which required a top-level decision. Arthur Cole believed that such a thing had come up.

Cole, the deputy news editor, sat opposite the editor's oversize white desk. On Cole's left was the reporter Kevin Hart; on his right was Mervyn Glazier, City editor.

The editor finished signing a pile of letters and looked up. 'What have we got?'

Cole said: 'Tim Fitzpeterson will live, the oil announcement's been delayed, the currency van raiders got away with more than a million, and England are all out for seventy-nine.'

'And?'

'And there's something going on.'

The editor lit a cigar. If the truth were known, he quite liked to have his administrative sludge interrupted by something exciting like a story. 'Go on.'

Cole said: 'You remember Kevin came in during the morning conference, a little overexcited about a phone call allegedly from Tim Fitzpeterson.'

The editor smiled indulgently. 'If young reporters don't get excited, what the hell will they be like when they get old?'

'Well, it's possible Kevin was right to say it was the big one. Remember the names of the people allegedly blackmailing Fitzpeterson? Cox and Laski.' Cole turned to Hart. 'Okay, Kevin.'

Hart uncrossed his legs and leaned forward. 'Another phone call, this time from a woman who gave her name and address. She said that her husband, William Johnson, had been on the currency van raid, that he had been shot and blinded, and that it was a Tony Cox job.'

The editor said: '*Tony* Cox! Did you follow it up?'

'There is a William Johnson in the hospital with shotgun wounds to the face. And there's a detective beside his bed, waiting for him to come round. I went to see the wife, but she wouldn't speak.'

The editor, who had once been a crime reporter, said: 'Tony Cox is a very big fish. I'd believe anything of him. Not at all a nice man. Go on.'

Cole said: 'The next bit is Mervyn's.'

'There's a bank in trouble,' the City editor said.

'The Cotton Bank of Jamaica – it's a foreign bank with a branch in London. Does a lot of UK business. Anyway, it's owned by a man called Felix Laski.'

'How do we know?' the editor asked. 'That it's in trouble, I mean.'

'Well, I got a tip from a contact. I rang Threadneedle Street to check it out. Of course, they won't give a straight answer, but the noises they made tended to confirm the tip.'

'Tell me exactly what was said.'

Glazier pulled out his pad. He could write shorthand at 150 words per minute, and his notes were always immaculate. 'I spoke to a man called Ley, who is most likely to be dealing with it. I happen to know him, because—'

'Skip the commercial, Mervyn,' the editor interrupted. 'We all know how good your contacts are.'

Glazier grinned. 'Sorry. First, I asked him if he knew anything about the Cotton Bank of Jamaica. He said: "The Bank of England knows a good deal about every bank in London."

'I said: "Then you'll know just how viable the Cotton Bank is at the moment."

'He said: "Of course. Which is not to say that I'm going to tell you."

'I said: "They're about to go under – true or false?"

'He said: "Pass."

'I said: "Come on, Donald, this isn't *Mastermind* – it's people's money."

'He said: "You know I can't talk about that sort

of thing. Banks are our customers. We respect their trust."

'I said: "I am going to print a story saying that the Cotton Bank is about to fold. Are you or are you not telling me that such a story would be false?"

'He said: "I'm telling you to check your facts first." That's about it.' Glazier closed his notebook. 'If the bank was okay, he would have said so.'

The editor nodded. 'I have never liked that kind of reasoning, but in this case you're probably right.' He tapped his cigar on a large glass ashtray. 'Where does it get us?'

Cole summed up. 'Cox and Laski blackmail Fitzpeterson. Fitzpeterson tries to kill himself. Cox does a raid. Laski goes bust.' He shrugged. 'There's something going on.'

'What do you want to do?'

'Find out. Isn't that what we're here for?'

The editor got up and went to the window, as if to make time in which to consider. He made a small adjustment to his blinds, and the room became slightly brighter. Slats of sunshine appeared on the rich blue carpet, picking out the sculptured pattern. He returned to his desk and sat down.

'No,' he said. 'We're going to leave it, and I'm going to tell you why. One: we can't predict the collapse of a bank, because our prediction on its own would be enough to cause that collapse. Just to ask questions about the bank's viability would set the City all a-tremble.

'Two: we can't try to detect the perpetrators of a currency raid. That's the police force's job. Anyway, anything we discover can't be printed for fear of prejudicing a trial. I mean, if we know it's Tony Cox, the police must know; and the law says that if we know an arrest is imminent or likely, the story becomes *sub judice*.

'Three: Tim Fitzpeterson is not going to die. If we blunder around London asking about his sex life, before you know it there will be questions in Parliament about *Evening Post* reporters scouring the country for dirt on politicians. We leave that sort of thing to the Sunday rags.'

He laid his hands on his desk, palms down. 'Sorry, boys.'

Cole got up. 'Okay, let's get back to work.'

The three journalists left. When they got back to the newsroom, Kevin Hart said: 'If he was editor of *The Washington Post*, Nixon would still be winning elections on a law-and-order ticket.'

Nobody laughed.

Three p.m.

Chapter Twenty-Nine

'I have Smith and Bernstein for you, Mr Laski.'

'Thank you, Carol. Put him on. Hello, George?'

'Felix, how are you?'

Laski put a smile into his voice. It was not easy. 'On top of the world. Has your service improved any?' George Bernstein played tennis.

'Not a bit. You know I was teaching George junior to play?'

'Yes.'

'Now he beats me.'

Laski laughed. 'And how's Rachel?'

'No thinner. We were talking about you last night. She said you ought to be married. I said: "Didn't you know? Felix is gay." She said: "Gay? So why can't happy people be married?" I said: "No, I mean he's a homosexual, Rachel." She dropped her knitting. She believed me, Felix! Would you credit it?'

Laski forced another laugh. He was not sure how much longer he could keep this up. 'I'm thinking about it, George.'

'Marriage? Don't do it! Don't do it! Is that what you called to say?'

'No, that's just a little thought hovering around in the back of my mind.'

'So what can I tell you?'

'It's a little thing. I want a million pounds for twenty-four hours, and I thought I'd put the business your way.' Laski held his breath.

There was a short silence. 'A million. For how long has Felix Laski been in the money market?'

'Since I found out how to make a real profit overnight.'

'Let me in on the secret, will you?'

'All right. After you lend me the money. No kidding, George: can you do it?'

'Sure we can. What's your collateral?'

'Uh – surely you don't normally ask for collateral against twenty-four-hour money?' Laski's fist tightened on the phone until the knuckles bulged whitely.

'You're right. And we don't normally lend sums like this to banks like yours.'

'Okay. My collateral is five hundred and ten thousand shares in Hamilton Holdings.'

'Just a minute.'

There was a silence. Laski pictured George Bernstein: a thickset man with a large head, a big nose, and a permanent broad grin; sitting at an old desk in a poky office with a view of St Paul's; checking figures in the *Financial Times*, his fingers playing lightly over the keys of a desktop computer.

Bernstein came back on the line. 'At today's price it's not nearly enough, Felix.'

'Oh, come on, this is a formality. You know I'm not going to screw you. This is me – Felix – your friend.' He wiped his brow with his sleeve.

'I'd like to do it, but I've got a partner.'

'Your partner is sleeping so heavily there's a rumour he's dead.'

'A deal like this would wake him if he was in his grave. Try Larry Wakely, Felix. He might do something for you.'

Laski had already tried Larry Wakely, but he did not say so. 'I will. How about a game this weekend?'

'Love to!' The relief in Bernstein's voice was obvious. 'Saturday morning at the club?'

'Ten pounds a game?'

'It'll break my heart to take your money.'

'Look forward to it. Good-bye, George.'

'Take care.'

Laski closed his eyes for a moment, letting the phone dangle from his hand. He had known that Bernstein would not lend him the money: he was just trying anything now. He rubbed his face with his fingers. He was not beaten yet.

He depressed the cradle and got a purring tone. He dialled with a chewed pencil.

The number rang for a long time. Laski was about to dial again when it answered. 'Department of Energy.'

'Press Office,' Laski said.

'Trying to connect you.'

Another woman's voice. 'Press Office.'

'Good afternoon,' Laski said. 'Can you tell me when the Secretary of State is going to make the announcement about the oil—'

'The Secretary of State has been delayed,' the woman interrupted. 'Your news desk has been told, and there is a full explanation on the PA wire.' She hung up.

Laski sat back in his chair. He was running scared, and he did not like it. It was his role to dominate situations such as this: he liked to be the only one in the know, the manipulator who had everyone else running around trying to figure out what was going on. Going cap in hand to money-lenders was not his style.

The phone rang again. Carol said: 'A Mr Hart on the line.'

'Am I supposed to know him?'

'No, but he says it's in connection with the money the Cotton Bank needs.'

'Put him on. Hello, Laski here.'

'Good afternoon, Mr Laski.' It was the voice of a young man. 'I'm Kevin Hart of the *Evening Post*.'

Laski was startled. 'I thought she said— Never mind.'

'The money the Cotton Bank needs. Yes, well, a bank in trouble needs money, doesn't it?'

Laski said: 'I don't think I want to talk to you, young man.'

Before Laski could hang up, Hart said: 'Tim Fitzpeterson.'

Laski paled. 'What?'

'Do the Cotton Bank's troubles have anything to do with the attempted suicide of Tim Fitzpeterson?'

How the hell did they know? Laski's mind raced. Maybe they didn't know. They might be guessing – flying a kite, they called it; pretending to know something in order to see whether people would deny it. Laski said: 'Does your editor know you're making this call?'

'Um – of course not.'

Something in the reporter's voice told Laski he had struck a chord of fear. He pressed the point home. 'I don't know what kind of game you're playing, young man, but if I hear any more about all this nonsense, I'll know from where the rumours originated.'

Hart said: 'What is your relationship with Tony Cox?'

'Who? Good-bye, young man.' Laski put the phone down.

He looked at his wristwatch: it was a quarter past three. There was no way he could raise a million pounds in fifteen minutes. It looked as if it was all over.

The bank was going to go under; Laski's reputation was to be destroyed; and he would probably be involved in criminal proceedings. He contemplated leaving the country, this afternoon. He would be able to take nothing with him. Start all over again, in New York or Beirut? He was too old. If he stayed, he would be able to salvage enough from his empire to live on for the rest of his life. But what the hell kind of a life would it be?

He swivelled around in his chair and looked out of the window. The day was cooling; after all, it was not summer. The high buildings of the City were casting long shadows, and both sides of the street below were shaded. Laski watched the traffic and thought about Ellen Hamilton.

Today, of all days, he had decided to marry her. It was a painful irony. For twenty years he could have had his pick of women: models, actresses, debs, even princesses. And when at last he chose one, he went broke. A superstitious man would take that as a sign that he should not marry.

The option might no longer be open to him. Felix Laski, millionaire playboy, was one thing; Felix Laski, bankrupt ex-convict, was quite another. He was sure his relationship with Ellen was not the kind of love that could survive that level of disaster. Their love was a sensual, self-indulgent, hedonistic thing, quite different from the eternal devotion of the *Book of Common Prayer.*

At least, that was how it always had been. Laski had theorized that the permanent affection might come, later, from simply living together and sharing things; after all, the near-hysterical lust that had brought them together was sure to fade, in time.

I shouldn't be theorizing, he thought: at my age I should know.

This morning, the decision to marry her had seemed

like a choice he could make coolly, lightly, even cynically, figuring what he would get out of it as if it were just another stock market coup. But now that he was no longer in command of the situation, he realized – and the thought hit him like a physical blow – that he needed her quite desperately. He *wanted* eternal devotion: he wanted someone to care about him, and to like his company, and to touch his shoulder with affection as she passed his chair; someone who would always be there, someone who would say 'I love you', someone who would share his old age. He had been alone all his life: it was quite long enough.

Having admitted that much to himself, he went farther. If he could have her, he would cheerfully see his empire crumble, the Hamilton Holdings deal collapse, his reputation destroyed. He would even go to gaol with Tony Cox if he thought she would be waiting when he got out.

He wished he had never met Tony Cox.

Laski had imagined it would be easy to control a two-bit hoodlum like Cox. The man might be enormously powerful inside his own little world, but he surely could not touch a respectable businessman. Maybe not: but when that businessman went into partnership – however informal – with the hoodlum, he ceased to be respectable. It was Laski, not Cox, who was compromised by the association.

Laski heard the office door open, and swung around in his chair to see Tony Cox walk in.

Laski stared open-mouthed. It was like seeing a ghost.

Carol scuttled in behind Cox, worrying him like a terrier. She said to Laski: 'I asked him to wait, but he wouldn't – he just walked in!'

'All right, Carol, I'll deal with it,' Laski said.

The girl went out and shut the door.

Laski exploded. 'What the devil are you doing here? Nothing could be more dangerous! I've already had the newspapers on, asking me about you and about Fitzpeterson – did you know he tried to kill himself?'

'Calm down. Keep your hair on,' Cox told him.

'Calm down? The whole thing is a disaster! I've lost everything, and if I'm seen with you I'll end up in gaol—'

Cox took a long stride forward, grabbed Laski by the throat, and shook him. 'Shut your mouth,' he growled. He threw him backwards in his chair. 'Now, listen. I want your help.'

'No way,' Laski muttered.

'Shut up! I want your help, and you're going to give it, or I'll make bloody sure you do go to gaol. Now you know I done this job this morning – a currency van.'

'I know no such thing.'

Cox ignored that. 'Well, I've got nowhere to hide the money, so I'm going to put it in your bank.'

'Don't be ridiculous,' Laski said lightly. Then he frowned. 'How much is it?'

'Just over a million.'

'Where?'

'Outside in the van.'

Laski jumped to his feet. 'You've got a million pounds in stolen money, outside here in a fucking *van*?'

'Yes.'

'You are insane.' Laski's thoughts were racing. 'What form is the money in?'

'Assorted used notes.'

'Are they in the original containers?'

'I'm not that daft. They've been transferred to packing cases.'

'Serial numbers out of sequence?'

'You're getting the idea slowly. If you don't get a move on they'll tow the van away for parking on a yellow line.'

Laski scratched his head. 'How will you carry it into the vault?'

'I got six of the boys out there.'

'I can't let six of your roughnecks carry all that money into my vault! The staff will suspect—'

'They're in uniform – Navy surplus jackets, trousers, shirts and ties. They look like security guards, Felix. If you want to play twenty questions, leave it till afterwards, eh?'

Laski decided. 'All right, get moving.' He ushered Cox out and followed him as far as Carol's desk. 'Ring down to the vault,' he told the girl. 'Tell them to prepare to take in a consignment of cash immediately. I will be dealing with the paperwork personally. And give me an outside line on my phone.'

He strode back into his office, picked up the phone, and dialled the Bank of England. He looked at his watch. It was three twenty-five. He got through to Mr Ley.

'It's Laski here,' he said.

'Ah, yes?' The banker was cautious.

Laski forced himself to sound calm. 'I've sorted out this little problem, Ley. The necessary cash is in my vault. Now I can arrange delivery immediately, as you suggested earlier; or you can inspect today and take delivery tomorrow.'

'Um.' Ley thought for a moment. 'I don't think either will be necessary, Laski. It would rather throw us to have to count so much money this late in the afternoon. If you can deliver first thing in the morning, we'll clear the cheque tomorrow.'

'Thank you.' Laski decided to rub salt in the wound. 'I'm sorry to have irritated you so much, earlier today.'

'Perhaps I was a little brusque. Goodbye, Laski.'

Laski hung up. He was still thinking fast. He reckoned he could drum up about a hundred thousand in cash overnight. Cox could probably equal that from his clubs. They could swap that cash for two hundred thousand of the stolen notes. It was just another precaution: if *all* the notes he delivered tomorrow were too worn to be reissued, someone might wonder at the coincidence of a theft one day and a deposit the next. A leavening of good-condition currency would allay that suspicion.

He seemed to have covered everything. He allowed himself to relax for a moment. I've done it again, he thought: I've won. A laugh of sheer triumph escaped from his throat.

Now to supervise the details. He had better go down to the vault to provide reassurance to his no-doubt bemused staff. And he wanted to see Cox and his crew off the premises fast.

Then he would phone Ellen.

Chapter Thirty

Ellen Hamilton had been at home almost all day. The shopping trip she had told Felix about was invented: she just needed an excuse for going to see him. She was a very bored woman. The trip to London had not taken long: on her return she had changed her clothes, redone her hair, and taken much longer than necessary to prepare a lunch of cottage cheese, salad, fruit, and black coffee without sugar. She had washed her dishes, scorning the dishwasher for so few items and sending Mrs Tremlett upstairs to vacuum-clean. She watched the news and a soap opera on television; began to read an historical novel, and put it down after five pages; went from room to room in the house tidying things that did not need to be tidied; and went down to the pool for a swim, changing her mind at the last minute.

Now she stood naked on the tiled floor of the cool summerhouse, her swimsuit in one hand and her dress in the other, thinking: If I can't make up my mind whether or not to go swimming, how will I ever summon the will-power to leave my husband?

She dropped the clothes and let her shoulders sag. There was a full-length mirror on the wall, but she did not look in it. She took care of her appearance out of scruple, not vanity: she found mirrors quite resistible.

She wondered what it would be like to swim in the nude. Such things had been unheard-of when she was young: besides, she had always been inhibited. She knew this, and did not fight it, for she actually liked her inhibitions – they gave to her lifestyle a shape and constancy which she needed.

The floor was deliciously cool. She was tempted to lie down and roll over, enjoying the feel of the cold tiles on her hot skin. She calculated the risk of Pritchard or Mrs Tremlett walking in on her, and decided it was too great. She got dressed again.

The summerhouse was quite high up. From its door one could see most of the grounds – there were nine acres. It was a delightful garden, created at the beginning of the last century; eccentrically landscaped and planted with dozens of different species of trees. It had given her much pleasure, but lately it had palled, like everything else.

The place was at its best in the cool of the afternoon. A light breeze set Ellen's printed cotton dress flapping like a flag. She walked past the pool into a copse, where the leaves filtered the sunlight and made shifting patterns on the dry earth.

Felix said she was uninhibited, but of course he was wrong. She had simply made an area in her life where constancy was sacrificed for the sake of joy. Besides, it was no longer gauche to have a lover, provided one was discreet; and she was extremely discreet.

The trouble was, she liked the taste of freedom. She realized that she was at a dangerous age. The women's magazines she flicked through (but never actually read) were constantly telling her that this was when a woman added up the years she had left, decided they were shockingly few, and determined to fill them with all the things she had missed so far. The trendy, liberated young writers warned her that disappointment lay in that direction. How would they know? They were just guessing, like everyone else.

She suspected it was nothing to do with age. When she was seventy she would be able to find a lively nonagenarian to lust after her, if at that age she still cared. Nor was it anything to do with the menopause, which was well behind her. It was simply that every day she found Derek a little less attractive and Felix a little more. It had reached the point where the contrast was too much to bear.

She had let both of them know what the situation was, in her indirect manner. She smiled as she recalled how thoughtful each had looked after she had delivered her veiled ultimatums. She knew her men: each would analyse what she had said, understand after a while, and congratulate himself on his perspicacity. Neither would know he was being threatened.

She emerged from the copse and leaned on a fence at the edge of a field. The pasture was shared by a donkey and an old mare: the donkey was there for the grandchildren and the mare because she had once been Ellen's favourite hunter. It was all right for them – they did not know they were getting old.

She crossed the field and climbed the embankment to the disused railway line. Steam engines had puffed along here when she and Derek were gay young socialites, dancing to jazz music and drinking too much champagne, giving parties they could not really afford. She walked along between the rusty lines, jumping from sleeper to sleeper, until something small and furry ran out from under the rotting black wood and scared her. She scampered down the bank and walked back towards the house, following the stream through rough woodland. She did not want to be a gay young thing again; but she still wanted to be in love.

Well, she had laid her cards on the table, as it were, with both men. Derek had been told that his work was edging his wife out of his life, and that he would have to change his ways if he was to keep her. Felix had been warned that she would not be his fancy piece for ever.

Both men might bow to her will, which would leave her still with the problem of choice. Or they might both decide they could do without her, in which case there would be nothing for her to do except to become *désolée*, like a girl in a novel by Françoise Sagan; and she knew that would not suit her.

Well, suppose they both were prepared to do as she wished: whom would she choose? As she rounded the corner of the house she thought: Felix, probably.

She realized with a shock that the car was in the drive, and Derek was getting out of it. Why was he home so early? He waved to her. He seemed happy.

She ran to him across the gravel and, full of guilt, she kissed him.

Chapter Thirty-One

Kevin Hart should have been worrying, but somehow he could not summon up the energy.

The editor had quite explicitly told them not to investigate the Cotton Bank. Kevin had disobeyed, and Laski had asked: 'Does your editor know you are making this call?' The question was often asked by outraged interviewees, and the answer was always an unworried No – unless, of course, the editor had forbidden the call. So, if Laski should take it into his head to ring the editor – or even the Chairman – Kevin was in trouble.

So why wasn't he worried?

He decided that he did not care for his job as much as he had this morning. The editor had good reasons for killing the story, of course; there were always good reasons for cowardice. Everyone seemed to accept that 'It's against the law' was a final argument; but the great newspapers of the past had always broken the laws: laws at once harsher and more strictly applied than those of today. Kevin believed that newspapers should publish and be sued, or even arrested. It was easy for him to believe this, for he was not an editor.

So he sat in the newsroom, close to the news desk, sipping machine tea and reading his own paper's gossip column, composing the heroic speech he would like to have made to the editor. It was the fag-end of the day as far as the paper was concerned. Nothing less than a major assassination or a multiple-death disaster would get in the paper now. Half the reporters – those on eight-hour shifts – had gone home. Kevin worked ten hours, four days a week. The industrial correspondent, having taken eight pints of Guinness at lunch, was asleep in a corner. A lone typewriter clacked desultorily as a girl reporter in jeans wrote an undated story for tomorrow's first edition. The copytakers were arguing about football and the sub-editors were composing joke captions for spiked pictures, laughing uproariously at each other's wit. Arthur Cole was pacing up and down, resisting the temptation to smoke and secretly hoping for a fire at Buckingham Palace. Every so often he would stop and leaf through the sheets of copy impaled on his spike, as if worrying that he might have overlooked the big story of the day.

After a while Mervyn Glazier sauntered across from his own small kingdom. His shirt was hanging out. He sat down beside Kevin, lighting a steel-stemmed pipe and resting one scuffed shoe on the rim of the wastepaper basket.

'The Cotton Bank of Jamaica,' he said by way of preamble. He spoke quietly.

Kevin grinned. 'Have you been a naughty boy, too?'

Mervyn shrugged. 'I can't help it if people ring me up with information. Anyway, if the bank ever was in danger, it's out now.'

'How do you know?'

'My tight-lipped contact at Threadneedle Street. "I have looked more closely at the Cotton Bank since your call, and I find it to be in excellent financial health." Unquote. In other words, it's been quietly rescued.'

Kevin finished his tea and crumpled the plastic-paper cup noisily. 'So much for that.'

'I also hear, from a quite separate source not a million miles from the Council of the Stock Exchange, that Felix Laski has bought a controlling share in Hamilton Holdings.'

'He can't be short of a few bob, then. Is the Council interested?'

'No. They know, and they don't mind.'

'Do you think we made a big fuss over nothing?'

Mervyn shook his head slowly. 'By no means.'

'Nor do I.'

Mervyn's pipe had gone out. He tapped it into the waste-paper basket. The two journalists looked helplessly at each other for a moment, then Mervyn got up and went away.

Kevin returned his attention to the gossip column, but he could not concentrate. He read a paragraph four times without understanding it, then gave up.

Some large piece of skulduggery had gone on today, and he itched to know what it was; the more so because he felt so close to understanding it.

Arthur called him. 'Sit behind here while I go to the lav, will you?'

Kevin walked around the news desk and took a seat behind the news editor's bank of telephones and switchboards. It gave him no thrill: he had the job because, at this time of day, it hardly mattered. He was just the nearest idle man.

Idleness was inevitable on newspapers, Kevin mused. The staff had to be sufficiently many to cope on a big day, so they were bound to be too many on a normal day. On some papers they gave you silly jobs to do just to keep you busy: writing stories from publicity handouts and local government press releases, stuff that would never get in the paper. It was demoralizing, time-wasting work, and only the more insecure of newspaper executives demanded it.

A lad came across from the teleprinter room, carrying a Press Association story on a long sheet of paper. Kevin took it from him and glanced at it.

He read it with a growing sense of shock and elation.

> A syndicate headed by Hamilton Holdings today won the licence to drill for oil in the last North Sea oil field, Shield.
>
> The Secretary of State for Energy, Mr Carl Wrightment, announced the name of the winning

contender at a Press conference overshadowed by the sudden illness of his Junior Minister, Mr Tim Fitzpeterson.

The announcement was expected to provide a much-needed fillip to the ailing shares of the Hamilton print group, whose half-year results, published yesterday, were disappointing.

Shield is estimated to hold oil reserves which could ultimately amount to half a million barrels a week.

The Hamilton group's partners in the syndicate include Scan, the engineering giant, and British Organic Chemicals.

After making the announcement Mr Wrightment added: 'It is with sadness that I have to tell you of the sudden illness of Tim Fitzpeterson, whose work on the Government's oil policy has been so invaluable.'

Kevin read the story three times, hardly able to believe its implications. Fitzpeterson, Cox, Laski, the raid, the bank crisis, the take-over – all leading in a great, frightening circle, back to Tim Fitzpeterson.

'It can't be that,' he said aloud.

'What have you got?' Arthur's voice came from behind him. 'Is it worth a fudge?' The fudge was what the public called the Stop Press.

Kevin passed him the story and vacated his chair. 'I think,' he said slowly, 'that story will persuade the editor to change his mind.'

Arthur sat down to read. Kevin watched him eagerly. He wanted the older man to react; to jump up and shout 'Hold the front page!' or something; but Arthur stayed cool.

Eventually he dropped the sheet of paper on the desk. He looked coldly at Kevin. 'So what?' he said.

'Isn't it obvious?' Kevin said excitedly.

'No. Tell me.'

'Look. Laski and Cox blackmail Fitzpeterson into telling them who has won the Shield licence. Cox, maybe with Laski's help, raids the currency van and gets a million pounds. Cox gives the money to Laski, who uses it to buy the company that got the oil licence.'

'So what would you like us all to do about it?'

'For Christ's sake! We could drop hints, or mount an investigation, or tell the police – at least tell the police! We're the only people who know it all – we can't let the bastards get away with it!'

'Don't you know anything?' Arthur said bitterly.

'What do you mean?'

Arthur's voice was as sombre as the grave. 'Hamilton Holdings is the parent company of the *Evening Post*.' He paused, then looked Kevin in the eye. 'Felix Laski is your new boss.'

Four p.m.

Chapter Thirty-Two

They sat down in the small dining room, on either side of the little circular table, and he said: 'I've sold the company.'

She smiled, and said calmly: 'Derek, I'm so glad.' Then, against her will, tears came to her eyes, and her icy self-control weakened and crumbled for the first time since the birth of Andrew. She saw, through the tears, the shock in his expression as he realized how much it meant to her. She stood up and opened a cupboard, saying: 'I think this calls for a drink.'

'I got a million pounds for it,' he said, knowing she was not interested.

'Is that good?'

'As it happens, yes. But more importantly, it's enough to keep us comfortably well off for as long as we're likely to live.'

She made gin-and-tonic for herself. 'Would you like a drink?'

'Perrier, please. I've decided to go on the wagon for a bit.'

She gave him his drink and sat opposite him again. 'What made you decide?'

'No single thing. Talking to you, and talking to

Nathaniel.' He sipped his mineral water. 'Talking to you, mainly. The things you said about our lifestyle.'

'When does it become final?'

'It already has. I shan't go back to the office, ever.' He looked away from her, out through the French windows across the lawn. 'I resigned at twelve noon, and I haven't felt the ulcer since. Isn't that marvellous?'

'Yes.' She followed his gaze, and saw the sun shining redly through the branches of her favourite tree, the Scots pine. 'Have you made any plans?'

'I thought we could do that together.' He smiled directly at her. 'But I shall get up late; and eat three small meals a day, always at the same times; and watch television; and see whether I can remember how to paint.'

She nodded. She felt awkward; they both did. Suddenly there was a new relationship between them, and they were feeling their way, unsure what to say or how to behave. For him, the situation was simple: he had made the sacrifice she asked, given her his soul; and now he wanted her to acknowledge it, to accept the gift with some gesture. But for her, that gesture would mean letting Felix go out of her life. I can't do it, she thought; and the words rang in her head like the echoing syllables of a curse.

He said: 'What would you like us to do?'

It was as if he knew of her dilemma, and wanted to force her hand, to make her talk about the two of them as a unit. 'I would like us to take a long time deciding,' she said.

'Good idea.' He got to his feet. 'I'm going to change my clothes.'

'I'll come up with you.' She picked up her drink and followed him. He looked surprised, and in truth she too was a little shocked: it was thirty years since they had been in the habit of watching one another undress.

They went through the hall and climbed the main staircase together. He panted with the effort, and said: 'In six months' time I shall be running up here.' He was looking to the future with so much pleasure; she with so much dread. For him, life was beginning again. If only he had done this before she met Felix!

He held the bedroom door open for her, and her heart missed a beat. This had once been a ritual; a sign between them; a lovers' code. It had started when they were young. She had noticed that he became almost embarrassingly courteous to her when he felt lustful, and she said as a joke: 'You only open doors for me when you want to make love.' Then, of course, they thought of sex every time he opened a door for her, and it became his way of letting her know he wanted it. One felt the need of such signals in those days: nowadays she felt quite happy about saying to Felix: 'Let's do it on the floor.'

Did Derek remember? Was he now telling her that this was the acknowledgment he wanted? It had been years; and he was so gross. Was it possible?

He went into the bathroom and turned on the taps. She sat at her dressing table and brushed her hair. In the mirror she watched him come out of the bathroom and begin to take off his clothes. He still did it the same way: first shoes, then trousers, then jacket. He had told her, once, that this was the way it had to be; for the trousers went on the hanger before the jacket, and the shoes had to come off before the trousers would. She had told him how peculiar a man looked in his shirt, tie, and socks. They had both laughed.

He removed his tie and unbuttoned his shirt collar with a sigh of relief. Collars always bothered him. Perhaps he need not wear them buttoned any more.

He took off his shirt, then his socks, then his vest, and finally his underwear shorts. Then he caught her eye in the mirror. There was something close to defiance in his gaze, as if he were saying: 'This is what an old man looks like, so you'd better get used to it.' She met his eyes for a moment, then looked away. He went into the bathroom, and she heard the surge of the water as he climbed into the bath.

Now that he was out of sight she felt freer to think, as if before he might have overheard her thoughts. Her dilemma had been posed in the most brutal way: could she, or could she not, face the thought of sex with Derek? A few months ago she might have – no, not 'might', but 'would', and eagerly – but since then she had touched the firm, muscular body of Felix, and rediscovered her own body in the sheer physicality of their relationship.

She forced herself to visualize Derek's naked body: the thick neck, the fatty breasts with tufts of grey-white hair at the nipples, the huge belly with its arrow of hair widening to the groin, and there – well, at least he and Felix were much the same there.

She imagined herself in bed with Derek, and thought of how he would touch her, and kiss her, and what she would do to him – and suddenly she realized she *could* do it, and take pleasure in it, because of what it meant: Felix's fingers might be skilful and knowing, but Derek's were the hands she had held for years; she might scratch Felix's shoulders in passion, but she knew she could lean on Derek's; Felix had dashing good looks, but in Derek's face there were years of kindness and comfort, of compassion and understanding.

Perhaps she loved Derek. And perhaps she was just too old to change.

She heard him stand up in the bath, and she panicked. She had not had enough time; she was not yet ready to make an irrevocable decision. She could not, right here and now, accept the thought of never having Felix inside her again. It was too soon.

She must talk to Derek. She must change the subject; break his mood and hers. What could she say? He stepped out of the bath: now he would be towelling himself, and in a moment he would be here.

She called out: 'Who bought the company?'

His reply was inaudible; and at that moment, the phone rang.

As she crossed the room to pick it up, she repeated: 'Who bought the company?' She lifted the receiver.

Derek shouted: 'A man called Felix Laski. You've met him. Remember?'

She stood frozen, with the phone to her ear, not speaking. It was too much to take in: the implications, the irony, the treachery.

The voice from the telephone said in her ear: 'Hello, hello?'

It was Felix.

She whispered: 'Oh, God, no.'

'Ellen?' he said. 'Is that you?'

'Yes.'

'I've a lot I want to talk to you about. Can we meet?'

She stammered: 'I – I don't think so.'

'Don't be like that.' His deep, Shakespearian voice was like the music from a cello. 'I want you to marry me.'

'Oh, God!'

'Ellen, speak to me. Will you marry me?'

Suddenly she knew what she wanted, and with the realization came the beginning of calm. She took a deep breath. 'No, I most certainly will not,' she said.

She hung up the phone, and stood staring at it for several moments.

Slowly and deliberately, she took off all her clothes and placed them in a neat pile on a chair.

Then she got into bed and lay waiting for her husband.

Chapter Thirty-Three

Tony Cox was a happy man. He played the radio as he drove slowly home through the streets of East London in the Rolls. He was thinking how well everything had gone, and he was forgetting what had happened to Deaf Willie. He drummed his fingers on the steering wheel in time to a pop song with a bouncy beat. It was cooler now. The sun was low, and there were streamers of high white clouds in the blue sky. The traffic was getting heavier as the rush hour approached, but Tony had all the patience in the world this evening.

It *had* gone well, in the end. The boys had had their shares, and Tony had explained how the rest of the money had been hidden in a bank, and why. He had promised them another payout in a couple of months' time, and they had been happy.

Laski had accepted the stolen money more readily than Tony expected. Maybe the crafty sod thought he could embezzle some of it: just let him try. The two of them would have to cook up some scheme for concealing the true nature of any withdrawals Tony made from the funds. That couldn't be difficult.

Tonight, nothing could be difficult. He wondered

what to do with the evening. Perhaps he would go to a gay bar and pick up a friend for the night. He would dress up, put on some fancy jewellery, and stuff a roll of tenners into his pocket. He would find a boy a couple of years younger than himself, and shower him with kindness: a wonderful meal, a show, champagne – then back to the Barbican flat. He would knock the boy about a bit, just to soften him up, and then . . .

It would be a good night. In the morning the boy would go away with his pockets full of money, bruised but happy. Tony enjoyed making people happy.

On impulse, he pulled up outside a corner shop and went in. It was a newsagent's, with bright modern decor and new racking along the walls for magazines and books. Tony asked for the biggest box of chocolates in the shop.

The young girl behind the counter was fat, spotty and cheeky. She reached up for the chocolates, letting her nylon overalls ride up almost to her bottom. Tony looked away.

'Who's the lucky lady, then?' the girl asked him.

'My mum.'

'Pull the other one.'

Tony paid and got out fast. There was nothing more revolting than a revolting woman.

As he drove away he thought: really, with a million pounds I should do something more than just going out for a night on the town. But there was nothing else he wanted. He could buy a house in Spain, but he got too hot out there. He had enough cars; world cruises bored him; he did not want a mansion in the country; there was nothing he collected. It made him laugh when he thought of it this way: he had become a millionaire in a day, and the only thing he could think of to buy was a three-pound box of chocolates.

The money *was* security, though. If he went through a bad patch – even if, God forbid, he did a stretch – he could look after the boys more or less indefinitely. Running the firm could be expensive at times. There were about twenty blokes in all, and each of them looked to him for a few quid every Friday, whether they had had a tickle or not. He sighed. Yes, his responsibilities would weigh less heavily now. It was worth it for that.

He pulled up outside his mother's house. The dashboard clock said four thirty-five. Ma would have tea ready soon: perhaps a bit of cheese on toast, or a plate of baked beans; then some fruit cake or Battenberg; and tinned pears with Ideal milk to finish off. Or she might have got him his favourite – crumpets and jam. He would eat again later tonight. He had always had a good appetite.

He entered the house and closed the front door behind him. The hall was untidy. The vacuum cleaner stood unattended halfway up the stairs, a raincoat had fallen from the hall stand on to the tiled floor, and there was some kind of mess by the kitchen door. It looked as if Ma had been called away suddenly: he hoped there wasn't bad news.

He picked up the raincoat and hung it on a hook. The dog was out, too; there was no welcoming bark.

He went into the kitchen, and stopped with one foot still in the hall.

The mess was awful. At first he could not figure out what it was. Then he smelled the blood.

It was everywhere: walls, floor, ceiling; all over the fridge, the cooker, and the draining board. The stench of the abattoir filled his nostrils, and he felt sick. But where had it all come from? What had caused it? He looked around wildly for some clue, but there was nothing; just the blood.

He crossed the kitchen in two big, squelching strides, and flung open the back door.

Then he understood.

His dog lay on her back in the middle of the little concrete yard. The knife was still in her – the same knife he had sharpened too much this morning. Tony knelt beside the mutilated corpse. The body looked shrunken, like a balloon with a leak.

A string of soft, blasphemous curses came from Tony's lips. He stared at the multiple cuts, and the bits of cloth between the dog's bared teeth, and whispered: 'You put up a fight, girl.'

He went to the garden gate and looked out, as if the killer might still be there. All he could see was a large pink wad of chewed bubblegum on the ground, casually thrown away by a child.

Obviously, Ma had been out when it happened, which was a mercy. Tony decided to clear up before she got back.

He got a spade from the outhouse. Between the yard and the garden gate was a small patch of poor soil which the old man used to cultivate intermittently. Now it was overgrown. Tony took off his jacket, marked out a small square of ground, and began to dig.

The grave did not take him long. He was strong, and angry too. He trod the spade viciously and thought about what he would do to the killer if he ever found him. And he would find him. The bastard had done it out of spite, and when people did things like that they had to boast about it, either before or afterwards, otherwise they would have proved their point to nobody but themselves, and that was never enough. He knew the type. Somebody would hear something, and tell one of the boys in the hope of a reward.

It crossed his mind that the Old Bill might be behind it. It was unlikely: this was not their style. Who, then? He had plenty of enemies, but none of them possessed both the hatred and the guts to do a number like this. When Tony met somebody with that much front he usually hired the bloke.

He wrapped the dead dog in his jacket and placed the bundle gently in the hole. He shovelled the earth back in and made the surface even with the flat of the spade. You didn't say prayers for dogs, did you? No.

He went back into the kitchen. The mess was awful. There was no way he could clean it up alone. Ma would be back any minute – it was a bloody miracle she had stayed out this long. He had to have help. He decided to ring his sister-in-law.

He went through the kitchen, trying not to spread the blood around. It seemed an awful lot of blood, even for a boxer dog.

He went into the parlour to use the phone, and there she was.

She must have been trying to reach the phone. A thin trail of blood led from the door to the body, lying stretched full length on the carpet. She had been stabbed only once, but the cut had been fatal.

The look of horror frozen on Tony's face changed slowly as his features contorted, like a squeezed cushion, into an expression of despair. He raised his arms slowly upwards and pressed his palms against his cheeks. His mouth opened.

At last words came, and he roared like a bull. 'Ma!' he cried. 'Oh God, Ma!'

He fell to his knees beside the body and cried: huge, loud, racking sobs, like the cries of a child in total misery.

Outside in the street a crowd gathered around the parlour window, but no one dared to come in.

Chapter Thirty-Four

The City Tennis Club was an establishment which had nothing to do with tennis and everything to do with afternoon drinking. Kevin Hart was often struck with the implausibility of its title. In an alley off Fleet Street, squeezed in between a church and an office block, there was hardly room to play table tennis, let alone the real thing. If all they wanted was an excuse to serve drinks when the pubs were shut, Kevin thought, they could surely have found something more credible, like philately or model railways. As it was, the nearest they could get to tennis was a coin-in-the-slot machine which displayed a miniature tennis court on a television screen: you moved your player by twiddling a knob.

However, it did have three bars and a restaurant, and it was a good place to meet people from the *Daily Mail* or the *Mirror* who might one day give you a job.

Kevin got there shortly before five o'clock. He bought a pint of draught beer and sat at a table, talking idly to a reporter from the *Evening News* whom he knew vaguely. But his mind was not on the conversation: inside, he was still seething. The reporter went away after a little while, and Kevin saw Arthur Cole come in and go to the bar.

To Kevin's surprise, the deputy news editor brought his drink across to the table and sat down.

By way of greeting Arthur said: 'Quite a day.'

Kevin nodded. He really did not want the older man's company: he wanted to be alone to sort out how he felt.

Arthur sank half his beer in one, and set his glass down with a sigh of satisfaction. 'I didn't get one at lunch-time,' he explained.

Just to be polite, Kevin said: 'You've been holding the fort on your own.'

'Yes.' Cole took out a packet of cigarettes and a lighter, and put them on the table. 'I've said no to those all day. I wonder how long I can keep it up.'

Kevin looked surreptitiously at his watch, and wondered whether to move on to El Vino's.

Arthur said: 'You're probably thinking you made a mistake ever to join this profession.'

Kevin was startled. He had not credited Cole with that much perspicacity. 'I am.'

'You might be right.'

'That's very encouraging.'

Cole sighed. 'That's your trouble, you know. You will come out with these clever remarks.'

'If I've got to lick boots, I am in the wrong profession.'

Arthur reached for the cigarettes, then changed his mind. 'You've learned something today, haven't you?

You're beginning to understand what it's all about, and if there's anything to you at all, you've acquired a trace of humility.'

Kevin was angered by the patronizing tone. 'It amazes me that after what's happened today there is nobody around here with a sense of failure!'

Cole laughed bitterly, and Kevin realized he had struck a chord: Arthur's sense of failure must be more or less permanent.

The older man said: 'You people are a new breed, and I suppose we need you. The old way – making everyone start at the bottom and work their way up slowly – was better at producing reporters than executives. God knows there's a shortage of brains in newspaper management. I hope you'll stick it out. Want another pint?'

'Thanks.'

Arthur went to the bar. Kevin was somewhat bemused. He had never had anything but criticism from Cole, yet now the man was asking him to stay in newspapers and become a manager. That was not in his plans, but only because he had never thought of it. It was not what he wanted: he liked finding things out, writing, working for the truth.

He was not sure. He would think about it.

When Arthur came back with the drinks, Kevin said: 'If this is what happens when I get a big story, how am I ever going to get anywhere?'

Arthur gave that bitter laugh again. 'You think you're alone? Do you realize I was news editor today?

At least, for you, there will be another story.' He reached for the packet of cigarettes, and this time he lit one.

Kevin watched him inhale. Yes, he thought, for me there will be another story.

For Arthur, there won't.

Encompassing all the passion and rage of a long forgotten time,* A Place Called Freedom *is a magnificent adventure from master storyteller Ken Follett

Ken Follett

A Place Called Freedom £6.99

Hidden in the shadows of a Scottish river bank in the winter of 1767, a young woman watches a figure emerging from the icy water. Lizzie Hallim has never seen a naked man before. But her excitement is tinged with fear. The man is a slave, and she is helping him to escape. From that moment on, in the Old World and the New their destinies will become irrevocably entwined.

Cruelty rules the Scottish coalfields as powerful landlords value black gold more than human life. Lizzie's fiancé, Jay Jamisson, presides over the mine where men, women and children toil underground, prevented by law from ever leaving the village.

Charismatic rebel miner Mack McAsh challenges the mighty Jamisson family, armed with only his wits, his physical strength and his irrepressible bravery. When Jay tries to enforce the law binding him to the mine for life, Mack defies him and flees to London.

Swallowed up in the city's seething, violent underworld, Mack becomes a leader in the famous poor uprising of 1768, only to find himself sentenced to death for a crime he did not commit. Rescued from the hangman, he is transported to America, where once again he struggles for freedom on the vast and dangerous frontier of the New World . . .

Ken Follett
The Pillars of the Earth £7.99

A timeless story of passion and idealism set in the mists of the Middle Ages

It begins with a curse, a song and a hanging and it builds into a magnificent adventure no reader will ever forget. At once a sensuous and enduring love story and an epic that shines with the fierce spirit of a passionate age, *The Pillars of the Earth* is without doubt Ken Follett's masterpiece, and a story for all time . . .

'Enormous and brilliant . . . No summary can do justice to this mammoth tale, which seems to touch all human emotion – love and hate, loyalty and treachery, hope and despair. See for yourself. This is truly a novel to get lost in and one of the marvels of the publishing year'
Cosmopolitan

'Action and intrigue, violence and passion . . . a novel that entertains on a very grand scale'
Publishers Weekly

'A highly enjoyable tale . . . this book evokes its period brilliantly'
Sunday Times

'Follett succeeds brilliantly in combining hugeness and detail to create a novel imbued with the rawness, violence and blind faith of the era'
Sunday Express

Ken Follett

A Dangerous Fortune £6.99

From the master storyteller – a breathtaking saga of love, power and revenge set amidst the wealth and decadence of Victorian England . . .

By the 1860s, the Pilasters ae one of the world's great banking families. But their fortune is jeopardized by ambition and greed. As the bank's tentacles spread from the City of London to the colonies, the Pilasters grow rich in the shadow of tragedy. The shocking secret behind a young boy's death will lead to three generations of treachery.

'A compulsively readable, enjoyable thriller-cum-saga'
Sunday Times

'Banks, brothels and a high body count . . . it's all there'
Financial Times

'Is this new one as exciting as his best? The answer, happily, is yes!'
Daily Mail

Ken Follett
Night Over Water £6.99

A night you'll never forget . . .

Night Over Water, the action-filled, romantic adventure from Ken Follett, author of the worldwide bestsellers, *The Eye of the Needle* and *The Pillars of the Earth*. A night aboard the most luxurious airliner ever built – the Pan Am Clipper, bound for New York. A night of drama and suspense, as panic-driven men and women flee to save their fortunes . . . their families . . . and the lives . . .

'The opulent interior of the first airliner, on a transatlantic flight from England to New York, in war-darkened 1939, is the setting for Follett's high-flying caper, guaranteed to hold the reader in their seat . . . the master of epic suspense spins an excruciatingly taut drama . . . a whirlwind of ramance and intrigue . . . his best since *The Eye of the Needle*'
Publishers Weekly

'Master of the romantic thriller'
Daily Telegraph